A TALE
of
BLOOD
and
TEARS

MENI SEA
MENINÏN
THE HIGH ISLAND
THE SHADOW SEA
LAST STAND OUTLOOK
DEERDROP
TWISTED TROUT
THE REMNA
FOREST ABRIG
Westerly Road
THE CITADEL THE HIGH CITY
CITHRIL
The High Road
MORGANDUM
The Low Road
THE CACIAN HINTERLAND
THE PORTAL

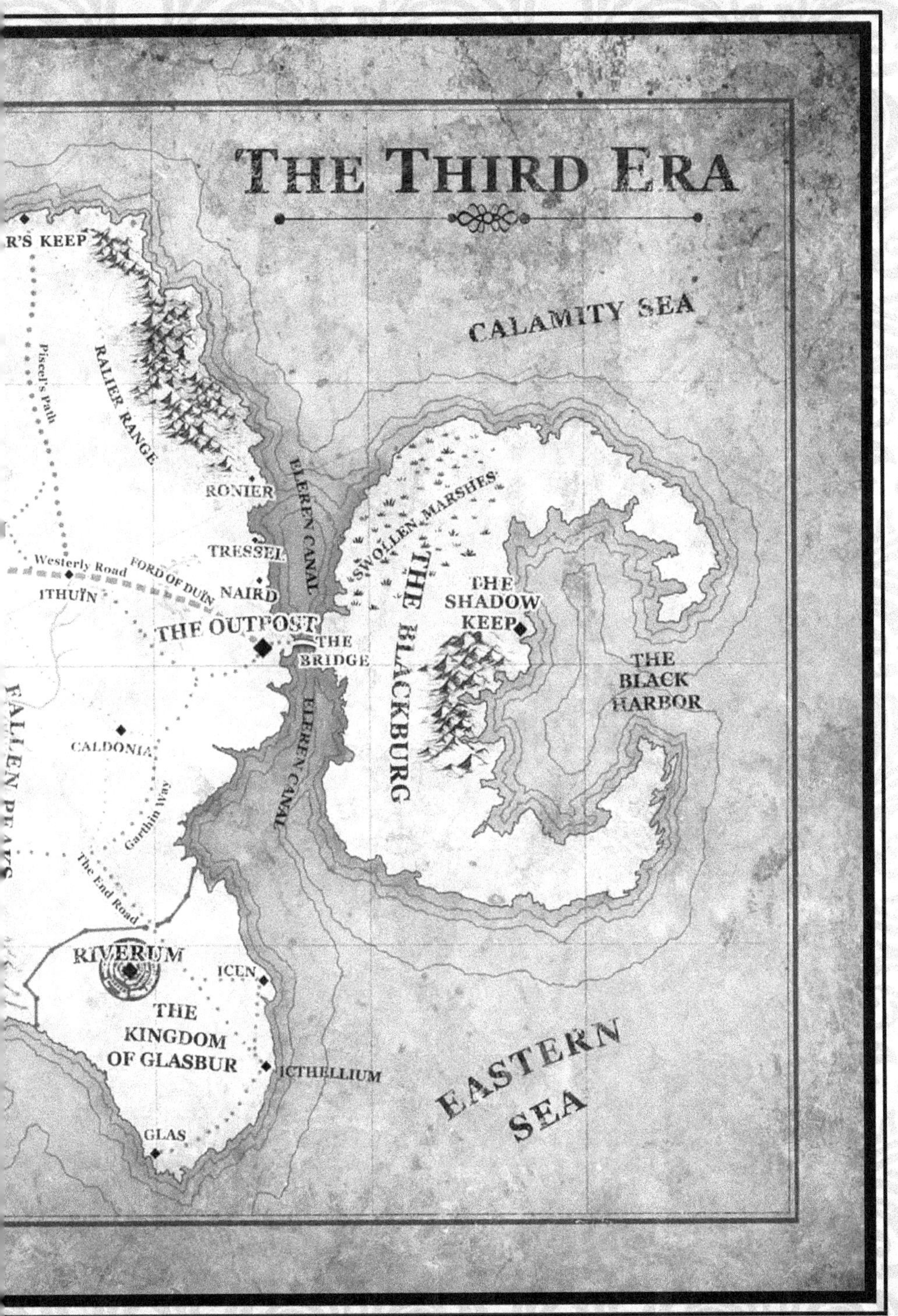

THE THIRD ERA
CALAMITY SEA
R'S KEEP
Piscel's Path
RALIER RANGE
RONIER
ELEREN CANAL
SWOLLEN MARSHES
THE BLACKBURG
THE SHADOW KEEP
THE BLACK HARBOR
TRESSEL
Westerly Road
FORD OF DUIN
NAIRD
ITHUIN
THE OUTPOST
THE BRIDGE
ELEREN CANAL
FALLEN PEAKS
CALDONIA
Garthin Way
The End Road
RIVERUM
ICEN
THE KINGDOM OF GLASBUR
ICTHELLIUM
EASTERN SEA
GLAS

THE FALLEN VEIL

BOOK TWO

Robert Scheck

Credit to the Editor: Molly Spain
Credit to the Book Front and Back Cover Artist: David Leahey
Credit for the Ëonë Map: David Leahey
Credit for the Character Headshots: Arthur Bowling
Credit for Formatting of Book/Artwork: Glen Edelstein

Robert Scheck
14:28

ISBNs and their formats:

979-8-9873978-3-1 (ebook)
979-8-9873978-4-8 (paperback)
979-8-9873978-5-5 (hardcover)
979-8-9873978-6-2 (hardcover with dust jacket)

CONTENTS

Phoenix Dunnigan Rather

Katherine (Katy) Chase

Timothy (Tim) Brestdon

William (Will) Gree

FOREWARD

A HUGE THANK YOU TO NOAH for his patience as I ranted long into the night about story elements and plot twists. Sometimes all you need for a good story, is someone who listens.

While it has been a long while since the first book came out, at this point four years, my resolve at telling a story worth the fantasy name has not changed. Within these pages, you'll find a story that is steeped in tears and reeks of death. Proceed with caution. Not all nightmares happen at the edge of a pillow. Not all evil beings lurk in your basement's shadows. Some hide in the very pages you now hold and will do their best to whisper to you. Take care you do not listen.

The sword shall shatter and the shield shall yield
In the darkest days on the blood-soaked field
When his broken gaze on her corpse thus steals
And the Elfinian throne bends the crown and kneels
As the battle rages in unending steel

PROLOGUE

The Lay of Ëonë

Her eyes moonlit lights of old sparkle as memories grow cold
Depths of time and eras unfold ere the darkness curse her soul

Her hair in golden light doth bathe the stars around her as a crown
Golden robes ascend the throne as deceit plunders all around

Her footprint goes throughout all time as armies clash for her name
Death defiles and tribulation triumphs over all who claim that fame

Those to battle and those to care for the future hope she sees
A grassland erect and proud engulfed by rotten splintered trees

Her image is one of timeless beauty against the choler of woe
Darkness may shield the light from all and corrupt the depraved foe

Her eyes moonlit lights of old sparkle as memories grow cold
Depths of time and eras unfold ere the darkness curse her soul

Robert Scheck

Her fame as time began in old side by side through halls of gold
Before the world extinguish and time snuffs out the stories therein told

Her love of life and laughter issues forth as the wind on a stormy day
Trees for miles and rolling hills bring love of life to those who play

As the final battle rages on and death destroys the green of life
And in shadowed lair extends a hand to take her as his wife

Her pain and fear increase in woe as the suffered demented cries
What should be done before our time as the world corrupted lies

Her eyes moonlit lights of old sparkle as memories grow cold
Depths of time and eras unfold ere the darkness curse her soul

Her fame and fortune cast aside as time twists every dream
The world into the madness of her captors in hatred seem

Her light goes out and her hope dies down as the black corrupted night
Extends its bloodlust upon the moors and extinguishes the brazen light

Fevered song and dreadful dance lift high the splintered pity
The sun arises morning splendor the valley glowing the city

in light of hope and prayer the whispering grass and dew strewn leaves
Heaven's voice in harmony as the blood runs free over darkened eaves

A warm touch a stricken smile on the battlefield before the odors rise
In constant motion as death's dreadful denial screams and hysterically cries

Death through curved steel flesh rent asunder in a bloodbath
A mist arises shadows grow and the sun sets down its iron-forged path

Her eyes moonlit lights of old sparkle as memories grow cold
Depths of time and eras unfold ere the darkness curse her soul

xvi

Chapter 1

Darkness on the Eastern Front

M Y BLOOD RACED IN RHYTHM with the undulating ocean. The cresting waves pummeled the shore and crashed over partially submerged boulders as I leapt high over a slab of stone and rolled to a stop with a gasp. Gravel spewed about, disturbed by my sudden appearance. An arrow hissed past my shoulder, missing my cloak by inches. Salty sea spray sprung high into the air, and I let it rain down on me, conscious of the heavy weight which hung palpable in the misty air. I spat in anger and heaved, pushing off and following the faint sounds of scuffling and snarling in front of me. The guttural growls moved from bush to bush. Heat beat down. Hot. Cold. Dry. Wet. It did not matter. Dagger between my teeth, sword in my hand, I was hunting. I looked out, observing the thick black clouds which slowly advanced on the shores of the gloomy island far out over the angry waters of the Eleren Canal, visible only thanks to the red flashes pulsating in thick thunderheads. The ominous burgundy light sent flickers down to the reflective surface below.

The toe of my boot caught against a rock. My muscles clenched from the continuous strain of a full sprint over miles of hilly terrain. I took my second fall with an annoyed snarl. The flashes of red illuminated the peaks of a far-off mountain range. I couldn't place whether it was the choppy, uneven patterns of the ocean, the foreboding shoreline of the BlackBurg, the name of the island beyond the sea, or the feeling I'd forgotten something very important, but my stomach churned uneasily. A tree shook barely twenty yards from where I lay sprawled, and the Varglarian I'd been hunting sprinted out into sunlight. It was alone and poorly armed. A perfect target.

I grinned, feeling the adrenaline return in waves as I shoved off the ground and picked up my pace, falling behind the vermin as it wove between trees and pillars of ancient moss-covered stone. It looked back as I closed in. Behind its iron mask, its fiery eyes glowed in fear and rage. *And they said being a scout was more boring than a watchman.* The creature took aim and fired. The projectile sang wild. Not even close. I ran up the side of a stone outcropping and, sword in both hands, aimed it point down as if I was going to plunge it into my own breast. I leapt out over clear space . . . down onto the creature's back. We tumbled against the brush as I wrestled to pin the creature down. The wet metal was slippery as the Varg's tar-like blood oozed down my palm. The creature roared and tried to plunge its own blade into my heart.

"Outpost cur," it growled as I gripped its wrist with both hands. The creature was fully armored in spiked black steel. Its fiery eyes drilled into me. "Your use is at an end. You will fall and we will feast on your flesh! My shadow king will rule all these lands. He will put the torch to every homestead and warrior who defies him!"

I leapt up and back, slamming the handle of my blade into the Varg's helmet. It staggered to its feet and swiped viciously with the edge of its blade. We were battling at the edge of a cliff that dropped a hundred feet into the frothing ocean below. Wind whipped about us as we fought hand and dagger to avoid death. My cloak snapped and threatened to trip me as the Varg shoved me inches from the edge of the cliff. I gritted my teeth and kicked at its legs. The Varg reached for an arrow, but I kicked the bow from its armored hand. I aimed my sword but cried out in pain as the creature headbutted me. I watched as my only source for defense spun pummel over point into the black waters and out of sight.

"Your time is nigh, DarkBairn." The Varglarian straddled me about the hips and readied to plunge its sword into my heart. My left arm was pinned down by its right knee. I groaned under the strain of keeping the blade away with my free hand. The muscles therein shook tremendously. Sweat beaded on my forehead. My face grew red with effort as the dagger point moved incrementally, inch by inch, toward my chest. The tip pushed ever so against my leather breastplate. *I told him the leather would be useless! Who equips scouts with leather armor?*

The wind changed course then and howled into the Varg's face with a ferocity I was thankful for. For a split second, the monster paused in its murderous efforts to adjust accordingly. I wrenched my left arm free and, fingers digging into a small scabbard strapped against my thigh, yanked out a small knife then plunged it into the creature's chest. For a long moment, nothing happened as realization flickered in the dying embers of its eyes. The Varglarian suddenly slumped against me, and with great effort I heaved it off. It didn't snarl anymore. My breath came and went in gulping gratefulness. My head rushed with the surge of adrenaline, and I laughed like a sojourner who'd drunk too much in the tavern. Sweat dripped into my eyes. I raised my shaking hands to stare at the blood as it slipped off in drips.

Two years had crept past since first I fell, rather unceremoniously, onto these grim shores. I hadn't even processed I was now an adult. What I may have added in form of built-in muscle and determination, and that in and of itself was a necessity to survive the grueling winters and steamy summers of the Outpost, had also claimed many memories and from them portions of my past identity. Time itself had not been kind to me. Where once youthful exuberance radiated from my face, now I sported a tanned chiseled visage, partly covered in pale stubble that failed to flourish to a full beard. The only freedom I received anymore were my scouting trips along the southern shores.

My leather armor was worn and passed down from the older watchmen. My clothes were worn, little more than a tunic, comically oversized shirt, too tight britches, and a cloak sewn together by the hand of the oldest watchman, Gilsworth, which allowed for the privacy of decency and little else. They itched something awful. Time alone could not save my raw skin from the constant scratching till my flesh became redder than the blood beneath it. It made the cool nights of bathing in the strait relaxing and peaceful. Despite the tumultuous waves crashing down around, and the frigid waters, nothing compared to standing atop the knolls and inhaling the smell of the ocean.

I slowly lowered my hands and rubbed them against the coarse grass. A year ago, what I'd just done would have seemed impossible. Taking the life of another being, no matter how corrupt and evil, would have seemed ridiculous at best and unfathomable at worst. Every inch of my body protested and ached. Here on the edge of the precipice, the ocean to one side and the rolling hills of the Eastern Ward on the other, I steadied my breathing. The butterflies came and went. Remnants of a past. A forgotten past. They still fluttered deep when I was least expecting them. I wish I could remember why.

Ever since I'd arrived in Ëonë, a heavy feeling of guilt had claimed residence. I chalked it up to my inability to remember things, for in the beginning most of my memories ended with my parents' kidnapping and began with me laying on my back here, in Ëonë, with DarSheer's blade inches from my chest. I'd recalled much since that fateful day. The fog had cleared, but my mind remained somewhat muddied. My lost memory was a source of great interest to our brooding Lord of the Outpost, Lord Malziek. Even DarSheer found me an oddity, but one to be humored.

No matter how I strained to recall, on sleepless nights beneath the unfamiliar stars, I could not force it. My past was a landscape of uncertainty save for two things which I held onto and repeated before I would finally fall asleep from pure exhaustion. I remembered my parents. Their smiling faces soothed my soul when I stewed, depressed and cold on the walls of the Outpost. It was comforting knowing that I was not alone. Somewhere, out there, people who knew and loved me were alive. I wasn't just a cursed bairn. I wasn't just an answer to a prophecy that spelt the doom of all. Or so I hoped. I recalled their kidnappings, but not how the ordeal had ended, if it ever had. The other memory that resurfaced when I was at my lowest was that of a face. It was a beautiful face that made my stomach hurt. I knew I cared deeply for her. But I didn't remember why. With the face came a name. Katy. While my parents gave me comfort, she gave me hope. And hope was worth fighting for.

The once green fields of spring were now a decaying brown under the withering frown of the beating sun. White clouds unfurled in mass against the shiny blue sky. They offered no moisture from the flowing riverbeds south of the Westerly Road or indeed the sea itself east of the main gate. All around, hours' hard ride from the Outpost, the fields bore only grisly twisted remains of ancient trees and crusted rock. My route took me up and down the ivory coast where the white beaches were assailed daily by the waves of royal blue and spring greens. The white-capped foam led the charge against the unyielding land yet was always repelled by the marching grains of sand. The old bark and driftwood left behind came in handy to fuel our warmth during the colder months, when harsh storm clouds brought thick deluges upon the wooded realm around our secluded home.

I rolled the Varg's body over the edge of the grassy cliff and watched with mild content at the ripples which moved out from the point of impact. The content was brief. Across the strait, the black clouds flashed ominously. Vivid evocations haunted my dreams. A single peak, silhouetted against a blue sky. A mountain with dark winding paths. Friends. Laughter. An old man with a smiling kindness. A throb in my chest increased, and I gripped my breast. I had made allies here, yes, but nothing more. All my friends and loved ones were a world away from me. I had lost something dearer than a lifetime here could provide. I would have stewed in my thoughts, but at that moment a horse's hooves kicked up stones as its rider cantered near and then proceeded to dismount. Underfoot, the sound of gravel crunched louder till I could feel the presence behind me and ignore it no longer. My disturbed brooding would have to wait.

"You're wanted by the council, stranger."

The voice behind me felicitated great joy as I turned. His simple looks deceived many, but beneath his burlap clothing, the stable boy had intelligence and with it the beginnings of muscle had begun to spawn. When I'd first arrived, he'd been one of the few to show any kindness. Most saw me as an outsider and thus shuffled away from me. His emerald eyes were full of childlike innocence mixed with mirthful mischief. He was never afraid to get his hands dirty and had bailed me out of trouble on numerous occasions. The journey from the Outpost had been a long one, and I could tell he'd already endured a grueling day. I grasped both his forearms and smiled.

"Do you know what they'll be jabbering about today, Brenneth?" I inquired in mock seriousness. "I've already told them all I know. I can't conjure a new memory before it comes; they should understand that."

"They don't talk to me about any of that mystical jargon." His eyes twinkled. "I'm just the stable lad, remember?"

"Right," I snorted, "everyone knows you're where secrets go to die. Spill the bistri."

"I don't know if I should tell you," he said. "I mean you are the 'DarkBairn' and all, least that's what they say." He clapped a hand to his mouth the moment he finished speaking, eyes wide in shock.

"The 'DarkBairn'? Any conversation including that cursed name must be important." My smile faltered as I grimaced and hurried toward the horse Brenneth had brought. "We'd better return quickly. Lord Malziek doesn't like to convene a council with the main attraction missing."

The journey back was quiet. As the horse's hooves thudded against the uneven path of tightly packed dirt, I resigned myself to quiet despair. Much remained a mystery to me, and the constant attempts to access my forgotten memories were taking a toll. My despair only convinced me that more memories lay hidden, concealed beneath a thin surface and just waiting for me to poke a hole. I knew within this shroud of unknown, something important was waiting. Brenneth had been kind where others saw isolation and ignorance a fairer gesturer. Even the lowliest of the servants regarded me as an unwanted omen of ill times ahead. DarSheer, who had brought me to Malziek the day he'd found me, hadn't trusted me and had petitioned for me to be shipped back to the city called Avalon. Malziek was indignant. He said he'd never send away a body that could be posted on the walls. It had only come through these grueling years of slaving alongside the men at the Outpost that I'd earned my right to scout and only through DarSheer's personal avouchment, despite his previous hesitations. Months of training and a few close calls slowly thawed the distrust around me. When Malziek had refused to send me away, DarSheer, in good step, had stuck close by. He was a reminder of the strange way in which I'd arrived, and I often grilled him for the finer details.

A familiar shape ahead jutted its dominance into the sky in the form of a grey tower with a pointed top. Surrounded by bland walls, the Outpost was the first defense against the dark forces Malziek and DarSheer believed teemed over the ocean, east of Ëonë, in the Black-Burg. The Outpost sat like a scrummage in an alleyway. The Westerly Road pierced the walls like a stake through a heart. The road to the single, small gate went from gravel to hard clay to mud as the walls loomed overhead in foreboding fashion. Several guards peered down; their hands gripped their smooth spears. One turned and called down behind the wall. Before we'd even attempted to notify them of our arrival, the small gate lumbered open. The oak wood groaned as we passed through it. All around, men stopped to stare at me, their breath ballooned in front of them as the cold air, which whipped off the ocean top, sunk into their clothing.

Horses stamped and whinnied as we passed. Several massive bonfires in the courtyard before the Grey Tower burned with an intense heat of crackles and pops. The braziers they blazed in seemed to shimmer with the heat. Clouds scuttled overhead, masking the sun from sight, preparing us for a dark winter to come. Brenneth, his arms around my waist, shook either from the cold or nerves; I could not tell. I patted his hand as we trotted to a stop and glanced toward the stables.

Bustling importantly from its rotting doors, a tall man who smelled as bad as his stables glared at my companion.

"Brenneth!" he growled, his massive beard quavering beneath his deep boom. "It's all well and fine for you to meander off on a dalliance along the shore, but we've important guests to tidy up after."

Brenneth scrambled off the horse's back and grasped its reigns. I swung over and down. Three boys hurried from the stable's entrance, gossiping with eager glee. When they spotted me, they hushed and averted their eyes. Two years and I was still the black sheep of the company. They carried the saddle of a Messenger. It bore the familiar red stripes running from front to back. We didn't get many if any visitors out this far east, let alone dignitaries from The High City, so it was quite the occasion when one was seen here. That journey alone took months, and much of it was over unprotected wastelands rimmed with potential dangers.

"Who's here, Altruic?" I inquired curiously as Brenneth moved out of earshot.

"A Messenger from The High City arrived just an hour ago amidst much pomp and circumstance," Altruic grimaced as if the thought pained him. He gave me a withering glance. "Horns blew and flowers flew. It's as if a blasted wedding was happening on our doorstep! Probably here for you." *No need to rub it in, old codger.*

Brenneth gasped where he stood, ear to a hole in the stable boards. Altruic shouted after him until he had scrambled once again out of earshot and through the creaking doors. The old stable master turned back.

"What do they want?" I asked.

"What does The High City always want these days?" Altruic reached to flick mud flecks off his boots. "From what I've been told they've finally decided to send someone to check on us. It'd be the first blasted time they cared. I've never seen nor sensed an iota of caring from our great and mighty Custodian. Winds can howl and the ocean beyond smack its fury down before he'd so much as remember us. Lost a good number of these sniffling stable rats to the harshness of these lands. But have some child drop from the sky and suddenly you're the most important location in Ëonë. Suddenly, you're good enough for one of the Custodian's personal Messengers. Makes you wonder why." Again, he stared at me, distrust oozing out of him. I shifted awkwardly.

"Surely, it might have something to do with the bizarre way I arrived here," I said sarcastically.

"No need to get your tight pants in a squeeze over me," Altruic snorted. It was the friendliest he'd been to me in a long while. "Save your wit for the council. I don't envy any man who has to endure those pompous elite. They think themselves the epitome of what Men can achieve. I've seen farmers in the droppings of their sows with more potential and honor than the highborn."

Interest renewed, I turned to gaze up the erect pillar of marble where even now, Malziek and the mysterious Messenger most likely brooded.

"Malziek won't like how long this has taken," I murmured.

"Malziek doesn't like waking up with less than a flagon of ale to greet him. Don't keep them wondering. You know those Messenger lot hate waiting." Altruic turned and hurried back toward the stables. "These cursed stable boys have no inkling of what they're doing."

I thought to rebuke his insult of Malziek but thought better of it. Why add more reasons to be shunned by the old codger. The single platform at the foot of the tower was accessible only by a flight of stairs which ended at the feet of a burly guard. Brute-faced with a bulging neck, the man stood stiffly, his hand always resting on his sword hilt, cloak flitting in the wind. His harsh eyes found mine as he surveyed my approach.

"They're waiting for you, DarkBairn," he rumbled. Voice deeper and louder than a drumbeat, he towered over, presenting an intimidating welcome.

"Greetings, Dwaith." I climbed the steps and whisked past, allowing myself to glance sidelong as I passed. Several of the guards had begun to spread the rumor that beneath Dwaith's heavy protection, he was scrawny and pale. It was a rumor that he did nothing to mask, choosing to ignore the verbal jabs and focus on the physical ones.

Hand on the thick door, I pushed through. The interior was dimly lit. A suffocating atmosphere hung drab and weighted as the sun broke through the thickly cut glass and meandered around. Several long bookshelves with musty manuscripts sat in the far corner. A heavy coating of dust masked their titles, and I often wondered what I'd find if I picked up one. I wondered but never looked. My only trips to this tower involved a council meeting, for when I wasn't sitting through

Malziek's reports, I was on patrol or watch duty. I hoped that a Messenger meant change was on its way. I didn't like the way some of these soldiers eyed me, with wariness in their eyes.

The curved staircase twisted impossibly high as my calves began to burn and my breath became labored. The occasional window allowed me to gauge my progress, and it felt like a long day had passed before I ascended the final step and, shaking, stood before a door. Already, the loud disagreeing cries oozed through the cracks in the frame as Malziek's temper got the better of him.

"Long have my people waited under the banner of our enemies and long have they been rewarded with silence from the Citadel and The High City. On the fronts and plains, we suffer constant raids. Nightshades and Varglarians burn and pillage unchallenged through many of the outlying towns and villages. We have stood as sentinels against the old evil, and the new, for in time we knew it would return. What hell came as my people were slaughtered and our villages burned at the command of darkness? Where was the Custodian then when we sent messages of bloodshed and warning and they turned their backs and forsook us to the arrow and sword of Mordën? Yet now on the case of a simple bairn, you are here?"

"Take care, Lord Malziek, that in your anger you do not insult he who has allowed you your position of power."

"Power over blocks of stone? You act as if anyone else would have taken this assignment! Perhaps you wish to remove your clean cloak and command the mud and grime? How long before the fancy in you cries over the harsh winters and fear?"

I inhaled deeply and pushed into the room. Firm and unmoving, Malziek stood at the head of a wide wooden table where six others sat in various positions of unease. Spittle flying and face red, he glowered down the table's length to a man in white garb. The single red stripe down both sleeves of the white cloak signaled the Messenger's vocation.

"The Citadel already lies on the brink of chaos!" the man retorted with an emphatic toss of his arms. "What would you have me do? Distrust brews as Mordën's return has sparked rumors of a great war on the horizon, a war we cannot hope to win. If we could send help do you not think we would have brought our greatest host from the west to your aid? Do you think us so ignorant that we cannot comprehend the threat now posed here? That we'd rather twiddle our thumbs in the peace of protection provided by the Elfins? Those blasted goldens who make transit a pain every day. Three hundred gold thruki, Malziek, to simply sail over the Ethero Basin. Travel is not easy, and the roads are less kind than last I was this far east. Even you, my old friend, have changed, though you do not wish to admit it."

"*Friend*?" Malziek swore and pounded a great meaty fist on the table. Clothed in a simple leather tunic overtop of a blue buttoned shirt, he turned his back on the Messenger. The table's surface, thick as it was, shuddered at the impact and a goblet of wine toppled and rolled to the floor. The other men, seated in dread, exclaimed their loyalty to Malziek and began bickering with the Messenger. It was common knowledge you didn't disagree with the hand that defended you. At the end of the room, DarSheer sat, head in his hand.

I cleared my throat and Malziek turned slightly, just enough for him to see me. His enraged exterior melted with hidden relief. The Messenger also turned. A thin wiry man with a tuft of hair atop his domed head, he peered at me. He kept his hands folded in the sleeves of his cloak as his eyes took in my appearance. I felt his eyes prodding my every bone and organ, as if judging me against his ideals for a prophetic answer, as some liked to call me.

"So, this is the DarkBairn?" he murmured softly. His voice was like a serpent slithering from ear to ear. It was both soothing and grating. "How can you be sure?"

"The boy appeared on the plains south of here. He quite literally dropped down from the sky. What more of a sign do you want? Should we demand Erëthuïl himself appear?" Malziek's tone dropped to a resigned level.

"He could be a fraud." The Messenger shook his head and waved one hand loftily. "Erëthuïl knows there have been many of them recently. Half the Citadel's court is packed with brutish outliers, a child in one hand, demanding to be shown before the Custodian. If we entertained every child for what their simpleminded owners claim them to be, we'd have a thousand answers to this prophecy."

"And how many of these children can claim they fell from the sky on the eve when our greatest enemy returned?" Malziek cursed. "Blast you Citadel folk. He dropped from the bloody sky! Last I checked, your bairns didn't grow wings and flutter about like a butterfly over a daisy. Open your eyes. You fancy folk have been proclaiming your support of us whilst secretly derailing any attempt at aid."

"Watch your tone in the presence of a Messenger," the man hissed sharply. His gaze glittered dangerously. "Our past does not give you right to scream in an undignified manner to a representative of the Custodian, no matter what your outlandish allies claim. We are not your enemy. Our perceived lack of action is not attributable to a lack of desire. One cannot move until one knows what one is moving against. Your word ever has been enough for me. Yet I do not stand here, before you all, for myself alone but as an extension of the Custodian himself. Stories can be rehearsed . . . made up. He will need more proof than your word."

"I was there." DarSheer rose, and the room went quiet. He gave me a confident nod. "I was there when Phoenix dropped from the sky. I saw it as sure as we speak now. The bairn is not a part of this world, and I believe the rumors of Mordën's return, which began a mere day after his arrival, are proof to that fact. We cannot ignore that the day he showed, the once dormant island sprang back to life. Long have we been cursed to watch those shores. We know what to expect and what is out of place. Mordën has returned. The boy was his means."

"Does he speak?" The Messenger squinted at me and advanced slowly.

"I do." I backed away, feeling a sudden nervousness. "You must be the Messenger everyone is in a tizzy over."

"Are they really? I suppose what with living in this dreadful place, any type of change is entertainment, no matter how mundane."

"Do you still refute it? Does your master claim ignorance to the undeniable yet again?" Malziek demanded firmly. The Messenger met his gaze, and for a few moments some unspoken battle raged between them.

"There is no way to prove Mordën's return. Your increased reports on Varglarian raids can be chalked up to time of the year. They thrive in cold and misery. A simple glance out that window will show you that we are not in the warmth of summer anymore. Even Nightshades are not a cause for pandemonium. Some still survived, I'm sure, from the war of old. If they band together with the Varglarians it may appear to be a host from the past. Has anyone here actually seen Mordën? Do not bemoan our hesitation. I agree that there is a peculiarity to how he arrived." He stared back at me. "Of course, DarSheer also makes a valid point. The Custodian sent me to decide if the threat was real. I believe I shall be returning."

DarSheer tilted his head in confusion as Malziek stormed forward.

"You're leaving? Already? Barely an hour since we opened our gates to you, fed you our finest, and now with a single glance you're gone? Months of travel and you'd take those harsh and cruel roads over a bed in my Outpost?" If I'd been the Messenger, I would not have looked so calm before Malziek's threatening gaze. It was like staring into the maw of a beast before it bit your head off. But the Messenger didn't seem phased, or if he was, he didn't show it.

"My mission is accomplished, and I do believe the Custodian would like to hear the results. Have your stable boys prepare my horse. Or have you now changed your mind and this bairn is not the one we've been looking for?"

He left the room with a practiced calm. Documents flew off the table as small containers of ink spilled and sent their black goo oozing over the hardened table. The torches set at regular intervals along the table center flickered as their fires were nearly extinguished with the sudden breeze. The small window set into the stone wall let next to no light through. Even the half-eaten horse flesh on wooden dishes seemed unappealing.

Malziek bowed his head and sunk into the chair at the head of the table. His exhalation was one of resignation as he covered his face. A posture uncommon to him, he appeared defeated.

"My Lord?" I spoke as the door to the chamber slammed shut, leaving only Malziek, DarSheer, and myself to bask in the Messenger's enigmatic words.

"You have done well, Broadsword." Malziek glanced toward Dar-Sheer, his once powerful eyes now quieted with sadness. "Though the Citadel and by means The High City have denied those I need, we still have time to prepare."

"I but serve you, my Lord Malziek, as it is my duty." DarSheer bowed. "I would die as would all my brothers if it meant preventing the return of that spawn of darkness. My sword and my loyalty have never wavered." His words brought a hint of a smile to Malziek's face.

"The blood of our people has protected these lands, and again shall it flow, I fear, before our very gates ere the Citadel realizes the true danger. Laziness trumps action until the sword is at your throat and not a thousand miles away." Malziek stood and paced to the window, allowing the few and scattered rays of sun to warm his face. "The Citadel will not help us. They have abandoned us. They send their own to entertain my brash outbursts. He will return with news of . . . *nothing*."

His words struck forebodingly as I realized the intense feelings Malziek had for those in the Outpost. While to many it was just a station of duty, he felt personally tied to this land and those on it. I'd heard the story of his commanding bravery during one of the many sword lessons DarSheer had been giving me in our free moments between patrols.

"I know I am the case for much of this controversy," I said quietly. "I know I'm a stranger in a land who would rather I be a bad dream if it meant the rumors were false. I will do my part to see Mordën's reign end before it begins. My loyalty is to you and the Outpost and, in turn, to Ëonë. You have nothing to fear from me."

"If only that were true," Malziek sighed, and for the first time I saw him for the weary old man he was. His visage of powerful leader had faded and was replaced with the wrinkles and labored breathing akin to men his age. "Your very existence is to be feared, for as long as the people believe you to be alive, then there is a chance their darkest thoughts are coming true. We could barely hold back the scattered forces of darkness centuries ago. Now, with their master returned, we do not stand a chance. We shall be as a sandcastle on the beach before a great and mighty wave. You have damned us all, Phoenix DarkBairn."

He retreated from the window, and I allowed myself to swallow the feeling of guilt that had been balled up inside. His words stabbed deep, and it was all I could muster to keep from breaking form. I remained stationary as DarSheer stepped forward.

"My Lord?" He tilted his head, cautious to speak. Malziek wordlessly signaled his approval. "Phoenix's arrival may spell doom for us but only if we refuse to act. I do not hold that your men will do anything but stand by your side. Your men love you. The very gates of darkness can open before us and not one man will waver. They fear death, my lord, but they love you more. The words written eons ago in the Second Era are but words on an ancient parchment. The ink is nothing but the blood of dead thoughts. You command these men, not a prophecy written in the hubris of prophets for the betterment of their craft. If you tell these men to march across the Bridge itself, they would do it. I plead with you to fortify these walls and stand bold and true as Phoenix does. He stands with us because he is one of us."

I didn't realize I'd stopped breathing until DarSheer finished speaking, and I glanced quickly at Malziek. Face partially covered by the growing shadows as the torches began to fade, he smiled. The fire danced in his eyes, and he leaned back.

"Forgive my old folly," Malziek murmured as he placed a weathered hand atop my shoulder. "I am but a voice for the weak. You are not to blame for the evil spawned beyond the ocean. Mordën would have found another. Forgive an old man his weariness."

With that he turned and retreated from the chamber, the sword at his hip thudding against his thigh. DarSheer waited for him to leave the room entirely before turning to gaze out the window. The night had already drawn nigh as the sun dipped into its slumber.

"Do you think he truly considers me to be the cause for all of this?" I murmured.

"Are you not?"

"You and I and the rest of Ëonë believe so. But does he?"

"Malziek has seen many things and through his eyes might we also see. Do not take his despair for anger, Phoenix. I did not speak falsely when I said his men would follow him to their graves. There is fight left in his aged bones and their loyalty knows no limitations."

We strode from the room as the last torch died and the room was cast into shadows. Even the faint paleness of the sky was unable to brighten the chamber. The stairs felt equally long to descend but when we reached the doorway and Dwaith's looming figure ahead, I realized how much I'd come to cherish the Outpost. From the squabbling stable boys to the two kitchen girls and the men who stood in direct defiance to the blackness beyond, I understood their plight. Despite my alienation, I knew they were fighting for their homeland as I'd seen, or at least as far as my memory allowed me to see, the evil which Mordën contained.

DarSheer leaned against the edge of the table. He'd been unrelenting the last five hours in my studious exploration of history. I had found it fascinating, but it irked him I wasn't picking it up at the speed he needed. He exhaled slowly and for the fifth time, pointed a long finger at the small black splotch on the scroll.

"And what is important about Avalon?" his voice coached me. His eyes drilled into me.

"Avalon is the last city made by the Drucodians in the First Era?" I answered hesitantly.

"Is that a question?"

"It is the last city made by the Drucodians in the First Era," I amended with more confidence.

"And what's important about the Drucodians?" He placed his hands behind his back and paced the edge of the table as a fire roared in the fireplace.

"They were the first race made by Erëthuïl at the dawn of time. When he awoke from his eternal peaceful slumber, he realized he was exhausted with loneliness and desired company. So, he made the Luthi, beings of power tasked with the creation of Ëonë. Their names are forgot-

ten to time but before the first creature walked these plains, they made the water, the trees, the rock, and Erëthuïl was pleased. He sculpted from all the good emotions he'd created a race of beings with lesser power than the Luthi, for while he was proud of all they'd accomplished, they were not what he was entirely looking for. Right?"

"Historians and bards differ on that point," DarSheer cleared his throat, "but for the most part, yes. The Luthi were made to be perfect beings of light and helped Erëthuïl to form all that we now interact with our senses. But they were too similar to him. He desired others. Of a lesser strength."

"Thus, he made the Drucodians."

"And they look like?"

"Beings of grey skin with a cleft in their face running from their temple to just above their mouth. Their eyes are large, larger than a Human's, and are colored with sky-grey irises. They do not have hair but heads ridged with bone pushing up against their flesh. They do not have ears, but holes located where ears would be."

"Do you remember why this is?"

"Erëthuïl was still experimenting."

"No," he sighed exasperatedly. "Again."

"Ears were not . . . a thing, yet?" I probed for the right answer as the heat from the fireplace began to climb up my tunic. Sweat beaded on my back.

He finally relented. "In a way. It is believed that Erëthuïl does not hear sound the way we do. Therefore, ears were not something he deemed important."

"So why do Elfins and the rest of the exotic races here have them?"

"If you'd been listening when I told you," DarSheer returned to pacing about the table, "Mordën is actually the root cause of that. Mordën sculpted his own race, his master race, known as the Varglarian. To him, the screams and cries of the dying and oppressed were music, a foul delight. He wanted his creations to be able to absorb this sound. When Erëthuïl made the other races during the start of the Second Era, he also fashioned ears but this he did not for the purpose of sound, but to let Mordën know that everything he did, Erëthuïl was superior at."

"Wait, can Drucodians hear, then?"

He nodded. "They tell us they can hear muted versions of what we hear."

I scribbled in a blank parchment with the quill I'd been loaned. The smell of the ink drying on the parchment and the crackle of flames added to the atmosphere.

"What's next?"

"You've gotten ahead of yourself," he cautioned. "Finish up what we know about Drucodians."

"Drucodians were the only race to exist during the entirety of the First Era and fought in the First Great War when Mordën used his armies to march on the creation of his once fellow Luthi. They repelled him at the close of the First Era, though, and he nursed his wounds on the BlackBurg for centuries while he rebuilt power. Then, five years into the turn of the Second Era, he sent out a single messenger to Avalon, then known as Avalonenburg, ruled over by one of the three Drucodian kings, demanding that the Drucodians bow before him and reject Erëthuil. They refused, and he once again marched on the lands. But he had been smart and in his time on the island, he crafted a new weapon. Drakes and Rachnadons. The former were drakes of great strength and size, and the latter were arachnids of gigantic height and width. Some say that a Rachnadon's body is the size of a tavern and one can walk clear under it without stooping."

"This is all good and well, but what about the Creation of the Three?"

I wracked my brain for the event and inwardly cursed at my poor memory. The name jogged nothing. I shrugged.

"The Creation of the Three . . . races," DarSheer prompted.

"What about the Elfins?" I countered. "You forgot them. To combat the great threat to his world, Erëthuil made a second race, Elfins. He sculpted them to be proud but fair, noble but kind. They came to the aid of the Drucodian armies and helped keep Mordën from taking the Eastern Ward. But even with their addition, they couldn't keep him at bay for long. Mordën pushed them to their edge and was nearly victorious."

DarSheer smiled. "Good catch. I guess your memory isn't as bad as you claim. Now, of the Creation of the Three?"

"*The Creation of the Three was Erëthuil's final attempt to stop his old creation, the fallen Luthi Mordën. Twenty years after the creation of the Elfins, Erëthuil made Humans, Ebyians, and Inclings. Into Men he put stubbornness, loyalty, and a desire to be working. Ebyians, he tasked with the high places of the world, cities built into the sides of mountains and a single royal burgh at the tip of the peak reserved for each Ebyian clan's king. The working Ebyian were in their great rock cities far in the high reaches of mountains where they'd mine for the rare 'sky' jewels to sell to those below. He fueled into this race a quiet introverted desire to remain free in their halls and care little for the outside world but the trades and imports that fueled their kingdoms. There are two main clans today, the Northlings and the Southers, which care little for each other. He made Inclings to be peaceful and keep the world grounded once the war was over.*

"*A century or two passed as the three races adjusted to the world they'd been birthed into. In that time, Avalonenburg stemmed the tide of evil. But the Drucodians and Elfin numbers dropped drastically. It was clear they would fail to stop Mordën, yet they continued to fight. Once they had been readied, these three races marched in great host to Avalon. To do this they had to cross the Fallen Peaks in what was known as "The Advance of Misery" where a third of the force died due to Mordën's attempts to bury them under avalanches and snowstorms. They did this because the plan was to circle around and attack Mordën's rear forces, effectively sandwiching him between two armies.*

"*When they finally made it to Avalonenburg, the Elfins and Drucodians were retreating in full force. The Humans, led by their fourth High King, the High King Temporal, rallied together his forces and charged. The Ebyians chose to abandon the fight as did the Inclings, both races deeming it beyond their desires. Thankfully, the Humans were all that was needed, and the tide of the battle turned quickly. Mordën was defeated and on the steps of The High City, he was banished. With him, the High King also went into banishment for use of the Portal requires an equal offering of good as it does evil. Since then, the Humans have gone without a High King as Temporal took his heir with him.*"

"Do you remember why?"

"Only the king's firstborn or only born could command the Grey Cloaks."

"And why did the heir go with him?"

"His son could not stand to see his father banished alone, so he and all his loyal Cloaksmen went with him."

"Good, continue."

"Well, after the High King was banished, the people needed some form of ruler, but they chose against a king. The Custodian manages his role in these hallowed times of peace for the belief is a king is only needed in times of fear and war."

Near the end, my words had begun to slur as the warmth in the room and the lulling crackles and pops from the fireplace seemed to place anchors on my eyelids. DarSheer rolled up the map that was opened on the table. The words "The Third Era" had been scribed centuries ago in dramatic font. As he folded the map up, he gestured toward the door.

"You've mastered the art of identifying the races and their origins." DarSheer rolled up a scroll and dropped a large map, nearly the entire size of the table, down. He scrunched his nose and arranged it. "Ëonë is arranged into bits and pieces to make it easier to track where one is and where one is headed. See this mountain range?" He pointed to a long line of trudging triangles in the center of the map which went from the top to bottom of the continent, essentially dividing the lands in and equal measure. "Ëonë is split in half by the Fallen Peaks, a mountain range running from the northern coastal tip here, to the southernmost point, near the western walls of Glasbur. Two years into the start of the Second Era, the Council of Choices convened in the Citadel and chose to divide all the known world into areas easier to defend. The Eastern Ward is somewhat hilly, and its expanse lies along the coast and the occasional farms further inland. But where its wealth truly lies is Avalon, The Golden City. Though praised for its shimmering splendor, it serves a darker purpose, as the defense against an invasion from the east. It lies at the breadth of the only truly passable area through the Fallen Peaks."

"This is Glasbur?" I ran a finger over the small title that had been inked in gold.

"Glasbur there, Avalon here at the end of the Ethero Basin, and far in the west, free from the tribulations that plague the Eastern Ward, lies The High City. West of the mountains lies the Western Ward. East lies the Eastern Wards."

"Seems easy enough," I yawned. DarSheer took note of it.

"Lessons are over. Your time on the wall begins soon."

"The watch?" All weariness fled. "Am I ready? The others do not trust me."

"I wouldn't put you in that position if I didn't fully trust you. Mine is the only person's trust you should care for, besides Lord Malziek." He placed the scroll into a cubby then stepped back and surveyed the small library of resources that had been stored here.

Since my arrival, he'd been tasked by Malziek to instruct me in the history and rich lore of this world. It went by slowly, but each new battle logged into my mind dislodged a piece of my past, so I delved in with great haste, discovering both my past and his.

I yelped as the padded training sword thwacked mercilessly against my buttocks. My cry was accompanied by the snickering taunts of the guards watching as DarSheer chuckled. I rubbed at the stinging with chagrin. I lowered my blade and motioned for a moment to breathe as sweat beaded down my face and soaked my collar. The leather chest plate and armbands already reeked of sweat. DarSheer aimed for a stinging prod as the tip of his sword jabbed into my ribs. I lowered my blade and raised my hands in defeat.

"There's no honor in striking an opponent in a match when he is unarmed." I tried to use one of DarSheer's lines against him but he merely grinned.

"You are armed," he pointed out, "or do you imagine that training sword to be your walking stick? Never assume your opponent will treat you mercifully on the battlefield, least of all when he smells weakness. A Varg or Shade will not loiter around as you take your sweet time to read a book, water your flowers, and flirt with the tavern wench." His comical tone turned serious as he aimed his sword at my chest and let the gravity of his next words fall hard. "They'll go for your weak spots and strike hard. They will show *no mercy*."

"If your goal is to put me out of commission, you're doing a splendid job," I grumbled and prepared to deflect the next flurry of attacks.

"Consider yourself blessed by Erëthuïl if you can avoid using this training," DarSheer steadied his hand as he crouched, peering for a vulnerable spot in my defense. He feinted right and caused me to stumble over my own feet. With a painful jab he let his sword mark the spot of my death. We set up again, and he stomped forward in a flurry of hard attacks and slashes. I parried a slash and countered with a few vicious moves which sent him stumbling backward. He grinned his approval.

"Have you recovered any more memories?" He lowered his blade, and I mimed the same action, keeping a cautious eye on him as he approached.

"Just those." I acted calmly as he approached within arm's reach. In a sudden burst of energy, I lifted my blade and brought it down on him like a hammer over a nail. Equally quickly, he rolled to one side, his blade slicing at my unprotected legs and swiping me off my feet. I gasped as the breath was knocked from my lungs and stars danced before me.

"Your enemy will have tricks up his sleeve." DarSheer was unable to contain his boisterous laughter. "Just because he acts defenseless does not mean a dagger does not wait beneath his cloak. If they are in your embrace, they can kill you with haste. Keep your enemies at an arm's distance, *always*." He bit down on the last word and helped me to my feet.

"What about Malziek?" I inquired as we trudged wearily to the weapon building. "You haven't talked much about him since you first brought me here. What's his mystical tale? Once a bard, now a lord?"

"Malziek?" DarSheer seemed to lose himself in his thoughts, and as we walked, he stared up at the curling smoke which coiled into the dark night sky. Shadows of the men leaning against the stone walls as they warmed themselves around the braziers flickered thrice their size along the courtyard. Atop the walls, the huddled forms of frozen men stood watch. The Outpost's gold and white banners hung lazily from their wooden poles. Even the single mountain which had been hand stitched onto each banner couldn't muster the spirits of the fabric to blow bold into the night.

"The men seem to respect him," I prompted, "but I haven't seen him do much. Two years I've explored every inch of the grounds and yet am none the wiser when it comes to Malziek."

"Malziek comes from an offshoot of the High Kings, a line given longer life than the average man. It's said his sire was there the day Temporal banished Mordën and in silence watched his cousin, Temporal, enter the Portal. Whether or not this is but the exaggerated sweetness on the lips of tipsy bards is beyond the knowledge of any here present. But nonetheless it makes for good gossip. He holds a commanding presence, doesn't he? He's as secretive with his past as he is good with a blade. Most hide in their self-inflicted ignorance. For most, it is easier to blot out the parts of that past that bring horror and fear. Mordën once ruled the hearts and minds of every man, woman, and child west of the Bridge," DarSheer said softly. "Rumor has it, Mordën laughed hysterically as the High King Temporal banned him from Ëonë and sent him through the Portal. He was banished for good, with no chance to return and all the monster could do was laugh. Who knows if Malziek was there? He has done nothing to encourage the songs nor has he blotted out the scrolls that mention his name. The lines show his age, and he is mentioned by name in ancient texts. Unless another by his title lived, it is him."

"I always get the impression he is sad," I acknowledged as we placed the swords point first into a small bucket. Brenneth toiled in one corner with several other boys, scrubbing saddles vigorously. He waved as we strode from the small house. I returned the gesture in kind.

"If the rumors are true," DarSheer's face darkened, "he has very good reason. The horror and devastation Mordën wreaked in the First and Second Great Wars of both the First and Second Eras is lost on the succeeding generations of youth. We've nested too long in the bosom of peace. Many now forget what should never have been forgotten. Malziek asked to be repositioned to the Outpost. He knew what Mordën's return would mean. At the time, this place was an abandoned fortress from the First Era when Drucodians were the sole race. It was rebuilt and now stands an eyesore to our enemy. Lord Malziek said he wanted to be the first thing Mordën saw when he marched across the Bridge. The first face the damned 'Shadow King' saw when he took first blood."

"If Malziek is a descendent of royalty, why would he not be crowned the High King? He lives in a remote Outpost far from the trappings of a king. Here, he is a mere lord."

"When the High King Temporal was banished, his line was removed from the throne," DarSheer said darkly. "They were replaced with Custodians, watchmen of the realm. They but feed the linings of their pockets with the wealth from their people and speak in long flowery tones to those less intelligent than they. There have been a few good Custodians, don't get me wrong, but the one that currently occupies The High City is a farce. It was deemed kings would not be needed in a time of peace and prosperity. I believe kings are needed now more than ever."

We walked down the courtyard's faded cobblestones as a guard announced the watch change. The men who had been monitoring our duel had vanished, presumably taking their turn to watch over the wall and east to the Bridge. Ever since my arrival, Malziek had ordered twice the men to man the walls and thrice the normal amount per patrol. Even the stable boys, when they hurried out to fetch water from the small stream which trickled, were escorted by armed guards.

"Do you think it's possible all is true, including the rumors?" I asked quietly as we entered the small home which had been constructed for me on my arrival. My narrow cot at one end signaled the end to my pain and weariness as I stripped off my shirt. It protested and stuck to every inch of my chest with sweaty determination before I was able to peel it off.

DarSheer sat on his own bed on the other end of the hut and gazed at the single torch which lit the room. "I think we'd all be fools to believe it isn't. You yourself said the day I found you that he had returned. The light and rumbles across the Eleren Canal on the BlackBurg have not been seen since well before our time. Only records on faded parchment tell what happened the last time those furnaces were lit."

"And?"

"And what?"

"What do the records say? What happened to the world last time?"

DarSheer stared darkly into the flickering orange light. When he responded his voice was barely above a whisper. "The world burned until the ashes on the plains outnumbered the sands on the shore."

We spoke no more that night as he turned and began reading the small book he kept beneath his pillow. The moon shone down on my face through the narrow window above me as I drifted off, allowing the thin comfiness of the mattress to guide me in a dreamless sleep.

The days and weeks passed in drizzling slowness. On the northern plains, a few rogue battles broke out between scouts and bands of Varg, but for the most part, all was quiet. A foreboding sensation awoke me one grey morning. My breath plumed before me, and I coughed under the thin blanket. It was around the time DarSheer would be on watch duty, so I had the hut to myself. With trembling fingers, I reached for the torch, which had since burned low, and replaced it with another. Welcome heat spilled over me, hungrily attacking the cold spots. A knock on the door jolted me upright.

"Phoenix?" The small voice was both excited and urgent.

It had been a fortnight since the Messenger's departure and in that time, nothing had seemed to bring Brenneth joy. He slaved under

Altruic's harsh watch, and though he was not the only one to receive the brunt force of the stable master's displeasure, he seemed to be targeted more than the others. The excitement in his tone had me swinging my legs over the edge of the cot and striding to the door. I opened it enough for him to slip through before closing it. His cheeks were flushed from the cold, and he blew into his hands.

"What is so urgent that you wake me before the sun rises?" I yawned.

"Visitors!" He beamed. His unbridled enthusiasm at this ungodly hour was both impressive and annoying.

"The Messenger?" I gripped his shoulders. Could it be The High City believed us and was sending aid? Could it be Malziek had misunderstood?

"No." Brenneth's posture slumped slightly. Then he returned with a wide grin. "DarSheer made friends in Avalon on his last venture west. They're a band of musicians."

"You woke me from my sleep to tell me someone better than Topper with his out-of-tune gloshee is here?" I stared at him with a deadpan expression. I contemplated throttling him for a brief moment.

"Will you clear the cobwebs from your mind?" He slapped my chest indignantly. "This is a professional bard and his troupe. You know how rare it is for visitors, let alone those with news and song, to make it this far east."

"This still could have waited at least for the sun to wake." I rolled my eyes, but his smile was infectious. "How do you know they're any good?"

"They're in the tavern with Marian." He bounced from foot to foot. "I got a glimpse of them and heard some song they're gonna play for us all tonight, Lord Malziek willing."

"Malziek is not fond of strangers," I pointed out as hunger gnawed suddenly at my stomach. "Are they there now?"

"Yeah, being fed and quarters assigned."

"And DarSheer invited them here?"

"Yes."

"Be at peace." I placed a restraining hand on his shoulder, and he stopped bouncing. "Thank you for these tidings. You better return to the stables before Altruic finds more reasons to humiliate you."

He was gone from the hut faster than I could blink. I sighed. There were times his youthful eagerness was appreciated against the usual grim stares and silent patrols. Then there were times when I wish he'd leave me well enough alone. I exhaled, clearing my lungs. I was low on friends so I couldn't very well scare him off. The good with the bad. Something of that nature.

The short walk to the tavern was cold and wet. A faint drizzle pitter-pattered against the cobblestones with plunks and drips. Puddles reflected the sky perfectly so at the corner of my gaze, it seemed like a hole to a grey pit. Some guards leaned against the walls, protected by the overhang of the battlements. They eyed me with mild disinterest. Ever since DarSheer had gotten me started on practice drills, they'd become less hostile toward me. Some even cheered me on as I got a lucky jab in. Today, however, on this dreary morning, such comradery was not to be had. Their hoods ended just above their eyes. Some inhaled on long black pipes. The grey smoke spiraled up until it blended in with the low clouds. Others spoke in hushed tones to each other, hands and backs pressed to lit braziers of crackling light. With the sun still an hour or two from rising, the dark morning was abysmally cold.

I crossed the muddy courtyard and noted the fresh horse prints. Altruic would be worse than usual now that he had to be up so early on account of musicians. He always hated bards. Considered them worse than traitors since they embellished every story into unrecognizable jargon. Sure enough, his hoarse shouts filled the barns and stables. Brenneth scurried into sight. He frowned when he saw me.

"He's not in a great mood." The stable boy massaged his arm. "Apparently, one of the girls in the troupe is extra picky about the conditions for her mount."

"And I'm sure you're doing absolutely everything in your power to keep your head low and not call attention to yourself," I chuckled and rustled his hair.

He grinned. "A model stable lad." Then he was off into the shadows, leaping over patches of mud and puddles.

The tavern was the only place in the visible area that seemed to have any hopeful light to it. Many had dubbed it the "Eastward Inn." Orange light percolated from the slats over the windows. The stocky man on guard duty outside the door sniffed and stared about as if wishing he was inside and not cursed to stand in the cold. I crossed the last remaining distance until he noticed me and came to attention. Not out of respect for me, of course. Malziek did not look highly upon anyone slouching at their posts.

"Bairn." The man nodded.

"Cioness," I replied. I opened the door and stepped into the embracing warmth and merriment.

Smoke curled about the rafters. Mugs of ale and mead were being carried on platters. Marian, her smile radiant, turned at my approach. Her eyes softened when she spotted me. While most of the people here had taken to my sudden arrival with hesitant speculation, she was one of the few to show any kindness to me. Her motherly chuckle filled the room. Traverse, the owner of the tavern and a well-built man with muscular arms and a tanned visage, grinned through his bushy beard. He raised a glass and roared out. The room filled with resounding calls, and I took notice of the five strangers cooped up about the fireplace.

"You're up early, bairn." Traverse upended the drink and wiped droplets from his chin.

"Couldn't sleep." I sat down at one of the barstools and leaned in, conspiratorially. "Spill the ale. Who are the newcomers?"

He leaned in equally quiet and murmured conspiratorially. "Strange folk from Avalon, or so they'll say to any who ask. I think, though, by their garb and talk, them lots from the Cacian Hinterlands they are. Funny times we're in, bairn. First you come crawling to us on the eve of doom, and now these lot. I'm fine with a little added mystery but we've had more visitors these past weeks than I'm blasted comfortable with."

"I hear that DarSheer invited them here. They can't be bad if he was willing to send out an invite, right?"

"Then you've heard more than I," he snorted gruffly, but some of the lines lessened in his face. "All I knows is they've been asking about for a song. The tall chap, ugly looking bloke with the hood over his face, claims that they want to sing a song for our fine lads."

"Nothing harmful about some music." I shrugged and accepted the mug of piping hot ale. Steam floated about and I inhaled the pungent smell.

"No, there is none," he retorted softly, "but these aren't any musicians I've ever seen before. But that's not saying much. When Topper is your only exposure to their breed, well you can't be prepared for anything then, can you?" He strolled off to help Marian in the back and I was left alone to the bubbling giggles and bursts of laughter as the group at the fireplace huddled close.

The taller man Traverse had singled out finally stirred and removed his hood. His hair was cut ragged and hung below his ears. His short beard and perfectly trimmed mustache gave him a villainous appearance. He broke into a smile when he saw me. He spread his arms wide.

"Apologies, master bairn." His voice was thick and nasally. The other four stopped their conversation and stared at me. "My name is Blukarnon. I am a famed ballad writer, decorated poet, and lover of a good tale mixed with ale. We've traveled far to reach here."

I raised the mug slightly so as to not appear rude. "Greetings, Blukarnon and company. I wish you luck around here. These lot are grumpy as they are gloomy. The cold addles their humor, so be warned."

Blukarnon threw back his head and laughed a throaty laugh. At his neckline, a gold pendant danced. "They have not met my troupe, then. The three girls sing better than a siren at sea. Their haunted vocals have stirred tears from the worst murderer of The High City. That bairn there is my son, Coliver." Coliver bowed his head dramatically.

"A pleasure to meet you all. When do we get the honor of hearing your talent?" I sipped the drink.

"We've been told the leader of your company is still in his ivory tower. Apparently, we're in limbo until he approves our presence." He snorted to make clear his thoughts on that matter. "We look to play tonight."

"Well, may Erëthuïl shine on your efforts." I downed the last of the drink and stood. I was considerably warmer and happier than when I'd walked in.

"Yours as well, fine bairn." Blukarnon bowed low.

"If you happen to meet Topper, give him some leeway," I said as if in afterthought.

"I welcome this advice. Who is this Topper?"

"It's complicated." I stopped at the door and gave Marian a wave as she bustled from the back. "But you'll know him when you hear him."

With that, I left a puzzled grin on the bard's face and exited into the harsh cold of the courtyard. On the horizon, a pale pink was creeping up and chasing the dark blue and deep black of the night. I didn't realize how long I'd been in the tavern. The watch had already changed and DarSheer trudged wearily toward our hut. He was intercepted almost immediately by a small man with a floppy hat on his head and a vibrant purple shirt. His stringed instrument, known as a gloshee, was already in his hands. The small fiddle-like instrument had three strings which were held tight by the carved mouths of two lionesses. At one end, the strings curved upward into the small drums which sat smaller than a thumb. Played to perfection, a beautiful melody of drums and strings could entrap anyone who heard it.

"Morning, Broadsword." Topper leapt in front of DarSheer, using the man's familiar nickname. "I have much to inquire from you."

"Mornin', Topper," DarSheer sighed as he came to a stop. "I'm not in the mood to humor your latest poem nor do I care to hear again of the tales surrounding the start of our time."

Topper frowned, his exaggerated features lit by the flickering torch-light. "I hear tell of strangers. Even worse, strange bards. They say you brought them in. Tell me you would not do this dishonor to me, your source of entertainment. It is a great insult." His eyes narrowed as he fondled his instrument with coveted admiration.

"They're in the tavern. Their presence is not meant to detract from your skill, merely add to it. Now move aside, please. It's been a long watch, and I fear if I don't find a bed I'll sleep on my feet."

He pushed past the stuttering musician and into our hut. I closed the distance. "There will be time for merriment and jest later," I comforted Topper as his shoulders sank in defeat.

He slowly walked off, the gloshee hanging at his side in silent sadness. The fires sent shadows racing up and down the looming walls. Standing at the mouth of my hut, the tavern lurked to the far right, under a large overhang of stone. Directly in front was the training grounds. To the left ran the small trail to the gate and the two staircases that hiked up the stone wall to the ramparts above. In the center of the entire thing, the tower stood gleaming and proud. From its top, one could see in all directions, most importantly toward the Bridge where enemy forces were likely to come from and to the west where visitors could be seen still a far way off.

My time to take over the watch had arrived. I walked the steps to the battlements and greeted the shivering kid on watch. KcNuck, as he was called, greeted me with a frozen nod.

"About time you showed up," he stuttered. The wind and cold increased tenfold as the thick walls no longer protected me. Atop the stoned divider, all eyes could see you and nothing hindered the icy touch of the ocean breeze. Goosebumps raced up and down my arms.

"I lost track of time bantering with the new bard and his traveling troupe," I returned in greeting.

"Is that who all the commotion was about this morning?"

"You saw them?" I shivered as the cold seeped through my garments. Not even the thick padded leather held the cold at bay up here.

"They came riding with a procession of horns as if they intended to bequeath titles of royalty to all," KcNuck snorted. "You'd have to be deafer than a dumb brick to not hear them. I'm surprised Lord Malziek didn't awake instantly."

"Let's hope they don't cause a ruckus," I sniffed as he removed the coat from around his shoulders and handed to me. He rubbed his arms as fog ballooned from his exhalations. "Where were you yesterday? Altruic was in knots over the state of the stables. I imagine he has a special word for you when you return."

"Some of the men on the West Wall were playing their hand at Chancing." KcNuck grinned sheepishly. "I made a rich bet that Tolard, the daft bloke, couldn't last without his coat up here more than a few minutes. I'm now a richer lad and Tolard a colder idiot." He laughed.

He shivered as I slipped beneath the warm embrace of the fur-lined coat. A necessity atop the wall, the coats were covered on the exterior with thick pads to prevent arrows from sticking. A hood even hung along my back, which if thrown over my head, could, in theory, prevent some damage from projectiles. Beneath, the coat was lined with the heat-holding fur.

I watched as the boy moved his way closer to a torch, using its slight radius of warmth to momentarily break the ice on his arms. At the tender age of thirteen, he held as much responsibility as the oldest man, and it showed. Shoulders slumped, body held close against the winds, he looked miserable. "I gained five thruki, and he's forced to take up my watch next fortnight. The men, they actually laughed." His face adopted a distant expression. "I haven't seen them so happy since I started my time on the walls. They laughed, Phoenix, like not the laugh that comes at the bottom of an ale. It was a genuine hopeful heart-warming chuckle. Who knew a sound could rekindle such hope."

"Five thruki?" I smiled. "Such wealth and nothing to spend it on?"

"DarSheer promised me I could have whatever I wanted from Avalon on his next venture. You know how much five thruki goes for in The Golden City?"

I shook my head. "I've not been, same as you. But if DarSheer's rumors are true, that could buy a fancy set of clothing or a new sword. Tolard must've been fuming."

"His exhalations created more cloud than the smoke from the fire." KcNuck grinned wide.

He turned once again and descended out of sight. My heart throbbed with pained sympathy. I breathed deeply and faced the expanding plateau which vanished into the darkness beyond. Above me, the banner now snapped in the growing wind and the fires flickered in response. Spaced every fourth crenel, the somber-faced men stood motionless. Only our eyes swept across the land before us. Some of the men had come to learn quickly that a moving target is easier to see. Even the torches were placed to cast their shadows over the guarding forms so as to conceal our locations. To an approaching horde, no man was visible on the wall. Only the fires signaled the inhabitance of the Outpost and the occasional shout or cry from someone inside.

A thick fog shifted off the ocean and enveloped the Outpost in its moist hug. For once, the muted sounds of conversations in the courtyard were no longer audible as each eye stared about apprehensively. Even the horses and wind had gone silent. I reached slowly for the sword at my waist as I moved my head from the courtyard to the far reaches of the opposite fortress wall, nearly obstructed by mist.

A few feet to my right, I heard Throbb's steady voice. "Do you think we should wake Lord Malziek?"

He was met with a faint response. "It's a simple case of fog. Quit your whining," Kissinger said.

"Since when did fog decide to drape itself about us like a low-cut cloth over a seductive bosom, ehh Kissinger?" Throbb snapped back, his calm voice breaking.

A thick silence hung off our coats and draped itself over the Outpost battlements. The flags hung lifelessly along their stands. The wind had died completely. It was as if all of Ëonë held its breath for whatever was about to happen. I shivered and buried myself deeper into the coat. The fog crept closer like a white blanket. I stepped back as the first touches of the mist reached out, like thin fingers, at me. Instinctively, as DarSheer's training had drilled in, I drew my sword. The faint glint of steel shone as I readied it. Across the wall, similar sounds of metal against leather could be heard. Someone grabbed a torch and began waving it about. Shadows danced against the haunted wines of the wind and swirling cloud.

"I've never seen anything like this," Throbb muttered nervously as he batted away a tendril of fog. "DarkBairn? You think this might be some more of your doing?"

"Yeah," my eyes were glued to the approaching fog, "I brought this wall of impenetrable fog just so I could be asked if it's some of my doing. For my next act I'm going to do a backflip off the wall and land with nary a scratch."

"I'd pay good money to see that," a voice spoke as the fog continued to advance.

"Hush!"

"I just thought I'd ask," Throbb retorted. "This isn't exactly normal. It usually holds at the shoreline. Someone get me DarSheer!"

Below, people had begun to take note of the odd phenomenon and DarSheer appeared at the doorway to our hut. Candlelight flickered on in some of the officers' windows as they appeared in their doorways. The long sprawling barracks butted against the West Wall as the fog curled toward them.

Several men began to talk, and some lit more torches. Movement began to waken on the battlements as additional watchmen hurried to their posts. In a time like this, safety was paramount and Malziek, having doubled the watch, was not one for taking chances. Even the distant windows of the single tall building jutting into the sky were glowing softly as Malziek's face appeared. All the Outpost, old and young, animal and human, held their collective breath.

A small beast, covered in bristling spines with glowing beady red eyes, rushed past, his twitching nose sending several of the younger members of the watch on a backpedaling panic as he leapt over the battlements. I let out a shaky laugh. The air hung thick then dissipated. The shoreline returned and we could see the waves crashing against the sand. I let out the breath I'd been holding.

"Back to work everyone," came the call below. The entire Outpost stirred as most slowly drifted back into shuttered rooms or returned to their soft talk over raging fires.

"You'd think by now I'd know a bloody ferrek when I see one," Throbb muttered, thoroughly annoyed with himself.

"That's what you call that thing?" I exhaled. "I've seen several on my shoreline scouting ventures.

"They're perfectly harmless, unless you're a stuck-up golden." A large man bit out a bitter laugh.

"Watch your mouth, Othrain." Throbb shook his head.

"Golden?" I whispered out of the side of my mouth, turning back to the front of the keep.

"A term used to describe those unfortunate souls to be born an Elfin." Throbb gritted his teeth and exhaled slowly.

I let them divert into bickering, something a lot of watchmen did to pass the time, as I gazed back out at the ocean lapping at the shores beyond.

The black water, its glistening spray licking at the shimmering sands, rose and fell. The solid stone bridge which jutted out and into the darkness with no end in sight seemed the sole evidence of a civilized era. Rolling hills on all three sides of the Outpost were met only with thick forests of lush green pines and spruces. The winding road behind the Outpost, dubbed "the Westerly Road," was rarely trod on this far east, but when carts of supplies or the eager young faces of new recruits would show, suddenly it became the most important road in all of Ëonë, garnering attention from the lowest to the highest. Since I'd been made a watchmen and scout along the eastern shorelines between the Prickly Rocks and Valley Swamps far south, the road had brought action only thrice, in two years. Now in the manner of a month, it had been traveled twice. What with the last line of trees and the gap between there to our rear-located gates, it was easy to spot a traveler miles before his arrival.

I leaned against the battlement, feeling it support me. The fog sent rivulets of water down my leather tunic. What guilt I'd held when I first arrived, or felt spawn at any mention of my supposed cursed arrival, had vanished. All that was left was the haunting cry of the ocean beyond and beyond even that, the gloomy mountains and black-stoned shores of the BlackBurg. I could see its shoreline and the faint outlines of a black peak against a salmon-pink sky.

"Anyone ever gone across the Bridge?" I finally asked. Throbb paused in his arguing and turned, standing next to me.

"And what man would be crazy to so much as think about that?" he scoffed. "Any young lad sets a toe on those ancient stones finds himself whisked into an early grave."

"Or old codger perhaps?"

"Watch your tongue lest you have it severed." He glared at me and placed one hand on his sword hilt.

"Wisdom is often despised coming from an old codger." I winked at him and avoided the slap I knew was coming.

"Watch it, bairn," he snorted. "Plenty of good men have died on this side of the Bridge. No reason to add that number on the other side. Fools and idiots, I say. Only a moron tests the patience of that simmering volcano. If all these rumors are true of *his* return, the danger is even greater."

He turned back and began hurling insults at the other watchmen. I gazed once again across the ocean. Two years I'd been here and, in that time, few raiding parties of Varglarian had dared cross the Bridge. Each time they'd been kept back with minimal casualties. Corus had been the last to fall, a blond bairn with a tuft of hair sprouting beneath his chin. He'd been standing right where I stood when he died. However, recently, we'd had as many as six attacks. The movement on the black shore was growing and with it, an increased amount of danger. The grim thought settled in and for the remainder of the watch I felt the hot points of a dozen arrows on my body. I twitched at a soft rustle of my cloak or the itch of my blanket. If I didn't die from an arrow, my own anticipation would do my heart in.

A soft gloved hand shook my shoulder and with a jolt of panicked realization, I jerked upwards. Falling asleep on the watch was expressly forbidden and it had happened only once since I'd been here. The older man had been stripped and flogged as a reminder of the importance of the watch. But the bright and eager eyes piercing the cold fog of morning was not the watchmaster ready to beat me upside the head.

Neither was it Malziek swearing he'd throw me hide and all into the ocean.

"Hey, Phoenix." Brenneth's grin was enough to form a smile on my own face as I shook the once relaxing waves of sleep away.

"Brenneth, blasted, you terrified me." I brushed my jacket's creases out and noticed his unprotected arms, shivering in the cold of the morning light. Yet somehow, his grin remained.

"Marian downstairs been brewing us all a fine pot of coffee," the eager stable boy chirped. "And besides, it's the end of your watch. I figured I'd wake you before the shift change."

I glanced up at the blue sky dotted with grey clouds. The sun was nearly fully over the horizon. I had been asleep a while and yet no one had seemed to notice. Each were tuned in only to their own miserable existence.

"The gesture is much appreciated," I exhaled, my breath ballooning out. "I owe you. Now get on before they ask to know your reasons for being up here. I'll see you downstairs."

Brenneth's speedy exist sent me yawning as I glanced over to where Throbb appeared to be standing stoically into the face of the frigid dawn, his shoulders slumped. I walked over, grabbing one shoulder and shaking it lightly. If I'd had the kindness done to me, best to forward it on. Throbb's jolt before turning was an answer enough.

"Blast it," he chided softly, holding his blanket tighter around him. "No need to shake an old man, bairn."

"For the last time, Throbb," I said casually as the men for the next watch arrived, "it's Phoenix. You can call me Phoenix."

I handed my jacket to a short stubby boy, no older than twelve, who took it. His lips were already blue as the ocean air wafted over. There were advantages to being near the coast, but on days like this there were very many disadvantages.

I stomped down the steep flight of stone steps and felt the softer ground of grass and mud. My steps squelched and I knew with a sigh that half my day would be spent cleaning mud off them. Outside, only one place in the entire area seemed to be rejecting the dismal attitude.

Set with its circular sides, the building belched friendly smoke from its one chimney.

The tail end of the morning saw the tavern's door swinging every few seconds as many came and went in search of hot beverages and a steaming breakfast. The door swung open and laughter and boisterous clamoring thundered out. It was like being hit in the face with a warm sound.

I entered, minding my way as I avoided stomping on feet or tripping over pointy elbows. Scabbards stuck at awkward angles out of tables and chairs. The curling haze of smoke above as men smoked and the fire burning in the center of the room twirled about in a mesmerizing flashy dance. A merry cry for more ale sent a ripple of cheers through the small room. A boy no older than I raised a wooden mug and downed the contents in a single swig. A second roar of approval filled the room as hands slapped his back and a gruff voice bellowed out:

"He's a man now I tell yer! That bloomin' youngin's a man now!" Laughter filled the room.

In one corner, a group of shivering boys, presumably from the stables, sat huddled around the fireplace. They held hands out to the roaring flames as if they intended to burn the cold off. I moved past them, careful not to step on the feet which protruded into the walkways.

"Another ale?" The friendly voice of Marian somehow managed to reach me over the commotion. Behind her, roaring in mutual laughter with a group of watchmen, stood Traverse. He was wearing his thick brown cloak, which hung around his shoulders and made him appear twice as large as he was.

"You know it, Marian." I smiled back, finding an empty table and sliding in.

As per their time-honored tradition, Traverse and Marian had set the tables with food prior to its occupancy, allowing patrons to eat the moment they sat. While some crumbs and slices of cheese found their way into leaving pockets, most found itself in the bellies of hungry boys and starving watchmen.

I dug hungrily into the freshly baked brown loaf of bread. Breaking the crust with a single soft tug sent small steams of hot air up. The smell. I inhaled and let my weariness drift off. The smell of Marian's bread was enough to fill the most famished traveler. The loaf was enough to lend fighting strength to any for days on end. Famed for its hard shell of a crust but softer doughier interior, it was a staple of the inn. The platter next to it contained juicy fruits and salty dried meat.

I spread a small cube of hand-churned butter over a slice of the bread, letting the warm butter melt into the doughy center before popping it into my mouth. Marian made her way over in an efficient fashion as only she could do in a room full of men. Her nimble figure allowed her to slip between patrons, her long arms to hold trays above their heads. She placed a wooden plate of vegetables, eggs, sausages, and what appeared to be some unidentified meat. At the far end of the room, a song had broken out. The boy who had downed the ale before was standing atop a table and belting out a familiar tune. Every time he finished his verse, tankards would thump against the hard wood tables and feet would stomp as voices spoke in unison.

So, tell me a tale as old as time

To which the crowd roared back: *Oh, tell us a tale of the king in his prime!*

He stood chest abroad no ill will to blame

The room belted in response: *Oh, tell us a tale of the king and his fame!*

When freedom was threatened his sword he would draw

A man's deep tenor rang out: *Oh, tell us a tale of the king and his claw!*

A tempest his swings overhead would cleave

The entire room including Marian and Traverse bellowed out: *Oh, tell us a tale of the king whose victims he'd leave!*

Yo, over the dangerous road a tale for a bard to rhyme

To which the crowd roared back: *Oh, tell us a tale of the king in his prime!*

The room thundered its approval as the boy dismounted the table and blushed. Outstretched hands shook him and clapped his small shoulders. Feet drummed again and a dozen mugs were thrust high into the air. Their contents sloshed out the sides and rained on the patrons. Some clamored for more song while others just sat and wiped the wetness from their eyes and beards.

"Three cheers for the bairn!"

"He's a man now he is, not a bairn!"

"That's what I said."

"You said bairn."

"Oh, hush and be at peace ya imbecile. Three cheers!" The room roared with approval.

"You know that song has more verses than years I've lived," Marian laughed merrily.

"They seemed to love it." I nodded, mouth full of bread. "I've heard it on the lips of many a weary watchman, but I do not know its meaning. Who was he? This king?"

"It's a ballad for the High King Temporal, of the Second Era. It's because of him that we're free to begin with. He ended Mordën's war of terror and banished the shadow prince to lands beyond our sight," she responded softly. "With rumors of Mordën's return, some believe that the High King himself will return as well. All wishful thoughts formed from the dregs found in the bottom of a mug, I'm afraid."

I cupped my hands around the tankard and felt the smoothed wood in my hands, letting the heat simmer through. I glanced around. Spread out in a circular spread, the twenty tables allowed nearly forty patrons in at one time. I sipped the strong ale. Like a magical elixir, my eyes widened, and I felt warmth flowing through me. Leave it to Traverse and Marian to wake up even the most zombified of watchmen. Marian gave me a small smile and bustled off. As she meandered through the sprawling appendages and cloaks, she was greeted with high praise and well wishes. There wasn't a man in the Outpost who didn't consider her their savior, for her food and warmth gave them strength. Even the five musicians cheered as she passed and the wiry Blukarnon called for more ale. He didn't seem frustrated by his inability to perform last night. In fact, he seemed happier and more outgoing than the night prior.

Brenneth slid across from me, his own smaller version of my meal in his hands. He set a mug of ale down. I gave him a nod, still entrapped in my breakfast. We sat for a few moments, infatuated with our food until he burped and pushed his empty plate aside.

"You know," he said as I buttered a slice of rich bread, "you wouldn't fall asleep if you just slept."

"A fine observation, Brenneth," I murmured over the edge of my cup. "Next time DarSheer tries to grab me for my seventh practice of the day, I'll tell him that."

The boy wrinkled his nose. "Why do you think he's putting you through all those sessions?"

He gulped down his ale. Far too young for such a beverage, he'd nevertheless convinced Traverse of his manly status, spinning stories until he coaxed the beverage out of its cask and into a mug. If Brenneth could do anything with his skilled maneuvering, it was convincing someone of something they shouldn't do.

"I'm not a warrior." I took a bite of the bread and rolled my eyes in ecstasy. "Mordën has left me no choice and I am abysmal with any sort of weapon. DarSheer agreed to give me training to improve this deficiency within me."

"Well, you're getting good. Not great, mind you. Even I could defeat you. I've been training since I could stand. DarSheer says my father was a great swordsman, and I'm to take after him." He wolfed down a portion of my bread.

I eyed him thoughtfully. DarSheer had pulled me aside one warm summer morning and spoke of Brenneth's past. His father had been a watchman and his mother used to be one of the tavern maids. Interactions of those sort between watchers and the tavern folk were expressly forbidden but Brenneth's dad had been taken with her beauty. They'd kept it a secret, believing their love a tantalizing mystery to enjoy. When his father had gone out on a scouting mission, he'd fallen to a surprise raid by Varglarians. They never recovered the body. Upon hearing these tidings, Brenneth's mother was inconsolable and took to walking the ramparts without coat or fire to warm her. Despite the other scouts, who had been able to retreat and live, speaking plainly of his death, she believed them all wrong.

Brenneth had been just a few months old, and his own mother was unable to nurse him or take care of him. At long last, driven mad by her grief, she'd ridden out from the protection of the Outpost and was never seen again. DarSheer theorized she'd gone looking for her love and had also fallen to the curved blades of Varglarian scouts. When Brenneth was old enough to question about his parents, Lord Malziek and DarSheer thought it best to tell the boy they lived in luxury in The High City instead of telling him they'd died. Brenneth lived every daydreaming he might someday meet his parents, but he never would. This knowledge made my heart fracture every time he mentioned finding his father or traveling one day to The High City in search of them. I spun my spoon about thick portions of stew in deep reverie, wondering if I should break the news to him. But when I saw the glint of excitement in his eyes and remembered how despite the conditions here, he managed to keep himself upbeat, I couldn't bring myself to tell him. It wasn't right for a stranger to know more about his family than him. So, I let him live in ignorant bliss.

"DarSheer says I'll be ready for the wall, and he's selected you to train me."

"Is that why you're being so nice to me?" I asked, amused as he dug into my uneaten tray of fruit.

"I figure, why not learn from the bbest?" His smile was warming. I turned away, the guilt racking me.

"I hardly qualify as that, but if DarSheer commands it, it shall be done."

"You do not wish this burden?" His voice fell. I saw the hurt in his eyes.

"Do not believe this," I said hastily. "I simply meant that I am no great teacher, but I will endeavor to instruct in what I know."

He leapt away from the table, his emptied mug falling with a thud and rolling under the table. Before I could call after him, he was off, speeding out the door. The stable boys by the fire raced after him. I watched them holler and shout out the door, and I drowned my discomfort in the bottoms of the tankard. I shook off the feeling of unease and was about to leave but nearly leapt out of my skin at the hand that grasped my shoulder abrasively.

"Have you learned nothing?" DarSheer's voice whispered behind me.

I calmed my beating heart. "Like?"

"Like keeping your back to a wall and monitoring the windows and door?" He slipped into the spot recently vacated by Brenneth and shook his head.

"Why would I need to do that here? Are you trying to make me jump at shadows? Paranoid of the friendliest touch? Should I sound the alarm next time Marian smiles at me?"

"I'm trying to bolster your senses, Phoenix. You can't be expected to survive this far east if you're slumbering with daggers in your back."

I leaned back, finishing off the ale in a large swill, before it got lukewarm. Setting the heavy mug down, I stared into my friend's eyes.

"You really, really, need to let me enjoy my breakfast before terrifying me for the rest of the day. My heart can only take so many life-threatening jolts."

He smiled, a rare sight these days. "The raids are becoming more and more commonplace. We've repelled how many Bridge attempts in the last two months?"

"Six," I admitted. The Varglarian had become increasingly bold, not even attempting to hide themselves as they marched over the stone Bridge. When I'd first arrived, raids were so rare that some watchmen believed the previous raid had killed off the entire Varg race, before inevitably months later another band would be spotted. Now, the rarity was to go a month without at least two raids.

They'd come in the night, whispering and hissing in their dark language. Their eyes burned like red hot embers, and while it created a horrifying appearance, it did not assist them in secrecy. We could often see their hunting groups long before they reached the gate. The call to arms would be sounded and minutes later, our bowmen would be atop the wall taking shots at any movement. Hours of quiet grey would pass before any survivors would charge the walls. I never understood their suicidal abandon. Five Varg could not take on several hundred well-armed men who sat fortified behind their walls. Yet time after time, sometimes in larger sometimes in smaller groups, they would assail the walls only to be repelled or completely wiped out.

"Six on our front alone." He frowned. "I have reports of fishing villages far north along the Curved Coast. Or rather I should say I've lost any contact with them. They rely on us for food and information. They wouldn't willingly close a line. I've sent my best scouts to see if any survived but if these raids pick up, soon even our walls won't repel them. It concerns me that they have found a way to the mainland that does not traverse the Bridge."

"Perhaps they've realized boats are a thing." I shrugged.

"Cheery thought, Broadsword." Marian brought a fresh platter of bread and cheese, a small bowl of horse stew, and a mug of ale next to it. The nickname "Broadsword" was well earned. DarSheer's weapon of choice dealt memorable damage in combat or practice. I massaged a hidden bruise.

"Fair Marian," DarSheer grinned and began slurping up the stew, "saltier than last time but a blessing evermore."

She faked offense then chortled as she hurried off. I watched her go, feeling for the first time a sense of familiarity. What mini squabbles the men got into, or the stable boys bickered over, always ended when they stepped foot here. No one could continue a grudge, no matter how deeply seeded, when Marian and her bowls of stew were presented or Traverse with his bottomless mugs of ale and cider.

"She catches your fancy?" DarSheer never missed any gaze, no matter how miniscule.

My face flamed. I feigned interest in the wooden beams above. "DarSheer . . ."

"Don't take offense, young master," he chuckled, "lots of bairns find Marian to be their first kindle. She's a fine woman, not to mention one of the only ones here, but she is a busy one. You know the rules in place are there for good reason. You'd do better to wait. Marian is a nice enough lass but annoy her or Traverse and you're eating cold mushrooms for weeks with double the watch duty."

"I didn't mean it like that," I bit out tightly. "I was simply pondering how much you all have become to be my family. But if such thoughts are to be misconstrued then I shall be forced to consider you all barbarians."

"A fair trade!" He laughed. "I meant no harm, a simple notice. Nothing to be ashamed of. Young Brenneth there seems to believe he will court her till she finally gives in."

"Court her?" I rolled my eyes. "He also believes he is Erëthuïl's gift to stable boys and that he will one day become Custodian and bring his parents back into his life." It was a shameful jab and I felt awful the moment it left my lips.

DarSheer hid his face behind his mug as he gulped down his ale. We stewed in silence over the bowls of stew before he finally spoke again. "We did what we thought would keep his spirits up. No one fights when they believe they have nothing left to live for. Hope is our last great weapon. Every man here has reason to hope. It was not in our ability to deny that to the young stable boy. He nears manhood and has earned the right to feign interest in the wench. She knows it. As do us all. Even Brenneth himself knows it. A harmless attempt at stealing a third morsel."

I brushed off the feeling and looked about. "Speaking of our esteemed stable boy, he tells me I'm to instruct him in the ways of the watch? Would this not be better handled by say Throbb or even the foul-mouthed Othrain?"

"You've personally seen Mordën. You've said yourself you remember Nightshades. The last time Mordën stepped foot in Ëonë was hundreds of years ago at the closing of the Second Era when Temporal banished him. Over four hundred years has passed since those days and at long last we hear rumors of his return. The iron forges of the BlackBurg burn hot as they did centuries ago. Raids have increased in frequency, and you sit before us, a stranger to our lands. Some men are blinded by their disbelief. Others don't even have eyes. There are still some among us who pass down the tales and legends, embellished though they may be, of those dark times when we lived in fear. We must fear the worst now. If he has returned, and we are to fight against him, we will need every resource in our armory. You are not the only living being to know him, but those scattered handful that have lived are beyond our messages. Only the Drucodians know more, and they hide in their hidden city in the north. I say all this to enlighten you. While many here possess far greater physical ability in the art of swordplay, it is not a sword in hand that will keep us alive. Knowledge of our foe shall be our savior. Some Drucodians have lived since the beginning of our world and those ancient beings live in the deep reaches of the mountains. We know not any longer where their hidden city lies. In the short time we have, you are the only one, and this Lord Malziek agrees with, that can properly prepare us."

"What of the distrust the watchmen all feel for me?" I pushed crumbs about on the table. "I know their looks and feel their disdain. I train him and he will adopt that same distance from them."

"Any distrust is the topsoil of their lives, Phoenix. The men here are too busy to wonder, though they may think they have time. You've been here two years and I've never seen such a close-knit group accept someone out of the blue like they've done to you. To you it may feel like they are distant, but truly you would know if they did not accept you. Do not confuse stray glances and whispers behind gloved hands to mean enmity and distrust are the only things they feel. Wherever you come from you may feel left out, but trust me when I say, this is more of a welcome than I would have hoped for."

"Fine." I gritted my teeth. I stood and began stacking dishes before a girl, roughly a year younger than I, scurried over. She wore a simple dress and an apron strung about. She was sent here to help Marian.

"You best be on then, Phoenix." DarSheer thanked the girl with a nod. "The fog bank from last night is perfect cover for a surprise raid. I fear they may have come across the Bridge without warning."

"Yes. Who needs sleep anyway?" I stood as the girl took our dishes. "My humble gratitude, Annika." I bowed slightly to the girl. She blushed and tripped over herself as she carried the dishes out of sight and into the backroom.

"If not Marian, perhaps her?" DarSheer's eyes twinkled merrily. I smacked him aggressively.

"What is with you trying to get me entangled with every female this side of the Fallen Peaks? Rules . . . policies? Have you heard of them?" I hissed as we stepped outside the bustling tavern. Lord Malziek stood at the training grounds, chewing out some unfortunate sod.

"I do it for my amusement." He shrugged nonchalantly.

I shook my head as we headed toward the stable. My mount, a dappled grey chestnut mare with a flowing mane that tickled my nose when we moved at fast-paced gallops, was waiting for me. Her large eyes watched me as I approached, and she whinnied her greeting. I patted her soft neck and felt her muscles tense then relax. When we'd first met, she was skittish and standoffish. Even the apples I brought couldn't get her to permit me on her back. Here in the dimly lit stables, I'd finally made peace with her. Brenneth appeared and smiled his toothy grin. He'd seemingly forgotten that I'd offended him earlier.

"We've been spoiling her," he said proudly. "Best-fed horse this side of the Fallen Peaks. When do we start my training?"

"We'll take watch tonight or tomorrow's dawn." I kissed the mare's long nose, and she bucked her head softly in protest.

"Yes!" He spun in place and bolted back into the dimly lit stable.

His enthusiasm was infectious. The promise of a ballad tonight only added to that excitement. But before I could do any of that, I needed sleep. It was a short trudge to my hut and a shorter stroll to my cot. The nightmares began as soon as I closed my eyes.

I gasped and sat up. The talons reaching for me faded with the wakeful jolt. I forced back the memories of pain that constantly assailed me. They were the same every night. *Her* face. *Her* smile. *Her* eyes. In every fearful dream she turned in fear and shouted something. It was as if the world moved in slow motion. In each moment, I fought against the restraints of memory and tried to call out to her. But she always vanished into the shadows of tunnels. Dark tunnels and caves. It wasn't the images of death and ruination, of indescribable pain tearing through my body as I gasped on a bed of sharp objects, that made me curse the few tears I allowed in the darkest shadows where no one could see. All that paled in comparison to *her*. I wiped the sweat away and stood. My legs shook. I could take all the fear and pain this world had to offer. But that one pain, I could not live with. I remembered her smile, her hair, the warmth in her hug. Then it was torn from me and all I felt was cold grief.

In practiced manner, I slipped into my tunic and tightened the belt around my waist. Then I slipped my boots on. For a long breath I just sat there, head in my hands.

"Then I am happy this is not a fictional world." She giggled. *"If it was, who knows what might happen?"*

A tear fell down my cheek. I did nothing to stop it. A second and a third joined it. It was all so wrong.

Of course, something is wrong. I'm walking with you and can't seem to create a sentence without looking like a dork.

The flames in the torch before me flickered suddenly and in the hottest parts of the fire, I saw her, once again turning back while being pushed forward. Her mouth opened in a silent scream and the image vanished.

"Why have you left me?" I murmured softly. Tears flowed like a stream. My breath was raspy, and I hiccupped. "Blast it all, Katy. I miss you so much. My heart breaks and I do not know how to heal the fractures. It's so cold here. I'm so alone. He has given me a plan, a way out, if I but bend the knee."

"Well, so long as you have a plan." She winked and bounded away.

"A plan, yes," I whispered into my fingers, "but at what cost?"

I buried my head in my hands and wept until I had no tears left. My hair stood on end and goosebumps covered my arms. Still, I sat in miserable silence. These people had accepted me as one of their own, but I knew with a horrible certainty, I would always be an outcast here. I was nothing more than an answer to a prophecy. My chest throbbed and I inhaled deeply. A sharp rap on the door signaled Brenneth's arrival. Quickly, I inhaled and rubbed any trace of tears from my face.

Brenneth was already waiting outside, his stable outfit replaced with a simple tunic and worn britches. A massive jacket draped about him. He stared up at me expectantly and I laughed. It felt good to laugh.

"You look ridiculous," I snorted.

"You're one to talk," he smirked. "Your eyes are redder than a Varg's."

I ran my fingers through my greasy hair and rubbed my eyes. Warmth returned to my chest, and I playfully pushed him.

"They're tuning up in the tavern," he said as he stumbled back.

"Any idea what they plan to play?"

"I doubt anyone cares. Who would want to listen to cheesy ballads knowing an army of Varglarian could be slipping unseen toward us?"

"Ah, you've heard the report?"

"As has everyone else."

"How? It was meant to be a secret."

"You forget, I'm where secrets go to die."

Already the tavern was bursting to the seams as watchmen pushed to get inside. Tense or not, entertainment like this did not come often. Lively music wafted out and cheers filled the air momentarily. Thruki were exchanged as bets were made on how good the bards would be. The smells of baked bread, sizzling meat, and Marian's famous stew wafted out. My nose twitched. Good music or not, I never turned down food, even if I'd just eaten. By the glare of the falling sun, I'd slept far into the afternoon.

We grabbed a spot near the back as the five musicians sat by the fire. The two men were strumming gloshees with focus while two of the women were stretching and practicing dance moves. The third woman was clearing her throat and humming.

"Quite the crowd." I leaned against the bar. Traverse wiped an empty glass clean and nodded.

"May I have your undivided attention." Blukarnon stood on one of the tables. His instrument hung at his side. The room went silent of casual conversation and waited in anticipation.

In one corner, Topper sulked. He had brought his own gloshee and his fingers ran over the strings listlessly as he watched his competition. The room hushed as all eyes turned to Blukarnon. Outside, shouts conveyed the start of the entertainment. Boots thudded as watchman slid in last minute. Marian and Annika stood at the entrance of the backroom. Marian dried plates with a faded towel. Annika bit her lip as she cast her eyes toward DarSheer, who leaned against an upright beam in the center of the tavern. He was ignorant of her, or feigned it, for his gaze never drifted from the troupe.

"Welcome." Blukarnon swept his arm out dramatically. "Thank you, kind folk, for having 'The Blukarnons' here to play in your humble tavern."

"There is no way they call themselves that," Brenneth snorted loudly.

"Before your eyes and ears, we shall take you back centuries and beyond to times of darkness and trepidation and before the night is over, we shall play our masterpiece: 'The Lay of the Maiden Elswire,' detailing the most tragic love story of all time." He paused dramatically as the room applauded awkwardly and sporadically.

They started with some ballads about the First Era and the "Grief of the Drucodians." We all listened intently as they sang about the curse of Primrod and Femright, the first two beings to ever exist, made by Erëthuïl's own hands. Their love was shattered when Mordën made a mockery of Primrod and showed his dead body to Femright so she would despair and side with him. Femright gave secrets to him on how to create and from her song the first Shade was born. It was a sick story of grief and deceit, and the onlookers ate it up with cheers. Some mugs slammed against tables. Blukarnon raised both hands and chuckled.

"The evening is long, and our last ballad is nigh. The tale of Elswire and Rëlios, star-crossed lovers, is a touching, albeit cautionary tale of trust. For the Lord Rëlios trusted too deeply and gave too much. In the end it was naught for the damned dame Elswire became an ally of Mordën and butchered those around her. Take care that you do not fall into the same trap. Our lovely Winter shall sing this ballad so please give her your full attention."

He sat back and slowly strummed the instrument. A haunting melody drifted out over the crowd as the other man joined in and in tandem, they played a spiraling course of notes that made my heart ache for a time I'd never seen. Around the room, the men leaned in various positions of depression and thought. Some drank their problems away while others picked aimlessly at their food and stared without focus into the flickering fire. It was a very different atmosphere to the previous songs, and I felt the change instantly. Even Traverse stopped drying cups to listen in.

Winter, the girl who had been humming when we first walked in, opened her mouth and began singing. She sounded how I imagined a mourning siren at sea would. Her haunting vocals filled the room from floor to ceiling. Even the shadows paused their dance to listened.

A tale of love betrayed by time
under pretense of heartbreaking song
Night silver's maiden sings the tune
of her fairy thoughts in this tale of woe
This broken ballad burdened down
by miles of grief and tangled words
Dressed by the layers of pain he wrought
Beware this is not a tale of love but a dirge

A cosmic swirl shifting reality a form of blackness
Demented by time and corrupted beyond redemption
His song twists and his words puncture
The lines in his eyes cut her to ribbons

The barrier is gone for her laughter keeps it at bay
There's something to say for the lilting tilt of her tune
Attracted all from around the Wards to see her beauty
To offer her their sons and their lands but she never took
For her only love was the world in her eyes

Here her words rose in pitch and fervor. She shut her eyes as the fire sprang into a mesmerizing swirl.

Spinning till her heart near burst and her mind imploded
At peace was she for she had all she needed
Till he came and in his eyes she fell like a boulder in the sea
Her world was drowned and her soul was contained in the chains
He wrought with his warm hands and beating heart

Lord Rëlios was her curse and her promised dream
He was her gift and her greatest weakness
Where once the beaming faces of sun kissed lilies
Turned her mind here he turned her heart

Where once she graced the world with her song
No more were such words heard for she was asleep
In a dream of passion and a world of possibilities
Where once she kissed the flowers here she plucked them for him

The gates were swung wide for all were welcome
Till that fated day arrived on horseback's call
The blackened heart burst her lily pure
And killed her lover dear, his eyes black orbs of death

A thousand nights she wept, a thousand first tears from her
Go down he sung for this world was no more and her delusion
Was a dream for those sleeping not for those awake
Her voice shook but her hands obeyed and she locked all inside

She tugged on the war in her body and tried behind the ivory gates
But sweat though she did and sing as she might her people slept
She burnt a new passion, a new song down deep where he couldn't see
Her fiery gaze turned icy and her soul hardened into battle armor
She rose, he'll fall, she wept, he crowed, but she waited

Her hands rose slowly as if she was accepting a basket handed down.
The musicians strummed their instruments softly, letting her words
and the wind outside send goosebumps down our arms.

Fall she fell but rise she will and when she does
The walls will crumble and the towers topple
Gone is her mind and corrupted her heart as ever she strolls
She yearns for the mercy of a swift demise but is kept alive in
The peaks beyond the aid or tears of her own, her lover lost

Away her rusty sword rots in the rubble of her home
Away the vines grow over stone and corpse alone
The roads now gone, hidden by time's unkind touch
She walks in grief over her child's aisle
A siren on land, a ghost in the emptiness of her mind

Her melody weaves vines and her tears grow the salmon sweetbrier
Her bare feet feel no pain as she strains over jagged edges
Only her heart yearns with torment for she has lost all
She has lost what Erëthuïl blessed her with
She has lost her will to live and feels no comfort anymore
But twisted cruelty keeps her alive walking the mountain peaks

*Roaming the range . . . as she roams her thoughts
Cursed to live in stricken grief*

Winter's vocals petered off until only the crackle of the fire remained. For a long moment the room was silent. I wiped the tears from my eyes and glanced about. I was not the only one who had been moved so, for the old and young alike stared in sadness. I sniffed. Life returned to those staring vacantly ahead and chairs scraped against the ground as their occupants stood. Blukarnon lowered his gloshee and the troupe stood together as the applause began in quiet trickle until it soared to a crescendo of roaring approval. Traverse wiped the moistness from his own wise eyes as he slammed his meaty hands together. Annika had her head on Marian's shoulder and was crying into the woman's apron. DarSheer watched the flickering fire as one deep in thought. Even Blukarnon himself seemed moved by the song and his usual bravado was lessened.

"Thank you all for *letting* . . ." His voice cracked and he flushed. "Thank you for your time. Donations accepted! We leave on dawn's first light. How about Winter, eh folks? That full voice?" He rubbed his eyes and his cocky smile returned as coins began to trickle into a bowl.

I pulled my jacket close as Brenneth tugged at my arm. He gave me a small smile. "It's time for the watch." His youthful eagerness made me feel old. I remembered my first time being told about the watch. It sounded thrilling until you realized that it meant standing in one place and staring at nothing for six hours. I thought about divulging this factoid but chose to internalize it instead. A common saying among the watchmen is "never interrupt or remove that which gives someone peace and joy for such feelings are nigh impossible to grow here let alone to flourish."

"I'm sorry, Brenneth. Our session will have to wait until tomorrow morning." I shook my head. "The important thing to do now is to mentally prepare. Go practice your fearsome faces and tomorrow I'll be by your bed to take you to the ramparts."

Brenneth hurried away, his face a tilted smile. Again, I wondered if I should spoil the big secret, why most try out for scouts before ending up on the watch. Ask any man which was preferable: freedom on a horse with the wind in your face or remaining isolated atop a stone wall for hours. My better judgement prevailed.

"You're that bairn," the foul-mouthed watchman, Othrain, stumbled into me. He reeked of ale. He was stout and tall, muscles hidden beneath his great cloak. His beard tickled my forehead as he leaned against me. "The dark one. Causer of evil. Birther of our enemy. Deliverer of . . . chaos!"

"And you're the watchman who likes causing issues," I grunted under his weight. I'd had no problem keeping my distance from him. His brashness was unliked by most.

"Kissinger, come check this one out," Othrain slurred as he wiped his hand over his mouth and burped.

Traverse had already eyed us and was waiting for my signal to take Othrain away. Othrain's harmless grin and good-naturedness could turn sour fast, as many had witnessed. A young boy, a year or two younger than I, peered over from his plate of pies and bistri. His long hair hung lightly around his ears. His simple leather tunic was hidden by the large fur coat that he had thrown about his wide shoulders. Either he'd just slipped in from the watch or he was always cold. The warmth of the tavern reached sweating peaks as exhibited by those nearest the fire.

Kissinger raised his glass and brow. "Othrain, be a good watchman and leave the poor boy alone."

"You're no fun, you know that?" Othrain rubbed his nose and heaved himself off me. "Don't you know who this is? The bairn I've been telling you about on the watch. You know? *The* DarkBairn."

I tried not to let my frustration show. Two years had passed and that nickname had remained prominent. Kissinger tilted his head as he surveyed me. His hands gripped his flagon like he was afraid Marian would sweep it away before he was finished.

"Yes, you've made your point and harassed the poor lad." He shook his head. "Now get back here."

Othrain mumbled something and patted me on the head before staggering off to collapse at Kissinger's table. His great back was nearly twice the width of mine. He stood a good foot taller than me. Kissinger on the other hand was thin and short, his body toned from months on the wall. His eyes were a misty green and rimmed with his long black hair. The room was interrupted by Othrain vomiting into a pail at his seat. When Kissinger was sure his friend was sufficiently occupied, he walked over.

"Sorry about that." He bowed his head forward.

"Trust me," I said wryly, "he's not the first, nor will he be the last."

"He's had some issues in his past," Kissinger glanced back at the lumbering bear snoring in his furs, "that were left unresolved. I do my best to care for him but it's like caring for a ferrek. I hope he did no lasting damage."

I shrugged and relief spilled over his face as he ran a hand through his black locks. "I'm Kissinger, by the way, in case it wasn't obvious."

"Yeah." I nodded. "You're the newest member of the Outpost. I watched them induct you two weeks ago."

"Guilty." He rubbed a hand on his shoulder as if massaging the memories. "For some reason he's taken a sudden liking to me. Now I'm the ally to bail him out of his drunken mistakes."

"My condolences," I snorted. "I doubt I need to introduce myself. I'm *the* DarkBairn, in case you didn't catch that part."

"The stable boy?"

"Real funny."

"Didn't you clean my boots the night before?"

"You think they'd make the 'Causer of Chaos' clean your muddy boots?"

He shrugged. "My first chore here was to clean Lord Malziek's waste from his chamber pot. We must all do that we do not enjoy for the betterment of this hellhole."

"It's always the new people who get that job," I agreed, remembering my first few days.

"So, we agree you cleaned my boots?"

"You forget you are the new one. I have been here more years than I've ever wished."

"This is true. I may be new, but my humor is as ancient as my grandsire."

"I birthed evil."

"Well, I doubt I will forget that. Phoenix Rather, Birther of Evil. It does roll off the tongue, doesn't it?"

I shrugged and tried to not appear rattled. "You know of my real name? Even my surname? Color me impressed."

"I'm observant." He mimicked my shrug. "DarSheer speaks very highly of you, even when you are nowhere to be found. He has been teaching me in the ways of the watch, and often in our long spells of boredom we discuss the controversial DarkBairn. Most on the watch are unsure of your allegiances and consider you at best to be strange and at worst . . . a spy for Mordën. There are a handful, myself included, who believe you to be much more than that. While many have troubled histories and are here to hide from them, I volunteered to take this assignment. Others drown their past in ale. I chose to learn from each lesson in my past."

"I see why DarSheer took you under his wing." I raised one brow. "Words of a wise man. Let me guess, you hail from The High City?"

He winced. "Is it so obvious?"

"You're not the only observant one, or one to be instructed in all things by DarSheer. Broadsword is a man of many talents spanning many subjects. Often have we holed up in my hut and explored the ancient scrolls and texts dating millennium past."

"Impressive. You've been here but two years and already know more than most self-proclaimed learned men."

"I have a good instructor."

"So, it would seem. Allow me to apologize again for my friend's rash outburst."

"Consider the matter forgotten. You know me and my story, it would seem, so please, indulge me. What's yours?"

"Where to start," he chortled. "Where else is a troubled bairn like myself to go except the furthest reaches of humanity a world away from where I grew up? Do you think a city of golde—I mean, Elfins—will keep me safe?"

"A criminal?" I tried not to make an obvious step away.

"You take 'troubled' and make quite a leap in logic. Criminal? Of not wanting to help a deadbeat mother?" His eyes narrowed. "Of not agreeing to live a life of thievery and politics? Is this so bad?"

"You come from a life of nobility."

"I come from a life of betrayal and backstabbing. Everyone wishes the life of wealth and prosperity until they live it. I fear the corruption is deep and beyond my aid. My privileged mother desired I break the leg of an opponent who was en route to the High Island city of Morgandum. I refused. The man was then found drowned by his now widow. Because I had, failed, my mother, as she put it, had to resort to this new low. I watched the widow hold his body and grieve, believing it to be a crime of the circumstance. I had to stand there and pretend like I had no clue what really happened."

We were silent as Othrain dry heaved and muttered to himself. The room was cleared of most of the inhabitants save for Annika and Traverse, who spoke in hushed tones behind the bar counter; a group of weary watchmen, who spoke with deep reverence over the ballad; and Blukarnon. Blukarnon was the last member of the troupe still in the room and before he stepped out of the tavern, he turned and raised an empty glass.

"Innith Inine." His simple words were innocent in tone yet deep in meaning.

"Onward till we're ashes!" Traverse and Annika said in unison.

"Onward till we're ashes!" The watchmen turned and raised goblets.

"Onward . . . till we're . . . ashes," Othrain mumbled sleepily.

"Words of a survivor," I murmured.

Kissinger smiled faintly as the bard left. "Words of a warrior. It's an old saying dating to the primordial days of writing on stone. People back then were never buried, you see, for that put them closer to Mordën and further from the hallowed halls. They were always burned. So, their ashes would ascend to meet Erëthuïl."

Othrain wiped his mouth as he stirred and leaned back in his chair. "Intriguing concept to be sure. But were they aware ashes eventually fall back to the ground, like little black snowflakes? A trip to the heavens only to fall back down to the cursed land they died in. A tragedy. To die because of an illusion." His voice was broken with coughs.

"You question the proven ideology yet worship the golden ale that flows from Avalon?" Kissinger bridged his fingers.

Othrain grumbled and his head slumped onto his chest. Within moments, he was snoring.

"Innith Inine," Kissinger said with reverence. "The battle cry of the Drucodian Anguish. Such words are never spoken lightly. Hallowed phrase of olden days."

"The people here say it with reverence. It is our duty. It is our calling. You are one younger than I yet older in language and memory. You cannot be reaching your adult years?" I asked.

"Two years prior. I'm still a bairn, as Othrain likes to remind me," he chuckled. "Never before has one so alien to our ways and peoples been so in understanding. Tell me, why?"

"I yearn to return to the place where I belong. It is safe now, far from Mordën's ability to corrupt beyond what it can bare. I cannot return to it, but I rest easy knowing it is safe. Here, surrounded by darkness and fear, you cannot say the same. The men of this outpost have welcomed me though they did so with cold glances. I've learned much, and I believe I understand the severity of what is to come. I have brought this evil to your shores and if I can, I will defeat it."

"You believe, then, you are the answer to our qualms?"

"I believe I will do what I can with what I have, in the manner given me."

"A diplomatic answer that answers nothing and leaves all else vague." He shook his head and turned to watch Othrain snore loudly. "I should return to my companion and ensure he makes it to the barracks. He has watch tomorrow morning and he'd have my hide if he overslept."

"Great," I sighed, "we have watch together. Can you perhaps convince him to refrain from showing me off like some prized jewel?"

"I said I have humor, good sir, but I am not a miracle worker." His eyes twinkled mischievously.

"One more thing," I said as he stood to go, "the ballad that the troupe sang . . . who is it of? I have never heard it before."

Kissinger paused. "It speaks of the Lady Ëvilithiel, a princess of legend. She was beautiful as the sun is bright, as the mountains are tall, and as the night is long. Most of what we know are from ballads like that, but a few scrolls made it this far. Her tale of woe brings even the strongest to their knees. She had everything and lost it all. It is a story of warning and grief. I'd recommend you read on it when you have a free moment."

"And what do you think of her?" I inquired, standing.

"People love to romanticize the stories of old. The bards craft you out to be a hero of legend or a heartless villain. So, tell me, Phoenix DarkBairn, which one will the bards make you out to be?"

Overhead, thunder rumbled. Chills traveled down my back, and I glanced to the door. Suddenly, my vision swirled. I leaned against the table for stability. I needed to get some air. It was like a great pressure had settled on my chest and wasn't letting up. My nostrils flared.

"I should go," I managed before walking out the door. Kissinger eyed me as I left, his friendly gaze darkening to a suspicious grimace as the door slammed shut behind me.

I inhaled the beautiful fragrance that came when a rain shower was imminent. Black clouds floated overhead and occasionally lit up with pale white lightning. Men rushed about in various stages of disarray as they prepared for the pending downpour. Horses were led from one stable to another, and atop the walls, those on watch huddled even deeper beneath their cloaks and coats. Torches were put out and braziers extinguished.

"Move it, you lot," Altruic snapped as he stomped past me.

DarSheer was waiting for me when I finally opened our hut door. He slid a stone down the edge of his sword. I cursed as I struggled to untie my boot and slammed it into the wall with great force. I breathed to calm the butterflies racing in my stomach. A voice hissed in the back of my head.

And what are you, DarkBairn? Hero? Or villain? What will the bards sing of you? The birther of evil. The causer of chaos. The lord of darkness!

Tears threatened to fall but I would not give Mordën the satisfaction of sensing my mind in turmoil. My chest heaved in rhythm with growing thunder peals. Under the bottom of the door, the darkness lit for a flash before going dark. Droplets fell slowly at first then with great intensity until it became a waterfall flowing down our roof.

"You know," DarSheer said carefully, "when I find things make my head ache, whether from being bottled up or a secret kept too long, I find it good to divulge this. Letting things simmer like a pot before it boils is damaging."

"It's nothing." I dropped my trousers and removed my tunic. It was itchy as it clung to my forearms on its way over my head. I wanted to scream. I'd been so good at concealing when these attacks came but I could feel something in my head, a presence that was not there in the previous escapades. A dark occupant standing in the shadows of my mind. I wondered daily whether a sliver of Mordën still resided within me, or if it was the emptiness left behind.

"Well, your 'nothing' left a dent in my wall." He raised an eyebrow and returned to his sword sharpening.

"I am soon for the watch." I felt an overwhelming dread and gripped my chest. "Please, let me . . ." I couldn't finish.

Then it began again. A voice. First, it was a soothing hiss like a serpent as it slithers along a path. My ears prickled. I massaged my head. The muscles in my arm flexed. I had balled up my fist and let it go.

Have you taken into consideration my generous proposal? You have done what no others could for me.

"No," I snapped. DarSheer looked up.

"I didn't say anything." His eyes spoke to his bemused state. "Are you okay?"

Do not cut off that which you've sought since your arrival here. I have no reason to recant my own oath. Having you here proves an obstacle to my plans. With you safely returned to your void of life, that which you call The Peak, I may return to my kingdom and you to yours.

Then I remembered something. It struck me later that at the strangest moments, memories would resurface. I could be in the fight of my life with a Varglarian intent on decapitating me with its giant sword, and a memory of Will walking through the great doors of a library would spontaneously appear as a mental snapshot in my mind's eye. A woman's voice spoke softly. It occupied the same space that the figure in my head did. They waged some inexplicable war.

It's just your heart flitting about and your stomach's nerves. Butterflies. Butterflies are harmless, my child. Nothing more, nothing less. Just breathe, in and out. They're just great beautiful colorful butterflies. See how the sun shines on the flowers below and gives them sustenance. How the flowers then in turn take care of the butterflies. A gorgeous thing, a butterfly. And they do not even know their own beauty.

A calmness returned and I almost laughed. The dark presence in my mind was gone, leaving a feeling of peace. It was the first new remembrance of my mother since I'd arrived. All the previous recollections I had were from what I retained when I'd been dropped rather unceremoniously onto a grassy knoll. Somewhere deep inside me, something changed.

"That was very interesting to watch." DarSheer sheathed his blade and leaned it against the wall. "I don't mean to pry, Phoenix, but what in the blasted ferreks is going on?"

I wanted to tell him about the darkness, the nightmares. How every time I let my guard down, Mordën or one of his followers found a way to invade my mind and destroy it. The pent-up, suppressed, stress and anxiety that assailed me constantly wanted to explode out and all it would take is letting DarSheer listen. Then a cold certainty set in. I looked across the small confines of the hut, the distance between us, and knew beyond reasonable certainty that I could never divulge it. Fabricated masks replaced the honesty that wanted to be told. It was an illusion, well-crafted by years of torment and I knew it was exactly what *he* wanted. He needed me trapped in the dungeons of my mind, jailed by my uncertainty. It was his own words after all. . . . *an obstacle to my plans . . .* Instead of the warm fuzzy feeling I'd expected when I heard those words, that I was a thorn in his side, someone able to upend everything he'd planned, it only intensified my fear. I wanted to tell my closest confidant about Mordën's offer. But I knew the moment it slipped out, I'd be on the chopping block for why I didn't tell them earlier he could get into my thoughts. It would be my word against theirs that I would not succumb to his dark promises. Or maybe it was my word against me. He had broken me once before. Could he do it again? This only sowed more doubt which grew into oaks of anger, of self-doubt.

"Phoenix?"

Somehow, surrounded by people who had taken me in and let me join their outpost, I was more alone than when I'd been flattened onto that torture bed in the tunnels. Then, I'd had the luxury of knowing my friends were in need. That I could possibly do something to save them. My noble sacrifice would lend wings to their feet, and they would, could, escape. Sure, I would pay the ultimate price. No one would ever find out about me, about how I'd died. But what mattered most was saving the ones I loved. There had been a passion that had burned in me even at my most pained, depressed moment. There had been hope.

"Phoenix?" He was standing now and moving toward me.

What did I have now? I was stuck in a world where I was a dangerous object not to be meddled with. I was a curse on the lips of those who struck their finger with their hammer. If I lived in a city, mothers would close the doors of their homes as I passed. Shutters would be up. No child would be allowed to frolic in the gardens. My friends, if they still survived, lived a life without me. Wasn't that what I'd wanted when I turned back to confront *him*? For them to live a life of normality even if it meant giving up my life?

My own words to run were burned into my brain with searing blindness. Had I not achieved the very thing I had set out to? My family and my friends were safe, free. A few seconds was all I'd had with my mother and father before I'd sent them sprinting into the darkness alone. It had been the right thing to do . . . right? Katy had pleaded and I'd refused. Better to be safe than dead. And *the* vision? My parents, dead. Katy? What did I have when she was beyond my grasp?

The weakness inside me grew its long spindly fingers and dug deep. On my scouting missions, I'd returned to the same spot DarSheer had found me. I'd paced in circles. I'd shouted up, cursed Mordën, and wept into the isolation of my thoughts. I was alone. I had no reason to hope. The kindness of those here could not be measured. When I lay awake at night listening to DarSheer's snores and pondering my life, I often realized that if they hadn't taken me in, or if the Portal hadn't dropped me where it had, I might be dead. Leave it up to a population incentivized by an ancient prophecy and their fears to take me as an ill omen and burn me at the stake or cut my head off. Like follows like. Cities would have hunted for me. My blood spilt would have been the only answer to end the words that haunted them. Was it by pure luck I landed in the one spot where I was welcomed? An outcast among outcasts. My head pulsated and I gripped my temple.

"Phoenix, look at me. What's going on?" DarSheer's entire face filled my vision. I stared ahead without blinking.

I owed everything to these people, even the ones who looked at me strange. Deep inside it meant nothing. DarSheer was not Tim. Brenneth was not Will. No one could ever be *her*. My chest ached with grief. Her smile. The way her hair rimmed her eyes. I felt the tears brimming. I couldn't stop them. They fell of their own accord. I would never see those I loved again. The people here were not my friends, not my family. They were allies, individuals of like-mindedness united of one cause. Unity in desperation and fear is not a great basis for friendship. So that was that? I had no friends. None here, anyway. Or was this more of Mordën meddling with my thoughts as if he owned me? Did he? He controlled me before. Or was that me? No, it was him, I remembered moving without my control. I saw my body act as if I was an observer in the passenger's seat.

I controlled you once like the pawn you are. I will do it again. I know your greatest fears. I know the depths your love will go to. I know everything

I need to to bring you down. You have one final opportunity to accept my offer. After that, I will use you in whatever fashion I need: to betray your allies, end what few strands of peace you still cling to, or perhaps let the simple minds of these people stick in their beliefs. Nothing is more deadly and powerful than a man stuck in his own misinterpretation.

I came to as if I'd blacked out. DarSheer sat at the bottom of my bed, his eyes focused on the torchlight. My face was covered in sweat, my hair plastered to my head. He turned with a start at the slight groan that escaped my clammy lips.

"It's okay, I've called for the healer. Just hang in there."

"No," I mumbled. My tongue was so fat I couldn't get the words around it.

"Your skin is warm and your eyes rolled back." He pressed my arms down when I tried to sit up.

The door burst open and Lëuthorn stepped in. His long hair dripped from the rainfall, and he removed his thick coat. Behind him, giant puddles pooled on the oaken threshold.

"Again?" He strolled to the bedside in the blink of an eye, his tanned hands tearing back the thin blanket. "DarkBairn, do you know the meaning of rest? Must I replace you limb by limb till you stand a new creation? First, the twisted ankle unfit for a boot for months, then the crack on your skull from that Varg's hammer, and don't think I haven't forgotten your damaging burn from spilling Marian's stew."

DarSheer cleared his throat. "He was staring into nothingness and collapsed. He began convulsing and speaking about Mordën." There was genuine concern in his voice.

"Convulsed? Like a tremor?"

Lëuthorn placed the back of his hand to my temple and whistled. He began to remove plants and tubes from his pocket.

"I need a bowl, perhaps a mortar with a pestle."

"It's not much." DarSheer handed him a curved dish with a thin clay device I didn't recognize.

Lëuthorn didn't answer as he got hard to work. The plants all looked the same, green leaves and stems uprooted as though all at once and in haste. He ground them first into a pulp then into a paste as he sprinkled what looked like dust into the curved bowl. With the clay pestle, he meaded them until he lifted one finger with the concoction in a lump.

"This will not taste good," he warned.

Before I could protest, he had shoved it into my mouth. At first, I wanted to gag, more because of his dirty finger than the paste. Then the flavor hit, and I dry heaved. He sat back and gestured DarSheer to do the same. They watched me as for a few minutes I silently begged my stomach to vomit. But the urge died, and I collapsed back onto my bed. The fog in my brain was gone. I could see and think clearly.

"What was that?" I shakily sat up.

"Careful now, Phoenix." DarSheer placed a steadying hand on my shoulder.

"A very interesting blend of herbs, which, when mixed together, heal a poison of the mind," Lëuthorn explained.

"No poison addles my thoughts," I protested, "merely constant exposure . . ." I grunted.

"He was speaking of Mordën and gripping his skull," DarSheer said.

Lëuthorn shook his head. "You delved too deep into your own mind and listened to *him*." He bit out the last word. "It's as I was concerned about, Broadsword. He's still listening to our enemy. He might even be a spy in our midst."

"Careful, Lëuthorn. Accusations like that are not to be made lightly."

"Mordën does not control me nor will he ever again!" I couldn't believe what I was hearing.

"He got in your mind and twisted you so badly you convulsed into what could very well have been your death rattle." Lëuthorn picked up his supplies. "Is this commonplace?"

"It happens but not frequently."

"Spare me the time and speak clearly."

"Several times a month."

Lëuthorn shook his head again and hoisted his coat back over his bony shoulders. "One who has consorted with our great foe may do so again. I caution the others as I do you, DarSheer, from believing every-thing that comes from his mouth.”

“He offered me a promise, a sworn oath in blood,” I bit out. The moment I said it, I wished I had remained silent.

“Offered you?” Even DarSheer seemed wary, and I realized how it must sound. He had been the primary advocate for my acceptance into the Outpost. If it turned out I was controlled by Mordën, he would be the cause for the damage I would be capable of. He would be seen as an enemy himself. Lëuthorn did not move.

“He thinks because I am in a world foreign to my own that I will be weak enough to meddle with. He once controlled me but that is when I had everything to lose. I am a boat broken on the rocks. He has nothing he can hold over me now. I have nothing to lose. Mordën offered me a chance to return home. I denied it.”

“The promise of a time and place without his talons is too good to be true.” DarSheer’s frown drilled into me like it was my own mother scolding me.

“He said if I didn’t accept, he would see to it that I perished along-side you lot. I will not, nor will I ever, let him control me again. Too much damage has happened because I gave in.” I felt stupid. “I gave in. I was not strong enough to stop him. I admit that.”

“It’s hard to admit when you’re weak.” Lëuthorn no longer seemed sure of himself. He stepped back, a shadow passing across his face. “But acknowledgement of a weakness does not mean it can’t happen again.”

“I told him no.” The words were as welcome to me as they were to them. “I have paid in blood and tears, and the loss of everyone I love. He murdered my parents, tortured my friends, and took the love of my life from me. I have every right to be weak. But I chose to fight. Here. Among you all.”

There was silence for a moment. “Fight whom?” They seemed to hang intently on my next words.

“*Him*. I’m not going to side with him. Because of him I have lost everything. I will fight him to my dying breath. When there is peace, I will still be fighting. There is not a particle within me that does not resist him at every step. He thinks because he can whisper in my mind that I am susceptible to his suggestions. He fears what I might be able to do when I finally free myself from him."

"You're not?" Lëuthorn sounded doubtful.

"Do you not all have cravings or whisperings in your mind, egging you to do that which you know is wrong? Do you entertain them?"

"That's different." Lëuthorn folded his arms. "Those cravings are of our own desires and intents. Yours come from a possessive demonic Luthi who seeks to burn all."

"So, they're not identical." I ground my teeth. "If anything, that makes what I'm going through far more important. You have no reason to believe me, Lëuthorn, but DarSheer, we've known each other for two years now. Have I ever once exhibited any indication that my loyalty is not fully with this outpost? Have I ever said or done anything to make you question my motives?"

"No," DarSheer said slowly. He turned to Lëuthorn. "I know that tonight may make you question trusting Phoenix, but if you trust me, it should be enough. He's a good bairn, troubled sure, upset yes. But after what he's gone through . . . I'll stake everything I've achieved to this point that he would not return to Mordën."

"I give you my solemn oath," I said quietly. "I would rather risk death than ever let him control me again. Whatever he could promise me, he would not follow through. He would betray me, and I would end up a corrupted version of myself in his ranks. I am not enslaved to his will any longer. The day will come when he and I must face each other, and that day will be his last. Mordën, I don't know how but I know you can hear me. I reject your offer and with great disdain for the coward you are. Let us meet on the battlefield so you may answer for the evil you have done in my life and all those present."

So be it.

Lëuthorn and DarSheer eyed each other as if unsure how to continue. I knew I looked insane speaking to the air as of expecting a verbal response from the table. However, for now at least, they both looked slightly more confident.

"Any friend of DarSheer is a friend of mine." Lëuthorn extended a hand. "I know the conflicts involved in mental struggles. Know you can come to me should he try to assail you again and you require sleep."

I nodded gratefully.

"However," DarSheer sat and leaned forward, his hands clasped together, "Lord Malziek will be troubled by this information. He must know, for the safety of those here."

"Of course." My shoulders sagged. "I will speak with him tomorrow."

"Tonight. If something happens, he'll need to know the root cause."

"Nothing will happen." My voice dropped to a whisper. "Nothing *can* happen. It can't."

"Phoenix," DarSheer stared directly into my eyes and gave me a sympathetic grimace, "even those with the best intentions often fall short of success. You can stamp your foot down and proclaim as loudly as you want to the mountains above and caverns below that you are a free man, rid of the trauma that has stalked you this far. But Mordën is crafty, cunning. I doubt words will destroy him."

"You think it's hopeless." I buried my head in my hands. "That I should surrender to any hope of freedom from his invasive games."

"Not in the slightest. I think it is important and a sign of manhood to admit one's weakness. I don't want you to regret what could have been done when it's too late to now do it. If Mordën knows we are all aware of his tactics and probing, he may cease."

"Perhaps from a mental barrage." Lëuthorn folded his arms and leaned against the doorframe. Behind him the wind had picked up and lashed the rain against the walls. "I fear that if he fails here, he will simply shift to a physical assault."

"Physical we can beat." I surprised myself with the confidence in my voice. "But if he continues to probe and milk my self-doubts and fears, he can do it to all. If he wages a battle of the minds, is there any who can resist?"

"None." They both shook their heads.

"Then let us prepare for what is to come." I brushed my tunic clean. "I will meet with Lord Malziek and accept his judgement as it is overdue. Thank you." They smiled awkwardly at me. "Thank you for being the allies I need."

DarSheer folded his arms. "There's a natural goodness in us all, and try as we might, the evil and darkness can never change that. All it can do is deceive us into thinking we are forgotten. The moment we listen to the fell whispers of chaos, is the moment we yield to his authority."

"Sorry, for calling you a spy." Lëuthorn glanced awkwardly at me. "You do not bear the mark of evil nor the scent of him who wishes the creation of Erëthuïl to burn."

"This is good." I stood and felt the last surge of dizziness wash over. When it was gone, I took a step toward the door. "Keep your enemies where you can see them. I speak firsthand of their deadly strength in the shadows."

I stepped from the hut. My first thought was the harsh smell of pine being burnt. The wood stock must be low. Soot cascaded down around us from the centralmost brazier. A few watchmen, cloaks tucked tightly around themselves, coughed into their fists. One tossed a new log in. They mumbled something to each other. The rain dug the weak flames.

Dwaith gazed at me and stepped in front as I moved to open the door to the tower. His size meant I had no choice but to explain myself.

"Lord Malziek is in thought," he said firmly.

"I have news that Lord Malziek must hear, concerning myself and Mordën."

The man glowered at me as if trying to judge which was worse, letting in someone Malziek potentially didn't want to meet with and hadn't approved, or forbidding someone from entering that held information Malziek considered vital. In the end, he simply snorted and stepped aside. The climb up was as brutal as it always was. I found myself huffing and gasping as I climbed the last step. Sweat beaded on my brow, which I wiped at in hopes I didn't appear weak. Years of being in shape still had not prepared me for this ultimate challenge. I gave the top step a rough kick to prove my point. The door was cracked, and voices petered out like streams of water from a river.

"The watch must be bolstered." I recognized Malziek's deep tenor.

"With what? The horses?" This was Throbb. He cursed loudly and I imagined him flopping back in his chair. "We're severely depleted in terms of resources. Three more Varg attack in one week. *Three!*"

"I can send DarSheer to Avalon in search of recruits."

I knew whatever was going on, I didn't need to hear so I simply knocked loudly and let the door swing in. At the fireplace, Malziek had rotated to see who was entering. Throbb and a smaller boy sat in the large chairs. They both shifted in their seats.

"DarkBairn." The boy's eyes went wide. I recognized him. He was one of Brenneth's friends.

"What brings you my way this late at night?" Malziek rumbled. His words carried a hint of warning.

"I must confess some things I've withheld from you."

The room crackled with sounds of wood popping and fingers drumming on the tabletop. Throbb turned to Malziek and raised one brow. The boy sat on his hands and seemed to find the fireplace of great interest.

"Throbb, we can continue this later. Return to the watch."

"Aye, Lord Malziek." Throbb and the boy stood simultaneously. Both seemed eager to be anywhere I was not as they skirted around me and vanished into the darkness of the stairwell.

"Speak plainly." Malziek rubbed his nose. He was tired again. His eyelids hung dangerously low. Wrinkles bagged beneath his eyes.

I did not conceal any longer that which troubled me deepest. He sat and listened with no outward reaction to the news. When I reached the nightmare I'd had where I was promised freedom, he slowly sank deeper into his chair.

"What hope do we have?" His words cut like a knife. "We stand not as a witness of our people's defiance, but as a future testament to his reckless abandon."

"Lord Malziek, sir," nerves fluttered in my gut, "respectfully, I disagree. Hope is the one thing we have and he doesn't. He can't hope.

Or so I believe. He knows it's our greatest weapon against him for where there is hope, there is a chance at survival. Haven't you heard the great stories of a handful of men beating whole armies? If they looked at their obstacle not as a mountain to climb but as a cliff to fall off of, then they would bear no more importance than a name scribbled in a ledger. They fought. They had hope."

"I wish more had the courage you do." He smiled at the flames. There was a great sadness in his tone. "If all the old men like me stopped despairing and held on to such values, we would be a free world. My heart grieves, for I fear that freedom from this will not come in my lifetime. Why do we fight?"

"For a future our own youth can enjoy." I knelt at his side. "Just because we do not reap the benefits does not mean we stop the fight. I have no reason to fight. If I stuck true to what I wanted, I'd accept Mordën's offer. I'd be gone, living in ignorant bliss worlds away while you all suffered. Tempting or not, I have a duty. It's because of me you're all in this mess. If I leave now, I must confront that I am a coward and unworthy to live."

"You're far better than we deserve." It was the first time Malziek had truly acknowledged to my face that he accepted me as the answer to the prophecy. "I will stand with hope as my banner even if it does not surge through my veins like it does yours. Forgive me. I thank you for giving me this information. Mordën has long used his persuasive powers to get what he wants. This is a good sign. If he sees people are beginning to resist him, he may realize Ëonë is not yet his."

I stood. "Agreed, sir. I will return to my quarters and you to your thoughts."

"Phoenix?"

"Yes, my lord?"

"Tell DarSheer to prepare for company tomorrow. A delegate from some of the northernmost villages in Fiscer's Keep are journeying down. What they wish to discuss is beyond even my considerable knowledge, but our scouts say they come with news of evil. We should prepare.

The road sees many boots where before it felt nothing. I believe we are nearing the end of the beginning."

"I will do so." I bowed slightly and exited the chamber.

DarSheer was splayed out on his cot. His chest rose and fell evenly. I regretted having to wake him, but Malziek's words hung like a millstone about my neck. DarSheer sighed as I conveyed the information.

"More and more these days it seems the Varg grow in strength. If they've reached Fiscer's Keep . . ."

"Then we may have lost the Ralier Range and the coastline to them," I agreed.

"Get some sleep." He rolled over on one side and closed his eyes. "Tomorrow will be a long day."

A month had passed since I was abandoned here. I thought it would become easier as time went but in truth, I only felt a growing sickness in my chest. As the waning stars glowed through gaps in the growing bank of clouds, I made my way along the courtyard, boots squelching in mud. I flicked specs of dirt and dust off my shoulders. The peaceful beams of soft moonlight were interrupted as a deep cloud fell over the moon. Dawn was hours away still. Trees and clothing and person and stone were hidden in its shadow. Ash and embers continued to softly descend. As I made my curved route, following the rather uneven manner of the most trod-upon path, I could hear the drums, far off. Lights flickered in the open window in the tower. I picked up my speed and nodded to the guardian as I entered the winding staircase of the tower. Uneven stone along the rickety planks, it was a grueling climb. I passed by several windows, all of which showed the ground steadily falling beneath my visage. Out along the plains, the moonlight had all but vanished, and in its place, a glowing fog seemed to hover. It was as if the very foul breath of Mordën had been expelled and drifted over the land. Coming through the fog like flames, embers rained down.

The last flight of stairs gave way to the door, which was partially opened. Orange light streamed out and with a hesitant knock, I pushed it in. Around the table sat eight individuals, all in attire fresh from travel. I could smell the stench of unwashed bodies and soiled clothing. Mud and dirt caked their boots and the bottoms of their cloaks. Swords hung at their sides. Along the far edge of the table, three burly men, all in chain mail, sat stoically, goblets of wine and plates of fine venison at their rounded stomachs. Across from them, in equally matured manner, sat four thin and pale figures. Their hair sat in undulating patterns around their shoulders, as if a sea of white fell from their heads. Seated next to DarSheer, a young woman watched. A hood hid her face and the shadows flickering about the room covered her visage. DarSheer, leaning against the open window, had his cloak tightly wound around his body, his hood all but hiding his eyes. He glanced up at my entrance and his look conveyed a weary relief.

"You ask for the word and here it comes meandering in as if called," he pointed a callused finger at me. All eyes turned, mouths shut, food momentarily forgotten.

"The bairn? This is him?" one of the large men asked. His curly beard, illustrated like a dying fire, was large and his bushy eyebrows nearly obscured his beady black eyes. Skin scarred with obvious past injuries, he was intimidating as he was heavyset. "The one the prophecy speaks of?"

"He is." For the first time, Lord Malziek spoke.

I hadn't noticed him for he stood shadowed against the edge of the fireplace. The flames which licked up eagerly, cast massive shadows throughout the room and Malziek's choice of position had him in the darkest one. But he stepped forward and I noticed the gauntlets around his forearms, the iron around his body. He was dressed for battle.

"What is the meaning of this?" I cleared my throat.

"Perhaps you can explain yourself," the man in chain mail, his hands twitching, demanded. "You come to disturb our tranquility with your ways? Long have we fought for the peace we earned. Hundreds of years our families have lived without fear. They let their children run in gay mirth along the plains and moors. Alliances were made and the old treaties signed. Never again, was said, would an enemy like Mordën rule

our hearts with fear. Yet now you arrive as a harbinger of death. A cry of anguish; a wolf's mournful howl. Speak."

"You claim I am a representative of evil?" I glanced at DarSheer, but he offered me no consolation.

"Do you deny it?"

"That is enough, Culkraith." Malziek shook his head. "The bairn is old enough to withstand your constant desire for accusations, for he knows no more than what I've told you."

"If that's the case, let him speak for himself."

"Lord Malziek speaks truth. My first clear memory is arriving here. I was found on the northern plains an hour's hard ride from here by DarSheer. I've been regaining many memories since then, but none to answer your questions about this prophecy. Surely, it is as alien to me as the concept that my intentions are anything but loyal to the Outpost."

The room was hushed again as none seemed able to keep my gaze. Only Culkraith, glowering as he did, held my eyes. I abruptly found the ornately carved tabletop of magnified interest.

"You speak as one with practiced rehearsal," he snorted and leaned back. "Fine, if you are as innocent as you say of ruining our peace, then who is to blame?"

"All I know," I shot back, "is I was brought here against my will. Surely, that is enough to prove the villain. Mordën is as a serpent, hissing his deceit and mockery of you."

"Watch your tongue, bairn. You speak to Lord Culkraith of Deer-drop." He wagged a finger at me.

"A threat to make grown men quake in their boots," DarSheer snorted. His voice was barely above a whisper. "Perhaps next, you'd like to pull at a loose string in his tunic and aim to disrobe the bairn and show his immodesty to the great lords of the northern fishing villages?" Culkraith said nothing.

"You were all brought here because the signs are not wrong," Malziek stepped in. "Ash. It has fallen."

"Ash? What, is Mordën planning on forcing us all to die of inhaling smoke?" This was brought up by the second man, who while softer in

demeanor, seemed crueler in his eyes. His smaller beard hid his face and curled at the edges. Eyes blacker than the night, he had not moved them from DarSheer.

"You may be too young to recall the words spoken of the Elder Days," Malziek stepped forward again. "But not all of us are. There are several who still recall those black words. Of armored bodies in the night, illuminated only through the burning of men, animals, and homesteads. Veneth, you should be more cautious with your mockery."

"Truly, you misunderstand my intentions, Lord Malziek," Veneth raised one brow. "I meant no disrespect. While young, I am much learned in the days following the end of the Second Era. The texts are very . . . descriptive on such matters."

"And well they should be," one of the pale men seated across from them murmured. His long fingers, twirled in his hair, moved like oars brushing through water. "The Elfins have not forgotten. We still write of the bloodshed that came from the failures of the Drucodians and the lack of awareness by Men. If I'm not mistaken, it was the ancestor of your leaders who allowed Mordën to burn my peoples' homes. We do not forget such things. Time may sully your wits but ours only grow."

"Word was sent by our own kin, yet it was forgotten during the butchering of our people by that disgrace you called a king. Defenseless, Breoth, they were women and children still on the dawn of life. Butchered like animals on the word of YOUR king! And what does his son do? Hide in his great halls of luxury and turn a blind eye to our suffering." Veneth wiped the spittle from his mouth, hand at his side where his dagger hung. Culkraith clenched his fists and hit them against the table.

"Quiet!" Malziek bellowed. "The actions of the past are in the past. What was then a travesty has become a learning moment. Both our races failed and so it is together we can repair those damages. But not so at each other's throat. Bereth, calm your companions and remember why I called you here. Mordën is on the move and the bairn cannot be held for his part in this prophecy. Rarely are those who prophecies speak of inclined to participate or agree with their part. Yet such is not for them to decide. All we must do now is respond accordingly. The fact of the matter is evident

and arguing will only allow our foe to creep up on us like a wolf in sheep's clothing."

"War is a messy business," Bereth murmured. "One day you're filling your belly with the comforts of home and the next you're marching in line like condemned criminals to be executed. It robs the rich of their wealth, the poor of their home. It drains the young of their life and prolongs the sleep of the elders. It destroys beauty and replaces it with grief. Ash and embers from the ever-burning furnace. Bairns beg for war. Codgers pray for peace."

The room was silent as he spoke, his wooden chair creaking beneath him. DarSheer moved slightly, his head remained covered, but from his seat, he watched the room. The smoke in the room swirled and a thick odor of wet oak hung in the air. Along one end of the council table, goblets of wine and flagons of rich steaming ale sat invitingly. Loafs of freshly made bread sat sizzling to themselves on platters. DarSheer, quiet during the outburst of before, looked up and gave me a smile. It was all he could muster, though, for he quickly fell back into his reclusive manner. Malziek, on the other hand, seemed to be on a mission to shout his loudest yet.

"And what news from the north?" he growled. His eyes flashed and the cloak around his shoulders swayed mesmerizingly over his great form.

"No Varg spotted in the assigned areas, Lord Malziek," a young woman returned. "The enemy is unusually quiet. I believe they are gearing up for a significant assault."

DarSheer sighed. "This is just more ill news on the tidal wave of war. I've received word from Icksbane and Trals that their constant run-ins with Vargs and Shades are at an all-time low. Even the meager attempts at harassment by a band of two or three Vargs have been ended. It is as I've been saying for a year, Malziek, Mordën is preparing for war. He's recalling his forces to his island and their numbers shall again sweep the world. If we no longer fear him, we should march across the Bridge and burn his last stronghold."

"What is the point of this outpost?" Malziek said evenly. "You despair without remembering why we are here."

"The purpose is to prevent . . ."

"Wrong!" The room went suddenly silent. "The purpose is to bring early warning to the Kingdoms of Ëonë and the alliances forged in times of peace. We are not to be the dam against the wave. We're merely the leaf alerting of the first ripple. Our mission, DarSheer, is exactly what we are doing."

"Drums beat in unison while fire falls on our uncovered heads. The enemy has to funnel his forces through a small bridge set up specifically to limit his numbers," DarSheer argued. "Sure, we can alert the free kingdoms, but it is within our sworn oaths as soldiers of The High City to defend. Every man and boy here trained by my hand as you requested can put up their own."

"Our mission is alert; our goal is defense," I said. They both looked at me. "One acts as if the other is unable to be there. Why not do both? After we alert, are we expected to lay down our arms and succumb to the knife wounds and arrow piercings?"

"Of course not," Malziek reported, though he seemed less uptight. "I simply mean the duty this outpost has to The High City is still intact no matter what happens. If Mordën, curse his name, decides to launch an attempt at a bid for power, he will be met with people who remember what he did before. Not all of us have allowed our minds to be sullied by the fragrant berries of peace. While some whittle their days away in the extravagance of wealthy life, there are others who take their post in the mud and grime. We'll be ready."

"If I may." The woman reached for her cowl.

"Of course, Arabella." Malziek returned to his shadowed corner.

She stood and her face entered the warm light. She was incredibly beautiful, her small nose set beneath her sea green eyes. Brown hair tumbled down around her shoulders as she let go of her cowl.

"When the call was made to bring the leaders of the peoples yet unyoked by toil and strife to come here and speak, I journeyed. When I was challenged by my people over my dedication to this, I gave no response. Lord Malziek, while heart in hand, is right, the terror and absolute horror that was reigned down a thousand years ago by the very enemy,

which now moves to march on these lands, is about to fill the hearts and minds of this world for a third time. Broken, we can hope to prolong our inevitable death but united we stand a chance. Bairn or not, prophecy or not, if we give in to the finality of dead words, we're no more learned than the people before Mordën first arrived. Folk love to speak ill of the Drucodians for their failures but I don't believe for a moment any one of you would have done better in their place. We can stand here and bicker all we want for as long as we want but like the bairn said, embers and smoke rain down around us. Drums beat their war song. It is coming and it won't be stopped by political bickering and revival of old wounds. When I return to my people, I will tell them of all I saw and heard here. I will have them arm every man, woman, and child and we will be ready. If you're telling me they, who are but farmers and fishermen in your eyes, are ready to do what brave guided warriors like yourselves are not, then perhaps it will come to no surprise when this world falls."

"Curb your loose tongue, lass," Malziek growled. "You may speak on behalf of your people, but I've been forbidden to speak on behalf of The High City. Don't lump their indecision and attempts to appease the beast over the waters with our choices here. As for the Elfinian race, they still swim in riches and fame. You did not think it would take one meeting to change their stance?"

"One meeting where the crimes of our enemy were laid on a parchment for all to see?" Arabella's voice rose.

"You speak as one learned of these crimes," Culkraith remarked. "How does one so young come to know the past?"

"Because unlike the powerful in The High City, Culkraith," she retorted, "we value the importance of history. Mordën took the world by surprise because weak-minded people like yourself refused to see what was coming."

Veneth stood aggressively, finger pointed. "You would do well to remember your place amidst the strong and wise, commoner filth," he snapped.

"Enough," Malziek raised a gloved hand. "Bairn, what would you say?"

"The signs are as clear as the hostility in this room," I said. "You know I claim no desire to be a part of this danger, but I am here. I chose not my fate and likewise none here or anywhere chose to be the creature Mordën plans to raze on. Yet Mordën will attack and when he does, he will find his first massive hurdle right out of the Bridge. His crippling weakness is his confidence. It will serve him well in the long run, but he overlooks or underestimates the strength of his enemies before his very nose. We must hold him here. If we can give warning to the rest of Ëonë when he marches, we will have fulfilled our duty and may have given the world a chance at victory. If we continue to bicker and barter like children over their toys, our own heated quarrels will serve better to blind us than placing a blanket over our heads."

We sat silently around the table. Candles flickered along the table and at one end of the room, a fire blazed intently. On the far wall, an aged map hung, within the bindings of an animal hide. The light which almost made it glow, showed the boundaries of a continent facing a single small island. To the far east, where the island sat, the creator of the map had drawn high-tiered waves and dangerous rocks, upon which many ships had been dashed in times past. The BlackBurg it was known. Its southernmost tip along the western coast bore marshes which hung in thick odorous density. Their heavy fumes were toxic to all but the healthiest of men. Along the eastern curve of the islands two pronged tips rode a moun-tain range. Closest to the west, foothills of motley curves rose and fell before the feet of tall black peaks. No snow nor form of life could survive on the nearly pure rock of these mountains. A sickness had taken their pointed forms and it all dwelt in the Shadow Keep. A fortress of black rock and fiery plumes, the tombstone to all life on the island itself, it remained a single reminder of the pain and horrors the peoples of Ëonë had gone through. It was a defiant slur in the face of a slumbering world.

"We must also be ready to admit that we are not enough to hold off a significant force," I continued. "I do not doubt the courage of any man here, but they are simply not enough for the darkness on that island. I've seen—though I don't remember much—what Mordën is capable of. He is black as his fortress, and he will not let anything stop him. Of that, I am

sure. He is counting on this. He knows that we cannot stop him and thus we would despair and lay down for the slaughter. Lord Malziek speaks truth: our goal is to alert. But so does DarSheer. If all lived by the conditions placed upon them and did nothing else, there would be no freedom. Imagine if the Drucodians, who were never meant to fight, decided it was not in their origins to defend this great continent. What if they had simply hidden themselves and lived how they perceived they were supposed to? It is because they had hope and loved this world that they beat Mordën in the First Era. Yes, they failed to stop him in the Second Era, but he was still beaten in the end. Against all odds, he was banished. It has happened before, that you lot overcame immense difficulties. It will happen again!"

"Wise words are great in a chamber of diplomacy," Culkraith gave me a cold smile, "but often fail to find footing among the more . . . physical. You have a career in The High City, bairn, should you ever come."

The room descended into bickering and snarls at his words. Half the room seemed to side with DarSheer and I while the other half, notably those in finer wear, battled for Malziek. It was an almost even split and it was clear that we would get nowhere.

"We will do our duty and that which is placed upon us, even if all others would quake. We will not abandon our posts. DarSheer?" Malziek turned. "What news from The Remnant?"

"They have refused our call for aid. They say it is a problem of man and that enough blood has been spilled on their accord. They did send a representative to meet with me in Avalon, but I fear it was only to remind us of our ancestors' failures."

"Blast those confounded rabble." Malziek rolled his eyes and crushed a grouping of grapes in his meaty hands. "They'll be the death of all of us. Of all the unrighteous, self-conniving—"

"Who are they?" I didn't like being kept out of the loop.

"The ancient race of the Drucodians." DarSheer puffed on a long pipe, the smoke curling about his head. "Once they were the sole race to live in Ëonë. They were the first to defy Mordën and incur his wrath. They faced extinction in the Second Era and nearly were had Erëthuïl not made the Elfin and Human race to defend them. Once, all we knew

was made and crafted by the hardened gaze and hammer of the Druco-dians. Avalon, the main Elfinian city, is known by another name."

"The Last Great Drucodian Burg." Malziek nodded as we settled in for the history lesson. The other men took to their drinks and thoughts.

"Once there were five great cities to rule. In the east, on the Isle of Primdon where the BlackBurg now sits, was the fortress of Ilsam. It was run by the chosen race of Drucodians, first formed by the mind and will of Erëthuil. Those first people consecrated the ground and there made the city to honor the beginning of time. From there, various families and lines moved out and began to populate the land created for them. In the center of the continent, they formed Avalonenburg. A hub of prosperity and bustling peace, it was destroyed and partly burnt in that great time of conflict of the First Era. When the Elfin finally defeated the enemy with the help of the last Drucodians, they called the city Avalon, The City of Gold. It stands the last great piece of architecture from that era and personally made by the hands of the Drucodians. To the west and far over the mountain range, sat Heltsburg, a great city of iron and ivory. Tales speak of its awe and of the noble bloodlines to dwell there. It stood and with-stood the test of time for centuries until Mordën and his forces demolished it. In its ashes now stands The High City, given to the peoples of men. Far south, along the shorelines, the city of Glasbur was built. Youngest of the five but first to fall, it served as the kingdom of the last Drucodian king. The king, in his final days, ordered the gates to be shut and for all trade to cease. No one knows why and all inside were never seen nor heard from again. Thousands of years have passed since that city opened its gates and equally now as then are we bewildered by this. Rumors flew that he had made a treaty with Mordën for the Dark Luthi never attacked them. The city, to this very day, remains intact and lost to time. None has gone in nor out since that day and although from far mountains you can see the rubble and emptiness, no one has set foot in it. Finally, north, sat the second oldest city of Frishburg. Almost nothing is known of it, for it was the target of Mordën's early wars and little was written of it. Its precise location is known only by a handful of Drucodian descendants, for those who built it were all killed and their maps and writings burned to ashes."

As DarSheer spoke in soft remembering, I watched the lights of the candles flicker off the map. The shadows there seemed to play out all that DarSheer named. I saw the Drucodians fall and the eventual making of the Elfin and Human race.

"And these Drucodians?" I asked. "Do any remain?"

"There was made a city of refuge for the remaining survivors. They fled there after the end of the war and little travel abroad now. It is said their last female died out a century ago. They now live in isolated peace, waiting their fate of extinction. It is considered good fortune should one be seen on the road with you. They are a secretive people now, hidden in fear of failure."

"And despite an offering to redeem their old honor," Malziek interrupted, "they turn our messengers away."

"Perhaps they are fighting their own battles," DarSheer interjected. "Much goes on behind walls we on the outside know not. The Varglarian have attacked as far deep as the Fallen Peaks before."

"Whatever the reason, they have abandoned us."

We sat in silence for a long while after. The figures at the table watched the flames lick the walls as Arabella eyed me. No one spoke after that. Outside, the night had fallen in full and torches from the courtyard and along the walls were the only source of light. Far off voices of men in jest wafted up, carried on a harsh breeze. The world was sunk in forgotten thought as the night deepened and the cold gale howled its mournful dirge.

The cold bit at my cheeks, drove its talons into the deep places of my cloak, and sank its fangs into my boots so that my toes seemed like solid blocks of ice. We didn't know how long it had been morning, for a bank of dirty grey clouds scuffled over the sun. A great shadow was creping out from the BlackBurg. We all felt it. Some denied it. Most dreaded it. A few, like myself, prepared for it.

It wasn't long before figures could be seen on the crest of the road. I squinted my eyes, gripping my halberd tightly. A call went up on the wall. Men gripped bows and hastily drew arrows. Muscles tensed.

"All hands on point!" Throbb bellowed as he stalked up and down the stone ramparts. "Arrows first, you buffoons, then swords. KcNuck, where are you, you blasted imp?"

"Not Varglarian!" Brenneth bellowed as he pointed a long arm. "Friendly. Friendly!"

"Friendly!" Kissinger echoed back several spots down from me.

One of the figures coming toward us was limping, borne on the arms of two others. There was no mistaking the grim, foreboding nature of their arrival. A strong wind shrieked like ghouls off the ocean front. The waves, barely visible on the horizon, crested in tall arcs of absolute destruction.

"It had to be today?" Brenneth chattered loudly. Up here, unprotected by the ancient walls around us, we were thoroughly exposed to the elements. "Today of all days, Erëthuïl had to test me with a miserable day."

"First lesson," I shouted, "the winds bring the cold fury of the sea, and it spares none. Rich or poor alike, stranger to this land, it whips a curse to your tongue and brings tears to your eyes. I'd recommend finding some furs to shove in your boots too or you'll need your little toes amputated by the medic." He gave me a look of great alarm.

"This is no curse from Erëthuïl," Throbb bellowed. "It comes from the blackness beyond. Men, keep your weapons handy. This could be a trick. I want fires going and arrows in hand. Someone alert Lord Malziek!"

The flags overhead snapped in the gale, and what fires could be kept alive whipped about like a snake's tongue. The figures were much closer now, and we spotted our scouts riding next to them. Lord Malziek soon arrived with his personal guard and stood to my right while DarSheer stood on my left. Both were quiet.

I felt something fall on my face and reached up, brushing it aside as casually as one might a wisp of hair. But a second fell and a third as well. All around, the men on watch had begun to take notice of the strange phenomena. Shouts carried over the battlements. It appeared to be snow, for it fell from the swirling clouds overhead.

"There is something amiss in the Eastern Ward. Black ash, black ash is falling," Malziek finally spoke. "Call the horsemen to arms and have Altruic prepare my stallion."

"Riders, to your places!" DarSheer bellowed.

A stable boy was dispatched to the thatched stable below. The scouts had dismounted and let the newcomers ride instead. The way they moved told us that danger was not far behind. I made out a female on the closest horse. Her hair whipped about her face, obscuring it. A child huddled against her back. On an adjacent steed, a younger woman was speaking to the man walking her mount.

"Open the gates!" Malziek commanded. `

Dutifully, the men in the courtyard below began cranking on the wheel and the door slowly swung open. Directly over the gate, bowmen notched arrows and placed the string near their cheek. Every man, be he young or old, bore a weapon today. We always did. But today, they were ready in weathered and tanned hands.

"Ash, from the lava flats of the BlackBurg," DarSheer said as he brushed a fleck from his tunic and shook his head, dislodging several glowing embers from his locks. "War is here. Even the most insistent naysayer cannot hope to decry this now. Why do the embers fall if not to herald their lord's arrival? Blood will be spilt this night and the red light of old will once again dance in the skies."

Across the seething waves, a black thunderhead had begun to expand from the far island's shores. In its black embrace hung flashing orange and red streaks like blood running down a hard surface. From the lifeless shores beyond, we all heard the first drumbeat. One single beat. Then silence. Goosebumps raced down my back and I felt my hair stand up.

"What's going on?" Brenneth asked worriedly.

Below, the newcomers had finally entered the courtyard. Without waiting for Malziek's command, the men rushed to close the gate. Ash rained down all around in a steady display. The ground below grew in patches of grey, swallowing up the mud and grass.

"My lord?" a man shouted up.

Malziek gestured for DarSheer and me to follow him. He turned with a swift pivot and hurried down the staircase.

"Stay here," I cautioned Brenneth. "Keep your sword in your hand, and remember your brothers are here to defend you."

I joined the others in the courtyard and came to a stop. The female removed her hood; her cheeks were stained with tears and her skin pale as the waning moon. Wrinkles hugged the bottoms of her eyes and her long nose seemed to wilt over her lips. The child behind her was nesting his head in the small of her back. The woman spoke softly to Malziek and her words became clear as I hesitantly stepped into earshot.

"They came from the shadows. Beings of darkness and evil. Nightshades. From living shadow, they appeared. They were nothing. One moment we were on our daily routines of fishing and harvesting the last of our catch before the first snowfall. Then a scream. Two more. A hut was lit on fire. They came marching from all directions laughing and singing a song of death."

"Where are you from?" Malziek apparently hadn't noticed the woman.

"Fiscer's Peak, the conglomerate of fishing villages in the far north. We were massacred." She lifted her head and spoke stoically, "There was much bloodshed. They spared few to tell the tale. Man, woman, and bairn all fell to the curved blades of the Nightshade savagery. There was no chance to even call for aid. We had nothing but pitchforks and tools for our harvest. It *wasn't even a fight*." Her voice finally cracked, and she turned away.

"They let you live?" Malziek lifted her chin.

"They didn't have the choice, but I imagine if they didn't want us to escape, we'd be headless corpses on the ground with our skulls stuck on the end of a pike. This is one of my sister's friends, Eskgard. My name is Glysperia." She ran her fingers through the boy's hair.

"I'm Elënya, the town's healer," the younger woman said, wringing her hands. "I was on the outskirts of town finding herbs for this sick bairn. Poor thing. I heard screams and the sounds of swords cutting flesh. I ran before I knew the truth to the sounds."

"We met up on the road here," Glysperia murmured.

"It is a long way to travel when Avalon is closer." DarSheer glanced at Malziek.

"Not for those who know these lands," Glysperia countered. "There are trails and paths hidden to the eyes of many. But those of us who still till the earth and claim our bounty on the sea know our way around hills and forests. We had a mount. One of the wild ones that we let loose every year in our festival. It was only a few miles, grazing outside the city. It took some convincing, but it let me put them on its back and we moved with greater speed. But we were . . . waylaid."

"A band of Varg spotted us and gave chase," Elënya sighed. Her hair was cut in various lengths and tied into a loose bun on the top of her head. Her dress was simple but effective. She had a rugged beauty that came with a tan in the fields. "They shot arrows through the poor beast but eventually we were rid of them."

"We've been running for six nights without rest and little food," Glysperia continued. "We've come to bring tidings of an ancient evil. It has awoken. But it appears we are too late for even now his gates are swung wide and his legions muster at the call of their shadow king."

"I must look after the bairn." Elënya took the boy's arm and checked his forehead. She dug into a small pouch which hung on her belt.

"Our own healer, Lëuthorn, will aid you," Malziek gestured.

"My lord," DarSheer pulled Malziek aside, "we must read the signs. Call for aid! Call the Elfin to send their best bowmen and strengthen our walls."

"I fear we are beyond the aid of the West," Malziek murmured slowly. He turned and let the ashes fall on his face. "Gone is peace in the fell chasms below. Clouds cover the sun and drums announce his call. Mordën has arrived."

Suddenly, cries came for all to man the wall. Swords were drawn, the metal scraping against the leather as the glinting blades reflected the torchlight. Men dislodged their heavy cloaks about their shoulders and raced up the narrow stairs. Altruic had called the stable boys to attention and had a long line of ready-to-go mounts waiting outside the dull stable doors. The day had begun to grow dark and heavy around us, suffocating conversation. A drumbeat. One beat. Two. A second joined it. Three beats. Four. A third. Five beats. Six. A great sound split the air. The Horn Asunder was sounded. Not in my time here had it ever been sounded. Malziek often reminded me it sounded to signal the beginning of the end.

"SHADOWS ON THE BRIDGE!" Throbb thundered. "Arm yourselves. They're coming!"

Malziek drew his blade, and his cloak billowed in the gale. The past couple of weeks I'd seen him defeated and in the comfort of isolation. Here, surrounded by fear-stricken faces and falling ash, his grim face was proud, and his hair flowed behind him. His cloak floated several feet until it landed half in a brazier. Flames licked it greedily. He turned to the newcomers.

"Our hospitality is lessened of late, my friends, of this I apologize. I must reinforce the walls and stand with my men. I'd recommend you flee while you still can. Once our enemy arrives, none are escaping."

"Some *must*!" DarSheer argued as they hurried to the stairs. "We are to alert others. Your words!"

"I know my words," Malziek said gruffly.

"Send some of our swiftest mounts and riders to Avalon. King Elharan must be warned!"

"And so, he shall," Malziek nodded. "I leave these choices in your trusted hands. You've never failed me in the past. You certainly won't now."

I didn't know what to say so I simply sprinted after them. We appeared on the wall. Malziek's eyes were heavy with determination. At his side, he held his massive hammer and peered out intently.

"When was the last time the lava flats erupted?" I didn't know if I actually wanted the answer.

"Not in our lifetime has such smoke and fire been seen," the response came back short. "The drums on the midday's currents speak of a force preparing to move. Listen!"

In the distance, as if in our heads, came a chant accompanied by hundreds of boots thudding against stone. The black fog above multiplied, moving over the water as if to cover whatever was beneath them. Drums rumbled. Nearly lost to the din, dark chants rose again and again. They sang of a new king and a new darkness. Tall halberds bore aloft a midnight grey banner which flowed behind them. Varg marched and stumbled and limped their way across the Bridge and toward the only visible obstacle in their path.

I drew the sword at my side. Red light forked through the day's blackness like a serpent's tongue hungry for the scent of its prey. The thunder of the drums drowned the pounding of the ocean beyond. Shivering and pathetic, I stood atop the unyielding stone of the bulwark gazing out at the sea of death before us. Snarling abominations held thousands of torches aloft. Across the battlements, the watchmen were hastily putting out the fires, casting the walls in growing patches of darkness. High above, the silver and green of The High City's banner snapped and danced to the tune of the howling wind. Down on the fields below, the Varglarian drew curved swords of black steel. Some bore shields, others pikes, whose pointed tips rose ten feet above their helmeted heads. On their banner, a black backdrop drew the eye instantly to a bloodred hourglass with seven orbiting eyes. Seven for the Hourglass.

"Othrain, Kissinger!" Malziek bellowed. "Take your bowmen and ready on my mark."

"Yes, sir!"

The two peeled themselves from the walls and dashed down the stairs into the courtyard. I turned slightly to where I could catch a glimpse of the leader of the Outpost. Malziek stood, unwavering, his hair flowing in the wind. Some crouched in fear but not him. In one hand he bore a golden spear, tip aimed for the night sky. In the other hand, he gripped the hammer nearly the size of his head. The light of a dream come true shone in his eyes.

"Now shall my people be avenged," he murmured. "Long have we sat here, pacifying the demands of the rich and the fat. They require proof. They shall have it. My blood will be the catalyst to unifying the peoples of Ëonë in this war. Mark my words, the fight didn't begin, for it never ended. As long as Mordën is allowed to roam free, we will always be imprisoned by his will."

"My lord," I hesitated, "what of Marian and Traverse? The newcomers? Surely, they should be given the order to retreat. Have them scale the rear wall."

"The order was given at the first horn blast," came the response. "Traverse and Marian refuse to leave. The westerlings and their entourage head west with our full blessings. I pray they ride fast enough to outride the tsunami about to hit these walls."

"And Glysperia?" I inquired.

"She went with them," Malziek promised.

Chants of death and darkness rose over the walls, slithering into the ears of any listening and gripping the hearts of the inexperienced fighter. Old and young alike shook in their boots. Two boys dropped their arms and fled to the stairs. An older man with deep wrinkles beneath his tanned brow dropped his spear and covered his face.

"Hold!" Malziek roared. He raised his weapon.

"Here we give our last to serve as a beacon to the aging that they may not join the dead!" DarSheer roared. He turned to look at the faces of those nearest him. "Our lands have been won hard by toil, and though this burden was not on our shoulders but those of our forebears, this responsibility now rests with us. Stand with us. Stand while the gates hold and your strength does not waver. If even one of us falters, we all fall. United together, together united!"

"This is the beginning of war," Malziek grimaced. "Mordën is not interested in resting in his shadowy lair any longer. The world shall know his name, and once again he will grip the hearts of all with crippling fear. We stand a pebble before a rushing river. Ours is now to be a beacon alerting."

"You mean we have *no* chance?" my voice cracked.

Far off, along the coastal beach, the ground began to rumble and with it came zigzagging cracks of glowing red. The hordes of Varglarian scattered, leaving a wide-open space where dirt and rocks began to fly like projectiles high into the night sky. Over the Bridge, a second group of shadowed individuals crested the rise. My throat seized and my eyes widened.

"Nightshades!"

The cry rose like a siren's wail. Malziek didn't move, but I couldn't help but notice that he gripped the hammer tighter. DarSheer, broadsword now in hand, gestured to Brenneth and a group of boys.

"Take every mount able and saddle them up!"

"Are you now in charge?" Malziek retorted. "Hold your posts, bairns."

"My lord." DarSheer stepped forward. He gazed deep into Malziek's burning eyes. "We can maybe hold the Varg for a day or so, but we will fall. Accompanied by Shades, they will have us choking on our own blood and joining the halls of our forebearers in an hour. It is true: alone they are easy pickings. The Varg are a pest alone. But Nightshades are far worse."

"We do not retreat." Malziek glared back. "I have stood, enduring the withering gaze of those far over the Fallen Peaks since I was a young lad assigned this cursed outpost. I will not sully the sacrifices my fathers made by retreating."

A figure stepped to the front of the dark lines and raised his head. His face was a line of scars and holes and his black eyes glared up at us with deep-seated hatred. His voice floated up onto the ramparts.

"Now shall the world of the living be replaced by those who came before! It was promised to us, and it shall be ours. The world shall know the name of Raoul, harbinger of doom and darkness. Go forth and do our master's bidding. I, Raoul, demand it!"

Raoul roared. Below, the Varg stopped their shouting and the entire field sat in silence. The Nightshades stopped their advance at the edge of the Bridge.

"It appears Mordën has found his first lieutenant." Malziek turned to his men and all eyes found him. For a golden moment, the enemy was forgotten as their leader rallied them with his commanding presence. "These are ill days. Death and ruin are our future. But I tell you this as surely as this will end in death, I welcome it. Here the very hordes of hell are unleashed and even if Mordën himself stood before me, I would gladly fall. I hold no man to their post for it is clear to be a lost cause. Any who remain shall perish alongside me but such an end it will be. The bards will be fueled with songs for centuries to come. Around tables of glowing maidens and eager young bairns shall our names be scribed in the Annals of Ëonë. When they speak of courage and honor, of bravery and nobility, of loyalty to their lord and land, no names save for the greats of old shall be held in higher esteem. If you choose to stay, I hold you as a brother. Our blood shall water the ground. Rank means naught here, henceforth, for we are all common blood. If you stand now with me against the face of hopelessness and despair, I make this solemn oath to you that you shall see your great reward, for tonight we dine in the halls of our fathers! Who stands with me?"

For a moment no one moved save for the flags on their posts. One could have heard a strand of hair hit the stone. Then a single figure stepped forward from the shadows along the walls.

"I, Tire, third generation of my father, shall stand with you, Lord Malziek. Of old was my great-grandsire a man of noble blood. He fought with the noble warriors of his day and Mordën was vanquished, banished. If our great foe has forgotten his place, it is up to us to remind him. You have my allegiance to the bitter end."

"And gladly do I take it," Malziek gave the man a nod of gratitude.

"I have nothing left to live for." A boy stepped forward. His entire body shook like a leaf in a gale. "I am named Scupe, but here I've been known only as a stable boy. I've done no great deeds nor have my family been worthy of song. I know now my father and his father through the lines of our lineage would stand here and give their lives. I am no different. On this my oath I give to you, Lord Malziek! And here I shall stand with the powerful men of my time."

Malziek pursed his lips together as his eyes grew moist.

"A fisherman," a skinny bloke with a large beard advanced a hesitant step, "by trade. That was the job I was born for. Since my first glimpse of this world, I've known fish and ocean and little else. I am proud to stand here doing what matters. I stand by my pledge as a watchman of the Outpost."

"And I!" Othrain growled up from the courtyard. His bushy brow was furrowed. "If the blasted Varg think they'll find me on my back waiting my death with the cowardice of a dog displaying its belly, they'll be quite surprised. We shall cut down enough that if we stacked their bodies on top of each other, we could reach the blasted heavens and *tell Erëthuil himself of our feats*!" He bellowed out the last part and cheers rang true. Men clapped him on the back and shouted his name. He practically glowed with their cheers.

"I live a bairn," Brenneth's small voice cut through the ruckus as all hushed in anticipation, "but I'll die a man!" His cheeks blushed red as several of the nearest bowmen uprooted him and planted him on their broad shoulders. Emboldened by their actions, he cried out loudly. "Where once reins and saddles were all I held, now sword and dagger be my tools of trade! To die a man of the Outpost is to die . . . with *honor*!"

In like fashion, nearly every man atop the walls pledged again their unwavering loyalty in oaths of fealty. Some knelt, others slammed their fists against their chests. Malziek gazed upon them, and if I didn't know him better, I'd think he was gazing with pride and humility.

"They are willing to go to the grave with you, my lord," DarSheer murmured.

"And you, my old friend?" Malziek murmured softly in stark contrast to the hoots and hollers around. "Will you follow me, an old joyless codger made cruel by too many winters, to the bitter end?"

"My sword is yours to command, as is my life." DarSheer bowed his head. "Once a watchman . . ."

" . . . always a watchman." They clasped forearms and grunted. The moment was touching but brief.

"Your command?" Throbb ducked. Several stray arrows flew overhead, far from any target but a signal the fight was about to commence.

Malziek cleared his throat and stuck out his chest with pride. "ARROWS . . . FIRE!"

From the courtyard, an answering hailstorm of flaming tipped arrows launched overhead. We watched in silent awe as, if in slow motion, the path of the projectiles went from an upward trajectory to a downward whistle toward the horde before us. Many arrows sunk their fangs into the mud and exposed bark of trees. A few soft cries of victory sounded as Varg after Varg collapsed, an arrow quivering in their neck, blood squirting onto their armor. Malziek cursed. A section of beach, riddled with arrows, began to glow a venomous amber. The Varg nearby scattered.

The horde beyond the walls roared in a sudden movement; bows were drawn from their backs and arrows knocked. I gripped the merlon in front of me. The air was positively tinged with electric current. At that moment, the glowing section of beach exploded outward. Sand and particles plumed out like a volcanic eruption. Debris rained down around us, sand coating my head. Varg near the eruption were engulfed and dragged beneath the sand as a long black tube jutted up and into sight. A second and third and fourth tube appeared. The red forks of lightning above flashed brighter and in the occasional bursts of red light, I watched as a black body the size of a large house heaved up from its sandy tomb. For once, neither DarSheer nor Malziek seemed to find words.

The Varglarian began jeering and chanting again, slamming sword against shield and waving their spears. Their drummers beat even more as the shape, joined by four more black poles, rose to its full height above the beach. Their ugly speech filled my ears.

"Rachnadon . . . Rachnadon . . . Rachnadon!"

"Spiders. They have massive spiders. Of course they do," Malziek sighed.

Chapter 2
The Ford of Duïn

CRIMSON STREAKS FILLED THE clouds with peppered flashes. A boulder, seemingly defying gravity, launched from the quivering jaws of a particularly ginormous Rachnadon. The stone hurtled toward the walls. Even as I watched it approach, I couldn't help myself.

"This is going to hurt," I muttered.

Less than a dozen yards from where I stood, the hunk of stone slammed into the wall. That section of battlements seemed to explode. Shrapnel flew every which direction. The few guards in the vicinity of the blast were reduced to screaming shapes as they were flung over the wall. I ducked but not before the blinding pain.

The sounds of war faded. My vision blurred. Blood flowed down my face as I shook my head. Several men were shouting but it was like listening to screams underwater. The blast had laid me out on my back, dust filling my lungs. The night sky above filled with projectiles like a meteor shower. A second boulder fell toward me. It aimed to land directly on me. I could almost smell the dirt and grime caked on the stone as it sailed, but it landed with a sickening crunch in the courtyard a few feet away, barely missing the battlements. I opened my eyes for a few moments, feeling my limbs and head to ensure I was whole. The boulder had landed on one of the officers' huts. There was no time to wonder if any unlucky souls were now jelly. I saw two wooden poles appear in a crenel. Sound returned with a rush, and I was aware of the roar of voices and the thud of boots on the ramparts. Men ran toward and away from me. Some shot arrows from their bows. Metal clanged and above me, gripping the poles, the first of the creatures appeared. It heaved its quivering body over the crenel and landed, iron boots first, onto the stone. With a roar, it turned to face me and raised its long curved black blade.

No matter how many times I was forced face-to-face with these creatures, they still took me by surprise. When I found the creature standing close to me, dagger drawn, I couldn't help but stare at it. DarSheer had explained during practice that the Varglarian began as corrupted husks during the early age of Ëonë. When Erëthuïl told the Luthi to spread out over the world and create, he had given them his blessing to do what they wished provided they did not create a race of living beings such as themselves, for that power was reserved for Erëthuïl alone. Mordën, in secret, took an example from his creator and tried to make his own race. He used forbidden chants crafted by his own chaotic soul and entrusted to no one else. The creatures had come to life, but he twisted the words so that a desire for destruction haunted them every moment of their miserable lives. He poured his being into making them and showed them to Erëthuïl. He expected to be rewarded with great mention and a place in the heavenly halls where Erëthuïl dwelt. Instead, in great sadness at this discovery, Erëthuïl banished the abominations to the lowest chasms beneath the Fallen Peaks in hopes they would never return to the good lands he had made. Because of his betrayal, Mordën was stripped of his title of "Luthi" and cast out into the darkness. In secrecy, he continued to breed and corrupt these life forms till he had formed an army and with them he marched on Ëonë in the First Great War. The first Nightshades came to be in the Second

Era, twisted, changed, and scarred versions of Humans and Elfin and Drucodians alike who had accepted offers of peace and longevity if they swore oaths to Mordën and resided on the BlackBurg. In the darkness of his fortress, Mordën had begun using them for terrible experiments. He would poison them, test their limits of pain, and in so doing discovered the weaknesses of each race. He improved steadily upon their weakness, adding the additional six eyes which made them so distinguishable. He had planned to use this to his advantage in his great war. What happened to the original people who had accepted the invitations, no one knew. Legend told they died horrible deaths burning alive in the lava pits. DarSheer believed Mordën killed them all after the experiments were done and he was ready to march on the world. With his knowledge from his experiments, he'd made the true-blooded Nightshades: dark, shadowy figures who could slip in and out of reality wherever shadows slept.

No one had really seen what a Varglarian looked like underneath their black armor or faceplate, but illustrations in ancient texts showed them to have misshapen bodies, as if they were cobbled together by parts from different-sized beings. Bones stuck out at odd angles. Their flesh was in a constant state of decay. It rotted even as they lived. Ears had been burnt off and their hair scalped. There was nothing remotely human about them. Mordën had reserved the worst for last. It is said the eyes are the window to the soul. Instead of normal balls of white with colored irises, or even solid black orbs like Mordën and the Nightshades, the Varglarian's eyes were simply balls of glowing fiery hatred, like embers burning in the night. At night, they were positively horrifying. They lived in a perpetual state of agony and anger, fueled by a hatred seeded thousands of years ago.

I rolled as the dagger rang off the stone. The Varg snarled. If I could have seen its face, I imagined it bared its teeth. Instead, I was forced to stare directly into its glowing eyes. My sword lay yards away in the shadows where I had dropped it upon being laid flat out on my back. The black steel glinted as a third boulder roared overhead. I didn't see where it landed but felt the heat as a fiery explosion rocked the courtyard.

"They send a bairn to fight where a man cannot?" the creature snarled with glee. Through the slits in the helmet, its voice sounded echoey like a snarl through a long tunnel. "Perhaps they hope such an offering will appease the hunger of the mighty Varglarian warrior?"

With a single flick of his wrist, DarSheer decapitated the beast and kicked its body over the edge of the wall. He gave me a look and, using his foot under the blade, kicked me my sword.

"Recommendation," he shouted over the noise, "have a weapon on you in the middle of a battle."

"I was taunting it." I wiped the sweat from my brow and tried to forget that I had been seconds away from death.

On the plains before the wall, they moved as a horde. And their boots sounded like thunder rolling in the deep. They chanted as they swarmed the front gates and with their weight, they slammed body and shield against the creaking door. Fell ranks moved with purpose, for they had one common goal. They cared not for their own dead but used them as shields, propped on the flat surfaces of shields or held up, two Varg hiding crouched behind till the corpse they gripped was filled with spears and arrows. Several commanded their like and ladders of great height were hoisted above armor and shoulder. Torches lit the scene as flashes of amber light gave us horrifying glimpses of how large their number was. Four Varg wheeled up a large device and aimed it toward the catapult that stood ready along the southern wall and with a howl of glee, a large arrow hurtled through the air. It slammed into the catapult and sent the device, wood splintering and all, over the edge of the wall and into the darkness beyond. Men hurried to and fro, ducking as they passed the clear shot of the crenels. Some crawled on their hands and knees to avoid being shot as hundreds of arrows filled the sky.

A second Varglarian appeared over a ladder propped against the merlon. Before it could step one hairy twisted foot over the crenel, an arrow appeared in its throat. Othrain jogged into view, a bow in one hand.

"You need help, Broadsword?" He grinned a crooked smirk of manic thrill. "Are these fat cretins providing too much of a challenge for ya?"

"If I needed help, Othrain," DarSheer responded, peering over the wall and squinting, "I would not have asked *you*, and if I did have to ask, I'd be greatly disappointed." DarSheer stepped aside and pointed. Othrain cackled and took aim. He waited for a Varg to stick its head over the edge of the battlements and fired at point-blank range. The arrow entered the creature's eye, and the Varg teetered back, falling off the ladder and down into the convulsing mass of armor and weapons below.

Malziek strode into sight, blood dripping from his blade, a vengeful look in his eyes. The wind whipped about his head and sent his hair flopping from shoulder to shoulder. On his chest, a small fire had begun to spread. He dismissed the worst of it with a slap of his meaty hand. The last tendril of fire he flicked with his gloved hand and glowered.

"They're swarming the southern and eastern walls," Malziek snarled. "Half the men are dead by sword or rock. Those Rachnadons need to be brought down. Othrain, why haven't you been using the catapult?"

"That was the source of their first target, my Lord," Othrain's humor was absent, and he stood stiffly. "I lost half my reserves manning that station. The rest are dealing with small parties of roving Varg who made it down into the courtyard."

"DarSheer, do you remember what we discussed?" Malziek's tone left no room for protest.

"I do," DarSheer responded cautiously.

A Varglarian appeared over the wall and leapt at Malziek. Without looking, Malziek reached a hand out and grasped the creature by the throat. The Varg struggled against his iron grip but ultimately expired as Malziek squeezed. He tossed the limp body over the ramparts with little concern, as if he were tossing a rock into a lake.

"Enact it. Take who you can and spread the news. Escort him to the city and be sure the golden king knows everything that transpired here." Again, his tone was final.

A ball of flame soared like a comet overhead, landing in the courtyard. It demolished the stables and inn, sending wood and stone into the air. Stable boys and men ran in pandemonium. Groups of Varglarian preyed from the shadows between huts on unsuspecting soldiers. Kissinger slid into view, blood running down his temple.

"My Lord, the front gates are being overrun! They attack from above and a battering ram is moving up the road. For every Varg our arrows kill, five more take its place. We will be completely breached in minutes!"

"They have a ram!"

The alerting cry went up as an arrow appeared from the blackness and lodged into the caller's throat. The boy, younger than Brenneth, toppled over the edge of the wall and Malziek looked on grimly. Throbb rushed to the spot and battled back a Varg who had leapt down on top of the boy's body and had begun hacking at it. The creature growled but fell back, Throbb's sword pressed firmly into its neck. The older watchman cried out and withdrew the blade, swinging it and severing a nearby Varg's foot from below the knee. From there, the aged man swung his sword and howled like a banshee.

"My lord!" he bellowed as he beheaded three enemies in an intense foray. "They're about to breach the gate." He gurgled as a knife imbedded in his eye and he dropped to his knees. The Varg that had delivered the blow grabbed Throbb's skull between its armored hands and crushed it. Throbb sank into a pool of blood and brain matter on the wall. One eye had popped free of its socket and dangled by a fleshy cord. I looked away. Kissinger dry heaved and gripped his stomach. Othrain glared.

"So comes the end of my time," Malziek said tiredly. "Ensure that those who fight do not forget what happened here nor forget the courage and bravery all displayed. Remember the Outpost."

"It will be a rallying cry, my lord, but surely there can be another path," DarSheer protested. "We've already sent some along the Westerly Road. Why don't we follow them?"

His voice carried a hint of desperation mixed with grief. It was clear now that the battlements were being demolished as additional ladders were thrown with relish against the crumbling stone and waves of snarling Varg swarmed the few defenders. It was only a matter of time before they would reach where we stood. Fires burned in blood reds and in the mournful blacks of the sky, I saw the lumbering Rachnadon step one long leg over the wall and into the courtyard. It was like a scene from some apocalyptic ballad. Men screamed as they were stabbed or beheaded. Several Varg took to feasting on the corpses which lay hewn about.

Othrain glanced over as a young man, in his early twenties at most, staggered into view and dropped to both knees. His left arm was caked in blood. His face was ashen and his lips pale.

"They've knocked down the gate. I did as you commanded, my lord. There are none now left to defend the courtyard. It is over." The man fell on his back and choked up blood. He expired soon after.

"Kissinger," DarSheer shouted briskly. "Pack what supplies were stashed at the western wall and meet us . . . where we discussed."

Kissinger, who'd been kneeling not far off, glanced between the four of us uncertainly. His clear hesitation mounted as Malziek gestured for the order to be carried out. But as a trained watchman under the rules of the Outpost, he did not question his commands and turned. I watched him hurry away into the darkness.

"Make for Avalon," I heard Malziek whisper to DarSheer. "Make for The Golden City. Remember not our grievances. We must forget the trials of our past. Old bloods *must* be rekindled if we are to survive. I task this last to you my most loyal of warriors. My brother. What was once strong will be strong again."

He clasped DarSheer's forearms and leaned his temple to touch his. For a brief second, they held the pose. Then Malziek kissed DarSheer's forehead in farewell and turned to me. Behind him, a Varg approached. With his back to the creature, I knew he would react too late. With a leap forward, I brought my sword up and under his outstretched arm and directly into the chest plate of the snarling vermin. Black blood spurted out, caking my face and drenching my hair. I choked on the sour liquid. A second and third Varg leapt over the walls and landed to my left.

"We have worn out our mockery of them," Malziek noted with morbid pride. He slashed both arms off one creature. "Perhaps we should not gloat any longer."

Kissinger reappeared from the blackness and gestured. Othrain and DarSheer turned to run. I needed no encouragement to follow. Explosions boomed along the walls, lighting the courtyard in brief flashes. In the brief spurts of light, I witnessed the end of my home. All around, bodies stacked high, and shadows ran from brazier to brazier. A deep bellow roared out as the shadow of Traverse was chased by a stream of black bodies until his form fell over the edge of the wall. His death was illuminated by a flash of red light. Marian's scream of grief was cut abrupt as she was crushed under a large boulder. The walls were nearly void of our own, now overpopulated by the enemy. The Rachnadon who had stepped into the courtyard was busy feasting on a corpse. I tried not to vomit when I saw Dwaith hanging from the spider's jaws. As the firelight flickered, I saw the wrinkled apron and dress of one of the kitchen girls in the pile of bodies.

"Flock to me you hideous heathens of cursed creation!" Malziek swung his hammer in wide circles. His spear in the other, he began slashing and hewing approaching Varg. Like a tsunami to a beach, they came crashing in a tidal wave of bodies. Yet he hacked and he hewed. Boisterous was his laughter. Savage were his howls. Against the backdrop of red and black and fiery orange, he stood like a proud warrior of old. His hair flowed about his shoulders as he swung his weapons with mighty precision. Heads flew like balls into the night. Bodies dropped like millstones in the sea.

A horrible pain erupted behind my eyes, and I dropped to one knee, crying out and gripping my temple.

"At long last, we shall march on what was promised us. At long last we shall have our due!"

In the air above the battlements, the air twisted and an odor like the smell before a lightning strike filled the air. DarSheer grabbed me by the arm and heaved me toward a hidden staircase behind the inn. It was still in darkness and seemed to be void of enemies. But my mind was drawn back to the walls.

As if a knife had cut a slit in the sky itself, a hooded figure floated into view. It hovered several feet above the walls. The Varg climbing the ladders and chanting nearby stopped and froze in clear terror. Six other such hooded and floating forms appeared behind it and fanned out until they were in one long line. Together, in raspy haunting melody, they chanted as they glided forward.

"What grew in plenty now dies barren. What stood for centuries, crumbles before us. None shall stop nor halt nor delay the kingdom of shadow. Behold what was once born in darkness is now birthed again. Ride the wave of chaos. Bow before the black helm!"

A heart-wrenching shriek split the very foundations beneath our feet. Cracks appeared in blocks of stone. Dust fell. DarSheer crammed his fingers into his ears as he bent over. The walls shook violently. Varg were cast off into the darkness and screamed their way to their demise on the plains below.

"Move!" DarSheer shoved me down the stairs and followed, accompanied by Othrain and Kissinger. He turned back, eyes never wavering from his lord. "Malziek! We must go! Now! Do not be foolish."

The clouds above Malziek swirled in a circle. They illuminated more frequently with bright red flashes. A small section of wall cracked and tumbled toward us. I ducked back but was too late as a rock slammed into my shoulder and sent me spinning off the edge of the stairs. My limbs floundered about for some grip, some purchase to stop my fall. I landed with a thud in the churned-up mud of the courtyard. I couldn't breathe. My mouth opened and closed like a fish as I inhaled and inhaled, silently begging my lungs to fill. My vision blurred and spots danced before my eyes. I reached automatically for my weapon but found it gone. Only the small blade at my belt left me from being completely defenseless.

The Rachnadon had by now made its way completely into the courtyard and was stomping and bellowing about with all eight of its spiked legs. The hut I'd called home for so many months was a pile of rubble. The Eastward Inn burned in the night. The figure on the arachnid's back roared in victory as all around Varglarian poured into view. They climbed over the walls like hungry spiders or stomped through the broken gate. Malziek leapt over the battlements, slid down a crumpled beam, and rolled to a stop, on one knee, in the courtyard. The host of advancing Varg came to a stop before him. He and he alone held the enemy at bay as he roared out a laugh. He slowly stood and readied his weapons at his side. The Varglarians snarled and sneered yet made no move against him. Lord Malziek turned to DarSheer.

"Go now!" he roared with a proud determination, light glinting in his eyes. "Ride for Avalon and bring tidings of our misfortune. Leave me to teach these failures what becomes of those who batter down my gates and kill my men. Go!" With that, he turned and bared his teeth. Atop the Rachnadon, Raoul, silhouetted against the red light, gestured and the Varg raced toward Malziek, their eyes glowing bright behind their emotionless helmets. Malziek swung his hammer into the chin of the first Varg to reach him and with a twist and pivot, he stabbed his spear into the second. The wood of his shaft splintered and broke in two as a third foe slammed its sword down. Malziek ducked the second stab and spun in place. His hammer arched through the air and bashed the Varg in the face, lifting the creature off its feet and hurling it back at those who stood nearby. With each hit, Malziek cackled and crowed. His muscles bulged against iron bands as he swung again and again. And again, and again, the bodies began to pile up around him till only his shoulders and head were visible over the scene. His hammer sang its metallic *swoosh* and the following *ding* against metal rang out like the beginning notes of a song. Blood trickled down his face.

I staggered to my feet and toward the back of the courtyard where a previous missile had battered a hole into the wall. The clear night air and the Westerly Road gleamed into view. DarSheer stooped to aid me as I hobbled along, even as Othrain and Kissinger sprinted toward the gap.

We stumbled along, dodging bodies and plumes of flames. The hungry tongues of fire licked greedily at our clothing as we passed. The faces of the dead stared up at me. Boys with horrified looks in their young eyes. Men with twisted grimaces, arms at various angles. Some bore bite marks and others were missing most of their faces, whether to feasting Varg or a rock I did not know. The darkness suffocated me as I stumbled along behind DarSheer. He'd made it through the opening as I tripped over a motionless body. I cursed as the move sent me sprawling. Mud clung to my eyebrows and dug into my eyes. I pawed at my face so I could see.

As I scrambled up, I glanced down at the face of the body I'd tripped over and felt the wind leave my lungs for a second time. Denial demanded I take a second look. Brenneth's waxlike face stared up in the miserable defeat of death. His eyes, glassy, held no light. His cheeks were pale, his lips purple. Blood caked one side of his face. It looked like he'd been leading several people out through the wall but had turned around to return to the battle. *What insanity sent him back?* Whatever it had been, it had cost him the highest price. My hand flew to my mouth, and I froze. No tears came. My eyes couldn't avert. My soul took in the small body and a piece of me cracked. I knelt to close his eyes, give him some piece from the carnage about, but DarSheer was at my side and pulled hard on my arm.

"We need to move!" he spat as he watched the mass of limbs and swords moving toward us. "We can mourn later. The dead gave all so we could live. Do not let his sacrifice be an end to us."

My fingers fluttered briefly over his eyelids as I closed them and strained against DarSheer's powerful grip.

"Come on, Brenneth, we're going. You'll be okay." My breath came out in shaky gasps as I shook off DarSheer. "DarSheer, you need to help me. His face. There's blood. Help him! The horse can carry the both of us. Come on! Please!" I stared at the others with disbelief. No one moved save for DarSheer who wrenched me away from the body.

"Come now!"

"He was a child!" The drums and chants of the Varg were closing in. I could almost feel their boots thudding on the ground as they rushed toward us.

"And he was as brave as any man who fell on those walls," Othrain gave over the reins of a stallion to DarSheer. He glanced at me. "Old and young alike, they will all perish before this is over. You would do wise to remember the cost of war."

"Careful," Kissinger chided Othrain. "You and I can stomach what comes at the sweep of a blade. Forget not he is new to this world and not used to the atrocities of battle nor the brutality that comes with the Varg."

"I know all too well," I said so only I could hear. I shut my eyes and saw an older man turn at the mouth of a tunnel; his eyes wide with energy but deep with grief. He gave me a small smile before dozens of blades pierced him. Even as he fell to his death, I'd somehow known he was at peace.

We sprinted out through the opening in the stone wall. The moment I set foot on the matted damp grass beyond, I let out a cry as DarSheer hoisted me up onto a broad mare's back and before I had time to protest, we were thundering down the Westerly Road. Othrain and Kissinger led the charge, urging their mounts to top speed. The fire surged in demonic possession as it danced, tendrils flailing about like hands in the air. A wind sent the smoke low over the ground to choke us out while trees, grass, and bush became fodder for the flames. The entire Outpost was ablaze, one giant torch in the night.

Before long we'd left the grass of the Westward Plains behind and begun traversing over the cobbled roads that connected us to the rest of civilized world. The wind whipped into a frenzy and dug into our nostrils and eyes as we galloped. The cold seized my lungs and twisted them as moisture leaked from my face. I buried my head against the horse's neck and trusted it would follow the others. It was a road none of us, save for DarSheer, had ventured far down. Only the most trusted were sent with missions to Avalon and beyond. Despite having lived most of their lives here, Othrain couldn't help but crane their necks about to soak in the vistas about us. Directly outside the Outpost, it had been sweeping forests tripped up at times by rolling hills or marshes that stretched into the distance. Here where evidence of a society began with a cobbled road instead of dirt and clay, I instantly felt out of place. All around, the world grew and twisted in various displays of nature. Giant rock formations presented imposing figures that stood tall into the sky. The ground was steadily climbing and finally we reached the top of a tall hill and paused.

DarSheer bent over his mount's sweaty neck as he let loose a grieving cry and wept. I glanced back at what was now a raging fire. We must have been riding for ten minutes and still it was visible, even more so now. The clouds and flashing red light were restricted to just above the smoking ruins of the buildings. Here, the starlight twinkled merrily through whisps of pale white cloud. Flowers dotted the sides of the road and fruits hung in thick allure from the bows of several trees. Our gaze remained fixated on the desecration far east. The Outpost was in shambles and disarray as riderless horses thundered in circles with utter terror and the shadowy forms of Varg and Shade did battle, their forms enhanced by the fires behind them. Shadows danced a horrific dirge and the clang of metal and gnashing of teeth echoed up to our ears. Only the White Tower in the center stood tall and unblemished as smoke curled around its form like a grey tunic. DarSheer turned to gaze back. Wet streaks ran from eye to chin as he silently beheld the end of everything he'd known. Everything he'd known now smoked in the fires of defeat. The horrid flames licked the sky and sent clouds of smoke spiraling up.

"All shed your tears for the victorious fallen," DarSheer's voice was full of bitterness. I hadn't realized just how much pain he'd been in as he'd torn me away from Brenneth. "Let their deaths be a rallying point so the rest of this world may see Mordën in the light of his own fire.

They shall be avenged, or I shall die trying. This is my oath and this I declare to the ashes of my allies and the ears of the living. Be at peace, Lord Malziek of the Outpost."

"Be at peace, Brenneth, stable boy," I whispered.

Othrain turned in his saddle and sheathed his blade. I hadn't realized he'd been keeping his naked blade out the entire ride, as if prepared to fight the very trees around us. I knew he wanted to shout some insult or make a gesture to the enemy below. But even he understood. This was different. Kissinger found great interest in the weeds and flowers at the feet of his mount. We were silent as DarSheer mourned. My chest heaved but I shoved it down. I could not, would not, entertain the grief that was threatening to override my mind. I'd given up all I loved. I could not do it again. In this manner, my stomach aching at the pain, I waited till DarSheer finally turned and gave a gesture.

"We ride for The Golden City. It was Lord Malziek's last wish, and I swore to him I'd see the bairn there, safe. I know you all are not familiar with the lands here for Malziek was strict about keeping us disengaged from the doings of the rest of Ëonë. It's time you visited the plains and fields beyond the Outpost. Avalon is a hard ride from here covering many leagues of ground, not all of which are as pleasant as here. As the horse gallops, it is a multi-week journey through several towns and a city called Ithuïn. That is where we make our first stop of any lengthy duration. These roads are not safe any longer. Does anyone wish to protest this action?"

We all shook our heads unwilling to speak either from grief or weariness or simple shock. I wanted to get as far away as possible from the constant reminder of my failure. *His* face lit in the light of burning bodies, pale and bloodied. *So young.* But wasn't that why Mordën was here? To dominate and claim these lands as his own dark kingdom? His Varg were proven capable of just about everything. Was it so strange to think he'd stoop to murdering children, not just fighting men?

The ground was moist with the growing dusk as the clouds reveled in their shadowy addition. The darkness of the night spread its tendrils into the West and as we rode, I couldn't help but despair. For two years

I'd trained and forced myself to remember I was not a part of this world, that I'd return home the moment I got a chance. I'd wanted to keep distant from everyone to keep my mission sole focus. Now, I'd let people back into my life and they'd been wrenched from me and cast on the pile of dead. Even as I felt the mare beneath me gallop and the sounds of battle faded into the chirps of hidden insects and snorts of the occasional animal, my every thought sounded like a child's scream in my head. Like the way I imagined the stable boy screamed as he died alone and frightened. The greens of the grass and hills to the north seemed masked by shadow, and the browns and reds of the forests ahead tainted by the bloodshed. Ëonë had seen its first bloodshed in one thousand years. The chaos of old had returned. The night had taken its first kill. Mordën had begun his great campaign and my home, the Outpost, was now only a jutting tombstone for the victorious fallen.

I ducked the blade meant for my side and spun along the ground. The move had gotten me out of more than one sticky situation but this time, DarSheer was ready for it. As I twisted away, he suddenly leapt forward and brought his sword down harshly. I cried out in pain as the training blade thudded against my back.

"You jest with me," I moaned in protest as I lay in the grass and let the pain dissipate before rising. "How did you know I would do that?"

"Just because a choice works for you in one instance, do not expect your adversary to be unaware of its existence, for he will counter accordingly at the next." His eyes twinkled as he held back a laugh. "We have a phrase here: Allow it once without shame but come round again the same way and prove the fool you are."

"You've got me there." I coughed and mimicked stretching whilst eyeing for a prime moment to strike. "But I think I'd like to rest. By the time the next Varglarian attack comes around, you'll have done more damage to me than all of them combined."

"To the tavern then?" DarSheer lowered his blade and turned to toss it into the cart.

In a single leap, I slashed the light wooden sword at his hindquarters. I expected to connect painfully with flesh but instead, my sword clacked against his. In the blink of an eye, he had pivoted about and deflected the blow. In his eyes, I noted the surprise give way to gloating.

"How did you know?" I dodged his next attack.

"You think you're the first to try attacking me behind my back? You think no one else has tried to be sneaky and wave a flag of surrender all the while readying for the death blow?"

"Let me guess, you disagree with it because it's distasteful to attack an enemy with their back turned?"

"Far from it," he snorted. "Many fights are won through dishonorable tactics. Your enemy will happily employ all of them at once he if could. I encourage the use of any tactics when it comes to survival. The Varg, and by extension Nightshades, will not fight as man against man. In such combat of man against man, honor should be observed, and trickery bared. But in a fight for your life against those abominations? Sometimes you must fight dishonor with dishonor. Be careful with your eyes. They seek to reveal your deepest secrets. A seasoned warrior will not be confounded. I'm just surprised you got as close to hitting me as you did."

"You're getting slow, old man," I teased, swinging the blade around while circling him.

DarSheer lowered himself into a light stance, rocking on the balls of his feet. He gave my defense a quick test then rolled forward. I leapt up and over him, letting my blade click near to his neck. I landed a foot away and whirled about. He stood but an inch from my nose, eyes glinting darkly. His practice blade was a centimeter from my throat.

"Well done," he approved. "You're dead. But you've come a long way since the bumbling idiot you were before. The bairn then couldn't even hold a sword let along preform the acrobatics you've displayed here."

"It's the grey in the banner motivating me," I joked. A banner above us snapped as if to make its point. The wind rippled through the fabric.

"You mock our banner?"

"Merely noting its odd design." I shrugged as I picked up my sword.

"It was made that way to be a beacon to the injured or lost." DarSheer dusted off his boots and sighed. "Anyone who had gotten led astray would look up and see the white mountain, and the blood of their ancestral warriors would flow through them."

"Don't get me wrong, I admire it." I eyed again for a chance to strike.

"Yet, in your attempt to appease while trying to find a weakness in me, I can sense your hesitation," he snorted back.

I lowered my sword and shrugged nonchalantly. "Not hesitation."

I stepped backward but as my left foot hit the ground, I instantly pushed off it, resulting in a leap backward followed by a lunge forward. DarSheer, momentarily distracted by our talk, reacted only to the rear leap. He lowered his sword to advance on me. His eyes went wide as I grew suddenly near and swung. The hard wood of the practice blade connected against his side with a solid thwack. Tears welled up in his eyes and he doubled over, coughing. He looked now like an old crone, helpless. But I kept my distance for I remembered his teaching and held my blade at the ready.

"Like I said." He stood, no longer a pitiful elder putting on a display of pain to draw me unsuspecting into his reach. He smiled widely. "You have improved. Once your kind heart would have mistaken my pain for truth. I dare say even yesterday you would have. What tipped you off?"

"Don't you think the tears were a bit dramatic?" I grinned back. "To anyone who knows you, they'd instantly see through that move. Besides, you have abs of steel. I doubt a training blade would even make you flinch. But I give points for the theatrical reaction. Perhaps one of a less intelligent nature would have fallen for it."

"Careful, bairn, keep your pride in check. Just days ago, you would be the same unintelligent bairn you mention. It's a good thing I don't make a habit of befriending Varglarians. I wouldn't want them aware of my most devious feints." He tossed his blade into the training cart, signaling the actual end of the training.

"I could go for some bistri." I added my blade to the cart and brushed the mud and grass stains on my tunic. DarSheer gestured and a stable boy hurried forward, his head down as he took the cart.

We strode into the inn. Behind a low counter, Traverse beamed at us. His face was red as a cherry and his hair stuck out in varying degrees. Over his cloth tunic, he had a small apron stretched to fit over his impressive girth. Laughter emanated from the few round tables as men, relived of their watch, enjoyed mugs of ale and wooden platters of bistri and salted meat. Even at its busiest, the inn held no more than forty men. Most chose to sit in silent exhaustion.

"You do me proud, lads," Traverse roared as he spotted us. "I'd thought the rumors of another Varg attack had scared off my favorite watchmen. What with blades ringing their song of war off each other . . ." He winked at his female counterpart as she strode past, and she shook her head. Always the seriousness to his humor, tonight Marian refused to play along. Traverse always scolded her for sullying his company and the two played off each other in this manner much to the amusement of all. Tonight, it appeared, Marian had had enough of his glee and didn't even humor his joke with the usual sigh and eye roll, to the usual roaring laughter of all present, drunk, or otherwise.

"Tough night?" I sympathized as Traverse hurried around his make-shift counter and stood before us.

"Oh, don't let Marian burn your spirits," he chuckled. "The usual?"

DarSheer and I nodded as he banged the table and Marian reappeared. She gave me a soft smile and a polite nod to DarSheer before vanishing into the backrooms, presumably to find any morsels she could for us. As the rumors had begun, more came to the tavern to discuss and the more they came the more Traverse found himself out of stock. Recently, with the next shipment of goods delayed due to Varg attacks in the neighboring villages, he'd been unable to maintain his usual cheeriness and had to turn away many to the cold unforgiving nights.

"Three bistri to split," Marian appeared at my side and set a plate of the brown crusty pie and two bowls of steaming porridge, "and a nice helping of my porridge. Don't ask me what's inside." She winked and bustled off to help a particularly drunk man who'd found a sudden fascination with the warts on his hands and was busy skewering them with the tip of a knife.

Traverse brought two mugs of his best ale and slammed them down before us. He spread his arms and bowed. DarSheer flicked him two thruki and with the pleasure of a man having made a profitable sale, the tender removed himself from our presence.

I sipped on the bubbling ale. "How long do you think before the next attack?"

"Our scouts say a small force has made its way to their side of the Bridge." DarSheer took a deep gulp of the ale and wiped his mouth. "Liqthuïn and Thraon have not yet reported back from their northern seaside excursion. Malziek is beginning to worry, but their report time has not yet passed so I'm biding my time."

"Shouldn't we worry?" I scooped a handful of the delicious beef pie into my mouth, letting the succulent slabs of meat clash with the sweet tangs of the bread. Marian's bistri pies always left their consumer satisfied and tonight was no different. "It's been over a week since they last even tried."

"Worry about what?" DarSheer snorted as he too filled his mouth with bistri. "We know the Varg hate crossing the water by boat. They will come by means of the Bridge and we will be ready and repel them as we always do. Malziek has doubled and tripled the scouting runs. It's why you've been trained so fast." He chuckled.

"All the same," I let the ale rest in my stomach, "I'd rather be safe than sorry." I stared intently at the small candle which sat in the center of our table. Wax dripped down the side and pooled at the base before hardening. The process was repeated over and over, the pile of wax growing taller with every passing minute.

"Remember any new memories?" DarSheer asked hopefully as he emptied his mug.

"None," I shook my head, "since yesterday. But it doesn't matter because what I do remember is enough to set the hairs on the back of my neck standing tall and erect. DarSheer, Mordën, in my world, was powerful yet crippled. I cannot imagine what he is like now when he has his resources to pull from."

DarSheer shifted uncomfortably in his seat, even ignoring the flirtatious look Elacious, one of the kitchen girls, sent him. He was doing her a favor, after the new policy Traverse had put into effect. She often found herself smitten with any man able to wield a sword and DarSheer was her latest target. Despite her recent advances, he'd usually been kind and returned with a smile or wave.

"We can only hope what you remember is tainted beyond recovery," he finally said. I stared at him and wrinkled my brow. "I know that seems wrong to say, especially after Malziek places such a high prize on your memories, but from what you've told me, we will gain nothing good from your mind."

"I wish all that was evil had been forgotten." I closed my eyes and let all the memories flood over me like a beginning storm over a helpless traveler. The force of the emotions rained down as I remembered her. Our final words had plagued my waking and dream-filled thoughts. I felt an emptiness where once my friends had filled.

"Phoenix?" DarSheer lightly shook my hand, concern in his eyes. "Perhaps we should move onto less painful subjects. Dwelling on the past is helpful, but only at a time you are ready."

"But what if my memories could help us destroy Mordën before he has any chance to launch his armies?"

DarSheer leaned forward with kind concern. "Do not feel I diminish your worth by saying this, Phoenix, but Mordën is careful. There is no known way to destroy him, certainly none that he would have so brazenly put on a pedestal in your world. Your memories, important as they are, will not bring an end to the potential chaos on the horizon. You must not put this weight on yourself. You will be crushed."

I felt stupid, like I was baring my soul to a stranger. "I was the one who brought him here. I fulfilled that inane prophecy, right? What if my role is not over? If in the depths of my darkest nightmares, I know a way to destroy him? And that's why he constantly attacks me in my sleep. I've lost almost everything. I'm afraid of losing what small hope I have."

"Malziek does place heavy emphasis on those thoughts." DarSheer sipped his ale. "Deep down he knows those will not be what brings about victory. It is good to remember, but it is fatal to remember too much. If you remember something that could help us, by all means tell us. But do

not beat yourself up if you don't. Your worth is not in what you bring to the table, but in how you act."

Maybe it was the ale murmuring comfortingly in my mind, but the words made sense. "Thank you."

"Don't let him take one more from your world," DarSheer said firmly. "You may have brought him here, but he will not destroy you. Have courage, my friend. Be at peace."

"But what if I can't? What if through my failures, the Outpost falls?" I allowed the silence to grow between us and the ears closest to us turned heads to listen to our conversation. Even Traverse had stopped scrubbing down the ale barrels and eyed DarSheer cautiously. The entire tavern held its breath. DarSheer took a bit of the bistri and let himself think. Only the sound of a faint buzzing broke the silence.

"Should we fall, Avalon would need to be notified. And a plan is already in place for such an occurrence. Malziek would not let even the most doubtful of avenues go unchecked. He would not let someone in our circle if he didn't trust them to hold their own. You value yourself as an object. I don't."

The tavern broke into soft conversations as backs were turned once more to us and heads swiveled back toward the center of their tables. Smoke from pipes spiraled up to the ceiling and there gathered like storm clouds. Traverse shook his disproval of our conversation and bustled out of the room.

"Of course. Avalon?" I sat back, letting my satisfaction with the meal linger. "The Golden City?"

"The same." DarSheer cleaned the ale from his beard and moved to stand. I pulled him back down.

"Why?" I stared deeply into his eyes. "The men on the wall tell me Avalon would not answer the call if Mordën's greatest host were knocking on their walls. They say the divide between Elfin and Human is too great to repair. What makes you think we should call on them and not The High City?"

"Don't let the disgruntled words of men with too much time on their hands sway you," DarSheer spoke determinedly. "Avalon will answer the

call; they swore an oath after the Second Great War. They are bound by blood to respond on the day when Mordën marches once more on Ëonë. Behind their white banners, The High City will rally. Hope is not a thing of the past, Phoenix, until we let it be. Avalon will answer. Promise me this: if the day comes when the Outpost falls, you must ride with the wind of a thousand dying breaths at your back to Avalon. Swear it to me as I have sworn to Lord Malziek. If we fall, the rest of the world must know what is coming for them."

I leaned back from his sudden urgency. A mere moment ago he'd dismissed my concerns with the ease of a man full of his meal and thoughts of his bed for his future.

"I promise." I let the words hang as Traverse waddled over.

"Are you lads done scaring off the people in my tavern?" His voice was gruff, but a mirthful twinkle shined in his eyes.

"Calm your bistri." DarSheer yawned and pushed back from the table. "Phoenix and I just stayed to drink our fill and grumble off to bed like the old men we are."

At that, Traverse grinned widely and chuckled. He ensured he had everyone's attention before responding.

"I appreciate your kindness, DarSheer Broadsword." His belly jiggled with his laughter as the men in the room forced out chuckles of their own.

We excused ourselves from the tavern and entered once more into the chilliness of the night watch. The sullen forms of men on duty shone against the brilliance of the moon overhead. In the distance, I could hear the almost rhythmic soft slaps of the water as if lulling all to sleep. There were some amongst the watchmen who believed the ocean was a servant of evil too. That every trickle was a limb extending from the form Mordën might take. The wind whispered his foul name. The air hung rich with his scent. No one would sleep tonight.

The night was heavy with the weight of spilt blood as we rode, letting the mounts trample plant and rock and leaf underfoot over the uneven ground. Damp with the dawn's coming glow, the laden bows of trees bore dew drops which sparkled like the night stars. The water droplets imploded as we trotted over them like mini explosions. The weight of my sword, as it thudded rhythmically against my thigh, pulled at my tunic. The implication of the previous night's attack troubled my mind and I turned to DarSheer who, at my side, kept up stride for stride.

"What does this mean? The end of the Outpost?" I had to force each word out between labored breath. Frigid air whipped about us and made moisture drip from my eyes and nose. Faint ghostly screams still haunted my hearing and every swish of a tree's foliage sent shivers down my spine.

The response came equally ragged. "With the Outpost razed, the gateway to all of the Eastern Ward, and by means Ëonë itself, is now largely unprotected. If the peoples who call this ward their home are not warned, they will be no better than livestock led to the slaughterhouse."

The air whipped by my face as we ascended the side of a steep hill and ducked beneath the occasional tree. Far behind, the dim light of fire against the clouds was still visible, sending constant reminders of what had just transpired.

"Avalon must be forewarned, for in them shall our hope continue. No one in the Eastern Ward now possesses the strength to defend against Mordën's armies since the Kingdom of Glasbur closed its gates eons ago."

He coughed and we rode in silence for several miles as the ground steadily rose and fell from the ocean plains to the hilly terrain which seemed more common this far inland. The morning grew bright as the sun peeked its form above the northern plains. It was not much further, and my muscles were aching to the breaking point as DarSheer's eyes drooped. The sounds of creatures in the underbrush sent goosebumps racing down my back. The slightest sound possessed the threat of a Varg. I found myself reaching for my blade, fingers itching against the smooth metal.

"We must rest," I mumbled. "I cannot live in this terror."

"We cannot rest." Othrain looked back. He still led the pace but even his eyes were red with exhaustion.

"Mordën's forces now hold the eastern territory we once protected." Kissinger ran his fingers through his hair. "With that they can strike the northern fishing villages. They'll not be expecting it. The longer we rest the more will die before a sufficient army can be raised to slow his advances. We're not merely saving our own lives by moving on without rest, we're saving thousands of others."

"All noble causes." DarSheer came to a stop and dismounted. He walked to a berm and gazed north and south.

"The closest village is at the Ford of Duïn." Othrain rode up to his side and looked down. "But what of the city of Ithuïn? Or Caldonia down south?"

"To get to Caldonia would require us to deviate far south, adding maybe ten days' ride to our trek." DarSheer shook his head.

"By the time word reaches Avalon," Othrain protested, "they'd be unable to respond anyway. I do not think Mordën means to sit and let his enemies armor up before he strikes. What if we split up? One rider to each major city?"

"Avalon is where we must ride." DarSheer glowered at him. "I gave my oath to Lord Malziek. We split up, we become vulnerable to surprise Nightshade raids. I shouldn't have to remind anyone that if we fail in this endeavor, all of Ëonë is doomed."

"Why not Ithuïn?" Kissinger asked. "It is along our road, and we must pass almost through their town center. Send a group of their finest messengers to warn Caldonia. We slaughter two ferreks with one arrow, I believe is how the saying goes."

I couldn't help but smile at the looks of confusion on the other men's faces. Kissinger caught my look and grinned back. He leaned toward me conspiratorially and said, "Leave all the thinking to these old codgers? Not likely, I say." His humor was appreciated, and I snorted.

"Alright, lay off us." DarSheer broke into a relaxed chuckle. "If it answers both of our quarrels, we can send word through Ithuïn to Caldonia. But then we continue to Avalon."

"Works for me." Othrain grimaced. "How much distance to cover before we reach the ford?"

"We might reach it by nightfall," DarSheer answered. "Longer if this weather is any indicator. If I recall, the last time I came through here, there was a small village resting on its banks we may rest at. There we shall find warmth and drink for the night."

DarSheer remounted and clicked his tongue as the mounts, grazing from the nearby fields, stamped their hooves and broke into a gallop. To the west, the clear blue sky shone brilliantly. Behind us, an ominous black thunderhead that lit with red flashes had begun to converge on the eastern horizon. Wind grew in intensity and gusted along the plains and hills. It howled and screamed like someone being tortured. I heard the screams of the dying, and it took all my restraint not to shove my fingers into my ears. Before long, we had to ride with our heads buried in our cloaks, for the wind threatened to gouge our eyes out. Clouds above formed conical spirals and pulsated with flashing light. I began to wonder if it wasn't a living shadow. We crested a tall hill, and I turned back. A ridge of small hills lined the black horizon behind us. Small spots of light moved down them like ants. My stomach clenched.

The movement behind us filled us with trepidation and we picked up our speed. The road was heavy beneath our horses' hooves. At high noon, we'd doubled our distance such that DarSheer became optimistic we might reach the village before nightfall.

The dark clouds and fog now swept past and above us. To keep my thoughts free from the fears that would control it, I soaked in the landscape as we rode. The terrain shifted to hills which were now rolling like waves around us. In the flashes of light, I could see the trees being tossed about and animals scurrying for cover. A ferrek dove in front of Kissinger's mount. The horse came to a stop, gravel spewing from under its hooves, and nearly tossed its rider over its head. The steed reared up on its hind legs and tossed its head.

"Easy, boy!" Othrain rode to a stop next to him and tried to grab the flailing reins as Kissinger gripped his mount's neck tight. "Be at peace, you blasted mule."

"Be kinder to the steeds, Othrain," DarSheer warned. "They sense their riders' moods."

The ferrek bolted into the shadows beneath a group of bushes. My own horse skittered about nervously. I massaged its neck with a calming rub. Kissinger's horse finally returned to four legs under the control of both DarSheer and Othrain.

"This thing will be the death of me!" Kissinger roared into the gale.

"Have more optimism," DarSheer frowned as he looked forward. "We're only a few hours from the Ford. We just need to keep it together."

Encouraged and rejuvenated by this hope, we continued the gallop down a grassy hill and up another. The Westerly Road went from gravel to clay to grass with sudden bursts of broken stone. But no matter the substance our trail was made of, it guided us hoof over hoof toward the village.

To the right of the road, a large circle of stones appeared in the gloom and fog. In the center of the stones, a tall tower jutted brokenly into the sky. I wondered how long it had stood there, resisting the natural elements. Empty windows and broken rubble told of its age. Moss covered almost every visible side. Behind it, a grove of trees surrounded a number of stone boxes placed neatly side by side. Moss covered them too and the wind moved around it like an invisible ward protecting the space.

"That's one of the many old towers." DarSheer leaned toward me so I could hear him better. Kissinger and Othrain pulled ahead.

"And the stone boxes?"

"Tombs. Tombs from one of the battles in the Second Era. These are quite common occurrences on the landscapes east of the mountains. You'll see many of them, seemingly placed with no contextual clues as to why. I once found a hundred of them in the middle of a field dozens of miles from any civilization."

"And those they hold have slept in slumber since then?"

"We respect our dead and so we haven't moved them, even if the cities or villages they were buried near were eroded by time long ago. They serve as a reminder to us of the price and source of our freedom."

It was sadly beautiful, and true to his word, as we rode along, more and more small boxes hugged the hills and small groupings of rock. Kissinger and Othrain spoke on their own so that we slipped into two groups of riders. They led the pace and DarSheer and I kept watch on our rear approach. In this manner, dusk finally sprouted as we rounded a bend in the road and saw the gates to a village. The clouds above us finally let loose their vengeance. Rain thundered down in pounding severity. It drenched our cloaks, and water flowed off our hoods and down over our faces. The road became muddied and the various holes in the uneven stones sought to twist ankles or force our steeds off balance.

I spit out the river that was flowing in my mouth and tried to cover my eyes with a hand to see. The hood of my cloak covered the tops of my eyes as we cantered to a stop outside the village's gate. The center of a long wooden wall, the gate was clearly a formality, for one thrust with a ram would send it toppling over. Even the walls on either side were barely thicker than the width of a man. The wall itself stood barely a head taller than DarSheer and glistened in the rain.

Othrain dismounted and pounded on the gate's entrance with both fists as I huddled beneath what small overhang the edge of the gate provided.

"Blasted doorkeeper," Othrain swore as he breathed into his hands.

"We don't want you," the voice behind the gate snarled and a heavy object thudded against the door. "Tell those damned villagers they can find another hideout. Keep your Varg and your problems out of our town."

"Are you going to speak nonsense while four soaked travelers stand on your doorstep getting ill from the cold?" Othrain retorted. "Let us in!"

The latch was unlocked, and the gate swung open. An aged man stood in the doorway and gawked at us. His grey hair was mostly stuffed beneath a cloak that was clearly too small for his considerable girth. He peered down the road and along the length of the wall before facing us again with disgruntled bewilderment.

"Truly, what strange people to receive on the Westerly Road." He glowered suspiciously. "Four men and by your garb, if my eyes don't deceive me, members of the Outpost. I thought your kind remained stationed . . ."

"Perhaps I may provide some clarity." DarSheer removed his hood.

"Broadsword?" The man's frown was replaced by a grin. "I didn't recognize you. Are you back for more ale? I'm afraid our last shipment is out already. We've none left, save that of our own taverns."

"No, no ale needed, thank you, Bastion." DarSheer shook his head and brushed his hair from his eyes. "We seek supplies and shelter till this downpour passes."

"You and these . . . strangers?"

"They come with me from the Outpost. We can explain, perhaps, in the dryness of Alforith's residence?"

"Please, come in," the gatekeeper shuffled back and swung the door wide. The stone of the Westerly Road was replaced by churned mud. Kissinger saluted him with two fingers and shouldered past. The village itself consisted of a low tavern, one inn, and a grouping of huts placed in the far corner opposite the gate itself. Troughs overflowed as sows and sheep drank or slept. A few men stood in the yard and pretended to ignore us. They held crooks and stood motionless. I felt them watching, their eyes raising the hairs on the back of my neck.

"Lovely village," I muttered.

The villagers peeked from taverns and homesteads. Rain streamed down windows and wind sent tavern and inn signs creaking. The clay and stone huts sat circled around a giant pit of fire and ash in the center. Spikes had been driven into the ground, and buckets of burning coals were spaced about the various huts. They offered meager warmth against the frigid rainfall.

DarSheer directed us down a well-trodden path, and I gazed at each building as we walked past. First, was an elaborate structure low to the ground but wide out the back. It was only distinguishable from the other low buildings as two men with swords in their hands stood on either doorpost. A welcoming light emanated from the cracked door. From the building came merriment and the sounds of lavish eating. It proved a stark difference from the rest of the gloomy atmosphere and because of that made me think of the Eastward Inn. On either side, two abandoned shacks sat bolted. Further down came the tavern, and was, as it proved, the tallest structure in the entire village. Twice the height of the inn, it sat shouldered between the edge of the village and a grey home. From the home, a man stepped out, a dagger in his hand. He narrowed his eyes.

"What brings you to our village?" he blustered.

"We're traveling through." DarSheer displayed his arms from the secrecy of his cloak. "Tell Alforith four men from the Outpost have arrived with urgent news. And do not loiter about. Your master will not take kindly to delaying us once he hears our words. We'll be in the tavern awaiting him."

The gatekeeper shuffled off. Above the tavern's door, the faded words "Minstril Tavern" shone dimly in the low light. Laughter echoed again from the cracks in the door. I opened it and stepped inside, the others not far behind me. It wasn't the heat or mirth that first brought me joy, but the lack of water pouring down my shoulders and face. Cloak or not, my clothes were soaked through. I shivered and removed the heavy garment from around my shoulders. Faces turned from their mugs and studied us.

"Greetings, strangers." A cheery woman finished drying the inside of a flagon and set it down. She placed her large hands firmly on the edge of the counter. "What might I get for four fine travelers like yourselves?"

"Ale for them and some tobacco for me." DarSheer bowed his head.

"By the light of the fires," the woman beamed, "I didn't recognize you, Broadsword. What are you doing out so soon since your last visit? Don't mistake my curiosity for anything other than excitement at your presence. Things have been dreary without you to keep us laughing."

"I'm afraid my laughter is limited these days, Bryna." DarSheer pulled a thick wooden chair from its table and sat down in it.

Kissinger and Othrain accepted the steaming mugs of ale from Bryna as she wiped down the countertop and listened with fascination to the stories DarSheer conveyed. Her eyes saddened when he regaled the destruction of the Outpost and dimmed when he mentioned Malziek's supposed death.

"I never much cared for the way he ran that place," she admitted. "But I'll be a blasted ferrek if I wished him any ill will. He knew how to keep a place functioning, and to be candid with you lot, we could use some of that stern guidance 'round here."

Kissinger and Othrain sat next to me, heads together as they watched the occupants of the tavern. Some of the tension from the battle still coursed through them in the way their eyes flitted to the dark corners, for nearby exits, and how neither let his hand stray far from his weapon. The villagers still sober enough to stand clearly distrusted the strangers in their humble abode, but no one so far presented enough courage to say something. I drank my ale and let the steam warm my frozen nose.

"Him?" Bryna tilted her head.

My thoughts plummeted back to reality at the word. Bryna had ceased her cleaning and stared at me with wide eyes. Othrain's hand moved faster than the eye could follow to his sword hilt. His fingers grew white with his strength.

"Be at peace," DarSheer warned him. "We only speak of Phoenix to encourage the less enthusiastic to action."

"You bring the cause of our problems into our village and expect us to receive you with warm welcome?" Bryna placed one hand on her hip.

"You do not fault the bowl the hot liquid sits in seconds before it flows in your eyes. The DarkBairn is not evil, nor does he carry any shred of loyalty to Mordën. Isn't that correct, Phoenix?"

"Of course." I nodded absentmindedly. The rumors had spread even to small villages like this. It made my stomach hurt. Her outburst caused some of the nearby eavesdroppers to stand aggressively and glare at us.

Othrain was on his feet, sword in full display, before I blinked. Kissinger had a dagger ready a moment after that. The room hissed with the sounds of swords being drawn from scabbards. DarSheer sighed.

The door swung open with a thud and a balding man stepped to the doorway. His eyes narrowed when he saw DarSheer and the black leather tunic he wore. The man himself wore a flowing shirt with tight pants hemmed at the tops of black boots. His lack of hair and the wrinkles around his eyes showed his age.

"You better follow me," the man grunted. "Put your blasted swords away. Is this how you treat my courtesy, Broadsword? If I had any sense rattling around between my bloomin' ears, I'd have you tossed hide and all into this cloudburst here."

"No." DarSheer gestured to the others. "Sheath your blades and tongues. I apologize for their actions, Alforith."

Alforith snorted and rubbed his nose till it turned bright red. He brushed stray droplets from his shoulders and thwacked the hood of his cloak, dislodging water. "I can imagine this will be pleasant if the Outpost has sent four of its meanest to deliver what one should be able to do alone. It must be dire indeed for a legendary Swordsmaster, a mysterious bairn, and two traveling troublemakers to show up on my doorstep. Come now, hastily!"

He ushered us briskly from the tavern back out into the pouring rain and across the yard into one of the homes we'd passed. The door was locked tight behind us by a man with a broken and swollen nose. His left eye was clouded, and his right was crisscrossed with red veins. As we were escorted inside, I observed several guards stationed throughout the home. On the muted purple walls, portraits of a single face were hung at even and measured spots. They all sported the identically long nose and brooding eyes of the leader of this village. Alforith stared at us in the flesh and through the paint over his younger eyes.

"A shrine to me from the locals." Alforith waved a hand as if he cared little for such things. "May Erëthuïl bless their minds for such small gestures. Surely, you understand this, Broadsword."

"Yes, I often find myself overwhelmed by Kissinger and Phoenix's mutual admiration for me." DarSheer rolled his eyes when Alforith turned his back. "I tell them to cease their ogling and they bow the knee at every turn. Othrain tried to have me molded into a statue."

"Right, right!" Alforith chuckled. "Solid ivory, no doubt?"

"They insisted." DarSheer smiled slightly at Othrain, who made a rude gesture in return.

We entered a small cozy room with a round table layered with old fruit, flaky bread, and an ancient-looking barrel of ale, the stopper having just been pulled as a short plump woman in a white dress poured the fragrant liquid into a wooden tankard. Alforith slumped into a wide cushioned chair. "Well, speak, Broadsword, but converse plainly for I am not in the mood to entertain foolish banter. Three of my hunters have grown ill and several members of our livestock perished in the night."

"Alforith, accept my sincere apologies for our unannounced arrival. Still, I believe we have worn off the welcome I've come to enjoy from this fine place. Tell me, is it the horrid cold and rain that has sullied your once generous greeting or the fat that now jiggles in your stomach?" DarSheer's eyes seemed to flash in the low light; Alforith frowned. I'd experienced DarSheer's moods switch from mirthful to angry when I failed to remember a location or to deflect a jab. It was nice to see it turned on someone else.

"Curb your tongue, Broadsword. Be careful how you address to your host," he said. "My girth may have grown, and the weather is mightily dreadful, this is all true, but it does not stand as the cause for my sour mood. You speak of an enjoyment for past welcomes, but the welcomes have been for you, not your mysterious comrades." Alforith's glare narrowed. He sat at the table where a maid had just readied a platter of smoked venison and ale. A bowl of old bread and wrinkly grapes twisted its week-old aroma into my nostrils and my stomach growled a second time. I covered my gut and tried to seem disinterested.

"Your men lie in their huts injured, maybe even at death's doorstep, and your livestock, which this villages relies on to survive, perish, yet here you sit filling your considerable gut with the foods your peoples' thruki can purchase from Avalon. You have grown complacent, *old friend*."

"You do not tell me how to run my village." Alforith lowered the pastry he'd been about to bite into. His voice descended dangerously.

"I am their leader because they needed one. No one else stepped up. Do I need to remind you, it's been me who has sanctioned your abrupt arrivals all because that lazy idiot, Malziek, feels the urge for butter on his bread? Without me, I dare say you would be feasting on dust and little else."

"The Outpost has fallen! Lord Malziek is dead. Mordën marches with a great host from his war furnaces and is but a day or so from your very little village. They put all they saw to the torch!" DarSheer placed both hands on the table and leaned forward. "So, forgive me if I dispense with the pleasantries and get straight to the point."

Alforith gagged as he inhaled the swig of ale. One hand pressed firmly against the table, he coughed and spluttered as one of the men stepped forward and moved to thwack his back. Alforith shoved him away and, eyes watering, he stabbed his fork into the wood. He inhaled deeply till he could regain his composure.

"Do you think tonight of all nights is the time for your style of humor? I should have my men cast you out for such blatant disrespect. *They* may not know who I am, but *you* do!" He pointed at the three of us and then DarSheer next.

"You and I both know I could take your strongest man," DarSheer returned calmly. "My words are not a jest. You yourself said it was odd for four to deliver one message and now you have why. We are the sole survivors and even as we sit here while you fatten yourself on luxuries your people cannot afford, Varglarian and Nightshade forces amass on the eastern border in the ashes of our dead. The Bridge is overrun and the Outpost lies in ruins beneath the heat of fire and steel."

"You mean to tell me you failed the one job you were there for? You stand with nary a scratch on your flesh and expect me to believe the Shadow Prince's forces march again on Ëonë? I call balderdash and poppycock on your waste of breath." Alforith guffawed. "I've said it time and time again, you folk are wastes of space and effort. I could have defended your walls with the men I have."

Othrain drew a dagger and gripped it. "You mistake our words of warning for a joke? We could have continued past this wretched grouping of huts and on to Ithuïn. They have men of steel and experience there. You and your malnourished stable hands could not hope to keep a pebble from its journey down the side of a mountain. Oh, that you had defended our walls so I could visualize your head severed from your body by Varglarian steel."

"You would do well to silence the tongue of your entourage in the presence of me and my sons," Alforith snarled nastily. He stood with a fork gripped like a dagger in his right hand. His face was redder than a tomato at harvest.

"I do not ask you to debate my message, Alforith," DarSheer returned evenly. He gave Othrain a scathing look and gestured for the other to sit down. "We could all debate their existence if we had the time, but a horde of the Lord of Chaos's forces march over the Bridge. We did our duty to Custodian and Ward. Our job was not to defend against thousands, but to cry the bell of alarm the moment Mordën tried anything. We did not fail. Those who perished at The Battle of the Outpost did not fail. The smell of human flesh is but a sweet aroma to the Varg and Shade's wretched nostrils and you will be their next target. Do you not think one as filled as you will not be prime choice for their insatiable hunger? They march boot over boot toward us as we speak. This downpour is not of normal creation. Its sudden approach should have tipped you off."

A sudden headache pressed down on my temples, and I let a groan escape. Kissinger gave me a concerned look.

"What ails the bairn?" Alforith demanded.

"Have you heard of *the* prophecy?" DarSheer's voice was powerful. "This is Phoenix, the DarkBairn. He is one from beyond our world."

"*The* bairn?" Alforith cried out in dismay. He stood abruptly and the dishes around him clattered noisily to the stone floor. "You think parading this boy before me will make things change? What would you have me do? We're a remote village. If the Varglarian come here in the numbers and intensity you're hinting at, there is no stopping them. The fools here are my sons and between our hushed company they know nothing, especially how to fight."

"Now you change your thoughts," Othrain laughed without mirth. "First, you insult us and say you and your men could defend what we could not and now you say there would have been no hope either way. Which tune do you dance to now?"

"Fortify your walls and call your countrymen to arms." DarSheer ignored Othrain. "There is no chance you will be victorious, but it will give us time to reach Avalon ahead of the host and warn the Elfin king. There are some villagers beyond your walls. Bring them inside. When you reach your breaking point, simply turn tail and run."

"Should be a move you're familiar with." Othrain grinned toothily.

"You'd have me lay down and die as a distraction," Alforith spluttered. His face reddened and he balled his fists. Spittle flew. "Are you absolutely insane?"

"Do something useful with your miserable life," DarSheer spat angrily. "For ages you've kept this place up by usurping the valuables from unfortunate travelers who pass through your gates. Call all your able-bodied men into a fighting force and meet the Varglarian at the Ford of Duïn. Hold them there if you can and, if you must break and flee, then do so. Even a day's delay would aid us greatly. I call upon the name of the *Oathkeys* if nothing else will make you see why this our only hope." He placed both hands on the table and leaned forward.

"Those keys hold sway over strategically important cities not a village at a random river. I hold no allegiance to those outdated keys." Alforith grinned nastily and waved a hand.

"If you don't," Othrain leapt over the table and placed his dagger at the jiggling throat of the man, "you will be replaced by one who can."

The room was silent as Kissinger, hand on his half-drawn sword, eyed the guards warningly. They too had their hands on their blades. A thick tension filled the room. DarSheer raised both hands.

"Let this not become a violent reminder of our fractured loyalties," he murmured. "Mordën is counting on our inability to become unified. He knows if we come together as a people, that all Ëonë could eventually repel even his largest hosts. But if we cannot even come to agree to honor those promises made in the past then we have already lost. This exact event is the reason the councils of old met."

"Given time and a great deal of bribery," Alforith resigned, "I could muster a hundred men. Not a hundred of the type you might expect, though. The women and children shall be moved south to the safety of Caldonia. Mark my words, Broadsword, if we ever meet again, it shall not be to your liking. You are not welcome here henceforth. You are *not* wanted. We will fulfil an ancient oath and be done with you."

"This is agreeable to me." DarSheer nodded.

"We shall also need provisions if you can spare any," Kissinger spoke calmly. "The road is long and unforgiving. Our travel shall prove arduous, and time is not our ally."

Alforith glared at him but then sighed, defeated. He whistled and spoke to one of his sons, who excused himself. "My boy will see to your needs. But we are low ourselves and our next shipment comes in the waning hours of the night. There's an empty hut in the corner of the village you may rest in till this deluge passes and the morning dawns. But mark my words, I want you out of my town before the sun reaches the top of its climb or you will find I can be as brutal as the Varg."

"I understand the risk you have accepted. We thank you for your generosity in both supplies and lodging. If all goes well, we'll be out of your mind soon." DarSheer let his tone move soothingly.

"I very much doubt that. I'd watch him!" Alforith pointed at Othrain accusingly as we strode from the room. "He's trouble and there's no denying it. He'll either be the death of you or of himself."

We stepped into the drenching rain and, hoods once more cast over our faces, we hurried along the road. Alforith's son led us to a hut and showed us through the open front door to a dusty living space. In the middle, a brazier of glowing coals lit the room and filled it with warmth. Several cots were placed along the walls. That was all the décor we clearly warranted for the walls and floor were bare. DarSheer thanked him and slipped him a thruki, which the man pocketed greedily, and dashed off. He was no doubt headed to the tavern to spill the tea to those willing to listen. Before long, if it wasn't the case already, the entire village would know exactly what had happened. We'd go from strangers to fearmongers.

"You're in pain," Kissinger murmured to me as we chose our beds.

I grimaced and gritted my teeth. The buzz which seemed to drill into my skull had abated and only tremors remained. I walked shakily but with determined purpose.

"I'm remembering," I murmured so only he could hear. "Dark hills and leering faces in the night. I see Nightshades and I see . . . *him* in the rippling mirror of a pool."

"DarSheer said you rejected his offer of returning to your world. Should this not have banished him from the recesses of your mind?"

"I haven't changed anything," I said mildly insulted. "He is gone from my mind, or I thought he was, but this pain was only present in the past when he was near enough to influence me. And with this pain comes with memories I know are not mine. When he had control of my body and brought me here, I was aware of what was going on. I could smell, see, hear, and feel, but nothing I did was my choice. He controlled my mind, and my mind commanded my reaction. It's like that but with memories. I am me, aware and alert, but memories that do not belong to me surface in places they shouldn't."

"He's inserting his memories into your thoughts? What does this gain him?"

"I'm probably wrong." I groaned at the soreness in my limbs and lay down.

"Get some rest." DarSheer said, looking over and frowning like he had overheard our conversation. "We leave as soon as supplies can be arranged. Storm or not, we can't afford to let it slow our progress."

Othrain was already snoring in one of the cots, his arm over his eyes and one leg limp over the edge. Kissinger padded his cot so it wasn't thin and knocked out in record time. DarSheer stood at the doorway.

"Get some sleep." He didn't look at me. A hundred unspoken words passed between us.

I laid down on the bed and closed my eyes. My mind hummed with a million thoughts until I found a single to relax and began my breathing exercises. I inhaled deeply in and out. Katy's face filled my mind's eye and before I was even aware, I had drifted off and the night-mare began.

M

I stood in a dark chamber. The walls and ceiling were made entirely of stone, with torches stuck in small sconces every few feet. The empty doorway opened into a long tunnel outside. Light flickered and projected shadows up against the cold stone. I wanted to cry for joy. I was back under the mountain. I was in the same tunnels, probably in the same room, I had been tortured in before Mordën had taken control. Had he been good to his word despite my refusal? Someone groaned a foot to my left and I nearly jumped out of my skin. But no matter how much I tried to move my arms or even turn my head to see what the source of the sound was, my body didn't respond. Then, as if sensing my desire, my head finally turned to stare at a familiar person stretched out over a bed of nails. The figure on the platform mumbled in delirium. His hair was plastered to his face and his skin was pale.

Will! But I couldn't quite form the words. My throat refused to make sound. Frustration surged and I began struggling to make any motion or sound. Finally, I moved forward and looked down at my old friend. His face was ashen and his eyes rolled back in his head. Small holes covered his left arm.

It appeared Raoul had obtained the needed intel to lure the bairn here. My jaw would have dropped had I been in control of it. That memory wasn't mine. Why did I think that?

"Hello, William Gree," I said in a deep silky manner. I raised my hand and ran it over his jawline. Only, I didn't do any of that.

That's when I realized. It was so obvious. The stale air over my skin, the unfamiliar stench of my clothes, and a memory that wasn't mine.

"Who are you?" Will mumbled through parched lips. He didn't open his eyes.

"I am Mordën, the Lost Heir to Ëonë, the Shadow King, among many other titles. All this is irrelevant. But I believe you and your folk

call me 'The Black Widow.' Again, titles in this event are not important. To you, I am simply the last chance you may have to survive."

"I don't know." Sweat beaded on his forehead as even an infinitesimal adjustment drew blood from the curved barbs he lay on. "You won't convince me of anything."

"All in good time." I smiled and felt the tightness in the action. I hated smiling. "I am here to offer you the answer. You lay here, a prisoner in my domain. Your allies will be unsuccessful in their attempts to save you."

"You underestimate them." Will gurgled out a laugh. A tiny stream of blood trickled down from the corner of his mouth.

"I've given them what they want." I moved around from his right side to just above his head. "I brought something meaningful into Phoenix's life. I gave him a purpose. He'll find his parents and like the dutiful offspring he is, he will insist on sending them to freedom while remaining behind and losing his life. It's a bittersweet tale sung by ballads millennium at a time."

"You didn't give him anything." Will sounded bewildered.

"You think he has made it this far without notice? That I didn't let him witness my Hourglass show the way into these wretched tunnels? That I didn't send a token force to ensure he thought I was fighting with everything I had? The Old One's death was simply convenient. It is ironic. He banished me in hopes I would meet my demise and he could return. In the end, he fell to the blades of my Shades, and I am on the cusp of reclaiming all I lost."

Will rolled his head over and coughed. It was clear he was drifting in and out of consciousness. I had to get my answers quickly. I leaned forward and wiped the trail of blood from his cheek and licked my finger.

"I can get you out of these chains, safely down the mountainside, and returned to the monotonous life you so prefer. I do not ask for much in return."

"Please, end the pain. I can't feel my legs. Help. Someone, help!" The last two words he whispered hoarsely.

"I can do that." I darted down till my cheek rested against his. I closed my eyes and inhaled. "Just do what I need, and all this pain will be over."

"What." His voice was so quiet I had to strain my ears to hear.

"Tell me what the bairn is about to do."

"Bairn?"

"Phoenix."

"We split up."

"Yes," I rubbed my chin, "this I know. You split up and he has met with Quire. He will be led to my makeshift prison and there discover his family. All this, I know. I need to know, what does he know about me?"

"Know? You're an evil word stuck in the back of his mind, but he has stood firm and resolute in his desire to save his family and bring you down."

"How disappointing," I murmured with genuine regret. "I make a masterful scheme and he still believes I am ignorant. He will find his way to me and before the end, he will be defeated. He must understand his importance to me."

"You kidnapped his parents. That's all he cares about." Will spit a dried ball of phlegm up into my eye.

I didn't react at first, mainly because I was more impressed he had any energy to spit. I wiped my face with the black fabric that made up my suit.

"You've told me far more than even you are aware of." I turned away from the bed as Raoul stepped into view with a wide man next to him.

"Greetings, my lord." Raoul stood coldly at the entrance of the room. He bore no love for me after what I'd done to him and that gave me relish. I preferred my resources hating me as much as the prey we feasted on.

"The bairn here has finished being useful to me." I brushed my hands of the foul odor the human boy had rubbed off on me. "Dispose of him."

"Yes, my king." Raoul bowed stiffly.

I exited the room as Will gave a jolt on the bed. In the shadows of the hallway, hidden far from him, I listened.

"Who are you?" he moaned.

"You are loyal and determined, William Gree," Raoul grimaced. "Some might call you a true friend."

"Where am I?"

"Let us not concern ourselves with that just yet, my friend. As to your first question, I am Raoul."

"I need some water." He hacked a wet spluttering cough that sent blood into the air.

"I'm afraid I cannot give you any." Raoul crossed to the edge of his platform.

"What do you want from me?" Will whimpered. Tears trickled down his face as he groaned in agony.

"A nice blood meat," Raoul said. "Oh, the possibilities if I had the time."

They bantered back and forth while Will gnashed his teeth and begged for an answer to where he was. I felt nothing but disdain for the bairn. He was weak. He deserved death. I watched as Raoul each took a needle and stabbed Will's arm from one side to the other, the tips of the needles protruding from his flesh. Will stiffened and I reached my hands to my mouth and sung out in a haunting tone that bounced from the low walls.

"You are a failure, William Gree, you always have been. You do not deserve to live. I hate you." This voice was my own, I realized as I shook inconsolable in the confines of my mind. No matter how much I tried to follow those words up with my own, it was like I'd forgotten how to speak.

Will's eyelids fluttered as a tear trickled down his cheek. He went from slowly moving to motionless but breathing . . . to breathing his last on the barbed bed. He'd died alone, horrified, in agony, and it was all my fault.

I sat up in my bed. Sweat covered my body and the threadbare tunic stuck to my chest. I took a few moments to steady my breathing so it didn't sound like I'd just been sprinting. Outside, wind tossed the tops of trees and rattled the door like a ghost trying to seep through the cracks. In the moonlight that pierced the edges of the door, a black shape leaned against the door jam. I wiped the bleariness away and swung my legs over the edge to a sitting position. The figure moved at the shuffle.

"You were having a nightmare," Kissinger murmured softly.

"Nothing worse than what I've endured in the past." I rubbed my eyes.

"Who is Will? You've never mentioned him."

I stared at the dusty floor. Every time I closed my eyes, his face stared from the dark places in my mind. His lips pressed tight in grief at my betrayal. *You do not deserve to live . . . I hate you.* When I'd first landed here, all I'd remembered of him was his exuberant attitude and desire to aid me in my quest. I had not remembered his brutal demise. Who else now lay as a rotting corpse beneath tons of motionless, cold, unyielding stone? Who else perished because of my failure? Overwhelming guilt assailed me as I realized the sacrifice Will had made. I'd barely remembered him, cast his memories aside like he was nothing more than a long-forgotten friend from the past. Not just died. Was brutally killed. My hands shook like I'd been the one to plunge the needles into his arm. My legs shook like I'd dashed across miles of rocky hills.

"He was a friend. *No.* He was a brother." I looked up as a ray of moonlight spilled over my face. The soft pale light revealed the tears streaming down my face.

Kissinger eyed me carefully. "If he was your kin, I'm sure whatever befell him, he was strong and unwavering till his end. He will find his way to Erëthuïl's Hall and there be a celebrated warrior among the glorious fallen."

"He didn't die a warrior's death." I shook with the tears. "He died on a bed of nails, *tortured* by servants of Mordën. I saw his face tonight, pale and twisted in *agony*. After all this time, I now know it was *I who caused his death*. There is much merriment in the songs of these lands, Kissinger, but also deep-rooted grief. Here I have laughed and shared in the wealth of your people, eaten your foods, and stood as one of the Outpost. There, he lay, unwanted, in pain, alone. If there was any who betrayed their own . . . I must claim that guilt. Your people are right: I am a harbinger of doom. I was weak and because of that, all shall perish. I must admit, this fills me with great sadness."

"Could you have stopped it?"

"What?"

"Could you have prevented Mordën from killing him? Or from entering the lands he'd spent decades preparing for? Are you stronger than the bones of the mountains against the howling winds?"

I massaged my temples. "No. But I remember more. Will chose to lead the horde of Nightshades behind us down a false tunnel. He gave himself up so I wouldn't be captured." I looked up. "He acted, knowing it would end him."

"He sounds headstrong, a man who would do whatever it took to protect those he loved. There is no greater love than this."

I let out a shaky laugh. "I could not have stopped him from what he did. He was determined."

"Could you have stopped the Shadow King from ending his life?" Kissinger pressed.

"*No.*" The word bounced about the walls of the room before landing in the brazier and sending a plume of heat out.

"He made his choice; he knew the risks. He died to protect those he loved so you would have a chance at saving those *you* loved."

"He did."

"There is no greater compassion and warmth than a brother who dies for another. You claim he has not died a warrior's death. I say, this is a perfect example of one. Not all deaths on the battlefield are source for song. Not all great men of old die as a soldier. Not all of us perish with a sword in hand and a mug of ale in the other, as Othrain seems to believe. Not all die with honor and their previous actions to speak for them, like DarSheer believes. Some succumb to the injuries inflicted in the deep places of the world and there is nothing we could have done to stop it. A warrior's end is not always an end of glory and fire. Some expire beyond the recognition of bards and hidden under miles of stone. Do not despair. Be at peace, Phoenix DarkBairn."

We let the fire crackle and pop, embers glowing like small pinpricks of light in the darkness. A log collapsed in as the tongues of flame burnt through it. A wave of heat wrapped itself around me like a blanket. A lump rose in my throat. It battled the flashes of guilt that washed over me every minute. He had died for me, diverted the enemy, with no personal gain for himself.

"He died a warrior's death," I finally agreed hollowly.

Kissinger smiled faintly. "It is an honor reserved for the greatest. Some suffer in their lack of action or even their cowardice. Will was brave. He did what many never achieve. There are too few in this world and yours who would give up their future, their chances, their life, for another. Hold his memory strong in your mind as a beacon of what you ought to become. Do not let his memory became a thing of the past because long after the ending of our cities, towns, and freedom, the day we let Mordën control fully what we know and remember, is the day he has achieved victory."

The warmth was no longer against my flesh but spreading inside me. Suddenly, sleepiness returned as I yawned. "You speak as one familiar with such concepts. Have you lost anyone?"

Kissinger stared into the depths of the fire. I almost missed his sad smile in the shadows that flickered over his face.

"No," he murmured. "I never have."

With that, he returned to his post and continued to count the stars in the sky. I realized then for the first time that the pounding din of the rain was gone. Moonlight meant clouds were no longer covering our heads. Moonlight also meant . . .

"We've stayed here too long!" I slid from the bed and reached for my belt. My tunic flowed about my knees. "It's nightfall. We have to go."

"Be at peace, Phoenix," DarSheer mumbled from his cot. "The night is deep and the cold is deeper. We have all endured a battle, lost people, lost a piece of ourselves. This warrants a few extra hours of sleep. We are no good if we fall from exhaustion or frailty ere we arrive at the feet of Avalon."

Othrain agreed with a loud snore as he rolled from his right to left side. He shuffled about and pulled the thin blanket over his broad shoulders. His beard quivered as he exhaled but he did not wake. At least one of us slept peacefully. I sat back down on the bed.

"You should be asleep, DarSheer." Kissinger turned his gaze back to the cracks in the door.

"Like you two," he returned, "sleep does not come easily for me. Nightmares wrestle with every sleeping moment till I wake feeling more exhausted than when I laid my head down."

I lowered myself onto my back and stared up at the dark ceiling. A few stray rays of moonlight broke through the thick thatch roof. Dust wafted down. Crickets chirped. The fire crackled. I yawned. Sleep overcame me.

DarSheer shook my shoulder softly until I snorted myself awake. His eyes were gentle, though there was a hidden concern behind them. He gestured for me to rise and ready myself and then pointed at the door where Othrain and Kissinger stood waiting. It was still dark outside; however, there was a softening in the blackness. The moon was gone, and the stars twinkled less brightly.

"We must ride while the village sleeps," DarSheer whispered. "The fewer eyes to follow our departure, the less word can spread to our enemies."

A strange man wrapped his knuckles on the door and Kissinger let him in. They spoke in hushed tones as Kissinger handed him a pouch, probably filled with thruki. The man waved for us to follow him. I slid into my boots, laced them, and tightened my belt. We moved in unison from the comforting warmth into a chilling draft. A few dogs chained to stakes slumbered peacefully. Torches lit the yard but there was no one on watch. I craned my neck about hoping to see someone, anyone, with a weapon on duty.

"Where's the watchman?" I hissed to DarSheer.

"They do not set one," he responded tightly. The stranger next to us didn't respond, but I noted his shoulders tensed.

"Do they know how close the enemy is?" I tried to clear the cobwebs of weariness from my mind to make sense of this.

"The words of crazy folk are not treated as undeniable proof," the man finally spoke. His voice was husky and rasped out. "Take these supplies and mounts and be gone. You're lucky Alforith was in such a good mood and didn't burn you for your insults."

"You will send the men? To the Ford?"

"Here." The man reached out to four mounts who blinked at us and shook their manes in greeting. "Leave our village and spread your fearmongering to those with less intelligence and less to lose."

DarSheer tightened the saddle on the closest horse and mounted up. We all mimicked him and soon, thanks to our elevated position, our gaze stretched over the entire yard. There was an even smaller gate on the opposing side of the wall. There, an old man with a long grey beard bowed till his hairs tickled the dust on the ground.

"I don't rightly know what your purpose is, Broadsword." He yawned. "But I'm not as dumb as many. A rations supplier man like myself is no idiot, I've always said, and here I am, consorting with strange folk from the Outpost. I have no doubt I shall be the center of gossip once more, but this time ale shall be my poison of choice and the intent ears of my fellow villagers will be turned to me. Where do you mind heading if you don't mind my old nose in your business?"

"I do not doubt that our private conversation shall become the widespread news of the day," DarSheer responded grimly. "At least give us till sunrise before you go spreading your rumors, Bastion. We are heading west to Avalon."

"Blast," Bastion nodded as if he guessed as much, "and I expect you intend to take the DarkBairn with you?"

"Word spreads fast." Othrain reached for his dagger.

"It's too early for threatening tones, Master Othrain. Besides, can you blame them? Not many pass before our eyes. We're pretty isolated after all. But your DarkBairn marks the third stranger to come through our gates in the last week. I know I shouldn't prod; it's not my concern what young strange travelers are up and about in the dark secrecy of the night. That is their business. Yet I'm an old soul. There is no harm in telling a weary man who shall soon be in the Halls."

"Strangers? Anyone of noteworthy mention?" DarSheer checked the straps on his mount.

Kissinger patted his horse's flank and murmured softly into the steed's twitching ear. Othrain moved his horse so he could gaze into the village behind us. He kept his eyes on the yard and empty doors of the grouping of huts as if he expected a Nightshade to burst from the shadows. His weathered hand gripped the hilt of his sword.

Bastion handed a satchel to Kissinger. "I don't believe they were from these parts, or for that matter were very bright. A young woman, a bairn, and a rather tipsy fellow who drank more than he spoke. They asked about Glasbur and how to get to it. I laughed till my belly jiggled, yet they did not crack one smile. Of course, I told them how to get there but I warned them, I did. I said, 'You lot are strange folk, but I will help none the less. Take the roads to Caldonia and then further south on the *End Road*. Can't miss the gates,' I said. 'They stretch from boot to the heavens itself.' They took my goodwill, and I overheard them muttering about speaking to the people there. Who doesn't know the fate of that city? Why would anyone try to journey to a tomb? I watched them ride west a week ago. Don't ask where they are now or how. I've not seen nor heard news since. Still, mighty strange. And now you come through with the DarkBairn. Forgive the wandering eyes and wagging tongues of the folk here but you can see why it draws their attention where usually naught but dust and animals pass through our gates?"

"Many shall appreciate you and your kind before the end." DarSheer dipped his head in gratitude. "You've helped us beyond our ways of gratitude. Now let us on our way. The mind of your mayor seems twisted and intent on enjoying the pleasantries of his own house while letting you all become fodder to approaching armies. If you take anything from me, Bastion my old friend, take your family and things and set out west on the road. Take it as far south or past Avalon. Mordën will not spare you or your family. If Alforith will not ride to the ford, then you must be far away from here. Stay true, my friend. Be at peace."

"And those two?" The man pointed at Othrain and Kissinger, who up until this point had been speaking softly off to one side. They turned to stare at him. "What of them?"

"You ask too many questions," DarSheer warned.

"Fine, fine, no need to turn your tongue so." Bastion shook his head. "Be at peace, Broadsword. I can't say I look forward to your return if there remains a place to return to. Thank you for your news. Be at peace, strangers of the Outpost and you, DarkBairn."

The man watched us ride with haste through the small gate. He watched us long after we'd become specks on the horizon before he closed the door with the gatekeeper at his side.

"He's a strange one," I muttered as soon as we were out of earshot. The cool morning was refreshing. The breeze on my face woke me more than a mug of ale would. Animals and creatures sprung from bush to blade of grass and under the watchful eye of trees older than the stars that twinkled through whisps of cloud overhead. A pack of ferreks sprinted off when we got too close to the animal carcass, they'd been stripping clean. The furry rodent was more bone than meat now.

"I know Bastion." DarSheer held the reins loosely and huddled under his cloak. "He's a bit eccentric but he means well. It concerns me that others before us have traversed this village. This village is almost as isolated as us, save for the shipments of food and ale they receive from Ithuïn. Not many know of their simple existence. It's always been my first stop whenever I am ordered on a mission to The Golden City. In all my years, once or twice has a traveler been in the village at the same time."

"Do you think these strangers ride with the crimson banner behind them?" Kissinger inquired. His hair flowed behind him. He made no discernable effort to stay warm.

"Servants of Mordën are not fair to look upon. Unless he's created a new race, then the only possibility I can conjure is that corrupted men are moving out from his wall, not as his creations, but as cloaks under his spell. The same way he's prodded into Phoenix's mind, he does this to others till they break and become his."

"Great, spies that look as normal as us," Othrain grumbled. His hand stroked the pommel of his sword.

"We must be careful of who we talk to and who we share out important intel with," DarSheer continued. "If spies of Mordën discover who we are and the message we bring, they may try to ambush us so our message dies long before it reaches anyone who can do anything. When we ride through or into towns, keep to your mounts unless I say otherwise. The people east of Avalon are not a trusting type. They've long been forced to live with the threats from the eastern shores. Varglarian raiding parties have made it deep into the continent before. Trust little, or better yet, trust none."

"Shouldn't we be spreading the word, ordering people to flee while they can?" I pondered.

"Yes, this is our dilemma." DarSheer gripped the reins tightly now. His brow creased with thought. "We can worry later. For now, heads low, and voices silent. We must make good headway after our lengthy rest."

Kissinger urged his stallion to a nice trot. We all fell into file behind him and soon the village was long behind us. Well-tended fields stretched off on either side of the road. The first rays of sunlight broke the edge of the world and shone down on the frost-layered leaves and grass around us. The tended fields meant we passed farms. Occasionally, we passed a farmer on the road, his cows trudging behind him while he walked with a long staff in one hand. These locals always watched us distrustfully. Still, we made good progress over the Westerly. The patches of broken cobblestone yielded to smooth stone as the road itself continued through the center of village after village. We didn't bother stopping as faces gawked at us. Children played games in wide expanses of land and watched us, hands to eyes, as we passed. The sun was a ball of fire in the sky nearly overhead and had dried up the morning moistness. I kept my arms around the neck of the horse as we rode hard down the road. It became obvious to me how far from anything interesting the Outpost really was. The few villages we passed were still small communities well outside the outskirts of any notable city. Seconds became hours which became miles traveled with nearly no change in scenery to impress us. The once-flat plains turned to hills. As the soft glow of eventide broke through the bows of tall greenery, we approached a clearing that sat snuggled in the arms of a copse of oak trees. The dying sun's peeking gaze barely reached the rounded tip of the hill behind us. Twilight had approached far quicker than any of us were willing to accept, yet our exhaustion could not pass up the opportunity to sleep.

"Tell me more about Ëonë," I said to DarSheer as I began building a small fire. "Beyond what you taught me in our sessions."

Othrain and Kissinger were off hunting, so I had taken the task of making crude beds with the few blankets we had been graciously given. DarSheer was sharpening his sword with a rock and glanced up.

"What more do you want to know? I've told you of the most important historical events."

"This Avalon, The Golden City, what makes it so important?"

"Back when Erëthuïl first sculpted the land, he found it in his innermost desire to create a people like him in wisdom, strength, and appearances to live in the world he had formed. He tried with the trees and the animals before he formed the first race to walk this world. Erëthuïl sculpted Drucodians and gave them breath."

"Continue," I prompted as the first signs of fire erupted in the kindling.

"According to the stories handed down to the surviving Drucodians they tell their origin story as such: Not a wind stirred, and a chill was in the air as the first Drucodian felt mud beneath its feet and its eyes opened for the first time and beheld the green beauty before it. The sky was garbed in blue expanse and waters purer than the Luthi themselves lapped against the shoreline of the luscious fields and sprawling mountains. Some say that the first words spoken before the hushed patience of Erëthuïl's creation was a song of adoration, though its words now lay hidden to that world of forgetfulness. Erëthuïl blessed his new creation with eternal life, should the Drucodians desire it. Long did the oldest race of Erëthuïl live in peace and rest. For hundreds of years, they farmed and built and traded and grew in population. They expanded far beyond the confines of their creation point. Many went to construct some of the most splendid cities the world has ever seen. Even the oldest Elfin and most of the remaining Drucodians remember those times only in tales handed down. Of their great cities, Avalon, or in their tongue Avalonenburg, was the chiefess and fairest. It rose tall and proud. It was a staple to their ingenuity and craftiness. The walls were paved with gold mined from the Fallen Peaks. Buildings were polished marble. Water gushed in plenty along designed troughs. It was said you could hear laughter and joy around every corner. People broke into dance and merriment for the lightest of reasons. Reading and writing were encouraged. It's why we have so many surviving scrolls of what life was like back then. Though the authors' names are lost to time, their work remains pivotal in understanding what happened. When Mordën marched in the dark beginnings of the First Great War with Varglarians, he was met with Drucodian strength. The scrolls say that Mordën fought the Chief Elder personally and they smote each other over and over. The hardness and sturdiness of the Drucodian Chief rivaled Mordën. He struck him down from a high place and broke Mordën's body. Again, that's just according to scrolls. You must always proceed with care when taking scrolls as literal truth. Some writers tended to take liberties and exaggerate. We cross-referenced similar tales from different perspectives and found this one, however, to be true.

"Whatever happened, the Drucodians managed to force Mordën back to his new fortress he'd built on the isle called the BlackBurg. Guards were placed and a bridge built to ensure there was only one way to enter the mainland and from that point, they could defend their world from invasion. It's from this era that many outposts sprang up, one even sat where ours used to rest. During this time of peace, Mordën studied and sculpted a new race of beings darker and eviler than even the Varg. He called them Nightshades. Nearly two thousand years passed between the First Great War and the Second Great War. Scholars believe this was the time frame when he spent the most in the fell dungeons below his fortress mutilating and experimenting on those unlucky enough to have been captured. When he'd finally succeeded in making this subservient slave, he called it Nightshade, and gave it the gift of shaderian travel, or shadow travel. He let a few at a time out into the night and they wreaked havoc on the outposts around the eastern shores. The same Chief Elder who fought him back all those thousands of years ago marshalled an alliance of kin to rid their lands of his stench once and for all. The great names of Drucodian legend banded together and the number of warriors stretched beyond count. They were filled with pride, and it betrayed them. The same bridge they'd built to keep Mordën trapped meant their forces were whittled down to single file march over the ocean. With his new creation, Mordën let his Varg archers pick them off long before they touched his soil while his Nightshades appeared behind the backs of the Drucodians and torched entire camps. The Chief Elder, and this is where history is fuzzy, supposedly marched himself over the Bridge to challenge Mordën. The Shadow King agreed but of course he was deceitful. During the face-off, he planted nightshades in the shadows of the arena and after he'd been forced to his back, the blade of the Drucodian inches from his chest, he cried out. There was much bloodshed that day and the Chief Elder's head was severed from his body. The texts like to claim the head of the Chief Elder still resides, mummified, in the BlackBurg as a trophy.

"After the death of their chief, the Drucodian armies disbanded and fled to their homelands. Mordën moved with little resistance. He displayed his latest creation, a host of Rever Drakes. With the combined powers of Varglarian numbers, Nightshade shadow travel, and the dragons overhead, he was unstoppable. Millions lost their lives in a few days in what is known as *The Nights of Grief*, when mournful cries outweighed anything else."

The fire crackled with flourish. I'd been leaning against the trunk of a tree while DarSheer spoke and sharpened his sword simultaneously. Shadows danced about and seemed to bring to life his words.

"That's horrible," was all I could manage. I imagined the slaughter that had taken place and felt sick to my stomach. *Millions.* I glanced about and wondered how many bodies the earth covered. How much blood fueled the growth of ancient trees? It was horrible to stomach.

"Erëthuïl realized his first creation was going to be wiped out if he didn't step in and change it. Records are confused on why he didn't just stop Mordën, but most seem to agree he didn't meddle in the affairs of Ëonë. He let his Luthi command that. But now, he could no longer turn a blind eye. He made a new race, Elfins. But the number of Drakes and Shades still continued to grow as the number of Drucodians dwindled. The Elfin tried their best, even the most cynical of scrolls does them honorably. Yet they were newly awoken from slumber and new to combat. Erëthuïl had given them traits of warriors, so they were able to fight bravely. In the end, it was for naught. Avalonenburg was invaded and taken as the Shadow King's stronghold on the mainland. He split half his forces to engage what he thought would be an army from Glasbur. But the Kingdom of Glasbur was silent. The gates remained locked. To this day, no one knows what happened or why their king closed off his city to the outside. Hundreds of years later, no one has stepped foot past the main gates. For all we know, the city was burnt to the ground and only the walls remain. We simply don't know."

"That's why you reacted when Bastion mentioned the strangers asking how to get there." It hit me.

"While I do not doubt many scavengers and thieves have attempted to break in and steal the wealth of the once-richest kingdom to exist, the gates have remained impassable for hundreds of years for a reason. Glasbur's wealth came from their docks and proud fleet. Many now have tried to sail to the southern shores but whatever caused Glasbur to shut its gates permanently also made sea travel an impossibility. The wrecks of hundreds of ships and a minefield of boulders destroy all vessels who draw close, long before their occupants can catch a glimpse of the forbidden shores.

"Only through the creation of the Elfins did Mordën face his second great conflict. And I suppose you know the result of that war by now. After the Drucodians were nearly wiped out, many of their great cities were abandoned. The last female Drucodian was killed at the prominent battle of that war. Only three cities built from those times are still standing and those are Avalon, The High City, and the once great Kingdom of Glasbur, though most now believe that latter city has long since faded into legend."

"You said 'most of the Drucodians' remember only through tales handed down," I murmured in deep interest. "Are there some who remember it differently?"

"As I said before," DarSheer returned, "most remember it that way because even their long life does not extend that far back. But several remember, because they were there, the glorious days when the Drucodians lived in peace and the green pastures, and the buildings of elegance were their greatest calamities. There are some who have existed since the first city was built. They are not old enough to have been there since the first night and day and of those number, more than a handful lived in black armor on the Isle itself, for they are known as *The Stygian Spears*, a group of Drucodians who turned on their own race to aid Mordën. One even rose to the rank of second-in-command of all Mordën's armies. His name has long since been lost to time but a few texts mention 'a Drucodian of noble birth now cursed to serve a master of evil.' There are very few sources to confirm his existence, yet the Drucodians now will not speak of him or that group, if you inquire after it."

"A Drucodian so evil he was made to be Mordën's second-in-command? What would cause one to turn on his own people?"

"The same reason many betray their own blood or banner—power. Some crave it so much; they'd give anything to have it. Those Drucodians now are either ashamed of it or affronted by the idea of it. They have lived long enough to know the truth, yet they do not confirm or deny his or the group's existence."

"They truly were blessed by long life then?"

"Aye, though many consider it a curse. To be forced to live centuries knowing your race is doomed and not able to continue your legacy or the legacy of your ancestors is a horrible thing. I'd rather die after living a prosperous life than have to endure the daily reminders of all those I'd left behind for a wretched existence."

"Where do these Drucodians reside?" I warmed my hands against the flames.

"There's a place north of the Abrigath Forest. It's called 'The Remnant.' Rumor is they have built an entire city of their remaining number and keep it concealed from any others. The city's name is not even known. We don't even know if their number has dwindled since the last time someone took count."

"How miserable," I murmured as I stood. "To be cursed with a fate beyond your control."

DarSheer eyed me for a moment then lowered his blade. He set the stone aside and leaned back. I tossed a twig into the popping flames and watched the flames soar with renewed vigor before dying back down to a soft burn.

"Speak your mind, bairn."

"Being stuck here is not as easy as I may make it seem. I wrestle every morning if I should continue aiding you or if I should be dedicating my efforts to finding a way home. I'm tired of feeling this yoke of guilt. Of wondering if I'm making a mistake."

"There comes a day when every man must face the quarrels of his inner thoughts; when he fights his darkest battles and sees if he wins or loses. Every man who wakes up and faces the demons inside and outside is a true hero, though lacking fame from folktale and lore he is as brave as a kingly man atop his great throne. Though no bard may sing his song, if only all men won their battles as such and bore their victory as kindness and grace. Do not despair because you feel these things. Despair when you succumb to them."

"So, there is hope then?" I glanced at him. "That the polluted fight in my mind can be won? That I'm not lost or a servant of evil? Mordën visited me in my nightmares last night. I didn't tell you because I felt shame. I witnessed an old friend perish in a brutal manner and I wonder if the hold he has over me is more than I once thought."

"The only moment when hope is truly lost is when you give up all else." DarSheer smiled slightly. "And you, Phoenix, have never given up. You have such courage and bravery like men of old. Legends will one day be spun to paint you as a man of stature and bravery. Do not doubt yourself, for such is an action of a fool, not a wise man."

"What if deep inside, he's planted a seed of doubt?" I murmured. "We ride from death. A black horde of horrible creatures on the borders and we have lost so many allies already. Two years I stood guard, you all much longer, and what did it amount to? I have no reason to hope. I'm afraid, DarSheer. Truly afraid. Afraid that Mordën has control of me like he did long ago. I'm afraid that unknowingly, I serve him. I see his face leering from the darkness, and I realize all my past was a game for his pleasure. He kidnapped those I cared about and set up an elaborate ruse. He sacrificed my friends. He somehow knew every step I'd take, and I led him here. I'm afraid of what I've done. I'm afraid of who I am becoming."

"Fear is not in and of itself an evil," DarSheer said softly. "For it merely invigorates a heightened awareness and defends from death itself. You are not weak for being afraid. You are strong for recognizing it resides within you. Do not let it control you; merely let it guide you. You, more than any here, hold a burden across your young shoulders that I would not wish on any. You feel a used vessel to Mordën and once you may have been but even the crudest vessel can be shaped into something beautiful. Do not give up, for while the blood of Erëthuïl and the strength of Humans and Elfins run through the deep veins of this world, and while courage of outsiders like yourself hold true, then we have nothing to fear. All this, the darkness and death, is but a miserable prelude to a feast in paradise. All that is good comes with a heavy price. And those who pay the price do so so those we love live happily. We do not take their sacrifice lightly, but we do not let it ruin our lives."

"I do not know if I want this burden or the cost placed on me." I stared deeply into the fire. "Yet it appears like much in my life, I have no say. I shall stand alongside all of you even though, if I'm being candid, I wish the opposite. I wish I could leave everything in my past, travel home, and see those I started this cruel joke of an adventure with. I want it all to be over."

"You are not bound by oath to see this through. Should you wish to depart I would not blame you. Many stronger men than you or I would have fled long ago. Here at this pivotal moment, you must decide if you stand with us *by your own choice*, or if you wish to find a way home. I would have you know you have my blessing either way." His words touched me.

I offered a smile. "I cannot decide in whole right now but a part of me knows that while I live and breathe here in this world, I have a duty, as a bringer of evil, to right the wrong. It was through me that evil was allowed to endure. It weighs me down. I am the reason Brenneth now lies in the mud amidst the death and carnage that once was home. I'm the reason thousands will perish, and the young will never become fathers and mothers. The call of the animal becomes the horn of the hunter. Shadows are as safe as the heat of fire itself."

"And through it all, your friends will be by your side. We made our choices, even when we knew the likely outcome. Your friend, Will, was the same way. I overheard your and Kissinger's and talk late into the night. You cannot stumble under the weight of that. He died knowing he was dying for a cause, for a good reason. Many cannot claim this at their own demise. You cannot help what happened, for it was not your decision. Though faced with death and grief you have chosen to stand and fight. Oh, if only the bards were here to see this. The words the trees would sing if they had a voice. I believe a ballad about you would bring a tear to all. An outsider, who despite the odds cast against him and his past, would rather honor that which was thrust upon him over letting the darkness take hold. I am truly honored to be at your side, for this is not the end. It is the beginning."

He poked a stick into the fire. For the first time in a long while, I felt a reason to keep fighting. The internal battle had been surging the last few nights. The doubts and constant fears that have assailed me since I'd arrived here seemed less potent. The sting of grief didn't sting as much.

"You speak of nightmares like they assail you regularly," DarSheer continued. "What do they contain exactly?"

The cold returned and I looked down. "Darkness. I see rooms and pits of darkness. A looming pale face bloodless and sneering. There are bodies with holes, bodies with no limbs, headless corpses, bloodless in the night. I march down troughs of blood and bathe in the bodies of a thousand spiders. And through it all, pain flows through me as fresh as if it was truly happening. They say you can't feel pain in a dream, but I can feel every prick, every stab, every bite, every *cruel* action.

"I also dream of another, a girl. My mind is fuzzy, but I know this above all else, I loved her and now I will never see her again."

"That is a great loss on its own." DarSheer placed a hand on my shoulder. "It pains the heart to lose someone to death; it aches the soul to lose them while they still live."

We continued to brood in silence, content to be left alone in our respective thoughts. Him to whatever world consumed him, and me to the wistful longings of the past. He pulled out a thin wooden pipe and placed brittle brown leaves into the small cup at the end. With a grunt, he lit it and puffed out a spiral of smoke that sailed up into the glistening sky. He offered the pipe to me, but I rejected the offer. The night was full, and a cold had set in. The others returned, grunting and heaving.

A rustle stirred us from our thoughts and DarSheer stood. He brushed the bristles and dirt from his pants, eyes alert. Othrain and Kissinger stepped from the long-reaching branches of an oak tree. Between them, they carried a massive animal. Antlers stuck out behind Othrain's back as he grunted and set the head of the beast down. He rubbed his hands with the satisfaction of a job well done. Kissinger lowered the rear end and grinned.

"Behold, the food has arrived," Kissinger announced with a flourish of his wrist and a deep bow. "I tried to get some options, but it was either this massive buck or some berries I'm pretty sure are poisonous."

"They're poisonous," Othrain droned as he drew a large knife from his belt.

"And how'd you figure that out?" Kissinger shot back playfully. "Did you try them?"

They dissolved into a battle of wits back and forth while Othrain used his knife to skin the deer. He started from the neck and worked his way down, exchanging humor with the others. DarSheer drew a second knife and helped while I watched at the edge of the fire.

"Get over here and skin the thing," Othrain grunted at me. He held out his knife.

I stood and moved cautiously over to the carcass. For once, the bloated body and glassy eyes didn't send shivers down my back. For once, the empty stare of death did not rattle me to my core. DarSheer mimed the next cut and let me perform it, so that my knife slid down the side with ease. I marveled at the entire ordeal. My hands were bloody, and heaps of fur lay about my feet before DarSheer began cutting slabs of meat off the body. Kissinger and Othrain skewered them with long sharpened sticks and placed them over the flames. The fire was low.

"How'd you manage to kill this thing?" DarSheer voiced my incredulity.

"It was already dead. Skilled hunters have been through this terrain as recent as a night ago. I saw boot prints half a mile south. There was an arrow in this buck's eye. Tip of it probably skewered the brain. Either they couldn't find it or didn't want it." Othrain adjusted how he sat and grinned contentedly. He looked like he wore red gloves.

"Because that's not incredibly ominous," I deadpanned.

"You have a deer and all its meat." Othrain leveled his blade at me. "Don't question it."

DarSheer frowned. "We cannot afford to not question things, Othrain. Mordën and his armies march abroad with little to no resistance. I don't believe even he could have followed us this fast, but there is no limit to his power, none that I know of. His scouts roam far and deep into the void of night. Do not lower your alertness for a bite to eat."

"Be at peace. If it was Varg, they'd have eaten it. If it was Nightshades . . . well it couldn't be. They don't waste their efforts on animals." Othrain rolled his eyes, but I noted the glance he gave Kissinger. The other ducked his head as if intently focused on piece of wood he was suddenly whittling.

By the time the meat was sizzling on the makeshift spit, our mouths were watering, and no one questioned the choice to dig into the hot dinner. We stewed in silence letting the juice drip from our lips. Othrain wiped grease from his fingers on his tunic as he finished his last drumstick. His belly full, he leaned back and began picking at his teeth. Kissinger and DarSheer ate far less but were equally satisfied with the meal. I felt like even Traverse would have been proud of this meal. My stomach grumbled for a bistri pie and Marian's warm smile.

DarSheer covered himself in his cloak and began to hum. His deep tenor rumbled and soon Kissinger began to sing a lilting tune that in light of recent events seemed to hold a sinister angle.

For joy I cry and my love your face has shown my life
Grieve not for I am here and blessed I am to see your laughter
Cry not lift up oh lift up your smile and share your joy
Come my child lift up your face for I am here and all have staid
Their ancient darkness is shattered and your mind at rest
A night beyond my time a world out of sight
Would the eyes of her gaze and the warmth of her touch
Starve even the bravest warrior to walk oh hallowed halls
Her scent of lilacs on a breaking dawn a promise unfulfilled
Beauty rarely comes bottled in human form yet there she verily stood
Complexation of a goddess her heart rich with love for seasons divined
Yet merely a thought in my head is how her memory lives on
For a night beyond my time a world out of sight
Is the Princess of Glasbur singing her ballad of brokenness
A haunting melody drenching all our ears in a siren's silky cry
Away far away in a kingdom of plenty where I cannot go
Gates once wide allowed all to ride now shut forever from me
Sunlight bright once burned with light now gone from my sight
Oh Princess of Glasbur rays from my heart reveal my intent for you
Though rays can hardly pierce the thunderhead you've created against me
So pass like stars in the night never to speak and never to touch

A face of familiarity hovered on the fringe, hidden by a veil shadowy in form yet no thicker than a strand of hair. After eating my meager share, I laid down and started to doze off to the crickets chirping and the trees whispering their nightly ballad. Kissinger's youthful but deep voice seemed to send the lyrics launching into the night sky and twirling about like a fairy. The fire crackled and popped and the shadows danced a lively jig. Where once the starlight above was foreign to me, now it sparkled in sadness.

"All these songs speak of sad times," I murmured sleepily. "Do you not have merry ballads that can bring a fire to our veins?"

"Many such songs exist, bairn," Othrain said, "yet these times are unfit for them."

Malziek breathed deeply. Blood ran down his temple and spilled into his mouth. Cuts covered his heaving body and spittle hung in suspension from his cracked lips. He slowly looked up as a dark shape advanced, parting the Varglarian like a boulder in a river. Their jeers hushed and their eyes intently trained on his every move; the figure approached and stopped. Malziek coughed blood and grimaced. The two brutish Night-shades holding his arms in a restrictive grip kneed him. He bit his tongue for he would not cry out in the face of his death. He would not give his foe that satisfaction.

"Lord Malziek," the blurred figure before him murmured. The voice slithered into his ears.

"If you'd have any honor, you'd let your cur release me and die at the edge of my blade," Malziek snarled. He was determined to fuel his fire.

To his surprise, the two Nightshades let go of him and stepped back. His sword clattered into view. Malziek looked up and into the pure black eyes of the pale man facing him. There was nothing pleasant about him, for he reeked of death, and his crisply pressed cloak and black tunic and hugged his form tightly. His hair was perfectly positioned, and his face was unblemished.

"*Mordën.*" *Malziek realized with concern. He gripped his sword feeling the first scent of fear settle in. He did not like it. It unsettled him.*

"I'm not surprised you know me, after what I did to these lands, to your people." Mordën grinned. His teeth were pearly white and sharpened like a sword's point. "I am more surprised how much people have forgotten. They remember only the stories of my banishment. Perhaps, it is time to remind them who their real king is. I have returned: your victorious lord to liberate you from Erëthuil's deceit. Bow before me and all you see shall be yours. I know how your own kin betrayed you, banished you out here to this cold rock. You've been blinded by tales founded on lies. Join forces with me and together we will build a new world."

All around, the Outpost sat in burning silence. All around, bodies covered the ground. Glassy eyes stared back in frozen agony. Blood pooled and fires ravaged the buildings of the place he'd called home. Bands of Varglarian were going about and systematically killing off any of the injured. A single cry rose like a whip on the wind and was silenced in gurgling death. Through all that, Mordën's eyes never strayed from Malziek. He never broke his gaze. He drew a curved blade of black steel. The hilt was blood red with golden tassels and formed in the shape of an hourglass.

Malziek exhaled. "You are dirt unfit to grow the vilest of weeds."

Mordën let out a snarl. "I am Mordën, Heir to Ëonë. I have come to reclaim these lands from the vile usurpers who stole them from me." He clenched his gloved fist as his eyes flashed with rage.

Malziek stood, shakily. He hoped it wasn't obvious how terrified he was. When he spoke, his voice was soft and deep. "Your power has dwindled, cur, and legends of your deeds revealed as exaggerated falsehoods. You've underestimated the people's fighting spirit. As long as people like me stand in your way, you will never be welcomed here. You will have to burn and slaughter for every inch of ground. The blood of your monsters will flow all the way back to your fortress till you are carried back. You misjudged us once, and you'll do it again. You are a relic of a forgotten time."

Mordën gestured and Raoul slid down the Rachnadon's leg. He drew his dagger and approached Malziek, who regarded him with mild disgust.

"Send a lackey to kill me?" Malziek growled. "Are you afraid to spill blood? So afraid to take the lives of the people you torture that you'd send a mutilated beast to do the job? Fear does not look good in a king."

Raoul paused as Mordën raised a hand. He regarded Malziek with a level of thinly veiled disdain. Malziek stared up at him. The air above them warped and shook as seven figures descended. Malziek's hesitant defiance shattered as he realized what they were. The Hourglass, robes flowing, landed and circled around him. Their hoods covered their eyes completely and their gloved hands prevented any recognizable feature. They drew seven blades of fire and raised them high. Malziek dove for his sword and spun into a crouch and prepared himself for where he predicted the attack would originate. Mordën drew a small knife and pointed it at the Outpost's leader.

"Fight me!"

Malziek roared and stepped forward. He swung the blade with great strength as it arched through the air and glinted the sunlight off its steel. Mordën took a single step to the side, caught Malziek's left arm with a sure jab, and plunged the knife into Malziek's neck. Only the handle was visible as Malziek dropped to one knee. Blood flowed down his neck.

"I bid you depart for the halls of your blessed Erëthuïl," Mordën knelt next to him and traced a finger in the blood that ran down Malziek's throat. "When you see him . . . tell him I am coming for him. I expect quite the banquet." He yanked the knife out and kicked Malziek's body.

Malziek choked and his eyes rolled up as he toppled onto his back. The courtyard was quiet as every Varg and Shade observed thin silence. Mordën licked the blood off the blade as he turned to his forces.

"Consume the dead and desecrate these hallowed lands but this one, the lord of this outpost, he shall remain. I have plans for him. Feast tonight, for tomorrow, we march on the rest of Ëonë."

Raoul stepped forward. "The DarkBairn escaped, my king, along with three others. They've been spotted by our scouts approaching Ithuïn."

"Good." Mordën sheathed his blade. "Send out Nien Thrass and his company to hunt them down, but ensure they reach visible walls before they are massacred. We want the people to have their martyr."

"I am your servant." Raoul bowed then paused. "It shall be as you command."

Mordën's scowl fiercened. "You will command my scouts on the hunt for the bairn."

"Yes, my king." Raoul bowed slowly.

"I do not need to remind you again of the price of failure."

Raoul touched the black lines in his face. "No . . . my king."

"Go in chaos." Mordën turned to watch the thousands of bodies march in unison past him. There was nothing more thrilling than hearing thousands of boots slam against the ground sending shock waves to all the races that populated this cursed continent. Let it be their warning. They had defied him and exiled him. He would not be so merciful.

Lightning forked overhead and in the flashes of deep amber, red . . . his calm shattered. He screamed a wild howl like a wounded banshee. His perfectly kept hair let lose a single strand that hung over his eyes as he whirled about. The air was thick with a burning odor and ashes rained down around him.

"Curse you!" he snarled in a high pitch and grabbed ahold of Malziek's neck. With little to no visible effort, he lifted the massive man up till Malziek's boots swayed over the dirt. "Curse you all!"

A ferrek, untouched by the ravaging and pillaging, sped off into the darkness.

Chapter 3
News from the South

THE BREAK OF THE wet dawn couldn't cure my aching thoughts or my belly, which grumbled its tempestuous complaints. Not even my thin blanket could provide menial comfort. Long had we ridden and long still did we ride. The deer we'd feasted on nights past was but a distant memory, and a particularly haunting one to my empty belly. The bags which had been gifted us by Bastion hung unopened and remained that way for DarSheer would not let anyone so much as touch the fabric. Tantalizing promises of a hearty breakfast rose in tempting fashion from the cracks in the cloth and a fair bit of thought was had if I should attempt to unfasten one of them.

"Dawn is near, and I don't want to be seen," DarSheer clicked his tongue. "I fear the Shadow King has sent his bloodthirsty demons out into the world and now waits to see the resistance formed. Blackness and a world of shadow will hasten to engulf our world if we do not fulfill our mission. We must make haste to Ithuïn. They will have fresh mounts there. Mounts and new supplies."

He'd been muttering this way for the past day, like a crazed man, about where to stop and what Mordën was up to. Kissinger and Othrain took to his new peculiar manner with quiet concern. I, on the other hand, watched him intently. His eyes danced about the deep valleys and climbing hills as we traversed plain and field and eminence which commanded a vista of the distant mountains. Vermillion blooms dotted a nearby knoll which seemed to sway in the soft breeze as grass and tree danced. A pack of ferreks watched us from a neighboring knoll, their beady eyes waiting for us to drop a morsel of food.

"How much longer are we going to endure this torture?" Othrain hissed to Kissinger when DarSheer was out of earshot. "He rides like a madman with little intent behind his actions. We've meandered thrice now away from our target city."

"He's leading us down paths the enemy might not expect," I responded. Othrain glanced at me.

"A nice theory if it was backed with evidence. He's going mad. Someone needs to slap some sense into him. We should have arrived at the gates by now. Have we asked ourselves if Broadsword is as innocent of evil intent as we all believe? I say we sit him down and interrogate him."

"Perhaps while we're there," Kissinger shot back, "we can sit you down and open your thick skull to see if you have a brain. Lord Malziek trusted him more than anyone else in the blasted place. You're fishing, but you forget, fishing on land is ridiculous."

Othrain's face went red as a tomato, but he quieted down. The frozen dawn warmed to a chilly morning before a bank of impenetrable fog lifted and we could see, far off, a large settlement. This city put to shame every village, farm, and outlying town we'd passed many days prior. DarSheer leaned excitedly in his saddle and placed a hand to his brow. His frown, all we'd seen for the last four days and nights, was replaced now with a broad smile. He pressed his lips tightly together and patted the mount's neck.

"Ithuïn," he crowed. "Behold, friends and allies, the last city east of Avalon."

It was immediately obvious how impressive the place was. Thick stone walls towered over the road. At various intervals, towers jutted from the stone where bowmen could rain hell down on invading attackers. Smoke curled up and into the sky, dispersing in the wind. A steady stream of arriving and departing travelers made the entrance congested. Soldiers stood and checked goods and materials being imported. Carts jostled along, hitting nearly every pothole in the mud they could. Disgruntled dogs barked and snarled at each other as they wove between legs and wheels. Piles of horse defecation steamed in the face of the sun. Children giggled and darted about, a pack of wild boys intent on lifting coins from the richer travelers who stomped their way across the Westerly Road. Women walked with baskets perched precariously on their shoulders. They whispered to each other as soldiers cantered by, mounted on broad-chested mares. Large banners snapped royally over the heads of passersby as the city of Ithuïn opened its massive gates to all who wished to pass.

DarSheer led the way down the hill and back onto solid road. My mount tossed its head as we passed a younger woman guiding a colt clomping east. She shaded her eyes as I passed and blushed. Behind her, carting barrels of ale and cider, merchants dressed in rich greens and blues sang their way toward the gates.

The cask is empty our bairns are young
Grab a mug and crack another
The barrel is rolling emptily away
But our stores are deep so crack another
Our tankards are dryer than a sandy desert
Pop the seal on the nearest keg
Your goblet to fill your eyes to see
Sing for the richest hogshead of the Drasmorian Guild

They roared with laughter despite the looks of haughty strangers that followed them. I recognized the small painted circle on the side of one of the vessels. The Ebyian troupe pushed their way forward as we joined the line of winding stragglers.

"This place looks important." Kissinger nodded sagely. "Haven't seen this many people since . . . ever. Is Avalon like this?"

"This place is to Avalon as the Outpost is to The High City," DarSheer said. "Ithuïn is a crucial role for the import of sea trade from the northern and eastern shores."

We began cantering toward the gates. Soon we were passing those who trod on foot. To our right, several carts of fruits sat on the side of the road as their owner haggled with another over pricing. An Incling grunted his disapproval of the price and threw his hands up in the air. The owner of the cart wheezed and tried again. We quickly moved past them as I stared about like a babe seeing with their eyes for the first time. Everything was so lively and vibrant in color. An excited tension hummed beneath the ground. Kissinger was right: I had not seen so many people in one area before. The Outpost was quiet, and while it housed several hundred men, most kept to their huts when they were off duty.

"At the heart of the city is a major intersection which branches off to Piscel's Path in the north," DarSheer continued. "It's a small road leading to Fiscer's Keep. Ever since Glasbur closed its walls, Fiscer's has been the primary importer of eastern sea trade. Ithuïn moderates the intake and outtake to ensure piracy and theft are as regulated as possible. All goods then go through Avalon, which is why the Elfinian king allowed Men to found this city in the Eastern Ward."

"Regulated?" I tried not to stare in the eyes of a skinny stranger who watched us hungrily. "Shouldn't they be fighting piracy? Why is it allowed?"

We passed a group of merchants on the side of the road, squabbling. They paused to stare up at us and one murmured to another. They watched us ride off as the city gates drew near and I couldn't help but feel a wave of cold wash over me.

"On the contrary," Othrain picked up the tale, glowering, "piracy is encouraged so the fat in The High City can have their fill. Blasted goldens. According to official regulation, it's discouraged, but simply slip a coin under the nose of the watchman and thrice the number of fish makes its way onto barges. They claim it's to help those who cannot afford their steep prices, but they conveniently forget it's they who set the damned prices in the first place. A happy watchman is a happy kingdom."

The smell of unwashed bodies and rotting fish wafted across the road. Donkeys and miniature horses chomped lazily at the tufts of grass that bordered the road. One man tugged a cart full of cages. Inside, we could hear loud shrieking and snarling. As we rode, we had to wave off several insistent traders who swore up and down that their silk furs and spices were the rarest in the lands. Through their thick beards, they promised us wealth and riches if we only trusted them. Othrain drew a dagger on them more than once until they finally let us go, though they grumbled about the rudeness of it all.

We approached the gate itself where a man in a cart was being stopped. Atop the walls, several armored bowmen monitored the road. A minstrel leaned against a box and was bellowing an out-of-tune tale. The entire scene seemed bizarre after the relative calmness and isolation that we'd come to enjoy at the Outpost. I found myself shrinking into the cloak that covered my shoulders. My head tumbled with the dozens of voices that shouted, shrieked, snarled, belted, roared, and thundered out in a cacophony of chaos. Animals hissed, carts thudded, boxes cracked, fires spat, and the flags that snapped proudly atop the wall whacked aside any doubt of the grandness of this city.

"Oi? What brings you lot to Ithuïn, kind sirs?" a guard atop the wall shouted down. His voice was pleasant though guarded. "If mischief be on your mind, you'd best make haste and off into the hills with ya."

"Such is the greeting from an ally to another?" DarSheer challenged merrily. "I'd heard more of the hospitality of this once great city and yet here I am being asked if I mean to rob you like I'm a common swindler."

"No harm meant, kind sirs," the man returned. His head vanished.

On the other side of the wall, several guards greeted us and after a thorough check of our persons and horses, they let us through. The man from the wall stood at regal attention but when he laid eyes on DarSheer he broke into a toothy grin and embraced him. Othrain, Kissinger, and I watched in surprise.

"And what of Brenneth?" he asked as he took DarSheer's calloused hands in his own. "Tell me of that boy. Does he carry the Outpost's banner proud and true like his father wanted? I haven't seen him since he was but a wee lad on my last visit to your home."

In that moment an uncomfortable silence followed. Kissinger and Othrain found the churned-up clay at their mount's hooves to be of considerable interest.

"The Outpost is actually the reason I have traveled this far, Eridon." DarSheer let his hands fall to his side. "This is no place for quiet talk where ears of all sorts listen in. Do you have a place we can shelter, perhaps a tavern? My stomach does rumble something fierce, and young Phoenix here has complained of his hunger from the ford hither."

Eridon focused on me.

"All are welcome if coin is in your pocket and mirth on your mind," he cried jovially. "Should you be wanting for trouble, let this serve as a reminder, we don't tolerate rats, thieves, and murderers. All else welcome."

"They don't tolerate them unless they offer a few thruki," Othrain muttered.

"Take us somewhere away from the public eye, somewhere safe." DarSheer lowered his voice. Urgency had replaced friendliness. "We have much to discuss, my old ally."

Eridon led us down the road as it dipped and climbed, turned, and meandered between home and inn alike. Light streamed from windows and laughter echoed as various folk, all arrayed in brown or grey garb, moved from alley to road to inn. Some huddled in dark corners, their patched faces peering out. Others hawked their wares as they pushed carts laden with pies, kegs of ale, and the occasional basket overflowing with leafy greens. A medicine worker bathed her hands in a steaming green liquid and rubbed it down a groaning Ebyian's back. A few boys in ragged clothes that clearly were handed down from larger men, danced about and shrieked their joy as a ball passed between them. Cats slunk between brush and watched the scene unfold. Dusk nigh, the entire city had a deep glow, as if the road itself glowed with energy. Folk moved this way and that with clear purpose. The sky itself was clear of veils as the stars twinkled.

I kept my head low to avoid the curious glances sent my way. It did not take long to realize that we made the locals uneasy. I'd hoped by now the incessant whispers and stares would dwindle but as we drew toward the center of the city, they only seemed to grow.

"You lot be careful around these parts," Eridon cautioned. "Folk here don't take kindly to snooping. Newcomers are tolerated but not trusted. Don't go accepting any food, money, or jobs that require you to leave the sight of the public. And do not ever go into an alleyway without a weapon. I said we don't take kindly to thieves, but we're few against many unruly strangers. We can't afford to tip the balance back in our favor. It's a miserable existence it is."

"Newcomers?" Kissinger mused. "Are there not strangers passing your gates every day? I know Othrain is probably the ugliest brute these lot have seen, but what makes us so different?"

"Hey!" Othrain thwacked the back of Kissinger's head.

Eridon smiled. "You dress as warriors, blades hidden in plain view. Your mounts are not garbed in the colors of the city nor of any major cities this side of the mountains. Your tongue is one with a slight accent. Most easy to identify, though, is your own dress. You wear the clothes of men of the Outpost. The folk here are wary, untrusting. Can you blame them?"

"Where are you taking us?" DarSheer inquired as we strode down the road. An aged crone grinned toothily at us from the dusty windows of a small shop. She waggled her crooked fingers at me and pursed her lips. Her eyes twinkled.

"Right," I leaned toward Kissinger, "are we sure that we're safer here surrounded by thieves and ill-doers over the road where a Varg or Shade might attack at any moment?"

Eridon overheard. "The people here are suspicious by nature, but no harm will come to ya if you keep your nose clean. Stick to the main roads, do not talk unless you know the other."

Eridon's cloak fluttered in the wind and his regal clothing snapped proudly as he turned corners abruptly or climbed steps hills. Passersby eyed him but no one seemed bold enough to harass us. Perhaps the meager soldiers here did command some intimidation. Guards at various crossroads nodded to him as he passed. Even the lighting of the setting sun seemed to cover him in a glow. His gloved hands gestured wildly as he explained the various buildings and where the nearest shops were and who to go to if you found yourself in a spell. I studied his face, impressed that anyone so outgoing and honorable could survive in this cesspool of mirk and seedy activity. From the outside, the city was bold and intimidating. The walls and towers boasted their impenetrability. Yet upon crossing the threshold, it became evident order was kept by a shaky truce between lawless and lawgiver. Shady deals were made and bribery was encouraged. While most were disheveled and hairy, Eridon wore his beard well, keeping it trimmed to the perfect length. It covered his mouth and chin. His long hair flowed down to his shoulders and bounced about with every step.

"Don't you be worrying yourselves, Broadsword." He grinned finally. "I know just the place for travelers like you."

I began to feel unsure of his honor as the trip continued and no end to the city or the road itself lay in sight. Ere the sun had about laid its head and let the night take the watch, we arrived at a long comfortable lodge where a sign, which creaked back and forth, bore the words *The Ilkspun Tavern*. The last word was faded, its blue and gold paint having dimmed from its constant years exposed to the elements. Next to the tavern, welcome light laid out as a carpet and the sounds of relaxed and excited voices issued out into the open air. The city seemed at peace, for men hurried along their way and did their business before the hours of darkness fell. Women tugged at the slender arms of their youth and hushed the cries of complaints. A few slender men gripped the hips of their consorts and spoke dark words in their ears, to which the maidens squealed in delight. Even the animals seemed content to live their lives as they chased fallen morsels or slunk between buildings and out of sight. Smoke curled from chimneys and faded into the sky.

We came to a stop outside the long building. The street bustled with merchants hawking their wares from various carts garbed in yellows and reds. Long bolts of silk were hung from bronze hooks. Here, the clay paths were replaced with cobblestone roads, these still being hard to cover on foot due to their inconsistent spacing and tilted nature. Boots thudded over the uneven cobbled road and cloaks rustled over the bodies of Elfinian, Ebyian, and Human alike. There was even a rare spotting of a group of Inclings, which Eridon proudly pointed out. The old sign above creaked and groaned in the wind.

"Behold my pride and joy: The Ilkspun Tavern." Eridon beamed. He hurried up to tavern and pulled the door wide.

I ducked my head, for the doorframe was built low, and couldn't help but feel infected by the sudden mood. A bubbling feeling of humor and tricks seemed glued to the atmosphere for all around, men and women enjoyed tankards of ale and beer and roared with laughter. Smoke wafted about from the lit ends of smoke pipes. A group of burly men huddled around a chest and exchanged gold coins. Their aggressive looks deterred even the most curious of patrons. Some chose to sit in relaxation after a hard day's bartering, their feet up on stools and pipes in their mouths. Grey and white smoke collected at the ceiling, so it appeared like a cloud layer floated above us. Some travelers chattered and danced, others sang and called. Some slapped their plump bellies and chortled with merriment as a troupe of elegantly clad folk in green costumes of leafy design danced on tables. Music curled its way between broad shoulders and beneath the outstretched boots and the swaying cloaks of the dancers.

Beyond the spires of darkness lies . . . the crashing ocean and the
plains in light
The grass doth breathe and the hills doth sing . . . their chorus cast
off the darkest night
Away and close the weary lie . . . foot by foot o'er their squinted sight
The tramp of feet and the creak of wheels . . . as carts round bends
in the mountain height
Sing forth brave brethren of the past . . . of the cries of men
as they fall in the fight

Sing forth brave brethren of the past . . . as the shadow falls
and the steel doth bite
We march to death's sweet touch . . . for our spears descend s
harpened from above
The horns doth blow and the men doth cry . . . wounded they lie
like a fallen dove
Do you remember the feel of life on the trees . . . and the bittersweet
touch of the maiden we love
Our breasts are heavy with weighted steel . . . as the light once
more is barren of
For the darkness brings its fearsome call . . . as the maidens their
tears they brokenly wove
Sing forth brave brethren of the past . . . of the cries of men as they
fall in the fight
Sing forth brave brethren of the past . . . as the shadow falls and the
steel doth bite

As the final chorus was bellowed, the room was filled with thunderous applause as bodies were slapped and tables shook. Goblets of wine and mead spilled onto the ground, but no one paid them any mind. Spirits were lifted high and loud voices proclaimed their admiration. Several gloshee were strummed, and their piercing hums sent the crowd into another round of whistling and a call for an encore. The dancing troupe on a small circular stage in the center of the room bowed and once again broke into song.

Ol' Belly does jiggle and his fiddle does riddle
As his garments he tore and his sword he draws for war . . .

The crowd, clearly aware of the song, broke into a chorus as the instruments strummed.

They bellow with glee and tear their wounds . . . asunder!!
They flash in anger like lightning and rumble like . . . thunder!!

The musicians on the stage laughed gaily and geared the crowd up for another raucous stanza as Eridon maneuvered his way around the tables and beefiest forms. We followed, careful not to step on any boot or tread on any loose cloak. Several tall and elegant figures leaned against the far wall, their fair blue eyes watching the troupe. Golden was their hair and it flowed around their backs in curls and pops. Each figure bore a dagger curved with handles of intricately carved wood.

"Are they . . .?" I breathed as they caught sight of me.

"Elfin," DarSheer murmured back. "They are most likely merchants from the Ethero Basin on business east, though I'm surprised to find them hanging out here. There are taverns here more suited to them. They distrust these people, as well they should. So why they would willingly put themselves here is beyond me."

"And why shouldn't they?" Eridon boomed. He'd slipped into a back room and gestured for us to follow.

The room was tight but comfortable. Along one wall a comfy couch had been readied for its next occupant. Paintings of mythical beings hung along the walls and a small circular window had been placed at eye level when sitting. Several candles burned and flickered on the table. Wax collected in clumps. The sounds and din outside dimmed to far-off shouts.

"We are safe to talk here," Eridon leaned back. "My family owns this place and I trust my guards. Tell me, Broadsword, what news from the East? How fares Lord Malziek? It has been many years since I was able to journey out there."

"It despairs me to have to bring such tidings to you now, my old ally."

"I don't like the sound of that," Eridon shook his head.

"The Outpost was attacked by Varglarian and Nightshade forces not nine days past. None save present company made it out alive."

For a moment Eridon said nothing, choosing to gaze distractedly out the window. On the other side of the thick glass, the last stragglers before night could be seen bustling around. Vendors finished their last sales as customers made their final purchases. A shred of light remained as individuals came along with torches and lit the braziers along the streets and candles in the windows. Finally, Eridon stirred.

"Long has it been prophesied," he spoke, "of the Shadow King's return. I've heard tales, ones I hoped made exaggerated by the wagging tongues of ill-reputed bards. Tell me of the bright-eyed stable boy who was so eager last I was there."

I considered telling him about Brenneth's lifeless corpse but the more I watched his greyed face, hopeful, the less I could muster the willpower to say it.

"He perished in battle," DarSheer responded instead. "I last saw him fighting off a legion of well-armed Varglarian. They had begun to burn the stables and Brenneth and several other of his stable boys had grabbed their barn equipment and begun attacking the creatures."

"If it helps," I breathed shakily, "Brenneth was a true friend to me. Alienated by my strange arrival, the others chose to keep me at arm's length, but not Brenneth. He spoke to me the first day we met, and I'll never forget what he said. 'Good evening to you, whoever you are. You look lost. Might I recommend Traverse's bistri? They're mighty fine when deep thought is needed, as I believe you desire.' After that we talked, and he shared his love of the countryside and the Outpost."

Throughout it all, Eridon sat still, his eyes turned down as he sat deep in thought. The fires outside glowed now through the window and the candle on the table sent his shadow against the wall. He was less regal and proud here, like he'd shed some exterior and revealed the soft underbelly.

"What you say is news of the worst sort," he buzzed. "What is your plan?"

"We make for Avalon, and there we shall hold King Elharan to his oath his ancestor made with the High King, millennium past."

"You'll find the Elfin have grown more possessive and secret of late." Eridon glowered out the window. "You'll be hard-pressed to make them consider anything they don't wish."

"Phoenix, you mentioned your hunger prior," DarSheer prompted toward the door. He raised both eyebrows. "Now would be an excellent time to obtain sustenance and let Eridon and I discuss matters in the privacy of this chamber. Kissinger, Othrain, you as well. Stay together."

For a moment I was too stunned to respond, believing I'd misheard. A pang of annoyance stabbed in my chest, but I exhaled it away and rose. I bowed politely to Eridon and nodded to DarSheer, closing the door behind, and retreating into the tavern space. Kissinger was already off, making a beeline for the bar where he began flirting with a maiden who poured ale from great barrels. She tossed her thick locks over her shoulders and giggled at whatever joke he'd made. Her cheeks were pink and her eyes glistening green. Othrain grunted a half wave and disappeared into the smoke and cloaks toward an empty table. *So much for staying together*, I thought darkly.

There was an infectious bustle of chattering voices as travelers from all corners of Ëonë discussed matters both secretive and not. Elfins murmured to each other in the far corners of the room. More in the center, Men, Ebyians, and Inclings prattled noisily drunk in the success of their trade. Stews simmered in thick wooden bowls and braziers burned bright on the walls. Apart from the brief comings and goings as the door revolved this way and that, the room remained warm and comforting. Ebyians in their thick cloaks with wide hoods cast low over their beady little eyes spent thruki at random tables where various games had begun. A band of Inclings, possibly the same one we'd spotted earlier, entered to the curious stares of many in the room. DarSheer had once told me Inclings were a quiet species, content living far from the prying eyes of seedy folk. Their homelands were southwest of the Fallen Peaks in a land known only as the Cacian Hinterlands.

Outside, a forceful wind had begun howling down along the streets and alleys. Rain lashed against the small windows and every time the door was shoved opened, puddles would begin to trickle along the ground and a lash of cold wind would snap about those closest to the door.

I carefully moved to a corner table by the roaring fireplace. A small man with a musical instrument glanced up, and at my approach he scurried away like a mouse into the shadows. A few men in black cloaks sat huddled in a nearby booth. They glanced at me as small bags were exchanged. Daggers hung on their waists. A foreign emblem of a rat with gold whiskers was embraided on their tunics. The closest grunted and bared his teeth at me. He half-drew his dagger just to show me he meant business.

A girl moseyed her way to my table and smiled at me. Her eyes were cheerfully bright and her thick, long hair dangled about her waist. A necklace of sparkling emeralds hung around her plump neck and danced alluringly over her bosom. She touched these jewels every few moments, as if in absent thought.

"Hello, love," she murmured sweetly. "Today's special is the Cairn the huntsmen brought in from their travels. What piece you'll be having, and shall I toss some ale on it? Age don't mind in a fine place like this, my dear."

From what DarSheer had told me during our many training lessons, Cairn was a rare beast which resided only in the furthest reaches of the mountains. It was considered a delicacy and often cost more thruki than some saw in a year.

"No, thanks." I raised one hand in rejection. "I'll take bistri and a tankard of warm cider, if you please."

"Suit yourself, love." The girl shrugged and winked at a passing Ebyian who grinned cheekily at her with a broad smile filled with brown teeth. She winked. He chortled and drew her close. She ran a long finger down his hairy chin, and he leaned up. I turned away and tried not to stare as they began kissing in a passionate display that made me wonder if my food would ever be delivered.

The tavern door creaked open against the gales and torrential downpour outside, and a stranger stepped in. A purple hood hid his face. After she'd had her fun, the girl brought me a plate and mug and set them down, eying the new arrivals as if sizing them up. I watched as the cloaked newcomer slapped away the groping hands of a man who had come for their cloak. Water flowed down the figure's dark mauve cloak and pooled about on the floor under their black boots. As the torchlight flickered, I saw that the arrival was a female, though her face was mostly hidden beneath her hood. On her back, slung over one arm, she carried a bow and an elegant quiver. The lack of arrows was notable. Brown tangled hair flowed from underneath her hood and when the fabric shifted just enough, I could make out a ruby-hilted dagger sheathed at her waist. The intrusion was not enough to deter any from their jovial conversations. In fact, many seemed completely oblivious to her or, at the least, content to ignore her. They roared displeasure as dice were thrown high. A fistfight broke out between two heavy men and was settled only when one was knocked unconscious into the wall. The figure cast her eyes about the room and paused when she laid her gaze me. I swallowed some cider, feeling the hairs on my neck tingle. A wave of familiarity rushed over me. She approached the counter where the tavern girl, whose name I later discovered was Ësha, was rubbing down a keg of newly arrived mead. They spoke in hushed tones as the girl waved a casual gloved hand at me. Ësha nodded and said something under her breath, leaning forward. The figure removed her hood and turned. The firelight lit up her pretty features and I nearly dropped the mug in my hand. I jolted to my feet, upsetting the table, and sending the plate of bistri spilling onto the floor. Steam spiraled up as several cried out in indignation. The men next door to me cried out and drew their blades.

"Watch your clumsy hands, you oaf!" one snarled.

"My only good tunic," another growled. "That's three thruki for that."

I blushed and sat back down. I was to keep a low profile and here was the entire tavern shouting at me. The girl made her way toward my table and stopped only when she was a foot in front of me. I brushed scraps of bistri off the table as Arabella Sky gave me a pained smile. Her crystal blue eyes reflected the dancing light. There was no denying her beauty. Nestled comfortably above her dark grey tunic, a leather breastplate hugged her form. Her long pants were stuffed rather unceremoniously into her tall black boots. The men who had been about to take me out and lynch me grumbled and returned to their business, not wanting to engage in a fight with an armed stranger.

"Truly we have fallen on ill times if the DarkBairn wanders alone on our roads," she said softly. Ësha brought food and Arabella sat. She removed her quiver and bow and placed them against the edge of the table. She ran a hand through her hair. I accepted an outstretched plate of bistri with a nod of thanks. Ësha scrambled away, not wanting to be seen engaging with the troublesome duo any longer than she had to.

"I thought you'd perished by Varglarian steel." I couldn't break my gaze from her rosy cheeks. "Glysperia and the last of your city came to the Outpost moments before it was besieged by the full strength of Mordën's forces."

"I was not in Fiscer's Keep when they butchered my people, not exactly," Arabella said darkly. "I was in the bay of brackish water, hunting. My sister...my family...my people...all were lost to the consumption of fire and steel, yet I was cursed to live on and witness their end. I know now his vision and I see his hunger. It takes all. It shows no mercy." Her eyes flashed in pained remembrance.

"You've no home now." I realized rather belatedly.

She stared at me. "You and I bear more similarity than we may wish to admit."

"Join our company," I said suddenly. "Four of us made it out alive. The rest were cut down. DarSheer, Othrain, and Kissinger are nearby . . . I can inquire."

She smiled. "I wish this. There is strength in numbers. It pains me to hear of the falling of the Outpost. It addles my already irked mind to hear the strength of our enemy grows. Tell me, friend, why do you dwell now in Ithuïn?"

DarSheer's face appeared in my head, a disapproving look in his pale eyes.

I bit back the curse that sat on the tip of my tongue. Pain seared from my buttocks as I rubbed them. DarSheer's training blade swung through the air again. This time, aware of the pending agony, I sidestepped and

brought my own sword down with a vengeful passion. My anger betrayed me, for my own strength sent me stumbling off-balance as DarSheer, readjusting his stance, hit me hard in the ribs. His disapproving stare sunk deep.

"You're not trying anymore," he pointed out. "In the space of five seconds, I've killed you twice. What addles your mind, bairn? Why is it not focused on your training?"

I wanted to snap back the painful memories kept resurfacing. The nightmares that haunted my every thought and Mordën's whispers that commanded my obedience. I glowered at him; aware I was not winning myself any goodwill.

"Do not share with strangers that which can be used against you. Very good. Silence will get you far." He smiled for the first time in the session. "Keep your tongue, then. But know this: you will be fodder on the battle-field if you continue to do so poorly. Excelling in your history lessons will not aid you when it comes to a fight to the death."

"He'll bore them to death with lessons on the Drucodian Expansion of the First Era," Brenneth called from the wall.

DarSheer tried to hide the smile that flitted over his face. I leapt forward and aimed for his heart, but he had spun away faster than my eyes could follow. The training blade hit my rear end for a second time, and I tumbled to the ground. My blade fell feet away in the dirt. DarSheer placed one boot over the handle and glanced at me.

"Do you yield?" he inquired.

"I yield," I muttered. "I blasted yield."

Do not share with strangers that which can be used against you! The line rang in my head. Her steely gaze bore into me with a weight. What was the saying? The enemy of my enemy was my friend? Was she an ally?

"I head to Avalon to speak with their king," I chose my words carefully.

"I see." She sat back in her chair. "You wish to warn the peoples of this age of their pending doom and in so doing, unify the last powers that could hope to defy Mordën? If he were to know of your mission and your location . . ."

The hairs on my neck raised as I slowly inched my hand for my blade. Perhaps she was not as fair in mind as she was in form. DarSheer exited at that moment from the backroom and stopped when he spotted Arabella.

"And I'd thought we were all out of friends to meet, maiden," he said dryly.

She cracked another weak smile. "I've been called better. Good to see you alive and mostly well, Broadsword."

We conversed and Arabella proposed joining our band. I thought DarSheer would be overjoyed at the prospect of another sword to defend us, but here his eyes darkened and his mood soured.

"You may have come too late." He sounded annoyed. "Phoenix, come hither. Word has reached Eridon of an advance Varg scout seen on the hills just outside the city. Behind the lone Varg march a horde. Pikes ten feet tall wreathed in living flame. They carry a crimson banner and sing a song of death. Mordën advances through night and day and will be here much sooner than I'd anticipated. What wonders it does for morale when you can march so openly with no fear. I must away down south to meet with someone. You must continue your task and head to Avalon. There you must inform King Elharan of all that's befallen us. Speak candidly and offer no veil. If we are to gain any allies, it will not be with threats or secrecy."

"I say it again, let me join," Arabella pressed. "I am good in a pinch, and my skills with a blade nearly match yours, Broadsword."

"But why must you go now?" I spluttered. "Can you not come to Avalon first?"

"Caldonia is unaware and must be warned," DarSheer said, mostly to Arabella. "The roads will be closely guarded by spies and the shadows will be brimming with teeth and sword. Eridon will handle what the city needs. As it is partly owned by the Elfinian Merchant's

Guild, they will be able to bolster the walls with Elfinian warriors from nearby outposts. If all goes well, it might be enough to delay Mordën's advance."

"Mordën will not be stopped forever." Arabella shook her head warily. "We can only hope to delay him, not stop him. What will you do once you've warned the southern city?"

"Then let us hope that The Golden City is enough to stop him." DarSheer's voice was deep. "Avalon holds the high ground, walls of great thickness and towering height. Thousands of well-trained warriors reside there and its place in the mountains will require great effort and manpower to breach. Once I bring word to Commander Scion of Caldonia, I will ride to Avalon myself, if it is not too late. Which is why I leave before dawn. Othrain will ride with me."

We stopped as the tavern's door opened. A flash of lightning revealed a figure unlike any I'd previously seen. His broad shoulders sported sculpted arms. A silver tunic tightened over his chest and on each arm, thick gold bands hugged his biceps. His eyes were silver and hair blacker than night. A brownish red scar cut right through his clouded left eye. Across one shoulder was strapped a sword in a starry grey scabbard. He stepped forward, his thick boots thudding over the wooden ground. Ësha stared up at him in what could have been deciphered as either absolute horror or complete and utter infatuation. Her bottom lip trembled, and she stood frozen in spot.

"I am Stavon of Inïn." The figure gritted its teeth. His voice was like thunderheads rumbling far off. "I come looking for one from the Outpost."

For a long moment he gazed about the room. He stopped when he reached me. He turned back as DarSheer cleared his throat. For a moment the two stared at each other, sizing the other up. Stavon seemed to study DarSheer's weaponry before giving a snort of dismissal.

"Broadsword," Stavon spoke loudly.

"Stavon." DarSheer bowed slightly. "I see you got my message."

The newcomer's tunic was a pale silver save for a single patch on the chest where a tree, hugged by a wreath of stars, stood proud. It was not an emblem I recognized.

"Word travels quick." The other shrugged like a mountain rising and falling. "I came before any message was needed."

"Your haste is greatly appreciated," DarSheer said as the men in the booth next to us began to move.

The travelers in black cloaks stood slowly and one, reaching for his blade, moved toward the visitor. The closest one grinned a nasty smile. He was missing many teeth and the ones he clung to were yellowed with age.

"Aye, look what walks in dripping his disgrace over the ground. Who let you in, cripple? You should have been accosted at the gates. Why have you come here?"

"You'll find my past makes for less interesting conversation than you're used to." Stavon slowly turned around. His gloved hand rested with purpose on his hilt.

"I didn't ask if I'd find it interesting. I asked what your purpose is here. You're built like a bear. Are we to skin you alive and place your hide on the floors of our noble keeps?"

"Perhaps. Shall I also thank you for your generous hospitality? I was about to raze Ithuïn to the ground but have since thought otherwise after receiving your warmth."

"Watch your tongue, snake! You High City doting folk have no allies here."

DarSheer reached for his own sword but stopped at Stavon's grunt. The great man glanced at DarSheer.

"I need no allies and I hold no loyalty to The High City," Stavon rumbled. He gripped his sword's hilt and drew it so a few inches of steel were visible. The blade was deep blue in color.

A second man lightly grasped the first's shoulder and shook it slightly.

"That there is cerulean steel, buffoon. You know . . . the Isle of Meninïn? The watch is calling, and a new wave of travelers has approached the gates, Imslath," he murmured.

I watched as they left. The one named Imslath walked with his back to the door until he slipped out.

"Now that all our introductions have been completed," Arabella rose, startling the room, "and Stavon has nearly gotten us into a fight, shall I introduce myself?"

"You need no introducing, Arabella Sky of Fiscer's Keep," Stavon released his hold on his weapon and turned to her. His voice rasped like metal over stone. "The tales of the Maiden in the North have reached even my isle, isolated as it may be."

She seemed taken aback and for a long moment was unable to respond. DarSheer tried not to smile as he spoke.

"And it appears none need introducing to Stavon save perhaps for the bairn. Phoenix, meet Stavon Gnar, latest in blood relation to the great line of Meninïn seers."

Up until this point, Eridon had been content to watch the giant rumble his words clear across the common area. He'd taken up a post behind the bar drying mugs and tankards while Ësha, who by now had figured out how to walk again, stood at his side. Eridon now broke out a small pipe and began smoking. His hand shook and I wasn't sure if that was from fear of Stavon or his love of the pipe.

"Now spill your secrets, Arabella." DarSheer turned to her, acknowledging her presence for the first time. "We've met before but not to great depth."

"I have seen parts of this world not allowed to many others. My people forged goodwill with the last remnant of Drucodians and men from across the sea. My excursions, at the will of my father, have led me to meet and make friends with all sorts. I come here now on the heels of a great battle of blood. Hosts of evil crossed the ruins of Fiscer's Keep but a few nights past," Arabella said tightly.

"Your father is the keep's ruler." DarSheer rubbed his chin as if everything made perfect sense.

"He *was* the mayor," she returned. "He now resides as ashes on the fields we once tended as bairns."

"I offer my condolences."

"As do I. The DarkBairn has informed me of the loss of the Outpost. Many great men resided there. I'm glad to see you survived."

"DarkBairn?" Stavon glanced around with the first signs of interest. "Where is he?"

"It is I," I stood.

"Phoenix?" His voice cracked. "You? The DarkBairn of lore? Rumored to be the reason Mordën has returned?" Everyone parted to let him stare his massive eyes at me. I squirmed under his harsh glare, trying to gauge the distance to the door against the weight of this human troll.

"You are the one my people prophesied of?" Stavon folded his great arms.

All fear fled as his words took hold. I forgot what I'd been thinking about before and simply let my jaw drop.

"You? Your people? The prophecy?"

"Once in darker times," DarSheer began, "long, long in the past, Stavon's people regularly traded with The High City. But they were betrayed in their trust. Humans themselves, they had come to rely on the High King BarVissur and his Grey Cloaks in disputes across their lands. It is from the line of Inïn that the great minds of their time developed. The last prophecy to come from their halls was the one of which you've answered. The men of Inïn are the oldest dated line of humans. The stories tell they can trace their ancestors to the first humans to walk the lands of Ëonë. In early times they were made to come to the Drucodian's defense but turned their backs. Erëthuïl punished them by making an island far from shore and placing them on it. It wasn't until much later they were able to finally make their way back, in time to aid in the banishment of Mordën by the High King at the end of the Second Great War."

"My people face a curse of their own," Stavon rumbled. "The blood in our veins is older than most alive. We can feel things others can't, sense what others ignore. We've felt this war like a strange scent on the wind centuries ago. King Ashdon will have his war."

"I know a way through the Fallen Peaks unbeknownst to most. It was a path for us when we could not afford the high toll for crossing the basin," Arabella offered.

"The Kestro Pass is weeks south of the Ethero Basin, and treacherous." DarSheer locked eyes with her. "By the time we will have crossed, the world would be burning. Phoenix must make for Avalon and convince them to fortify for an invasion."

"Then it is decided." Stavon wiped his chin of the ale and stood. His massive sword hung against his back. "Phoenix and others move as soon as the dawn breaks."

"And what of you?"

"I will ride to my isle and plead your case before my king. He is fair and I doubt he wishes to commit a similar error as his past ancestor did."

"It is decided. Othrain will journey with me, Stavon will journey west and from there north, and Kissinger with you and Arabella, Phoenix. Eridon has rooms for you all already." DarSheer gestured for the man then glanced about.

The tavern's doors flew open as Kissinger staggered in. Water trickled off him as thunder rumbled. He coughed and leaned over, hacking up water. Othrain appeared behind him. I hadn't even realized they'd left the tavern.

"I told you to stop chasing them, idiot bairn. It's a wonder you're not dead on the table of a hag's herb closet." Othrain thwacked Kissinger's head and walked in. He stopped at the sight of the new arrivals. For a long, happy moment, he gazed at Stavon slowly from boot to head.

"Well, I'll be," he grinned widely, "I'm gone for a mere hour and a lady fair as the night sky and a beast of a man able to rival a Rachnadon show up? Do you even need us? Shall we offer our services? I the joker and my comrade here your minstrel?"

"Jest not with them, Othrain you cow." Kissinger stumbled drunkenly. "You're clearly the minstrel and I the joker!"

He was met with an awkward silence before DarSheer chuckled. "Arabella, Stavon, meet my somewhat misguided traveling companions: Othrain and Kissinger. They're the only others to survive The Battle of the Outpost."

"Fair maiden," Othrain bowed low, sweeping a hand wide, "forgive my intrusion but you seem familiar."

She smiled tightly. "I may have passed through the Outpost's gates on more than one occasion. But I must admit, I fail to remember you."

She turned and left the table as Kissinger laughed till tears ran down his rosy face. Othrain scowled after her and adjusted his belt and sword. Stavon snorted. Even Eridon covered his mouth to hide the smile blooming there.

"Truly the fool, never the jester," Kissinger wiped his eyes, "for some laugh with the jester and his bag of tricks, but everyone laughs at the fool."

The two sat down and began helping themselves to remaining food whilst Eridon led Stavon led into the night. Arabella had her fill of Othrain's jokes and Kissinger's loud burps and had moved to a reclined place by the fire. I rose and departed as DarSheer brought Othrain up-to-date on the plan. I moved to Arabella's side.

"What's bothering you?" I asked gently.

"It's my people . . . slaughtered where they slept, like a beast for that cacodemon's table. Their screams of pain are more vivid with every waking second. I see their blood running in my nightmares. If only I had been there. . . . Even the children. A young boy not three years of age, brought under the sick hilt of those Nightshades. Blood and anguish and death are all that await us. Is there none who possess such strength to defeat this evil? Or are we abandoned to walk atop the graveyard gloom like specters of the past lost in doom?"

"I was just dreaming of the people I've lost." I stared into the flickering flames as they soared. "There's my friends from back home. This girl I'd learned to love. Her laughter sounds like a giggling brook. I could stare into her eyes long past feeling. When I was with her, I felt this strength, like I could alone put an end to the madness of the world. My family. My mother. She's the reason I even left the comfort of my village and journeyed abroad. He killed them, or so I think. My mind is muddied in that regard. He's killed most of those I love, so why should they be any different? Mordën took all of them. I wish with every fiber of my being I could say I do not relate to your pain, but Arabella Sky, I fear as time progresses, more and more shall be able to sympathize.

"We will end his rule of terror so the sun may once again warm the people below. To a time when the clouds bring water not death. When far-off flashes of light mean rain, not fire. The young will rise like stalks on a hillside, and each will bear the arms of their houses, and the courage that comes from defending one's home will light such a fire in their blood as has not been seen in an age. These atrocities will only serve to destroy his momentum, to start the pebble rolling which will lead to an avalanche. Those who died in our villages and towns did not die in vain. Their loss will be what convinces those still blinded in their complacency to lay aside their fears and embrace the only reason left for living. Mordën rules by fear and carnage. There is no world where such a life is possible. If the people don't stand now, they will soon have no legs to stand upon. If the people of our time must face their greatest fear and do so with no training to prepare, then my own personal concerns are but chaff on the wind. If it is what is asked of me, I will gladly walk stride by stride with these brave folks who are the stuff of legend."

"Do not so swiftly dispose of your concerns, Phoenix." Arabella brushed a strand of her hair out of her eyes as her voice shook with weariness. "So wise for one who owes this world no loyalty. What ignites this fire in your blood?"

"Sometimes we're called upon for things greater than our own lives." I swallowed. "You know? I cannot return home knowing a world suffers under the iron boot and sword of oppression and evil. Though it shakes me to my very core, and every waking moment I battle the temptation to flee, I will see this through. I feel, sometimes, that if I don't, my friends and family will have died for nothing . . . for me, which I cannot help but fear is worse than nothing."

"What courage lies in you. If only all men of Ëonë possessed it, then this world would truly be a force to reckon with. Sadly, honor and loyalty are words traded flippantly as political niceties. Too long have people dressed in clothes of freedom and safety. They've forgotten what war brings, Phoenix. I fear for my people . . . for Ëonë."

"If I was a betting man," I smiled and took her hand, "after all I've been through and the strength and brutality I've seen personally, I'd bet without a doubt on people like you. It's easy to march on lands and burn all in your path. Why care when you've no attachment? But a man who defends his own home is a man to be feared indeed. Mordën will soon realize his mistake when he moves from cornfields and cottages to great cities of men and Elfinian craft. He will be forced to face his delusion when the pitchforks of farmers are replaced by sword and bow of trained warriors."

"You're very sweet, Phoenix." Arabella laughed lightly and gazed fondly at me. The light from the fire danced over her face. "It is good and promising to see the ruins of war have not yet taken that passion from you." She placed a callused hand on my arm. "Guard it and let it be your strongest ally. There is much to be said when the honor of strangers exceeds the bravery of our own people. Whoever this girl was . . . I'm sure she'd be proud knowing how you turned out."

Warmth spread to my cheeks, and I looked back at the flames. They danced and bowed and castrated themselves on the ground before the looming threat to come. A chill raced down my back.

"It's decided," DarSheer was saying. "We continue the goal Lord Malziek sent us out for. Lady Arabella of Fiscer's Keep and Kissinger of the Outpost will join you, Phoenix, as far as Avalon. Othrain of the Outpost will accompany me south. Heed my warning, there is no place in this world where Mordën will not eventually control if we do not work together. Ride with haste."

"You sure you don't want me with you while you journey south?" Kissinger asked. "What danger will be on the Westerly Road west of here while the Elfins still gather strength? But further south the roads are wild and unguarded."

"If danger meets us on the road, I fear no strength or weapon will protect me." DarSheer shook his head. "Travel to Avalon, and there aid the city in its defense. By the end they will need every able-bodied man there to fight. If I reach Caldonia in time, I will get the use of their forces and we will march to the Golden Gates. Do not expect much, but it might be enough to change the tide of battle."

"So, it is written in the annals of our minds." Othrain stood. He yawned. "All this talk of death and destruction has made me weary. We move out at first light. It would be wise for us all to sleep. Farewell, Phoenix DarkBairn and you, my old friend Kissinger."

He clasped my forearms in his own and nodded. Kissinger, for a moment lost in thought, simply nodded at him.

DarSheer looked about. "Get some sleep. You'll be needed in fine shape as well. The three of you have an early start. Get rest, and if all goes well, I'll see you in the coming days."

I rose and hurried over as he made for the door.

"DarSheer, you're just . . . leaving?" I asked. "After all we've been through, all the training, the painful reminders not to turn my back on my enemy, all of it?"

"We all must part ways at some point," came the response. "Yet for you I've reserved a more solemn farewell. Since we met, you've come far and grown to be one of the finest young men I've met. The Outpost would have fallen no matter who protected its walls, but having you there meant we took a few more cursed wretches with us. Trust me. Follow them to Avalon and there prepare for war. You think you've tasted true bloodshed, but what was had at the Outpost was trivial in comparison. I imagine The Battle of Avalon will ring in the storybooks for the rest of time. Take care not to lose yourself in the fight. Remember who you are and where you've come from. And above all . . ." here he choked up as his eyes watered ". . . trust your allies. In this world, it may seem easy to believe everything a trick of Mordën's."

I wiped my own tears away and embraced him. "I never thought I'd see the day we parted ways. For some reason I always envisioned us fighting side by side till I found a way home."

"You will find your own home soon." He ruffled my hair. "All good things come at their own pace. You cannot rush them or speed up the process anymore then you can clear the clouds above us. When this whole conflict is over, I promise you by my blood and honor, I will aid you in finding your way home."

"An oath of such proportions from you is one I can trust implicitly." I sniffed and smiled. "Take care you old codger. The rain and winds on the road will do their worst, but I know what hides in wait for you once you clear the safety of the bowmen atop the walls. Promise me, we'll meet again in Avalon."

"You know I can promise nothing of the sort." DarSheer stepped back and grabbed a bag which Ësha had thrown onto the corner. Inside, she'd placed food and blankets and a spare dagger. I tried not to display my sadness as he spoke. "But I tell you this, nothing short of my own death will keep me from finding you again. Besides, I have Othrain to ensure I don't die."

With that, he turned and was out the door into the raining night. Stavon shouldered his large bag of weapons and folded his monstrous cloak about his broad shoulders. He saluted with two fingers and stepped out into the night. Othrain, giving Kissinger a brotherly punch to the shoulder, stopped in front of me and glanced down.

"Look, kid, for what it's worth, I think you're a fine bairn. Take care of Kissinger for me. He may have a head filled with wild uncouth thoughts, and he may need help with his swordplay, but he's like a son to me. See to it he keeps his minds on the things to come." He leaned in conspiratorially. "And if you can play a few pranks on him in my honor, I'd be grateful. His head gets larger every day."

I laughed and gave him a quick hug. He stood there waiting for my response, so I hardened my gut and rotated.

"I tend to get overly attached to people." I forced a laugh. "You have my oath I will protect him as well as Arabella. You all have become family to me. It is as DarSheer says, we embark on tales which will be told for centuries to come. I am truly glad you ride with DarSheer."

"One day this will end." Othrain checked his sword and tightened his tunic. He turned to go.

"Othrain," I said.

He turned. "Yes?"

"Keep him safe."

"You have my word."

Arabella touched my arm and gave me a small smile. "We should rest."

Othrain vanished into the howling gloom. I found a small source of comfort knowing that the three together were better fighters than half of Mordën's forces. Still, I inhaled deeply.

The torches were soon extinguished, and we were led to our rooms. They were sparse with a single cot and a small pail of water. On one wall hung a rugged rag which had clearly seen better days. Several small candles burned steadily and cast their long arms of darkness along the walls. I bid Arabella goodnight and closed the door. I held the small pillow to my chest and let its presence soothe my worries. Before long, I knew I'd yearn for this moment, for a time when the grief of war did not fully plague every inch of my mind and pain was but a promise not a reality.

"Phoenix, help me! HELP!"

"DARKBAIRN! You think they care? You think anyone does? NO ONE CARES! THEY NEVER CARED!"

"My sweet one, please, don't leave me! I'm hurt. I'm in pain. Please!"

"Homeless, wandering filth under the eye of a great power this land will grow to fear with every waking moment. A person dancing by the strings of his master. You are worthless, cur. You are feared by no one. You are loved by no one. You are a waste of space, a speck in the eye of greatness."

"My sweet one, come to me, please! On my breast, rest your head. Let my embrace fill you with warmth. Do not hold back your tears. Come to me and be at peace."

In the distance, the long coastal view stretched into infinity. Black waves of frigid waters crashed against the pale white shores. Her voice carried over the winds like a siren crying out to passing seamen. I heard the bitter weeping and tears ran down my face. For some reason, I felt a horrible emptiness. I had to find her. I had to make this pain cease. Birds flocked overhead, their long wings graceful and grey. DarSheer used the word "kolst" when he described them. Their cries of agony reached the heavens as the siren sang a haunting melody of pain and suffering.

Before me, dark clouds moved with lightning speed. They surrounded me, and from them seven figures stepped. They all were figures of horrible nature: Their eyes were pure black orbs of death. From their backs sprouted great wings of shimmering shadow. They wore long black cloaks with burning fiery breastplates. They did not have faces as one would expect from a creature. No mouth nor nose nor ears were visible, just haunting black eyes.

"You are forsaken," the figure in the middle hissed. The words did not come verbally, but through my thoughts. "Left, abandoned, in a cold world. Cursed under the boot of the Shadow King. We've met once, bairn, outside a cave, though you had no clue I was aware of you. Remember this?"

The figure raised a gloved hand from under its cloak and I felt the pain in my head reach an indescribable level. Spots danced before my eyes and I cried out, clutching at my temple.

"Before this over," the figure before me said, removing its hood, "the one you love will be no more and through this, shall you finally be let go. Your service to the Shadow King will be complete. It is as I, Ashnogrold of old, have said: The end of the free and the death of their liberators will be swift."

Ashnogrold reached out and, with a finger so long it seemed to defy logic, touched my forehead. I blacked out, hearing nothing but the screams and weeping of a female's voice as blackness swirled about.

"Help!"

I gasped and sat up, slamming my forehead into the bottom of a slanted ceiling. Eridon had put us up in rooms but failed to mention they were for people, or a race, far smaller than us. The bed ended where my calves reached. I'd shoved my traveling cloak on the ground to cushion my feet but even so, only nightmares and broken sleep had been my companion. Already, the first soft light of dawn had begun to creep over the horizon. Outside, the city was coming to life as merchants began to fill their stalls and men found their way to taverns for a warm and hearty breakfast. Strange travelers in cloaks with hoods over their heads marched past my window. Boots splashed in puddles left behind.

I nearly fell off the bed at the stern knocking. My heart raced so fast I wondered if I was having some sort of heart attack. I gripped my sheathed sword in alarm.

"Phoenix?" Kissinger's voice boomed through the thick wooden door.

"I'm coming, yes, I'm coming," I called. Flashes of the nightmare danced across my eyelids. I calmed my racing heart.

A cock crowed its prideful, shrill call as the first ray of sunlight broke the horizon. The orange light painted the road in hope and a promise of a new day. I swallowed heavily, knowing what was to soon become of this place.

In one corner of the room, my trousers and tunic had been neatly folded the day prior by Ësha. Her soft hands had cleaned all our traveling gear, save for my cloak. This and this alone I'd refused to turn over for it still held some dried blood from when I'd fallen over Brenneth. I knew it was foolish, but I couldn't clean it just yet. I hadn't told this to the others.

I opened the door and behind its oaken barrier stood Kissinger, his eyes drifted lazily, and he leaned heavily against the wall.

"Good morning, bairn," he greeted me with a grunt. "It's time for breakfast. My head ails me something fierce."

"The drinks catching up to you?" I tried for a laugh.

He groaned. "If a beautiful lass tells you she has a place she wants to take you and escorts you into a dark alleyway where four of her grimy friends are waiting . . . don't believe her. It's all too good to be true. The sooner we leave this place the better."

"Don't get tricked by a maiden into being robbed senseless," I said blandly. "Got it. Duly noted."

The morning was sweet, and dawn had vanquished the cold of the night. The sun rose in splendor, rays touching the faces of the upturned and warming them. The streets were once more filled with bustling crowds, intent on their own agendas. Beaming peddlers shuffled their carts, hawking their steaming goods. Already, Arabella and Eridon stood waiting. Kissinger hoisted up a sack filled to the brim with food. Our weapons were freshly cleaned and sharpened. Arabella's cloak hung about her shoulders, and she blinked drowsily. She gave me a small smile and yawned as I exited the inn. Even Eridon seemed in a better mood.

"Buy some great sloppy gobs of these 'ere pies and I betcha won't get up off your bed for a 'undred years," one peddler called loudly as he pushed a cart of bistri past.

"Taste the water of the Ethero Basin," said a rare Elfin vendor who strode by. He carried a tray with small glasses of sparkling water. "Taste and see the might of The Golden City, pride of the Elfinian Kingdom."

We shuffled into The Ilkspun and Eridon presented a tray of delicious breakfast meats and bistri, topped off with a bubbling tankard of his best beer. I stuck a wooden fork into the first massive link, impressed with the juiciness and tenderness of the meat.

"Let me know if I can be your servant in anything," Eridon said as he bustled off to help another patron who'd entered the tavern. "Your traveling companions left late last night, and Broadsword told me to tell you, "Do not be slow; move with haste as soon as you might.""

As I ate, I watched a hooded traveler who had followed us into the establishment. The cloak on his back was a dark green with a blue fish stabbed through its heart by a long pike. down the center. Many eyes followed his progress around the tables as Eridon showed the man to a corner booth. Some whispered and eyed him under the guise of picking up a dropped utensil or handkerchief. The less nosy patrons chattered as they enjoyed the early dawn and warm sun. The blue sky was as merry a sign as anything, for the mood of the city was lifted since our arrival at dusk. Even the animals which roamed the streets seemed to sulk less and beg more. Smiles overcame frowns and laughter replaced annoyed glares.

Kissinger massaged his temples and sulked under his hood. The ailments of the ale the night prior had caught up to him. He groaned after every loud noise and muttered after every chair's scrape against the floor.

"I'm surprised to see it is your inability to hold liquor that does you in and not a sword to the chest." Arabella grinned.

"Less talking and more . . . no, just less of everything," he moaned and buried his head in his hands. "Why is it so loud in here?"

"We must keep our senses and wit about us. That means no more ale or beer until we are safe behind the walls of Avalon," I admonished him lightly.

"Phoenix has a point." Arabella sipped her ale then shrugged at my stare. "A single pint won't hurt. But we must be careful. The road can sweep you off to adventures your mind can only imagine. One day you stretch out admiring the Fallen Peaks from afar, a walking stick in hand and a smile on your face, the next you're fighting Varglarians with every ounce of strength."

"This has really been a treat to behold, I mean an absolute honor to witness you two bond," Kissinger dug his fingers into his ears, "but must you? If nothing else, I will be the one to remind you lot that DarSheer did order us to not dawdle."

The mood turned cold again. "He's right." I bit my lip and looked out the window. "DarSheer and his lot will be on the road to Caldonia, and we as well must be outside these walls before the sun rises completely. The fate of millions rests in our hands. We cannot delay now."

"What of the people here?" Arabella bit off a long stringy piece of meat. "Are they to perish?"

"If we could save every soul we've come across," Kissinger looked up, his eyes red and moist, "then we would. But we can't. Eridon knows of the threat, and he will fortify the walls as best he can. This is a stronghold, you remember. The High City placed it here. They will not lightly lose it. That must be sufficient."

Breakfast and the morning sullied, we put on our cloaks and buckled our weapons to our belts. Arabella adjusted the straps of her breastplate and Kissinger moved his cloak about his shoulders. Eridon and Ësha fussed over the smaller details like who would carry the provisions pack and where we must go to find out mounts. Finally, we left the tavern, after much advice from Eridon concerning where ferreks like to hide and the places between here and Avalon where one could be easily ambushed. We began walking from each section of the city, ending at a small courtyard where peddlers had set up shop for the day. My stomach hurt when I realized how much morning we'd wasted. The sun was nearly over the edge of the fields. Merchants of Elfinian and Ebyian type mesmerized their onlookers and spun great tales of what their wares could do. The Elfinian folk from the tavern the night before stood surrounded by eager faces of young children. One Elfin spoke softly and a bright light appeared in his hand, a ball of starlight. The light radiated in flickering light and the children *oohed* and *aahed* in indulged satisfaction. They giggled and clapped as the ball of light exploded into mini lights.

We moved through the square and at long last, the western gate stood elegantly before us, towering and domineering. Men in grey armor stood stoically atop the walls, spears in one hand and a bow over their backs. I closed my eyes and heard the heavy snap of banners overhead. The grey color illustrated the now familiar mountain with the tall tower at its center, the sigil of The High City. It was mesmerizing to watch the fabric fold and unfurl in the breeze atop the ramparts. Goosebumps scaled my arms as I remembered looking up at that very banner on the eastern shore, moments before the arrows launched.

"We must go," Arabella called to me as she mounted a brilliant white mare. "Come, Phoenix. We cannot delay."

Two other horses stood waiting. Kissinger leapt onto the back of his sleek stallion, the horse's black sides heaving with excitement. It tossed its head and neighed loudly. I grappled with the last steed's reigns and put one foot in the stirrup. The mount sidestepped away, as if afraid. A guard nearby hurried over and held onto the horse's harness so I could mount without further difficulty. I looked down at the young, armored man. His grey helmet and breastplate were clearly too large for him. Behind his confident gaze, I saw fear deep in his eyes.

"There are many who deem you an omen of evil," the guard spoke freely, "but not all. We will gladly give our lives for your message to ride west. Be at peace and succeed. All Ëonë waits with bated breath."

"Thank you," I replied. *No pressure or anything.*

"Open the gates!" the guard roared. He stepped back as the western gate creaked loudly in protest.

The chains rang metallically against the stone of the wall as they were pulled, and the doors swung wide. I wondered if Ithuïn would still be standing the next time I saw it. We thundered under the wall and out the gate; we picked up speed as we hurtled along. Kissinger led the pack as we galloped up an embankment and down the other side, always remaining on the sure footing of the Westerly Road. I couldn't help but glance back. The banners flew proudly over the walls and the grey armored men atop the battlements looked like light flecks in a black sky. In the far distant east, the black clouds blotted out all light save for the flashes of red light. They were dangerously close.

Dew from the early morning dried into crystals as the hooves of our steeds rumbled over pebbles and flaky clay. The Westerly Road was little better than uneven ground at this point. It constantly shifted from stretches of clean cobblestone to muddy pools of clay and debris to tracks of pressed grass meandering through tall bulbous crops. It served more as a directional guide than a road. With little else to do on the journey than stew in my thoughts, I'd taken to deciding a name for my steed. The one I wrestled with currently was "Fidget" due to its overly cautious nature. He would toss his head when we neared any rocks or large outcroppings of branches that stretched over the road like claws as if he half expected them to grab him. He skittered about and shook his flowing mane at every inconvenience. As we ascended a large hill in the road, I patted his sweaty neck.

The rock and gravel strip were now interrupted by boulders and tree roots. We took longer leaving the countryside than I felt comfortable with. Hours after we'd slogged our way past deep pools of mirky water and crooked trees with long flowing leaves, Ithuïn was still visible in the distance. I began to wonder belatedly if we'd been handed bad mounts on purpose. Arabella was struggling, though less openly, to control her mare who kept drifting off the road and into thickets of thorns. Her legs, protected by her leather boots, were mercifully spared the insistent scratching by the thorns.

"Come on, Snowstir," she murmured comfortingly to her mount as she narrowly avoided being unseated for the tenth time. The horse whickered softly and rolled its eyes, flattening its long fuzzy ears back against its head. "No, no don't, Snowstir the road is over there."

Only Kissinger seemed unbothered by his mount who stared ahead with little concern over the passing of trees and brush. The two moved ahead as one, eyes searching the terrain. His sword was drawn in open defiance of the shadows that lingered about.

"I hope DarSheer knows what he's doing," Arabella muttered. She clicked her tongue and dug her right heel into Snowstir trying to keep it from heading toward a bush of blushing berries.

"DarSheer is strong and smart." I gritted my teeth at the constant jolts and shocks as we clomped over loose stones.

Finally, Snowstir returned, albeit grudgingly, to the road. We rode side by side as the ground, once hilly, became level again. This allowed us to make good time, weaving between trees and small dips in the path. Several remote streams trickled underfoot as we crossed them in small splashes. For the first time that day, when I glanced back, I finally didn't see the walls or buildings of Ithuïn. We'd officially left it behind. It was comforting. The sun guided us and served a constant reminder of how slow we were progressing. Already it was sinking toward the mist ahead. *Mist.*

For a long while we rode in silence. Far ahead, Kissinger scouted, his own long hair flowed about him. A particularly strong gust of wind forced him to cover his face as gravel and dust sprayed about. Low cloud cover and debris bogged down the once clear air. We chose to ignore the signs as the road changed to cobblestone once again. Some of the stones were missing, meaning we had to navigate slowly around holes where water and creature hid. The afternoon's breeze increased in intensity. Trees along the road bent under the force of the wind, and above, in the sky, the sun began to slowly lose warmth as clouds appeared seemingly from nowhere. I wrapped my cloak about me and shivered. A deep cold replaced the warmth of the day. I was reminded, not for the last time, of the Outpost and its frozen watch.

We stopped for a quick bite and then we were back on the road again. Kissinger continued to lead the way. He spoke very little, content with acting as scout and guide. Often, I caught him muttering to himself and his steed who responded by licking its lips. We let Kissinger be the de facto guide even though I was pretty sure he knew less about our road ahead than Arabella did. As the day continued, and the ground returned to a hillier state with deep tree cover. We passed small towns where caravans of people had begun to flee their homes. Men who kept glancing nervously back east rushed by with their groupings of carts. Children gripped the tops and sides of the carts and women in shawls and cloaks rushed along behind them. Several animals pranced about as if finding the whole ordeal very amusing. A goose honked loudly as it chased after a baby. A woman in a long green shawl cursed loudly as she swung a reed at the animal.

We passed them by and, unhindered by anything, soon were at the front. Each group we passed sent my heart sinking a bit more. A small cart bore a shivering woman with a newborn in her arms. As we rode past, I heard the babe's cry and the mother's weak response. It appeared word spread far faster than some thought. A second cart bore a weeping girl no older than ten who begged her mother to take her home.

"We can't, my sweet darling," the woman tried to console her. She looked up at us as we rode by. "I've told you, my love, we are going on a small journey west."

"It tugs at your heartstrings," Arabella said after we passed the third such weeping bairn.

"How is it these poor folks will heed the warning cry of steel but not so great cities like Ithuïn?"

"Ithuïn is to be attacked," she returned. "Eridon is a noble warrior. He will do his best to ensure that the families and weak are moved west to Avalon. He must have sent word by messenger for them to flee but I fear for them. People grow startled by the length of their own shadows." She inhaled the cold air.

We rode in silence as dusk cast its long grey blanket over the tree-tops and plunged the valleys into shadow. Weariness pulled at the bags under my eyes. Wolves howled, far off, at the moon, which hung like a glowing disk in the sky.

In this manner, four days came and went, the sun completing its climb, and the moon chasing it back only to be scared itself into hiding. Banks of dark clouds scurried like bats over the sun. On one day, a harsh pelting rain that was aided by gusts of strong wind drenched us. We rode miserably and wet through three towns and past many farms which showed no sign of life. On the next day, a great heat dried all of us up, including our desire to converse. We did not speak one word the entire trek until we'd collapsed wearily at dusk.

At the edge of a creek on the fifth day, sun high overhead, Arabella leapt over the water and hurried up the side of the steep embankment. Her tangled, dirty hair was kept tight against her skull. We'd all grown to reek of horse smell and ash. I knelt against the slippery edge of the creek and drank greedily. When Arabella turned, her eyes were wide.

"You guys need to see this," she shouted.

I hurried over the babbling brook and up the grassy bank, coming to a stop at her side. My heart fell like a boulder over a cliff. Kissinger cursed loudly next to me. His sword was in his hand, and he held it ready.

The ruins of what once had been a fighting force of golden clad warriors were castrated about. Horses with bloodied flanks lay on the ground. Flags waving mournfully atop pikes that had been imbedded in the chest of their bearer. We watched as a single banner tossed about and revealed the yellow fabric and golden archer of Avalon.

I raced down the side of the hill and over to inspect one of the fallen Elfin. Kissinger shouted at me to stop but my head buzzed. I couldn't hear anything but the beating of my heart in my ears. The sun reflected off their golden armor in a blinding display. The deceased lay in their death throes. Some had their eyes wide open with looks of horror and others lay peacefully in the mud as if they'd died in their sleep. Blood sat stagnant in pools around carts and bodies of younger figures were seen butchered. Heads had been left on stakes. The golden hair which flowed from their skulls was cut crudely and left fallen at the base of the pikes.

The silence was heavier and louder than a grieving mother's scream. Smoke curled around various fires which dotted the field. Carts that had been forced onto their sides spilled out bags of grain and barrels of beer. Cloak and banner and horsehair flitted about in the breeze. A horrible stench hovered over the ground.

"What fresh madness is this?" I picked up a golden breastplate and gazed at it. "Is not our foe behind us? Do they also ride these hills before us?"

Kissinger dropped a helmet with thinly veiled disgust as a head fell out. It rolled to a stop at his feet, the mouth falling open and a tongue slipping between the blue lips.

"Over here!" Arabella shouted with urgency. "COME!"

We rushed over the field and knelt at the side of what appeared to be the most well-dressed Elfin. The markings on his shoulders and the pendant around his neck identified him as someone important. His once golden hair was now red with his own blood. Deep cuts covered his armor and body. The Elfin choked and blood bubbled up from a gash right below his chin.

"What happened?" I demanded harshly and gripped his arm.

"With ease," Arabella cautioned.

"They came from the shadows," gasped the Elfin. His eyes fluttered weakly. "They were primed with weapons of dark origins. Cloaked figures with eyes like coals burning in a dying fire. Wings of ash and smoke. They cut us down with ease. We stood no chance. It was a bloodbath. They bore such bottled-up rage. I saw them. I couldn't look away as they butchered my men. Black wings and *breastplates of fire.*"

The Elfin gurgled as blood oozed from his wounds and the light left his eyes. Kissinger closed his eyelids and glanced up.

"So passes this company of Elfins. What group could cause such rampant destruction? Varglarian and Nightshades do not bear wings. This is a well-trained band of Elfinian warriors. Their tactics and prowess do not allow themselves to be surprised. Yet here now lies evidence to the contrary."

"Mordën is not limited to Varg and Shade, for he has many other servants to do his bidding." I gripped my head as memories surfaced in a disorganized manner. I pictured the seven figures of my dreams, their long black wings touched points. "We must double our pace, and now!"

"If they could not survive, we are like sheep on a hillside surrounded by wolves," Arabella argued. "What hope is there now where trained warriors fail?"

Kissinger, leading all three mounts by their reins, hurried up. "We've overstayed our welcome." He pointed to a distant hill where a series of black clouds spiraled in a funnel shape. "We need to go, now! Enemies! On the ridge!"

Seven figures descended from the heavens toward the visible rounded point of a grassy knoll. Chills raced down my spine. My eyes were glued to the figures in horrified fascination. Was this just another nightmare? Wind howled in my ears and thunder rumbled from the center of the clouds. Red lightning forked through small thunderheads and a freezing cold pierced my heart.

"Everyone, get down!" Arabella hissed and dropped to her chest behind a bush. "Phoenix!"

I took a step toward the Hourglass, their seven cloaks billowing out behind them. I heard their whispers, felt their hunger. I felt drawn to them in some inexplicable way. Old beyond the tell of time. The lead's feet finally touched the grass. The green withered into death. Screams and metal clashing rang out across the gap. The six spread out behind their leader, three on each side. They displayed massive black wings of smoke and threw back their cloaks. I gasped and fell back onto my rear as pain surged through my head. *Breastplates of fire*!

"You are persistent." The lead Hourglass's voice was like drums rumbling in the distance.

Kissinger's hands were on my britches as he yanked me close. The air fled my lungs, so I lay like a fish out of water, gasping for air. The edges of my vision went red as the lead figure reached a hand toward me.

"These are the fallen Luthi in their fair form," Arabella murmured in shock.

"I doubt it matters who they are if they kill us," Kissinger ground out.

The lead Hourglass screeched out a cry that ached in my head. My heart beat faster and my body seemed sluggish. My eyes drooped and I felt a pain I had never felt before. Blood began to drip from every orifice, and I felt it push against the veins in my body, as if trying to burst free and fly high into the sky.

"*Ash . . . fire . . . murk . . . death!*" I whispered.

"What is he saying?" Arabella hissed.

"Who cares?" Kissinger bit back. He stared at me in horror. "He's bleeding! How?"

"All this chaos is not yours to bear, Phoenix Dunnigan Rather!" The voice snaked into my mind and gripped it like a man's hands around a bull's horns. "Bend your knee and he will send you home."

I cried out as cracks began to form on my flesh. Blood trickled down and blackness swirled around me.

"Never," I muttered. "I will die before I kneel at the feet of death."

"Then you shall die alone; he has promised this! Enjoy what you can for soon it will all be blood!"

The wind howled in intensity and the shapes soared like missiles up into the clouds. The swirling thunderheads dissipated, and the sun once again returned. I felt the intense pressure inside me abate and my mind cleared. Sweat mixed with blood.

"Phoenix?" Arabella held my head as the darkness took me.

Chapter 4:
Blades on the Moors

I PARRIED THE LONG slash and sidestepped his next attack. My boots were oversized, and I'd already received a fair number of blisters from the constant friction. I was determined that neither that nor the continuous pain from being hit repeatedly with the training sword would make me cry out. DarSheer had so far taken every meager jab and successful hit with barely a flutter of his eyelids or frown. A round of raucous laughter spilled from the battlements as the guards, bored of their watch, had instead turned to watch me. I'd arrived at the Outpost only a week prior and already I'd become the center of attention. I couldn't piss behind the barracks without eyes following me.

"You stepped aside too soon." DarSheer spoke gruffly. Outwardly, he displayed a confident disdainful attitude toward me, but he always took extra care to ensure I was well-fed, rested, and learning at a pace I was comfortable with. There was kindness in his eyes while his mouth spouted retorts.

He had brought the edge of his blade to my throat. I winced and lowered my own weapon. I'd been "killed" in such a manner six times and the day had just begun. If I wasn't falling for tricks the enemy might be likely to employ and thus perishing, I was being flung onto my back and skewered through the heart like a pig for the bonfire.

"Go again!"

The instruction had been given for the seventh time. I settled into my defensive posture, feet shaped like an L. Left hand behind my back. I calmed my breathing to help ignore the stinging pain. I'd had so many nightmares in the past few nights that I preferred this type of pain. I welcomed it. It grounded me. I'd thrown myself into training when I wasn't on watch. I found these were the rare moments I could breathe without fear.

We dueled about the courtyard and Brenneth, consuming a plate of bistri, cheered from the sidelines. He said a few choice words to DarSheer. I tried not to smirk. DarSheer allowed those around us to stay as it made for good training. To survive, you had to put your all into fighting. Distractions, even for a second, could end with death. One of his first lessons for me was to filter out the distractions. In battle, there was plenty of bodies and screams and flashes around to throw a seasoned veteran off-balance if he didn't learn to block it out.

I leapt forward and parried his first move. He backed a step and spun, ducking under my next attack, and bringing his blade up and down like a hammer. I sidestepped and kicked out. My boot slammed into his side, and he staggered back. For a moment it appeared like I'd truly injured him as he doubled over. As I lowered my sword to ask him if he was alright, though, his sword found its way to my throat. He looked up through his tangled mess of hair and grinned. He turned to walk off. I grunted and slashed down till the blade bounced off his back. He stopped. The courtyard was silent. All eyes tracked his next response.

Sweat poured down my face and stung my eyes. I wiped my hair away. DarSheer turned about and bowed politely.

"This training is over. Your time of watching the walls is nigh. Suit up and report to the watchmaster."

"But how did I . . ." I began.

DarSheer was already aggressively pushing the training cart off. Brenneth waved back, a forkful of bistri inches from his mouth. His wide smile and youthful eyes radiated excitement.

The rays of light slowly forced their way into my groggy mind. I snorted and groaned.

"Phoenix?" Arabella hugged me tight. "I thought . . ."

"I'm fine," I mumbled. My tongue was thick in my mouth and my head ached. "What happened? How long have we been here?"

"A few moments." Kissinger stared down at me. "The Hourglass are gone. They just stared at you as if trying to kill you with their eyes. You stared back. Then they left."

I rubbed my face and was surprised at the lack of blood. Arabella showed me the cloth she'd used and smiled awkwardly.

"You look as good as you did before," she promised.

"I still look like a starving unwashed mongrel?"

"Sorry." She shrugged. "I can clean blood, not work miracles."

"We need to move, if you're up to it." Kissinger reached out a hand and hoisted me up.

I let the sudden rush of dizziness abate and climbed onto Fidget's broad back. *Then you shall perish!* I glanced back. The bodies of the fallen and the dead patch of grass were the only reminders of what had happened here. Bushes moved lazily in the breeze and trees stood tall. Fidget dipped his head in greeting and continued to chew at the grass in his mouth. I patted his side. Arabella led the way. She kept low in her saddle, a hand up to signal advancement or a fist to stop our movement. Through this means, we soon came across a hill encircled in stones. They had been placed in an obviously unnatural state among the dirt and rocks. There was no vegetation and no animals meandered between the stone.

"The Crown of Oxly," Arabella said reverently.

"The Site of the Ancient Tombs," Kissinger said at the same time. "I thought we'd be too far south of this place."

Arabella continued, "Here lies from ancient times the tombs of the fallen. During the Last Great Battle of the Second Era, forces of good and light battled the darkness brought from the shores beyond. Blood and tears were spilled here beyond count. It's said the sun didn't shine for a year and after the battle was won, nothing grew, for the trees and foliage themselves considered it too sacred a site to lay root. They entombed those of royal blood who perished here, the rest it is said were left until the wind had blown their ashes to the heavens."

Arabella's words were quiet but sad. I noticed now that the rocks arranged in various angles were in fact stone structures barely taller than a man standing. Atop their lids were letters of a forgotten tongue.

"It's said that the fair-eyed Heiress of Avalon and the last High Prince stood back-to-back and for hours, together, drove off the snarling Varg. Hours they dueled until the bodies became a wall around them. And still they fought. She took arrow after arrow, and he was stabbed beyond count."

"What happened to them?" I stepped closer so I could read the stones. I ran a hand over the faded lettering. Though centuries old, I could still make out very faint lettering. Mirky water from a past rainfall made it easier to spell out the name of the tomb I stood nearest to.

Here lies in the throes of death, a sword in hand, helm tarnished with the blood of his enemies,
The High Prince of The High City, Carthire. His end was glorious, and he rests now in the halls of Erëthuïl, free from this earthly bondage.
All hail the last High Prince.
At the Turn of the Second Era.

"Mordën himself slaughtered them." I'd expected Arabella to respond but it was Kissinger who spoke.

I felt my heart squeeze for a moment. The entire hilltop seemed to be filled with a sadness beyond words. The trees that grew around the foot of the hill hung their branches and leaves low like they mourned in eternal grief. The air felt colder and thinner here. The wind sang a dirge for the fallen and mourned their passing. Amidst the old stone markers, rusted swords and cracked shields sat wasting away.

"There was a time when the peoples of Avalon and The High City considered each other blood brothers. One could not live without the other. We did not always quarrel and bicker with another. It is my hope one day to see these walls torn down and once again free-flowing goodwill between our cities," Arabella said. "No one knows where the princess lay, for she was taken into the dungeons of darkness on the BlackBurg. Bards sing songs of her prolonged death and the torture she endured for she refused to yield to him. *Are her eyes so mystically proud, so defiantly bold? Hail the ones who yield not. Hail the defiant dead.*" She sang the last part in a soft tone.

I rested a hand on the edge of Carthire's tomb and felt a pang. Here, surrounded by death and grief, he had remained strong. My own qualms resurfaced, and I stared bleary-eyed about. All these tombs. Warriors who had stood against a timeless evil. They were strong. They were true.

Kissinger was silent but I saw him staring at Arabella with a look I'd not yet seen. Some who did not know him at all might take it as sadness, the ways his eyes turned, the way his face sagged.

"This is a sacred site," she continued. "A place to remind those why they defy such reckless chaos. It is meant to bring hope, though in times of peace it is forgotten."

Kissinger began moving down the side of the hill and as I moved after him, a gnawing feeling began to take root in my chest. The clouds above dispersed and soft blue moonlight lit the area. A single butterfly fluttered its thin translucent wings over the sleeping dead as it moved wistfully from tomb to tomb. We watched it go until it landed on top of a tomb that rested at the center of the group. All other tombs had been laid out around it like a circle with this one as the eye.

We dismounted and walked toward it. Arabella stopped to read the name off one of the tombs in the circle while Kissinger crouched down and placed his fingers in the soil. I kept moving till I came close to the butterfly. It stood atop the first name etched in the stone. Its blue and green wings moved rhythmically and slowly up and down like it was meant to move the air.

"Who are you?" I murmured into the face of the stone. The more I stood, the more I wanted to weep. It was like the hill was infused with something beyond our knowledge.

The butterfly took flight and was gone, taken by the shadow. Only the etched words remained visible. I reached a hand out and dusted them off so I could read clearly.

Here lies Oasted, brother-in-arms to the High Prince.
His golden hair and grey eyes will look on these lands no longer and this
shall be his legacy. As brave as any warriors of old. As loving as a bairn
in his family. Ëonë itself weeps at his passing.
At the Turn of the Second Era.

"We must keep moving," Arabella said from her spot at the edge of the tomb. "Night will not last, and I do not trust the shadows. Nightshades may lurk even here in this sacred place. Kissinger and Phoenix, prepare the mounts. We ride through the night."

"I feel sad here," I said.

"It would be wrong to not feel the grief that plagues these tombs." Kissinger tightened the saddle on his mount. "At the same time, I feel joy, knowing that the strength and pride of my people stood without wavering against an insurmountable obstacle. Those who died here deserve the respect of the entire continent. Without them, we would all have perished and sleep in eternal torment under the steel and cries of Mordën."

"Imagine being a prince, garbed with the lush trappings of royalty, and giving it all up to die."

"Imagine being a prince and fighting," he returned darkly. "Such concepts of honor and nobility are lost now. Those who reside in The High City would sooner rather flee to their protected walls than stand in open defiance of the shadows that march toward them. Cowardice and fear are the banners of my people now. It is a source of great shame for me."

The moon was once again covered by dark clouds as we traversed over the rocky countryside and wooded glades. As the terrain grew flat and the trees were replaced with cold stones and unyielding boulders, the temperature changed. We rode for hours under the watchful eye of the world. Animals flitted about the roots of trees and kestro soared with wings wide overhead. The early morning chill evolved into growing warmth as the plains grew lit with a gloomy light. Dawn was coming.

"If I remember correctly," Kissinger called back, "we are but a few hours from an Elfinian outpost. I passed through it not long ago on my journeys to be a watchman."

The darkness was scattered and soon the orange glow of sunlight lit the misty fields. Dew dripped from leafy trees and on to lush bushes below. Arabella grumbled in consternation that we'd drifted north. The path we had been following was no longer the Westerly Road but an offshoot made by trackers and hunters. Every turn in the road, hidden or not, held the potential for a wave of enemy taunts and attacks. Shadows creeped everywhere. Every tree, which sent its drooped form over the road and let its fingers brush the tops of our heads, was a potential concealed spot with visage to prepare an ambush. The soft whines of the wind rustling the leaves made even Kissinger's mount skittish as we urged them forward, reins taut in one hand and eyes fixed firmly ahead. Hours passed as we moved between foliage and over long stretches of grassy fields. My frustration grew more potent as we went on. It seemed we were doomed to ride forever and come no closer to Avalon than the day we set out.

"We are arriving at a place known for harboring bandits and cutpurses." Arabella gestured with the small dagger she kept in her hands. "DarSheer mentioned we should keep our eye on it. Everyone should have a blade in hand."

"Cessation Row, as it is known," Kissinger cracked his knuckles and let his dagger spin between his fingers, "is a well-hidden niche inside of several toppled boulders from the mountainside. They hover directly over the road and can house as many as ten men inside. Keep your sword ready, for if such an ambush will be attempted, it is here."

The road curved ahead. We continued to advance. My right hand never strayed from my hilt as my left hand gripped the reins. The howling was silenced as the wind banked off and did battle elsewhere. The grass blades lay low, their hesitant forms pressed to the ground. Quiet. Watching. The sounds of the horses' hooves clomping on stone grew steadily louder till it thundered out in commanding precision, proclaiming us at the doorstep. We rounded the corner, eyes glued high. I slowly drew my blade and let the tip hover over the saddle horn. Not a voice broke, even the ground held its breath.

We moved beneath the overhanging outcrop of rocks, their pointed ends hovering a mere foot above our heads. Silence continued to dominate, an eerie quiet but for the crunch of gravel and scrape of stone. I thought I saw beady eyes, eyes of darkness and hate, eyes hell-bent on seeing us destroyed. At every howl of the distant wind, I heard a howl of war as Varglarian leapt down upon us, as sword found flesh. A rock was kicked by my steed's hoof, and I fantasized the clamor for blood on the lips of Nightshades as they materialized from shadow.

As we passed the end of boulders and they began to drift behind us, sullen reminders of how unsafe the area was, I turned and let out the breath which I'd kept bottled in. Kissinger visibly relaxed, his back going somewhat slack as he loosened his tight grip on the knotted end of his sword. We sheathed our weapons except notably for Arabella who was not yet willing to trust the lack of ambush as sign that there was no one about.

"The worst is behind us." Kissinger rode forward fast.

"How much further to this Elfinian outpost?" Arabella clicked her tongue.

"Beyond that ridge," Kissinger pointed, "if it endures."

The road dipped far south, and we parted from its clean path. Animals scampered out of our way as if surprised to see anything of our size this far from the Westerly Road. Some sat on their haunches, watching long after we'd moved on. Their noses quivered as they drew in long inhalations. A ferrek lurked in the recesses of a copse of trees, its eyes watching us. I heard the snarl.

The scent of smoke assailed my nostrils, and I cursed in moaning disgust. The trees here were scarred with scorch marks like long gashes slashed into the ancient wood.

"Our enemy is both behind and in front of us," Kissinger growled irritably. "They continue to send us warnings. A defiant reminder that they know where we are."

"It could be completely coincidental," Arabella piped up. "Varg bands have made it this far west before."

"Before, they didn't march as a host of locust to the farmlands." Kissinger shook his head.

"I do not like this. We must move quickly." I leaned forward and moved to a full gallop. The others followed example until we became as blurs of color on a cold dark background.

His breath was labored as they approached the massive gates. The towering walls of stone stared down on them like mountains from afar. He'd heard rumors of their size but always chalked them up to exaggeration after a few too many pints. Darkness held its sway as the moon rolled behind clouds. The icy wind off the nearby ocean howled its intensity and sent debris rolling along the moors. What vegetation did survive here did so out of sheer desperation, for the ground was not much more than uneven rocks, pebbles, and boulders. Even the End Road, upon which they'd been traveling the last day, was full of holes and the occasional root from a brazen tree intent on uprooting them from their mounts. Several stringy trees clung to life as they burrowed deep into the ground. A bush, brown with hunger, drooped along the uneven path. It was almost mournful. Even the stonework and gates themselves seemed to have given up and perished, for the weathered mortar crumbled at his touch and the hinges that held the mighty gates shut groaned like ghosts in the wind. Several torn remnants of cerulean and cyan stitched flags fluttered on the ramparts. They still waved proudly—reminders of a time long forgotten. The years may not have been kind to this place, he decided as they approached the last few feet of the road, but it was altogether sad. If he listened, the young man could almost hear the haunting echoes of war horns blowing their charge, cries on the wind. He could imagine the hundreds of bows being pulled tight, the wood creaking, and then a twang as a thousand arrows took flight. He wondered what it looked like in its heyday, proud bowmen atop the walls, warriors in gleaming armor standing guard as thousands of merchants and sojourners traversed the wild lands to enter the splendor and glory of the Kingdom of Glasbur. Now, stones lay crumbled at the feet of the vine-covered walls. Banners had holes and while they still waved atop the ramparts, they did so with less and less fervor. Even the mighty wooden gates before them splintered and were broken in places.

A fly flitted into his ear, and he waved aggressively, shaking his head. His companion ignored him. A single piece of tangled and beaten teal fabric lay along the base of the wall. It was torn and some dark stain covered most of it. He reached down and lifted back the corner. The image stitched on with blue thread was of a horn. The horn was curved and glistened with gold and silver coins falling from one end. The fabric made the horn almost seem like it was floating in a sea.

"Are you sure this is the place?" He turned to his companion who lifted the hood from her clouded eyes. She was searching again, as if unaware he was before her. He'd noticed as they drew closer to that forsaken village that her mannerisms had changed, and their conversations had suffered. When she did this, he felt more alone than he ever had. It hurt him. Ached deep. A bitter reminder that no matter where he was or who he was with, he'd never regain the happiness of old. *Forgotten and abandoned.* That was the song of his tale. He folded his arms.

"That Elfinian merchant seemed dubious at best," he said. "I'm beginning to think he sent us here in jest. Did you hear the way he said, 'Do they not know? Have they not heard?' like we weren't in front of him?"

"Relax," she responded swiftly and knelt to pick up the torn fabric, "if it's wrong we return the way we came. Besides, the Elfinian merchant is held in high repute with the Herb Master. She says he's good to his word, then I'm convinced. I'm sure if this all turns out to be a wild ferrek chase, then she'll be more than happy to reprimand the Elfin and return our thruki. What other leads can we follow? He's somewhere here. I know it. Can you not feel the tips of anticipation? It courses through me." She rubbed her fingers over the fabric and looked up, arching her neck so she could view the tops of the behemoth walls.

"Just because the blasted merchant had an illuminated manuscript with fancy fonts and glittery paint doesn't mean he knows anything," he grumbled as she leaned her weight hesitantly against the imposing gates. "At some point, my dear, we have to conclude that we're going in circles. Have we not been this far south only months prior? The search is dried up. We've been as far north as Fiscer's Keep and along the eastern seaboard. That crone from Ronier said she'd heard rumors, but rumors be damned."

"What of the scouts from the Outpost?"

"We hunted down that path, and it led us nowhere," he argued.

"Or that maiden from Naird?"

He paused. "This is our what third attempt in our search? In these wild and tangled lands, he could be hundreds of miles away or just over the next mound of dirt. We'd be no more the wiser. Besides, this city is abandoned. You heard the merchant. 'The great Kingdom of Glasbur hasn't opened its gates in over half a millennium. All inside perished, or so the tales say. What takes you to such a forsaken land, cursed with spells beyond the mind's comprehension?'"

"And what makes you think that the rumors are true?" she snapped back. "I have been patient with your disbelief. Ever have I humored your constant jabs at my resolution. I did not ask you to follow me blindly. If you so wish it, I will continue alone."

The words hurt him worse than any sword. His chest sunk. She didn't mean it. She *couldn't* mean it. They'd been scouring these cursed lands for years. Did she not see how he was trying to aid her?

"You search with desperation," he said. "I do not desire to see you disappointed, is all."

"Or perhaps you wish it," she countered stiffly. "I know the sufferings you've been through. Trust me, I know. But he is here. I know this too."

The nearby walls groaned and creaked as wind shrieked overhead. It tore a branch from a tree and sent spiraling by, missing them by feet. He brushed past his thick hair and ground his stained teeth. *So much for trying to make her forget. Why was she being so stubborn?*

"I will not give up on him." The young woman turned, her eyes glistening. "He's still alive I know it. I feel it. There have been rumors of him since we reached the Ethero Basin. Merchants claimed they had heard tales of a stranger far to the east. I cannot give up now. I must have hope."

She does not care, the voice in his head hissed. He gritted his teeth.

"You imply I don't?" His shoulders drooped. "I simply don't wish to see your face fall when at the end of all this we are proven wrong. Face it, my dear, we've done our duty. He is not alive, or he is beyond our aid. Let us go home. Do you not yearn for the soft familiarity of home? The sounds of birds in the trees on a warm summer evening? Do you not yearn to be back with your mother and I mine? We are not welcome here. We are strangers on the run. These lands are not ours. They never will be."

"You would so quickly abandon him?"

"How can I abandon someone who is dead?" His voice rose higher than he meant, and he instantly regretted it.

"Just because you've lost all hope, doesn't mean I have," she said softly.

He reached a hand and brushed her arm with his fingertips, but she moved away. She'd grown so distracted in the years they'd been trekking across forsaken mountains and plains. The dirt and grime and time had begun to wear him down, yet she never lost her ever-hopeful gaze nor her proud mindset. His heart ached when he thought of what he'd become. What she'd become to him. She stumbled in the rubble, and he steadied her, hands on her hips. The wind sent her tangled hair flowing out behind her and what little sunlight pierced the thick bank of clouds was cast about her. He wanted more than anything to believe. He wanted to have hope. But every moment of his waking days he was plagued with suffering, mental and otherwise. Voices wove in his brains like serpents. He hadn't told her. He couldn't. She had to believe his loyalty was unwavering. He needed her to believe his intentions were true.

"You despair because you have no other choice," she continued sadly. "I know what we've been through has been hard on you, especially after what *you've* been through. Forgive my harsh words. I know this. Despair comes easier to some than others. I am obstinate and foolhardy."

He ducked his head and blinked back the tears. "You bless me, my dear, with your words. There is no apology needed." *It hurt.*

It will always hurt, the voice snarled.

Not always! This will be over soon! He forced his hands into fists behind his back.

You are alone. You are forgotten. You have been abandoned. This is your part.

He gazed at her as she slowly dropped the fabric and watched it blow away. Her behaviors were enigmatic to him.

For a long moment he wanted to bring her into a tight embrace but resisted. It wasn't right. He turned and approached the intimidating gates. From bottom to top, it was easily over fifty feet tall. Maybe he could use this as an opportunity to finally force her to give up her search. To give up on *him.* He wondered what would happen if they did not find their precious comrade. *He abandoned YOU!* He shook his head and cursed silently. He wasn't ready for that. Before he could suggest anything, she had reached the large iron handle and pulled on it. The gate remained shut. He didn't know what she'd expected.

"How are we to enter?" She cursed, "Blast it all."

"We could go through that hole," he said and pointed.

At the base of the gate, a small hole, wide enough for a dog to squeeze through, had been formed over time. With much sucking of his gut, he believed they could squeeze through.

He hunched over as the wind picked up and tore its icy fingers into his threadbare cloak. The nights had grown fearsomely cold. Not even the pair of cloaks they'd stolen from a sleeping traveler had kept the misery out.

Some fabric makers they turned out to be, he thought darkly as he wrapped the folds around his shivering arms. Despite the thin protection, he was still grateful for it. What cold he'd been accustomed to in his hometown was laughable to this. He'd never lived by a body of water. He'd never experienced the winter winds off the frozen and slushy seas. Yet now here he was, feeling its teeth gnaw at his warmth and consume it hungrily.

"Push me through!" she hissed as she began to force her upper half through the entrance.

He heaved against her and winced as she yelped. But her whole form passed through and in similar manner he too popped out on the other side. He felt the scrapes and cuts on his arms but chose to say nothing. *What would she care anyway?*

"Promise me this, if this end is a dead end, we give up the search." He sweated, feeling the beads of moisture harden even as they were created. Like small icicles, the balls fell with clinks to the ground, before vanishing beneath the pebbles and rubble, or borne aloft by the howling wind. He took a hesitant step under the watchful eye of the gate and stared down the now winding road ahead of them. The woman at his side let a small gasp escape her lips. The road wound toward a massive city, backlit by the silver clouds. The once mighty buildings were ghosts of their former glory. Armor and swords, rusted by time and exposure to the salty air, littered the road they stood upon. Vines and ivy covered the walls and disturbed the evenly spaced cobblestones. Holes, some as wide as the road itself, broke up the monotony of discarded weaponry and fallen debris.

"What happened to this place?" he whispered.

They both felt the feelings of sadness creep in. For every step they took, it was like they were invading upon the hallowedness of a graveyard. A long line of houses, their windows gaping holes of darkness, sat on the left. Their roofs had long since caved in and most of the walls had crumbled away. Trees and vegetation had retaken much of the area to the point that it appeared more nature than city. What confused him the most, however, was the sheer number of weapons and helmets and breastplates that lay discarded as though in haste. Some sported small holes evident of arrow piercings. Others were cloven in two by mighty swings. He knelt at the entrance of the gates and picked up a single blue helm. The proud visage stared back. It was deep blue in color with a single green fish above where the nose would have poked through. He turned it over in his hands. On the back, scratched faintly by a dagger point, the word "Rivëonas".

"A name?" She leaned over his shoulder.

He shrugged. "Or a company name."

"Whoever it belongs to must have been important," she observed. "The rest of the armor here is rusted steel brown."

Bordering the main road, clumps of clay bricks and thick stone slabs were stacked like someone had come through and cleaned the rubble away from gaps in the road. Wood boards leaned against what had once been a low building. The ceiling was long gone while the sides of the building remained erect, albeit covered in ivy and erosion. A weathered and dreary sign hung from the building's gaping hole where once the door had been. He squinted and read the words "Valire Inn and Tavern" in paint. He reached out and touched it and in a sudden flurry of movement, the sign, bolts board and all, fell from where they'd been attached and exploded into shards of dust and wood on the ground. He froze.

"What are you doing?" she hissed. "Do you mean to bring the entire city down on us?"

"Sorry."

Shields and spears, crusted rusty from constant exposure to the elements, lay scattered about. Breastplates, with many dents and battered holes, lay strewn under the moon's glare. In some senses it appeared things were preserved well, in others, they were ghosts of their former image. An old wheel leaned against the wall of what appeared to be an armory. Inside the broken wall, he spotted spears stacked in groups of five to a barrel. Shields hung from the wall. In another time, he would have loved this.

He stepped carefully, gingerly. He winced as a sword clanged against the stones. It rang out loudly into the hushed sky. The girl at his side gritted her teeth and placed a hand steadily on his arm. They waited, half expecting a Varglarian to burst from the shadows. But the city remained quiet. No shouts answered the alarm. No doors slammed shut. No kestro flew overhead. It was eerie.

"I don't like this," he murmured and took a careful step around an old helmet. The dented visor glared accusingly up at him as if blaming him for its owner's demise. "This is why that blasted merchant was so candid with his information. What could possibly be in a city of ghosts? Armor by the barrels? A battle happened here, I'm sure of it. Look, the buildings have eroded. Who could possibly live here? How could *he*? We're wasting our time."

"It's clear the place has been abandoned for some time." She ignored his concerns and walked along. "A sadness hangs over these spires like fog over a harbor. See the weapons of war and instruments of defense? They are laid about as if in hasty abandon. Where are the people?"

"Dead," he muttered so she couldn't hear. "They are long dead."

She ran a hand along the bricks of a half-crumbled wall. The shafts of spears remained in the clay at the feet of what once were steps. The wind lamented the deeds of the past as it wove from gaping window to creaking wooden door out into the empty streets. Scars dotted the walls, where once torches would have been burning. The sconces themselves littered the ground. All around was dreary and dark and desolate. As he strained his eyes, he caught sight of what obviously was once a very popular inn. Faded golden spirals had been painted on the sides of the building and laying face up in the gravel ditch, he saw the barely visible letters "Sp ys de nn."

"This is creepy," he murmured in growing agitation as they advanced carefully along the road's breadth. "That merchant warned us we would not like what we saw. The place is abandoned, my dear. Is this not proof enough he is not here? Would he not have come running like a dog to his master if he saw us?"

She continued to ignore him. "What could have caused all of this?"

"People have pondered this very question for centuries! We will not find an answer now if they have not already! See reason." She ignored him. *Again!*

Black shadows leered from empty windows and doors slammed on their hinges. A half decayed wooden sign swung from over a doorway, the painted characters faded long ago. Dust swirled about in the streets and the faint sounds of debris being moved by the wind could be heard. Several long banners remained at their post, their moth-eaten fabric snapping in the wind. On the right of the winding road, a circular structure sat under the heavy weight of time. It had once clearly been a watchtower of some sort, though now it resembled little more than a pile of rocks. Behind that, brown thorns from dead shrubs lined a field of dirt and rocks. The way the thorns wound and tumbled about, he wondered if it had been shaped into a maze.

They continued to cautiously move along the street, eyeing the remains of what once had been a considerate civilization. Carts lay useless in corners. Large stains covered the stones. Bones of fish and other creatures lay in heaps. They passed stores and inns, taverns, and herb huts. Swords and spears dangled from large trees like decorations. A suit of armor lay crumpled at the base of a bough. He swallowed as he saw the cord that hung directly above it.

"I wish I knew more about this place." She touched the tip of an ancient dagger. The metal was covered in rust. Flakes fell to the ground.

"I have a feeling this place did not rest peacefully." He pointed.

She followed his arm as they beheld another suit of armor, face down. A sword was impaled through the back, the handle having broken off. She reached out and prodded the helmet. Her companion slapped at her arm even as the helmet toppled off and clanged noisily down the street.

"What are you doing?" he snapped. "You'll get us captured!"

"From a ghost town?" she scoffed. "What of that building there? It looks . . . royal."

A large plateau rose in the center of the city with escarpments on all sides. Atop it, at the flat top, a large building slept in regal display. The walls were once a vibrant blue, now a faded mint. Grand arches and pointed peaks supported the thick stone. A stone path led up to the front door. All they'd seen so far had been in various stages of ruin. The building here seemed stuck in time, as regal and majestic as the day the gates closed. It gleamed in the pale moon beams.

"I've seen enough." He yanked at her arm. "We're clearly in the wrong spot. I don't see any reason to disturb the dead any longer."

"I would like to know what happened to them," she spoke as if in a trance. "They deserve to sleep in peace."

"Look at this place," he retorted as he followed her. "Why do you seek death so, woman?"

"I said if you wish to leave you may go!" she lashed back. He stared after her as she hurried along the path and toward the building. He raced to follow, though his gut churned angrily. *This is your part.*

"Can you hear it? *Whispers* in the wind. *Shapes* on the water." Her voice became dreamy and smooth.

"What are you talking about? The ghosts here are driving you mad. See reason!" He was about to force her to a stop and shake some sense into her.

"A great battle was fought here." She pointed to the grassy sides of the escarpment. Armor littered the ground. "It all ended . . . up there. Locked inside."

"What ended? Everyone's life? Then maybe we shouldn't go up there?" he pleaded, but his words fell on deaf ears. He followed her outstretched arm to the building atop the hill. Accompanied by the shrieks of the wind and the goosebumps on his arms, he made his choice. The ghosts of this mournful place would not haunt him nor his nightmares. He was over it. He turned to grab her arm and cursed. She was halfway up the pathway. She moved like a cloud across the sky. Her feet barely touched the stone. He hurried after her, leaping the stone steps two at a time. The sword at his side thwacked against his thigh. He brushed the hair from his eyes as they reached the door. Without waiting to comment, she reached out with her hand and wrapped her fingers around the "U" shaped handle of solid iron. The door was chained from the outside with thick iron links. She ran a finger over them. Great marks had been made into the door like fingernails had scratched the wood. An eerie feeling settled over him. His insides churned with nerves. This might be his last chance to keep her from making some big mistake.

"What if this city is cursed?" he pleaded. "What if they brought some great punishment on themselves and now, we too have taken it for disturbing the dead? The door is locked from the outside. Is that not sufficient reason to avoid opening it?"

She brought her sword up and, pummel first, began bashing it against the wood with great strength. The ancient wood began flaking and splintering. Encouraged by this, she hit harder and stared at him.

"Help me!"

He wrestled with the idea of grabbing her and forcing her to flee this place. The words he'd been hearing in his nightmares the past month returned. *Whispers in the wind. It's all ended on the roiling waves. Lives lost, for the grief of their age was too much. Songs like sirens singing on the sea. Believe their tears are real and don't fear. They are simply shapes on the water. They are broken on the stones.* He watched as she finally broke a sizeable hole in the door and joined her. Together they broke a gap large enough to sidle through.

The boom of their entry echoed down a long hall. At the end, she stood against a second set of doors. Colored stain glass windows let in red and orange light. Dust wafted through the beams of moonlight. He stepped out onto a thick carpet that must have been a rarity of its time. In their journeys across these lands, he'd found only the rich had such carpet. Tables stood at various intervals along the wall. Vases stood, their contents now reduced to dust. Faded paintings lined the walls.

"There's so much pain here," she whimpered as she reached for the second set of doors. "It hurts. They're screaming. Help them! The fingers of those asleep pry at the door."

He couldn't help it. As he moved past the paintings, he ogled up at them. The first was a beautiful display of the city at dusk, orange rays of light lighting up large ships in the harbor. On the docks, hundreds moved about in endless chaos. Seamen pushed off with great pikes as they set sail for the unknown. Dockworkers shuffled large crates of exotic animals and vats of fish. Fishermen, returning from their long day of fishing, lugged nets full of their day's catch off their boats. Soldiers walked casually through the crowds, five at a time. Dogs and horses meandered about in the foot traffic as a group of dignitaries, protected by guards, walked down a side road. Colors ranged from rose pinks and ocher browns, to sea blues and viridescent greens. It was a beautiful image. The next painting was of a Drucodian in royal attire, robes flowing about his feet. He held a sword in one hand, his mighty brow furrowed in thought. His eyes were strikingly clear, grey in color, separated by the cleft that was common to that race. The third painting was covered in slashes like someone had taken a knife to it. All he could see as he squinted in the soft light was a woman's face. He stared at her mesmerizing eyes and felt a stir in his heart. Her face, despite the slashes and cuts, was beautiful. He wondered what she was like. Had she been royalty as well? The wife of the man next to her? His daughter?

"Now!" she called back to him with an urgent tone. He turned and shook his head to clear it of the cobwebs.

They were soon inside the room. He craned his neck back to gaze at the beautiful architecture. Domes and flying buttresses interrupted the carved ships that rode the walls as if they were water. In the center of the room was a round table. Atop this, a mound of moth-eaten parchment and abandoned weapons. Furniture was strewn about haphazardly like someone had tossed it over in haste to get away from something. This unknown chewed at his mind. In the center of the room, a large slab of stone covered a vat. Before he could stop her, she was across the room and at its side.

"Have you had enough adventure?" he begged. "It's a big empty room. We must go!"

She didn't respond. Her eyes danced over a fancy script in the surface of the slab.

"Here contains the last memories of Drasmor of the Guild as well as his body. With him, in eternal slumber, lies the Princess Laylagail. There is no hope. They've breached the doors. Snarls and screams and ever clawing fingers. Mordën cursed us all and we now pay the price. Sirens in the sea. Voices on the water. They've come for us and there is no escape. We cannot refuse their call through the rain and torment of the angry sea."

"You shouldn't be here." the voice came from behind them. It was gravely with a snarl at the end. The voice spoke again. "Your mistake."

He heard the unmistakable sound of a bow being drawn.

Something was different. Unexpected. The cold draft wafted over me and soothed my nerves as a nursemaid to her charge. I opened my eyes, letting the early pale morning light peek in. Birds chirped in the branches of tall oaks and wide spruces that towered over us. The faint noises of conversations stirred in my ears, and I thought I made out Arabella's soft tone.

"I'm scared, Kissinger."

"Who wouldn't be. But of what, particularly?"

"Everything. We're banking *everything* that King Elharan will meet with us and discuss. Furthermore, we are hinging all our efforts on the fact that he'll believe us."

"You doubt their resolve?"

"I doubt their willingness to adhere to centuries-old scrolls written long ago in a younger world."

"Villages are being burned and people fleeing," he said soothingly. "How many towns did we pass through and see a great fleeing host of folk seeking the safety of Avalon? Word is spreading."

"Then what are we doing? What is our point? Why move with an urgency being displayed already by those around us? What are we doing with our time?"

"We are complying with what DarSheer asked of us."

"And if he was wrong? If our efforts could better be used to help the people here and around us?"

"Those on the plains are lost already. They've fortified their huts and towns and made long their defense, but all must perish before the fire and ash," I said as if in a trance.

There was a long silence as I stirred and sat up, rubbing my eyes, and looking about blearily. Arabella and Kissinger had made a fire and placed the remains of an animal on a long spit. The smell of sizzling fat and meat filled my nostrils. My stomach grumbled and I shoved off the thin blanket and sat up.

"Explain your meaning." Kissinger leaned against a stump and picked the flesh from his teeth.

"We ride as a ship sails with the full strength of a gale in its mainsail. Our mission is to alert the Elfins abroad of the threats encroaching on their boarders. Those fleeing the outlying towns and villages are being slaughtered as they flee. Do you think Nightshades spare the weak and mottled because those fleeing fear them? Mordën is not intent on enslaving this world but destroying it and rebuilding it to his design. All must burn before his anger is satiated. We ride to prevent this."

"Does this knowledge come because of your . . . interactions with him?" Kissinger asked.

"Much of my knowledge of him comes from this, yes," I said despite Arabella's look. "I feel his hunger grow. With every burg he demolishes, it grows. I feel it in my sleep. I know it when I wake."

"They will not heed the tidings of folk save for those garbed in Outpost attire." Kissinger sighed. "Phoenix speaks truth."

"What makes you two more inclined to truth than others?" Arabella challenged as she picked at the flesh of a crisp hare.

"We know better than to exaggerate our findings and explain the attacks to rogue bands," Kissinger returned. "Think about this: most of the people on this side of the mountains are farmers and fishermen, content with living away from the busy folk and cities abroad. That is why they came here. They are not warriors of old, strong as steel. They are not overly bright either, for their strength comes from their toils, not their minds. Most refuse to accept the truth that Mordën has returned. They will make it to the walls of Avalon and there claim refuge from 'a rouge band of Varg' who came upon them in the night."

"You belittle those less intelligent than you?" Arabella asked.

"Not belittling, merely explaining," Kissinger stated.

"I didn't intend for this to turn into an argument." She sighed and rubbed her temple. "Forgive my words, Kissinger. I will continue our quest despite my confusions."

"We must all do things we don't fully understand before the end."

"When was the last time we ate hot food?" I groaned in hunger. My stomach rumbled appreciatively, and I reached for a sizzling squirrel. "Did you cook this, Kissinger?"

"It's nothing." Kissinger grinned back, his mood broken. "I haven't been sleeping well so I decided to make use of my tossing and turning. Two hares, a squirrel, and the best catch of all, this half-eaten ferrek. Poor brute met his end in a tussle with some tusked creature. He was oozing out his entrails about half a mile north of us."

"I could get used to this," Arabella leaned her back against a thick tree. "No screams, no metal against metal. Just the kolst chittering their aimless chatter above us. Is this what peace is?"

"Your new home might turn out to be the Cacian Hinterland," Kissinger joked. "I hear this is their life every day.

"Don't tempt me." She smiled back as smoke flowed up into the sky. "Actually, go ahead. Tell me more."

"They say the Inclings there are a secretive bunch keeping to their huts of straw and mud. They are simple creatures who steer clear from matters outside their clans. Some humans and a rare Elfin have traveled to their lands and now live as adopted members. They wake with a pipe in mouth and a babbling brook to echo a kolst's song. The sun is always warm and the grass always green. Food is plentiful. They have it all: Fields of wheat to the east, a large forest filled with creatures to hunt for sport, and bushes of berries for the children to pick through on a midsummer's eve, all to the north. During the steamy summer nights, they'll lie on their backs and count the sparkling stars overhead.

It's said nowhere else in Ëonë do the stars shine so bright. To the south, they had great docks to trade with Glasbur before it shut its gates. Now they use that space for boating and sport. To their west, they have docks that elicit trade north with The High City and The High Island. Even merchants from the Isle of Meninïn can be found bartering with them. Some of the most renown bistri pies to rival even Marian's come from their furnaces. It's protected by the mountains to its east and The High City to the north. Some say it is the most well-protected point in all the continent. The sun rises and falls on content bellies and peaceful minds."

Arabella had a glazed expression as she picked a piece of meat from the rotating spit and popped it into her mouth. "After all this, I shall retire my bow and shield and live a life free of harm and danger."

"All alone?" Kissinger glanced at her as he continued to spin his sword over the fire.

Her eyes flitted to him. "Are we ever truly alone?"

"Some might feel it."

"You would end your warfaring days there as well?"

"Why not?"

"I don't know." She stared into the fire. "You seem the type to be restless without a Varg to skewer or a Nightshade to prick."

"I have a soft side," he teased. "Believe it or not, I did learn to play the gloshee. Topper wasn't keen on me usurping his craft, but he taught me a few simple melodies. I'm sure I'd be famous in that small corner of the world. *The Cacian Bard* people would call me. They'd say, 'He's the one who writes ballads not from the words of others but from his own experiences. Never in all of time has a bard done what he sung, but he has!'"

"And would you? Have adventures to sing of?" She raised one brow.

"Who's to say I haven't already." His smile was gone as he frowned into the embers.

"I'd listen to you." She hugged her arms tight. "Any man who can surrender the weight of the sword after it is no longer needed, for the sickle in the field or the gloshee in a tavern, is worth listening to."

I listened sleepily as they conversed. It was soothing to feel, for a moment, at peace. The kolst overhead chirped and launched into flight, soaring past us and into the clouds above. I watched until it was a speck on the horizon.

"Maybe one day I'll let you listen to my ballads." Kissinger smiled.

"You've written many?"

"Not yet."

"How can I listen to that which does not exist?"

"After we save Ëonë, song will be in plenty, for the tales will span coast to coast."

"You really think we have a chance, then?"

He took her hand in his. "I've never doubted it. I do doubt if I shall survive to see the end, though."

We were silent for a long while after that. The only sounds came from kolst fluttering about overhead and the spits from the food as it cooked. When it came time to eat the delicious food, we continued to do so in silence. I could feel the tension. Bumps covered my arms—whether from the cold, the nerves, or the endless stream of bugs everywhere, I knew not.

"We need to be on the move." Arabella checked the sun's position. "We've lost the morning."

The camp was packed and cleaned in record time before we trekked onward. Hours passed, or maybe it was minutes. The wind stung our eyes. Rocks and pebbles tripped up our progress. In the distance great peaks, white-capped mountains, jutted their dominance. Their green leafy capes swayed, and a milky glow hung low, painting the feet of the mountains in an angelic glow. Running along the base of the hills, bright green plains contrasted with dark foreboding clouds, which sank closer to the ground. A harsh wind had sprung up among the flowers and grown into a howling banshee, shrieking its displeasure across the treetops and down into valleys and crevices. My cloak snapped in the wind, and I clasped the small clip which kept the hood around my neck, letting the circular emblem rub over my pale, frozen fingers. Clenched now in my hand, I massaged its smooth side. I wished, not for the last time, for a mug of ale and a warm fire.

It didn't take long for the howling wind and bitter cold to force my eyes shut as I rested my face from the blurriness. I wrapped the cloak around me and let the soft fabric warm my face. I'd have to have a word with the craftsmen of such cloaks for the wind pierced its hide as if it were no more than a paper pocketed with holes. I sniffed as mucous trickled down and froze on my upper lip. As we rode, the terrain changed notably, flowing from the dirt browns of perished grass to soft flowering plains. The wind slowed as we left the valleys and hills behind. Great oak trees and twisting pines swayed to the lament of the breeze, their leaves clapping soft cheers. Water trickled in deep beds along the path.

Kissinger ground out, "It may be the birth of winter now, but I cannot recall a cold wind with such ferocity as this one in many years."

"We have crossed the Elfinian border," Arabella shouted to be heard as she pointed. "We can house ourselves at the next settlement, for we are safe from harm here. Not even Mordën would dare cross these borders, at least not yet. Even at the height of his powers, he lost a great deal of his host trying to force the Elfinian armies back. I have no doubt it is a sore spot in his memory. He won't be eager to chance his luck again. I'll wager the Elfin remain in firm control of these lands and wouldn't be against reminding him of his place."

Ahead, a single pinnacle of stone pushed past the branches of proud ancient trees whose leafy tops swayed with the wind. A single resplendent banner appeared. It snapped proudly, showcasing the golden Elfinian bow against a silver sea. The sigil of the Elfinian race was a welcome sight and we let out nervous laughter. Kissinger gripped my shoulder as we sat on our mounts, side by side, and shook it.

"See, bairn?" he crowed. "The darkness may be deep, its arm long and crooked, but not all come under his sway. Behold a friendly home at last."

"Keep together," Arabella whispered.

As we came to a stop before a low wall, a face peered from a curved buttress. A horn blew atop the wall and a small gate, barely taller than a man on horseback, swung open. A troupe of Elfinian guards rushed out, their spears glistening in the pale evening light.

"Speak and declare your purpose, outcast riders of the world," a deep voice boomed from the wall. The face glowed like a ray of moonlight, and I could see his flowing aureate hair and gold-yellow cloak, which swayed with the wind behind him. A bow was cast over one arm, and a barrel of arrows peeked their feathered ends over the wall.

"We are allies of The High City and Avalon," I shouted up to him. "We carry urgent tidings of fell creatures crossing the Ford of Duïn. Alas, they might even now be sieging Ithuïn. Most of the Eastern Ward suffers from much bloodshed and burning, and now it is at your own doorstep. We wish shelter from this wind before we continue to Avalon to warn King Elharan."

"We have seen some of this threat from afar," the Elfin atop the wall called down. "It is but a foraging party. It is not rare for them to cross the ford and roam along the coast. I'm sure it is an easy task to destroy them."

"The Outpost is burned and its people dead," Kissinger shouted back. "The one who just spoke is Phoenix, DarkBairn. Arabella stands behind me. I am Kissinger, of the Outpost."

The Elfin leaned forward, and the glow of the setting sun outlined his fair face, wreathed with stray hairs. "DarkBairn? The one prophesied? These are grim tidings indeed if the purveyor of evil now stands on our threshold."

"Careful, Elfin," Kissinger warned, his tone icy, "we have not battled many and come far to be insulted by you fair folk."

I placed a cautious hand on his arm and shook my head. Since arriving in Ëonë, I'd slowly come to terms with the fact that most people would not be glad to see me.

I cleared my throat. "I am not from this world and indeed was forcibly a host to Mordën's soul. I've battled him mentally and in my nightmares for the last two years. He has been mustering his forces these past two years, sheltered from the eyes of the world in his cursed keep. But he is no longer hiding now. In a moment of our weakness, he struck the Outpost. I saw with my own eyes the horrors unleashed there. Legions of Varglarian, hordes of Nightshades, giant arachnids so tall you could walk beneath them without bending over. Many of my friends perished there."

At the Shadow King's name, the Elfin drew back, head retracting into his hood. He listened to the rest of my speech with little movement until I finished.

"It is unwise to speak this name on the road," he muttered. "It is equally unwise to dispatch those unfortunates when they come seeking shelter. We Elfin are a proud and noble race. We will not tolerate Varg or Shade moving unchecked in our lands. Be at peace, for should any bearing the mark of evil cross our lands, they will be killed."

The Elfin on the wall beckoned with his fingers. "You are welcome to enter through the gate below but take care not to bring any evil with you. You may be fair in visage but corrupt at heart. We will not hesitate to do what we must, should this be true."

The group of armed Elfins stonily watched us as we passed through the open gate. The Elfin on the wall waited patiently in the small court-yard for us as we approached. He remained mute until the gate slammed shut and the locks and bolts were slid into place. The courtyard was tiny, nearly half the size of the Outpost's. He led us into a small square building, the ceiling barely tall enough for us to stand comfortably in.

"My name is Gisli, commander of this watchpost." The Elfin motioned for us to sit as he unpinned his cloak and draped it with care over the back of a cushioned seat. Two Elfinian guards brought curved jugs of mead and plates towering with berries and dried meat. "I know these are not the comforts of home for you, but they serve us well."

"Thank you for your kindness." I bowed slightly as Kissinger dug in. Arabella joined him, shoving her mouth with berries. I cleared my throat. "It is our belief spies have infiltrated the major cities. If we can make it to Avalon and inform King Elharan, then perhaps the unified armies of Ëonë can once again destroy this force of evil as it did in millennium past."

"Has it not occurred to you that the court of King Elharan could itself be infested with spies?" Gisli drank from a mug.

"You speak ill of your own king?" Kissinger's eyes narrowed. A slice of meat hovered inches from his moist lips. "I thought it against your creed to do so."

"King Elharan has brought nothing but good to my people, since the horrors of his sire," Gisli returned calmly. "I do not curse his name, nor would you catch such an insult passing my lips. I simply mean not all hold our morals as close as we'd like. They can hold their own agenda, whisper their own brand of poison in his court."

"If you would allow us," Arabella wiped her lips, "to spend the night we would be eternally grateful. You speak wisely. Long have we run over hill and plain and river and rock to reach here. The road is our only guide yet also our most potent challenge. Varg creep in the shadows of even your lands, despite your claim that you don't permit it."

"Mordën and in turn his hosts would not so boldly march across our borders," Gisli argued. "He may be waging a battle on the peoples further east, but he is still weak. The might of the Elfinian armies will match his own and end this facade of his. Do you not think it saying that his hosts of war, as you say, do not move in open combat against us? Long have they battled with the burgs closer to the shores. This risk those people accepted when they journeyed there."

"These attacks are no such raid." Kissinger shook his head.

"This is not an insult; stay your anger," I raised a hand. "We merely wish to illuminate the risks we face on the open road."

"He's faced, what, a band of men at an isolated outpost?" Gisli leaned forward. "They are commoners, rabble, largely leaderless, of no great lineage. I know you call them ally, so I apologize if my words rustle your nerves or blow afoul of your banners. But against the Elfinian kingdom, he would stand no chance. You would not show concern to a leaf taken by a weak stream. We are a boulder, master bairn, and your Outpost the leaf."

"If you do not fear the stream," Arabella sniffed, "then there should be no issue with aiding us."

"It is as you speak, perhaps." Gisli nodded absentmindedly. "While we do not fear weak currently, we cannot anger those around us. Besides, whom else has he battled? Peasants and farmers and fishermen? You claim he marches on Ithuïn. That is but a city with an ego. It believes itself to be important, but it has few guards and a weaker fighting force. It is a trading settlement, little more. No one you've spoken of has any chance to defy even a meager force. To you this may appear hopeless but when faced with the gold-tipped spears and flowing cloaks of the Elfinian race, he will realize it was all a fantasy he spun for himself. Be at ease, young masters. Sleep well, for your eyes wander with bleariness. This kindness I will not deny you, but you will be on your own come morning." Gisli folded his long fingers. "It would do you well to regain what elusive sleep you may. You can rest knowing you are protected for now."

"With all due respect . . ." Arabella pushed.

"I accept your respect, Lady Arabella," Gisli spoke firmly, "but my best bowmen are abroad, and I assure you should any creature come within a bowshot radius of this watchpost, they would be felled before they could escape. There is no proof any significant force moves against us. Until such a time comes, you will find that King Elharan will humor your intentions, but not your words of chaos. Do not believe for one moment that we who guard the Eastern Ward would surrender it easily. Should you be right, and not servants of chaos, we will stand as we did of old. Others in the courts of my king might have their agendas, but I remain true to the scrolls and texts signed centuries ago. You do not need to doubt my resolve nor that of my people."

"Commander Gisli honors us," I said diplomatically into the silence. "Kissinger, Arabella, let us retire to our beds." I quelled their pending outburst with a quick shake of my head.

"If we accept, will we also be allowed to continue our journey to Avalon and there put our tidings before the king, despite your belief?" Kissinger challenged.

"You may shout into a thunderstorm or to the world for all I mind." Gisli smiled faintly. "It is of no concern to me how my king responds, for I will obey his commands as is my duty."

Arabella took his hand and, smiling awkwardly, left the room. They headed toward a hut protected by two guards, one on each side of the door.

I gazed out into the night. "Evil is coming, Gisli, a great evil which has already begun its domination of the eastern shores. I've been in these lands for several years. The trees seem poisoned. The water is cold. I feel no warmth from the sun along the shores. The Outpost has fallen. Numbers uncounted flood over the plains with the crimson banner of the Hourglass. I do hope you excuse us for our rushed pleasantries. Our mission is one which may give time to the remaining peoples of Ëonë. You chose to cast our words to the wind and that is your place. This shred of hope we carry might be enough to stop Mordën's advance."

"I can see even at your tender age," Gisli sat back in his chair, "you have witnessed much. Rest now, for your task is thoroughly illuminated and the urgency of your actions are noble. You will receive only comfort and aid here, and when the sun rises will be sent off with a full belly, a rested horse to ride, and all the good wishes we can spare. Do not take my words to mean I do not believe danger awaits us. I simply do not believe it to be to the scale you say. Even if it were, the Elfinian race can extinguish the hottest of fires. Mordën may have spent the last two millennium growing in strength, but he'd be foolish to think we haven't as well. Be at peace, DarkBairn. The watch is ours."

He took my hand and squeezed it, letting the soft glow, which emanated from his eyes, spread over me. I stepped out of the building and into the cold, hurrying toward a low hut. I tried not to allow my frustration to be obvious. Before I stepped inside, I glanced out. Several Elfin stood proud at their posts, cloaks waving as nobly as their banners. Inside, Kissinger and Arabella argued in soft tones.

"They are lackadaisical by nature." Kissinger rubbed his eyes furiously.

"Sometimes, the only way for someone to believe the impossible is possible is for it to occur before their eyes." Arabella sighed as she looked up and smiled sadly at me.

As I found my bed and laid my head down, I felt the tension increase. My muscles ached like I'd run the distance from the Outpost instead of rode. The pain in my head, which had been quieted since Ithuïn, returned in a storm of darkness. The peace that should have come from watchful eyes instead fled itself and left me to gaze into the monstrous horror of a grinning Mordën. His laughter echoed in my nightmares.

Soon, you will die!

Chapter 5

The Last Great Drucodian Burg

MORDËN WATCHED AS RANKS upon ranks of spears passed smoothly and in unison before his gaze. Their bearers, snarling and snapping amongst their own, were the strongest and boldest the Pits had yet released. Legions of scarred, twisted faces hid beneath smooth black helmets. The Varglarians' bodies, mangled and deformed as they were, were hidden underneath obsidian armor, which itself was curved every few inches along the sides to nasty barbed points. Behind the spearmen, a horde of lesser Varglarian shrieked by. Their bows were draped from the meager belts that tightened over their metallic tunics, curved swords in hand. These Varg were bred differently: they were smarter, their vision extended far, and their aim was as yet unchallenged in perfection by the greatest Elfinian bowman. Where Mordën had gone for brute strength in the batch that had just passed, these archers he'd poured his cunning and mental strength. The Varglarian archers passed him by, some carrying the crimson banner at the end of long poles. The red fabric snapped above their heads. Behind them, Rachnadons thundered past. Their long, thin legs were heavily armored with steel points. Due to their size, they could travel comfortably over the heads of the Nightshades and Varglarian marching by with little effort. The effect meant that every hundred feet, a giant arachnid towered in the gloom and darkness, illu-minated by red flashes. Mordën couldn't resist a small smile, his black eyes reflecting the flashes of red.

"We were unsuccessful." A Nightshade in cerise armor approached humbly. "The vermin are restless. They desire blood. They've waited for thousands of years, my lord. I've lost three legions to a surprising resis-tance on our western flank. Ithuïn falls but with it one of our generals too. The troops are in chaos."

"I did not summon you here to entertain your failure, Nien Thrass." Mordën waved a finger slowly like he was drawing a painting in the air. "Ithuïn has fallen. My plans remain on track."

"Yes . . . my king." Nien Thrass again opened his mouth to continue.

"I know you stand at the precipice of asking a dangerous question." Mordën rotated his head just enough to bring the ugly brute into his peripheral. "I would not advise it. To question my command is to infer I know not what I am doing. Is this what you are suggesting?"

"Of course not." Nien Thrass had the good graces to cower before him, head cast down. He was easier to talk to when his hideousness couldn't be seen.

Mordën returned to watching his forces march past. "Behold, Nien-Thrass, the promised darkness once more marches against the light. Prepare your best men. I shall need you at the forefront."

"I obey, my king." Nien Thrass bowed stiffly and turned to go.

Mordën watched him go, keeping his simmering rage out of sight. *Failures. Abominations.* He had not come this far to be undone by decayed potential. He turned his mind to larger prospects. There were others who could do his bidding, when his most trusted servants failed. Other ways rooted in darker times that most had forgotten. He had not even remotely shown his full strength yet. To do so would mean he was worried. *Worried of the Elfin?* He was not. *Forget the past and you are doomed to repeat it. Intentionally ignore the past, and your future will crumble before your weak hold.* He let his mind travel far past the edges of his armies. Past the grimwolves, which raced in the dark, and through forests dark as his mind. The grimwolves wore iron collars studded with sharp points. From *their mouths hissed hot saliva. Their teeth were as thick and wide as a bairn's arm. Behind them raced Nightshades in the cool black flow of shadow. Worried about the DarkBairn? He chuckled to himself. He had ways of keeping control. Mental torture that the strongest Elfin would buckle under.*

"Before this is over," Mordën mused, "the blood of Men and Elfin will fill every hole and creek. The sun itself will burn. Hope is a thing of the past."

"'Scuse me, sirs," the voice slashed through my anxious ponderings like a knife through butter. I wiped the bleariness from my eyes and blinked through the gloomy fog encasing my thoughts. The voice belonged to a strangely thin Elfin in armor that was clearly made for someone much buffer. "I'm 'ere to let you know it's morning, sirs. Sun risen, it is."

I slapped my cheeks and yawned as Kissinger slowly sat up. I threw my legs over the edge of the bed, groaning inwardly at the spots where the cot had dug into my back. Beneath my bed, stacked one on top of the other, Arabella grumbled sleepily and turned over. I leapt down from the bunk and nodded to the pale Elfinian guard, who quickly pulled back from the doorway as if he couldn't leave fast enough.

"Is it night still?" Kissinger murmured drowsily. His eyes were shut tight as he began to keel back on to his side.

"Morning, actually," I gestured out the door to the grey sky.

"We've slept all night?" This time it was Arabella's surprised voice.

I splashed my face with refreshing water from a silver bowl and gazed into a dusty mirror. My hair was grimy. My face was bony and thin. At the Outpost, I took pride in my slowly growing beard and now I looked like a hermit. My eyes bore a haunted craze I couldn't shake. I knew it vain, but I couldn't help but appreciate how despite all that, I still looked good.

We stepped out into the courtyard which was still bathed in early morning darkness. I glanced to the north and felt my spirits lift at the orange glow which had begun to chase away the inky darkness. Even the clouds seemed to hesitate, as if confused. Two Elfins, garbed in thin robes with thick breastplates, stood on either side of the door, spears clutched firmly in their long hands. They eyed us as we moved to the center of the yard. Atop the walls, faces hid beneath helms stared down, their gazes intent. The wind had abated against the ground but was still strong as it gusted high over the wall, sending flags and capes snapping briskly. In one corner, a single Elfin strummed a curved horn and as the notes blew out, the sun crested the horizon and the morning seemed bathed in a crisp newness as the greens and blues of the world clashed in a battle of colors. Birds chirped merrily in their nests. The trees, which stood as sentinels along the southern wall, waved their armaments and weapons of bark and leaf, defiant against what might rail itself against the walls.

We crossed the courtyard to the gate and waited. I adjusted the clasp around my neck and felt my cloak flutter around my feet. The quiet tune from the horn was carried up on the wings of the wind. Gisli descended from the wall. With him, two others kept their hands in the deep recesses of their cloaks. He bowed in greeting.

"May warrior's fortune shine on you yet." He smiled politely. "Remember, evil only claims victory when you surrender hope. Accept these rested mounts and filled bags of food as a gesture of our goodwill. Should you make it to Avalon, and we meet again, I hope you do not hold this against me."

An Elfin guided three new mounts forward and handed us the reins. On the backs of the horses were packs slung on either side. For a long moment, the three of us stared at them.

"What happened to the horses we came with?" Kissinger finally inquired.

"They have seen much and been through a lifetime of pain," Gisli responded as if he'd prepared long for this question. "They will stay here until they have rested and are ready."

"Ready? For?" Arabella tilted her head. "How would they tell you?"

"Everything has the ability to speak if you but know how to listen." Gisli folded his hands into his cloak.

"Thank you," I said into the void of awkward silence, "for not just the mounts but everything you've done for us. I hope that you are correct, and all my concerns are nothing in the face of the great Elfinian kingdom."

"Your kindness will not be forgotten, Commander Gisli." Arabella recovered from her previous confusion.

"It is reward enough helping one so fair," he bowed in return. "Watch your backs on the road and do not stray off it. You might believe it to be your enemy, for surely your enemy is watching it. But these lands are untamed and only skilled Elfin scouts are able to distinguish the untrodden path. Keep to the Westerly Road and no harm will come to you. Do not stop for strangers on the road. We may yet be safe here from Nightshades and Varglarians but that does not mean all you meet are innocent or not under the yoke of the Shadow King. Trust only when you must. Do not take this wrong, but I hope to never meet again, for the next time we meet, I believe, will come at the turn of the tide. Farewell. Be at peace."

"It will be done." I mounted up. I was going to miss the mount that Bastion had given us, but secretly I was glad he would be able to enjoy some peace. "One day, I hope to return this favor. Farewell, Commander Gisli. May you and yours stand ever a defiant reminder to Mordën of the strength and bravery of the Elfins. Innith Inine!"

"Onward till we're ashes." The other bowed slightly. "The past remembers."

We turned and without any more word, rode from the courtyard and out onto the open road once more. The warm light of the sun sent the dew dripping off leaves. It gave the terrain a fresh scent. Mud sparkled with dewdrops and freshly hewn trees lay bundled at the side of the road. We passed several mounted Elfin as they no doubt ensured we rode far from their watchpost so they could return and report to Gisli.

As we all rode side by side, a thought gnawed at my mind. "Kissinger, you seem unhappy with our hosts, and I recall Othrain using the term 'goldens' whenever he talked of Elfins. Yet Gisli bore no ill will toward us nor did he treat us badly, despite knowing where we came from. Why is this? Why do he and you both quarrel with them?"

Kissinger gripped the reins and I saw the blood rush to his face. "This is not a tale for me to tell. It is Othrain's right."

"To those who have been listening, he has told already," Arabella pointed out. "He does not harbor it as a thief does a jewel in his den."

"What are you talking about?" I stared at her. She sighed.

Kissinger began. "An Elfinian warrior murdered Othrain's wife in cold blood. She begged for her life, and he still plunged the glimmering steel into her breast like she was made of water and he was poking it with a stick. Othrain begged him for mercy, and finally, the Elfin relented. This was all before I arrived at the Outpost, but as Arabella said, he does not hide his disdain for the Elfin and will speak his mind on the subject. I applaud him for his stance."

My eyes widened; aware of how uncomfortable the mood had become. The once beautiful morning glowed with a reddish tint as the story sank in.

"Why would an Elfin kill a woman?" I questioned.

"He was operating on behalf of the previous Elfinian king," Kissinger said. "We do not speak lightly of this matter. Sooner in our past than we care to remember, the Elfinian King Grasspear commanded Avalon and all his peoples' lands. After a disagreement with the Custodian, he charged some of his soldiers to launch a raid against the outlying villages and farms. He meant it to be a demonstration, a show to the Custodian of his strength. But those he charged with the act had bad blood for the villages. There existed, and still partially does, a dark past between the Elfin and Men. The Elfins are not proud of the fact that Humans had to come and bail them out of their failures at the end of the Second Era. Some took their disdain for Men a step too far. It was a vile crime and ended in many dead. Houses burned and fields of crops were reduced to ash. It escalated to a possible war. An army of men led by the Custodian himself marched to bring Grasspear to justice. They needn't have bothered. Grasspear's own flesh-and-blood heir, just a bairn at the time, snuck into his father's throne room and during supper, buried a blade into King Grasspear's rotund belly. That's what the stories say at least. Rumor continues that the king was so fat the lard of his belly covered the handle of the dagger completely. The king was carted off and buried and his son, King Elharan, assumed that which his father had disgraced."

"Wow," I murmured softly. "I understand Othrain's rage but surely he realizes that the damage is done, and the current king is not to blame, nor are the race of Elfins responsible for his wife's death and the actions of one single Elfin?"

Kissinger glanced at Arabella. "I do not hate nor despite the Elfins, especially those who are too young or had no part in these egregious actions. What was commanded under their watch is horrific and those responsible should be brought to justice. But not all see it this way. Othrain is too blinded by hurt and grief. As are we all when it comes to matters of family and love."

"We all bear our own stories of woe," Arabella sniffed back a tear, "but we all react differently. Still, it is wrong to accuse the whole for the actions of a part."

"He's just in pain." Kissinger defended his friend. "His wife was murdered by a supposed ally. He drinks now to forget. He begged for her life and was met with cold unyielding pain. You can see how this would breed distrust of all of them. Othrain must learn to come to terms with what happened, as we must. Mordën operates through many races, not just Varg and Shade."

"Mordën took everything from me." I let spill everything that had been bothering me since I woke up. "He took my parents, my friends, my family. In fact, he's the reason I'm here. I've seen what he can do at his weakest. Stripped of his power and forced to resort to commoner's tactics, he launched a war on my world. Second by second, he sought to drain the world of its force, create a veritable hell of his own design. He tricked me into doing exactly what he needed me to do and took over my body when I was at my weakest. I realize that as much as I want to forget him, he still holds a curved talon in my soul. His love of destroying my world was a mere playful thought next to his desire to wipe out all life here. Make no mistake: he will try. It has taken me several years to come to terms. The issues of the past, the blood spilled on behalf of words from dead people are nothing compared to the threat we now face. There will come a time when the valor and courage of the people of Ëonë will fail. We will turn on each other, Men on Elfin, Ebyian on Incling. He will use events like this, events he may have orchestrated, to turn what might be a unified threat into a bunch of squabbling nations. There is no crime in fear. There is nothing wrong with feeling hopeless. The real crime comes when you let those emotions command your actions. It is because of me that the entire situation we are in has spawned into play. I have fulfilled the thoughts of men long dead, completed a prophecy that they spent their lives writing. I could sit back and watch the world burn. This is not my home. I did not grow up here, did not spend my childhood here. In fact, I know next to nothing about anything here. My knowledge is limited to the Outpost and the lessons DarSheer gave me. I have asked myself, why do I care about the goings and comings of a world I am not a part of? It is easy to let the words of the black beings across the waters infiltrate and confuse me, disguised as well-meant words of my own creation. This is not a time to resort to bickering. I hope Othrain will realize this as I have. The death of those we love, by sudden happenstance or long-lived illness, is a tragedy, but if we fall to the tidal wave that is anger, we open ourselves to the prompts of the Shadow King. I do not ask any to cast aside their feelings, but to not let them command their actions. Let your memory live on but do not condemn a race for the actions of a few. There is a greater evil we now face. We cannot fight amongst ourselves or all we have fought for, all I have given up for, is naught."

"You speak carefully constructed words of well-meant nature, Phoenix," he murmured, "but the weight of a horrific death under such horrible circumstances cannot be so easily set aside by those like Othrain. Do you not think we wish to our core that we could forgive and forget? The bloodshed and agony brought on by people you trusted, by those who were supposed to be your allies? When you turn to see who placed the knife in your back, how should you react when you see your friend standing there in your enemy's place? Let us ride in silence now, for my mind grows weary of conversing."

"You have suffered, this much is clear," I called after him as he galloped ahead. "Kissinger, just talk to me. I'm sorry if I've offended you."

"It may not make sense," Arabella said. "Many things do not. Just give him time. I've found the best medicine for these complicated issues is patience. It will be worked out and Othrain and Kissinger will understand."

"You don't agree with him?" I glanced at her.

"We've all suffered losses, some more painful than others. I see this as a chance to fuel our fight against Mordën, not to fight among each other. That's how he wins. He commits egregious horrors and watches us commit atrocities toward each other instead of him. While I believe this, I can understand why Othrain and Kissinger act the way they do." She gave a pitiful shrug.

"What happened to Kissinger?" I rubbed my head. "He hides his past like he is ashamed of it, and at moments like now I get just a glimpse into his mind. Did the Elfin also kill someone he loved? All he's told me is that his mother was a member of The High City's political court and needed him to do something dishonorable. He's never mentioned any resentment held toward the Elfins."

Arabella didn't speak for a moment. We'd passed by the edges of a forest and over three streams before she finally spoke. "He hasn't confided in me either. I don't think he's told anyone. Our place now is to be there for him, not prod. An invasive probe into your life can be disconcerting."

After that, we rode in silence for many miles. These miles turned into days as we slept and rode under the stars and sun. I kept to myself and was content listening to the other two bicker between each other. Gisli was not wrong, for in those days we did not meet one foe. The horse's undulating body beneath me lulled me into deep thoughts. The terrain once again switched from plains to rolling hills with tall broad trees. Small streams ran crisscrossed, fed by some larger body of water.

The air was cooler and less moist here. Ahead, the road dipped into a valley before rising out of sight. As we entered the gulch and over a stream that was so shallow it barely reached higher than the mounts' hooves, I felt the hairs on my neck stand and twisted in the saddle. Shadows danced behind us, egged on by the clash of the waning moon and rising sun. From these depths, I got the unnerving feeling I was being watched. There was no proof, no Varg nor Shade standing there. It was just a feeling perhaps brought on by days on horseback and a mind running wild.

My horse worked hard to get up the steep opposing side of the gulch and back on to the road. I knew we had reached somewhere significant because the muddy trail, which acted as the road we were following whenever water was nearby, was replaced by smooth stone. Kissinger had pulled his steed to a stop at the top of the hill and pushed up in the saddle. A ray of sunlight burst in front of him. I squinted to see, as I joined him, and placed my arm up to my forehead. The sound of running water and crying birds filled the air. Wheels creaked against stone and voices lofted high. When my eyes adjusted to the sunlight, I gasped. We stood on a grassy knoll parallel to the actual Westerly Road. All the times we'd bickered about whether we were following the right road now fell by the wayside.

Before us, in full splendor, stood the purple Fallen Peaks. Their white-capped points vanished into a grey bank of fog. At their base, blankets of trees swept down and into the fields before them. Flocks of winged creatures soared overhead. From left to right, they marched onward ever without end. In all my studies, I'd never really thought about what they would look like and now my jaw dropped. I widened my eyes. Far off, sheltered into the side of the towering mountains, a glistening metropolis of shimmering buildings and walls jutted elegantly into the sky. Spires of gold reflected the sun and sent beams of light in all directions. The road wound like a meandering river as it moved to kneel at the feet of the monstrous walls. The Golden City. Avalon bathed in light, a feat of Drucodian engineering to marvel. The greens and whites of the mountain landscape behind set the city glowing with vibrant colors. Buildings of bloodred shimmered, intermixed with sea blues and sun yellows. The walls towered, a defensive force which would turn away even the most determined of invaders. Banners sporting the golden bow of the Elfin archer waved proudly. They cast their golden threads over the walls, supported by thick posts. Elfin garbed in the aureate of their armor stood atop the walls, stepping from one viewpoint to another. From base to top, the walls surpassed any structure I'd yet seen. The city was set into the side of the mountain, with a long base. The craftsmen who built it had dug high up into the mountain and formed the city to be divided into levels. Each level seemed ringed with walls. Far off, barely visible, high in the reaches of the mountains, near the tallest point in the city, water reflected light. The Ethero Basin. The plains swept up like a great quilt and were deposited at the feet of the city. Great lakes, water as clear as a summer sky, dotted the mountains' rolling sides. Hills sprang up from the weeds, and dried up tributaries ran down the sides like evidence of a great serpent's passing. Ancient trees spread their twisted boughs. Their roots dug deep. Their leaves waved tall. To the east, the Westerly Road vanished behind tightly grouped trees and boulders as large as a house. To the west, it marched along the base of Avalon and the lands beyond. To one side, perpendicular to the main road, it broke off and meandered south, no doubt to the lands of Caldonia. When DarSheer returned, this would most likely be his route.

"Behold!" Kissinger broke the silent awe as he swung out both arms in dramatic splendor. "Behold the great metropolis . . . The Golden City, the Last Great Drucodian Burg . . . Avalon!"

"I've read of the beauty of the city," Arabella exhaled faintly, "but to see it in person . . ."

"A formidable city whose occupants inhabit it proudly," Kissinger was unable to keep the respect leaking from his words. His sourness from several days ago was gone. "It is said no living force can rupture these walls. No flying creature could survive the thousands of bows atop the walls. Should any army, dimwitted as they be, decide to march on the city, the tier-structure allows for thousands upon thousands of added bowmen to have an unobstructed view of the plains before the city. It is built like a conifer, with the top point housing the royal Elfinian line and the wide base home to the thick and intimidating walls you see before you. The mountain itself aids in their sight. And should the unimaginable happen and the wall be breached; the enemy must fight uphill through several smaller walls and twists and turns known only by the Elfin continuously through ravines and crevices. A true feat of engineering and pride. Here lies the last standing Drucodian Burg of the First Era and Second Era. Oh, to have seen it in when the Drucodians ruled it."

We rode for a few more minutes till we joined the throng of travelers and merchants jostling about on the Westerly Road, eager to make it to the city and start selling their wares. A steady stream of travelers hiked along its smooth surface. A group of Ebyian miners trudged past, grumbling about the sores on their feet. Weary mules pulled carts laden with food. Children giggled as they danced about the feet of their parents. Animals of all sizes and shapes were led by a muzzle or rope. Farmers struggled to move their cattle due to the congested nature.

"Follow!" Kissinger called as he urged his mount forward.

Being on horseback, unlike the vast majority of those around us, we managed to quickly force our way closer to the gates. Despite the glares and occasional shouts of protest, most didn't hinder our progress. Horns sounded as a party of riders were dispatched from the open gates. The gates alone were a miracle of engineering, for each stood thirty feet tall, clad in thick iron and boasting curved points which jutted several feet into the road. The riders rode with the glory of their city behind, their capes fluttering behind them and their smaller flag riding over their helms. People scrambled to clear the road for them, even diving into the ditch on either side.

"Great riders of Avalon," Kissinger spoke as soon as they came within earshot, "we come in great need. We wish to speak to your king."

"Who shouts at the royal guard so?" the lead rider called as he passed us, reining his horse to a cantering stop. "Who are you?"

"We come from the Outpost," I joined the conversation.

"Outpost?" The Elfin narrowed his eyes. "Your arrival will send the city into a riot. You are the same who crossed our border but five days prior? We have received word of your plight from Gisli, commander of the Eastern Garrison." He looked at me and I felt a sudden cold mist spin into existence. "So, it is true. You travel with the DarkBairn." the Elfin rider tilted his head, removing the helm from his brow. His thick hair flowed back behind him, a slight blond shade. He eyed me distressingly. "A man of the Outpost in our city will stir the pot of rumors hot as lava, but the DarkBairn will tip the pot on its side and consume everything. What brings you to our city?"

"Mordën marches . . ." Arabella began.

"Do not speak those words here." The Elfin raised a hand abruptly and glanced behind him. His fellow riders had yet to make any motion. They sat in their saddles silently and stonily. People and carts moved around us like water around a rock. The Elfin leaned forward. "These matters are not for the casual traveler to overhear. Your news is best reserved to the Council Halls. Save your distress for the proper audience. King Elharan extends this branch of goodwill. He invites you to the King's Tier where he awaits your news. Beware, my friends, for not all eyes who gaze upon you here or in the city do so with joy and not all mouths report your goings to suitable company. Follow me. Be quick about it."

"You never mentioned your name," I spoke as he turned and began riding toward the city. Once again, people dove to avoid being trampled.

"We're walking here!" a man in a scruffy cloak snapped angrily.

"Do the commoners mean nothing?" An Ebyian gestured with both hands. "Our hard mining means nothing to you crazy riders!"

"That was my kid!" a woman screamed as the lead rider shoved aside her small bairn.

Two riders split the crowd before us, and the rest brought up the rear. It allowed us to ride confidently despite the throng of travelers.

"I am called Berëthelluïn, of the Elfinian Guard, in the Elfinian tongue." The Elfin sighed at my wrinkled nose. "Perhaps the common tongue would be preferred. You can call me Bereth."

"I wish it were under better circumstances that we met, Bereth." I tried to hide the awe in my voice as the city expanded in size before us. The walls seemed to grow taller with every yard we advanced.

"I wish we had never met, DarkBairn," Bereth spoke frankly. "Our meeting has set a prophecy in motion most deemed dead. Your arrival is the single scream before a party of raiders descend on a village. Your existence is the first cry from the hunter, the swish in the air as the arrow leaves the bow. You shall be the reason our young and fair perish before their time."

"Lovely people these Elfins," I muttered out of the side of my mouth to Kissinger who snorted. Arabella hid her smirk.

Side by side we rode, a burning sensation swelling up within me. Blood flowed to my limbs and my hair stood on end as the power of the city became evident. This wasn't simply a city of power; it was a city of history. Great forces of evil had thrown themselves at these exact walls twice before. At one time, the fate of Ëonë was in the hands of the Elfins. Their walls had been broken and their spirits dimmed as forces beyond number assailed their walls.

Great manualists stood atop pillars of stone. I gawked around me, letting the view sink in as we passed before the first pair of towers. Watchful eyes monitored us as we moved closer to the gate. The rumbling doors remained ajar, barely open the width of a single horse. Two massive statues stood at the gates, both with swords drawn and helms atop their fair visages. They stood in stances of defense, ready to fight for their city. They towered easily a hundred feet over us.

"Ëvidire and Bruïnsire, the first two Elfinian kings," Bereth narrated. "They've guarded this city in their stone watch since the days we claimed it as our own."

"Follow Bereth!" Kissinger murmured as we slipped into single file before the gates. "Keep your heads down. The less we attract, the less we have to worry."

Inside the walls, a bustling city sprang to life. People hurried over the cobbled roads, their cloaks kept tight around them. Many bore long staffs of dried wood. Some smoked from pipes of curved wood. They jested with each other and roared out deep laughter. Others clearly had alternative intentions. They eyed us carefully as we passed. Some were armed, others hid beneath their cloaks and gazed from under hoods. Various venders hawked their goods along the street and paused as they watched us ride by. They shouted merrily to us and those around them. Carts bore deep dishes of breaded jelly, cooked bistri, and steaming ferrek. Steam wafted the intoxicating smells across the narrow streets and into open windows. Houses of gold and green were pressed tightly together. Long ropes stretched from window to window and held up the weight of drying tunics and cloaks. Women walked by the side of the road with baskets of flowers and mugs of ale. A group of Elfinian bowmen jogged under an archway and into an alley. Doors clanged shut and shutters were closed as people went about their business. Steaming pots of soup sat over small fires. Some of the seedier individuals sat scrunched against walls and corners. They blew into their exposed fingers, watching us as we rode with the interest a tired man expresses to a bug as he passes over it on the roadway. Several men in white cloaks sang a haunting melody. They stood atop a platform in the center of a large square. Onlookers listened with either great approval or scorning disdain. Some threw flowers while others threw knives. A fight broke out and two of the singers shoved a rowdy onlooker. Fists were thrown and a dagger pulled. The rest of the group ignored the melee, even as the two singers who fought were overwhelmed under an angry mob, and their voices reached a feverous pitch as wind howled above. Before we'd passed out of sight, a group of Elfins rushed into view to break up the fight.

Taverns and inns stretched along one main road, aiming to be among the first locations that newcomers saw. It was set up so that the further into the city you went, the more you were met with. Just beyond the gates lay the places for sleep and drink. Past them came the medicinal tents and herb stands. Houses continued to interrupt the stages of winding road so that children running amok were as common as Elfin warriors. Travelers came and went in a steady flow. No one paid attention to anyone around them, for no one had the time to do so. Along the inner wall, torches flickered in golden sconces, sending beams of light into the dark recesses of the wall. At an open doorway of a tavern called *Far Quota*, three women sat knitting at a complex machine. They looked up and one held out a long quilt. The yarn she'd been using was frayed and brown. I looked away and stared up toward the heart of the city, which sat several hundred feet above us, nestled into the mountainside. Banners streamed out, spanning hundreds of feet in length. The golden-clad sides of buildings reflected the sunlight into blinding intensity.

The further into the city we rode, the more people filled the streets and the harder it became to keep our current pace. We slowed down to let a troupe of traveling bards scurry past.

"Sing, now, you imbeciles!" the lead bard snapped.

> *We're the worst the very very worst this side of The High City*
> *People listen to us not for love or adoration but crippling pity*
> *We cry when we perform because we're so hideous*
> *We're the traveling troupe of bumbling idiots*

If Topper had been here, he'd have been heralded the best musician around.

"Are you mad?" the lead bard cried out as we rode by.

"I'm taking you to the Glistening Hall on the King's Tier," Bereth said. "It's the top level of the city where his keep and the various buildings of lore and study reside. Take care not to anger our king, for he has graciously allowed what most of his court fought against."

"They don't want us there?" Kissinger prodded.

"This is true."

"It will be good to meet him," Arabella whispered to me. "He has reigned for the last ten years and in his place much of Avalon has grown in economic prosperity. He expanded the trade routes over the Ethero Basin and constructed new roads to better allow for movement of merchants. He is one of the first kings to move from warfare to peace. His father and grandfather lived on the bloodshed of their ancestors.

He is heralded as a noble and honorable ruler among his own people. Some say he is an answer from Erëthuïl for their cries for mercy."

We galloped down the road as it began to slowly climb higher and higher. A second wall stood tall before us. Although half the size of the exterior wall, it still was imposing to see. Chills raced down my back as we passed beneath its thick buttresses and ancient soaring stone. Vines and plants had covered the aged sides. The gates swung shut after we passed through, and their echo leant wings to our horses as we thundered along. Here in the inner sanctuary of the city, the citizens expanded their offering of goods. Several vendors with carts of illustriously spun silk and yarn raised them to the sun and let bystanders ogle the fabric, which against the sun seemed to glow as if it were on fire. Gold thruki was exchanged from table to table. Here, it seemed, was where the rich went. Glittering gems and glistening jewels hung from hooks. Most of the nobles passing by wore thick garments of silk and fur. Unlike the main level of the city below us, there was no intense rush of excitement and babble of conversations. Everyone moved quieter and with more purpose. At a nearby stand, a wide man, barely taller than the bottom of my horse, in bright red clothing smiled slyly. He caught my eye and hurried out before us, letting his beastly bulk block our way.

"Move aside!" Bereth ordered as two Elfin rode up and leveled their spears at the vendor.

"Oh, really," the man blustered as he was forced to take a step back, "is this the healing helpful hospitality I've heard so much about? Why, you make The High City seem like fun friendly felines. Stand back you, avast! I am no thief in the night to be treated like slippery sneaking swine. My name brings explosive and exhilarating excitement to all who hear. I am Leotard the Bard. I said avast, unhand me you big burly brigands!" He swiped at the sword of a third Elfin who had hurried up. Two others grabbed him by the arms and dragged him away as he spluttered his deep disapproval.

"Our apologies, Lord Berëthelluïn," the guard placed a fist to his chest plate and bowed, "the rabble are out in force today, even here.

We've got reports from all over the city. Something stirs that has not before. They can feel it. They're antsy. Clear the road, musician!"

The Elfin jabbed at Leotard who had made a quick turn and was back in front of us. The musician roared out his disdain and slapped the Elfin's hand aside.

"Really, this is quite unnecessary. I am happy and harmless, merely wishing to share my safe sensational songs with the world. Swords and muscles for a bard. I do declare that you lot are a worse audience than that time I ran into those trying tyrannical troublesome Ebyians. And they nearly killed me! Stop! Do not hurt me. Ouch!"

He went down with a splat as the same guards tackled him down. They placed the tip of their swords against the man's beet-red cheeks. Blood trickled down from the point and he howled. I opened my mouth, but we were once again moving quickly, despite the bard's screams which rang from behind. Even out of sight, he could still be heard snapping at those who restrained him.

"Do you want to know what the songs will speak . . . hands off, you mean man, that is not for you . . . of you? I shall be sure that all bards know the truth . . . I said away, that purple pricy purse is mine. It's coin I earned . . . you are not gregarious but a golden lot of grief. Absolutely not! Let a bard walk on his feet. I am not a bairn in his infancy!"

Finally, as we ascended beyond the fading cries, the air was free of his words. I glanced back the way we'd come, a heavy feeling in my gut.

"You disapprove, DarkBairn?" Bereth eyed me with subtle mirth.

I remained mute as we approached yet a third wall, this one a third the height of the main exterior wall and clearly the oldest. Vines were draped like decor over the crumbling stone. In one section, the wall had collapsed in on itself. No invading force would find this an obstacle. The guards atop this small wall monitored us with the formal watchfulness of bored soldiers. Buckets of arrows sat ready for use next to a flickering torch, and a long rack of spears was propped against the stone wall. Here the stone was yellowed and caked with dirt. Old scrapes on the jagged surface showed attacks from battles past. Whatever it had once served as, it was no longer that. Inside the walls, everything seemed to have aged a thousand years. The squat barracks and small tavern looked older than the wall itself. Even the air smelled older.

"This place . . . it feels ancient. What is it?" I gazed about.

"This was once the location of the original Drucodian stronghold back in the First Era, although its true name has long since been forgotten," Bereth answered. "It held back the tides of darkness at the expense of a race of people. Once it stood but a small wall and a few buildings. Now it stands a mighty reminder of the power of the Elfinian race. We've mastered that which the Drucodians failed to. We've placed our most important advisors and meetings in here. We shall plan the destruction of Mordën in the same place as last time. These walls have guarded the very prosperity and longevity that The High City flourishes in." Bereth rubbed his chin. "It has been peace for them while we mop up the eastern plains. Many texts lie on this level, detailing the wanton death that was dealt in the early days. We would not have that happen again. Varglarian have spawned north of the Outpost and raid regularly the fishing villages and unprotected towns. We, the Elfin, have stretched our own forces to protect that which The High City deems 'undesirable.' Some view it our lot in life for our failures of old. Would you punish the present for the sins of the past? I see it as our duty to Erëthuïl. Many here do not share this same outlook."

A feeling of respect had dawned on me as I felt the city grow more and more ancient the further we rode. Where once the gleaming towers and looming walls held power, thatched huts and crumbling garrisons gave way to abandoned town squares and inns turned into storage centers. Rubble from fallen homes lay strewn, hidden beneath tall coarse grass. Rusted weapons littered the cobblestone. An ancient burial yard slept peacefully under oaks whose long leafy fingers swept the faded markers below. Even the people seemed older, not by age but by sun with bleached skin and thinning hair. They moved with reverence, as if quieted by the magnitude of their surroundings. The only thing that seemed to give the place life was the main road, which traveled from the base of the Westerly Road up like a snake into the heart of the city and out to the Ethero Basin where a great host of ships awaited transit.

"It is in that very square," Kissinger gestured with awe, "that King Elharan met with his generals before marching on his own father. Rumor has it he took a spear from a fallen Elfin warrior that his father had personally beheaded and, jutting it firmly into the ground so as its handle quivered in the morning breeze, stated, 'Here shall the fortunes of my people advance under the banner of a unified kingdom. No longer shall we fracture under the weight of our failures.'"

Bereth glanced at him but made no correction. The city continued to fly past as we followed Bereth and his guards through streets, down alleys, and over hills. I began to wonder if the King's Glistening Hall was in the heart of the mountains themselves ere we rounded a bend and approached a single wooden wall, stuck between two monstrous mountain peaks. Of all the buildings and beauty of the city, this wooden wall was the most basic. If you'd been in a hurry, you'd have missed it completely. There were no fancy flags nor banners to indicate that behind this was where the king resided. Bereth motioned us to stop and dismount.

"Open the gate!" he bellowed as the door, cleverly hidden in the wall, swung open and two Elfin guards advanced, spears at the ready.

"Lord Berëthelluïn," the foremost guard saluted, "your arrival brings warmth to our hearts and stamina to our minds."

Bereth saluted similarly and we were escorted through the wall. The gate slammed shut with finality. I felt the hairs on my neck straighten. All around, leaning against walls or seated upon upturned barrels, wooden pegs in hand, guards lounged about. They hurried to their feet at Bereth's approach and saluted. Bereth turned to us and was about to speak when a door in the wooden wall thundered open.

I turned as a graceful Elfin with a flowing gold cloak stepped down the short flight of stone steps. At his side, a man was talking, engrossed in what looked to be an important matter. The Elfin paused from his discussion and glanced at me. For a moment we made eye contact. Upon the Elfin's brow was a single gold and silver band. There were no fancy armaments save for his breastplate which bore the golden bow. At my side, Bereth kneeled. I followed suit, quickly, as did my companions.

"My king," Bereth murmured in a hushed tone. He spoke in a soft voice, in a language I could not discern. The other gazed upon him and gestured for us to rise. "All behold King Elharan of the Elfinian people. Long may you reign, and your prosperity grow!"

"Well met, Berëthelluïn." King Elharan withdrew his long hands into the sleeves of his tunic.

"Thank you, sire." Bereth glanced at me. "This here is the Dark-Bairn you requested."

"Come, let us speak in the privacy of my hall." Elharan turned and escorted us up the steps and into the King's Hall.

Inside, orange light was abundant. Great fires burned hot in their iron braziers. Guards with red cloaks lined the walls. Their long hair hung neatly around their shoulders. Swords were sheathed at their belts and in their hands, they held a spear and shield. In the center of the room was a long table of thick oak. It ran the length of the entire hall and on either side from end to end were massive chairs, the backs of which stretched nearly six feet high. Candles also lined the table. Their light glowed over plates of bistri and breads. Bowls of fruit and jewel-encrusted armor on display covered the center of the wood. Plates of gold and silver and oak were set before each chair as if expecting a meal any moment. At the far end of the hall, seated atop a dais, was a simple wooden chair.

"Commander Gisli sends his respect and tidings from the Eastern Garrison," Bereth continued. "He bids me to inform you all is well and no raids have been conducted in the past month."

"This report is a song unto my ears." Elharan made eye contact with me and straightened. "Approach, bairn."

I moved hastily and bowed out of respect. "My apologies for keeping you waiting."

"Don't ask for apols." The other waved a broad hand as a group of stiff Elfins crowded the room. "This court is no stranger to your history. When the last High King exiled Mordën to the Beyond, he inadvertently, through some power of the Luthi, opened a portal to your lands. It should come to no surprise of us that at some point people of those lands would find their way here. But many are suspicious in their comfort. Our bellies grow fat with the prosperity that Erëthuïl has generously laden us with. Our location in Ëonë and the Ethero Basin ensures our status remains unchecked despite the centuries past."

"You've never really mentioned your world," Arabella spoke. She gazed questioningly at me as if wondering whether she should ask.

"It is of a time past," I murmured. "I would sooner forget it than remember what I've lost."

Elharan leaned back in his chair. "You are probably wondering why I would so eagerly welcome you to my court and listen to what most would perceive as ramblings of a lunatic."

"Ramblings of a what?" Kissinger snorted. "You can ask any east of Ithuïn about the status of the Outpost and they'll all back our statements."

"You misunderstand my meaning." The Elfinian royal stared at the Human. "Always quick to judge and slow to understand. Word has long since reached me of the prophecy unfolding. I've known longer than most of the goings on in the BlackBurg's furnaces. A bairn crosses the misty aisle and within a fortnight rumors of Mordën's return are sparked. Such coincidences do not simply happen without a connection. I sent spies east to discover if the rumors were true. They journeyed, brave souls, across the waters to the BlackBurg . . . and never returned. Now amidst turmoil from fleeing patrons of the many taverns in Ithuïn coming to my doorstep, the DarkBairn himself arrives in my city. What's more, he journeys with a female of northern descent by her tongue and a ragged uncouth Human from the east. Your disdain for my people is not as veiled as you may believe." The last part he directed to Kissinger in an almost amused observation.

Kissinger blushed red and found sudden interest in the stone floor. He bit into an apple. For a long moment no one spoke.

"Tell me, DarkBairn, of what tidings you bring from the Outpost. Why do a maiden from the north, a bairn originating from The High City, and the answer to a prophecy of old seek a council with me?"

I cleared my throat. "Mordën marches in open defiance of the peace of Ëonë. I was there on the walls when his forces marched across the Bridge and waged war against my brothers-in-arms. They slaughtered all, including children. I watched great creatures, spiders of monstrous size, break down stone walls with their armored legs. Nightshades used Shaderian Travel to appear on our walls before they'd even breached them. And the Varglarian were beyond count of numbers. They never seemed to end. Lord Malziek, leader of the Outpost, was the last to fall, defending that place with his dying breath. I would not see his death go in vain. I was charged by him and another to bring this news to Avalon in hopes it would burn a fire in your blood. Perhaps you know him? DarSheer. Mordën targets the race of Men but in time he will turn his focus on the Elfinian empire. He will utilize fear and hatred and fire against all who defy him. If you think your people are free of his spies and lies you are sadly mistaken."

The group of stuffy Elfins blustered about in indignant annoyance. They stopped when Elharan raised a hand.

"You accuse some in my own hall of betrayal?"

"Not accuse, merely warn." I shook my head. "The only way the Shadow King could return was through a bairn as prophesied of old. I am that bairn and through me he returned in full force with a host of blackness ready to march and cover all the lands in fire. I've had to live with my involvement in all this. Sleepless nights I lie awake wondering if I'd just had the courage to defy him, if all this would be over. There are others, I'd presume, who would be keen to respond to his calls. I saw a world of peace brought to its knees and beheaded by the battle axe of betrayal."

Elharan smiled slightly and raised one hand.

"You may save the passionate eloquent speeches for another day, Phoenix. I am on your side. I simply wished to hear it from you. There are many who've cried foul in the past. They've seen shadows rising in the east and some have gone so far as to curse their child to the part of the bairn. When I first heard the rumors, I placed you as one of the unfortunate souls trapped by your father's lies. But then my own did not return to me and word reached my ears of a great evil spreading in the eastern lands. Tree and stone do not lie. They've been here since before my birth and will be here after my death. Those who do not listen to their whispers fall. If you have but the ear to listen, you can hear their tales from the beginning of time. I listened and I heard of your plight. The Elfins were brought into this world to destroy Mordën in ages past. We were not strong enough then, but we will not fail again. History will not discuss the great failures of the House of Elharan but of their foresight and strength in the face of evil. You have the gratitude of a nation, DarkBairn. Be at peace."

"That's it?" My words rang hollow. "Just like that? What now?"

"Now?" Elharan stood. "Now you sleep and rest for your hard work is done. Messengers have been dispatched to The High City and the Custodian. I suppose you are free to do as you will. My city is yours to enjoy as are its riches. Should you wish to join our efforts against Mordën, as I feel you will before the end, we would gladly welcome your swords. But now, my young masters, your duty is over."

Several grunts rippled through the court around Elharan as his political advisors grumbled to themselves. Several eyed me as if hoping their king would reverse his choice and have me thrown in a dungeon for blubbering madness.

The single window in the room had gone dark as the last rays of dusk vanished behind the mountains. In the far courtyards below, a song hummed on the breeze. A musician strummed an instrument as the singer, a female, raised her voice. The torches in the room cast long shadows up the stone walls where great banners hung. On each banner sat a face of pride and nobleness. The woman's voice began to crescendo with haunting beauty.

At my far-off stare, the king smiled. "She is singing the 'Nightly Farewell,' an ancient tradition for Elfins. We bid the night a short hold on us and yearn for the peace of the morning's smile. I will leave you to your own." Elharan gestured to the door. "There are rooms in The King's Tavern on the second tier. You are my guests and if you wish to remain here you are welcome. Be at peace, travelers of the night. Sleep and eat. You are safe here. Goodnight."

The words were obvious enough a dismissal, so we stood and exited the old hall. Outside, the wind had picked up and a few white spots danced at the edges of the light. I reached out a hand and felt the moist flake melt. The song rose in pitch as the trees swayed softly. Merchants and travelers had stopped to listen as the final glimpse of day was extinguished and the world fell into darkness. A burning orange disk hovered over the tossing trees on the edges of mountains. My heart ached as the last glow fell to the long arm of night. Already, the moon had climbed high into the sky and settled into its nightly watch.

"I can't believe we completed our mission," Arabella was saying to Kissinger.

"I thought, somehow, it would feel different," he murmured. "Like a millstone released from 'round our necks."

"But instead," I picked up, "it feels like somehow we've more to go. That we haven't completed our task, merely finished a portion of it."

"This is folly." Arabella tossed her head. "The mission was to get the news of Mordën's advances to King Elharan. DarSheer tasked us as much."

"We should sail over the basin and into the safety of the Western Ward," Kissinger glanced at me. "Phoenix?"

I inhaled the sharp fragrance of baking bread and humid air. It intertwined with the noises of carts rolling over the stones on the nearby road. Travelers in vibrant colors moved listlessly through trees and out of sight on their personal missions. It all seemed so arbitrary, the comings and goings of this world. Ebyians mixed with Inclings, drinking their way into the night. Elfins laughing in mirth as Men from the western cities told tales mesmerizing in content. There was no order, or if there was, it was hidden behind chaos. *Ash*! I blinked at the grey fleck on my eyelashes. Another fell before I could move. It was a foreboding sight, the world gone dark with the clouds weighing oppressively down. The roads were soon covered by an inch of soot. All around marveled and uneasy eyes strayed to the east. We needed no extra urgings to find the inn and head indoors. The innkeeper, a fat Elfin who insisted on bowing every time someone spoke, glanced up from his desk as the oaken door shuddered open.

Inside, warm light and a raging fire sent shivers down my back. Travelers seeking the same comfort filled the tables. Laughter spilled from private booths and atop wide tables patrons played games. A skinny man shouted angrily as an Elfinian merchant clicked a peg into a corner hole of the board. The other shrugged and was congratulated by those around him.

"Damn near impossible to beat a cheating golden!" the man cried.

"Hey!" the innkeeper shouted over the din. "There'll be none of that here, Trogg. Save it for your misses. Either pay the debt owed or clear out. I'm sure the bed of ash will be mighty comfortable tonight over my downed pillows. Blimey waste of space."

Trogg glowered and caught my eye. He stared at me for a moment as we brushed the ash from our cloaks and stepped inside. Reluctantly, he handed the Elfin several gold thruki. He then stood and crossed the tavern to stand next to us. The fat Elfinian turned and eyed us.

"Three weary travelers," he mused. "What be your names?"

"Arabella, Kissinger, and my name is Phoenix," I said nervously. Trogg continued to stare at us.

"The three from the east." He rubbed his jiggling chin. "I was told to expect you. My name is Lathium, the trusted barkeep here, well barkeep and owner. Not often do I receive such esteemed guests. Three rooms are made in your fashion, or should I say the fashion of Men. Trogg, bugger off now, blimey! These guests are not for your wandering 'ands."

"Hello," Trogg stared at me. His breath reeked of ale. "What's a bairn like you doing in a place like this? Who are you fair folk? A maiden and a brute? Your garb is not Avalon by craft. You style your hair different. Your eyes are heavy with travel. Where did you say you came from?"

"We do not wish to discuss our travels," Arabella said curtly. "And we thank you for allowing us to pass untouched by your unwelcome probes."

"A fire in this one's blood," he chuckled as he staggered from the counter and toward the door. "Watch yourself in the city, love. Many things happen in the wee hours of morn. And many more to come in the dark days ahead. Not much good looking for trouble when it's already found you. Remember the name Trogg."

He yanked the door open and fell into the cobbled darkness beyond. Lathium sighed and shook his thick head. His awkward ears, which stuck out, flapped against his head.

"Apologies, young travelers, for this most uncordial of welcomes. Trogg has been plaguing my patrons with his thieving paws for the last two nights. I haven't the heart to kick him out. Word from some others is he used to be a great man in his day. Shame to see such blood reduced to a drunken wreck. Anyways, you didn't come here to listen to old Elfin blabber. Three rooms are ready for you on the eastern wing. If you've found the outhouse, you've gone too far."

"Thank you." I accepted a thick metal key. Arabella and Kissinger did likewise.

"We have ale and the finest of foods from all over Ëonë. Most who stay here do so by personal invitation of the king. I won't be prying my honkin nose into your business, and I'll kindly ask you to do the same of those around you. Secrets are a bag of green thruki: it's good to have but easy to spend. Bug no one around you, keep your heads low, and no one will bug yer bag."

"Thank you for the warm Elfinian welcome." I smiled. "I've heard many tales of this proud city."

"Your first time here?" He leaned against the counter. "You lot wouldn't happen to be Outpost folk would yer?"

"Now now," Kissinger grabbed my elbow and forced a smile, "we did promise you to keep our noses out, how about you return the favor, old man?"

"Kissinger!" Arabella protested.

"He meant no 'arm." Lathium snorted with a gruff grimace. "I was proddin' where my nose ain't needin' to poke. I just happened to have some folk here from that place and simply was curious. My apologies. Enjoy your stay!"

"Well, you were rather rude." Arabella nudged Kissinger as Lathium returned to his customers.

"And he was rather nosy," Kissinger muttered under his breath.

The atmosphere inside was unlike any other inn I'd visited. Conversations were kept quiet and furtive glances were cast around. Deals were made and quick exchanges of money were had under cloak and robe. Several Elfinian merchants handed a man, no taller than my chest, a bag of coins. He produced a silver dagger with gold and green lettering on the steel blade. They oohed and aahed as he displayed it. In another corner, a wiry man with beady eyes watched from behind his hood. The fire in the hearth cast shadows over his face but he leaned into the light and sniffed. His teeth were yellow and cracked and one eye was but an empty socket. A second figure in the booth with him yanked him back and they began conversing heatedly. But nothing in the room captured my attention more than the being at the center table. To look at him from behind, one might believe him to be a tall human with grey skin. His arms and torso were covered in iron. But from the front, the cleft in his face and the wild eyes gave him a sullen look. His ears twitched like a mount's. They swiveled about and he gave me the impression he'd heard every word spoken in hushed tones about him. Thick, coarse black hair covered the being's head and fell to his back.

"By my eyes," Kissinger breathed, "that's a Drucodian."

"His name is Khergdoc," Lathium stopped nearby and whispered. "Strange times these are indeed for a Drucodian to be this far south. He came here on business from the north. King Elharan personally escorted him here. Won't speak his business to the likes of me. Can't say I'm offended though. Some take it a good omen, a Drucodian in my tavern. Who am I to spurn such ideas, novel or otherwise? Rumor has it he's made a deal with a band of Inclings, and they mean to ride south and try their hands at entering Glasbur. Bunch of Ebyian-created nonsenses if you ask me. Why, might you ask? Well, I am glad you asked, I shall answer. Inclings are a very quiet and peaceful race. A band of them would never ride to the ancient gates in the south and try their hand at adventure. It's a wild tale and no doubt the Drucodian is doing naught to dissuade it. That lot are a dramatic type. Can't say they don't have a flair for imposing, at the very least."

"Nor you the ability to read a room," Kissinger muttered. "Come, let us find a table where we may discuss our next moves in secrecy."

The mood had greatly diminished as we meandered through the angled tables. I couldn't help but twist my head to soak in the strangeness of the Drucodian as we passed him. Atop his pointed head, bands of gems glinted in the firelight. His eyes were large, glassy, and seemed sad. His skin moved almost like an ocean, rising, and falling with the tide. The cleft in his head formed like you were staring down into a valley. When I passed directly in front of him, his scan shifted from a gambling group of giggling bards to meet my eyes. He followed me even as I averted my gaze.

We settled at a table near the fire and Lathium came around and set tankards of ale on the table. A platter of cheese and bread was also set in the center next to a flickering candle. Kissinger leaned in conspiratorially as if the tongues of fire would spill our secrets.

"It's odd seeing a Drucodian on the road," Kissinger glanced, "and sad, honestly, knowing that there is no hope for the future. Imagine waiting for the day the last of your kind perishes."

"They were cursed from the beginning," Arabella mourned softly, "a race doomed to fall."

The Drucodian turned as if hearing her words. I couldn't imagine he went anywhere where he wasn't the main topic of conversation. Every eye on him. Every mouth speaking in hushed awe. Reminded every day of his doomed existence.

"So, what now?" Arabella cleared her throat.

"We could journey south to meet up with DarSheer and Othrain," Kissinger said. He brought his tankard up to his lips.

"No." I shook my head. "He told us the roads were unsafe and he'd meet us here. It wouldn't be wise to risk it. I vote we remain here and stand the watch with the Elfinian warriors."

"We've fought our war." Kissinger stared at me. "Why must we fight theirs too?"

The room was silent as the flames popped and a log split in two. We watched the embers fly and smoke pour up the chimney. Warmth flooded the room, and the shadows were frightened off, temporarily. I glanced at Arabella who was gazing intently into the fire.

"All that awaits these people is death," Kissinger gritted his teeth.

"Then I shall share their fate," I said.

"How can anyone fight against death itself?" His voice was barely above a whisper. "You would so recklessly throw your life aside for a city that does not care?"

"King Elharan cares."

"Enough to lose your life?"

Her face appeared in my mind's eye and my voice broke. "What else have I to live for?"

Before long, the logs were hissing to themselves as the last of the flames died out and the glowing embers lit the shadows across my face. Kissinger puffed on a pipe brought to him by a sleepy Lathium and before long the less eager patrons had vanished into the dark recesses of the inn. Only some and a bard with his gloshee remained in the lights of the fire. Those who hugged the comfort of darkness listened as he strummed and began to sing. His voice rose in pitch as he seemingly commanded the air about him to swirl.

There's a tale to tell you see of a burg divided by rippling sea. What happened to the noble city of green?

Oh the bards like to harp on the hardships they faced
but no one knows for sure
One day those gates like fate shut tight so no light could
pierce their gaze
The road dried up, a river in the heat of summer, till
plunderers came to visit
What they found was gates locked shut by chains in a
kingless rain
No proof of war has ever been gathered nor exodus
from the docks beyond

The ships all sit in the salty spit, their masts all awry,
their hulls in the sky
The mystery of Glasbur has stumped the greatest
minds and their finds with literary binds
What happened to that fateful city of green?

The legend in his right, a warrior of fright, Drasmor
and his men entered that den
And none have seen them hence. Mighty an Elfin he
was brought low by the bow
And none have seen him since. No sword could save
what the shield couldn't block
The rock which led to our hero's abysmal and lonely
death
Gather near as I tell the tale of what happened to the
mythical city of green!

No sign or warning of times gone ill were their last and
final days
A mighty Drucodian city of old brought to its knees
again
Their banners run high in the amber sky, yet they wave
no liege lord today
The secrets they could say if only they could like a drop
of the sun's golden ray
But still it sits beside itself on the coast of the kingdom
dark
Hear this part, read this tale, of what happened to the
city of green.

The rumors run rampant round the taverns of ghosts
and banshees in the night
The fright they'd cause the light they'd dim in that
howling cursed sight

*Scrolls speak of specters shrouded on the sea, like sirens
singing spells
No one knows what happened that night on the nine-
teenth of 3400 TSE to the doomed city of green!*

*Was it spells that dwelled in haunting oceanic swells
Was it cries that lied and defied all reason and drove
the mad men to the docks
Was it darkness harking like a lark upon the city there
The scrolls end short, the letters run dry of what
happened to that coastal kingdom
The legend lives on, the rumors continue to spawn
I sing the tale of The Lost Kingdom of Glasbur
Let all else pale in comparison to the failure of the
mighty city of green!*

The morning brought with it a sliver of light into my room. I
stirred beneath the threadbare covers and yawned. The sun was warm
on my face and for a moment I forgot my troubles and felt content.
This all ended at the shouts that echoed from right outside the door.
I sighed and rubbed my eyes. In this manner and for many days to
come, a weary but relaxing comfort came from the quiet isolation of
my room. The sun rose and fell like the seasons and the warmth came
and went. All around seemed to pass by sleepily, for merchants sold
their wares and travelers journeyed across the Ethero Basin to visit the
great city. Ebyians trundled to and from great mines in the mountains. They were secretive but I managed to overhear a group of them
murmur about sinister news from the east. Messengers came and
went from The High City and guards paced the battlements cease-
lessly. On the outside, the city slept like normal, but underneath a
hive of activity was taking place. The mornings had gone from warm

and bright to dull and grey. Even the purple mountains capped in green flowing trees could not distract the eye.

It was on one of these grey mornings where the sun had hidden its shyness behind a bank of clouds that Arabella found me. I'd tucked up behind a tree, a great oak with widespread branches where the pitter patter of rainfall could drown out the din of vendors beyond. The scrolls in my hand were as boring as they were long, which was to say greatly. Yet it served its purpose for already I'd learned much in the ways of Avalon and the history of Ëonë.

"I thought I'd find you here," were the only words she said as she sat beside me.

We listened and let the fog roll from the tips of the mountains to the city below. Carts wheeled from street to street as children raced up and down alleys crying out and giggling. The sounds were mirthful, not anything like Ithuïn or the Outpost. One could almost imagine settling down where the daises grew and maybe even going out for an occasional stroll on the cobbled path. There was no starvation of views. To the north stood the tall mountains. Their snow-tipped peaks jutted into the cloudy sky and were hidden from our view. To the east were the sprawling plains and the Westerly Road itself. Folks of all shapes and sizes came and went with all types and manners of goods to sell. Parties of Ebyians seeking work and roving bands of Incling merchants were frequent guests of the road. Strangers from far east came bringing treasures of the sea. We'd seen no more of Khergdoc but there was a small group of Drucodians who, much to the intrigue of those around them, entered the city on business they would not divulge. Rivers and the occasional lake graced the plain and broke its green monotony. The south was a near mirror of the north and a bit west, save for the glistening shore of the Ethero Basin. It was the lifeblood of Avalon and without it there would be no city. I'd been told it was the only known way to cross the mountains without going thousands of miles to the northern and southern tips of the range. This one singular break meant the Elfinians held dominate sway over demand and transit. Their monopoly on this route ensured their ability to live in luxury.

"Not much else to do," I finally returned. "I just had to tell an Ebyian that I would not in fact bless his pickaxe and mining endeavors. He seemed to think I had an aura of luck."

"The day is splendid and the sun warm, when it breaks from the clouds," she chuckled. "I fear that before long poets and musicians will have blown your reality into famed legend. The Traveler from Beyond. It has a ring to it. I passed an Elfinian with a galosh stringing so loudly that everyone in the area had to shove their fingers into their ears."

"What was his song?"

"The mystery of the DarkBairn. What else?" She shrugged.

I leaned back against the curved trunk of the tree. There was a soft silence save for the rustling of the tree and drops of rain.

"I think you hold me to an esteem they do not." I closed my eyes. "I believe they would drive me from the city if I wasn't protected by King Elharan's own guard."

"That's not what I've heard from the meetings in Elharan's council" She leaned her head against my shoulder. "Many scouts have returned from the eastern shores and their tidings are grim. A black host moves at a fast pace toward these very walls. Some more cynical in the council have of course raised objections to these 'younger scouts' and their 'desired need for excitement.'"

"I cannot fault them," I said feeling a weight settle. "I wish it were but rumors to spur excitement. That all the helplessness and darkness I've felt was but my own insanity and not an omen of what's to come."

"How can one be so sad in a beautiful place like this?" Arabella gazed about.

"Beauty to some is sadness to others. You see a sprawling metropolis where I see a city doomed to die."

"Have you been talking to Ëberith again?" Arabella seemed genuinely concerned.

"No," I snorted. "Well, maybe. But he has a point. History proves itself. This is not unlike the beginnings of the Second Great Battle all those eons ago."

"If history proves itself true again," she stood, brushing leaves from her pants, "then we shall triumph over evil once more. Come now, I mean to whisk you away. You've sat and brewed in your own festering thoughts for nigh an age and a half. Come where it is warm, and the laughter of children force the dreariness away. You brood and let your thoughts command your mood."

I took her hand and she led me out from under that great tree. Its branches waved as if in farewell.

We moved over the hard roads, their uneven stones tripping horses and man alike. Those more familiar with the area kept to the sides of the road to avoid being run into by those less familiar. It didn't take long for my mind to clear of the shadows which had taken it. For all and around laughed a band of merry children, no older than ten. They danced and tossed a small sack, all whilst singing a tune. I laughed and Arabella nudged me, her eyes twinkling.

The breeze above took a less sinister look and the sun cast off the clouds. Its warmth returned and once again the beauty of Avalon was spelled out for me. Indeed, its glow was so bright I had to cover my eyes. From our vantage point in the highest tier of the city, we could see the buildings far below and beyond them the sprawling plains outside the walls.

My mind blanked when I saw the golden serpent winding its way from the foot of the nearest hill toward our gates. I immediately thought the enemy was upon us, but then realized they bore the arms of Elfinians and in that their golden armor was a testament.

"The gates! Our own return and they bring tiding!" the call went up and the children forgot their game.

"Who is it, do you think?" Arabella shielded her eyes with one hand.

"In these meetings you've been in, did they mention a force of riders?" I inquired.

"Only that the outlying villages and outposts were to be emptied upon the arrival of the black host itself. Oh my, do you think . . ." She covered her mouth.

"If these are them," I said grimly, "then war is upon us. Quick, the answer is very important."

I sprinted faster than I'd ever sprinted before, outpacing even the fastest youth as I made my way from gate to gate down toward the arriving mass. My stomach tossed and my side ached. In the depths of my soul I knew—beyond any logical reasoning—it had begun.

Chapter 6

The Scarlet Rider

D ODGE!" THE COMMAND WAS followed by the clang of metal as DarSheer advanced. The jeers and taunts of fellow guards
filled the barmkin.

"Aim for the legs, Phoenix!" One called. "He can't fight if he's legless."

"An astute observation, Freth." I laughed. "Perhaps you'd like to face
me after I send DarSheer crawling legless for his life?"

The courtyard itself seemed to roar with laughter as I parried another
strike. Even Topper had abandoned his string playing and joined in the
merriment. Atop the battlements, Malziek paused from his examination
of the guards and watched the action below. A small smile appeared on
his hairy face.

"He's weaker on his right side," Brenneth called. "He overextends to
compensate for it."

"Is this my lesson or do you mean to rile up the whole courtyard
against me?" DarSheer pleaded.

"I can't help it if my admirers wish to see me the victor." I knocked
his blade aside and slapped his wrist with the blunt edge. He cursed and
grabbed where the skin had turned red.

"Blast it all, Phoenix." He hopped from one leg to the other. "I said
sword combat only. I expressly said no bodily contact!"

"*An enemy won't stop while you suck on your wound like an infant.*"
I stepped forward. Before he could react, I'd driven the point to his chest. I stopped when he yelped. Brenneth cheered loudly, ever my supporter, as the onlookers descended into the training yard with triumph. They lifted me up onto their extended arms and carried me around, chanting my name.

"All hail the victorious bairn!" Dwaith blew into his horn.

Topper began to strum a tune and before long the men began to sing in a loud booming chorus.

> Well, we went to see the sea you see
> Yet what do you think we saw instead
> Cresting the sea we saw the bairn ahead
> And we shouted his name in triumph
> Oh hold back your steeds and shield your lads
> For the greater one they see
> Keep back your wives and your daughters too
> For their hearts now go to the bairn of the sea

I let loose a cheer and Brenneth approached. He laid a crown made from broken twigs upon my helm and I enjoyed one final roar of approval before they set me down.

"Riding high on the wave of pride, bairn?" DarSheer rubbed his chest but smiled good-naturedly. "I'm afraid I'm all out of medals."

"Your respect is the only medal I need." I squeezed his outstretched hand and the match officially ended. I picked up my cloak, which I'd cast into the mud. I now regretted that choice. The rain began to pelter down in small droplets. They plinked off the armor like small beads.

"It appears we best head to the tavern," Brenneth called. "The men wish to drink in your honor."

"Tell the men I appreciate their kind words." I waved dismissively. "However, I have a small rickety cot with my name on it."

"Good fighting!" KcNuck waved from across the courtyard.

"Well played, DarkBairn!" Another voice barked from the ramparts. I waved to both.

"You don't mean to sleep, do you?" DarSheer asked as he put the training swords in a bucket. "You've used that excuse once too many."

"Maybe I'm a weary codger," I challenged.

"Or maybe you're a man who is hiding something."

"It's nothing." I began walking toward the sleeping huts. "I just have been feeling off lately. I've had this headache and I went to the medicine room but Lëuthorn could not help. In fact, he said it was 'a mere fragment of your young imagination.' Blasted medics…"

"He means well. But if you truly feel this bad perhaps tomorrow when the sun dawns we can ride west for a small village. I know only one man who is better at the craft of medicine than Lëuthorn. Any idea what's been causing the headaches and nightmares? Maybe it has to do with your memories returning?"

"I don't know." I stared east where I knew, over the wall, the Black-Burg sat. "Every time I feel like something is about to happen, I get this splitting headache. It's only there for a minute at a time but it happens with enough frequency it's now a daily nuisance."

"You say before something is about to happen?" DarSheer rubbed his chin. "Do you know when exactly? Before a meal? Sleep?"

"No." I shook my head. "I'll try to come up with a better answer tomorrow. For now, I need some sleep if I am to properly man the wall tonight. I know the moment I close my eyes, I face a world of uncomfortable blackness, a suffocating truth. Every moment I see him!"

"My dear Phoenix," he exhaled, "relying on your emotions to guide you through the trials of life is no way to live. Emotions are good, but utilized as the fuel of your existence they can damage you beyond repair. Stick to your head, your smarts, and you will survive. On the battlefield, a Varg will not wait for you to come to terms with the many deaths you've inflicted. He will strike when your guard is at its lowest. You must be levelheaded, calm, and distance yourself from the viper inside you. At a tavern, sipping ale in honor of the victorious dead, then let the burning sensation of hope and honor stir your heart. Choose where you let your emotions run. But do not let them buck as an untamed mare."

We parted ways and I walked the remainder to our hut. I pushed through the door and walked across to my cot. As I did so, a sharp stinging began to penetrate my eye and, dizzy, I collapsed to the floor. The world spun and darkness adopted three new shades of black as I moaned and rolled on the floor. A voice as smooth as silk but as treacherous as a viper hissed in my head. I cried out and clapped my hands over my ears.

"No, begone!" I shouted.

"Your use is at an end."

"I said begone!"

"Watch as your host bleeds."

Before I fully lost consciousness I saw, standing before me, a man in black, a hood covering his ghostly pale face. The hood covered half his face, ending right above the nose. With lips a pale hue of scarlet he grinned. He withdrew the hood as tears flooded down my cheeks.

Arabella had to do her best to keep up with me, for I practically flew down the streets, leaping over carts, knocking aside unfortunate pedestrians, and crashing into elderly Elfin. They cursed at me in their tongue and gestured emphatically. I shouted many apologies but at my speed they hardly heard a word. Even if they had, the branches of trees and bushes did more damage to me than their undoubtedly harsh words. But the blood that trickled down my arm was forgotten as quickly as the scratch happened.

An immense cold filled my lungs as the wind whipped through my long hair. I skidded along the uneven stones nearly capsizing a small stand. Its owner cursed at me as I kept running. Again, the cold seized me and I tripped, this time rolling head over heels and tumbling into a small bush. In the sky overhead, a great suffocating cloud descended. Droplets tripped and toppled down. Shopkeepers hurriedly secured their wares and mothers urged their offspring indoors. Arabella came to a stop and stared down at me. I lay on my back, gasping for breath.

"The front gate is down there." She pointed slowly.

"Oh really?" I stood and brushed prickles from my shirt. "How good of you to know the way."

The final gate loomed high overhead. Atop the walls, bowmen rushed to and fro. They called down and some leapt high and over the edge, holding on to taut rope as they slid down them and came to stop at the base of the gate. Berëthelluïn was already commanding the scene as the ironclad gates swung slowly open. He turned at our approach. Over his head hung the impressive golden banners of the Elfinian nation. The golden archer stood proud, surveying the great city of Avalon. Except in addition, it rippled with palpable unease as horns blew atop the battlements. Drums beat feverishly.

We came to a stop as a host of bowmen hurried from the inner city and marched quickly up toward the top of the wall. Arabella held her hand across my chest. Behind them came a group of mounted spearmen. The foremost reined his mount to a stop and glanced down.

"My Lord Berëthelluïn," his voice was stiff but respectful, "the scouts beyond should be escorted in. Allow my host to act as a rear guard, ensure they are not attacked."

"Do not be hasty, Captain Aroditha," Bereth said calmly. "No black army can be seen and the green trees beyond speak of a neutral ground. These are simply our own returning from missions to bring us tidings. Tell your group to hold at the turn of the road."

I glanced at Arabella who was recovering her breath. She eyed me with an upturned brow. Upon the battlements a cry went up. It was repeated though barely audible.

"Shadows and death! Ruination has come!"

Berëthelluïn could no longer contain the men before him, and they galloped out of the open gate. Bereth watched them go, arms folded. He saw my stare and grimaced.

"They run as children to their play. Many here have experienced less war than you have, bairn. Their blood is green with newness."

"Yet surely their courage speaks for itself," I said. "They would die for this city. Look even now, they ride with the wind in their hair and a smile on their face."

"They ride for the exhilarating idea of war."

Horns blew again as I watched the arriving group straggle closer to the main gates. From afar they'd seem long and impressive, a golden snake winding through the valleys. Now, as they neared, I saw their wounds and fear. Some were supported by their compatriots whilst others were tossed over the backs of steeds. Those uninjured jogged at the edges and front of the host. Gasps escaped the onlookers' lips as they saw, behind the force, a black cloud seemingly moving toward the city. Red light flashed in its thick thunderhead.

"That is no ordinary thundercloud," Berëthelluïn growled. "The walls! To the walls, all of you!"

He leapt, two stone steps at a time, up the stairways. Elfins rushed the walls and drew arrows to cold wooden bows. They stood rank upon rank, their golden hair flowing in the breeze. Banners spaced evenly atop the walls fluttered majestically. Horns blew and now a deep drum issued from the deep of the mountains.

"They're sick, or injured," Arabella cursed as she stood motionless in the center of the road.

"Arabella!" I yanked her arm as the first of the weary Elfins crossed the gate.

As they staggered by, my mouth fell open. Blood caked the armor of nearly every single warrior. Some lay crying in agony, missing limbs. One particular Elfin was cursing the world as he held his hands to his face, where both eyes were missing. His once fair hair was tangled and matted with blood. This was not just a group of retreating villagers. Women, their cries loud as the men, rushed the wounded and instantly began carrying the most grievously injured toward medical huts.

"They came from the shadows," an Elfin gasped painfully, "like beings from the night. There was no hope. They've taken control of the eastern border."

"Aye," a man in tattered clothes wept into his weathered hands, "my bairn is ribbons on the moors. They've taken them, and I do not know where they have placed them."

The lead of the pack, followed closely by Aroditha, came to a stop before me. His one good eye flitted about frantically. The other socket was covered by a golden plate.

"Take me to the King's Guard," he spat. Blood was mixed with his saliva. "Will someone take me to the *blasted* Guard?"

"We should go back to the tavern," Arabella said uneasily. "This is not a matter for us. Leave this to the Elfins."

But her words fell on an empty space for I'd already begun to scrabble up the steep steps. The air seemed colder, if that was possible. The noises below faded to a soft whisper. Berëthelluïn was shouting orders to his men as they took aim at the growing cloud. It had stopped advancing but that had not kept it from growing. It shielded the entire city now in a black haze.

"Bereth!" I shouted over the drums and horns. He partially turned, his eyes grim.

"Bairn, this is not the place for you. Return to your tavern."

Before I could respond, from the cloud, seven whisps of smoke shot out like tendrils from a sea creature. They wove and dove through the air toward the city itself. A league or less spanned the edge of the cloud and the great gates below. The cloud itself was thicker than the darkness of a moonless night.

"Fire!" Berëthelluïn roared. He waved a flaming torch and hurled it over the edge of the walls. Hundreds of arrows were launched and sailed on their deadly mission. They arched over the plains below. They vanished into the black pillar. To the naked eye there seemed no discernable change. "Hold! Hold!" He raised his fist and squinted down.

Far below, a mounted rider cantered lazily from the mist. The horse was black, and it snorted, stamping the ground with one iron hoof. Its rider bore a red cloak which flowed out behind him. He turned his head slowly to stare up at us. Despite the great distance, I had no trouble making out his hissing voice. It was like the scales of a serpent slithering over pebbles.

"*I am the Messenger from Death itself,*" the voice rose over the wind.

"Begone, cur and scum!" Berëthelluïn bellowed. I wasn't sure if the rider below would even hear but he smiled in response.

"*You have been granted mercy from the Shadow King. All who fall and bend their knees to his touch shall find themselves free from the grip and weight of war.*"

As he spoke, the seven whisps of cloud shot down toward the ground and morphed into seven robed figures made entirely of ash and smoke. With the change of the wind, they reformed. Great cloaks flowed about them and in their fiery breastplates was carved a sinister shape. The Hourglass. Their red eyes glowed with hunger. In unison, the Seven drew their swords and raised them, point first, toward me. Not Berëthelluïn. Not Arabella. Nor any of the guards atop the stone walls. They pointed them directly at me.

"*I am the Scarlet Rider.*" The rider smiled. "*I will not waste words on fools who value their city over their life.*"

"You're equally a fool if you believe King Elharan, ruler of the mighty Elfinian nation, hero to the free peoples of the Eastern Ward, and always and ever a thorn in your master's side, will simply leave the protection of his walls." Berëthelluïn snorted derisively. "You would ask the king and his folk to walk unarmed in a valley of vipers."

"*I will not speak to your golden.*" The Scarlet Rider's cheeks widened. His teeth were blackened. His long red tongue licked out like a serpent's. "*I will speak only with the DarkBairn.*"

Berëthelluïn turned in shock and stared at me. Red lightning flashed off my face as I swallowed. All around the wind howled with a ferocity that sent banners tearing from their poles and flying over the city below.

Ever since I'd left the Outpost, I'd been beset with nightmares of a hooded figure smiling from a black ocean. Every night I'd battled with every skillset I had, barely surviving to see the sun rise. Now my time had arrived. I pivoted and set my shoulders.

"Open the gates!"

Berëthelluïn stepped close, his hair tangled. His eyes were wide with confusion, and I sensed that confusion mirrored in every soldier nearby.

"You must be mad," Bereth spat. "I will not open my gates to let any evil the chance at an easy victory. If they hope to defeat us, they better have brought an army the like of which this world has never seen. Our walls are tall, our honor unblemished. Stay fast, young bairn, for you have much to learn."

"I will not speak as equals," I turned and shouted down. "For you are but a slave. If you wish to converse with me, you will do it here and now."

Out on the main road, the single wall of black cloud was intimidating. The red lights pulsating sent shivers down my spine. Atop the wall it was easy to watch *him* with little fear; after all, what can kill over such a great distance? In my head, a voice began to sing a soft haunting melody. What were the lyrics? They seemed so familiar. As if they were more a part of me than words on a page. The Scarlet Rider spoke in lilting mockery.

"*Of the golden halls, none shall remain. Of the weeping city, all shall fade. The tales of glorious men shall cease and the age of the Elfin perish beneath ere the return of Mordën in darkness upon Ëonë in the soul of a bairn in shadowed crossing . . .*"

". . . o'er the misty aisle," I finished grimly. "I am the bairn. What now?"

"*The Shadow King's promise is still one of truth. I was once a mortal as yourself. I was enslaved. Now I stand, his voice, charged with bringing the destruction of this entire city. Must it come to that? The ruination of such ancient beauty?*"

"The people here, they won't simply let you raze it." I shook my head. My voice was hoarse.

"*I'm counting on it.*" The Scarlet Rider leaned forward.

My eyes widened and I took a step back. My head split in two as a horrible scream filled my ears. I dropped to one knee and gripped my skull. The shadowy figures advanced on me with cold urgency. My hearing lessened and I cried out. The scream. I knew her. In a flash, my vision went black.

The knife appeared in her chest and her scream filled the air. Blood ran down her shirt. She turned and her eyes were filled with the absolute horror that accompanied betrayal. I tried to wade through the cold water which lapped around my calves. Suddenly, in the distance, a great plume of fire erupted and I could see the outlines of buildings and even further off, the great wall itself. Sound returned fully and I could hear the anguished cries of the dying. Blood and tears ran down the street, mixed in one awful concoction. Children huddled in door frames, languishing in the horror around them. Bodies filled the gardens. Once beautiful flowers now lay strewn about the fallen bodies. Torchlight flickered and beyond the docks which I now stood upon, I saw an undulating horde of black forms running from house to house, skewering injured with relish and greed. Screams broke the crackling of flames. Wood snapped under its heat and whole houses fell into themselves. A single golden banner floated through the air like a feather from a forgotten creature. The fires gave me just enough light to see the archer as a single spark sent the entire piece ablaze. Bells and gongs and drums and horns rang out the call. Bodies floated in the water about me. Their dead faces stared up. Their pale skin seemed ghostly in the orange light. The closest body opened its eyes and gazed in morbid glee at my look of horror.

"Phoenix!" She wept bitterly as she fell to the ground.

It wasn't the cry of pain. It wasn't the cry of horror. It was the cry of inconsolable grief.

Behind her, a shadowy form stood. I couldn't make out its face or anything identifiable but even so, I waded forward until I came up on a dry portion of the docks. To my left, a great vessel slowly tilted on its side as flames ate away at it. Men leapt from the tallest portions of the masts and were no more. They screamed as they spun head over heels.

I looked up as a new figure stepped into the fading orange light. He stood but a few feet from me on the docks. His cloak flowed behind him. His pale face held the same stretched corpse-like appearance. The flesh was stretched over his bony visage. His black hair was almost perfectly set atop his temple. His lips were ashen and his eyes black as night. Somehow, despite the stench of fire and death all around us, his scent reached me. Like a freshly buried body. His tunic and pants seemed made of living shadow. They formed and reformed.

"I promised you a chance to return," he said softly. "You have made a jest of my offerings and so all these will pass."

Mordën grabbed my throat with his free hand. His skin was colder than ice. His gaze was deadlier than the sword he held. He exhaled close as I choked.

"Deliver this message and vision to the free peoples of this world. Their Shadow Prince has returned. My arm is long and my reach fills the depths of the caverns below the Fallen Peaks. My rule shall stretch from the Isle of Meninïn to the BlackBurg. All will submit before the rise of my kingdom. This is what awaits to those who foolishly resist: death and tears and bloodshed."

My hearing returned like a growing windstorm. I wiped the blood from my nose. My body was still in shock over what I'd seen. It was so real I felt as if I'd truly witnessed *it*. In my head, a woman's voice sang a haunting melody. Arabella was at my side, hands on my arms, as she spoke to me. But once again my hearing seemed to have failed me. All I could hear was someone shouting for the herbwoman.

"I am fine!" I swatted the prying hands of an old crone as she tried to grab me. "Leave me be, woman, I am fine."

Arabella stared at me with concern even as Kissinger rushed into view. His youthful exuberance was extinguished. His eyes flashed with anger.

"What happened, Phoenix?" Kissinger leaned against the wall. Arabella stood at my side. "The people of the city speak of a tempest about to break on these walls. What did you hear? Does he ail you more? Has he visited your mind?"

"It is happening as he foresaw." I blinked slowly. "Kissinger, I am not now so confident."

I glanced back out over the wall and was amazed to see the shadow of pulsating amber was gone. The grey clouds had returned, and rainfall was imminent. The rider below and his seven were also gone. Kissinger remained mute, which was unlike him, until I got to the end, then he fidgeted with his sword handle. I spoke of the burning city and vessels capsizing in the waters. I relayed the images of corpses floating in the water.

"Oh, Phoenix." Arabella gritted her teeth. "You must know all that was a nightmare of dark proportions. Mordën means to sow dissention and chaos before he attacks. He seeks to implant within you dismay so you will not fight him."

"Besides, even you must know we will not just lay our arms down and let that depraved shadow cover us." Kissinger spat into the dirt. "King Elharan has called a council to meet tonight. I think he means to launch an offensive. He cannot wait for an invasion. The peoples will look to their king in this darkening hour. If he appears weak then they shall despair."

"And I shall go as one of them." I felt the comforting presence of my sword hilt. "If this be my hour to show my honor, let it be laid bare. No whisperings of evil will sway me."

"And we will be there with you, from today until our final." Arabella smiled grimly.

"Together, forever." Kissinger stood in the torchlight.

And for a brief moment I felt a haunted memory of years past. There had been another time I'd spoken with such determination. There had been another time I'd set out on a quest to fight against a shadowy figure, and my friends then had also pledged to be there no matter what.

"I do not ask this of you. To follow me is to welcome unwanted attention from those who know me as the DarkBairn. Mordën has a way of finding me no matter where I go."

"Look around you," Kissinger snorted. "We're not exactly free of our own pasts. If Mordën wants you, he'll find a swifter defense than he'll have anticipated. I don't go down easy."

"I saw my entire village burned and mutilated." Arabella drew her dagger and held it. It reflected the flickering light. "I am no stranger to this game either. You have my oath that I will not waver. I welcome death, for what else do I have to live for?"

She glanced at Kissinger who gazed back unblinking. They exchanged thoughts. Without another word I stepped from the wall, down the stairs, and felt a cold chill from the evening breeze. The stars twinkled overhead. Torchlight filled the main road as it wound from the great wall toward the king's chambers. Bereth had already moved ahead of us and was presumably in the council. The figure on the mount and the seven shapes had not attacked and nothing more seemed to come of their sudden arrival.

It took long to weave our way to the final terrace. As we passed beneath the low walls and small door, the guards atop watched me. They didn't observe me as last time with an air of intrigue. Now they watched me with apprehension. The King's Hall was alive with hurried and frantic movement. Guards watched those who came and went with intense scrutiny. Scholars and Elfin of the court whispered darkly to each other as I moved past them.

Inside, a warmer light showed dozens of scrolls open on long tables. Thickly robed Elfin peered over them chattering intensely. Two warriors in the rich golden armor of the king's personal guard stopped us as we moved to open the throne room doors.

"We're here to join the council." I gestured.

"Forgive me, DarkBairn," one said, "we did not recognize you."

They swung the doors open and we entered. It was stiflingly hot as dozens of candles and several braziers billowed with hungry heat. King Elharan stood at the end of a long table. Dishes and scraps of food were being whisked away by servants as Berëthelluïn slammed a fist to the table.

"The coward ran before us like prey to the hunter's bow. They are weak. The shadow is gone and with it the threat of darkness. The sun shines as bright as before. There is hope."

"Such an act of aggression should be met in force," a stocky Elfin agreed. "He crossed our borders and has laid waste to our eastern garrisons and borders. If the others see we do not retaliate for such an action, we will become the laughingstock of our people. To allow this scum to walk freely over our lands is to allow tongues to wag of the incompetence and fear of their leader."

"Watch your tongue, Aroenal," a third Elfin with a silver breastplate spoke softly. "You speak of King Elharan as if he were a soldier beneath you."

"I can speak for myself, Kevdar." King Elharan raised two fingers. "Aroenal, despite his lack of political fineness, is not incorrect. The people will be looking to us now to see our reaction to such a clear invasion. I wished ignorance, that the words spoken from our newcomers were words of chaos. Such is not so. This foul . . . Phoenix!"

The entire room paused and turned. My cheeks flamed with the new attention. I stood tall and waited for Elharan to gesture me forward.

"My apologies, great lords, and King Elharan, for the intrusion." I bowed slightly. Kissinger and Arabella mimicked my move. "After today, I believe I have much to offer in the discussions to come."

The room was silent as each studied me. Parchment rustled in the distance as scholars pored over their rich illustrations.

"Please, someone offer chairs to our young friends." Elharan motioned. He sat down and the other Elfin did the same.

I allowed myself a few moments to calm myself as Arabella and Kissinger introduced themselves to the scowling scholars and spoke of the roles they'd played in getting me here safely.

I told them everything, from the first moments of my journey way back, years in my shadowed past. I told them of losing my mother. Those particular memories had begun to resurface. Others like Temper and Quire and the mountain had returned. Some areas were grey so I skipped over any details. When it came to the point of Mordën entering my soul and using me to open the Portal, Kevdar hissed inwardly.

"The fulfilling of the prophecy," he murmured. "This one is the DarkBairn of lore?" The others nodded in silent confirmation. They shuffled awkwardly as if distressed by my very presence in their hallowed chamber.

I moved on to the first few years I'd been at the Outpost. When I recalled the dead faces of the stable boys, of Brenneth, the room grew solemn.

"That foul cursed beast never knew the difference between innocent children and warriors," said one they called Jyrre; he scowled.

"There are times I wonder if I have the stomach for all of this," I said. "Sometimes I feel the fire in my veins but when I look upon the death and destruction that the BlackBurg has spawned, I yearn for a warm bed and the heavy weight of covers to hide beneath."

"Not all are so quick to take a life or find enjoyment in the destruction of war." Bereth leaned forward. "Take heart in this."

"I FOUND IT!" The words ricocheted off the stone walls as the doors burst open and a thin Elfin rushed in. He waved a scroll enthusiastically before slowly lowering his arm. His eyes widened as he realized who was all here.

"Please, step forward. You've found your motivation, now execute it with equal determination," Aroenal snorted. "What have you found that was important enough to disturb this council?"

"Yes, my lords and king." The Elfin bowed low to the ground. "We were charged, that is my booksmen and I, were charged with discovering the root of the Prophecy. We've found it. My king, it is far worse than we originally surmised."

"Leave the surmising to the warriors." Aroenal snatched the parchment from the other. "Begone."

The Elfin bowed again and hurried from the room, though his cheeks were as flushed as mine had been. I bit my tongue. Aroenal had no place speaking to him in this manner. Before I could speak my mind, he had unrolled it and spoke the all-too-familiar words. This time, there was more.

Of the golden halls none shall sing
Of the weeping city all shall fade
The tales of glorious men shall cease
And the age of the Elfin perish beneath

At the return of Mordën in darkness upon Ëonë
In the soul of a bairn in shadowed crossing o'er the misty aisle

For the sword shall shatter and the shield shall yield
In the darkest days on the blood-soaked field
When the golden gaze on the truth thus steals
And the Elfin throne bends the crown and kneels
As the battle rages in unending steel.

The bottom of the scroll was torn in half. The uneven edges of the tear taunted me.

"That last part, that's new," Kissinger said bluntly. "That last part wasn't mentioned before. What exactly does that mean?"

"It means, young Kissinger," Elharan exhaled, "it appears the end is just about to begin."

"My king," Berëthelluïn bowed, "I recommend we gather our forces of old. Call the banners to the city and rekindle old alliances. Send word to The Remnant in the north and The High City in the west. We are not alone. If Mordën wants to pit his own against our walls, he will find a larger force than he believed possible. He will find we do not forget the history of old."

"Aye, my king," a female Elfin they'd called Nemoia raised her mug, "my forces would rally to their banner lords. We have six thousand ready to come to the call of their king."

"Another three thousand who have been stationed near the Old City, sire." A new Elfin half stood. He toasted the king and sat back down.

"Half of my company is still in training." Kevdar shook his head with a glimmer in his eye. "But even recruits fresh from their teens will find their blood boils for a cause such as this. They will gladly give their lives for their lands and their king."

"I do not ask them to lay down their lives for me." Elharan raised one hand. "Yet for their family, their homes, this cause I would march with the very least of them into war. It seems we have no shortage of bravery here. Phoenix DarkBairn, what say you?"

"Only that in the long years I've been here, I have never felt at home. I've always been moving even if I never left. I watched the place closest to a home burn to the ground. I watched those closest to me cut down. If you would accept the sword of the bairn who brought this evil back, then I will stand with all these brave ones."

"You will find my blood boils as strong as any Elfin." Kissinger nodded. "There isn't a swordsman here who knows their weaknesses like I do. I've fought many Varg and dueled with more than my fair share of Nightshades. I can train where lack of experience might be your downfall."

"We have them on our doorstep," Berëthelluïn said bitterly. "You speak of rallying forces, but the attack could happen any moment."

"Our scouts relay the closest enemy host is still a day's ride from here," Trian, an Elfin noble in appearance, growled. His long flowing hair had dimmed from yellowish blond to a light grey, like a dying star. His eyes were old and his skin wrinkled.

"Such a truce is nonexistent. It might be to lure us into complacency!"

"I will not let this happen." Elharan folded his arms. He was regal against the background of fire and shadows. "Call your banners and recall your scouts. We are about to make the greatest stand since the Last Battle of the Second Era."

"A lot has changed in the five hundred years since then." Berëthelluïn gripped his sword.

"Our resolve has never wavered." Elharan gestured calmly. "There is no doubt in my heart nor my hall that you are as brave as any here. It's as the old adage says: 'I saw the pebble lying there and wondered from what mountain it had rolled.' Youth and the elderly will fight together."

The room filled with shouts of approval and mugs were slammed into the hard oak of the table. Servants brought forth kegs and refilled the glasses. Several brought out long pipes and lit them.

"I'll task my scouts with making first contact with the north." Kevdar sipped his last ale. "The Drucodians will not fight for their love of us, but they know all too well, especially their most ancient, of the harshness and fear Mordën brings."

"Very good, Lord Kevdar." Elharan approved. "Berëthelluïn, I command you to rally the forces nearest the city. Find every Elfin, young and old, male and female, able to wield a weapon. They are to begin their training if they are not already trained. Lord Aroenal, send word to the Eastern Garrison and the Hidden Hovel. I want them to return as soon as the message reaches them. We know not fully the ways Mordën means to push forward, but I'd imagine a great army is hard to miss. Jyrre, take your best huntsmen and tracksmen. Find the location of their body and report on its every move. They will not find a sleeping city here."

"If it please you, King Elharan," I ducked my head, "I offer my sword.

"Phoenix DarkBairn, curse and *bane* of my people," Elharan turned in a cold move before smiling and exuding a warmth, "I shall welcome such a sword. Long have you lived among a world not of your design. You have paid for your crimes tenfold and still wish to fight. It is good to see that you stand so. It speaks of the honor and bravery of your people. Your two comrades shall ride with you. Berëthelluïn, call the Midiheim! Let us all disperse. It has been a long evening and I still have many hours of planning to commit to. Phoenix, Arabella, and Kissinger, please retire to your quarters and rest. One of the guards outside will escort you."

The sounds of wooden chairs scraping against the stone floor filled the room. Servants sprinted nimbly around exiting lords as they cleaned the table.

"It feels *different*," Kissinger said as we stepped into the night.

"How?" Arabella took his hand in hers.

"I woke up to the smell of a damp rain on a spring morning. Now all I can smell is ash and fire."

The city stretched out below us like fireflies. Lights flickered and twinkled. Shapes moved to and fro. I calmed the butterflies in my gut for they were Elfins . . . not the cruel cold Varg and Shades. For now, the city slept in peace. How long would that last?

Fire dotted the city. Beneath the dark trees of the plateaus, wood crackled and light soared into the starry sky. On the battlements, torches blazed in their sconces and cast long shadows along the stone. In houses and tents, flickering light revealed the outlines of people, moving around with haste. Fire moved like an undulating snake, from road to field to battlement, borne on the hands of eager riders. It reflected off naked steel, aged wood, and the sweating flesh of Elfin.

"I always knew somehow I'd die sooner rather than later." Kissinger picked at his fingernails. "I just never thought I'd die in a city of Elfin."

"Always looking at the brighter side." Arabella nudged him playfully.

"Right, like a few thousand Elfin behind a wall will simply stump Mordën," he snorted derisively.

"More like slow him down," I murmured. I was a few feet away from them, watching the world sleep beyond the wall. "If we can deal enough damage, inflict enough casualties, then maybe we stand a chance in the long run. How many will answer the call of their ruler? Tens of thousands reside outside this city. There will be a great force behind these walls ere Mordën attacks."

"Great," Kissinger threw his arms in mock resignation, "the world is saved but I have to die first."

"So do most great warriors." I glanced at him.

"You hear that?" he said to Arabella as he pointed at me. "Dark-Bairn here thinks I'm a warrior of legend."

"I didn't say that." I rolled my eyes.

"I heard it." He shrugged and grinned. It was the first real smile he'd shown since we'd come here.

"Yes." I closed my eyes. I could already hear the screams of the dying. The smell of blood on a sweat-soaked field. "I'd like to imagine I'm wrong. One of the greatest motivators known to anyone for survival is defending one's home. It's possible I underestimate these Elfin. You both know them and their species leagues more than I do."

"It's been an age and a half since anyone had major conflict." Kissinger's tone softened. "I shouldn't judge their actions so harshly. I simply feel the hope slipping away."

"That is what Mordën needs." I stepped from Arabella's grasp and gripped Kissinger's shoulder. "He needs us to despair. No matter what happens or how lost we feel, we must never give up hope."

Far below, a minstrel strummed a gloshee and began singing to anyone who would listen. His words wafted up and we paused to listen.

> *There is no pain nor sorrow from the world I leave*
> *Our grief has fled and sorrows are lost in the peak*
> *Curling waves crash o'er breaking hills of ironclad stone*
> *As women cry in mourning and your young roam alone*
> *Dangers as darkness in shadows lie*
>
> *What hope has the fish when the sea monster thrives*
> *How will the fisherman fish with no will left alive*
> *How will the hunter catch his game after a grueling day*
> *When all the prey are poisoned and in death's arms lay*
> *What hope has blessed these hills like dew drops on the morn*
> *What hope remains in our blood from the blast of the war horn*
>
> *The future is dead as dead as our own*
> *If not from us, then our youth all alone*
> *In time the shadow will cover all*
> *Burry the blade of grass and mountain tall*
> *What hope remains as darkness in shadows lie*

The minstrel was eventually booed out of the square and he went off filled with drunken depression.

"What idiot thinks a song like that is helpful on a night like tonight?" Kissinger eyed the minstrel below.

We stood in silence as the clouds passed their watchful gaze down on the slumbering city. Even the last lit torches were being extinguished as guards made their patrols. The moon showed its glimmering face and from its blue light, I watched the rolling hills and far-off swaying treetops. How could a place so beautiful and peaceful be the deciding factor in this war?

"Woah." Kissinger grabbed my arm and pointed. "You all see what I see?"

The great sweeping plains and rolling valleys were broken by specks of light. The pale moonlight could not explain the phenomena. The nearest guards had spotted it already and two drew arrows to their long bows. We all watched in silent anticipation as, grueling minute by minute, the lights expanded. What was once a pinprick of orange in a sea of black became a dot which grew to show the riders that held it. Below the closest light, a figure in a hood rode hard. His mount tore the road like a Varglarian was slashing at its heels. Behind him, two smaller figures were huddled under a cloak on the same stallion. Bringing up the rear, another solo form held a torch high. He seemed to be waving it in hopes of attracting attention. It had worked. Elfin bowmen were racing down toward the gates. They shouted commands for the massive doors to be inched open. Their voices carried on the wind up to our straining ears.

"Whoever they are," I muttered, "they're riding fast. Too fast for a normal approach."

"Think they're one of us?" Kissinger leaned over the edge of the crenel. "They don't appear to be Varg, but trickery is not an alien tactic to our prestigious shadow prince."

Arabella led the way as we hurried down the long stairs. They cut back several times due to the height of the walls. The closer we got to the ground, the more distinct hoofprints on stone I heard. They were getting close. In tandem, the Elfin were shouting out to each other.

"Get Lord Berëthelluïn!"

"More wood for the fire. I can hardly see in this suffocating darkness."

Arabella brushed her hair from her eyes. "Those visitors are nearly here."

The Elfinian soldiers ran out over the Westerly Road and lowered long lance-like spears toward the oncoming riders. Horses snorted and hooves scuffed over gravel. We could distinctly make out the shouts of the riders to their mounts, the urgency in their tones. It was unmistakable. My worst fears surged in my throat and I batted them back down. If Mordën was about to attack, the call for Berëthelluïn had been made. This city could awaken fast.

"Phoenix!" Arabella gasped. "They're Men! Not Varg!"

I shook away the cobwebs of nerves and peered out into the night. The torchlight borne high by the mounted occupants revealed more of their visage. The lead rider was still shrouded in the gloom of his hood but behind him, the two riders atop the single stallion had cast off their hoods. It was still too dark to identify them completely, but I noted the lead rider was a girl. Her long hair flowed behind her and into the face of the male rider behind. He had his arms around her waist and head low. Their torch flickered dimly and for a split second I thought I saw something familiar. My mind raced with intrigue, and I pushed my way out of the safety of the walls and onto the road. Kissinger was at my side, his dagger out.

"Can't be too careful," he said. "You have your blade?"

"Always." I felt the familiar thwack of the scabbard against my thigh. "What are the odds this is a trick, and we end up dying?"

"I've never been one for odds and ends." Kissinger wiped his nose.

Arabella had a knife in her hands. "A million to one," she said softly.

"Good odds," I said with a raised brow.

"That was a million to one against us." She gave me a side eye.

"Remain behind the line!" Bereth called to me.

I ignored his pleas as my jaw slowly lowered, inch by inch. The lead rider finally raised his head and what joy I felt at the prospects of these riders soared into new heights. I cried out with elation, raising one fist in the air. Arabella eyed me with obvious concern, but I did not care who saw me. King Elharan himself could have been watching for all I cared.

"No blasted way." Kissinger lowered his dagger and stared. He too was open-mouthed, rendered speechless.

Behind the two mounts, the third rider removed his hood. I'd know his smirk anywhere. Kissinger sheathed his dagger and took a step forward. Tears stung his eyes. As the riders finally closed the distance, the Elfinian guards raised their pikes.

"Halt! You approach The Golden City. Speak your name and make known your identity. None who pass these gates may bring with them any evil, for it has no place in Avalon."

The lead rider cantered to a halt; his smile reached his ears. With a great exhalation of air, he dismounted and removed his hood. The others also dismounted. The two riders kept their heads down, as if they were waking from a long sleep.

"About blasted time." Kissinger laughed shakily.

"I did tell you we had an alliance to forge." DarSheer removed his riding gloves and turned to the Elfins. "Be at peace, my friends. I am DarSheer of the Outpost. With me rides Othrain also of the Outpost. The two in the far back are Elfinian escorts from Commander Gisli of the Eastern Garrison. And these . . ." DarSheer paused as the two smaller riders finally looked up into the flickering light.

What happiness I'd held at the welcome sight of DarSheer completely and utterly shattered. My brain filled with such an intense buzzing I couldn't hear anything. My mouth was dry. Then suddenly moist. Sweat soaked my armpits. Blood rushed to my face. *It isn't possible*, I reasoned to myself. *This is a dream. I'm dreaming and I'm about to be awoken.* My eyes and ears refused to accept what they beheld even as the girl spoke.

"My name is Katy Chase. This here is my traveling companion and dear friend, Tim Brestdon. We've journeyed far and wide. We are not from here nor are we from any world you can imagine. DarSheer agreed to bring us here to see someone we've been trying to find for two years now."

I realized I'd been shrouded by the darkness. Berëthelluïn arrived, panting, at that moment, a torch high and his sword drawn. He paused at the grouping and glanced at one of his men. They communicated wordlessly and he sheathed his blade. The fire he bore shed light to my face and this time it was Katy who noticed me. Her eyes went wide even as Tim, behind her, cursed loudly. Her eyes filled with tears, filled to the point of breaking. Her face drained of color and then she blushed. It was like my world was caving in. Mountains of sound and emotions and feeling erupted and fell away. I didn't know what to do with my hands. Should I walk forward? Embrace her? Demand to know why she was here when she couldn't possibly be here?

"Phoenix Dunnigan Rather," Katherine Chase breathed the words like they were worth more than all the gold in Ëonë.

His world was one of eerie calm. Despite the raucous rabble outside, and the overwhelming thuds of the Sicarack's legs in the underbrush beyond sight, Raoul paid them no heed. His goal, his mind, was focused on one thing and one thing only. Before him, seated atop an obsidian throne, Mordëngrold, the Shadow King, the True Heir of Ëonë, and First of the Fallen Luthi, smiled. It was not uncommon for his master to smile at the prospects to come or at the progress they had made. The Outpost had been but a bump in the roll of their mass. Raoul had taken personal pleasure in killing the weak soldiers stationed there. Ever since he'd been placed at the right hand of Mordën, and made commander over the shadow armies, he'd come to realize his growing disdain for the seated individual. The world opened before them like a flower receiving sunlight. It was ready to be snipped from its stem and placed in a note-worthy spot. Yet here they stood, ground to a complete stop. And for what? The misty ends of a plan erected centuries prior to unfold? Who needed old prophecies? In Raoul's opinion, they merely delayed what was right-fully taken.

"You believe me a fool." Mordën's voice slid from one ear to the other. Raoul resisted the urge to itch.

"I do." His own voice sounded odd in his ears. Like a shout under depths of water. "Our time can be utilized better." The spike of fear that surged through him was greater than any before as Mordën turned to stare at him.

"You wish to know why our great forces stand short of their victory!"

This wasn't a question so much a note of disdain at Raoul's incompetence.

"Forgive my brashness, master," he dipped his head, "but it is as you yourself have said. We are but a day's march from their chief city. Imagine the glory and splendor that could be ours if it falls."

"Not if, my young fool," Mordën licked his pale dead lips, "but when. I admire your hesitant bravery in these questions, even if I had to break it from you. Every step of my plan is as I desire. The vessel who brought me here is right where I need him. He despairs and it is sweet honey to my mind. There is much to be achieved through patience. Your simple mind cannot comprehend how long I have let this fester in the depths. Like a monster it will reveal its gaping maw and this world will be consumed in its fiery bite." His voice rose. "What was once denied me, my rightful claim, will be denied no longer. The almighty Erëthuïl shall withhold me my land of darkness no longer. You cannot hope to understand what the patience of thousands of years yields. I am in no hurry. I fear no defeat. Avalonenburg will burn and its ashes will be a reminder of my victory for eons to come. We will march from one city to the next until none stands alive. First Avalon, then all of the Eastern Ward. You ask for a sign for your faith. The words you planted in his mind will consume him until he drops dead. I have spoken."

The Hourglass morphed into a swirl around his throne. Seven voices whispered of the secrets of the world since the dawn of time. They hissed and snarled in and out of earshot. It was like a great windstorm but with voices from the past. Raoul understood this and he bowed to his master before leaving him. It was clear to him now that he must bide his patience. It did not hurt to let this play itself out. And when it ended, Raoul would be there to pick up what was left. Let Mordën think he reigned. He should never have brought him back from the dead those fated days ago. He should have been allowed to rest. Now he would plan and he would be as patient as his master.

Chapter 7

The Council of Banners

DARSHEER PARRIED THE STRIKE, *and I cried out as the wooden sword glanced off my fingers. I shook them and resisted the urge to suck them back to a painless feel. The courtyard watched intently. DarSheer's lessons had come and gone in intensity. The important thing was that the sword didn't feel so alien in my hand. The shield was no longer a cumbersome weight designed to throw me off-balance. He might have hit me, but his move was a tactical loss.*

With a cry of success, I swung my foot behind his knee and pulled. He tumbled to the ground. His weapon skittered a few feet away. When he looked up, the point of the sword touched his neck. Sweat poured down his temple and neck. We stared at each other. Neither one spoke. The courtyard was silent, holding its breath. It was as if the entire world waited for the outcome. Finally, the other slowly broke into a smile and stood.

"Phoenix DarkBairn, I offer you my sword as an equal. There is much I could still teach you if you'd have me as your instructor. But what you know will aid you well to come."

Lord Malziek walked over. The hushed tension from all eyes could have split a boulder. He gave me a gruff nod, which I realized was the closest thing to a sign of respect I'd ever seen him give me.

"It is not often I have the pleasure of seeing someone achieve respect in DarSheer Swordsmaster's eyes," he boomed. "You are one of us, bairn. From the sky you have come and you were but a stranger. Now, you have earned the right to say you're a bairn of the Outpost. Do you have any words you wish to share with all your brothers here?"

I cleared my throat and surveyed the grounds. From stable boys to iron workers to scouts to guards, all had paused to watch and despite my alienness and attachment to a horrible prophecy, they'd taken me in as a brother. They'd given me a bed and food. Brenneth had shown me how to ride skillfully so as to not embarrass myself. DarSheer was keen on training me the ways of battle and now, thanks to him, I felt confident with a blade. Topper held his gloshee at the ready. KcNuck poised to cheer. Even Altruic, his scowl present on his face, let some warmth melt his hard exterior through the cracks under his eyes. It was not easy earning your place as one of the Outpost. Despite all of that, they'd accepted me as one of their own, a brother not by blood but of fighting spirit.

"If this is to end in death then I welcome it," I said loudly. "If the very hordes of the Pit itself were unleashed and every Varglarian and Nightshade from here to the BlackBurg assailed our walls and meant to rent us asunder, I would gladly die. For you all, these walls, and this good earth beneath my boots was fought for. Blood was spilled here to water the future we see. I will not let it be taken by any evil that can be conjured under the sea, on the land, or in the heavens above." My words pierced the morning air.

"Is there then yet something to cling to?" Malziek cried loudly. "Outside, they march as a thunderhead in from the east. They are a clashing torrent of unbreakable waves. What is there we can do against that evil?"

"A darkness now lies on these lands. It's like a black poison seeping through every vein, into every cave, and up every steep mountainside. Those clouds are not of natural design, for they carry the foul stench of war. Over twig and boulder, they will stomp, burning and killing as they go. But we have something they can never defeat. We have something stronger than their lust for death."

"What," DarSheer said in his gravelly voice. The courtyard hung on every word.

"Hope." I smiled and turned to see the guards atop their stones grin back. "We fight for our home, our families. And we hope for a day when those born into this world do not have to live in fear of a cursed monster who should have died LONG AGO!"

I bellowed out the last words and the courtyard erupted into approval. Topper strummed his gloshee and, in his usual out-of-tune manner, sung a new rendition of his previous song. Brenneth and KcNuck danced about in the dirt. Guards and cooks and stable boys alike chanted "Phoenix DarkBairn". If I didn't know better, I'd have believed I saw respect and admiration radiating from Malziek's crinkly eyes. DarSheer took me by the shoulder and led me out of sight of the jubilant throng.

"You have given these men what they've sorely lacked." He clapped my arm. "They will not soon forget this."

"I meant every word," I exhaled shakily. "Back home . . . let's just say I wasn't exactly anyone. I was me. And that meant being harassed by bigger and meaner people. I constantly felt tired. I was not sure that I would find a friend again after the passing of my world. Yet here, among the stone and waves of this shoreline, I have found you and Brenneth. The light of Erëthuil may still shine where shadows take root."

"Do not so easily forsake the bonds of friendship," he warned. "Events like what you've gone through often bond two people closer together."

"Even so, I am glad they could not be here to see me like this." I kicked at a rock. "I have not always been a friend as they deserve. I have seen visions of one dying, and another chained to bare rock and whipped by metal. His blood watered the stones beneath him. It is because of me they endured this and at the utmost cost, too."

"With time you'll find peace of mind."

"It's not just the nightmares I speak of. I can feel Mordën in my head all the time. He whispers things to me. Dark things. He promises every day he will destroy all that is good and light. It's like a headache that never heals. And every day we fight off roving bands of Varglarian, he takes one step closer to raising his army. I can feel him growing in strength. I think *since I came across the bridge between my world and yours, a part of me was lost forever."*

"It's like you said, we have hope on our side. Besides, after your performance with that sword, I'm sure every Nightshade and Varglarian will be quivering in their iron boots. You never mentioned these friends before. The ones who survived, did they mean much to you?"

I thought of Tim, and Katy. I thought of Will, what he'd sacrificed. What they all had sacrificed for me. Guilt racked me. As time had progressed, so had my memories become clearer. I remembered that day when Katy rescued me from my bully and nemesis BB. I'd been so infatuated with an idea of what I thought was normal. Her beautiful eyes were a safe haven where I was free from the tyrannical clutches of boys bigger than me. And no matter what pickle I'd gotten myself into, I'd always had Will and Tim there to bail me out. DarSheer's question brought only sadness.

"They mean the world to me."

"Then do you believe they would, even for a heartbeat, abandon you? After all you've said you've been through?"

"I hope not," I said.

"Hope is a powerful igniter," DarSheer turned, "but it is only good if it fuels the right course of action. Your friends are safe and free from this world of pain. There is no reason to hope for them, for they live it. Be at peace. Wherever they are, your closest friends have not and will never forget or forsake you."

All I could see was her two brown eyes, like pools of tawny tinted chocolate. My gaze drifted over her, soaking in her beauty like the fields soak in a summer rain. Most notable, her hair had gone from its brown to a wispy silvery color. It was as if all the stars of the night sky had descended upon her. While different in color, it was pulled up in the same ponytail it had been all those memories ago. Her smile was there but it masked a deeper resignation. She took a step forward. The entire group remained motionless. The figure behind her, Tim, cleared his throat as if to speak, his eyes flashing in the glint of the torchlight. Then, with her emotion spilling out onto her face, she ran into my arms. The impact knocked my breath from me, and I staggered back, holding her like she'd vanish if I let go.

"I'm dreaming, this is a dream." I laughed as I held her face. She stared back, her familiar eyes pools of joy. Her tears dripped on my cheeks as we embraced. I shook with sobs but this time it wasn't because I thought I'd never see her again. It wasn't because I had to force myself to forget her face every night it appeared because it crippled me. Now, it was because the unthinkable was true. I knew it. I knew I wasn't sleeping. Her warmth filled me. Her laughter made my knees shake. Every part of me, the deepest part of me that had believed her forever beyond my reach, trembled with pure joy.

"It's been a long time," Tim began.

"If it is a dream, then we must both be sleeping." Katy sniffled and laughed and wept all at the same time. She covered her mouth as tears flooded down her cheeks. We hugged and I was content to hold her, letting the warmth of her body press down on me. We laughed together.

We snuggled, our faces inches apart. Her nose rubbed against my own and our lips were mere centimeters apart. Her breath was comforting. I felt the tension in my body release like a wave of water over a hill. Two years of ache and pain seemed to vanish. A weight like a millstone around my neck was gone. I hadn't even realized it had been there. What emotions I had contained in the deepest chasms of my soul now melted away, no more a threat than a heavy winter's snow under a burning sun. For a few moments I felt the urge to kiss her. But then the veil that seemed to ride between us reared its ugly head and the thought was shattered. It had been nearly two years since we'd last talked. I didn't know if those feelings which burned so bright in the past, still remained. What distance had time wrenched between us?

"Kiss me, you idiot." She laughed and cried at the same time.

Our lips pressed together. It was a wet kiss, full of confusion and embarrassment and pure bliss rolled into one. Her heart beat fiercely. I could feel it. A soft crimson filled her cheeks and when I slowly pulled back to gaze into her eyes, tears brimmed.

"I thought I'd never see you again." My words came out watery and hesitant.

She ran a hand through my dirty hair and down my neck. She looked me over from head to toe as if soaking me in for the first time. Her full lips shook slightly whether from exhaustion or the urge to kiss me again, I knew not.

"I never gave up looking," she breathed softly. "Even when all else failed, I never gave up hope." She pressed her forehead to mine.

"I'm so sorry," I held her head in my hands, my thumb rubbing her earlobe. "For everything I put you through. Not a day has gone by where I didn't curse myself in every language of this world."

She giggled and sniffed. "We searched from the far reaches of the Ralier Range and even as far south as Glasbur. I believe I overturned every rock and pebble in my path."

"She never turned her back on the thought of seeing you again." Tim's husky voice broke our passionate moment. "Not even when I begged her to see reason."

"Reason?" I held her tight. "Tim, thank you, for protecting her."

He dipped his head stiffly in a nod. "She came back for me in those wretched tunnels. I owe her my life."

"What are you talking about?" I turned to look at her.

"I can explain later." She wiped the tears from her eyes. "Perhaps in the safety of a walled city?"

"Yes," I heard his faint voice, "let us forget the past for now."

"Sorry to break this up, but am I welcome to join this reunion?" DarSheer grinned, in a wide stance, arms folded.

"Broadsword." I kept my hand in Katy's but spared him a huge smile. "I never doubted you. I thought your journey would be longer though. Kissinger and I believed you to be weeks from arriving here. What of your mission south?"

"This too can be spared for the warmth of a tavern and the brewing of ale." He smiled kindly. "We should move into the city. I do believe we are giving these poor warriors a heart attack."

"It would be best to return inside." Berëthelluïn gestured. "Phoenix, we are still in a state of caution. The gates cannot be opened for long."

"Of course, my apologies Lord Bereth," I said. "It is not safe to be out here. Let us return to safety and bask in the coziness of good light and a warm hearth where we may talk to our heart's delight."

The night was long, and it had just begun. Usually visible high in the sky, the Fallen Peaks hid behind the darkness. The sporadic torches throughout the city were the only things that indicated life. King Elharan had decreed that for the time being, light and their consequential shadows must be kept to a minimum. There was no reason to taunt the dangers outside.

Crowded around a thick mahogany table in The King's Tavern, after we were served piping hot mugs of cider and plates of meat and bistri, Katy was the first to reveal her secrets. Luckily, the tavern was empty at this time of night, and we had the common area to ourselves. Only Lathium stood within earshot, rubbing the inside of a tankard with a dirty cloth.

"The darkness swallowed you whole," she whispered. The firelight from the hearth danced dramatically over her face. "You told me to run and . . . I couldn't leave you behind. I urged Quire to safely escort the captives from the mountain."

Quire. My gut clenched. In all my remembering, I'd completely forgotten about Quire, Last Commander of The Grey Cloaks. His concealing cloak hid him from more than just eyes. The guilt ate away at the back of my head. I owed everything to him, and I'd completely forgotten his existence.

"We got to the exit, and I watched them run safely toward the sparkling lights of a city below us. But I could not leave you, or Will, or Tim, to the tormenting clutches of the terrors that seeped through the caverns. So, I turned and went back the way I'd come. It was hard finding the path again and I had to hide from several bands of Nightshades. I found him." Her voice cracked and tears brimmed her eyes.

"Who?" I felt the cold spread. "Who, Katy?"

"Will." She rubbed at her red eyes. Tim rubbed her back, and I felt a prickle of discomfort. "He was stretched out grotesquely on a .

. . bed of . . . nails. Most of the red was gone from his face and he was in and out of sleep. But he was awake when I found him. He told me he had failed, that he had been unable to, when the moment called for him to step up, stop Mordën. I watched him take his last breath. He died believing he was a failure; believing he was the reason the plan had failed."

Will was dead. He'd been dead this whole time. Yet the news still dug deep.

"He did not die as a failure," I said shakily. "Without him, we would not have found or gotten as far as we did. We all came together and not one of us could have done it on their own. Whatever happened in his final moments, unbeknownst to me, he was honorable and brave in the face of certain death. He now thrives in the halls above. Innith Inine."

"Onward till we're ashes," everyone in the room, save for Tim and Katy, echoed the words. Kissinger and Othrain had stopped talking at the onset of her tale and now looked as if they'd been hit by an avalanche.

DarSheer raised his mug. "To an honorable death, of a bairn I did not get to meet but still consider a brother. All hail the fallen hero!"

"All hail the fallen hero!" The others raised their glasses. The room was quiet.

Katy sniffed and put her arms around my waist. "After I found him . . . like that . . . I worried what had become of all of you. Tim was taken long before any of us entered the mountain and if that horrible death had become him as well, I did not have faith he would leave alive."

"But she did find me." Tim's voice had grown deep over the years. His hair was shorter but still a tangled mess. His sharp eyes pierced beneath two heavy brows which adorned his tanned visage. He'd been quiet up until this point, content to let what was to be said be said and listen. I'd almost forgotten his part in this tale. He gazed about stonily. "I suffered much to be here."

"What, I mean where were you?" I breathed through my fingertips.

"They took me to a chamber and strapped me down to one of those flesh-cleavers, that's what they called it. Some scum named Raoul visited me to torment me with the images of dead comrades, a failed quest. Another aged figure, I forget his name, spent hours drawing my blood and tearing wounds into my back. He whipped me with chains as thick as my fingers."

Tim stood and, back to us, raised his tunic. We gasped in unison. His back was riddled with scars. Some were deep, others a surface wound. Most came to a puckered point almost like the hole in a ring. The holes that had been cut deep had healed to scars but had not properly closed. Tim lowered his shirt and met Katy's concerned eyes. Something passed wordlessly between them. I was so taken with his scars I missed the look.

"I abandoned you." I turned to look at him. "I know this now."

"Yes, you did," he said softly. "Yet I am here and thus my story continues."

"I ask for your forgiveness, in all my failures."

"It is not easy for me." He held his arms close. "I am unable to accept."

Kissinger shifted awkwardly as Arabella sat down. She placed two more ciders on the table and looked around.

"Did I interrupt something?" She winced.

"Just the usual," Kissinger smiled, "happiness and joy."

"I had all but given up, clinging to a false hope that someone, literally anyone, would find me and rescue me," Tim continued. "I knew the odds, had made the choice to come on this journey . . . *I get that.* But there's something animalistic that comes over a man when he's faced with his mortality. It didn't take long for me to despair. I would die alone and cold and abandoned by those I'd called friends. For all I knew, you all were comfortably outside the mountain, laughing and hugging in reunion and forgetting me."

I was surprised at how bitter he sounded. His hands were clenched into fists. He didn't sound like the Tim I'd known. Time had not been kind to him. His past grin was gone. Katy took one of his hands in hers and smoothed his fist out. She intertwined her fingers in his and gave him a reassuring smile. His scowl softened slightly as he gazed at her. My eyes darted between the two of them. Tim's attitude was not the only thing, it appeared that had changed with time. *Could it be?* I pondered. Then Katy turned and gave me a smile. Her cheeks flushed and she averted her eyes, letting go of Tim's hand. He withdrew his hand into his sleeve.

"So how . . ." I began.

"How did I escape?" he interrupted and turned to stare at me. Again, his voice had a steel bite to it. "I heard a commotion outside in the corridor, so I cried out in a feeble hope that maybe I was wrong. Maybe all this time I had lost faith in you; you'd been out there in the tunnels tirelessly. When the others had wanted to go home, you'd said, 'No, Tim matters. He's my brother and I will not leave him to the wolves. I am not leaving him. I'm not abandoning him,' you'd told them off for their thoughts. I held on to the hope that you remembered me. Hope failed me that day."

"I was chained in a roo—" I began to feel my face heat.

"I was running back from the room with the strange pit," Katy interrupted, "and I heard his weak plea for help. My heart soared and I found him. He was barely alive, Phoenix. He looked as dead as Will. I got him free of his chains and wrapped him in his shirt. There was so much blood. The room reeked of it. I helped him, one arm over my shoulder, out. He begged me to find you, Phoenix. He said his life was forfeit and that the evil shadow was out for you."

"You said that?" I looked at my old friend. His scowl and harsh glare did not reflect the story being told.

"I said a great many things," he murmured. "One's mouth wags when one is delirious."

"Come now," Katy nudged him with her knee, "we spoke of this."

"What had you seen, Lady Katy?" Arabella cleared her throat.

"One of the Shades had taken a step over the edge of the pit, in the ground and just dropped, like a stone. He never came back."

"She convinced me to go check on it," Tim said, derision laced his words. "I was too *weak* to argue. So, we limped and dragged ourselves to this chamber."

"You knew, somehow, that it involved Phoenix," Katy corrected. "We came to the edge of the pit, and I saw you, Phoenix. Laying on a grassy knoll in the center of a rippling image at the bottom of the hole. There were rolling waves in the distance and a stranger with a sword standing over you. I didn't even think, I just scrambled for the edge and fell forward. I kind of pulled Tim with me."

"Cast unwillingly into a world of strife." DarSheer glanced at Othrain and Kissinger. "Does this ring bell towers?"

"The day the DarkBairn showed up." Othrain nodded. "The day the rumors started of Mordën's return."

"DarkBairn?" Tim cracked a smile.

"A nickname drummed up with many ballads." Othrain stared at him. "This prophecy has been in place for ages past."

"Phoenix showed up, practically on our doorstep." DarSheer bridged his fingers. "Our minds are slowed by peace but sharpened now with trust."

"Trust should not be so hastily handed out." Tim downed the dregs of his cider. "If Phoenix is this crazy answer to an old prophecy, why is Mordën still being allowed to run amok, killing and butchering as he pleases? Things may seem pleasant here, but we've journeyed long and far in two years. You're all living in ignorance if you think these walls will simply stop him."

"Phoenix is not so much an answer to a prophecy." Kissinger coughed. He glanced at me apologetically.

"So much as he is the result of one," Othrain finished.

"Pray, tell." Tim was taking high interest in this, I noted uneasily.

"The prophecy speaks of a bairn who would be the vessel for Mordën's return. One day, he would come back and invade the lands of Ëonë from his fortress on the BlackBurg."

"Phoenix swore an oath to remain at the Outpost till his death," Othrain murmured. "The code doesn't speak to the Outpost's eventual burn and demolition, but those of us lucky enough to escape with our lives have journeyed here."

"We have received word that Glysperia and Elënya crossed the Ethero Basin a week ago." DarSheer sat back. "They and theirs have journeyed into the Western Ward and into safety."

"Bless Erëthuïl," I breathed.

"How many survived?" Katy inquired. She touched a glimmering emerald fish at her neckline. It hung on a golden chain and clashed with her now tan skin. Othrain spread his arms wide.

"You're looking at us, sweetheart. We once spanned hundreds. Now there are less than two dozen."

"You've had too much to drink." Kissinger stared pointedly.

"It's cider." Othrain sounded genuinely offended. "This is cider. You can't get drunk from cider. Are you drunk? This is cider."

"I'm making a point." Kissinger rolled his eyes in exasperation. "You've been on the road too long, old friend."

"Drunk on *cider*," Othrain snorted into his mug.

"Can we get back on topic?" I raised one finger. "Katy, you said you saw me lying on a knoll. When you fell or stepped through the Portal, why did you not show up? You never were there."

Katy glanced uneasily at Tim who stared brazenly at me. More unspoken words passed silently between them. He sighed and hoisted himself to a fully seated position.

"I don't know how this … *Portal* … works. But when I was dragged in after Katy, we landed in a marshy spread. It was nighttime so clearly some time had passed. I thought we'd landed in some weird underground world. It took several days to realize I wasn't hallucinating on some poison. This wasn't our world. It became obvious when we met some short, weird creatures on the road."

"Short?" Arabella sat forward. "Were they Ebyians?"

He gave her a look like she was insane. "I didn't bother to ask. We hid as they trundled by, but it was clear nothing like that was in our world. We searched the coastline far north for signs or news of Phoenix. It was as if we had transported into a time long in our past. We thought we were at a place in our own world before our birth. It wasn't until we entered Fiscer's Keep and saw the banners and heard the news from a city called Avalon, that it hit us. For one and a half years we traversed rock and hill and plain looking for you, Phoenix. We neared the city of Caldonia when a grouping of armed soldiers on horseback cantered on. They had shields and swords and a banner. I remember one of them snapping at another saying something about 'The Lost City remains lost for a reason.'"

"He's right," Katy interjected. "The lead rider was having trouble corralling those behind him. They seemed awash with stories of the city they'd just left. One said, 'There's no way in. It's a sealed tomb in time. The last time those gates opened was well beyond any of our years.' The lead rider snapped back, 'And why should we care what's inside. The Lost City remains lost for a reason, per his orders.'"

Othrain glanced at DarSheer who ignored him. Kissinger practically buzzed in his seat. Behind us, Lathium dropped a dish and cursed in his tongue. He stared up sheepishly and apologized.

"If what they say is true," Othrain urged, "then this may be the time."

"It's not possible."

"Think of the treasures that remain behind, DarSheer. The weapons isolated by walls of stone so thick they could rival the mountains wide."

"Children's stories are not welcome at a table for adults," DarSheer scolded lightly. "The rider is right; The Lost City remains lost behind its walls for a reason. Tim, do you remember the banner the riders rode with?"

Tim scrunched his nose in thought. "A tall white tower in front of a triangle of sorts. Something like helmets lay scattered about the feet of the building."

"That's The High City's sigil," I murmured in thought. Katy stared at me.

"We heard the name pass the lips of many travelers." She sipped her cider. "We know not much else about it."

"A story for another day. Continue in your tale, Lady Katy." DarSheer inclined his head.

"Well, we didn't know the city of Glasbur was named that to begin with." Katy seemed uncertain now. "Tim reasoned a city like that though had to have rations and supplies. If we were stranded in a nightmare, we might as well look the part with full bellies. We followed the road the opposite direction of the riders for nearly two months. Rain fell and the marshlands slowly succumbed to rolling hills and forests of splendid green. We came upon fewer and fewer travelers on the road. They all stared at us something strange and one tall golden-haired individual asked us our purpose on the End Road. We told him we looked for The Lost City and he laughed at us but told us we were nearing our journey's end. He left without further mention."

"We can break here for nightfall." DarSheer rose tiredly. "We have much to ponder ere the dawn rises. I can pay for our rooms tonight but on the morrow, we must make for King Elharan's hall. He will be able to better understand these cryptic findings. Goodnight, fellow travelers."

The group disbanded and I hurried to his side. He seemed aged in a weary manner. He walked with a small limp, and I noticed the scars he tried to hide with his large cloak. He noted my prying eyes.

"I should have known better than to hide the obvious to you, Phoenix DarkBairn." He chuckled and gave me a hug.

"I didn't know if I'd see you or when," I confessed.

"I told you to look for my coming." He nodded to Lathium and handed five coins to the innkeeper. "My mission in Caldonia should prove successful. They still muster a formidable force of cavalry and bowmen from the old days. I talked long and hard with their commander. It's what took me so long. And good thing it did otherwise we'd have left before your friends entered the town. Take care of them, Phoenix. They are lost and looking for familiarity. I believe you hold the key to their lock."

"Of course, I'm glad you're mostly in one piece. I won't ask about the scars, not yet at least. Sleep well, Swordsmaster."

"May the blessings of Erëthuïl give you deep slumbers." DarSheer bowed and pivoted. He walked off to converse with Othrain and Kissinger.

Tim paused and stared at me. I felt that he was wrestling with some battle deep inside. His eyes still watered as if tears were moments from brimming.

"I'm sorry," I said. "I had no idea the suffering you went through."

"Yeah, I figured," he said bitterly. "It's easy to forget those who once stood as your brother under duress of weakness."

"What meaning hides behind your words?" Something cracked inside me.

"Do you remember the day I was captured?" He inhaled deeply.

"I remember much but not that day." I shook my head.

"I was taken by Shades on the mountainside. I thought you'd have come for me. Temper even. I thought anyone would come for me, but long did I spend straggling at the end of a line of prisoners. I was tortured nightly for their amusement, burned with iron lit by fire. My screams fueled their madness. One by one they began to kill and feast on those unable to keep up."

I said nothing.

"Do you know the only thing that kept me going?" He looked at me and the first tear fell. "I hoped somewhere out there, in the trees and dense foliage, you were waiting for a time to save me. My tongue dried from the lack of water. My mind was fuzzy without food. But my resolve never wavered."

I hung my head in shame. "Tim, I didn't . . ."

"I know, you claim to forget." He wiped the tear. "If only I could forget too."

He walked off and was soon vanishing up the stairwell toward his room. Arabella was arguing with Lathium over her room and gave me an exasperated eye roll and smile. I nodded back and felt the warm hand on my own. The warmth radiated up my arm and down my back. I inhaled deeply.

"Hey there, stranger," Katy murmured. "Can we talk?"

"I'm always good for a conversation." I smiled. Tim's words troubled my mind, but I pushed them down, far out of reach. "Outside?"

The night was in its deepest hour when the moon was pale and clouds covered the sky. Some called it the witching hour. Others feared dark spirits roamed the empty streets and played pranks of mischief on unsuspecting homes. From the cobbled streets, ghosts of shopkeepers shouted their wares across the roads to passing travelers. Boots thudded over the uneven stones and into puddles of water. To the far left, down the road from the inn, a copse of trees gave way to one of the prettiest views in the entire city. A plateau jutted out over the tier that sat below us and gave a breathtaking view of the mountains marching from left to right. The shimmering plains below seemed so far away. In the shadows of night, they were nothing more than a sea of mystery.

"I never gave up looking."

Her words cut through me. Goosebumps prickled on my skin. The wind tousled my hair with mock longing. We came to a stop and turned to look at each other. I really soaked her in for the first time. Her ponytail was slightly shorter than I remembered it. She wore a faded blue tunic with arm guards and a pair of leather britches that were clearly too large for her. Her clunky boots of grass green were flecked with patches of dried mud. She smelled like she'd been riding for several days with no bath. And yet she had somehow become more beautiful, like a corporeal figure from myth. I reached out and touched her cheek.

"I cannot fully grasp you are before me," I admitted. "Every second I see you; I fear that jolt as I wake. Like every dream before, every nightmare that you were in, I always woke to realize it was nothing but my deepest thoughts. I held to the belief you were safe, far from the clutches of this world. I came here with many memories forgotten but I've remembered so much about those days. When all else failed, I never forgot your face and name."

"You never gave up," she whispered. The wind tousled her silvery hair.

"If I let myself believe for a moment that you were laying injured in those tunnels or worse, dead, I would never have survived." Fear rippled through me. "That fear has now returned. War is coming, my love. I fear for you."

She stepped close to me, and her body radiated that same alluring heat. Her hand found my own and our eyes met.

"The only thing that kept me going was the hope of seeing you again." She smiled slightly. "I may not have been able to find you, but word travels fast. I later discovered we appeared, so to speak, in a long plain between Caldonia and the End Road. We spent much of our first few months in Caldonia finding what information we could bargain off of the travelers who visited. It cost a pretty sum and Tim had to find work in the villages outside the city. Daylight had broken on the four hundredth morning since we had arrived. A prophecy was coming true, or so the old bat outside her potion shop tried to make us all believe. I was actually quite indignant when she forced me into her shop to view the parchment that she swore came from Erëthuïl himself. It said that on the eastern front, a boy, or as they said 'bairn,' was living. He had seemingly 'arrived from the heavens.' My mind tumbled and I won't lie my stomach seized with the renewed hope. Tim thought I was being rash. He said we'd built a stable life in Caldonia. We had the trust of the locals, and we should put our energy into finding a way home. I refused and dragged him out of our hovel. There were many stories about the nearby Kingdom of Glasbur. Most spoke of it in awe so there I decided we should search first."

"Tim had every reason to lose hope in me." I stared into the few visible stars. "I can tell he resents me. He wishes he had not found me, and he would be right for it."

"He doesn't," she murmured. "He felt abandoned by his friends. When we found out we were nowhere near you and in a strange land, he got worse. For a long while he didn't even want to speak of you. When word spread of your existence, he asked what allegiance he had to someone who had left him to rot in the tunnels of a killer. But as time has gone by, I think he's clung to that idea that we weren't alone. His anger fades with the sun and returns at night when his mind wanders. Deep down, he misses you deeply, Phoenix. He may not admit it to himself or others, but he knows you didn't abandon him. You yourself underwent horrible, unspeakable acts. You were no more in control than he was. He had nothing but his thoughts to occupy him in that room with a hundred points tearing his flesh to ribbons. Your mind can be your worst enemy when left alone. For so long he's lived with his idea of who you were and now he has had a chance to hear your story, he will come around. Give him a chance to destroy his idea of you."

"Will we even have time? You spoke of rumors," I murmured conspiratorially. "Were they good? Like save the world kind or more end of the world, hide behind closed doors, kind?"

Her eyes twinkled. "Let's just say they spoke in equal part good and bad. Some praised you as the answer to a prophecy. If there was a way for an old enemy to return, the one who was cursed with bringing him could provide the solution to destroying him. Others clung to the more popular viewpoint that you are a curse brought to punish Ëonë."

"Curse? Wow. No mention of my bulging muscles or roguishly good looks?" I flexed.

"They sort of left that part out." She laughed.

"I miss that."

"What?"

"Your laughter."

She blushed. For a long time, it filled my dreams and the chasm in my heart. It was the most beautiful sound I'd ever heard. Then it faded.

I sucked in my gut and reached one hand out. Hesitant, I paused a fraction of an inch from her cheek. She leaned into my touch and her eyes closed. I pulled her in tight and we stood as one. She slipped her arms behind my back and held me. I never wanted this to end. For the first time since I'd arrived in this world, I felt happy. Sure, out there in the cold void, there was an army marching toward us with every intent to maim and castrate all who stood in their way, but that was in the future. For the present, I was content. Even the lurking shadows presented no real threat. They were merely shadows after all.

Fire blazed . . . screams howled in the pale sky . . . steel sang its deadly ballad. Clouds danced above the bloodbath and hid the breaking sun. What small hope had been brought by the dawn's light was dashed as the darkness, like a great fog, enclosed.

Gisli, commander of the Eastern Garrison, tasked with the protection of Elfinian borders from the growing threat in the east, had failed. He walked slowly along the upturned grass and dirt. The bodies of his men lay strewn about him. He avoided their glazed expressions and the blood that blanketed them. His cloak fell softly over their still-warm corpses. Steel clattered to the stone as his boots crunched over bone and shield. Arrows hissed through the air. Some fell noisily to the ground. Most found a breastplate or shield to stick in. All around, Varglarian roared as they beheaded and dismembered his kin. An Elfin not ten paces from him was whirled about by a savage punch and skewered with a long polearm. Gisli felt as if time had slowed and forced him to watch every single death. From the overhang of the battlements, a Nightshade appeared. It snarled and drew a long curved blade of blackened steel. Red jewels encrusted the handle. Gisli reached for his own sword but staggered back as the creature whipped him with the end of its weapon. He gasped and felt the blood trickle into his eyes. The shouts of battle dinned with a high pitch whine. He ducked the next parry and swung his blade. It vibrated off the other's and he was flung back. The Nightshade before him was stronger in muscle and warfare. The creature took a large step forward and snarled. Spittle flew into his face and Gisli had to cough to avoid the pungent odor. His mistake. The black steel sliced through his breastplate and deep into his chest. He coughed and dropped to one knee. He glanced down and nearly vomited at the torn flesh and open wound. The next blow hit him in the side of the head, knocking his helmet clean off. The blade sliced his cheek and now blood trickled into his eyes. He lay against the back of a hut, sword arm raised high to protect himself from the final blow. A metallic swish filled his ears and a body thudded to the ground.

"Commander!" Naveron, his second-in-command, rushed to his side. His helmet was dented and one eye was missing.

"Get those able out," Gisli gurgled. "Get them all out."

"Commander," again said Naveron. "They've abandoned the banner. Ezrya, his brothers, and their company retreated before the sun rose. Only Kestral and his company stand with their commander now."

"Order . . . them to . . . retreat." Gisli's chest heaved as blood trickled from his mouth. His voice caught. The few standing Elfin were beaten back. One beheaded a charging Varglarian before an arrow stuck in his head. The Elfin tumbled back. Blood stained his once fair hair.

"It was an honor serving with you, my commander," Naveron breathed.

Gisli growled and, with the help of his second, he drew his blade. The effort to stand nearly caused him to blackout. Dizziness assailed him worse than the sword. He blinked and squeezed his eyes shut and open. The din of the slaughter returned in full force as his adrenaline coursed through him. Naveron was struggling hand to hand with a Varglarian. The latter grabbed the Elfin's face and shoved it with full force into the point of a rock. Naveron moved no more. Gisli could count on one hand his remaining men. He had failed them. He had failed Ëonë and would now go to the halls of his fathers a disgraced member of his house. His banner would be the blood of his men. No. Commander Gisli stood tall. His cloak flowed behind him, and he raised his sigil once more. A Rachnadon towered over the walls. Its eight long legs were heavily armored and encased in blood. The rider controlling the beast was roaring with pleasure. Gisli staggered toward it and stabbed a wounded Nightshade just before the beast beheaded a fallen Elfin.

"Cursed beasts. Foul abominations, return to your Pit from whence you came!" he bellowed and hacked with all his might at the Sicarack's nearest leg. The sword contacted metal and flew from his hands. He cursed loudly at his torn hands. They shook as he looked about for a new weapon.

"Arrogant as the day you were made." The voice was soft, barely above a whisper. Gisli felt it in his head more than he heard it.

From the swirling shadows of chaos, a form appeared. Whatever it was, it was larger than anything he'd ever seen before. Its torso was as wide as three men fingertips to fingertips. It slammed down in front of him and a low rumble shook the ground. Gisli gaped at the scene unfolding and the figure atop this strange creature.

"*Begone, cur of this world!*" *He swung his fist at the hooded man.* "*The Elfins have been keepers of Ëonë after you lost all power. And we will be long after you are killed. You think you've won. You've only . . .*"

He never finished his statement as the hooded form slid down the trunk of the creature and came to rest a few feet from him. Gisli watched the other remove his hood and stare up. Something was wrong. This was no Varglarian chieftain or a Nightshade commander. The eyes . . . those haunting eyes he was unable to escape from . . . bore into him.

"*I am Mordën,*" *the form hissed and stepped forward.* "*You claim authorship of all this, yet it was I at the beginning of time who was entrusted to its creation.*"

"*Mordën.*" *Gisli's face drained of any remaining blood. The adrenaline fled and was replaced by crippling fear. Every inch of his wound flamed up in renewed pain. But nothing took his eyes off the other.* "*It is true.*"

"*Truth is hardly what's at stake here.*" *Mordën smiled. His lips were pale and twisted over bloodless gums. His skin seemed stretched tightly over his bony frame. Gisli got a good whiff of his odor. He smelled dead.*

"*All of Ëonë stands ready to defy you,*" *he stammered.* "*You might command a race of mindless beings, but Erëthuïl made us, and we will not let The Golden City fall. You've overestimated yourself.*"

"*Erëthuïl?*" *Mordën mused with mock seriousness.* "*I see a fractured and divided world. Its own creator hides in his heavenly halls. The Druco-dians are a sliver of their former selves and even at their best they were not enough to defeat me. Glasbur is a relic of time, preserved maybe from the outside but a tomb for the fallen inside. And The High City?*" *He snorted.* "*They have been leaderless since their king banished me. What threat is a herd without its leader?*" *He stroked Gisli's chin thoughtfully.*

Gisli tossed his head weakly. "*The men of that place have more honor and strength in their one city than you've all to your name. You forget, they defeated you all those millennium ago.*"

"*No.*" *Mordën smiled again and gripped Gisli's chin tightly. He forced the disgraced commander to stare into his eyes.* "*The Men, with the help of all other races and the aid of Erëthuïl himself, were what it took to banish me. You forget your place. The Elfin, after all, failed in defeating me too. Just like you failed here."*

Commander Gisli exhaled sharply as Mordën plunged a dagger into his chest. Blood flowed out of both his chest and mouth. He grinned feebly and looked up to the sky, finally free of those wretched black orbs. He was going home, maybe not on his shield to be mourned by his kin and folk. There would be no songs. No burial. Darkness closed around and suffocated his last breath.

King Elharan had summoned *the* council. Not since the Second Era had "The Banners Council" been called. Attendees from every race and nearly every city were invited. DarSheer informed us we'd see the likes of Drucodians from their hidden city in the northern parts of the Fallen Peaks. The Ebyians had agreed to send their three most influential, which loosely translated to richest, to speak. Of course, The High City had agreed without much urgency to send a great number of diplomats. I heard rumors even some of the Inclings from the Cacian Hinterlands were making the journey which was surprising considering how little they cared for the goings on outside their peaceful borders. Caldonia was busy with assailers on their borders and elected DarSheer as their trusted advisor.

The day was just breaking, and a heavy rainfall had cleansed the city of its grim and darkness. It seemed to sparkle with hope. Everyone's moods hung in the gutters as the cold sun rang out the clearer. Clouds hung delicately in the morning light. Trees displayed their plumage along the widely paved streets. The gates of the city were kept open, under a heavy watch, as travelers and refugees began streaming in from the eastward villages. Disturbing rumors came with them. The three main fishing villages responsible for three quarters of the trade on the eastern coastline had gone dark. A man spoke wildly in the city square of the fate of those who lived in a small village called Lilro.

"Like a sickness spread," he would tell any who listened. "One day everyone was fine, the next children dead as they're born. Old men toppled over and never got up. The ocean became uncrossable, and black beings were spotted moving over the Bridge. We got no help from the Outpost when those Varg sort ransacked and looted our neighboring towns. No help indeed. I fled myself to Tressel to warn them but found just as much destruction and wanton death as I had out my home window. No word came from Ronier either. Silence filled the coast. So needless to say, I came here as fast as my legs could carry me. Not in my sixty years have I seen such things."

He had drawn quite a crowd as I walked the roads with Katy and Kissinger. Arabella trailed a few feet behind, lost in thought.

"Any word from Fiscer's Keep?" a shout rang out.

"Word?" The old man peered, trying to find the person. "No word at all. Some folk, it appeared, fled into the Ralier Range, that forest in the northern corner. Not heard any word from the northern villages since I made my way past *Ithuïn*. Wouldn't surprise me if they were as dead as my chances at love." Several onlookers chuckled. "Laugh all you want, but the point remains: a shadow has come from the east and is spreading like a poison through these lands. Villages are seemingly vanishing from the face of Ëonë."

"They don't seem to think it's Mordën," I murmured to Kissinger.

"Many find comfort in their self-inflicted ignorance," he responded. "It's easier to label something as an 'unknown evil.' Hard to get frightened over something like that. The moment you admit that Mordën has returned, despair takes over."

Katy kept quiet. She slipped her hand in mine as we walked. I glanced at her and felt my courage return. All these words of chaos and evil burdened my soul yet here she lent my feet wings.

"If I were you," the man continued with enthusiasm at his audience, "Avalon is not a haven anymore. Take the ferries across the Ethero Basin and find refuge in the safe lands beyond."

"Where are you going?" a deep voice boomed.

"To every village and town that will listen to reason, of course." The man laughed like it was obvious. "If you were wise, you'd come along with. I hear tales tell of a Rever Drake seen on the outlying moors. Wings as wide as a city. It stands as large as a mountain. Great rumbling sounds."

Newcomers jostled to the front, curiosity overcoming whatever errands had taken them to the city square. Some jeered in disbelief, others clutched their youth to them like they expected Mordën to appear right there and then. Those just there for the public spectacle leaned against low-lying walls and against the sides of houses and taverns.

"They eat it up like its sizzling *cres*." Kissinger exhaled nervously.

"They should all be warned and moved for their safety." Katy gazed about. "There are children here. What about the elderly or those infirmed beyond fighting capability?"

"King Elharan's called the Council of Banners, hasn't he?" Kissinger pointed out. "Othrain says we're to discuss such a possible plan. He believes all will be evacuated and the city made ready for attack."

We made our way up the winding streets toward the upper tier of the city. Golds and reds flowed as merchants came and went. Some wrapped their banners about the posts that stood on each end of their carts. They seemed weary, less enthusiastic than when I'd first entered the city. A trembling Elfin bairn tried to grab a loaf of bread and run off, but the vendor grabbed the child's hand and began berating the kid. I turned my gaze away as two guards rushed to intervene. Trees hung their lazy bows of foliage over nearby walls like decorative banners. Several children had a ball and bounced it between them. It reminded me of games I played long ago. It reminded me there had been a time when I was as carefree as these bairns. Their rosy laughter was foreign. It had no place here, yet they somehow found merriment. I watched them dance from foot to foot, crying out with varying degrees of confusion and excitement. I watched as various folk of all strange sorts spilled from tavern doors and crept either in shame or exhaustion into seedy inns. A group of Ebyians, standing to the waist of a normal man, exploded with frustration at the ignorance of an Elfinian merchant. They spoke in a harsh tongue and jabbed various diamonds and rubies at the calm

Elfin. Though the jewel's size was not to be underappreciated, for it was the size of a fist, the vendor was not particularly impressed. After passing under the second to last gate, Arabella and Othrain moved through the crowd to our side. I greeted both with a hug.

"A council can mean a great many things." Arabella buzzed excitedly.

"Not the least of which is finally preparing for war," Othrain growled. His obvious discomfort of Elfins radiated. "The fair-haired goldens here seem to think they have all the time in the world. Just yesterday, I spoke to that stuck-up commander about cycling the watches as we did at the Outpost. He told me the words of a man who had failed to uphold his only directive were worth less than sand to him."

"Bereth means well by his account." I placed a weathered hand on his shoulder and gave a light squeeze. "Consider it from his perspective, my old friend. He commands these walls, not us. He is a respected leader amongst his warriors, and they ride high on the pride of their unbeatable city."

"They'd do well to respect the words of a man who's seen with his own two eyes the destruction that Mordën wrought! The Caldonians are a fearsome and strong lot. These goldens are weak."

Kissinger scratched the back of his head. "Respect is earned, Othrain. You of all people know this. How long before you trusted Phoenix?"

"If I recall correctly," I stifled the laugh, "you were one of the more outspoken against me remaining with you."

"No offense meant." He slapped my back.

"None taken," I gasped.

We approached the final gate where ten Elfinian bowmen watched our progress. The road twisted between houses and the rare farm of *velcri,* the succulent purple fruit which grew from the roots of these planted bushes. Outside the opened gates, groups of various peoples and races moved silently under the watchful gaze of the Elfinian soldiers. A group of Drucodians, all eyes marveling in their direction, moved seamlessly out of sight. Behind them, carrying their sigil of coin and axe, three Ebyians rode on small horses. Their shortness was nearly comical as the bottoms of their feet barely dipped below the saddle itself. Hands on the reigns, three Elfin guided the mounts into the gates and up the winding road. An entourage of men on brilliant white stallions carrying the banner of The High City moved slowly, behind us, from the bottom of the road up towards the gates. Several spectators threw them flowers. Traveling with little to no décor, a group of strangely garbed individuals walked up the road. They came in on no fancy rides or with any servants.

"Inclings," Kissinger said. "It's been a minute since I saw one of their race this far east, considering they do all their trade with The High City."

We followed this last group into the final tier. The gates thudded shut behind us with a finality and from outside the slight privacy the low walls offered, we heard the people singing.

> *The hall of the kings in darkness brings*
> *A light to our darkest dreams*
> *Their callous deeds of ancient times past*
> *Rushes blood through the veins and holds us fast*
> *Sing high sing low for the king we praise*
> *His manner is goldening his banner we raise*
> *The hall of kings in brightness brings*
> *A hope to our nightmarish dreams*

"They can feel that something big is about to happen," Arabella narrated. "The song is one of hope after King Grasspear was overthrown by his son. I've only ever heard them sing it when they had a need for hope."

"Don't we all," Othrain said in hushed tones.

He turned and stepped toward the glittering King's Hall. It stood out even more so than before. Or maybe that was just because I knew the importance of what was about to happen. The simple walls around the spires sent shivers down my spine. Green vegetation crept up toward the tops of their points. Behind them, and looming, the Fallen Peaks gave a glimpse at the impressive nature of Avalon. The mountainsides were strewn with boulders and the ground was unkind. To have delved deep into the sides and built this city was a testament to the Drucodians' persistent and impressive craftsmanship. I wondered if the Drucodian escort felt anything, any twinge of the past, being in this city. Our convoy stopped as the procession wound down and some of each race entered the King's Hall. I promised the others I would divulge all the happenings of the council. Othrain shook his head and expressed his clear distaste for the limited representatives, but Kissinger took him aside. The two squabbled about something and soon hurried off.

"Where's Tim?" I whispered to Katy before we were whisked off.

"He volunteered to stand watch on the gates," she said softly. Her concern showed clear. "He told me the likes of him was not meant for great halls and royalty. I'm worried, Phoenix. He's not himself, not since we came here. I worry that he has let darkness enter his thoughts. Please, talk to him."

"I will," I promised, "as soon as this council is completed. I know that burden and I do not wish it on any. If Mordën indeed holds sway on his thoughts, he will need a comforting hand."

After I was liberated from the security of my sword and dagger, DarSheer and I entered the throne room. The throne had been pushed aside in favor of the long wooden table. Its ebony surface shone under the stray rays of sun. On the left of the table, the Ebyians and Drucodians talked casually to each other whilst keeping wary eyes for the others in the room. To the right, the men from The High City milled about with Elfin and Incling dignitaries. We all found and took our spots as King Elharan appeared from a side chamber. His arrival was signaled by the echoing thud of the door closing and the scuffling of several of his advisors.

"Allies of the free peoples of this world and all others," he displayed both hands, "please come forth. Thank you for entertaining my request. Let this Council of Banners, the first of its kind in the Third

Era, commence." Elharan sat at the head of the table. "My letters were vague in the reason for bringing you all here, I know. Yet secrecy is a tool we must utilize for now. The spies of our enemy wander in open eyesight. However, it should come as no surprise that our foe of ancient origin moves in open war against all of us. The Western and Eastern Wards need to put aside their differences and unite under one banner. Only together do we stand a chance. We may all be new to the consequences of war, untested by the strength of the sword, but our strength stands nonetheless."

One of the robed men at the far end of the table stood with a patronizing smile. "I am Master Hendrix, voice and arm of the Custodian. I'd like to extend a greeting to all gathered here. Despite the reason for this summons, I'm sure our dignified allies from the east have good reason to maintain good relations in tone and manner to us. With me are Latherul and Endaya, my personal prodigies." He placed a hand on the shoulder of a young man and young woman in turn. They gave shy smiles.

"We've heard from The High City." Elharan moved on briskly. "Lord Berëthelluïn?"

Bereth rose and bowed to his king before speaking. "I am Lord Berëthelluïn, commander of the Elfinian forces in this fair city. May I first remark that the safety of all here is of paramount interest. Guards will be stationed at every street juncture and at every crenel on the battlements."

An Ebyian with thick glassy eyes peered up. "You speak riddles, my richly garbed friend. Now speak answers. We've heard this fear in your tone and note the shakiness of your hand."

"With me are the Lords Rygone and Parnethëlleon. We are honored to be here at this pivotal moment in our history." Berëthelluïn carefully finished and sat down.

"I am Rusbalz." The same Ebyian stood. The top of his head was only a foot above the bottom of the table. "We have paused a great harvesting of rare rock for this meeting and would like answers. Why do you demand an oath from the before days?"

"Your confusion is understood, and all will be explained shortly," Elharan mediated.

"To my left are Cleoz and Durtain," Rusbalz continued.

One of the Inclings, a rosy-faced man with short hair and a wide smile, stood hesitantly. He cleared his throat and brushed imaginary dirt from his perfect tunic. The room waited in silence.

"My name is Clayon, of the fields," he bowed low. The two others seated beside him gave a raucous cheer which died as awkwardly as it had begun. "Yes, well you've met my beloved children it seems. The pretty lass is Primula, and the other normal lass is Aega." The two Inclings stood and bowed deeply in turn. I couldn't help my eyebrows as they rose. *What a duo.* Primula bore a shy expression of intrigue and batted her eyes every few seconds. She blushed anytime she made eye contact with anyone. Aega, on the other hand, was built stockily with thick locks and a piercing gaze. Her arms were folded.

All eyes shifted to the Drucodians. The two seated quietly at their places stood. There was something sad about the way they gazed into each other's eyes and finally at the council.

"Fair greetings to those aforementioned," one of them spoke in a sing-song voice. "It is unusual for us to see so many strange faces or even to be from our coveted homes for so long. The words which were sent spoke of an evil abroad that caused our hairs to stand on end. We have seen much and been a part of much in our long lifespans. My name is Dhir, and my companion is Ynasha. We are the youngest surviving Drucodians, born not long before the Second Great War. It is an honor to be seated here amidst such respected peoples. We hope this dialogue enables us to come to a mutually agreed end, whatever the reason our being here entails. And we thank, with distinction, our Elfinian host for his kindness."

King Elharan stood and, smiling, bowed low. The room tittered with surprise. It wasn't often a king bowed to commoners. But there was no denying the respect the Elfins and Drucodians had for each other. All eyes turned once again, but this time coming to rest on me. Words were muttered softly around the table. DarSheer raised himself from his chair and placed both hands on the table. His voice was deep and his eyes wide as he nodded to the arrivals.

"My name is DarSheer. I come from the ill-fated Outpost. We were tasked with alerting all Ëonë of a nameless evil seen reigniting the forges of the BlackBurg." He turned and nodded to me. I stood.

"My name is Phoenix Rather, DarkBairn," I said. "I . . . I'm no proud warrior. I'm not even a part of your world. I come from a different . . . land . . . so to speak where Mordën was once banished to. The acts of the last High King sought to rid your lands of the evil that usurped it and for the last five hundred years you have lived in blissful peace because of it. It is because of us that you all are here, seated, and listening. Mordën, the dark princeling, has returned to these lands and even now burns the eastern lands."

"Impossible," Rusbalz snorted. Snot ran from his wide nostrils. "That dark chapter in our history has long been closed. I do not doubt Varglarian still run amok on the eastern shores and that despite our extensive destruction of that cursed isle, there might be some stones that were not fully turned over. Some lost villages do not amount to a full-scale invasion."

"Far beyond a small few," Berëthelluïn cleared his throat importantly. "Our scouts indicate that Ithuïn fell not two days past. Varglarian hosts marching under the banner of a red hourglass against a black field have been seen laying waste to the fields and villages between our eastern border and that once lively city. It is chaos out there. Law and order are things of the past and nothing but the long arm of bloody conflict controls the lands beyond our walls. We may sit here in peace thanks to the strength King Elharan has built up, but those who reside outside our walls will not find themselves so lucky. If he moves with—"

"All Elfinian propaganda." The Ebyian waved a hand as the room shifted uneasily.

"Do you not see who it is who stands there?" Master Hendrix pushed his wired glasses further up. "You would not only interrupt him but also accuse him of deception?"

"Not deception, honored dignitary from The High City." Rusbalz shook his head. "I simply wish proof of these wild claims before I pledge undying support. My people and I are not as trusting as most present, and for good reason. The more radical Drucodians and Elfins no doubt desire the glory days of past. It must ache them something to perish a death that is not suitable for a warrior. Who desires to expire on the bed of old age? Where are their warriors ending?"

"If I may finish." Berëthelluïn narrowed his eyes. "I've received word from the Eastern Garrison." He paused while the room quieted down. "Commander Gisli sent a message, and I was told to wait till this council convened to read it."

I leaned forward in my seat. Commander Gisli was a name I recognized well in this sea of unfamiliar titles. Bereth cleared his throat and broke the grey seal on the scroll. He read unwaveringly:

"The shadows are long, and my warriors grow restless. We can all feel it. It's palpable like a heavy fog rolling in off the tumultuous sea. A deep disturbance has settled over the trees and plants. Some die with no explanation. Once a healthy bow yesterday, today it is sickly and weak. I sent my best scouts abroad and they have not returned. I send more and they too fail to report back. Not a few days prior, a bairn and his allies passed through my walls, and I dismissed his words with little concern. Do not make the same foolish mistake I have, for I know now what the cost is. I am left with the fear that what we were apprehensive of is now approaching. It rumbles like a far-off thunderclap. I see shapes in the forest beyond. It is only a matter of time before the darkness that the DarkBairn promised reaches our doorstep. I have closed the gates and placed all on watch. We stand, loyal to the end. Our honor will not be blemished. We know our fates. We know the *future*. How does one prepare for his own death? It is too late for us but if this scroll can be delivered safely to Avalon, be forewarned . . . Mordën has reached us. He sullies the ground and corrupts the minds of every beast. Long live King Elharan. May my failure be not a stumbling block to the defense ahead. I can feel them. Their drums fill my every thought. Innith Inine! They are here."

Berëthelluïn placed the scroll down on the table. Candlelight flickered ominously over the upturned faces of the dignitaries as they processed the words in their own ways. Elharan leaned into his seat, one hand on the table, the other draped over his right knee. His eyes were clouded. Lord Rygone, an Elfinian lord to his left, raised both brows, revealing his golden irises.

"If we've lost the Eastern Garrison, we have no force outside these walls to defend us. We remain vulnerable to the evil that may come."

"Not true, my lords." DarSheer stood. "I have visited Caldonia in the south."

"Beyond . . . the . . . recommendation . . . of your . . . *Custodian*?" Master Hendrix drew out each word slowly and nasally. He dug into DarSheer with a disapproving scowl.

"Forgive my rudeness, Master Hendrix, but the urgency with which the situation required left no time to send a message. Some things must be done without waiting for proper channels to be completed."

"And what of Caldonia?" Rusbalz demanded. "Will they come to our aid?"

"Now it is *our* aid?" Lord Rygone scoffed. "You've changed sides rather hastily."

"I cannot deny something hunts freely over the lands." The Ebyian sniffed. "Do I think it is the princeling of old? That is balderdash. However, many other evils were put to sleep when he was banished. It is not without reason to believe some may have awakened in the centuries since. My people and I stand at the behest of King Elharan, ready to commit."

For the next several hours, the room was silent save for one or two voices as the entire nightmare was laid out. From the moment I'd appeared in Ëonë till now, we spared no detail. Occasionally, one of the delegates would ask a probing question and go silent when given their response. Even Hendrix had nothing snide to add as the timeline progressed. Faces creased when we told of the fall of the Outpost. Hands clenched and lips grew dry as the afternoon came and went. We talked about the movements of Rachnadons, Varglarian warbands, and Nightshades. The addition of Rachnadons did not seem to faze any present. These creatures had been used in wars past and whilst some more alarming than others on the field of combat, to talk in the comfort of an enclosed hall one might thing we were discussing what to eat the following morning. Had it not been for the earlier scroll, they might not have taken to the news so well. I could see the words sink in. Not all took it calmly, however. Rusbalz in particular took great exception to everything. He was unhappy about the ways Mordën had returned, calling it "fables of a prophetic fanatic." Silhouettes of night elongated along the wall and the candlelight grew bright before he had been talked into submission. Hendrix finally spoke up in support of the Ebyian's disbelief. He claimed it fit into the agenda of a warring faction of Elfin who yearned for the glory days of old. I had to hide the surge of rage that pulsed through me. It was as if he was intentionally waiting till everyone was on the same page before tossing out some potentially believable objection and causing everyone to become disunified. Anytime the group finally stopped asking questions about a certain topic, he would be right there to egg on those with the most disbelief. Many still bore skeptical looks or straight up confusion but at long last, when the sun settled into its bed below the horizon and the bewitching moon prowled high overhead in the sparkling sky, the council adjourned. Chairs scraped against the stone floor as tired dignitaries moved out of the hall toward where accommodations had been made to fit each specific race.

As DarSheer and I stepped into the night, I mentioned my concerns. He laughed them off when it came to Hendrix. He seemed to believe the other would come around when he realized the validity of our statements.

"Some folk cast doubt into the proceedings to give themselves more time to decide," he said as we walked down the road toward The King's Inn where the others would be waiting for us. "They stir the discussions in a circle so they may prolong the inevitable."

Streams trickled and the soft flow of water over stone made me feel relaxed. A warm breeze fell down from the tips of the mountains and sang its own relaxing tune to the aromas of flowers and wet wood. High overhead, rings of stars danced in harmony. For now, the night was young, and the world slept in comfort and peace. We strode down a lane bordered by young saplings. Their spongy bark and weak branches danced in the breeze. I twisted an offshoot and smelled the intoxicating aroma of pine. Flowers of all colors grouped about the bunches of perfectly kept flower beds. I wondered who from my party would be up to hear our news and who would have succumbed to exhaustion. I was mildly surprised when I saw Katy standing outside the thick wooden door of the tavern. She brightened at my approach and unstuck from the wall.

"Took you long enough," she joked half-heartedly. "We'd begun taking wagers on if the sun would make an appearance before old good King Elharan released you to sleep."

"The matters at hand are vital to the continent," DarSheer murmured darkly. "We shall discuss as long as it takes to protect those who entrust themselves to us. We may sleep once we have liberated these lands."

"Accept my sincerest apologies." Katy's face flushed pink.

"Now it is my turn to apologize, Lady Katy, for that is no way to speak to a maiden. The proceedings were long and made so by several intentional disruptions. My mind aches with the sounds of their voices."

"He's talking about The High City," I translated. "Their dignitary wants nothing but trouble."

"That's just men for you," she shrugged.

"Perhaps the rotten ones, though most harbor goodwill and a fighting spirit if only you can find it." DarSheer bowed slightly. "If you'll excuse me, my lady, I must recite for the others the day's events then retire to my bed. Until we meet again, Phoenix. Sleep well. I believe we are to resume at first light."

He opened the tavern door, and a sliver of orange light broke the dark greys and blues of the night. Laughter spilled out. The fires in the hearth were going strong as huddled forms sat at tables and shouted for more ale. Lathium seemed extra busy as he completed his delivery dance between tables. The door shut and with it the noise and light ceased as suddenly as they had begun. I stood awkwardly for a few moments as Katy nudged a small rock with her boot.

"The others are nice," she said softly with a small smile. "I like Arabella. Even her name is beautiful."

"I'm glad you're making friends."

"You should speak with Tim."

"Must we discuss him now?"

"He's acting strange, and I can feel something is happening. Please, just talk with him. Help him see reason."

"Still as beautiful as the day I left you." I reached out a finger, afraid to touch her like she was some priceless vase. Her dimples appeared as she turned pink from her nose to her ears.

"Flattery won't distract me, Phoenix," she murmured. "Please?"

"Alright," I sighed. "I do owe it to him to at least have a full conversation beyond the snippets of derision he's been sending me."

"He's had a rough go at it. We all have. I didn't know if my search was futile, if you were out there somewhere, or if I was putting all my trust into a fool's hope."

"I'm here, all alive," I said.

"I thought you were dead." Her voice was barely above a whisper as she took a step closer. She stepped into my touch. My finger traced her cheek where an electric current seemed to shoot from her to me. Goosebumps soared down my arm. My heart thumped excitedly. It was all I could do to simply remember to breathe. I hoped I appeared manly and not like a giddy buffoon.

"I've come close on many instances." I swallowed hard. "You have no idea how many times I nearly leapt off the walls when Topper would strum his gloshee." The intimate moment was broken. She let out a half snort, half laugh.

"Topper?"

"He was a terrible musician back at the Outpost."

"Always playing the wise guy."

"I was going for a deep brooding look with magnetic charm, but I'll take wise. I can do wise." I scrunched my nose mockingly and spoke deeply. "*You will find the one you are looking for. He is right in front of you. He is very handsome.*" She raised one eyebrow.

"You know for a wise guy, you can say some dumb things." She placed one hand on my arm. "Do you know how hard it was, living in a world where you were and not being able to find you? Wondering if you saw the same stars I fell asleep gazing at."

"Sometimes on watch," I swallowed the lump in my throat, "I'd gaze up at the night sky and wonder if the stars looking down were the same ones as back home. I wondered if you might be looking at them at the same instance and when one shot across the night sky, I'd wish with all my heart that I . . ."

"Do not stumble on your words, Phoenix, my love." She fluttered her eyelashes. "Speak candidly, for this honor I believe I have earned."

"I woke up every morning, sweat on my face because of a nightmare I'd just had. I dreamt you'd died in every way imaginable. There were times I wondered if you had been corrupted beyond saving, doomed to serve Mordën till the end of time, his poisoned twisted *creation* . . . I thought a lot of things. Some days you were alive and healthy and living life without me. I was okay with that because I knew you were happy. On darker days, you were pining after me, a siren lost at sea. And on my blackest nights, he held dominion over you."

"Hey," she took both her hands in mine as the first tear fell and gave them a soft squeeze, "I'm here, handsome. All glorious, one hundred percent of me. You're stuck with me."

"Let us not speak of losing what is found." My hands shifted to her hips, and I pulled her close. Our bodies were a fraction of an inch apart. I could feel her heart racing as her softness melted into me. Her hands found their way around to my back where she traced lines in my tunic.

"You were tortured too," she murmured. The breath of her words tickled my nose. She pushed some of my hair back. "You were tortured, and you were forced to be a part of something you never should have been. We all have suffered in our own ways."

"Must we waste our nights speaking of such ill times?" I sighed. "We have lost so much time and I find myself wanting to hear every tale you have lived."

"The pasts of these people will not be your future. I do not believe this to be your end." She cupped my cheek in her hand. "Do you remember back when I caught you being chased by BB?"

I blinked. *BB*. It felt odd hearing such a name here in this world. "I have lost much, but that memory remains firm."

"I found that even the thought of you being hurt bothered me profusely. Then when I was disturbed by Claire's constant drills, I only had to think of you and my chest settled. She leaned forward and kissed me."

My mind grew so lightheaded I wondered if I'd pass out. Drums in my ears sounded out the celebration and my ears blazed scarlet. Our heartbeats began to synchronize as she held me close. I hugged her tight, not wanting the moment to go. Her lips tasted of a summer morning under a cherry tree. We took a few small steps, her backwards and me forwards. I held her waist like she was a lifeline in the ocean. Her arms were like the comforting presence of bed right before you drift off. And her smell. I hadn't realized it before, but beneath the days of unwashed travel, she smelled heavenly. Her scent was more euphoric than all of Avalon. I knew in that instance she was who I'd go to war for. I'd been uncertain before, but now, beneath the arching arms of a weeping willow, I had found a reason for fighting. My reason. The realization sent flutters through my stomach. *Butterflies*, I thought.

I finally broke the kiss, our lips pulling apart slowly. She labored to keep her breath normal as she opened her eyes and we gazed at each other. And there, under that tree, there was no denying it any longer, not that I'd been trying. I hadn't said the words before for fear she'd fade into the sky like a ghost.

"I love you, Katy," I stroked her soft cheek and placed a strand of her silver hair behind her ear.

Tears brimmed in her eyes, and she giggled softly. Her eyes were wide, revealing her chocolate irises. They practically glowed. She glowed.

"I love you, Phoenix," she murmured and wiped the tears from her eyes with a slow intentional swipe.

The day had begun with a tedious council intent on fixing an unfixable puzzle. Now it was ending with the girl I loved, in my arms.

We stayed awhile, watching the stars twinkle merrily overhead. She kept an arm around my shoulder, and I kept one around her waist. We laughed at stories of merchants trying to sell her all sorts of bizarre products. Fluffy clouds floated lazily overhead. I laid my head in her lap as I spoke of Brenneth and the end of the Outpost. She ran her fingers through my hair and stared down at me. She almost missed the shooting star overhead.

"Make a wish." I pointed up.

"Done."

"So?" I teased. "What did you wish for?"

She raised one eyebrow. "I may not know everything about shooting stars, but I do know you're not supposed to share your wish. It's bad luck."

"Point taken." I sighed dramatically. "Humor me."

She looked up into the night. "I wished that this memory would be the one that glowed the brightest, no matter how much darkness Mordën threw at us. When I'm at my lowest point, the thing that brings me back is the memory of you in my arms. And I wish that I will always have you here to share in these moments."

"That's cheating," I said sleepily and yawned. "You can only have one wish."

"There were two shooting stars." She kissed the top of my head.

The door to the tavern was flung wide and Kissinger, nearly falling into the street with a bottle of ale in one hand, staggered into view. I turned and Katy jolted. He stared at us for a long silent moment. I sat up and rubbed my uneven hair back into place. He continued to stare at us.

"Wow." He ran a hand through his thick hair. "Can you guys hear me? Is it uncomfortably warm? I would use a cloak but that barmaid has it. Oh boy, the food is coming back."

I let go of Katy's hand, despite how much I wanted to hold her, and helped him to the side of the road where he wretched loudly and wetly for several long minutes. Katy gave me an apologetic look and entered the tavern. The light had greatly died down in the hearth. I supposed we'd been outside far longer than it had felt. My own weariness settled back familiarity into the knots in my back and I groaned.

"Alright, big guy," I wheezed, "we have to get you to bed."

"I got the dingus," Othrain stepped outside. "Get some rest, bairn. Tomorrow's a big day."

"Aren't they all?"

I carefully shifted Kissinger's weight over to Othrain, who eased the other onto the ground. My job done, I entered the tavern myself. True to my assumptions, most of the crowd were long asleep. A few drunken Elfin slumbered deeply in curled positions. Even one of the Ebyians from the council was snoring loudly at a corner table. I bid Lathium good night and trudged up to my room. I thought we'd be staying once again up on the final tier where Elharan had placed us earlier, but the dignitaries were being housed there. My bed welcomed me with comforting sheets and a thick down pillow. Before I'd even kicked off my boots, I was drifting off into a world of slumber. For the first time that I could remember, Mordën's nightmares did not visit me. It was altogether a dreamless sleep and the best I'd ever had.

A grey cloud slipped over the wet stones. To anyone inside, they felt the soft breeze of a moist mist. He brushed the droplets from his brow and brought low his cloak. Even with the soft light spilling from shuttered windows, not even the fairest-eyed Elfin would see him now. He ducked beneath an arch and hugged the soft hill to his left. An Elfinian patrol strolled past.

Of all the times to need him . . . why now. He remained motionless in the foggy shadows. The guards walked less than a foot by. The gold cloak around his shoulders shifted.

"*I heard those cursed Varglarian have attacked the eastern outposts.*" *The words came from a burly Elfin stumbling along the street. In one hand he held a tankard. The liquid sloshed around. At his side, a young girl hurried along. She supported the bulk of the older.*

"*Such rumors are nightmare fuel and no more,*" *she comforted.*

Hidden by the branches of a bush drooping low over his head, the figure smiled. Ever since his arrival in Ëonë, he'd found a weak crippled people brought low by centuries of unity. His master would find no resistance here. A generation bred in peace does not know the trials of war. He shook his head at the sudden thoughts that invaded him. Why was he doing this? What was wrong with him?

"*Tell that to the king's guard,*" *the Elfin grumbled. "Nemoia, how many times must I tell you not to let me drink this late at night?*"

"*Nothing can breach these walls, Father.*" *Nemoia rubbed his back, and they moved past him.*

Nothing yet. He felt for the hilt of his dagger and for a moment the urge to silence the two before him nearly overpowered him. The bloodlust had crept like a disease, first starting in his mind and as gravity claimed it, inching down to his heart. His arms had begun to twitch and every cursed Elfin he saw brought him one step closer to slitting their white pasty throats. He hated them. The blasted goldens! For a moment a part of him surged and he nearly dropped the curved blade. This wasn't him. He wasn't himself. But then as quickly as it had shown itself, the feeling evaporated like steam. The voice inside him reassured him. His eyes adjusted.

The two moved beyond and out of sight, turning down a brightly lit path. They were out of his reach but not out of his master's reach.

He moved from his spot. By now his cloak was soaked through with the heavy fog. The wind moved sluggishly, taking time to prod and stab every inch of exposed skin. What wasn't exposed was subjugated to the cold sappy touch of his cloak. Even his undershirt had begun to cling to his flesh. He hated and loved the cold.

The looming walls of the outer city towered above, arching into the night sky and vanishing as the fog covered them. No torchlight would pierce its grey fabric now. The few guards who patrolled on this side of the wall would be sleepy and unwilling to accept what was about to happen.

He came across an Elfin who leaned against a pole arm, head drooped in deep sleep. With a simple thrust, the guard was on the floor, a stain spreading through his golden breastplate. The torch on the wall went out. He felt a deep sense of satisfaction as he hurried by the fallen guard.

In a small recess of the wall, a single hole had been tunneled from one side to the other. It was nearly thirty feet long and less than a pinky size wide. He didn't know how they had managed to create this and frankly he didn't care. All that mattered was his mission.

"Hold on, fair stranger!" The voice sent his thoughts scampering into the dark places of his mind. He rotated carefully.

"Oh, it's you." The guard lowered his bow and stared, cockeyed. "What are you doing here this late at night? Your companions await you."

"A simple late-night wandering." His black pupils narrowed. He took several casual steps closer. "I felt stressed by the recent events and thought a walk would clear my head."

"It's still strange for a member of the . . ." The guard gurgled as a knife appeared in his throat. He collapsed, hands pawing weakly at his neck as his eyes bulged. The guard keeled over and was motionless.

A forced hoot distracted him, and he wiped the blood from the blade as he hurried to the wall.

"I am here," he hissed, lips pressed firmly against the gap.

"You know of the bairn?" the scratchy, grinding voice snarled.

"He resides on the royal tier of the city," he said. "Tell our master he may begin his assault. All those he wishes to destroy lay perfectly prepared behind their self-fabricated security."

"He will find a place in his reign over Ëonë and the lands beyond. Long live the Shadow King of the BlackBurg." The voice faded as its speaker hurried off.

"Long live the Shadow King," he murmured more to himself than anything else.

He cleared his hand of the dagger and let it fall beside the guard. The Elfin's pale face shown in the fog. His eyes were wide with horror, glazed and glassy. Blood still trickled down his torso and into the wet grass.

"How could . . . you?" the Elfin gurgled.

He tilted his head, as if admiring his work. He watched the Elfin expire in the lonely expanse of darkness. Killing came so easy now. He couldn't remember a time before the lust for death. His left eye twitched and for a moment he wanted to weep. But the feeling was quickly replaced with happiness.

All was in motion and soon the city would be in flames. If he was lucky, his would be the largest bonfire of them all.

\The day yawned before me, a great chasm of undeniable boredom. Time came and went along with the plates of food and tireless servants, their eyes always averted. I began to wonder if the point of this council was to unify the races of Ëonë or if it was to rehash old wounds. The Drucodians did not desire to ally with the Inclings thanks to their believed betrayal in the "early days" of the Second Great War.

"My people, the last bastion of hope for a free Ëonë, were beset by a horde of Varglarian scum and *your* people abandoned us . . . in our most dire need." Dhir's voice filled the hall.

"You must understand the will of my forebearers," Clayon protested. "We wish to not repeat the same bloodshed that culminated in the First Great War. Countless dead lay strewn about the battlefield. We have ballads which number our dead more than the sands in these shores."

Dhir stood. His full height towered over the Incling. "My people fought to their race's extinction for the good of these lands. You were afraid of a few deaths."

"Perhaps you should let go of the transgressions of the past," Clayon snarled. "The perceived sins of my forefathers were their choice, not mine. I should not be enslaved to their actions."

"Yet presented with a similar opportunity, you make the same grave error." Dhir grinned, a smile that was anything but happy.

"Please, gentlemen." Elharan leaned forward and tapped the

table with one finger. "This council is not to pit us at each other. If we cannot put aside those grievances caused by people well before our time, then we are all lost. Our only chance at defeating the evil in the east is to unify. Surely, the ill will between our great nations is not more important than our survival."

By the end of the morning, I could not take it any longer and excused myself to the battlements where I watched the fields of green and mountains of purple. An orange glow filled the sky, speckled with blue and white. Dawn was long past, yet the day still held an air of youth. Clouds floated lazily by. Men led horses by the great stables set into the side of this part of the city. Stable boys ran to and fro, cleaning hooves and brushing down the sleek glistening flanks of their lords' steeds. My stomach clenched thinking of Brenneth, and I practiced breathing again. Rivers flowed from unseen mouths high in the mountains. The water sparkled and glistened against the growing sun and gurgled from the mountain's head far along its feet until it vanished south towards the flowing fields of Caldonia. Beyond the horizon there, I knew, well beyond, the Lost Kingdom of Glasbur sat shrouded in a fog of mystery. To the east, along the road we'd come, I imagined Ithuïn in flames. Screams failed in the air as smoke stole their breath. Steel hissed against scabbard and bells tolled. Horses thudded frantically, full of utter panic, against the hands of their riders. They trampled enemy and foe alike. I swallowed and glanced at the horizon. The Westerly Road branched north at Ithuïn and headed up toward where Arabella called home. Those poor villages lay razed under the curved blade of the Varglarian.

The council continued, locked in the confines of the King's Hall, under the radiant splendor of its golden weight. Grey smoke wafted lazily toward the ceiling. Parchment rustled as scribes took notes. Throats swallowed mugs of ale thirstily and munched on thick loaves of freshly baked bread.

"The goings of the First Era are an equally humbling and proud moment for our races," Dhir said and stood. "Those of my clan who still remember the fire that came from the Pit those millennium ago when Mordën first made Varglarian will also remember the atrocities that the fallen Luthi committed. The world was young when Mordëngrold, once a Luthi himself, first caught the displeasure of Erëthuïl. With his creation of the corrupted race of Varglarian, he was cast from eternal bliss and made to dwell here with those who called the place home. He's always been an outsider, foreign, to the will of my people. Those dark mornings, the sun held no warmth and the night was long. The purging of my peoples' homes and the murders that took place before we rallied in strength still bring tears in 'The Great Passing.' We do not quickly forget nor do we forgive. With his return, Mordën desires power like he never did before. Some here question the legitimacy of his return. We do not. Where once he wished to see the death of all the good and purity that Erëthuïl had made, now he wishes to corrupt it into his own evil. This we will not tolerate, even if it means our own extinction. I have come to this council, called by my equals around this table, and hosted by the benevolent King Elharan, to pledge our allegiance. Once, Drucodians, Elfins, and Men stood shield to shield on the battlefield. Once we stood as allies. This day forward, you will have what remains of my people, their *krekites* sheathed at their side. Mordën will not so quickly have forgotten what my people did to him."

"Your wise words and allegiance are honored by all present." Elharan smiled warmly and bowed ever so politely. "The horrors your people have had enacted upon them countless times is a tale made longer by each passing millennium. Truly, you are strong. Allegiances of old will outstand the tests to come. Now for the Ebyians, will you also hold to old banners, take up the sword and spear and defend this great realm?"

Cleoz and Rusbalz pushed their great chairs back and stood. In the dying embers of the fire, they appeared mysterious. Shadows flickered over their aged features.

"We have no love for much of the events beyond our lives," Rusbalz admitted grudgingly. "But we cannot ignore the threats that brought this council together. Long have we desired to believe that all of this was a rumor. In my halls, the DarkBairn is a trophy for mockery. His words are as stale as bread under a sweltering midsummer's day. We may not have lived as long as our Drucodian comrades, but we are no stranger to the malevolent barbarity of the Shadow King. We too suffered in the old days. We are no stranger to war. Our own ancient scrolls remember what we have forgotten. Though it has been a millennium and a half since any of us held a blade or thought of anything beyond our work, it should be noted this does not delude our resolution. We were made to be a stone with which the great waters crash against but go no further. You have the banner and loyalty of my people." The two bowed again and sat down.

"Lovely fellows," I muttered.

"Don't hold their incredulity against them," DarSheer murmured back as the Inclings once again began talking. "Many wished you a madman, sprung from the bosom of a wayward tavern maiden. Accepting truth can be hard, even for the strongest of people."

"The words of this council are bittered by infighting and speculation." Clayon shook his head. "My people are a soft-spoken and rather mild-mannered group. We do not have any love for war nor the bloodshed that follows. I have been sent, along with those in my company, to speak on behalf of all Inclings who now have made the Cacian Hinterlands our home. We will not hold ill will toward any present here. But we will return to our home and tend to our crops. Should a time come when it is needed, we might consider sending food or supplies to aid any distressed. But we have lived our wars. Now is our time to rest."

"Blasted Incling!" Othrain burst from where he'd been leaning unnoticed in the shadows. "You claim you've lived your wars but the last great battle you fought in was nigh two millennium ago. The Drucodians have lost everything. Yet you do not see them grovel before the black words of the Shadow King. Even now, a race without a future, doomed to wait their remaining years, they wish to stand and fight. There is more honor in one drop of their blood than your entire people."

"Be at peace, Othrain of The High City!" Elharan's eyes flashed angrily. "There will be no hostilities in a court I have convened. You will do well to remember this."

Othrain bowed but his disgust smoldered beneath his beard. "Yes, sire."

"The purpose of this council has been completed." Elharan turned his attention back to the table. "Return to your homes so we may begin our duties of defense. The days of war have returned. The hour is at hand when blood and tears will flow as one. Protect your kin. Barricade your cities. Raise your banners. Lords Parnethëlleon, Rygone, and Berëthelluïn, if there yet remains one ounce of blood inside me that still boils at what the enemy has done, I shall defend my people. Sound the trumpets and muster the legions to respond to their king. The utter lawlessness Mordën wishes to spread will go no further than this realm."

Berëthelluïn knelt as the room stood. "If this is to end in death, then I welcome it. If the very hordes of hell itself were unleashed and every demon from east to west came to rent us asunder, I would gladly perish."

"And with your honor and sacrifice, you would see your kin and people in the Halls of Splendor, where Erëthuïl awaits all the victorious fallen."

The room was emptying fast as the dignitaries made plans to return and report on the decisions of the council. The Ebyians and Inclings were the first to leave as the others milled about. I found King Elharan alone by his throne, a simple chair considering his stature. His old eyes found mine and broke in a friendly look.

"Phoenix, forgive the mind-numbing nature of a court like this. Political bantering is but a norm and to be expected. Do not take the Ebyian's words personally."

"Of course, King Elharan." I bowed. "Hard as it may be, their desire to remain ignorant is at least understandable."

"It is to your credit." He sighed and blew out a stubby candle. "I had hoped to receive an oath from the Inclings as well, but overall, what's done is done."

"I do not blame them." I smiled. "I cannot curse a simple life. There's something pleasant in the average moments of the day. From the crow of the cock to the trundle of wheels over pressed dirt. Seeing bright flowers pay homage to the one who made them. The sounds of water over moss-covered stones. There truly is something alluring to this existence. The cries of battle and grief are not a burden all can carry."

"You are wiser than your years are young. Would that all held your optimism."

"I am hardly bereft of reasons to despair, King Elharan."

"Come now, why is one so young, so grim?" He smiled sadly. "Have the few years in this world darkened even you?"

"Where can anything but grimness grow in a field of hurt and anger?" I tucked my arms tight against my body. "When I feel like I finally know what I'm accomplishing, Mordën reminds me of my failures. How many more people will awaken for their last time before it is revealed? I was a vessel for the Shadow King. He used me in the same way he uses everyone's fear to act against them. Because of me, the entire continent faces an evil they should never have had to endure. Bairns trundle off for the last time. Old men are cast into fire and rubble."

"You were a vessel, that is where the emphasis ends. Do not weep for those of the past nor of your perceived lack of strength. None can resist the fell whispers of that shadow. His poison weakens even the strongest realms. Many great men of old succumbed. What differentiates us now from them is we have something they gave up on."

"What could we have that great kingdoms of Men and Elfin didn't?"

"An unselfish desire for peace and good."

"I wish I could believe there were truly pure or good intentions. Behind every good deed is a selfish lining. Whether it is the reward of a kind action or money reaped for services rendered. I sometimes worry hope is the same. It stands a banner for the light until an enemy force is raised. Then it perishes as easily as the tree and leaf do to fire."

Elharan took me by both shoulders. "It doesn't matter who you are or where you come from, bairn. Whether you were born a warrior, birthed into this world or a different one far beyond our means of reaching, or whether you grew up in rags. Today . . . today every Man, Elfin, Ebyian, and Drucodian prepares for the same goal. Rich and poor alike. King and commoner. Today, we defend our homes. You say hope flees at the first sight of an army. Hope is strengthened when you are with those you care for. Hope rallies to our banners. When all else fails, it still stands, a beacon to those suffering. Never give up hope."

My eyes welled up with tears and no matter how hard I forced them back or pinched my palm, they flowed down my cheeks. It was as if all of my fears surfaced in one single moment. The room was empty, thank goodness, as the final door shut.

"I feel weak," I confessed. "I cannot hide behind armor. I know I should be brave, be ready to face death, but I'm not like Bereth. I'm not brave, or strong. I'm sorry, if I fail you by confessing this, but it has weighed greatly on me since I arrived. Ever since I rolled into the fields south of the Outpost, I have felt it. A burden so great my mind shuts down. He visits me in my dreams. He walks with me in my worst moments. I want this hope you speak of. I wish to be garbed in it. Yet my grief betrays me. I am more of a thick bonehead than a man. What man weeps over such trivial matters?" The tears trickled freely now, and I inhaled shakily.

I half expected Elharan to look at me like I'd lost everything. Like I was an embarrassment. I was a bringer of doom. Why not add that to the list of traits I possessed? But when I lifted my face to meet his stare, I was surprised to see tears in his own eyes.

"My dear, Phoenix," he said gently, "it is a myth that tears in the eyes of a man show weakness. For one who weeps at the brutality and hideous nature of war is truly a man indeed. Your prior injustices . . . let them be put to rest. Be free of the past, for it holds no strength anymore. It is but a passing memory, a cloud on a spring breeze. The cloud may attempt to cover the sun, but it has no more strength to stay in one spot than the darkness does to stand against the light. You are strong, stronger than most. Do not give up when we stand at your side."

"Someday I will repay your kindness, King Elharan." I rubbed the last drop from my eye.

"The blood of war stains the purest of intentions. Do not lose that hopeful spirit. It may be the only light in your life. I cannot see through the shadow and mirk of the coming days, but if we have strong warriors like you to defend this realm, I am at peace. You honor me by fighting with me."

Bells rang in the distance. Their loud clangs echoed like gongs. Horns joined the cry and soon all of the evening was lit with the sounds of instruments. I turned to glance out the window. *They have come.*

"What . . ." I began.

"Those are the sounds of our scouts returning." The king raised himself to his full stature. "Mordën soon approaches, a mutt to the crumbs that cascade from his masters table."

DarSheer and Othrain shoved the hall's wide doors open. Weapons were drawn. Behind them, the Elfinian guards had their great swords in hand. The horns were loud now. Their stare was firm. There was no margin for misunderstanding. The days of peace had gone. The light was setting behind the horizon. War had come to these lands. What ballads would be made of the fallen if there was none living to make them?

"It is too soon." I moved toward the door. "We are not ready, never ready. What of the council? The Ebyians and Drucodians?"

"We have given time for the Western Ward to prepare." Elharan placed a glistening breastplate over his tunic. "That is all that matters."

Chapter 8
Ballad of Love

*S*HE STARED AT ME. *Words fell soundlessly off her parched lips. Where once her brown-crested eyes gazed back, now two swollen black eyeballs penetrated. Her hair was black as night and her veins bore a dark fluid. She walked along the docks. Her bare feet stepped without notice over splintered wood from sinking vessels half ablaze in the harbor. Embers rained down as a great blaze burned brilliantly in the background. A tall spire covered in golden spirals toppled over onto one side. A fresh furnace of heat arose. Her hair fluttered about, yet she walked on. Her clothes were not the usual britches and tunic I'd now grown accustomed to. She sported a long black cape about her rounded shoulders. A dress of velvet flowed about her ankles. Varglarian stopped their merciless slaughter of unfortunate fishermen and soldiers. They watched her in silent awe as she strode toward me. Her narrow lips spread in a pale smile.*

"There you go, DarkBairn, in the evening doom, walking atop this graveyard gloom."

My words caught in my throat, but I managed one. "Katy?"

"Like a moth unto a flame you've come. I always knew you would."

She stopped a foot from me, heat radiating off her. Katy's smile no longer bore the beauty I'd come to admire. It was twisted and sour with a wicked glee. Her hair was not the brown of old or silver of now, but a black matted tangle like a corpse's head after nights in the weeds. A familiar smell oozed off her in a cloud.

"This isn't real," I choked. "You're not real. None of this is."

"Look around, DarkBairn," she hissed as her hand shot out and snagged my throat. Her hand was icy cold.

All around, a city burned in hungry tongues of fire. Varglarian ran from building to building, their snarls and roars filling the night sky. A winged creature swooped between the clouds, too dark to make out what it was. Nightshades appeared from a side alley and beheaded a fleeing woman. Her body thudded to the ground as her child, hand now free, wept in the flickering light.

"This is your future, your prophetic destiny." She yanked my face to stare as a boy no older than Brenneth was hewn down where he cowered. "Watch the faces of those who trusted you burn in the almighty hailstorm to come. You brought this about. The grieving wails of childless mothers will haunt your waking moment till finally you are allowed to die."

Othrain cried out as an arrow found its mark in his throat. He staggered back as a second and third pierced his torso. Kissinger lay lifeless on the docks, a pool of blood circling his head like a halo. Arabella and DarSheer were scrambling on a ship no larger than a tub. Three Varglarian aimed their bows. They pulled back on the strings. I cried out. They released the arrows aimed directly toward the two.

I awoke from my nightmare with a jolt. Sweat glistened on my brow. My mind howled with a female's mournful wail. A tear hung poised to drop from my eye. The night outside had increased to a windy gale. Chimes swung crazily about, their soft sounds filling my ears. I leaned up on one elbow and brushed the moistness from my cheek. I thought I heard the same bitter sound. Was I still dreaming? But the pain from my slumber was all too real and my sheets were soaked with sweat.

Outside the world had begun to rise in bleary fashion. First the sun tipped its head over the southern horizon, peeked about, and charged the ranks of darkness. The battle was fierce but to every victory the sun obtained, a streak of orange seemed to lance through a patch of darkness. Before long a horn blew and the light was bright enough to see the streets beyond and the crying bairn snuggled against his mother's bosom as she walked the streets. Fog wafted over the battlements and its long tendrils sought out every living blade and leaf and petal. I stepped into the morning's sleepy light and stared about. At every crossroads, on every tier, robed Elfinian maidens stood. They held their hands in the sleeves of their robes and stared out over the rolling fields beyond the great gates. I listened as they sung a slow melody in a tongue I was unfamiliar with. From a side street, a maiden stepped into view. A hood covered her head. Behind her, two Elfinian warriors bore torches and protected her head from the sun's rays.

"They sing a final dirge for their city."

I hadn't even noticed Kissinger's presence. He stood shoulder to shoulder with me, bleary-eyed as if he'd also been abruptly woken up. His hair was messy and his eyes dark. My eyes were instantly drawn to the necklace about his throat.

"That's new," I gestured with a toss of my head.

He quickly shoved it under his tunic and began tying the laces on his boots. "It's nothing."

I shrugged and glanced out to the nearby battlements where Katy stood. Her pale hands crested the edge of the wall. Her hair fell like a cascading waterfall down around her shoulders. The Elfins had given her a sky-blue dress with a golden "half-mantle," so its soft silk underside kissed the small of her back. Even under the downcast hue of the sunrise, she outshone all who glimpsed her. Katy practically floated as she moved effortlessly under the watchful gaze of the purple mountains above. Their peaks watched her delicate features as she moved silently. A soft murmur broke against the mountainsides. Trees swayed in mesmerizing dance at some enigmatic tale. Their curved boughs dipped toward her, worshiping the "Silver Maiden." The title was one given to her by many and spoken breathlessly. Children stopped their games as she moved past. Guards turned from their duties, if only momentarily, to witness her passing.

My stomach clenched, not for the last time, as she came to rest at my side. The horns of war still rang in my ears. It had been less than three days since King Elharan's band of scouts had returned, harbingers of the bloodshed to come. Some had limbs which were hewn off in the heat of conflict. Others bore several arrows in their torso and legs. Not one rider returned unharmed. The message was clear as the cold reality settled in. Every day that passed, more and more fled to the Ethero Basin as word spread of the impending attack. Merchants wrapped their carts up while the sun was still high in the sky. Vendors closed their thatched doors and turned away all from serious investors to those suffering from idle curiosity.

"I picked a rose on my way up here. Despite all that is going on, the flowers and trees still grow as normal. The kestro fly overhead and the ferreks hunt at dusk."

"I wish I shared this optimism."

"You believe us to be lost?"

"I believe the fight will end in death." I tried not to sound too down but it was impossible not to. My stomach flipped. "I have seen a fraction of his strength, Katy. I fear for the next few days. King Elharan's scouts say he is but a day's ride from our gates."

"Today we admire the beauty of the flower. Tomorrow, we save this city." She smiled and her full lips parted in a dazzling display of glimmering teeth. I gently pressed one stray hair behind her ear.

"This world may have addled my mind, but not so the Silver Maiden's."

"The Silver Maiden," she said the words thoughtfully. "Arabella said that's what the people have been calling me behind my backs, in whispered conference."

"Arabella?" I raised one brow.

"The maiden you arrived with. She is strong for one so damaged. She's told me of the terror her people endured while being cut alive.

How can anyone bleed those memories and be as beautiful and fair-eyed as she is?"

"You see her as beautiful?"

"I do have two eyes." She smiled.

"As do I."

"And what do you think of her?"

"She serves her people in ways I understand. I carry the ghosts of my fallen brothers in different ways. She presses on even when she doesn't feel like it."

"Sound familiar?"

"As I said, I understand. But her beauty is a different type altogether. She is beautiful in her fighting spirit. Most would lay down their arms and cry as a babe fresh on the birthing bed. The Inclings still have not forgotten what millennium of time tried to conceal. Yet in as little as a month, she is still strong. Her beauty is admirable, for it does not let the scars of war disfigure it."

"You admire her?"

"I'd be a fool not to. I admire anyone who can go through such grief and come out the other side with as much fighting ambition as a fresh-faced lord who is eager to test his resolve."

She lay her head against my shoulder, and we took in the vista in front of us. On the far horizon, black clouds pulsated with red flickering light. They had appeared less than a day prior and grew larger with every waking hour. What had begun as a sliver of darkness no wider than a horsehair was now blotting out half the sky. A strong wind tousled our hair and played with the long banners. Their golden colors were matched by the radiant sun. Despite its beauty, the ball of fire had lost all warmth and so those in the city moved about as if winter was early. Hoods covered long hair and eyes were cast downward. None could deny the darkness marching on our doorstep. The Elfinian city, a proud capital of ancient origins, was diminishing as noticeably as the sun was losing its heat. King Elharan issued a decree stating any who could lift a sword or fire a bow were to prepare with haste. Those unable, the old and infirmed, had begun evacuating over the Ethero

Basin in the "Great Ships," noble vessels with high-sloped sides and golden sails. Vendors and merchants lined the creaking docks in masses. For many, the pains of the future were motivation enough. Others had witnessed firsthand the cruelty with which Mordën forged ahead, and those injured villagers were among the first to be granted access to the boats.

Not all was grim, for DarSheer had solidified aid from Caldonia. I watched the fields below the city where thousands of spears reflected the sunlight like wheat in a field. They'd arrived the hour prior and their lines still stretched beyond sight. muscular, tanned arms held shields as thick and tall as a man. In as little as a day, the Caldonanites had unified and marched to our aid. It was a testament to both DarSheer's prowess as a negotiator and their willingness to fight. The Caldonanites, boisterous bearded men, marched boot over laced boot into the city. And with them, their leader, a young man they called "Commander Scion" after the promise of his bloodline, fair-eyed and toned, slept with them and with no additional comfort. He was inspiring to watch. He rode and stood with his men in the mud and danger. He didn't ask any of them to do something he wasn't equally willing to do. It came as no surprise then, that those who had journeyed with him from Caldonia had an intense loyalty to him. He rode about often, a champion garbed in the ash grey colors of his city. His head remained free of a helm and often he could be seen with a torch in one hand and a sword in the other, calling down to his men and boosting their spirits. His cloak flowed behind him, and his hair bounced about his shoulders. Othrain and Kissinger were often seen riding with Scion during his frequent excursions to shore up their defensive lines and run battle plans by Berëthelluïn.

Word arrived that the Drucodians in the north were assembling. The messenger who brought the scroll to King Elharan on a clear day, spoke in awe of the sight. The Drucodians had forbidden any to see inside their city long ago, but upon allowing this one messenger in, they'd broken an eon-old decree. I'd watched him be sent away babbling about the "End of the Drucodians." His words were eagerly soaked in by the more impressionable nobles and lords of the court. He went to the local tavern with more than one maiden hanging on his words and an ensemble of jesters and bards trying to find fuel for a new ballad. Even King Elharan, despite his longer life, had never been inside that city. The messenger stated that over a thousand Drucodians were on their way south, following an unknown path which would soon merge with the Westerly Road. The last time such a number had been abroad was when the sun was far younger, five hundred years prior. Not since the Last Battle of the Second Era, had any force of Drucodians been seen period.

While the Inclings would send no aid, on the contrary, the Ebyians sent everything they could. Rusbalz had realized what the reality of a Mordën-infested occupation would mean for his people. They held great cities hidden by rock and tree high in the spires of the Fallen Peaks. While they were impervious to the darker evils hidden beneath the mountains, they were as mortal as the Elfins below. Rusbalz ordered the treasuries and stores his people had to be emptied and aid sent down to Avalon and the refugees still seeking asylum. Carts and barrels of food and ale were rolled in on the daily. Weapons of true iron appeared in shipments and were handed out to grateful Elfin and Men who held little else but a dagger. Rumors were bloodied by actuality as more and more streamed west along the Westerly Road. Their eyes were dried from tears they'd long since spent. Bodies began to replace the broken families. Carts of spoilt corpses wheeled under the watchful eye of the guards atop the walls. Even now, a long line stretched from the docks on the uppermost tier of the city to the main gates. Night and day, old and young trudged over rock and stone to reach Avalon in hopes of aid. Word came that all of the Eastern Ward was on fire, save for Caldonia in the south where even with the impressive force on the fields below Avalon, they held enough men to hold off the initial waves of invasion. Othrain recounted with fierce pride how the Caldonanites had apparently knocked the lead Nightshade off its mount and driven a stake through its breastplate. Its red armor was spoiled by its own black vapor. These accounts reached the ears of Elharan and he was troubled greatly by their tales. Mordën torched all he came across. Forests as old as Ëonë itself were consumed in the hungry flames. Bairn and codger were cut open and fed to the Varglarian. It was only truly thanks to Commandeer Scion and his forces that the Westerly Road remained a viable option of travel at all. Bands of Varglarian and troublesome Nightshades appeared at dusk upon weak travelers. The roads were watched by more than eyes and guarded by lesser steel, blackened with corruption. Banners bearing an hourglass on a red field stuck at haphazard angles in burning fields. Farmers were strung up and their torsos covered in seven red dots, done so with their own blood. They were turned into scarecrows and fed upon by the kestro that flew overhead. Those were only the reports that made it to my ears, and that alone made me sick to my stomach. Many more were considered not important and handled at Bereth's level.

The more troubling news trickled from a tribe of Ebyians who made their homes in Ralier Range, a small grouping of mountains along the eastern sea. The grumpy Ebyians spoke of a poison. Captured villagers were tested on and many screamed their own lungs out as the dark streams were imbedded in their veins. Other such practices were being made under the watchful gaze of "a red servant." The mixed accounts put him as a new servant of Mordën while others said he was a Shade elevated to this position. Those who chose to remain behind and defend their homes were easily cut down. As every hour passed, it became clear not one soul would remain if we failed. Caldonia could not hope to defend for much longer. Kissinger brooded that the only reason they hadn't been burned like the others was because it was too far south to devote the entire force. Mordën was choosing instead to toy with them and keep them occupied.

My thoughts had long gotten away from me, and I stirred in Katy's comfort. Her smooth breathing calmed my heart. Her silky touch kissed my skin. I let a strand of her argent hair run through my callused fingers. What was in the past, what guilt remained a burden around my neck, was washed away with every moment I spent with her. Many took notice but most said nothing. Only Othrain dared give me unfettered advice on the matters of love. I was just as happy to forget everything he told me.

"Do you think a time will come when we can enjoy a panorama like this?" She sounded tired.

"Evil may roar its hardest, and darkness spread its widest veil, but even that must come to pass. The shadows of night are frightened off by the light of dawn. During the soft hours of nightfall, we may despair, for the crying of animals and the thoughts in our heads prolong the hours into years and years into decades. What peace we seek in dreams is broken by nightmares. At their worst, they seem as powerful and intimidating as a raging river over a thousand-foot fall. But then the cock crows its blessed ballad, and the sun begins its warring stomp and the clouds part to reveal the light. What enemies we've made in our minds or the horrors we've witnessed in our nightmares are chased away, for even that intense evil drummed up in our thoughts cannot stand against the breaking of day."

"Did you memorize that whole dusty volume?" She let loose a giggle.

I shrugged. "Wise words are often found in pages of nonsense. This does not diminish their value; it only strengthens it."

"You said your mind was weak compared to that of 'The Silver Maiden.' You are wrong. I fear that this world has done great damage to you, but your intelligence remains intact. Not all can sit through this utter boredom you must endure to discover a few lines of precious wisdom."

It was my turn to chuckle as we stood atop the great battlements of Avalon. The horizon held nightmares to come but the city flourished below. I pivoted and waited till Katy stared up at me, a thought forming in the way she wrinkled her brow.

"Katy, I know I'm not flashy or brave or particularly wise. I don't have thousands to command. I'm not experienced like many. I'm simply a man in love with nothing to give but his heart."

"My dear Phoenix," she brushed my cheek and planted a kiss on my trembling lips, "there is nothing this world could offer that would make me stop loving you. I could be given kingdoms to rule and I'd turn it all down, for why would I wish to see this continent without you by my side? You have always been my mind and heart."

We stood, silhouetted by the cold sun. Its rays danced in battle with Katy's starry glow. And for that moment, I didn't care if Mordën himself were to split me in half. Every atom inside buzzed with the joy that only true love could bring. What I once feared dead, or at the very best, long out of my reach, was now here. This feeling only burned the fire of determination inside me.

"I stand here in your chest," she breathed, "but I cannot help but feel so much has changed."

"Water does not taste as crisp as it once was," I said without waiting for her to finish. "The air is ripe with tension to come. Even the smiles of these fair people stand before a hidden terror."

She stepped back and looked me over before hugging me tight. The sun was now tilting noticeably toward the westernmost peaks. We only had a few hours of daylight left. She took her leave, and I watched her descend the long set of wide stairs to the common grounds far below. The wind blew her tunic about, and her hair floated like a swan's wing. Shadows danced about her feet, and I realized why the people held her in such reverence. Even the guards descending or ascending around her took as wide a berth as possible. She was "The Silver Maiden" to all in this city and abroad. Her beauty was prominent against the brutish features of farmers and outliers. Before long, Katy was swept off and I leaned against the stone with nothing to occupy me but my thoughts.

It was in this deep reverie that DarSheer finally found me. I didn't know exactly how much time had passed but the sun was nearly gone, and a penetrating chill wound its way around the rocks.

"This city is beautiful," I murmured as he leaned against a crenel. "Far more lovely than anything else I've witnessed made by the hands of masons and the hearts of these people."

"If you think that Avalon is a city to behold, wait till you see The High City. The Elfin have it well here, but this place is a festering pit in the side of a dark mountain next to the shimmering glory of The

High City of Men." He spoke as a man does of a lover. His eyes were passionate and his gestures enthusiastic. "Walls higher than some mountains, whiter than snow, and broader than some cities are wide. From the great shipping yards in the west . . . to the southern farms ripe with purple and yellow fruits. You walk along a path hidden from sight by great rolling hills, greener than grass at first light. Animals move in the underbrush and sing their songs. Then you turn the corner and before you in great array lies my home. They say when the city's original founder discovered the rich lands before him, he pierced the thick soil with his spear and said, 'Here shall generations of kings prosper. Here shall the fate of my people be tied. Upon these lands as far as the eye might see do I claim for the right of my kin. Blood shall water what our bodies cannot bring forth. Darkness shall flee at the very thought of this place.'"

"I hope to one day visit."

"The coastal line crashes but half a mile west of the city and there a great bustling trade of all courts flourishes. Fish and undersea rocks of eye-opening colors can be found. In times past, great lords of mighty nations came to simply walk the streets and to behold its glory. Artists and musicians come to hone their craft in the bustling metropolis. Forges with fire so hot they'd melt your face off. Beds woven of such softness, you would sleep simply laying a hand on it. When you see the city, your jaw will drop for it is like a mirage. You will believe it is not possible what your eyes behold. It is fairer in beauty and greater in stature than the most beautiful of maidens or strongest of men. The flags run tall and proud, and her armored knights below stand as defenders of our hard-earned peace. Fields of crops more prosperous than any other area of the realm wave like a hundred hands to each passerby. The sun above warms the earth and many clouds let lose deluges to moisten the fertile ground. In the sea beyond, waters greener and bluer than you thought the color could be lap at sandy yellow beaches. The tallest spires stand high, and their pointed tips pierce the heavens. Fleets of prosperous ships run trading routes all over the coastal line, as far north as north can be and down where once the Kingdom of

Glasbur reined. Men have perished, their lifeblood flowing down the city they swore to protect. They died with honor and pride. The city is a fair sight to see, my lad, for she captures the heart of all who journey to her. If Mordën believes he can take even that jewel, he underestimates us."

"You speak now in a way I have not heard you utter before." I laughed. "Pray, tell, what brings this renewed love?"

"I have been a servant of the Outpost most of my days. Being here, surrounded by Elfinian art and works, I am reminded of my own. This is a place for traveling through, but it is not a home for me. Oh, my friend, to grasp the warmth of her bosom and rest my head in her welcoming embrace is to live a life worth living. Tell me, Phoenix Dark-Bairn, have you ever felt an emotion gripping your soul so deeply that you would bank your entire future on the outcome of this feeling? This feeling of intense loyalty and pride and love and passion and dedication that would send the very black heart of Mordën himself scuttling back to the bubbling holes of his accursed existence. To place a hand on the strength of the people and to see the joy on their faces. . . . Pray do not awaken me from the dream I now hold. I stand atop the walls. The wind is on my face, and it kisses me as I stare out over miles and miles of land, tethered to the working hands of farmers. Great cities, though smaller in size, reside on all points save for the sea. Above my head the fabric of a hundred seamstresses and the collection of years of storing brings the elegant sigil of my city to life. It folds and undulates as the sea it oversees. My child, you do not know beauty till you see the Harbors of Asgaloth or walk the streets of Miridean beneath the warm summer nights. Petals of rich purple and brilliant pinks line roads of pure silver starlight. I am honored to be asked to remain here and oversee the conflict, but I would be deceptive if I said I wished to remain here any longer than I must. I miss my home." He opened his eyes. I shifted and felt my heart singing along.

"Have I ever told you, Phoenix, the greatest bistri ever to be found in the corners of this world come directly from The High City? A fellow named AvReek resides in the Tempter's Tavern and if you tell him I sent you, oh just wait for the glory to flow from his kitchens. You shall salivate for the crunch of the crust. A warm heat shall radiate from the inner deliciousness and then in one massive bite Erëthuïl shall dip down and bless your meal. Oh, to be back in The High City where the maidens are more beautiful than our greatest songs are inspiring. Where laughter is more common than words. I pity the man who never strays far beyond his birth bed. The wonders he is missing . . ."

"It sounds like a fairytale," I exhaled. "Speak no more or I shall run now to the docks and be on my way."

"Sometimes I wonder if I remember it as it is, or as I wish it to be. When these days of war are over, and the water sings its chorus of peace once again, I shall take you. Aye!"

"I do believe we have a deal, Broadsword."

We watched the world fall into deep slumber and the pinprick lights of a thousand torches wink into view as the great egress continued the docks far above. Shouts wafted up on the night breeze and before long, I began to feel the deep fear return. Shadows flickered and taunted me even as I stood under the comfort of a warm brazier.

Raoul sat atop his great black stallion. The horse's mane sat against its corrupt flesh. The steed was long dead, but so were most of the creatures in his master's army. Only death would align itself with Mordën. Death and the black shadows of despair. A long line of slaves marched into view. Their shackles were pure iron, forged in the deepest fires of the Pit. Overhead, red light flashed periodically in the clouds. Thunder rumbled. There was no sound greater than the thud of tens of thousands of marching Varglarian. They passed him by, ranks upon ranks. Some held great spears of pointed malice. Others held shields, red as blood. Banners flowed behind pikes as their bearers sang in evil tongue.

To war! To war! For the Shadow King of old
To kill! To kill! Our enemies abroad

Darkness shall march before us and vanquish the light
Sword and shield are our message, death our fight
In the pits of shadow have we waited, the Pits we were bred
We go now on ash and fire with desire to be fed
To war! To kill! For the Shadow King to come

Raoul turned in the saddle and smiled. The dark blackness that flowed through his veins throbbed with eagerness. He could sense it as easily as he could feel the beat of his heart. The Last War was beginning. Blood ruled these lands now. Shadow covered hope. The farmers and fishermen they'd conquered labored in the depths and were made anew into the perfect evil. He flexed his fist and reached for his sword. The first glimpse of Mordën was the sudden rush of wings as a black shape flitted about in the sky. The second was the thundering roar which shook every tree to its roots. Dirt and rocks flew from their sleep and were cast aside by the great machines of war. He smiled.

The cackling fire spiraled up, high into the rafters. Embers drifted down like lazy fireflies. Oaken logs in the brazier popped and hissed. Tongues of flame pirouetted, great orange dancers. They wove between thought and vision. At one time they were objects of idle curiosity, others they became the focal point of deep reverie.

We sat around the brazier, all lost in our own thoughts. Kissinger and Othrain lounged on the floor, content to shave splinters off a statue they were carving. Arabella was chewing at the end of her hair, her eyes reflecting the flickering light. Tim stood against the far wall, his gaze cast outside the narrow window. A gentle wind wafted in and stirred his hair. DarSheer leaned forward in his iron chair and tossed another log on the fire. None knew how long before Mordën attacked. His forces were rumored to be a few hours march from the city gates. All sat in self-reflection and made peace with what was about to happen.

"Like my hopes and dreams," Kissinger said into the silence. We all stared at him, so he pointed at a log that was being consumed by greedy flames. "The log is young and new, see the green in it? But it burns anyway. It's suffocating me."

"You're but a few years my younger," I said.

"And I'll be a body on a spike in a few hours' time, so excuse my self-pity for just a few moments," he shot back, uncharacteristically bitter.

"Keep your head about you now, bairn," Othrain poked him with the sharpening tool. "What goes on in the coming hours and days will come to us all. You don't see DarSheer here pulling his hair out."

"Some hide their nerves better than others," Kissinger countered as he blew dust off his end of the statue. "What about you, Katy? You nervous, with this dark enemy coming to our doorstep?"

"Of course." Katy was sitting next to me, her hand in mine. Only I could feel the sweat in her palm or read the concern in her tone. She held herself as one more invested in the uneven edges of Kissinger's construction than the wall of steel and death marching toward us. "It would be folly to see the coming of war with no concern. But should the worst come about, we may retreat over the basin and fight with the force of a hundred thousand bannerman from The High City. I do not see a reason to give up hope, while it still exists." She glanced at me and her eyes told me all I needed to know.

"Lass has more bravery than you," Othrain snorted. Kissinger smacked his arm.

"Lass also has a name," Katy scowled. I squeezed her hand.

"You've never told us much about your past." I nudged DarSheer with the toe of one boot.

"Perhaps it's for a reason I've never told." He stared into the flames.

"I mean if we're all going to die soon . . ." I shrugged nonchalantly.

"Thanks for the optimism, DarkBairn." Othrain threw a scrap of wood at me.

The others chuckled as DarSheer lowered his tankard of ale and breathed. "I do not speak of my past, for I wish to forget it. Forgive me, for I know this is not the answer you seek."

"Mysterious." Katy's eyes twinkled with interest. "Why must you hide behind that which has already transpired?"

"Because it still affects me," he murmured darkly.

"Please, let us have some light tales," Arabella slurred her words and raised a goblet. "If I'm to perish at the hands of a black-steeled saber on the dawn's first light, at least let me have laughed and drunk my way to sleep the night prior."

"Tell of the time you two first met." Kissinger waved the sharp end of his knife at Katy and me. Katy smiled and sat up, the blanket she'd been snuggled under falling to her waist.

"Back in . . . our world . . ." she began awkwardly, "we have these buildings like long low taverns but for learning. Our two families had sent both him and I there. What were we, five?" This she directed to me.

"I believe so." I nodded in memory. "I'd grabbed a yellow block and was going to build myself a tower of epic stature when you walked up and asked—"

"I said, 'Hello. My name is Katy. My full name is Katherine, but if you call me that I shall leave. I need your yellow block. Please. May I have it?'"

"And I gave it to you." I brushed a hair from her face and kissed her nose.

"That is cute." Arabella smiled and glanced toward Kissinger. I was surprised to note he was already gazing at her.

Katy pushed me back playfully. "You said, and correct me if I've forgotten in my considerable old age, 'This is my block. Find your own, wench'?"

"Stop . . . the romance . . . it's turning even my stone heart into a real one." Othrain blew fake tears into his sleeve. We all laughed.

"We've been friends since that day," I said into the room. "There have certainly been times where we fought or argued or had our differences, but the best part of that friendship is no matter how much we argued, we always came back in the end. Because if you truly care about someone, despite their failures, you'll find a way to keep them in your life."

Arabella eyed the fire and played with her hair in a wistful manner. Kissinger cleared his throat.

"Aren't the lot of you going to have the decency to at least care to pretend when it comes to my history? So, I don't have a history of tangled romance with a maiden fair as the fire is hot. Am I to be abandoned by the wayside? Honestly, you people."

"Tell us!" we all shouted into the rafters, our spirits soaring. The fire surged slightly and we shielded our eyes. It might have been the ale speaking, but I felt at ease and a little giddy.

"You sure you want to hear this sob story?" Othrain chuckled. "He's been a bit of a mess ever since I first ran into him."

"Who's telling the story, you or me, you lugnut?" Kissinger jabbed him. "I may not have a tear-jerking story like the DarkBairn, but in my own right I've had a rough go of it."

"Yeah, he's had to go around life with that face," Othrain snorted into his mug.

"A right thorn in my blasted side you are," Kissinger glowered. He gripped his mug as his cheeks went red with embarrassment.

"Let the jests sleep," DarSheer said softly with a look to Othrain. "We all want to hear, Kissinger."

I lay my back against a post which went from the floor to ceiling. As Kissinger told his tale of growing up on in The High City, I turned to half-glance at Tim. Something about the way he stood had bothered me ever since we'd begun our talks. He had not added anything to the conversations and was merely content to watch the glowing moonlight. *You should go to him*, Katy had advised. I'd lied to her and told her I had and that things were as patched as they could, but truth be told, I hadn't found the nerve to. He was distant in a way I'd never seen him. Back when we were younger, we used to talk about how after prolonged absences, people drift apart. But this felt worse than that. Way worse. Every time he glanced at me, I felt I wasn't so much a thorn in his side as I was the reason he suffered. His eyes held the tears of a pained man, and it broke me to see him that way. The Tim I remembered from my world was outgoing and jovial. Whatever had transpired in the last two years had shattered him. Katy murmured in mild protest as I excused myself from the group and walked over to him.

Tim did not move as I leaned against the wall opposite him. I studied his features for a long while. His hair had once been thick and rich with dreadlocks. His style had often been the brunt of derogatory names. *Mophead. Curly Whirly my Twirly. Medusa.* Now his hair was smooth and hung about his shoulders. His skin, once pale white, was tanned.

"You going to stare at me all night or should we at least talk so Katy thinks her plan is working?" Tim broke the silence. He glanced at me. His eyes were red as if he'd been crying. He tried to hide it by gripping the windowsill, but I could see how his hands shook. His breathing was rapid.

"It has been long since we talked. Far too long. I take ownership for that error."

"I would have come to speak with you first, but I figured you had all the attention you needed."

"You speak as if we are different, but we are the same, my *brother*. Did we not grow up together and see the sun rise and fall for decades over the same mountains? What enmity you hold against me is warranted, for I failed as a brother. I left you to the wolves and steel of our enemy."

"You are mistaken, *stranger*. We are not the same, you and I. And we never have been. Will is dead because of you. How long did it take you to forget that? As easy as it was to forget me. Temper too. All those in this world, who because of you now sing their dirge in hallowed halls far beyond our reach instead of feasting at tables with their families. I respected you once, Phoenix. Loved you as family. My *brother*, aye, once. I never had anyone growing up what with my father not being present. It wasn't easy trusting, but you made it so easy, so outgoing. I got confidence and life seemed good. Now I don't know who to trust."

"You can trust me."

"Trust in you is the reason we are in this cursed mess to begin with. My trust was you finding me in those cursed caves. My trust in you is why we are in this place waiting for an evil we should never have had to deal with. I paid the price in blood. *My* blood. I want to return home, but I cannot because *she* follows you, a pup after its mother. You would not understand such a concept as loyalty. I cannot leave her to these lands. She is the reason I fight. You are the reason I have to fight."

The blood heated in my face. "I never made her follow me. She does so out of love."

"Love? Prize? Reward? You don't understand, do you. She was all I had. When I lost you to those caverns, I found her. For two years we grew close. She has barely spoken to me since we arrived. Two years of travels and memories. Did she tell you about the band of mercenaries we came across in Gottersam? How we had to fight tooth and nail to escape the wolves which fed on the corpses of criminals tossed out of Caldonia? Did she happen to mention between intense wet kisses, our time in Glasbur?"

"Glasbur . . . the Lost Kingdom of Glasbur? That's impossible! DarSheer says . . ."

"Well, your precious Swordsmaster is wrong. What does that say about the people you keep in your company? We entered the impenetrable walls. I know what lies on the other side. *Who* lies on the other side! This darkness that marches for our gates is not alone. There are fouler and worse things in the lost places of this world than you can possibly imagine. I've seen things, Phoenix. I've felt things. I've heard them all. In my mind. My heart. She and I endured much just so she could throw me away at the first sight of you. A wound healed with scar tissue can still be reopened. The night before the city, you both forgot I was even there. I did not. I saw you and was ready to forgive. A surge of weakness kept alive in a world of confusion. So infatuated were you both with the mere idea of the other that I became as bath water from a barn. Treat her well, my *brother*. She cares deeply for you. Her time here will be short and yours shorter. This world does not take kindly to outsiders. Invaders. Take care and always watch your back against the long shadows of the night. This evil that flows toward us . . . it can take many forms. It inhabits many people. Some do it unwillingly while others relish in the honor."

"Would you not at the least give me a chance to defend what honor I have?" I protested softly. The others broke into raucous laughter at the expense of Kissinger's dignity.

"Go back in time and don't abandon the people who left everything to help you." Tim smiled. There was no warmth in that look. It was icy. Unapproachable. "If I had the chance to go back and stop myself from agreeing to journey with you, I would. I wish we had never met, Phoenix. I wish you were a stranger to me."

"I know our connection is damaged." I tried to ignore the pain that surged. "I do not ask for that to be restored, for one does not rebuild a weak bridge that has crumbled into the river. You build a stronger one in its place. I am truly sorry, my brother. For all my perceived misjustices and injuries I've committed against you. If I could turn the wheel of time itself, I would and forbid you all from joining me on that cold morning. You do not think I wrestle with my choices too? That I could not go alone? You act as if Will's death has not crippled me. It has. I know the damage my choices made and not a day goes by I don't pay dearly for it. You are not the only one to suffer. Your ignorance in this blinds you worse than sand in your eyes."

"Finally, the truth comes out. I am weak. You are strong. Our suffering is not the same for you endured worse and I but child's play. Thank you for correcting me, *brother*. There is weakness in you. I can see it in your eyes. You may have fooled the others. But I see it."

"I spoke hastily and out of turn and disrupted your peace," I cursed myself for my own hurtful words. "Please, Tim . . ."

"I have found what scraps of peace I can in these cursed lands. It is you, DarkBairn, who must find peace. Peace with your actions and peace with the future. Remember this at the end of all things. If it's not enough you've ruined everything for me, now I must choke on my own blood and perish defending you. What bittersweet justice is that? You can tell Katy you did your best to bring me back around. I was obstinate. You were persuasive and kind. I was rude. Ever the fool who can't listen to reason. You two are perfect together. Farewell." His eyes filled with hateful tears, and he no longer tried to hide his shaking hands.

He stepped from the window and pushed past me. As he did so, I felt something shatter inside. There had been a shift, and I knew deep down, even if I didn't want to admit it, that that shift would never reverse. It was a sickly feeling. The room filled with laughter again as Othrain slapped the ground weakly and howled. Kissinger was grinning appreciatively at the reception to whatever he said. Even DarSheer was laughing, his head thrown back and his eyes to the heavens. Katy, giggling, met my eyes with a merry look that quickly frosted to a concerned twitch. I could not meet her sight any more than I could muster the courage to smile.

"And it's because of that moment, they called me Kissinger," Kissinger finished.

"So, all because you faceplanted into an inger?" Arabella snorted.

"A hog?" Katy clarified. Arabella nodded.

"Fell into a hog's mouth with his own mouth." Othrain grinned widely. "First I've heard him tell of this tale."

"And never likely to let me forget it," Kissinger rubbed the back of his neck with chagrin.

"Never, *brother*." Othrain clapped Kissinger on the back.

"Come now, Othrain." I rejoined the circle and shoved down the regret and bitterness from my voice. "Kissinger has told of this legendary pig smooch. Surely, you have some stories to brew over this fire."

"My life is no more pleasant than watching grass grow, bairn." Othrain shook his head.

"I believe we're entitled to a few embarrassing tales." Arabella leaned back in her chair.

"Nothing embarrassing here." The other shrugged.

"Save for the time you pissed yourself on watch duty because you thought a Varglarian was about to climb over the wall," Kissinger snickered.

"The mighty, standoffish Othrain wetting himself? Oh, now this I have to hear," Arabella covered her mouth, her eyes wide with glee.

"It wasn't wet, a mere jolt in my old muscles." He flexed one arm in demonstration. "Never worked properly. Why do you think they stuck me at the Outpost?"

"Definitely not for your inability to keep your trousers clean." Kissinger slapped his arm. "Careful, Othrain, that shadow moved. Might be a Nightshade."

"This coming from a sow romantic." Othrain slapped him back. I winced at the brutality in the hit.

"Boys." Katy raised both her hands. They turned to her. "I want to hear Othrain's story."

"I saw a black lump sliding down the front of the wall onto the battlements and like the good watchman I was—"

"He blew his horn and waved his torch and woke the entire camp all because Throbb couldn't keep his eyes open," Kissinger interrupted and howled with laughter. He fell back onto his side and the room filled with guffaws. Only Othrain stared about with narrowed eyes.

"Alright you lot," he growled and shook a fist, "just you watch. Our enemy will soon come along the battlements, and I won't blow any horn when you're struggling for your life. I might just fancy myself a nap."

"Is this why Throbb never liked you?" My jaw dropped. "You blew the horn on him and got him in hot water with Malziek?"

"Maybe the unofficial reason why," Othrain grumbled. "But Throbb was an old codger. He never liked anyone."

"He liked me." I shrugged.

Arabella gazed wistfully up at the ceiling. "I wish I had what you now own."

"A new pair of britches?" Kissinger was red in the face with mirth. He dodged the goblet aimed for his head and pranced out of reach of an enraged Othrain. The two danced about the room while DarSheer shouted out pointers.

"Watch the jab there, Kissinger. Oof. Othrain, try a kick!"

Katy leaned into my arm and gave me a small smile. "What was that about, with Tim? He wouldn't look at me as he left. Is everything okay?"

As I gazed at her hopeful stare, I wanted to speak truth but found my throat closing up. The longer I hesitated, the less her smile until finally she began to frown.

"Phoenix?" She was alert now.

"We exchanged words. I was rude. He has every reason to hate me, and I fear it has come to this."

"Why do you say these words? Did he admit as much?"

"He said if he could, he'd go back and prevent himself from joining me." I knew no matter how annoyed and grief-stricken I may be, I couldn't blame him.

"You mustn't take it to heart." She leaned her head against me, and I kissed her forehead. She yawned. "It's easy to feel abandoned, especially when the only people from your world are so close to each other and you feel left out. But Tim is strong. You should have seen him. He fought down bandits and wild creatures like he'd known how to swing a sword his whole life. He protected me with his life. I trust him. He will come to see reason before the end."

My gut dropped like a stone, and I covered by coughing into my fist. Tears threatened to fall but I forced them back down. Her optimism was not something I believed in. Othrain finally grabbed Kissinger and body slammed him into the ground. DarSheer and Arabella winced.

"Let's not break the floors," she called out. "We're borrowing this space."

"They're a proud and mighty people." Othrain grinned as sweat beaded on his forehead. "They can afford to fix a few floorboards in their fancy homes. The only thing broken is this whelp's dignity."

"Yes, you're a very strong man," Arabella sighed. "Your muscles bulge with your power. Can we save the acts of bravado? There are not maidens here to impress."

"I have muscles too," Kissinger panted. He gave her a side glance. "I let him win."

"Sure, you did." She smiled. "I never doubted you."

"What of your tales?" Katy inquired. "You've spoken some to me and I'm sure the others. Anything I'm missing?"

"I was born in Fiscer's Keep."

The firelight dimmed and we snuggled closer. Several blankets had been lumped into a pile against the far wall and DarSheer distributed them. After we were all cozy, Arabella continued. Her voice was fragile, but her body radiated a proud energy.

"One thing to know about Fiscer's Keep is everyone helps. There are no stipulations based on who you are or your status or who you knew elsewhere on the continent. We fished and farmed, and we were good at it. Fiscer's Keep is not proud and noble like your cities. It's a grimy hub of villages shoved near the northern coast. We'd catch great fish there and import them south to Ithuïn. It was how we made our money and the only reason we could afford to live where the snow rarely thawed. My parents grew up there. Their parents and their parents too. My kids will one day. . . . We often did trade even further north than us with the Drucodians, though we were sworn to secrecy about it. I guess it doesn't matter now."

"Didn't you also trade with the Outpost from time to time?" Kissinger squinted through the dim light.

"My people did make stops at the eastern villages and would occasionally make it far south as your outpost, yes. But it was not a priority. To be quite frank, we all thought you lot a bit strange. The idea of guarding a bridge to an empty island was one we could not understand. So, we traded occasionally but for the most part, our imports went to Ithuïn and from there to Avalon and Caldonia. In the olden days, our great shipments would make it as far as Glasbur in the south. One day, I was in the main village, known to us as Fiscer's Isle. It's an old run-down section with buildings older than some of the Elfin. The wood would creak something awful in the windy months and only those whose hearing was bad could stand to live there.

"They came out of the shadows. One moment I was laughing with my younger sister. It was her day to fish, and she asked me to join her. We were sitting on our small boat in the icy waters, and I heard screaming. The shores were dotted with growing fires and at first, I thought a building had caught fire. We rowed back to the shores and as soon as we hit sand . . . that's when I saw *it*. The brute was nearly twice as wide as anyone, and it stood half a foot above the tallest of my people. I learned a new hatred that day. He cut down Galbrought, our mayor, and his political advisors. My father and some of the townsfolk rushed him but from the shadows, a horde of creatures appeared."

"Nightshades?" Katy breathed.

"Varglarian. They didn't appear the way a Nightshade would. I'll never forget it. They wore black armor and wielded great black steel blades. They cut through wood and stone and flesh without discrimination. But what really stopped me in my tracks were the glowing red eyes. Their helmets were solid iron. My sister ran toward my fallen father, and they cut her down as easily as any of the others. We rallied, most of the uninjured, and were fought back until finally . . . I was forced . . . to flee." She cleared her throat. The room was silent for a long moment.

"The horrors you've witnessed are unspeakable," DarSheer murmured sympathetically. "These ancient terrors should have stayed dead long ago when that scum was banished from our shores. He shall find more than the casual farmer and untrained fisherman when he sieges Avalon."

"Gone are the days of peace." Othrain nodded sagely. "War is thrust upon us, and we shall answer."

Horns blew in the distance, and we were all on our feet faster than the blink of an eye. Arabella had her dagger as she bolted to the narrow window. DarSheer, sword in hand, was next to her. His fair eyes peered through the darkness toward where the main gates sat. The horns rang anew and even my ears could detect the distant crunch of gravel underneath boots. I found a spot to peer under DarSheer's arm and over Katy's shoulder. The winding road which led away from us and toward the towering wall was lit with torches.

DarSheer's frown was replaced by a wide grin. "Be at peace, my friends. They are not our enemy. Those are Caldonanite horns mixed with . . . a sound unheard of in our time. The Drucodians have arrived."

Shouts carried over the night breeze as the great gates rumbled open. Along the Westerly Road, a mass moved in perfect unison. Caldonanites who had previously been standing guard along the road stood at attention and monitored the Drucodians as they marched by them. Sporadic braziers lit the fields so the grey shapes moving in step seemed more shadow than real. Their lengthy procession stomped over root and dirt clump and stone. Banners were held every dozen rows. I squinted, trying to make out the icon but was foiled by the mirky air. Horns blew yet again, and this time drums rumbling in the deep answered. Torches moved along the top of the wall, as if on their own. Their bearers shouted down commands to the figures struggling to fully open the gates. It was as if every Elfin, Man, and Ebyian not yet on the docks was watching the arriving force. King Elharan stood at the top of the main road leading to the doors of his city. He sat proudly astride his great white stallion. The mount flicked its tail and shook its long neck. Its eyes glinted with the torchlight as it let a small sound pass. I saw now the Elfinian drummers, struggling laboriously under the weight of drums twice their size.

"They greet the newcomers," DarSheer translated as a dispatch of riders met the lead of the Drucodian force. "They will exchange brief pleasantries before moving into the city. King Elharan has chosen personally to meet them. This is a telling hour when Drucodians move in mass. There was once a day and time when the continent itself breathed them. They are rarer than gold now. Look your last upon the Drucodian race. I fear their existence hinges on the success of this battle."

It took them nearly an hour to finish their talks and move into the city. Eyes followed them from shuttered rooms and atop walls of stone. Elfinian warriors stared as the grey beings moved past rhythmically. They whispered in hallowed respect. Even I, a stranger to these lands and histories, couldn't find the words. It was clear the impact this war would have on the free peoples of Ëonë. The room was silent as our light dimmed into glowing embers. The warmth left the room. Ebyians, arms crossed, surveyed the arriving force with clear awe. They whispered to each other but there was no mistaking their wide eyes and open mouths for anything less than amazement. Even now, in the darkest night, hours before the end, there was still something ethereal about it all.

"I don't know why," Katy breathed, "but I feel sad."

"Me too." Arabella took her hand. "It's as if a remnant of people older than time itself march to their altar. They must know how hopeless the outcome is. They wield the knife to their own demise."

"They do not care for odds and victory," DarSheer spoke. "Their youngest was born in time to see the Second Great War. Their oldest . . . well legend has it their oldest can trace his line only a few generations to Primhald and Fethright themselves, the first two Drucodians. They walked and held council with them as easily as you and I do to each other. Long have they drawn breath from these lands. They labor under the harsh heat of the sun. Many in their ranks consider this their greatest honor, to die as their ancestors did long long ago."

"This brings me some peace." Katy looked at me. "It is good the peoples of this world are unifying under one banner."

"Should Mordën attack tonight," I agreed grimly, "he would find the people of this world are not so easily vanquished. His old enemies from time immortal stand spear tip to spear tip atop walls so thick he'd need the sea itself to break upon its walls."

"We are not wheat before the scythe, ripe for harvest." Kissinger gripped his sword hilt.

"We are not fish on the end of a fisherman's hook," Arabella murmured.

"We are not deer in the range of a skilled bowmen." Othrain inhaled sharply.

"Nor are we to be counted among the cowardly or written down as smitten with Mordën's ways." DarSheer sheathed his blade. "Come now, let us head to our rooms and sleep. The night is still long, and we do not yet know when Mordën plans to march on Avalon."

The dying embers shed just enough light for us to grab our belongings and exit in single file. I shoved open the thick wood door and stepped into a misty street. The building, atop the middle tier of the city, sat high above the other dwellings. Plants grew in ornate pots along small windows and banners of silk hung along the walls. The building pointed at its thatched peak so it mimicked the mountains high above.

It was altogether beautiful. The rich blues and royal purples of its sides shimmered in the shadows. DarSheer and Othrain broke left as Kissinger and Arabella took a right turn, toward our housing on the uppermost tier. I paused.

"Speak your mind to me." Katy embraced me. "For I can see that you wander in thought."

"I find myself growing weary of late." I flexed my hands. "It is one thing to wake, for it requires no effort. But to sleep . . . it is a task better suited to our elders. Who can sleep when they have drums in their heads and *the* song twisted by the laughter and cries of sirens long at sea?"

"What song do you speak of?" Her delicate fingers traced my jawline.

"Ever in my darkest dreams she sings me the lullaby my mother sang. Her voice is familiar yet barely beyond my recognition. I weep and beg for it to stop but my words are no more impactful than a water droplet on a boulder."

She leaned her head on my chest, and I inhaled her fragrance. She smelled of summer blossoms. Of white flowers extending their long petals. I remembered Brenneth's laughter. Topper's horrible music. Marian's radiant smile. Malziek's proud stance as he turned to face the hordes running to meet him. Temper's eyes returned to my mind. I saw again his sad smile before he was buried under the blades of the charging Nightshades. So much death. No reward.

"They talk much of what they do not know," I said more to myself than Katy. "It is not so easy for the weaker-minded to simply accept the dead have died and move on. It is not so easy for me to accept the death of a race any more than it was to accept the death of my friends."

"Walk with me." Katy intertwined her fingers in mine even as a single star shone down.

I had not been down this lane and instantly questioned why I hadn't. Silver flowers adorned the cobbled path. Trees with boughs of fruit so heavy they drooped, tempting. Torches were lit every few yards. Leaves spiraled about us as petals fell.

"You speak in long talks with King Elharan and DarSheer. I find walks in the wooded areas to be more my style. I can almost hear the songs the trees sing when they dance to the instructions of the gale. The flowers turn their faces to me, and their glory is more enchanting than any old books or airy speeches. The simple things of this world speak to me, and I listen. This blossom, long has she struggled to give forth her beauty and the others mock her." Katy gently touched a closed bud. "They call her slow, worthless. A flower's primary vocation is to present a beautiful image and she has not. She worries she will not outlive her compatriots and that all that will be remembered of her is her failures."

"For all the courage these Men, Elfin, Ebyian, and Drucodians possess, their failure will be all that is remembered of them." I stared at the bud. "Their screams for mercy will be the only thing remembered in the annals of time. Would you give a hope where there is none?"

"Can you stop the avalanche as it spirals toward a village? This flower cannot change who she is," Katy looked up, "yet she strives forward anyway. She ignores the side glances and hushed words of those around her. Do you not think she is well aware of what her role is and how she is not able to fulfill? Think then how this belle will be seen when her petals finally open and the moon and sun alike are in awe. Think of the jealousy when her late bloom reveals the most beautiful flower of all. To stop the very change of day into night is no miniscule feat. All she is owed is patience and trust. All she has is hope. Is this so different from us?"

"You speak of flowers whilst I wrestle with people. How do a few petals of a worthless flower compare to the unified peoples of an entire age?"

"Do you believe that this bud will become a flower given the right patience, nurture, and trust?"

"Of course."

"Then why do these Men and Elfin deserve any less? Are they not a great people birthed by the will and words of their maker? Is not a flower the creation of its maker? It may be small in stature, yet men fight for her to adorn their halls and fill their maiden's hair."

"Yet even a flower may wither under a harsh gaze. Sun or Mordën it makes no difference. You ask for time, but the sun will not be so kind when it burns it to a crisp."

Katy placed her arm behind my neck and gazed at me with a sad smile. "I remember once a young boy who would charge down imaginary foes with naught but a wooden stick and a smile. Times far bleaker than this did not shatter his resolve. Where is this boy now? Why do you despair so?"

"That boy was a naïve child," I murmured against the pit growing in my gut. "His imagination was his greatest ally. But they were all imaginary. He had not seen the true evils of which the world was capable."

"He had not seen yet he was ready to make his stand. When the darkness approaches, will this young boy back away? Should the flower fade before its bloom? Time may not be our ally, but we are not lost yet. Give them a chance, my love. Give *us* a chance before you mourn our death. We will laugh together one day in the summer bliss on a field of daisies, and you will wrap me in your arms and together we will spend all our days in peace. Does this not sound better than the fears that control you?"

"I will stand sword in hand at the end of my days, though I will not always be brave. If this is my future, then I will fight for it."

"Ever my brave knight in radiant white armor." She kissed me intensely. "Do not let this darkness destroy you. No matter what happens, hold on to that piece of you that was ready to resist the end of all things. Oh, to be young again when the worst of our fears was missing school or our parents finding us skipping class."

"You must have remembered another handsome knight," I joked. "I don't recall skipping class."

"First grade? Second grade?"

"I was sick!" I protested. "That's not skipping. I had a note. I had chicken pox."

"You were sick in love with a girl too blinded by her own future to see the boy at her side," she sniffed. "She was so concerned with making the squad or passing her next exam she failed to see the reason for her happiness. It did not come in the form of books or stories. It was right in front of her." I hugged her close.

"What about the day we met?" She had the other arm around my neck, and we moved in rhythmic symphony. If I strained my hearing,

I could hear a gloshee strum its song. Or maybe it was all in my head. Either way, as we danced in slow manner around the clearing, I never wanted this moment to end.

"You mean when you saw me lifting five blocks in one hand and you fell in love?" I said with a straight face. She stared at me. "Four? Three, and that's my final offer."

She laughed. "No, I mean the part we didn't tell the others."

It was my turn to stare. "I remember after I gave you the cube you smiled and said, 'I think we're going to be best of friends. Do you want to join me'?"

"To think it all came down to a block." She rested her head on my shoulder.

"I thought I'd never see you again." The tonal change caused us to stop our movements. She dropped her arms from around my neck.

"But you have. I'm right here. I'll always be right here. You have but to look."

Tears stung my eyes. "Two years I had to come to terms with the idea that you were happy and content in our world, probably in the arms of someone else laughing at his horrible jokes. Thoughts like these fueled my resolve to help DarSheer and the others. I knew I was ready to give my life because my life had no more meaning. Who mourns the passing of a weed when they have a flower to cherish? If even one particle in my body had thought you were here, I would have left all and scoured every inch of these lands for you."

"Do not dwell on the past, for its actions are beyond changing," she said. "Rather enjoy what is in the present. I knew you were out there and that fueled my resolve. Tim and I journeyed over many lands, up mountains, down valleys, and across waters. I must confess there was many a time when I myself lost faith. For how could anyone hope to stand in the path of Mordën and survive? In the beginning, it was Tim who kept me going. He told me if any of us could survive the hostility of these lands, it was you. He had hope when I was lost. As we traveled town to town, we got pieces and rumors of a bairn who had fulfilled a prophecy."

"Tim," I said.

"Tim," she responded.

"I know that bridge has been burnt completely but it does not erase the bitterness I feel."

"Many speak out of anger but that does not make them right. Tim has had a long time to relive his injuries both mental and physical. He's talked much with me. It has not been easy for him and being in this world, stuck with the reminders that haunted him for days in those tunnels . . . even strong men crumble. Do not blame him for his confusion. He needs time to sort through his thoughts."

"Time to hate me more? He is not the same Tim I last saw while we rode for the mountain with Will and Temper."

"That's because he is not the same Tim. While you battled it out on the Outpost walls, I rode with him. He would often wake sweaty in nightmares beyond his ability to explain. Dark shadows and whispers in the night kept him up long after the sun had fallen. He told me many times that he felt great pain, a quiet whispering in his mind. He would cry out your name and sit in the shadows at the edge of our fire afraid of what you might be going through. Months passed before he told me he knew what it was like to suffer beyond the limits of pain. He truly feared you lay in some dungeon on an isolated rock, at the whims of Shades and Varg. It fueled him almost more than me. Then one day, after we were forced to kill a Varg, he changed. He said it was a reminder that no matter who he was or who he became, a part of him would always be lost in those tunnels. Something had irrevocably changed. He had changed. He took to long walks in the night on guard. He wouldn't eat nor sleep nor drink water from the babbling brooks. The longer we rode, the worse he got, feverish in the night, cursing to himself. I thought I caught him speaking to the shadows and swearing, but when I questioned him, he made me believe I was seeing things."

"I am the cause of all of it." I looked down at my hands.

The night sky sang with the evacuating ships on the Basin and the thud of boots against mountain stone. Voices rumbled in deep places and songs filled the air, from the uppermost tier of the city down a winding street which broke off like a stream to its tributaries. The last of the merchants and those deemed unworthy for combat were making their last packing attempts. Guards rapped hardened knuckles on doors. Some occupants complained loudly and with great force but were eventually forced out to join the remaining throng. They mourned for Avalon, for all knew they would not see her like again. The air was heavy with grief and anger. The shadows themselves, once a servant of Mordën, shivered in their isolation. Torches adorned the sides of buildings and from their light the city glowed. Even at night, Avalon was as beautiful as the first time I'd seen it. In the square down the lane from us, where trees hung old, withered fruits yet to fall, a band of weary Elfin strummed gloshees and a new instrument I didn't recognize. They sang softly yet it was easy to hear their words. The wind moved their golden hair in flowing fashion, much like their cloaks.

"They sing the dirge for their city since none who remain shall live to sing it themselves. Their mournful cries rise high and shall echo in the halls of forgotten stone. Much like they themselves, all here shall fade into folklore. A shame, isn't it, all this beauty, to be burned?"

I turned as Tim approached. His leather pants and black tunic hid him well in the greyness of the night. His hair, now tied back in a tight ponytail, hung above the nape of his neck, and one hand was on the sleek dagger at his side. He stopped, still partially in the shadows, and glanced at me. The flickering torchlight lit only half his face as he spoke.

"What has been done cannot be undone. I do not ask forgiveness, for I know there would be none. If you will excuse us, Phoenix, while I still yet have the energy to talk."

I bowed ever so slightly and turned to Katy, kissing her forehead before returning the way I'd come. I hadn't even made it fifty steps before I heard Tim's voice. Against my better judgement, I halted and listened, a temporary fixture under the leafy gaze of an oak tree.

"Do not do this to me."

"I do not know what you speak of." Her voice was firm.

"Two years, and you're going to throw it all away. For *him*? What has he done any more than I? It was not him who protected you. It was not him who gave you hope."

"I know you speak tempered by anger. Am I to converse with you in a serious manner when every word you'll speak is slighted against him?"

"Ever the graceful orator. Your words will not stop the arrows that pierce his breast. They will not stop the blood that flows like water down his chest."

"But the shield I bear will. Speak plainly, Tim. Enough of this cloak and dagger. You know I love you, my brother I never had. There is nothing that could change that. Phoenix knows this. He knows how much you did for me. I have spoken candidly to him of our times abroad. You have changed and not for the better. There was once a time when you were a kind, considerate person. I don't know what you have done with him, but the Tim who stands before me is a constant reminder that you are not yourself. You are sick. He whispers in your mind. Do you think you could hide that from me? That I would be taken with Phoenix and ignore the signs so obvious in your eyes? You hold an anger and hatred toward him beyond what is warranted. No one could have predicted how things ended on that mountainside. We all agreed to the risks, even you. You cannot blame him for how things ended."

There was a long pause and then Tim spoke. "You wound me, my dear. Your wounds hurt more than a hundred cuts. I'm here. Right here. All of me. And yet it's like I've no more weight than a parchment atop water."

"You don't mean any of that!" she pleaded. "Phoenix is your brother. He has been so your whole life."

"Brother?" he snapped bitterly. "That word is meaningless. We were *friends* when it did not cost him any potential harm? You call me your brother, but the last two years show anything but that."

"You volunteered every bit as much as we all did, Timothy Brestdon!"

"I *volunteered* to help my friends. I took a brave step. I didn't actually expect to be tortured and scarred for life. You can't pretend you did either. You're good at many things, Katherine Chase, but deceit is not one of them. I became the way I am because I was left to rot in a blasted hole in the ground where nothing but the dripping of water and rattling of chains kept me grounded. Do you want to know why I am? Why I've 'changed,' as you chose to call it? You have nowhere to look but him. He made his choice. I deal with the repercussions. And ever loyal you remain, steadfast to the bastard who broke me. If it wasn't for my sacrifice, his parents would still be rotting their wretched lives at the bottom of a cell. But we'd be free. Free of this guilt of this torment. Free of this forsaken land. As soon as it became convenient for him, I was cast aside as vermin. He forgot me as easily as Temper. As easily as Will."

"Will was tortured too."

"And he *DIED*. Do you honestly think if he were here, he'd be preaching anything different than I?"

"Phoenix was tortured, and his body was used as a vessel for *him*!"

"That's because *he was weak*! At the first prod, he caved to phantom images while I gnashed my teeth to real pain wrought by metal instruments. You don't think I wasn't offered the same relief? A choice? You don't think Mordën didn't visit me in his corporal shell and give me the chance to aid him and be free of this misery? You think Phoenix was 'destined' to be the DarkBairn? Why, because he said so? That none other could do what had been prophesied but him? Phoenix Rather is no more important or special than Will or me. He simply crumbled first. Will gave his life to prevent Mordën's return. I suffered and would have gladly died. You don't think I wasn't shown images? That he didn't clearly detail the deaths and mutilations of everyone I loved? The things I saw would have sent that coward, Phoenix, crawling back from whence he came. My family. My friends. My future. Me. All rotten and bloated in the ray of his horrible gaze. I resisted. I was stronger than Phoenix blasted DarkBairn. Between my screams for death, he told me everything Will endured. He told me how easy it had been to convince all of us to walk right into his hand. It was all a part of his plan. We never controlled our destiny. He was two steps ahead every moment. Phoenix is no more a hero than I am. You see it's not that he simply abandoned me when I needed him most, it's that he's been gifted all this. He has friends and allies and respect where he does not deserve it. He has you. What did he do to deserve you? I slave in the heat of my misery. My own blood was drawn on my body. I sweated through nightmares. What did I get? I should be asking, what did I lose? Seeing you with him is harder than all that torture I endured. It sickens me. There is an evil we cannot escape marching toward us. Every second *he* gets closer. I feel him in my bones. There is no escape. You want to chase after Phoenix, be my guest."

"What are you talking about?" Her voice was soft, and I could feel the tears rolling down her cheeks.

"You are blind. Be the naïve little girl you've always been. Phoenix deserves to die. If he wants to be the noble hero he claims, he will lay down his life for his friends. I started this journey two years ago with three friends. I soon leave with *none*."

His steps crunched off into the silence of night. I heard her cries and resisted the part of me that wanted to run and hold her close. I dropped to my knees and held my head in my hands. A rift split my heart like a dagger through a drape. I knelt that way until a numbness was all that remained. When the dark greyed with morning, my tears dried to salt.

The rain came down in sheets. It filled the drainpipes till they overflowed and gushed down the streets with purpose. So intently did the heavens weep that I could not see more than a few feet in front of me and often found myself cursing the thin fabric which made up my cloak's hood. It seemed to succumb to the cold and rain faster than wood to fire. My neck and face were drenched even as I spit out water and rubbed my eyes repeatedly. I cursed loudly my choice to take the morning watch. What blasted thought had gone through my head to abandon the warmth of The King's Tavern where even now Katy and Arabella no doubt gossiped under dry blankets and were served ale so hot it steamed. I longed for that pleasure that came with a full stomach and a dry cloak. Grey clouds tumbled with ancient arguments against the unyielding stone on the mountain peaks. The water ran down roads and filled the ponds and grassy fields. Droplets poured from the large leafy overhangs of great trees older than the oldest Drucodian. The cold bit through my thin cloak and tossed it about my neck in an airy rampage. The few torches that managed to stay lit in the deluge flickered weakly and without warmth. I rested my red nose inches from the flitting flame and cursed loudly. *Blast this morn.* I marched down the uneven road, my boots splashing in the growing rivers. My britches were as muddy as they were soaked. Houses sat dark and empty; their windows thrown wide in the hastiness of their owners' retreat. Should their occupants ever return, they'd find their half-eaten food and unwashed dishes laid to soil in the mold that was to come. Dips in the ground became new pools where frogs and worms battled it out in the war of their time. The city was otherwise abandoned and quiet in the absence of its people. For what is a bunch of stones piled atop each other if there was none to call it home?

Every alleyway was the same: a misty haze hung in the dark air and swirled as I moved from entrance to exit. Deserted low-hanging plants in faded flowered pots swung like a lantern on a great ship's mast. White light flashed in the sky and an answering war cry of rumbling drums echoed in the distance. Every time the light lit up the shadows, the looming mountains glowered down as they wandered past to some unknown destination. Some of the Elfin believed that on certain nights, a new mountain peak would appear after a long rain shower and at the start of the next would be moved on. It comforted some and concerned others. For me, on this day, that place was underneath the most powerful thunderstorm in the Third Era, or so King Elharan claimed. To those just having awoken, it would appear the sun had never come up. The black clouds blotted out all rays of sunlight so it was as if night reigned supreme.

"Phoenix!" DarSheer had to practically bellow from his place a few feet away. "Phoenix!"

I winced and placed a hand over my brow so I could simply open my eyes. "DarSheer? Blessed am I to find you still alive."

"If Mordën wants me dead he'll have to cross 'attempted drowning' off his list and into his failures," DarSheer snorted. Water sprayed from his nose and lips. His cowl hung over the tops of his eyes.

"What of the reports?" I cried over the howl of the wind. "The scouts? What have they to say?"

"King Elharan seeks a council with the captains of Caldonia and our alliances," DarSheer roared back.

"He waits for my undergarments to soil with water before he calls this meeting?" I caterwauled miserably.

"Why do you think I braved this nightmarish storm?"

"I'll never shake this from my ears, or the recesses of my bones! Would that he had called this council hours ago."

We staggered up the winding road, leaning against the other 'er we lost each other in the fog. Trees bent with their tops kissing the ground. I focused on simply putting one boot in front of the other, which shouldn't have proved difficult but was akin to walking with a hundred pounds on my back. DarSheer didn't fare much better as he leaned forward, head toward the ground, his cloak tightly wrapped around his broad shoulders. Rainwater flew off him and spiraled into the abyss of darkness behind.

After what felt like an eternity but was in reality half an hour of forcing our way through howling wind, we arrived at the uppermost tier of the city where two guards stood atop the walls. They remained at their station, though I had no doubt inside they too cursed their luck to draw the watch. Our approach was heralded by the gates opening slowly. DarSheer led us into the outer courtyard and to the front doors of the King's Hall. Guards were there as well, and their grim expressions should have indicated to me the future outcome of the council. Orange light spilled abundantly from narrow windows where roaring fires warmed the hearth. As we stepped inside and felt the wind and rain stop immediately, voices took their place. Men in white robes spoke in hushed concern with larger forms shadowed by the firelight.

Elfin drank the dredges from flagons as they brooded in silence. King Elharan was busy staring at a large map placed on the long table. Dishware and banners had been removed to make way for it, candles lighting the aged parchment.

"DarSheer, Phoenix," he greeted wearily as the voices came to a mumbling stop. "We are all relieved to see our unannounced thunderstorm did not force you into less helpful accommodations."

"In truth, my lord king," DarSheer bowed, "it could not be a better time. Phoenix and I were assigned to walk the streets, but we do prefer the dryness here."

Elharan smiled faintly and turned his attention back to the map. I hovered next to him and in the midst of several burning candles, could make out the faint shape of Avalon. The walls and defensive placements were heavily focused on in grey boxes with fancily scribbled words. I mentally noted the locations of the tavern we stayed at, the King's Hall, the Ethero Basin, and the main walls. I shook my head wondering how much time and cost this city had been to build. I found new respect for the Drucodian people.

"My spies send word that our enemy marches west with little to no resistance. Some of our bowmen keep his outer flanks occupied and have spared the villages from being razed. Their occupants even now board our ships for the Western Ward. But it is not enough to deter him. I'm sure all of you noted our allies and their arrivals. Delegates from those forces are here tonight to speak their alliance into reality."

An Ebyian I did not recognize stepped forward. He was unusually short, even by his people's standards, and the top of his head stood even with the bottom of the table. He wore a red cloak lined with furs and a fierce glimmer hinted in his eyes.

"My name is Ir'Landi, the Princling." He puffed his chest and growled. "I speak for my people and come as a token of my father's loyalty to this union. Mordën will find my people do not so eagerly forget the way he burned and murdered at his height. It is because of him we found our love of the rock and moved our cities to the towering peaks which stare down on us now. Those Ebyians who were mustered to fight alongside me are dedicated to this cause. We will stand unwavering alongside our Elfin, Drucodian, and Human allies."

He sat down as a tall grey skinned creature bowed. His eyes shimmered. "We echo the sentiment of our mountain friends. My name is Parod. I have lived many generations, seen the sun age from its first light to a poisoned paleness without any warmth. I have fought against our foe many times and though most in this world cannot remember the atrocities he committed; I do. The Drucodians, once a mighty people, have been brought low. Our numbers once spanned in the millions, for we were the first creation of Erëthuïl. Through the hubris of my ancestors, we were humiliated and cast down from our pedestal. It took the creation of two new races to even win a war against a weakened foe. While the Inclings have chosen to remain in their peace in the Hinterlands, my people have left the comfort of our home and will stand as we did once long ago with Humans and Elfin. We gladly welcome the addition of our Ebyian neighbors. Together, we will do once and for all what we could not before. We will wipe this blight from our past though it cost our entire race. We will die a warrior's death."

The room was silent as we listened. To even be in the presence of someone who had been alive for thousands of years was awe-inspiring. I could feel the tangible uplifting of hope swell in the room. Drucodians were the stuff of legend, and though they failed in defeating Mordën at first, they succeeded in the end. To have the oldest-living creature in the room, someone who had been alive before anything that is . . . I wondered if it would be enough to keep Avalon's light glowing.

"We are truly honored to have the fabled Drucodians standing shoulder to shoulder on our front lines." Elharan dipped his head in an unkingly, humbled, manner. The rest of the room mimicked the gesture.

"We may not have a great past of a warrior's valor." Scion brushed his long hair from his eyes. He stood next to Elharan. "Caldonia is no meager collection of farmers and vendors, unlearned with the sword as they are inexperienced with sailing. Our roots span many generations of quiet houses and folk with little love of combat. It is true traced back far enough, my father's ancestors bartered with Mordën for our freedom. We paid to be left alone. For decades our people were shunned as *ilkwrathen*, 'lovers of evil.' When DarSheer arrived in our noble city and told us of the threat looming, I knew this was our chance to put to rest our shameful past. I, Commander Scion, will charge into the unknown with five thousand of my best. Our spears will bristle against the Shadow King so he does not even reach the walls."

"The honor of our southern allies is not in question," Elharan smiled. "You have aided my people and the people beyond the Ethero Basin on many occasions. My own house has committed grievous atrocities to yours. Your alliance is welcomed and shows the unity of the people of this continent against our foe. If there was any chance you would side with him as of old, as he hopes now, it is dashed. Five thousand spears are a hefty defense to attack if he truly wants Avalon. We will do what we must do for our people and the future generations."

"The Caldonanites will rest in graves away from their homeland before they kneel in his city. I will ensure our past is forgotten."

"To war!" Parod stood and drew a dagger. He stabbed it into the thick oaken table and grimaced.

"To war!" Ir'Landi growled.

"To war!" I tried to appear confident even as I knew I looked like a wet rat dragged from his hovel. DarSheer didn't look much better.

"Then we break, for our spies say that our great foe is a few hours from the city walls." Elharan cast forth his arms wide. His visage became dark as the others streamed from the now open doors out into the night. "DarSheer? Have you gathered the barrels I've requested?"

"Aye, King Elharan." DarSheer flexed his hand as if lost in thought. "They shall cover the fields and be a beacon of hope."

With little warning, noises erupted outside. Horns shaped like cornucopias straddled the gates at every level of the city and blew with alarmed fervor. Those still in their beds rose in fear and the already nervous crowd focused on evacuating the city began pushing forward, trampling those around them, as they overwhelmed the already full boats. Two of the great vessels tipped slowly onto their side and began sinking as people kicked and screamed in the water. The horns blew again. A fire erupted in the sails of the smallest ship and the docks swarmed with figures.

Elharan slammed his fist into the table. "Mordën is not days but hours from our walls. Blast our complacency. DarSheer, take my finest and fill the plains below."

Horns thundered the cry as torches were borne aloft by shouting soldiers and carried from gate to gate. Men, Drucodians, and Ebyians alike raced to their posts. The walls on the main level of the city bore the weight of thousands of warriors, ready to defend what was theirs. Where once a thunderstorm of impressive magnitude assailed the walls, now a deathly calm replaced it. It was as if the entire world was holding its breath. The mountains huddled together, gazing ever downward. The rainwater rushed into the garden beds and was gone. Cobblestones gleamed clean.

We raced from the chambers. It was finally about to happen. The Battle of Avalon would soon be underway. The fate of the Eastern Ward was about to be decided.

Chapter 9:
The Battle of Avalon

MORDËN RODE FORWARD. HIS armor reflected the maroon glow of the eyes watching him. Attached to his back, two massive spikes curved up and outward. His helm was simple and smooth, with two holes for his eyes and slits for his mouth. But unlike the commoner Varglarian around him, the rest of his armor showed his stature. His boots came to a point and curved up with a deadly point. His gloves creaked when he squeezed his hands together. The breastplate around him was made of living shadow and changed every time he blinked. One moment it appeared solid iron, the next it was wreathed in flame. In one hand, he held the massive scythe that was his weapon of choice. The black blade curved and at the end, green venom glistened. The shaft was solid ivory. A long black cloak flowed behind him marked with the red hourglass. Vermillion paint traced down his sides.

His steed, a bony malnourished stallion, whinnied softly. Eyes as deadly as the Varg around him, the mount nickered and stamped its iron hoof. The creatures around them moved to let him canter by. Their grossly beautiful visages were masked, unfortunately, beneath welded iron-spiked helmets. In their gloved hands, the Varg carried curved obsidian blades. The steel was black as the night. Garbed in grey and black clothing, the creatures milled about in disarray. They shoved each *other, snarled at each other, and when challenged, they even killed each other. Banners were hoisted high, and several drums beat out of rhythm in the distance. They were restless. He smiled under his helm.* Good! *They knew well enough to move aside for their Shadow King.*

From his position just inside the massive bank of fog and cloud, he stared toward Avalon's massive wall. Torches lined the front of it like small pinpricks of light. Visible between every merlon were rows upon rows of Elfinian bowmen. The tidings had reached his frontlines that the Drucodians and Ebyians had allied themselves with the goldens. He frowned. There would be a special place in his dark empire for them. He would turn them into perfection. Raoul, covered from head to toe in black spiked armor, rode up to his side.

"Caldonia has answered their call," he growled in a guttural grumble. His voice was somewhat muted due to his half-helm. It covered from the top of his skull to his nose, leaving his mouth exposed. It was a personal choice he'd demanded. His sharpened teeth bared, he glowered at the fields before the wall where a dark pool of water filled trenches and holes.

A Varglarian rode on his other side. Wide as the horse was tall, the obese abomination snorted into its helmet. Its beady red eyes glinted. Its fat pushed at the edges of its armor. Mordën shifted in the saddle.

"The walls are old and thick," the Varglarian whined. "They have the advantage as long as they can just fire down on us from their protected vantage. How are we to climb such obstacles? They have soiled our advance with bodies of water deep and cold."

"If I'd wanted your complaints, Vigathi," Mordën said coldly, "I'd have asked for it. Spare me your constant driveling snarls."

"My lord." The creature bowed.

Spears were raised and the scarlet banner fluttered over their heads. He stared about at the ranks of Varglarians and Nightshades. They numbered tens of thousands. He stared back up at the battlements where the figures appeared as small dots.

"Prepare my hordes, Raoul." He gestured with his scythe. The black steel projected from the ruby-red shaft. A protective guard was built right

above where he gripped the wood. "Summon my servants. We mustn't keep our Elfinian friends waiting. It's rude to ignore our host."

"Yes, my lord." Raoul bowed in his saddle and took out a horn that was more shadow than solid. It undulated from black to grey to light grey and back. He blew upon this horn and the sounds of a thousand echoing horns filled the air. The host behind him roared their challenges and stomped their feet. The fog bank swirled about as if mesmerized by the sounds and began to pull back, revealing them.

At that moment, arrows began appearing in the haze. Some found home in the sides of trees or stuck deep into mud. Others landed in necks and appendages. Mordën remained stationary, letting the arrows fly around him. One stuck into his saddle horn and quivered. He stared at it with mild fascination. His eyes, black as the night around him, glowed with an intense strength. Vigathi, silent at his side, suddenly cried out with an explosive gurgle as an arrow appeared in its throat. A second and third Nightshade collapsed with projectiles to their necks. Mordën watched as a great number around him began to fall with no more interest than a mutt gives a cloud.

A dark grey fog rolled with purpose from the hills right up to the edge of the walls. Then, with almost deliberate malice, it slowly climbed up and over the merlons into the battlements and down toward the city below. Shouts rang clear as we lost sight of each other. Where once we stood side by side, it now felt like we stood alone. I could barely spot DarSheer a few feet to my left. The drums rumbled. They resonated thick, ugly sounds like thunder booming across the mountains. With it came a deep raspy rumble as if thousands of voices were chanting from the backs of their throats. Far below the edge of the wall, the mist swirled as if a hidden wind parted it. It retreated back until it formed a great impenetrable wall of cloud. The Varglarian were never a threat in small numbers. They were reckless, stupid, and careless, even. Where most intelligent beings would run when outnumbered, they charged in even if they did not have a weapon to fight with. A few at a time, they were no worse than fighting a two-legged animal. My momentary relief stalled as from the wall of clouds, the host of shadow appeared. There weren't a few dozen or even a few hundred. Thousands upon thousands of Varglarian marched in organized step. They wore black armor with helmets that covered all but their glowing amber eyes. Small slits had been carved vertically where their mouths should've been. From their iron death masks, they chanted and sang and roared. Drums rumbled again and from the depths of the fog, a single fork of maroon lightning crackled out. The clouds had gone from storm grey to a midnight black, lit with occasional flashes of red light, against the cold blue above.

Katy took my hand. "As long as we stay together." I squeezed her hand. My stomach clenched in my gut. Sweat beaded at the nape of my neck. What altercations had been had at the Outpost were infinitesimally minute in comparison to the sheer number outside our front lines. My throat was parched, and I wished then to have a tankard of ale to wash it all away. I wished a lot of things.

"I've seen worse." Kissinger swallowed hard and grinned a toothy smile. He tossed his sword from hand to hand. "Just a couple million? I expect we'll be eating well tonight, lads, seated atop the bodies below us."

"Must you speak so rashly?" Othrain grunted.

"I merely seek to lift the moods, my grumpy brother." Kissinger swallowed again, and I saw the absolute fear in his eyes. "Why so grim?"

"We'll be eating a brilliant feast, alright," Lord Berëthelluïn murmured, "in Erëthuïl's hallowed halls."

"Ready arrows!" Elharan's deep voice boomed out like a whip cracking. Sounds of a thousand arrows being notched to a thousand bows rippled in the air. Shouts went from wall to wall. The main wall was filled with Elfinian and Caldonian bowmen, tensed with anticipation. The second level contained the Ebyians, who no doubt were biting at their bits to join the conflict. And far, far above us, hidden behind the ceremonial ancient walls of old, where it had all started for them centuries ago, the Drucodians waited. Their banners snapped tall and proud in the wind.

"All I want is peace. Peace and an end to this bloodshed." Kissinger's fragile exterior cracked as the enemy's drums thundered in the plains below and the Varglarian's war screams rose in intensity.

"Target the gaps in their armor!" Elharan roared. "Necks, below the shoulders! Their eyes!"

"I fear peace will not come again to these lands, bairn. Aye, it won't be seen again in our lifetime." Othrain checked his small quiver for the hundredth time. In his own way, he was exhibiting how terrified he was too. His once unmistakable confidence was gone. His eyes betrayed his gruff exterior.

"Berëthelluïn, tell your host to stand planted firm and unwavering over the gates themselves. Any who approach will find the teeth of a city biting down. Do not let them get close enough to break our walls!"

"You may have given up in your old age, you codger," Kissinger tossed his sword from hand to hand and flexed his neck and back, "not so the young Kissinger."

"Your will is my command, Lord King Elharan." Bereth saluted and hurried off.

"My heart fails me," Arabella confessed, "yet my mind remains stalwart."

"Like maggots unto a corpse, they come to feed on the still-warm flesh of my reign," Elharan said softly. "The time of my kin has gone down, a fiery fury of brimstone and chaos. The sun rises in the east and sets over a world mourning. So did my line rise from the beginning and now it will end, here at the darkest of times."

"You should go, my king." DarSheer pointed up toward the sparkling Ethero Basin. "Get out while you still can. The people need you to survive and lead them after this conflict is over."

"What king would I be, Broadsword, if I fled behind the protection of my dying people? You ask me to act cowardly. Nay, I tell you this: I will be the last one on those boats, or I will not go at all. Much grief has been caused. I will not let my father's failures decide the future of the

Elfinian race. That is his shameful past. A king should fight for those who cannot."

"If you fall on the field, my king," an Elfinian bowmen cleared his throat, "who shall our people follow?"

The stones beneath us, the very bones that formed the city, began to vibrate as if a great earthquake was imminent. From the thick fog, bolts of red lightning illuminated horrifying images of a moving sea of bodies. In one instance they were as clear as day, until the flash was gone and the black fog hid them. Every flash of light illuminated the apocalyptic scene. Stalking over the helmed hordes below, Rachnadons towered. Armor covered them from thorax to abdomen and along each of their eight legs. The steel pointed every few feet creating a barbed appearance. They tossed their heads like horses and roared.

Elharan looked at him, a deep sadness in his eyes. "Survival besets lineage, CorSire. Should we be victorious, the people shall decide their next king."

"I was really hoping those arachnid things wouldn't be here," Othrain cursed loudly. His face was ashen now and he abandoned any relaxed facade. Sweat ran down his forehead. He gripped his sword so tight his knuckles turned white.

Arabella, hand on her yew bow, nudged him. "Hey now, Othrain, don't faint now. You're the best swordsman in this city."

"Yeah, right." He nodded and inhaled deeply. "Who else is going to defend this city? The trees?"

"Maybe the thousands of . . ." Kissinger began. Arabella silenced him with a sharp look.

"Quiet your minds!" King Elharan had returned, a living symbol of power. His golden cloak billowed behind him. Underneath he wore a silver tunic emblazoned with archer bows. On his forearms were leather guards and in one hand he held a massive blade easily as long as his own height. His voice rang out the clearer in bold and deep resonation.

"Hold! Hold your ground! We will not give in, we will not back down before the darkness of our time! We will stand united, a proud people before this wave of darkness ere it drowns us all! Lift your faces to the light, and fear Mordën no more as we stand before the onset of chaos! Before the day of reckoning when we will make an account of ourselves let it be such an account as worthy of every ballad. Give the bards something worthy to remember. These monsters want a war? They shall have their war. Behind every stone they shall find Elfin, Drucodian, Man, and Ebyian armed with bow and sword. If it's a slaughter he wants, it's a decimation he's getting."

"Do you not also feel terror?" I squinted at DarSheer who had up until this point been silent.

"From them? I must admit I have come to terms with the outcome of this battle. Nay, I do not fear them."

"A man of solid stone." Arabella sounded awestruck. "What scares you?"

"What if, after all of this, our legacy is to be forgotten?" His voice shook. "A number in a scroll. After centuries past, how will we be remembered? That is my fear. To be forgotten. It's a curse that's plagued me since my first awakening. I do not desire to live a life only to be forgotten. It's as my father told me, 'We've been born to bring out change. How effective is change if it doesn't change anything? How effective are your actions if you acted only for yourself? How effective is your life if no one remembers you?' I'm afraid our actions here will be as useless as a twig stopping a howling windstorm."

With that somber thought, a low rumble filled the sky. The drums and chanting ceased abruptly as a guttural growl slithered out. On the plains below, the long line of Nightshades, Varglarians, and Rachnadons stood impatiently. From the depths of the clouds a shape moved. I blinked, thinking I'd made it up. But there it was again. A black shape the size of a mountain moved in the fog. A flash of light lit up one end of it and I felt my stomach drop. Goosebumps raced down my back as I stumbled back. I gripped my chest and squeezed. Red light again illuminated the mountainous form. It rumbled with a deep booming snarl.

"It's not possible," DarSheer exhaled. "*They're* not possible anymore." The clouds went black once again.

"Today does seem the day for the impossibility of legend to become reality," Berëthelluïn raised his sword as the entire fields below went silent and all eyes turned upward. Every bowman atop the walls trembled where they stood at the soft growl that emanated from the fog.

"Elca, light an arrow and lose it into that bank of fog!" Elharan commanded.

A stern-looking Elfin in gleaming armor nodded stiffly and grabbed for a spare arrow. With precision of a trained bowman, he lit the tip of the long arrow and brought the string of his bow to his fair cheek. With a half squint, he took aim and loosed the flaming arrow so that it sailed high and far. Below, the enemy host remained stationery and mute. No sound was uttered, no drum was played, no horns were blown. It was as if Mordën had turned off sound.

The arrow illuminated the cloudbank until, from the depths, it came to plink off a massive lumbering shape. We watched in silent horror as the arrow was lost and the form vanished again into the darkness.

"My king," an Elfin commander named Elsberry exhaled, "it is not possible."

"What is it?" I felt my blood drain as the red light forked once more through the fog and again the lumbering shape was backlit.

"ARM THE CATAPULTS!" Elharan bellowed.

At long last, the form appeared, a long neck bursting from the wall of fog. My first thought was that it was a serpent as wide in girth as the walls were tall. But then a claw the size of a tavern slammed into the dirt. A second claw appeared and crunched into a boulder, smashing it into dust. The snake slithered until I saw the massive torso it was attached to.

"DarSheer?" I swallowed shakily. He stared without speaking.

"*REVER DRAKE!*" A single despairing cry filled the air and then went silent.

A long snaking maw hissed up as two glowing eyes followed. Its teeth were long and pointed. It was a drake. It unhinged its gaping jaws, and I wondered if we were to be cooked in a fire hotter than any known flame could get. Instead of fire, however, sound gurgled up then bellowed out. The air spun like a cyclone and hit the edge of the wall where rock exploded inward, into the city. Screams filled the air and chaos descended as boulders slammed into our lines. Many broke formation, dropped their weapons, and ran for cover.

"That's a Rever Drake?" I felt the dizziness hit. "I thought they were horrors written up by Mordën to scare the Drucodians."

"Apparently, he's been busy." DarSheer glowered. "My king? King Elharan? It will not be long before they breach the gates if they march with such monsters. Order Scion to hold the courtyard before the gates whilst we rain down hell on them!"

Large curved black spikes ran down the drake's neck to a point along its back where a large grey saddle sat. There, upon the back of this fresh terror, sat Mordën. I knew if I was close enough, I'd smell the stench of death. A black helm covered his face, but I had no doubt he was smiling up in the sky. He turned in the saddle and raised a gloved fist. The drums returned, beating a new fast-paced rhythm. It was like the sounds of an avalanche growing louder and louder. The Varglarian slammed their swords and shields against their breastplates. They roared their savage hunger and shook their heads like madmen. To view it from the wall, it was like an undulating sea of spears and sound. Towering high above, like a tsunami frozen in time, the drake watched it all. Its long black tongue slithered out like a snake's. It bared its mouth and revealed the rows upon rows of razor-sharp teeth. Beneath it, miniscule in comparison, Rachnadons shook their heads and eagerly snapped their mandibles.

The sound was deafening. My ears ached with the continuous cacophony. I couldn't hear my own thoughts. Seven figures appeared from the fog over our heads. From their throats a raspy sound snaked about. They were laughing.

"I gave you a chance to serve me." A familiar voice filled my head. *"Behold what your failure has reaped."*

I blinked as an intense headache blossomed behind my eyes. On the fields below, obese Varglarian marched forward holding two long pikes.

But it wasn't the Varg that sent a dismayed cry rippling along the wall. It wasn't even Mordën's words that curdled my blood. Two figures were raised high, supported by the pikes. Brenneth and Malziek's lifeless corpses had been skewered from rectum to skull. Brenneth's eyes were wide, glassy. Malziek's eyes had been taken from his skull, leaving only two haunting holes.

"No!" I cried out in pain.

DarSheer cursed words I'd never heard him utter before. Othrain was silent and Kissinger's face was hardened into a mask of simmering rage. Katy gripped my hand tightly and looked away.

"They're . . ." she began.

". . . friends from the Outpost." The words hurt to say. No matter what I did, I was unable to force my eyes from the stable boy's body. He was so tiny on such an imposing pike. "And Mordën just made a crucial error."

"*These and more await those who ally themselves against my growing empire,*" the voice hissed out over the entire city. People covered their ears in pain as the booms filled their minds. "*Before this city burns you will face death and betrayal and you will remember that it was you who caused it all to happen.*"

"He's in your head, isn't he?" Katy said softly. "Mordën?"

"He's always in my head." It came out as a groan. "Always corrupting. Always deceiving."

Kissinger, skin white, clapped me on the back. "This is where we end it all, bairn. You and me and all these thousands who are here to defend against insurmountable odds. You read the tales?"

"Tales?"

"Yeah, you know, the big fanciful fairy ballads of maidens fair and warriors proud, where the good always come out victorious in the end. Surely, in your world they have tales like that. If not, blast, your world must be a sad place to live in."

"No, no, we do." I squeezed Katy's hand and resumed a posture of confidence, overlooking the fields below.

"And what happens in your stories? Do you always come out the victor?"

I stared down at the field as the wind played over my hair. "Always."

"Good." His voice cracked. "We could use some of that optimism about now."

The Hourglass, the seven hovering figures, drew blades made of dark cloud and underneath them, mounts made of convulsing fog appeared. They descended toward us. Mordën, atop his drake, leaned over to peer at his minions. His monologue was loud and heard by every soldier in the city.

"There is no freedom. A new age has been brought on these lands. The peoples who once banished me shall be the ones to crown me. There is no retreat. If you choose to die you will be granted this in a merciless manner. Avalon is a steppingstone to my dark empire. My hordes wish to feast, and I am a generous king. Farewell, golden light. Darkness shall reign over the Eastern Ward and soon all of Ëonë will know my mercy." He gripped the drake's reins and started to turn the lumbering beast.

"Mordën . . ." Lord King Elharan, ruler of the Elfinian race, stood arrayed in golden splendor. Banners snaked around him like silk on the bodies of dancers. His helmed brow was turned upward, letting what feeble sunlight remained, light his brow. There was a hush that descended as Mordën's eyes, black as they were, glimmered.

"King Elharan." He smiled. His tone dropped to a soft venomous murmur. Yet even then, it was still heard by all. "Come from your walled burg and face me."

"We will face each other," Elharan boomed. "I promise you that. But it will not be on your terms, and it *will* end with your head on my spear. *You* have one chance to turn around and retreat to the BlackBurg."

Ugly laughter rippled among the Varglarian and Nightshades. Fists slammed into chest plates, drums rumbled like thunder, and horns sounded like glass shattering. Thirty thousand fell voices rang out on the clear air. The drake opened its jaws and roared, not enough to generate a devastating wind, but enough to cause pain to all who heard it.

"Retreat?" Somehow Mordën could still be heard above the cacophony. He sounded amused. "I did retreat to a mockery of this world. For decades, I was in shame and banishment. Your people, self-proclaimed saviors of this city and this world, will understand soon enough. The time is over for you blessed Elfins, too proud to admit when they have fallen beyond disrepair. Men have corrupted all they touch with their deceit and trickery. Ebyians ruin all around them, drilling and destroying what was made in the beginning days. There is none left in this world to stop me. Do you think the peace-loving Inclings can defend your world? Will Erëthuïl himself and his doting Luthi stop me?" He looked around as if waiting for a heavenly response. None came.

"And what about us?" Parod asked behind me, his shoulders wide and his gaze powerful. He had somehow slipped from the top level to here without anyone noticing him. "What about the Last Remnant of Drucodians? Do you remember us, foul abomination? Do you remember . . . *me*?"

I knew on the uppermost level, the Drucodians would be standing proudly, with their long sleek grey bodies encased in brazen white armor. This was their dream, to stand against their old foe one last time. Parod's old eyes were resolute as he stared directly at Mordën.

"*You!*" Mordën spat vehemently. His eyes roiled with rage, and he screamed a ghoulish wail. "Cursed cur, vilest of living forms. You stand here now? NOW?"

"I've defeated you twice before," Parod said grimly. "I brought you to the High King. I banished you and I will defeat you again!"

"BURN THEM ALL! SPARE NO ONE! BRING ME THEIR HEADS!" Mordën screamed. Spittle flew from his helmet. He'd been transformed into a crazed madman atop the drake. His once black eyes glowed as if fire burned behind them.

Commander Scion raised his blade and shouted something to his men before glancing at DarSheer.

"They want flesh? I say let them have it."

"I knew he was a warrior of old," DarSheer murmured. "But I never imagined that was his secret. If that is not a sign of our fortune changing, I do not know what is."

In a split second, the scene changed. The mass of darkness, on the command of their king, charged. To hear thousands and thousands of metal boots thudding against the earth was a sound I never wished to hear again. Scion raised his powerful blade.

"Sires of lesser lords, aim your bows true and do not miss. Light the fields below so they may feel the weight of the sun. Burn them and rid us all their chaos. *FIRE*!"

A deep cheer went up as the Caldonanites raised their bows and launched a wave of fiery arrows down against the black liquids on the fields. I watched with grim satisfaction as the fields of oil, not water, roared into angry presence. The Varg and Shades unlucky enough to be wading through them were burnt to a crisp. Many came to a complete stop, unable to find a way around the fire and to their prey. A horn was blown frantically. Bellows filled the air. Riderless horses neighed. Shades perished. *Explosions boomed*! In the center of it all, a hysterical laugh echoed out.

"Elfins to the front!" Elharan bellowed. "Parod, return to the upper tier and make fast the gate there, should we need it."

"We've been ready for thousands of years," Parod returned evenly. "It is time to rid this world at long last of its parasite. Long may the Elfins, Ebyians, and Men live in peace. I retire now to my glory, for this end shall defy all legend!"

"Ëonë owes your people a debt it can never repay." Elharan gripped Parod's forearms. The Drucodian's grey skin meant it faded in and out of view with every bank of fog that rolled by.

"We may speak little of it," the Drucodian returned kindly, "for the Drucodians have owed a debt to the free peoples of this world the day we failed to stop Mordën. Now, after two millennium of waiting, it is finally over. Long ago you came to our aid and while together we were not strong enough, it is not just us two here now. The Drucodians shall stand in defiance . . . one last time. *The crimson flow was shed . . .*"

"*. . . so the green of this world could flourish,*" Elharan finished.

"DarSheer?" I checked.

"Present."

"What are they talking about?"

"The plan."

"Which is?"

"Commander Scion and King Elharan use their bowmen to kill as many of the charging horde as possible before they reach the gates. Once the foe reaches the great gates and begins trying to breach, our bowmen can continue pick off hundreds at a time whilst those on the wall make ready for the siege ladders."

"And what of Ir'Landi?"

"Ir'Landi and his Ebyians hold the second tier should we need to retreat. If we, by some miracle, start pushing our foe back, they will reinforce us."

Far below, a battering ram protected by black steel plating, was carried by sixteen rotund Nightshades. Eight to a side, they heaved it forward, step-by-step, through the turmoil and growing mud. Each of their eight eyes was trained on one thing: the gates.

"And should it come to that," I tried not to sound helpless, "the last of their race will perish here. How can they be so calm knowing this is their likely outcome?" I remembered Mordën's words and felt the guilt growing. Not for the last time, my mind flashed back to my days tied to the torture bed, in the belly of a mountain. If I hadn't given in, if I had only been stronger . . .

"Everyone here has made their choices. Do you not think the wise Parod knows he will not leave this city alive? Are his own any more deceived than us? It will be a slaughter but our purpose is not to completely defeat Mordën, but to delay his taking of the Eastern Ward." DarSheer grabbed a bow and notched an arrow to its sleek wood. "Mourn the dead when we wave the victorious banner."

"So, you believe we will fail in defending the city?" It was hard swallowing the lump in my throat. "Just like that? Already you've despaired?"

"*Innith Inine!*" a shaky voice called.

"*Innith Inine!*" a second voice rallied.

DarSheer smirked against the yew of his bow. "*Innith Inine!*" he roared, then turned to me. "The basin remains open should you wish to take it, bairn. But there are many here who would see this death a greater honor than any other end. The High City needs time to pull its forces together. They haven't been awakened or used in five hundred years. What happens here will change the course of history! We must simply delay." Soon the entire wall was chanting the inspirational saying.

"I will stand as all of you, but it burdens my heart knowing this." I drew my sword and felt its weight in my hand. Once that weight had comforted me, now it reminded me of the bloodshed to come.

"What does that mean: *Innith Inine*?" Katy whispered to me, but it was Othrain who graced her with a response.

"The oldest war cry we know," he snarled. "*Innith Inine* . . . it means 'onward till we're ashes.'"

"*Innith Inine*! ARROWS . . . FLY!" King Elharan pointed his sword toward the clouds and bellowed out the command with his chest.

A volley of arrows filled the sky with their whistling as they spiraled down toward the moving mass. Nightshades gurgled on their own blood as it misted into black steam and floated into the clouds. Varglarian snarled and tripped as they became pin cushions. I beheld dozens of them fall lifeless, only to be trampled by their own kind as they rushed toward the gates. The flames on the fields filled the air with an acrid, black smoke. The Varglarian archers raised crudely bent bows and aimed for the battlements. Elharan turned. His eyes were wide.

"*DOWN*! TAKE COVER! HIT THE STONE!"

As soon as the words left his mouth, hundreds of black feathered arrows arced through the air toward us. I dove from my perch and pressed my body against the unyielding stone. The Elfin behind me was not so lucky. He cried out as three arrows filled his torso. Blood flowed down his shirt as he tumbled backwards off the wall. In a similar fashion, those who had not heard the command or were otherwise occupied, fell to the pointed bringers of death. Bodies thudded lifelessly to the ground. Torches fell the distance to the ground. Shields clattered noisily, released from their bearer. Sporadic screams marked the newly injured. Red light forked hungrily across the growing cloud front. Drums roared. Across the battlements, fires went out in increasing blackness. High above, the golden archer snapped and danced to the tune of the howling wind.

Katy drew her blade as she lay next to me. I resisted the urge to reach a hand out and ask her if she was okay. Who could be okay when faced with impending death? At my side, she held a bow. A shield was strapped at her back and a dagger hung from her belt. Her hair was pulled up into a tight bun. I swallowed my fear and gave her a confident smile, for her eyes searched my face for some comfort.

"I miss home," she murmured shakily. "Is that wrong? To wish that I could abandon everyone here and retreat to safety?"

"Of course not," I took her hand as arrows clinked about on the stones and metal clanged against metal. The Caldonanites were now releasing arrows at will. Scion marched up and down the battlements, shouting encouragements to his men and pointing out targets. All sound about us seemed to fade to a far-off din. The Varg on the fields were quickly finding gaps in the flames and their charge of the walls drew them nearby. The Westerly Road had been cleared of debris and dangers and Nightshades with their battering ram rushed toward the gates. Elharan barked orders and DarSheer spoke reassuringly to those around him. It was all barely audible. A protective urge nearly swallowed me. I wished to run with her and flee this battle. Perhaps there was a place we could run where Mordën could never find us. Perhaps there was a place where we could be happy. Not for the last time, my thoughts turned to the ships still docked in the Ethero Basin. If we could only get there in time . . . I sighed.

"Forgive my despair." She gripped her bow tightly. "I waver on ground strong as stone. I question the sun when it falls and fear the moon as it rises. It is wrong of me to challenge that which happens."

"It is not wrong to despair." I tucked a strand of her hair behind her ear. "Mordën might seem as strong as a powerful gale, but remember, the howling wind fears the approach of that which might finally master it."

"What can control the elements?" She held my gaze. "What makes the wind fear so bad that its growls turn to weeping?"

"That which can stop the wind from its progress. What does the wind fear? The mountains, which stand a defiant example through time. Wind can uproot trees, roll boulders, destroy cities, but it cannot move mountains. Mordën might have a host from the depths and bowels of Ëonë itself, but there are yet a few here who might master him. The moment we lose our hope, he wins."

"Can you promise me we'll come out of this alive?" There was the question I was dreading to hear.

I opened my mouth to respond. A throb echoed dully in my ears. A single bead of sweat formed on my brow. It danced about the idea of falling, slightly dipping over the raise of my forehead but then slinking back. Finally, it tipped over the edge and ran down the bridge of my nose. It fell as a glittering gem, turning and diving its way to the ground. It plopped and shattered back into liquid as in its own little world, it spilled over the stone. Drums thudded nightmarishly in the dark, unceasingly, and naggingly. Deep voices snarled and torches flickered as they grew nearby. I heard the stomping of thousands of iron boots and the cry of the land as it yielded to the merciless charge of the Varglarian horde. A horn blew shrilly. Clouds congregated above to watch the conflict, whispering in their airy language. I exhaled. Sweat beaded on my brow.

At the onset, I'd been ready, eager almost, to see this come to an end. But now, having learned what I'd learned, I felt something different seeping into my veins. Flashes of recollection berated me, reading me of the failure that was the Outpost's last stand. I closed my eyes as the screams closed in. I . . . was . . . *terrified*!

We watched as the two funeral pyres were lit and the flames began their feasting. Wind forced its talons around exposed skin as the night grew. This was our third burning in as many days.

"*The Varglarian are getting bolder.*" *Lord Malziek snapped a twig in half. His eyes beheld the blaze. "Ironic, isn't it? The few times we get warmth beyond the wall, is at the cost of our own."*

A morbid chuckle rippled through the motionless men. Some clutched their thick cloaks around their bony shoulders. Others were content to simply watch. Topper, his gloshee at his side, was unusually quiet. There was no song or bad music coming from him tonight. Traverse's arms were wrapped protectively around Marian. We all watched as the nine bodies, wrapped in cloth by Marian's delicate hands and prepared by Altruic, succumbed to their fate, and began disappearing. The smoke was thick with their ashes, blown about by the wind. I wondered how much of the soot collecting on our cloaks was from the hewn logs versus the bodies.

At my side, Brenneth was breathing into his hands. Altruic had prevented him from seeing the last two funerals, but he'd weaseled his way into this display. His wide eyes brimmed with tears that he brushed at repeatedly. I gave him a comforting hug.

"What about all those who can't be buried or burned?" Brenneth murmured.

"Everyone gets buried or burned," I said reassuringly. "Their essence travels to join the feasting in the Hallowed Halls. All warriors are granted that right."

"Not everyone. What about the bairns and codgers who took it into their own hands to cross the Bridge? What about those who die in battle and lay to bloat and spoil under the sun's gaze?"

"All, especially warriors, head to the halls Erëthuïl has made for them," DarSheer spoke in the shadows behind us. We turned to stare at him. "Whether you're buried or not does not change that outcome."

"Still," the boy sniffled, "it's undignified."

"Much is, Brenneth." I shook my head.

"He's got a point," DarSheer murmured. "They all deserve a proper burial, the bold and young, weak and old, kind and foolish . . . even the cowardly. Truly, the cowards in the midst of war are far braver than the warriors of peace. War breeds peace and peace gives birth to complacency. Keep the watch and govern your decisions with the actions of the past as a

map to the future. Do not discount the words of the old or the feelings of the brokenhearted, for they are not weak, nor does a codger's failing vision mean he has no wisdom to give. Only a fool forgoes the whispering of a man who saw the world at its worst."

Sweat and ash covered my face as wind ruffled my hair. Brenneth was quiet as the last of the fire licked up its meal and slowly died itself. The embers brooded deep in the bowels of the pyre, glowing eyes in a shadowy forest. Most left to man the watch or prepare for the day's events. Only a handful, Brenneth and myself included, stayed behind to ruminate on the temporary nature that is life.

"Are you afraid of dying?" Brenneth asked.

I was surprised by the question and not at the same moment. "Sure. What makes you ask that?"

He pointed wordlessly at the last embers of the pyre. I gazed at the crumbling remains of the wood as it was blown into ashes by the wind. The waves broke furiously against the beach.

"The pyre on the left had Serle and Theodoric. They met you on your first day here. Remember?"

"Yeah, Serle was the big guy with the axe and Theodoric was his hairy brother?" That made him chuckle.

In all honesty, I'd clouded faces and names from my memory. We'd had countless funerals since I'd made this place my home. It was just easier not to remember.

"It's just one day you're here and the next . . . poof." He dropped some dirt for emphasis. "Every day more and more perish. How soon before it's my turn? I've thought about it. I think I'd want to die unconscious. I hear it's the least painful."

"You shouldn't be thinking about any of that stuff. You're young. You have your whole life ahead of you."

Out over the shores, the dark brooding clouds of the BlackBurg rumbled ominously. The wind whipped the waves into a frothing frenzy. My hair flung about, and I huddled in the warmth of my cloak.

"I don't want to die." His whispered words were as harsh as the wind was cold. "I'm scared, Phoenix. I'm so scared."

"Hey, stop thinking about that." I hugged him tight and smiled, hoping it was a reassuring smile and shedding none of the fear that harbored inside my own heart. "We'll destroy Mordën and before you know it, this Outpost will become obsolete, and you'll return to The High City. Think of the bistri and merrymaking that shall be had then, eh? Think of the warmth and the parties that shall be had on the day this world is free forever. No, don't think of fear for it is temporary. Now, move along and tell Marian we'll be ready for some of her famous cooking. I'm starving."

He was up and away in a bound, cloak snapping about his heels. As he vanished inside the gate, I turned back to stare at the Bridge. The side that sat on the beach of the BlackBurg was covered in a mist. My gut rumbled. I hoped this would be over soon, and I'd be back home ... wherever home was.

"... I hope," I added.

I stared at the pike bearing Brenneth. A quiet rage began to burn. He was just a bairn. He was just a bairn. *I don't want to die.*

He was just a bairn, I thought as I stared out toward the drake. Mordën's only visible indicator he'd heard me was his head turning for a moment.

He's the first of many.

A cry went up on the air as all watched the unfolding chaos below. The Varg advanced, now under protection of shields or the bodies of their own dead. I peered out into the haze and wondered why the Nightshades remained at a safe distance.

As the morning matured into midday, the scope of the battle was fully displayed. Our forces had been split into two groups on the walls. King Elharan and his bowmen occupied the northern stretch of rock while Scion and his archers took to the southern curve of the wall. Between their constant barrages, bodies stacked so high on the fields they became as walls in a maze. Varglarian and Nightshades.

"Their blood fills the field below so it might rival the depth of the basin," an encouraged Elfinian bowman cried. His eyes were wide with both glee and fear. "There may yet be a victory for us against this darkness!"

I craned my neck to glance back where Katy and Tim stood feet behind me. Katy's expression was blank, but Tim smiled. His eyes danced over the fields. I knew his joy at how much Scion had managed to kill was shared in grim satisfaction across the walls. Some laughed at the countless piles of Varglarian that had been hewed in half. It was not over yet. The battering ram was dragged step-by-step closer to the city gates. Rachnadons, burdened by hundreds of Varg clinging to ropes attached to the spiders' bodies, staggered toward the city. We were about to be assailed. Scion and his men could only hold a fraction of Mordën's attention when his true prize was sitting there ripe for the taking.

"Give up! Give up!" A chant began as the Varglarian on a nearby Rachnadon hurled ropes anchored with steel plates into the air. Some found footing against the merlons, and one by one, the Varg began the arduous task of climbing up the ropes toward us. "*We serve the Shadow King*. All hail his dark form and bow down. King Mordën will have his prize. *He will have his inheritance*. Surrender now and your death will be quick."

"Archers . . . swords! Draw and face!" DarSheer boomed. His own broadsword was ready and lethal in his grip. "Prepare for the charge!"

I drew my blade and stepped forward. My palm was greasy with sweat. I inhaled and exhaled. In perfect unison, a line of Elfin and Men drew their blades and stepped forward. Boots thudded rhythmically against stone. King Elharan, hair flowing in the breeze, aimed the tip of his golden blade toward the dying sun. The feeble rays of sunlight glinted off its impressive form. Shouts of unified determination rose amidst the ranks atop the walls. It was funny, I thought much later, how impending death can bring together a group of unlikely allies.

As the first of the ropes was severed, sending a handful of Varg shrieking to their deaths below, Elharan thundered out: "We rumble like thunder. We roar as lightning brightens the night. Our cry shall boom from the deep and echo in the valleys! We are bloodied and beaten names on scrolls forgotten as moths consume them. Herein we give the chance of freedom to those who'd spit on our corpses. Let the village hear your cry. Let the town feel your thunder. Let the city know your bravery. Let the world see your honor. Stand and face down the shadows before us. Know not the harsh sting of death. Erect your hearts and wield your blades. Now is the hour to repel evil and darkness!"

Through the gloom I saw quick movement as the battering ram, borne through the fray by the largest Nightshades, neared its destination. The ram was nearly twice as thick as any man and roughly thirty feet in length. A Varglarian's hideous helmed head stuck over the wall and was followed by the rest of his body. A second and third followed. They chanted in ugly unison as they withdrew curved blades of obsidian steel.

Behold his wings are wide, his vision far
Mordën grows in shadow's realm
Behold he nears, behold he sees
For all shall soon be his, on bended knee or buried down in graves!

"Ram! Ram!" I roared as I swung my sword in the air and gestured down. My first combat began as a Varg rolled over the edge of a crenel and barreled into me. I tumbled unceremoniously to the ground. With that, a wave of Varglarian reached us and we fully engaged them. Metal clashed against their curved steel. The battle had reached the city walls.

"Fire your arrows down there." DarSheer gestured emphatically to the secured bowmen. In the distance Elharan echoed the same words.

A bowman who'd been rushing forward stopped and for a moment stood motionless. He tipped backward, falling over the edge of the wall. An arrow had imbedded to the shaft between his eyes. Black feathers bristled as he tumbled off and crashed through the roof of a barracks far below. The Varg let out a horrific roar as they began climbing up the ropes faster. Rachnadons' long legs appeared through the low hanging mist as the cloud of fog advanced on the city. The spiders themselves began climbing up the walls. One placed its armored claw in a spot where the stone crumbled away. It let out a horrified shriek as it lost purchase and tumbled backward, crunching satisfyingly against a battalion of Nightshades in the fields below. Our archers returned several volleys but there seemed an endless flow of bodies to replace the fallen. Our battlements quickly grew sparse of men as they succumbed to the enemy's hunger. As quickly as they'd arrived, our forces were diminishing.

Katy stabbed her blade deep into the neck of a Varg and whipped it out, beheading it swiftly. Her hair was splattered with gore and her face was now grimy with her own blood. A cut on her temple flowed freely and she staggered. I fought through the bodies, hacking, and diving back to avoid being skewered like a boar.

"Katy!" I cried, but the din of the battle was too loud.

"She can't hear you," Tim murmured in my ear. I nearly leapt out of my skin. His voice was icy calm in stark contrast to the scene that played before us.

"Tim!"

"Focus on helping us get out of here alive, and not on the well-being of your love," he said.

"Tim, that's not . . ."

"I did not ask, nor do I care," he snorted. "Just fight."

And he was away, back spinning and slashing before I could respond. Five Nightshades made the mistake of challenging him and with a speed and agility I didn't know he had, he dispatched all five with ease. I glanced back at Katy and cried out as a Varg slammed its shield in her face and she fell back. The large creature, drool oozing out from its facial slits, stomped toward her and raised a large hammer. Before I could hew off its appendage, Kissinger had leapt onto its back and driven his small knife between its shoulder blades. Othrain charged at the head of a small grouping of men. DarSheer dropped to one knee and spun like a top on a smooth table. His blade sliced several Varg cleanly in half.

I paused at the edge of the wall and gazed about. The Varglarian, thanks to their Rachnadon mounts, had overwhelmed the middle of the wall and split it in half. Half our forces battled strenuously right of the gates and the other half, that I was a part of, staggered under the iron blows on the left side of the gate. Far below, now unburdened by arrows from above, the Nightshade battering force began slamming their ram against the massive gates. To their credit, the gates appeared to hold, albeit quivering and releasing pounds of dust after each hit.

Scion roared out as a Varg stabbed him between the shoulder blades. His voice was filled with grief as he dropped to one knee. His own men fell in similar fashion. From the wall of fog far below, endless streams of Varglarian hordes backed by Nightshades were marching into view. Rachnadons, with a hundred clinging Varg on their backs, rammed their long legs into ally and foe alike. Fires burned hot as once lush groupings of trees became kindling. The plains were no longer grassy expanses but a spread of mud and bodies. The Westerly Road was a current bringing the enemy closer and closer to the gates, like boulders somehow rolling on the tops of a mighty river.

"Why doesn't he just end us all?" Kissinger spat as he shoved the body of a Varg from his chest. "He's got a blasted a Rever Drake. He could end this whole conflict in two seconds."

"You overstate the powers of the cursed creature." DarSheer grabbed an abandoned bow from the ground and fitted it with a long arrow. He aimed and shot the tip directly between the eyes of a Nightshade who had morphed from the shadows. The creature stared for a second and all eight of its eyes rolled back as it clanged to the ground. "A Rever Drake can only produce such a howl after a lengthy time. It must build it up in the furnace that is its wind organ."

"How do you know so much about the thing?" I raced to help Kissinger who was being besieged by three brutes. We fought them off, but not before I'd gotten a deep gash on my arm. The blood flowed out as, cursing, I tore off parts of my cloak and tied it tightly just above the injury.

"Do you really want me to give you a history lesson?" DarSheer demanded incredulously.

"Save it for when someone cares!" Kissinger rolled to avoid being cut in two. "If the drake can't sing for a while, it still has talons and a maw full of teeth."

The answer dawned on me as I wiped grime from my forehead. "He wants to prove how easily he can defeat us. He doesn't need a mythical creature to win his battles for him."

"Great," Kissinger grimaced as he stood and spat blood on the face-plate of a dead Varg. "Any chance we can use his smug arrogance and confidence in his victory against him?"

"Arrows!" Elharan charged toward us. "Hit the ground!"

Kissinger and I dove for the stone as a wave of arrows hissed overhead, inches from scalping us. In our breathless conversation, we'd ignored the swarm of Varglarian archers who had climbed over the wall. I gave Elharan a brief nod of gratitude as we stood back up. The Elfinian king paused at our side as his entourage charged the edge of the wall and began hacking away at the ropes.

"How fare the gates?" King Elharan wiped the black blood from his blade. "Does Commander Scion still stand?"

"He has fallen." DarSheer fumbled about for spare arrows, his borrowed bow thwacking against his back. "Most of his bannermen too, but a small force still stands and for every one of them that falls, five Varg choke on steel."

I was in the middle of side-stepping a Varg's downward cut when I heard a scream.

"Phoenix!" Katy's voice cracked like a whip. "Phoenix?"

I pivoted, expecting to see her beaten down once again. She stood, hair flowing behind her in the wind. Her face was dripping with sweat, and she cradled her arm. Blood oozed from her nostrils. She wiped it away with one hand and met my eyes. She looked like a figure of legend, a warrior who had slain thousands of horrible beasts, a person of folk-tale. I hurried to her side.

"I can't . . . find . . . Tim!" Her words stumbled out.

"I'm sure he's fine." I grabbed her arms and squeezed. "Katy, he's fine. I saw him not too long ago. He's with Othrain and Arabella.

They're on the opposite side of the wall from us now, with the Caldonanites, separated by a horde of Varglarian. But he's okay. Are you okay?"

She nodded hastily. "I'm no stranger to killing these abominations. Tim and I faced down a few on our journeys looking for you. But they were always isolated to a measly few and weighed down with fear of being discovered. Here . . . I don't know . . . they fight with a savage desire."

I hugged her tight as screams filled the air. "We will get out of this, Katy." Her body shook. "I promise."

"Come on you two." Kissinger slapped a hand on my back. "THEY'RE BREACHING THE GATE!"

I whipped about and craned my neck to see over the edge of the wall. DarSheer was at my side.

"Defend the city!" DarSheer's voice was filled with an urgent pleading. "King Elharan, send the Ebyian hosts on the second level to defend the gates! All will be lost if the city is breached!"

Several dozen Elfinian archers took aim and let loose a storm of arrows, pinning down the enemy on the wall. Cheers erupted and each began fighting with renewed vigor. The Varg howled and retreated over their dead, some falling over the edges of the wall to their deaths below. I blocked a slash. The Nightshades responsible for lugging the battering ram were filled with arrows where they stood until they were little more than quivering mounds of flesh. A Varglarian in front of me choked on its own blood as Katy pulled her blade from its back. She grimaced. Kissinger, sword in hand, was standing a few feet off. He stared off toward the center of the wall and I knew his thoughts were for his old friend, Othrain, as no doubt Katy's were for Tim. In the moment of joy, the enemy had seized control of the right hand of the wall. We bathed in temporary rest while they continued to be battered to pieces. Dozens of Varglarian swarmed the stone, hacking and hewing everything in sight.

"The wall is lost," I gasped as I stared about. "We must prepare the retreat. DarSheer?"

"Stay your haste, young bairn," he snapped.

"We need to go!" I challenged him abrasively. "Now! Those who remain will be as good as dead."

"Don't say that!" Katy beat against my shoulder with her hand. "I know you've given up on Tim ever being as he was of old, and no matter whatever grudge the two of you hold, you must remember he is our friend. You leave them for dead you're leaving *him* for dead. What about Arabella? The silver maiden from the north? The old drunk? Othrain?"

"Katy, we're about to be overrun." I pointed to a large chunk of the wall as it crumbled under the weight of three Rachnadons. The men who had been hiding in its shadows screamed as they plummeted down to their deaths. This sudden shift allowed the Varglarian to push forward even faster. The wall thinned of Elfins. It was clear that within minutes we'd be facing down a large hungry horde of fangs and points. "We have to fall back."

"We've lost the main wall," DarSheer agreed heavily. "That much is clear. We can only hope to provide a retreat for those still on the right wall."

"How long do we have?" I asked.

"That depends on . . ." There was a sound of boots against stone. We watched as Scion staggered into view, with battered and bloodied men stumbling behind him.

"They are too strong," Scion despaired. "They cut us down and while we match them five to one, there is an endless supply of them. Even the greatest warriors eventually fall when the enemy never runs out."

"Tell your men to retreat to the courtyards!" Elharan barked. "Hold the gates as long as possible to cover for those who must retreat for the second level."

"Aye." Scion wiped blood that leaked from his mouth and turned to his men. "To the courtyard! Let's give these blasted curs another life whooping."

Varglarian began pouring over the walls, slamming into the remaining Elfin and Men. Blood trickled down the walls and crenels.

I whirled about as a Nightshade stabbed its blade right for my chest. Deflecting the attack, I fell into rhythm. I parried the next strike and ducked the following swing. Its blade scraped off the stone and, knocked off balance, it staggered backward. I drove both feet into the ground and like a frog leaping forward, forced the blade deep into the creature's guts. It let out a horrific scream and collapsed on its back. I forced the blade deeper, twisting as I pushed, and watched the movement in his eyes darken then die. Black mist flowed up as I twisted to avoid inhaling the toxic odor. I pivoted out of the path of a spear thrust as a Varg attempted to skewer me. It stepped forward and I stepped back. We danced like this, an ever-hesitating moment.

"What's this?" the creature sneered. "Are the goldens so desperate they send bairns to fight for them?"

I ducked and pushed off one foot. A second later the headless Varg toppled to the ground. In its wake came ten more, and before long I began to feel the weight of my sword and the pain of exhausted muscles. A blade glanced off mine, cutting slightly into my side. I dispatched the vermin, but the wound stung. Blood and sweat stained my shirt as I deflected yet another attack. Tripping over a body, I fell to my rear end and narrowly avoided my head being removed. Before the Nightshade could find an open spot to pierce me, I found a fallen arrow which still burned with flame and, covering my eyes, shoved it upward with all my strength. The eight eyed monster stopped and slowly crumbled to the ground, the tip of the arrow in one of its eye sockets. A ball of fire eagerly consumed the creature's head. DarSheer grabbed my shirt and hauled me to my feet. His face was grimy. One eye was black and the skin over his nose had been split open. Blood openly trickled down and into his mouth. His teeth were stained red as he grimaced.

"We near the breaking point of the bulge," I said forcefully. "We must fall back before they breach the gates. DarSheer!"

"This is true," DarSheer coughed. "The gates are near breaking. I fear Scion and his men will not hold them off for long. Head for the second terrace. Now!"

I sheathed my sword and began hurrying down the steps. Katy and Kissinger were right behind me as DarSheer stood, silhouetted in the roaring fingers of fire that flamed behind him. His mane of hair hung like a defeated banner. Blood caked his arms and breastplate and he finally turned, as shadows grew closer, and followed us.

As we skidded to a stop in the courtyard at the base of the walls, Varglarian and Nightshades had finally breached the once impressive gates. Scion and his host stood in a shield wall formation. They shouted insults and stabbed long spears through gaps in the shields as Varg threw themselves on the smooth surfaces.

Seeing me in the faint light, a Nightshade roared and cast a long spear at me. I dodged it and it clattered uselessly into the street. It drew its curved blade and charged. The first blow was strong, and I nearly dropped my own sword. The second came with an intense hatred as it slashed. The point of its sword cut through my shirt with ease. I sucked my gut in, and the Shade's next pass cut into my stomach.

"Mordën will enjoy seeing your carcass on my pike," the creature rumbled eagerly. "Your entrails shall make a fine meal."

"I hope he's patient!" I spat back. "Because he'll be waiting a long while." I swung my blade.

Like the sounds of cracking timber, a great black body fell from above. I staggered back as it slammed into the ground where the Nightshade had once stood. The Rachnadon was full of arrows, like a pincushion. It was missing several legs and multiple spears had been imbedded in its skull and underbelly. My relief was short-lived as the Nightshade burst from the belly of the creature. Guts and entrails hung on its shoulders and armor as thick blood oozed down the Shade's chest. The creature stomped clear of the carcass and knocked my sword from my hand. I inhaled sharply in pain at the vibrations which traveled up my arm. Blood pooled in my palm at a stuck sliver of steel which had broken off. The Shade's heavy boot slammed into my head, and I fell, gasping, to the ground. A thick wet liquid dripped from my chin. I grunted as the same boot stomped down on my back and knocked the air from my lungs. No matter how I struggled, the boot pressed down with unbelievable strength. The cold kiss of steel burned into my neck as the Shade lowered its sword. Before it had a chance to behead me, a female roared and leapt on the creature's back. I rolled free as the Shade bellowed and dropped to one knee, struggling to shake the girl from its back.

"I didn't think this through. Help!" Katy yelped as she clasped the abomination's neck like a rider on an untamed stallion.

With an ear-splitting roar, the Shade bucked her into the wall. She crumpled to the ground with a small squeak. I grabbed for my sword and thwacked the tip against a nearby wall.

"Hey, ugly," I shouted, "why don't you fight someone who can gouge all eight of your eyes out? Who rates higher on your precious master's list? Me? Or some Avalonian wench?"

"You talk fierce combat, but you'll die gasping on my blade," the Shade snarled.

We dueled back and forth for a long agonizing moment. Seconds before it had me again in a headlock, a flash of metal whisked by me and sunk its teeth into the Shade's neck. DarSheer hurried up and pulled his dagger free of the black mist. I cried out in relief and hugged him.

"I have never been so grateful to see you," I gushed weakly. "Katy needs help."

I dodged two separate fights between Nightshades and Elfinian swordsmen until I reached her side. She held her arm and grimaced under the pain. Her brown eyes flushed with fear at my approach and changed to relief.

"You're welcome for saving your life," she joked feebly.

"Don't you ever do that again." I hugged her tight and she gasped. "Thank you." Her eyes found mine.

As if to confirm my worst fears, a ball of flame larger than a house appeared over the wall moving at what appeared to be a slow spin before it exploded into the side of a tall building. The domicile erupted in dust and rubble and crumbling stone. Stone rained down around us. A Nightshade lost its head as a chunk of material slammed into it. A second and third ball of fire hit two other nearby buildings as the gates exploded in debris and splinters.

Kissinger slid to a stop next to me and together we carried Katy, who had drifted off into a mumbling state. DarSheer protected our rear as, like hundreds of defeated soldiers around us, we ran for the second tier. Through the broken remains of the gate, Scion and a handful of remaining Men stumbled back against the slashing blades of the Varglarian horde. I couldn't help but notice how few were left of the once impressive number of Men from the start of the battle.

We crossed paths with Elharan, as his personal guard slashed and stabbed the Nightshades that had used their shadow travel to bypass the line of Caldonanites. His face was bloody and his hair, once golden and smooth, had become tangled and knotted. He staggered back to my side as DarSheer turned and scooped Katy from our arms. Kissinger and I stood shoulder to shoulder with the Elfinian ruler. Slowly, despite the brave last stand by Scion, the Varglarian were pushing us deeper into the city. Rachnadons towered over us, silhouetted against the flashing red clouds that advanced over the city. Elharan sounded his horn and on the battlements, and illuminated by the flames on the wall, Elfin warriors responded.

"Where is the moron?" Othrain yelled, sprinting into view. "Kissinger? Blast you, golden lover. Where are you?"

"Over here, crazy eyes!" Kissinger waved a hand. His voice held a derogative tone, but I could see the immense relief in his eyes. "Where have you been? Dallying about the dead?"

I ducked as Elharan swung and cleaved the head off a charging Nightshade four times my width. The body fell with a wet thud. A fresh wave of reserve Elfins spilled into the street from both sides. Renewed with the support, we battled on. The avenues were full of bodies and the gutters which ran along them flowed red. Discarded armament littered the ground. A golden archer banner was torn and thrown aside. Its thin fabric had become snagged in a tree. Fires burned everywhere, started by accident from fallen braziers or sent intentionally by the advancing horde, we did not know. Overwhelming hot smoke and hungry flames consumed buildings quickly. Black acrid smoke wafted overhead and filled my every breath. Everything was hot. Burning hot.

"They advance with numbers beyond our ability to stop. I must admit: I begin to fear." Kissinger coughed into his hand. "Do you, Othrain?"

"Of course not," Othrain said as his hands trembled. "Fear is a game made for bairns still nursing." He cleared his throat as his voice cracked. "But you should ride for the basin while there is still time, and we control the upper levels."

"No chance if you're remaining here."

"Staying behind is not wise."

"Then I am without intelligence."

An animalistic roar shattered their conversation as a Rachnadon, towering above us, stampeded through the melee. Each of its eight spiked legs crunched a body beneath as it stomped around. Some of the spikes on its legs dragged the limp bodies of Elfin who had been unfortunate enough to be speared by them. I leapt back to avoid become jelly on the ground and in so doing tripped over a body. I fell back and gasped as once again I lost my air. For a moment I was like a fish out of water, my mouth open and my chest heaving.

"Get back up, master bairn." Elharan grabbed my arm and hoisted me back. I swung with determination and a Shade, which had tried to take advantage of the king's distraction, took a step forward. It was crushed by a massive leg, the Rachnadon above stomping in circles as it was egged on by its rider.

Without response, I stumbled like a drunken fool through the battle and down a side road. I shook my head to clear the echoes of slaughter and butchering. Several Elfin rushed past and dove into the fray. I ducked down an alleyway and found a moment to breath. All around, on morbid display, bodies lay. Severed hands, heads, and arms were strewn about. I covered my nose to the stench and forced down the desire to vomit. A headless Elfin toppled down from the roof behind me. I watched the thud and held a shaky hand over my white lips. A second later, the head spiraled into the air as a Varg leapt from roof to roof.

As I passed one of the fallen bodies, it jerked and reached for me. My heart jolted, and I scrambled away. I grasped for a dagger and pointed it at the creature. Shadows danced about and I realized how exposed I was. I was alone here with the dead and dying.

"Water, I need water!" A young Elfin, barely older than I, looked up, breathing laboriously. Broken and bloodied, his armor coated with red, the figure winced.

"I have none to offer," I said.

"I need water," the Elfin pressed in growing panic. "My love awaits me beyond the shores. I cannot remain here. It . . . was a mistake." His voice caught as his eyes rolled back.

I examined his body and found five arrows imbedded in his chest and legs. The wounds did not appear to be life-threatening, but it was clear he was dying from a loss of blood. Hesitantly, I grabbed a cloak and pressed it against as many of the wounds as I could. It was already too late. He made no move. His eyes no longer saw.

"Phoenix!" Othrain bellowed behind me.

I whirled about and instantly felt a hot pain in my hair as a shield slammed into my skull. Stars danced about my blackening vision as I was thrown several feet into a crumbling wall. A searing pain arched through my back. The Varglarian advanced with a hunger in its eyes. It reached for its iron helmet.

"A mouthful," it spoke to itself, "but a mouthful is better than naught. I prefer the blood still warm and the flesh pulsating with fear."

Before it had a chance to fulfil its desires, Othrain leapt into view and cleaved its head from its shoulders. The body thudded to the ground, just another number in the carcasses around us.

"Are you good, bairn?" Othrain demanded as he stepped over the corpse and reached a hand out.

Before I had a chance to respond, his eyes went wide, and he staggered forward. His face drained of its natural redness as we both stared at the arrow quivering in his back. A second hissed into view and stuck in his calf. He went down with a roar, kneeling. A third arrow arched over a nearby bonfire and despite my weak warning, landed with a sickening crunch in his arm.

"Run," he gasped. "Leave now while you still can."

I forced myself up to my feet and despite the spots filling my vision and the pain that came with a broken rib, I grabbed his hand and started dragging him toward a side alley. But he resisted. Stubbornly. I turned back as he yanked his hand free and grabbed the Varg's shield.

"What are you doing?" I cried out. "Othrain, you need aid. Come with me!"

"Othrain never runs from a fight," he snapped as his teeth turned red with blood. With that he turned back to face three creeping shadows. The three Varg raised their bows again.

"Othrain!" I screamed his name as an arrow narrowly avoided hitting me. "You won't win this one. Put down your ego. Run with me!"

"You want my blood?" Othrain staggered forward and dispatched the first Varg with ease. "You want my people?" He dropped to one knee before heaving himself back up and stabbing his sword into the second Varg's breastplate. "You want my world?"

My own blade lay on the ground and I limped for it. The third Varg was more intelligent and kept its distance, choosing to hold Othrain at bay with a primed arrow. A ball of flame roared overhead and, for a split second, illuminated the entire scene. Fire danced in the eyes of the dead and reflected off the armor all around us. It was a scene of chaos.

Weapon in hand, I charged the Varg. It loosed its arrow and in the confusion, I leapt forward and knocked the creature to the ground. My dagger quickly ended its wretched existence. Othrain, however, stood staring down at the fresh arrow in his chest. With a soft groan, he took a step back and collapsed.

"No!" Kissinger's voice cracked out like a whip. He rushed into view, his eyes wide, and pain clear in his voice.

Othrain heaved for every breath, as if the simple effort was more than he could muster. His nose was clearly broken, and a broken point of flesh and bone blocked where his left eye once was. Blood bubbled from his mouth. Tears streamed down his face as he chuckled.

"Who'd have thunk it, bairn?" He whispered as he closed his eyes. "I'm to die in the city of goldens."

Kissinger slid along the uneven ground and came to a stop at his side. He grabbed Othrain's large hand and held it tight.

"You absolute moron." Kissinger let tears drop. "I'm right here, you blasted ferrek. You are not . . . *dying*."

"I am beyond the repair of this world," he said softly. He opened his good eye.

"He came back for me," I said as the cold realization hit like a boulder. "He came back because he knew I was in danger."

"No." Othrain turned to glance at me, though his eye was glassy now, and I wondered if he saw anything. "I do not hide behind pretty walls of ancient stone. No golden will convince me there is honor in dying a cowardly death. I've met death on my terms. This is my perfect moment." He gave a watery snort. "I killed many of them." He opened his mouth and his tongue seemed to fall back into his throat. His voice was barely above a whisper. "I did my *duty* in defense of my nation. Tell the bards that, yeah?"

With a final wheeze, he went cold. The fires above danced over his face of pale white. Kissinger hung his head and bawled like a newborn. His voice cracked as he let the floodgates loose.

"I'm sorry." I tried to repress the guilt that surged up. "I lost track of where I was . . . I didn't mean . . ."

He looked up, eyes red, and nose full of dripping snot. For a moment I feared he would launch himself at me but all he did was wipe his face on his tunic and stand. With loving care, he placed Othrain's hands over his chest and closed his eyes.

"Find your way to Erëthuïl's Hall, my brother, that I may someday find you again. Our journey ends in this life, but we have all eternity ahead. Feast gloriously over your deeds today in the halls above. None shall forget your name; of that, I swear. The bards and minstrels shall sing of the fearless Othrain, one of the last defiant survivors. They shall herald your death as the beginning of the end for Mordën. Be at peace, Othrain of the Outpost."

The din of battle was growing near as Elharan and our force continued to retreat. All along the alleyway, Scion's men groaned as they bled out. Death was present on every approach and not for the last time, I was faced with my mortality.

A dull throb began in the recesses of my mind. I had experienced so much death in just two years that I feared for a moment I was getting used to it. Then the familiar ache blossomed in my chest, and I almost welcomed the feeling. In a matter of moments, the blood was gone from Othrain's face. He was so pale. So lifeless where just seconds before he'd been breathing. His hand curled, either from gravity or through some morbid spasm and for a long inhalation, I let the grief wash over me.

Kissinger gazed at him, for Othrain seemed asleep, lying crumpled on the stone steps. His hand slipped from his breast and fell on the hilt of his sword. Kissinger reached over and took it, placing it in his hand and pressing his fingers closed over it. They unclasped and he stubbornly tried again. Swords clanged and I jolted up as a host of Varglarian rushed down the alleyway toward us. We were losing ground fast. I didn't care anymore about the pain that wracked my ribs. I didn't mind the headache crackling behind my eyes.

"Shall we stand together?" Kissinger turned and I saw a rage in his face I'd never seen before. "Shall we send these vermin back to the halls of hell from whence they came?"

I gripped my sword and smiled. "*Innith Inine!*"

"Onward . . ." He swung his sword and clashed against the first Varg.

". . . till . . ." I sidestepped a parry and, reaching into the planter nearby, hurled a lump of dirt into a Varg's eyes. The creature howled and pawed at its helmet. I kicked it back as my sword glistened with black blood.

". . . we're . . ." Kissinger swung his sword powerfully and the Varglarian he was facing turned to run.

". . . ashes!" I roared the last word and hurled my dagger at the fleeing cur. The Varg toppled over and moved no more. In a second, though, the last Varg, whom I'd lost track of, crept up behind me and seized my neck with a strong grip.

"A prize to be taken, scalped, and lacerated, to our master!" the last

Varg hissed. "The blood meat DarkBairn is dead at last, by my hand." It raised its large sword, tip to my neck.

I grappled with the handle and choked against the iron grip. Spots danced at my vision. A memory surfaced of a time long, long ago. I almost smiled before I drove my heel up and back. The creature, dumb as it was strong, took a moment to register where my boot was headed. It was all I needed. With a howl of rage, it dropped me and staggered back, clutching its midriff. I swept it off its trembling legs and, raising my sword, plunged the blade deep into the monstrosity's chest. It shook violently, and blood spurted into my face and down my breastplate. Its legs thrashed around on the ground and its arms spasmed before going still. The glowing fiery light faded from its visor, and I gasped. The pain returned and I was very aware of every cut and bruise that now speckled my body.

"Come!" Kissinger grabbed my arm and we turned to run as another host of the Varglarians made their way toward us. These were large with a crueler laugh. Kissinger gave one final somber look to his fallen comrade, then we were shoving our way into the main streets of the city.

We ran from the alleyway. The main cobbled street was strewn with bodies and small crackling fires. Rogue bands of Elfin raced from alleyway to alleyway, spearing any Varg or Shade that had made it behind the frontlines. I ran into Katy first, limping along the main road. Her scalp bled and her dirty hair was cut to half its length. As soon as she spotted me, she cried out and threw herself into my arms. We both gasped from the pain.

"I'm covered in blood," I protested but hugged her tight. Her warmth spread over me. I felt her heartbeat and let my own beat alongside it.

"I just had the brains of a Varglarian explode on my face." She leaned back and winced. "I don't think a little blood will make me smell or look worse."

"You look disgusting," I amended.

"That's uncalled for."

"Othrain is dead." Kissinger's emotionless words brought us back to reality. "Perhaps we should focus on getting to safety?"

"Oh! I'm sorry." Katy gave him a hug as an Elfin rushed into view.

"They've broken through the main walls and now control everything from here down. King Elharan commands a full-scale retreat to the second wall. Now!"

We turned and bolted up the road. It was a long run, and we passed many piles of rubble where once gleaming taverns, stables, and forges had resided. The King's Tavern was in flames. The marketplace I'd walked so many afternoons was a field of bodies and a fountain of blood. Varglarian banded in hordes and moved through the city, placing everything they could to the torch. Fires roared into the sky and smoke filled my lungs. It became harder to breath the longer I ran. I blinked through the sharp stings which watered my eyes. The deeper into the city we ran, the less death and carnage was apparent. We rounded the corner and I found myself inches from losing my nose to a sharpened point.

"Friendly!" Kissinger waved his hands. "Don't shoot!"

"They're ours!" a voice called down. The arrow removed and I focused. The young woman who held the blade was a sight for sore eyes.

"Phoenix!" Arabella dropped the bow and hugged me. "You're alive! You absolute moronic fool. You're alive." She squeezed me close until I gasped in agony. "Kissinger!" She let me go and hugged him tighter.

"Aren't you going to call me a *fool*?" he demanded playfully, but I noticed how he leaned into her hug.

"I figured it was a given." She punched him in his shoulder. "Where have you two been? I was about to venture out looking for you."

"Have you seen Tim?" Katy asked.

"Or DarSheer?" I inquired.

She wiped the sweat from her eyes. "I'm doing great too, by the way. Tim was just along the northern section of the wall leading a group of Scion's men. DarSheer is in the second terrace because he's a good warrior and followed the fall-back command when it was issued. We were told to help the stragglers in, but I think most are dead, captured, or fled."

"Wait." Arabella glanced about. "Where is Othrain? He has not yet made it to the walls."

"He perished in a dark alleyway, bloody fool," Kissinger muttered to himself. "Always said we would die together. Can't keep an oath to save his life." His voice cracked as he inhaled and stared at us. "We need to move."

"Wait, just like that?" Arabella demanded, surprised. "That's all you will say on it?"

"He knew the risks. We all did. None here expected any less. We'd be fools to. If we stop to grieve all who perish we will soon join them ourselves. There is a time and a place for tears, and it is not on the field of war."

"How can you say that about him? He was like your brother!"

"Do you not think I know this? Will reiterating it to me heal the wound in my chest? Do you wish me to ask Mordën kindly to pause his invasion so we may sing a dirge for him? Standing here mourning will not save us."

"I didn't mean to offend you," her voice dropped noticeably.

He sighed and rubbed his fingers through his hair. "You did not. My mind wanders to places it shouldn't. Come now, we must head into the second level."

We approached the main gates of the second terrace walls at a sprint and were waved through. Dozens of Ebyian bowmen perched atop the wall, their gazes trained at every moving shape, imagined or otherwise. Spearmen bristled as the gates opened, preparing in case our arrival was a trap. Eyes stalked us for the seconds it took to cross beneath the wall and as the small gates slammed shut and a wooden beam was thudded into place, they turned back. Cots of injured filled the courtyard directly inside the wall.

DarSheer hurried towards us, and his face melted in relief. "I thought you all had perished when you didn't arrive. Thank Erëthuïl you survived."

"Well, not all of us. A bit premature for celebratory cheers don't you think?" Kissinger shoved past him.

"Othrain came back for me and was killed in the process," I explained to the puzzled Swordsmaster. "He died a hero. There were more bodies than I could count around him."

DarSheer tried to appear as if the news didn't affect him, but any who knew him could spot the slight sag in his shoulders and distant look in his eyes. I knew he'd wait to grieve till the time was safe. Kissinger's words were more and more the wise way out.

"Phoenix." DarSheer gestured that we should stand alone. We moved to a copse of evergreens. The odor of burning flesh and smoke drowned the smell of pine. He spoke in a low tone. "The Varglarian have taken the first tier and with it our best defenses. I just talked to Berëthelluïn and he told me the second wall was never meant to repel a major force. It's a design meant to impress dignitaries and ambassadors. It's not means to hold off a full-scale invasion."

"What are you saying?"

"I'm saying, if we could not hold the first wall, we will lose this one faster. The Ebyians here will reinforce our dwindling numbers and so we may survive a little longer. I no longer see our outcome of victory, but a prolonged defeat. King Elharan wishes us to make our last stand here. The Drucodians are already marching out from the third level of the city. They will be here within the hour. I do not despair easily, but I can see no other alternative. Look around us: the city burns. It is *over*." His voice was strained to the point of breaking, and for a moment I didn't recognize the man before me. He had always been the voice of confident assuredness. We'd fled from the Outpost and not once had he seemed to let it affect his judgement. Now, his eyes were wet with hopelessness.

"The men who died out there did not die so we would accept defeat," I said and pointed. "Weak wall or not it is still a wall and with it comes a higher chance of defense." I leaned in. "The outlook is bleak. But we simply cannot allow this city to fall. It is the key to holding the Eastern Ward and further preventing Mordën's forces from moving west. If we cannot stand, we condemn all Ëonë to fall alongside us. Mordën knows the strategic importance of this city. He's not simply attacking it because it happens to be here. He's attacking it because it is quite literally the only way for him to destroy this world. If we let it fall, we open the only way through the mountains. He will have secured his spot for the next phase of his plans. Surely, you understand this. What of the main host? Did enough survive to hold this wall? Have you counted the dead?"

"You assume much, bairn." He shook his head. "I see this and much more. King Elharan means to fight to the death. Commander Scion and a few hundred of his men survived and are safely behind our walls. The Princling and all his own stand at the gates to give rest to those who need it. They are strong, Phoenix, but low in number. We counted the Ebyian's ranks in the thousands, fresh and ready for combat. Thousands against tens of thousands. Parod and the last of his folk will arrive soon. Our dead number beyond our worst calculations. We lost far more than we should have when we lost the main level."

We were silent for a long time amidst the din and cries in the distance. We listened to the imploding homes and taverns as fire claimed their supports. The clang of metal was less and less frequent as the streets went unchallenged against the hordes that patrolled them. The smoke from the fire hugged the top of the city like a blanket. Occasionally, a scream would fill the air, a flurry of sword against shield, and then silence. Some removed their helmets every time this occurred while others simply stared vacantly at the fires below. Due to the layer of ash and smoke above us, we could not see the expansive plains below or the tops of the mountain. It was hard not to be filled with dejection. Every fiber of my being desired it.

"I have not lost hope, not while any man in this city still fights," DarSheer finally responded. "My mind merely examines one of many possibilities. We must prepare for the worst, and hope for the best."

I turned to ask him what he meant but stopped at the approach of King Elharan and his guard. There were no smiles, nor loud greetings. It was too grim a time for those.

"DarkBairn? It warms my heart to see you live, as do most in your party. DarSheer, I've lost all my captains capable of leading them. Gorg perished on the retreat. Elca, Tunithuïn, and Elsberry all died at the breaking of the main gates. I have none now to lead the splinters of my command. Will you take a part in this responsibility?"

"What of Bereth?"

"He is injured and sleeps in fevered fits. He's lost a leg to poison, and I worry he will not last the night. DarSheer, do not take this as a command but a hopeful request. Please."

"I will do as you desire, my Lord King," Broadsword nodded, "but I would at least ask for thorough consideration in this choice. I know very little in the art of command."

"None who have their first command find it easy," he said sadly. "Great warriors have fallen, and it is now up to us to ensure more blood is not spilt. You will lead the garrison at the walls while I take our last remaining bowmen and set up at a decent vantage point to cover a possible last retreat to the docks. When they breach the gates, you will unload our wrath and fury into their writhing miserable mass." Spittle flew from the Elfinian's lips in an unusual display of rage. "We shall make them regret the deaths today. We shall make Mordën mourn his return to our land. Are you with me?"

"It shall be done," we all spoke in unison. My stomach did a summersault.

"Aye," Kissinger spoke up without emotion. "I have a score to settle. An eye for an eye. A life for a life."

"Take care your emotions do not blind you to the task at hand," Elharan cautioned.

"My emotions are not a cause for concern," he said in a monotone voice.

For a moment, Elharan eyed him as if waiting for a *but*. However, Kissinger remained mute, eyes averted to the cobblestones. The Elfinian ruler turned and with a flourish of the leaves above us, was off. I waited to see if DarSheer meant to spill some secret adventure to me now the king was out of earshot, but my old friend merely nodded to me and grabbed for the attention of a passing Elfinian warrior. Commands were recited and at once the square before the gates was a bustling metropolis of activity. Shouts echoed up and down the roads as Elfin rolled barrels, carried planks of wood, and heaved stones along.

"Your direction?" Katy stood behind me. Her cheeks were flushed pink. On one shoulder a long bow hung. Strapped to her back, a quiver full of arrows bristled. Her ponytail bobbed up and down.

"What do you mean?" I cleared my throat uneasily. "I command no one."

"We're here at your side, and we always have been," Arabella checked the weapons on her belt. "DarSheer commands them, but we are a tight-knit group. We've all decided."

"We have." Kissinger stepped forward. "Out of all of us, you have the most experience with Mordën. We trust you."

I pivoted and stared at them. Kissinger stood proud but broken. Arabella was confused but stoic. Katy? She was beautiful but hurting. Her eyes constantly roved about, and I knew who she looked for. I cursed myself inwardly for forgetting him again. I truly was a horrible ally and even worse friend.

"It would best assist them for us to fortify the range up the road from here. Elharan and his Elfin will hold the main road but when they need to fall back, they will want someone to cover their return. We will be among the last to fall back, and this you need to be ready for. The docks are our last way out of this city and the only way to a world yet unplagued by the fires here."

"Are we not the mighty and strong of the free peoples of this world?" Arabella asked. "Why do all prepare so readily for retreat?"

"King Elharan knows, as do you all beneath your pride, that this wall is not meant to withstand attack, let alone an invasion. We lost the great and mighty walls of this city in a few hours. How long do you think it will take him to pummel this stone and turn it into rubble? We may not enjoy the thought of fleeing like thieves into the night with no reward to show for our mischief. There is no glory in journeying for a great hunt and coming back with no game to show for it. Where is the honor in throwing your lives away with reckless abandon? Yet sometimes retreat is necessary."

"There are times when to win the war you must lose a battle." Kissinger said.

"What?" I turned to where Kissinger stood. He slowly raised his head.

"Kissinger . . ." He held up his palm to me.

"This is what we face." His words were directed with great volume to the others. "You think this a chance to claim honor, to hold onto your pride like it's a blasted banner. Wave it from the ramparts. Wave it and count your glory like coins on a tavern table. What good will your pride do for you when you choke on your own blood and *his* foot is pressing down on your chest? He's not just taken lives of people I know; he's nearly eradicated an entire race and demolished one of the strongest cities. His hold on the Eastern Ward is all but secured. All that stands between him and this achievement is us.

"I know we may not look like much. Some of us are but newly into manhood. Most of them have never been in battle before. Half of these lot are wet behind the ears with exaggerated stories proclaimed of their ancestor's might. The Ebyians are but crafters high in their mountain cities. These Elfin are not the same who stood against him before. They are the offspring bred in peace. Their forebears are dead. The men who marched in the Second Great War are gone. We are all that remain. Mordën will not cower when you say their names of lore. This is an hour of death and destruction, but let it not be the hour of your prideful fall.

"It is the way of this world: that greatness often be beset by peril and emptiness. There is nothing you or I nor any great kings of legend can do to stop it. Our grief and dismay do not stem the tide that comes any more than a pebble stops a mighty wave. It arrives on its own with a mind of its own. But even the wave must recede at some point. It's powerful for one awful second and then it's over. We may not want to admit that we are at a point where failure and defeat is the only outcome, especially when we see the lives lost to get here. How can we be defeated when the Drucodians are all but gone and thousands of our own, men we called *brother*, lay in the gruesome throes of death? But you see it is this deceit on ourselves that Mordën uses to prey on us. Crippled by our pride we are weak, a herd dispersed by its flaws. But together, banded united, even a Rever Drake cannot stop us.

"This is what he fears—that we will not give up hope. That we will focus only on our pride. When a man loses his fear of death, then he is a man to be feared. We fight for the living, but we will never forget the fallen. They died not so we would lose this war, but so we would stand a chance. It is a strange thing, this torment. It lasts an age in one's mind, but it is as swiftly passing as the seasons. It can be cold and harsh as winter, blinding and suffocatingly hot as summer. The brief moments of respite end as quickly as they began. But do you know why we keep pushing? Why we retreat when we know we're defeated? Why we don't let our pride get in the way of what matters? Because even the most miserable and hellish winters come to an end. The sun wakes from behind its cloudy blanket and the cold melts from every orifice till the land, healed and growing, sprouts anew what the darkness tried to snuff out. Through the mound of snow, that first green leaf juts out. It's a defiant reminder to that cursed cold that even surrounded by death and misery and pain on all sides, there is still something of great value. There is *hope*. There will always be *hope*! But hope dies when we fail to live. Our bodies will not be the ground over which Mordën walks as he secures his realm. Hail and more to those beyond our watch. Hail and more to the fallen who fall no more."

"Hail and more to the fallen who fall no more!" all around us, a group of Elfins chanted softly. "Hail and a kingly feast to those who rest in peaceful slumber!"

For a long exhalation, the clearing was mute as every ear bent to his words and every eye beheld him anew. Some stirred in agreement while others bowed their heads. I couldn't help but stare at him. In such a short time, he'd aged. Maybe not in visible years but in expansion of his thoughts. Still younger by years, he was growing older in wisdom. I felt a pang in my chest and realized some of my own doubts had been squashed. There was hope and there always would be if we still trusted each other and continued the fight.

"I don't intend to dishonor the dead by retreating," an Elfin bowman called out.

"We shall stand a wall of spears," another cried out.

"Words spoken as a man, no longer a bairn." King Elharan stood behind Kissinger, hands behind his back, a tired look in his eyes. "The lesson is as powerful as the sword in your hand." He turned to the hesitant Elfins. "I understand your qualms about the coming hours. But look to your left and right. We are proof that the peoples of this world will not give up without a fight. Whatever happens, whoever comes through our gates, and no matter the cost, we will not surrender. Let no record of Men, Ebyian, Incling, Drucodian, or Elfinian show that in their most desperate hour, the Elfinian race bowed to defeat. We stand on our feet over perishing on our backs."

The clearing clamored out its agreement and the grouping of Elfins and Ebyians began to move about with purpose. There was a clarity to the air. No one was deceived of the potential outcome, yet here and now, boldened by the words of a stranger and their king, they were ready once again to stand against the odds.

"Well, well, well," Arabella stepped smoothly forward, "a speech fit for the royal halls of The High City."

He rubbed the back of his head. "I meant every word. Othrain, if he were here, would have cursed me for letting the sacrifices of all here go in vain. Now, I can't stand the idea of blemishing his memory by doing the one thing he never did. I cannot let him down now."

Arabella took him in her arms and hugged him tight. His body trembled and began to shake with grief as he sobbed into her shoulder.

"Shall we away for a minute?" Katy had her hand on my elbow. "Maybe give them a moment?"

The evening grew gloomy as we strolled along a side path. Up here, protected by the second-tier walls, the damage to the city was minimal. At various crossroads, homes and trees were blackened by fire. Randomly, small flames feasted on vegetation and the occasional body. A slight breeze swept away smoke and clouds. The leaves of trees danced mesmerizingly. It was a sweltering night. My skin crawled as if dozens of spiders ran up and down my arms and legs. The shadows leered at me with empty promises of Nightshades spilling out. Blast those abominations and their shadow travel. Even up here, far from the main gates, my nerves sought to get the better of me.

"What are you thinking about?" Katy took my hand and squeezed it reassuringly.

"Why is he waiting?" I wracked my brain. "He has the city. He knows we cannot hope to succeed yet he waits. Does he wish the sun to reveal our corpses? Is the night not suitable enough an ally to his cause?"

"You forget while he may be a being of unimaginable power, his forces are still governed by the same weariness as we are. At least, I'd imagine. His forces need rest. If he knows he has the city, he may be giving his troops time to recuperate before the final thrust."

"I would be more concerned if he attacked right now." I leaned forward against a crumbled sidewall, placing my palms on its surprisingly cool surface.

"We must keep up our vigilant watch and make ready the ships," she said.

"Our priority should be preparing for his next assault, not already admitting defeat." I stubbornly shook my head.

"Phoenix, we cannot hope to win." She touched a single finger to my chin. "Kissinger was right: we have to watch our pride that it does not blind us to reality. Mordën is stronger than he was back in our world. Back then he had a few paltry Nightshades and wolves to do his dirty work. Here . . .?"

"Back then we had no allies. We were just a couple of kids. We didn't fare so bad then and we won't lose now."

"Phoenix, you have to come back to reality." Her voice caught. "We *were* a couple of kids, well out of their depth. Will and Temper paid the ultimate price. Tim is mentally damaged beyond my ability to help. I fear for him every day. His mind is fractured, and he awakens in the morning in tears. We marched directly into Mordën's arms and now we are paying the price for our mistakes. He manipulated our every step and that was at his weakest point. He is strong now."

"Do not speak of his strength to me!" My own voice sounded bitter and filled with regret. "He reminds me of this fact on a nightly basis. I live with his reminders that I am nothing but a pawn of his. I do not hide behind a reality you believe. I know our chances of success. I am constantly reminded of that." Anger stained my words.

"Come to me." She opened her arms and I stiffly stepped into her warmth. The pain in my ribs had subsided but her arms still sent shivers of pain down my side.

We were both covered in sweat, bruises, scabbed cuts, and dried blood and yet she continued to shine with a strange radiance. In a flash of nostalgia, I felt as if we were back in the school hallway. The home-room buzzer was about to be sounded. Kids pushed and scrambled left and right. Their bodies twisted and turned like the moving currents of a hurricane. And in the center of it all, in its eye, Katy and I stood. My body shook as I inhaled her smell and felt the comforting touch of her skin. She made no move to pull away and I felt a wetness on my shoulder. I do not know how long we stood and frankly, I did not care.

"Othrain died because of me."

"Why do you say this?"

"I was a fool and wandered away from the main group. He is the only reason I am alive. He died for me. Will died for me. Temper died for me. Brenneth and the others at the Outpost died because I allowed Mordën to return. I do not know how long my strength shall stand, for I waver with every passing death. I'm a mosaic of everyone I've loved. Each person who dies takes back their piece. How soon before I exist only as a memory of them?"

"You cannot hold such a burden on your young shoulders," she pleaded with me.

"Yet it weighs down. Always."

She pulled away just enough so we could look into each other's eyes. Hers were still damp from her tears. Over one brow, a cut was still healing. Her hair fell over her cheeks. My own tears mixed with the pain I'm sure was written on my face.

"Shall we dance?" Katy asked.

"To the fire burning? The screams of the dying? What happiness is left to boost our spirits?"

"I can provide some music," a voice said casually. Kissinger sat on the edge of the crumbling wall, feet crossed, one hand behind his head as he leaned against a tree while the other hand picked at his teeth.

"Kissinger . . . what, where is Arabella?" I calmed my breathing at the sudden jolt his appearance caused.

"She's gone on to talk DarSheer."

"Are you doing . . . are you . . . okay?" I stumbled over the words.

His face flushed with something like regret before he smiled. "Who isn't doing amazing right now? Enough about me—this is all about you two. I know a few beats from the Outpost. Topper was never shy about teaching me. Might I entertain while you dance to the tunes of dying heroes?"

"Not when you put it that way." Katy hugged her body.

"Relax," he sat up and reached down to a slab of wood, "I'm messing with you. Frankly, I think we could all do with some merriment to clear our minds. Katy, do you have anything in mind?"

"Something with a slow and soft melody."

"I can do that." He cleared his throat grimly began to hit the wooden plank with a growing and dying tempo. Despite the unorthodox nature of it all, it became music to us.

"Are we really going to do this?" I asked. Nerves assailed me. I'd fought Varglarian, been taunted by the darkest being known to exist, seen heads and arms cut off, watched Othrain die, and had to kill beyond count; yet here in a clearing of trees faced with the prospect of dancing, I felt nervous. Butterflies flitted about in my stomach. *Butterflies*.

She took my hand in hers and placed her other hand on my shoulder. Dutifully, I placed my free hand on her waist and as we danced, or more like as I stumbled about trying to find a beat to move to and she gracefully didn't say anything; she gazed into my very soul.

"Do you remember when we graduated middle school and were readying for high school?" She said so only I could hear. Kissinger was busy in his own world of playing the board. "Do you remember when it all began?"

I leaned against my grey bedspread and sighed. The brochure for the place of education sat open. The faces of young teenagers grinned happily back. Some stood in a field, uniforms showing their sport. Others sat at desks, books open in clear interruption of their reading. It was all so fake it made me want to wretch.

"I wonder what she's thinking." Katy pointed at a blond, blue-eyed girl with one hand keeping a textbook from closing. The girl's teeth were pearly white, and her face was perfectly captured without a single blemish to note.

"I'd imagine she's the type to freak out if she gets less than an A." I shrugged. My loose jacket hung baggily around my shoulders. I wore Will's "Stand Strong and Be the Nerd" shirt beneath it.

"I like to think at this moment she's delving intently into the world of . . . psychology." Katy hesitated to read the title of the book. "And this photographer rushes up and demands she pose for a photo. He's probably in love with her and the school promised him the chance to get her photo."

"That's creepy." I wrinkled my nose and tilted my head like an owl.

"Her smile tells a different story. I believe she loves him too; she's just too nervous to say anything." Katy pulled her pink hoodie tighter to her body and glanced at me.

"You can tell all that by a smile?" I felt my heart beat a bit faster.

"It's a girl thing," she stated and smiled sheepishly.

I matched the rhythm of my heartbeat, tapping away at the wood floor beneath me. Boom, badum, bap, beet, bop. I could swear my deodorant had failed me and my armpits were now toxic pools of teenager sweat. Her face was caught in a ray of light and a few wavy strands of hair escaped her ponytail as she leaned close.

"Are you an angel?" I asked in a slightly higher-pitched tone.

"What?" She pushed away and laughed.

"It's a guy thing." I grinned sheepishly.

In that moment I felt something shift. My heart pounded and my stomach tossed itself in fits. Anxiety began hissing in my ears. I'd missed something. Something crucial. She sat further from me, almost unnoticeably. She hugged her arms close to her body and only glanced at my face a few times.

"I should probably head home," she said. "My mom will my expecting me."

"Katherine dear," my mom stuck her head past the partially closed door, "are you staying for supper? Ted is putting a steak on the grill and your mother is bringing her famous potato salad."

My mother was the only person who could call Katy "Katherine" without incurring a look of wrath and a snappy retort. Not even I had that right.

"No thank you, Mrs. Rather." Katy scrambled up and grabbed for her book bag. "My mom invited guests over and she expects me to actually show up."

"Oh, no worries." Mom held the door for her as she slid by and hurried down the hallway.

"Bye, Phoenix!" Katy's voice faded.

"Goodbye, Katy." I held back the feeling of regret as long as I could.

"She's a sweet girl," Mom said as she smiled at me. "You've got the love blush, you have."

"Mom!" I hugged my pillow to my chest and flopped back on my bed.

"Alright, alright." She raised one hand in defeat. "Supper soon, be down in five."

"Yeah, the day we looked over the school brochure," I murmured into her ear. "Why?"

Kissinger changed the tempo of the beat, and we moved slightly faster. He started humming a fast-paced climax. The board thwacked against his hand and thigh in rhythm. The clouds overhead had moved past the peaks of the mountains. Finally, the stars twinkled down like small fairies above. I spun her around at arm's length, letting her twirl about and giggle before pulling her back. I rested my hands on her waist and pulled her till our bodies pressed against each other. Laughter seemed both incredibly wrong and perfectly right in these lands. It was a sound I wish I'd heard more often. She wrapped both her arms around my neck. Our lips brushed together.

"I wanted you to be thinking of a good memory." She inhaled shakily. "We're pretty much bathing and sleeping in nothing but horrible memories. Sometimes I think you forget you're only eighteen, barely an adult. You've had so much placed on your shoulders, and you've stood strong."

"I've faltered many times." I swallowed the bile of regret. "It's because of me that Mordën returned here. It's because of me that we're stuck here in the first place. I heard Tim say as much."

Her smile tilted. "You heard that?"

"Can't mistake the sound of my name being dragged through the rubble and barbed wire." I tried for a winning wince.

"Tim . . . it's complicated. He's been through a lot and from his vantage point . . ."

"From his vantage point, he let himself get captured for me and I never came back for him, and it appears as if I forgot he existed completely," I finished.

"Everyone has a different point of view." Tears filled her eyes, but they did not fall. "We've—the three of us—have had different experiences throughout this whole ordeal. If Will were here, who would know what he'd say but himself?"

"Do you ever regret it?" This had been the question that had occupied me for so long. Ever since I'd found myself staring up at a night sky that wasn't mine, I'd pondered the answer. Maybe I'd wept at the possible response.

"Regret?"

"Regret agreeing *to come with* me on this whole crazy thing?" I cleared my throat and breathed but no matter how I said it, my voice cracked. "Do you ever *regret* knowing me in the first place?" There it was. My worst fears laid out all at once. I blinked rapidly.

Finally, her tears spilled down her cheeks. She ran her fingers in my hair, and we kissed. I pulled her close and hugged her so tightly I feared she might be unable to breath. Our cheeks were squished, noses pressed at an awkward angle. A blubbering moisture covered our faces. I didn't even realize Kissinger had stopped playing. Nor for a moment was I aware of the presence next to him.

"Why would I regret knowing you?" Katy hiccupped and giggled. She wiped her eyes with her thumb. "You stupid, beautiful, strong, tired, handsome, broken man?"

Laughter burbled out of my lips like a deranged man's guffaw. "I don't know. I guess with everything that has happened, I wouldn't blame you." We were laughing together now till our sides ached. She curled her long fingers into my hair again and forced me to stare at her.

"I consider knowing you the only good thing about my life. When I broke my arm and leg doing cheer in middle school, you were the only 'friend' who visited me in the hospital. When I was getting over Dameon, you comforted me. Through practices with Claire, the only reason I was able to put up with her and her goonies was because I knew after every practice, you'd be there, leaning against the bleachers, ready to make some inane joke. I saw you help Will out even though simply associating with him meant you lost any 'coolness.' It's not easy making the right choice when peer pressure is like a tidal wave taking you in the other direction. When Tim was freaking out over losing his basketball scholarship because his grades were failing, you spent countless nights making sure he passed. *You are the only person I want to spend my life with.*" Here her voice cracked. "Regret is the last feeling I will ever associate with you. And no . . . I do not regret journeying along with you to save your parents. I don't regret the last two years of searching for you. You've done so much for everyone. You've been a leader when we needed one. The deaths that precede this moment should not control you. It's led us to this moment. If I was given the chance to return home and never depart with you and Temper and the others, if I was offered a chance at a normal life, to see the sun rise and fall on a typical summer morning . . . I *wouldn't* take it. Nothing could be offered to make me change the past. It's *our* past. Our story. This is our story, my love."

"Wow." Suddenly, the stars burned brighter. The voice that had been hissing doubt in the back of my mind vanished. I felt a bubble burst.

"Does that answer your question?" She kissed me again.

"Yeah," was all I could manage.

"I want something like that," Arabella muttered.

"Seriously, who's next? Who's just going to magically appear? DarSheer? You hiding in the trees? King Elharan?" I sighed dramatically before winking at Katy.

Kissinger stood; the board abandoned at his feet. His eyes were red. He hurried off into the trees. In the midst of my happiness, I felt the familiar feeling of guilt return.

"Go." Katy smiled reassuringly at me. "We girls have to talk anyway. I've been meaning to have a little chat with the northern one."

"Be with him; he needs you." Arabella shoved me gently. "We'll make sure the bowmen are ready on the ridge for the next assault, whenever it should come."

I thanked them and stumbled through the trees after him. His head was buried in his hands, but his cheeks were dry.

"Hey." I sat down next to him and fiddled with a twig, unsure how to continue.

"This image I've constructed of a fearless bairn facing down all of the evils of this world with no more concern than if I were deciding between a brown or black tunic is a carefully crafted lie," he said without glancing at me. "It's an illusion to paint over my fear, my concerns. And now I've lost the only person whom I truly knew. Othrain is gone. What is the point in fighting when all is lost?"

"Did you forget your own rallying cry?" I asked.

"Fancy words to motivate the commoner rabble." He shook his head. "Those with true wisdom know its fallacy. I have no more strength left in me, DarkBairn. I have none left on this continent that I call family. I have no friends. These are dark times."

"I know how you feel."

"How is that possible?" He snorted derisively. "The girl from beyond this world seems pretty infatuated with you."

"Before that." I shook my head. "When I first arrived here, dropped like a sack of potatoes on the ground, I knew no one. Even DarSheer, the first person to find me, kept his distance from me. I was alienated, alone."

"I'm sorry," Kissinger stared at his fingers, "I forget myself. I wallow in my own self-pity and forget that all around me suffer as well. At least you have someone who cares for you. I'd never admit it to the blasted drunken idiot, but I cared deeply about him. He was always a fool, rushing headlong into altercations with no thought for what he was leaving behind. He was so stupid, one day the rain was falling on our hut, and he thought it was arrows raining down. Woke me in the middle of the forsaken night trying to convince me we were under siege. Blasted idiot. But he was like a father to me."

"I wish there were a way I could ease your pain." I rested a hand on his shoulder and was surprised that he did not immediately cast it off.

"You know, he spoke very highly of you." Kissinger looked up at the stars overhead. "He didn't do that with many. There were many nights in the tavern when he swore Malziek was as smart as Topper." We shared a chuckle.

"The bard could only play one song well, the rest he bloodied his fingers for our enjoyment." I laughed.

"Enjoyment?" Kissinger said. "You took satisfaction in his playing?"

"I was being lenient in the definition of the word." I shrugged. He snorted.

"Thanks for being here for me." He leaned against the edge of the building we sat next to and covered his eyes with one hand. "I'm not used to this, talking and stuff. Othrain enjoyed the more manly action of getting drunk and starting brawls to this quieter conversing."

"Othrain was unique." I couldn't lie.

"He was a damned crazy man." Kissinger laughed till he shook. "Did I tell you of the time he tried to woo a horse?"

"And *he* made fun of *you* for smooching a sow?" I laughed.

"He was so drunk, Marian had to have him carried by six men out of the tavern. They deposited him next to the stables. Altruic was not happy, and he voiced it clear enough. Othrain apologized and was about to leave when one of the stable hands brought in a chestnut mare from a scouting mission. The look on Othrain's eyes as he bowed low and called the mare 'madam.'" Kissinger wiped the tears from his eyes. "I'll never forget Altruic's bewildered face as the lunatic danced his jig of idiocy. I miss him, Phoenix! I miss Marian. I miss Traverse. Altruic. Topper. KcNuck. Throbb."

"Brenneth. Malziek." I picked up where he paused.

"Othrain," we said in unison.

"You've had a rough start of life ever since you joined the Outpost." I steered the conversation.

"No worse than others. Men out there fight even though their children, wives, and brothers perished. Here I am sopping like an old widow at the headstone. Forgive me."

"You are new to all this, as most here are." I shook my head. "There is nothing to forgive. I don't know what I'd do if DarSheer or you or Katy or Arabella came to harm."

In front of us, the broken city yawned out in groupings of intense flames and midnight darkness. Plumes of hot fire burst high into the night. There were scattered pockets of sound ringing out. Metal clanged against stone. Boots thudded. Cries rang faint and desperate. The Rever Drake was no longer visible but, in the distance, I heard its soft bellow. The sound still made my hair stand on end. It was hard to fathom, that out there in the darkness, were countless slain and more injured, just waiting for a Varg to find them and kill them.

"You know, I don't know much about Othrain's past, other than what he shared before this whole mess began," I said. "I do know how proud of you he was. You were once a bairn, but manhood suits you well."

"I don't often feel a man. I've made rash choices and he's always been there to bail me out. He pretty much took me under his wing. I was a troubled brat running rings around Altruic's ancient ankles. I was the instigator of every practical joke. Instead of despising me and being content to sit back and watch Altruic beat me like the rest of the watchmen did, Othrain stepped in and prevented the old codger from skinning me alive. I'd never had that. My parents . . . they never cared. Or they wouldn't have sent me to that cursehole. I don't know them. *Didn't* know them. Frankly, I'm glad I don't. Can't be disappointed by a ghost. I was perfectly fine living my life of bad choices. I didn't rely on anyone, and no one relied on me. I didn't care about the numbered bonfires we had to mourn the dead. I watched with passive interest in the burnings of bodies. It meant nothing to me, for they were all ignorant of me. I liked living that way. I was protected. Then that fool had to stop Altruic from hitting me. That blasted fool. Had to make me care about someone finally. I couldn't just be left alone to rot in isolation." Here, Kissinger lowered his head, and I thought I heard the beginnings of a sob. I sat like a statue, unsure how to continue. For a long moment, we just sat as he wept. "And now I fear he has caused something worse than the love of a brother."

"What do you mean?"

"I find myself falling for her, Phoenix." He looked up at me through the tears.

"Arabella?"

"No, the old sow of legend I once smooched . . . of course, Arabella! I love her but I do not know if I should. I could not bear to lose another person I care for. I am weak."

"We weren't meant to live alone. Men, humans, were meant to live with others and spring forth with merriment and bravery. We weren't meant to live lives away from each other. It protects the heart at the cost of the soul. Othrain knew what he was doing. He saw a bairn alone and knew it wasn't right. He had a rough exterior, but what can you expect of someone posted at the Outpost? And Arabella? Have you seen the way she looks at you? Commit to courting her!"

"You think she'd fall for a bumpkin like me?" He sniffled.

"I don't *think* she would because she already has, trust me." I gave him a comforting thwack on his back. "Othrain would be proud. A bairn . . . now a man."

"I imagine he's already drunk at Erëthuïl's table."

"Probably the first thing he went for." I let out a watery laugh. "Pushed right past Erëthuïl himself in his eagerness."

"Think he's chugging a cider?" Kissinger asked.

"Cider? Up there in the hallowed halls? He'd rather come back down and die again. He'll have gone straight for the ale kegs. Probably is bragging to the great kings of old of his conquests on Ëonë." We shared a laugh.

"I'm sure he's bragging above of the greatest warrior he ever met," I said and gave him a comforting smile.

His eyes twinkled. "Topper?" He couldn't hold back the snorts of laughter at his own joke.

I dried the moistness from my eyes as the last chuckle died down. "I'm serious, ya blasted codger."

"Do you think he was proud of me?" Kissinger wiped his eyes dry and cleared his nose on his tunic.

"Without a doubt. He said so himself. You know Othrain better than I. When was the last time he said he was ever proud of anyone?"

Some color returned to Kissinger's cheeks as he rubbed his hands together. He gave me a small smile and inhaled sharply.

"The poor bard." He hiccupped.

"Poor, Topper," I agreed. "When this is all over, we'll find a place and bury his sword. Proper like."

"Like a funeral?"

"He deserved it. He died with the blood of two Varg on his blade. He deserves to be in the scrolls that will contain all the heroic names of the Third Great War. He was just as much a hero as any man here.”

“I’d like that. He wasn’t the sentimental type. But I think he’d like it too.”

“Shall we head back to the proceedings?” I stood and brushed dirt from my rear. “I wouldn’t put it past Mordën to attack whilst we sit here.”

“I meant what I said back in the clearing,” Kissinger said as he took my offered hand and stood, “when I told those bowmen why we would not give up hope. Forgive my momentary stumble before. I still believe it; I just needed a reason to.”

“What are brothers for?” I smiled as we began walking back the way we’d come.

“Brothers.” Kissinger smiled broadly as he shook my hand and then shoved me back. “Come on, *brother*! Those Elfin don’t know how to set up a defensive line if their pretty golden city depended on it.”

I stomped through debris behind him and couldn’t help but feel my spirits lift. *Brothers.*

The one they’d called Othrain lay in a half-twisted crescent. His body was stiff and his skin cold. His eyes were glassy, and his hair flowed in the wind. The figure over him removed his hood and stared down. A grim smile replaced the prior frown.

“The rabble have retreated into their second city.” Raoul stared at him, hinting.

“Their peace is momentary.” He raised one of his thick boots. “But this . . . this satisfaction will last.” With a single hard stomp, he planted his boot squarely in the center of Othrain’s blank face.

Raoul didn’t flinch. “You serve the Shadow King. Remember that.”

“And without me, you will lose more than you can afford to.” He turned and wiped the flecks of blood from his face. “Remember that. I can get you inside the gates. I will deliver to him the prize he so desires.”

Overhead, the sounds of great wings beating down against the wind howled. They both looked up and tensed. Mordën had gone from maniac to calm since the start of the conflict and had dwelled far behind the front lines. Something was changing for him to be this far forward.

Back in the courtyard, the defensive proceedings were well underway. Torches shed light as rubble was carried and stacked against the gates. In this low light, the gates looked feeble and weak, brittle. I ran my fingers through my greasy hair and tried not to imagine the thousand different ways Mordën could break through. King Elharan stood atop the walls. He spoke in hushed tones with DarSheer and Bereth. The latter two looked on in grim focus and didn't even turn when a boulder was dropped behind them and burst into several chunks. The remaining fighting Men and Elfin peered vigilantly into the darkness. Ebyians stalked up and down the edge of the wall. Hands never strayed far from the hilts of their swords. Helmets never came off. Spears were stacked against walls and braziers full of arrows were kept ready. A dozen spare bows hung from hooks near the small building next to the gates. Elfin went in and out of this small hut, heads low and cloaks billowing out behind them. There was an air of anticipation in every exhalation. They waited for the inevitable charge.

"Behind!" An Elfin cried out and blew his horn.

Coming up the road behind us, garbed in their white armor, the Drucodians had arrived. They were met with a mixture of excitement and stony silence. Those still uninjured hung to their spears and shields like they were lifelines. They stared at the approaching grey mass without word or comment. Parod walked at their head, his proud face high against the night sky overhead.

"Well met." King Elharan descended the stairs from the wall and bowed low.

"The cries of the injured wail too loud on our ears for us to sit by and do naught." Parod bowed in return. "We ask only one honor: place us in the courtyard so we are the first to meet his charging horde."

"It shall be as you ask. DarSheer? Take those behind the gates and move them up to your watch."

"Aye, King Elharan. Phoenix?"

"Here." I waved a hand. He gestured for me to come.

"Movement! Enemy spotted!" Bereth roared as he swung his sword in the air.

As I crested the last uneven step, King Elharan behind me, the bowmen nearby drew arrows and aimed. The air was filled with a crackling tension.

Ahead and cantering down the road, a hooded rider atop a black skeletal mount stopped. The sigils of red and black were evident on his wrinkled cloak. Rain began falling. It wasn't a cleansing rain. It carried a foul stench. The droplets plinked off the tops of helmets and rolled slowly down the sides of buildings. The filth on the road began to slowly vanish like an invisible mop wiped it away. Born by unknown enigmatic commands, the rider dismounted. All atop the wall held their breath as with great authority, he turned and out of the shadows a Nightshade appeared. In an instant, a dozen spears were lowered toward the newcomer. Bows were pulled taut and arrows readied to launch. Shouts carried to the courtyard, and it was a mess of activity as the Drucodians marched to bolster the gates. Parod commanded his force and stood at the very front, a sword in hand. The Nightshade accepted the reins offered him. With arrows trained to loose at his command, Elharan narrowed his eyes. The figure, now standing in two thick boots on the cobbled road, looked up. Water ran in rivulets down Elharan's sweaty face and the golden flecks in his irises glowed with anger. His hair, coarse and long, hung about his shoulders.

"Why do you approach our gates, rider of the night?" He boomed. The figure made no comment. "Do you wish to meet? Perhaps you have your terms for your surrender? If that is the case, then I heartily accept."

The rider chuckled an ugly laugh and reached to pull his hood back. The simple gesture was met with the hissing of swords being drawn and the murmured preparedness of the bowmen.

"Prepare below!" a soldier shouted to the waiting Elfin in the courtyard. "The gates! To the gates! Defend the city!"

"Hold!" Elharan almost imperceivably gestured at his men. They did so, though I felt the unease alone would snap a few bowstrings.

"You ask for surrender, yet you cower behind walls of stone whilst I stand here, unarmed, and undefended?" The rider let his hood fall and stared up. His face was ringed in black as though his veins were filled with shadow. His eyes were orbs of obsidian. His pointed nose and drooping chin reminded me of a cartoony villain. I wondered whether he meant to command respect or illicit confusion.

"These walls can withstand much," Elharan returned calmly. "Long have they kept Avalon strong."

"Yet here we stand. It does not take the brain of a king to realize you have lost the city. I have but to command these hordes and the last great Drucodian burg fades to ash. Your legacy is fodder for greater kings."

"If you merely mean to exchange joyless banter, perhaps I may interest you in the points of my arrows? As you noted, you are undefended." Elharan turned and with a viscous cut of his hand, a dozen arrows were launched. The volley aimed with deadly accuracy. I blinked. When I reopened my eyes, the figure below stood in the same spot as if he'd never moved, the arrows clinking uselessly on the cobbled road behind him.

"If we are done playing games," he replied with little concern, "I come before you on behalf of Mordën, Shadow King, the true heir of Ëonë. He has given me power to speak on his behalf."

"They went right through him," one man muttered.

"Through him or around?" another countered.

"Neither. They vanished and reappeared behind him," yet a third spat.

"Who are you?" Elharan asked.

"I am Raoul, commander of the Shadow Army, and right-hand chief to he who needs no introduction." He raised a finger.

The air morphed into swirls. It was as if the atmosphere were no more than a painted canvas and a wet brush had begun stroking circles.

The clear paint began to blend and merge with the colors around until the sky was altogether strange. Raoul raised his hand and from the clouds and seven figures strode. They moved as if from a far distance, small at first then growing larger each second. On their brows a ring of fire burned steadily. Their black cloaks swished as they moved. They wore breastplates of fire. Where the eyes would be, two blood red orbs burned. It felt as though a hundred fists were pummeling the inside of my skull. A red hue adhered to the edge of my vision. Raoul turned and stared directly into my eyes. His own, black, and unreadable, seemed to pierce like a lance.

"DarkBairn. You remember."

"Who *are you*?" I snarled through my gritted teeth. DarSheer stepped toward me out of concern, but I waved him away.

"We've met before, many times. But I pale in importance compared to the Hourglass. You all believe you've seen the might of Mordën. You might be able to identify between the drake and the giant spiders, but you know in your feeble minds his strength grows. What you've seen today, the carnage that has been spilled in his name, will continue. Up until now, he's kept his strongest allies in reserve. He has not unleashed his full anger. All this has been a demonstration."

"The Fallen Luthi." DarSheer exhaled. Elharan slammed his fist angrily.

"Quiet," Elharan barked and DarSheer hung his head.

"The human knows." Raoul grinned a toothy smile. "Then you also know what they can do."

Elharan growled. "It was said in the Annals of Ëonë, the Fallen Luthi, banished from Erëthuïl and forbidden to create and build because they followed Mordën, twisted their art into darkness."

"And out of that darkness?" Raoul prompted.

"They can corrupt the minds of their enemies and sow dismay and fear in their hearts." I'd never seen Elharan look weak. Now he appeared an old form shook against the darkness.

"Mordën has been gracious in letting you feel like you've made a difference here. You want hope where there is none. This is admirable.

But why throw away the lives that still remain when they could just as easily survive in his name?"

"You insult us all," DarSheer snarled. "Every race here stands in direct defiance of your cursed master. We would no sooner bend the knee in fealty or turn on our brothers than we would slit our own throats. You've come expecting weak and traumatized warriors, but you will find our resolve has never been stronger."

"Does the human speak for all present?" The figure's voice dropped an octave. The air grew colder.

"For every living being here." Elharan stood tall. "We've done great damage to Mordën's forces, and we're prepared to do far worse to him. You can spew your fearmongering here, but it will not change our outcome. Take this message back to your master, witless servant of shadow: begone from these lands and put to the torch no more. 'Ere we stand in strength till your crowned usurper becomes a forgotten page of history! We will not yield this terrace. We will not admit what is a falsehood. Bring your drake. Unleash your Seven. The High City and Elfinian race stand ready. The Ebyians and Inclings and Drucodians will meet him. We are ready." The Men and Elfin on the wall bellowed out in joy. The Ebyians cheered and shook their bows. Below, Parod and his force rumbled a deep song.

"So be it. Let your last moments be filled with only the worst kind of fear." Raoul turned and mounted his steed. The skeletal mount whickered, and Raoul directed it to start cantering back down the street. The Nightshade next to him vanished into the shadow. The figure was about to move out of earshot when he paused. He turned in the saddle. Despite his distance, we all heard his next words as clearly as if he whispered them in our ears.

"Do you want to know the identity of the one who will betray you when you need him most? He sits on your own council. He eats your food and stands watch over your sleeping body. And soon Mordën will call on him to fulfill his oath. You speak of honor, yet he who lives with none is held among you as one of the strongest." With that he faded into the night.

"Hear not his poisonous words. He seeks to sow fear among us. Set up the night's watch," Elharan commanded tersely and began descending down the stairs. "I want as many men as possible to patrol these walls. Not one blasted finger gets passed our defenses. Get me Ir'Landi, Scion, and Parod. DarSheer and Phoenix, we have much to discuss. With me!"

The walls erupted into a flurry of activity. I turned and my heart nearly leapt out of my throat. Tim stood not five inches behind me. Face-to-face, our noses nearly touched. He shook his head as if coming out of a trance and took a step back. I cleared my throat and waited for him to say something, anything. He said nothing as he rubbed his back with one hand. Bowmen ran from crenel to crenel on the wall, finding the best angles from which to deliver a killing shot. Spearmen rushed into and out of sight carrying weapons and buckets of water. Still, we didn't say anything. He opened his mouth several times, as if trying to find courage to say something. His eyes were sickly looking, the skin a greenish yellow like a bruise. Scars covered one side of his face and dried blood caked his hair.

"What happened to you?" I tried my best not to stare.

"We're in a war. War happened to me."

"Are you . . . okay?"

"We're in a war. Bodies are bloating and rotting all around. Blood is in my hair. I just spent the last several hours killing."

"Tim, you should go to one of the med tents. You don't look so good. Your cuts could get infected."

"He mentioned betrayal."

"Who? Raoul? Like King Elharan said, he said it to create confusion and fear in the ranks."

"I don't know." For a moment Tim seemed to weaken as he took a step back. His usual smirk was gone. Weariness shown in his eyes. "There could be betrayal. You would know a thing or two about it, wouldn't you? About friends betraying others." There was almost a sadness in his tone.

"What do you mean?"

For a long pause it seemed like he was fighting to get words out. In the end, he hung his head and gripped the stone of the wall. A single tear. A hiccup. He looked up.

"I'm just saying, loyalties are divided and Mordën's influence is strong. Be careful."

It was so unlike our other interactions it took me a moment to register his words. His hair was tousled by the wind and his dark eyes were lit with some unknown emotion. It pulled at my heartstrings. I wanted to pull him into a hug, to apologize again for everything that had happened. But I failed to find the courage to. He stood feet from me, and I couldn't.

"Thank you. You be careful too. We are weak while we fight fractured."

"Yes," he said as if in a trance. "I know. Goodbye, Phoenix."

I watched as he turned and descended to the courtyard level. He sidled past the unmoving ranks of stony-faced Drucodians. The wind picked up intensity and I had to cover my eyes with my hand to see. I watched him step out toward a long line of trees and pause, turn, and gaze back before looking up and making eye contact. He tipped his head once and vanished into the shadows beyond. In this manner, I watched the spot where he'd gone for a long period.

"Phoenix?" Katy was sat my side and saying something, but it was garbled, like hearing words at the end of a long tunnel. "Phoenix, hello?"

"Sorry." I shook my head. "Tim is acting weird. I think the cuts and injuries he's sustained have damaged him worse than I believed."

"DarSheer is ready."

I hurried after her. The night would be long and dark, but it would also hide the guilt flaming in my cheeks. For the first time in my memory, I welcomed the blackness and dreaded the dawn's first ray.

Chapter 10
The Ends Burning

WILLIAM GREE SAT AT *a large table. Upon it the contents of a vast feast were arrayed in kingly splendor. Torches burnt brightly in sconces lined at even intervals. There were no windows. There were no doors. It was a circular room of black walls and ruby ceiling. There were only two chairs, despite the size of the table. Will took up one, at the head of the table. The other, at the midsection of the table, faced the wall. I sat in that chair.*

"Hello, Phoenix." Will smiled sadly. His eyes crinkled in that grandfatherly manner that made you feel cozy and at home. Except this wasn't home.

From the shadows, seven figures stepped forward. They were robed in the darkness. If I looked directly at them, they became nothing more than flickering shadow, but from the corner of my eye they hovered like ghosts.

"Will." A thousand words flooded to mind. I wanted to tell him how much I missed him. I wanted to laugh with him and talk of Katy and all that he had not been there for. Will was dead. It struck me as a nail in my palm. Painful and surprising.

"Yes, I imagine this is an unusual nightmare for you." He took a pale hand and picked up a fork. It was made of smooth glass and sparkled in the torchlight.

My heart sank. "This is a nightmare. I should have guessed. Mordën?"

"Fear not, I am simply here to speak with you. I apologize if my presence brings up any unwanted . . . feelings of grief." He gave me an almost hopeful stare.

"Will, I . . ." Again, the words caught in my throat.

He waved a hand dismissively and scooped up a helping of some purple vegetable. The food crunched in his slimy teeth and that's when I noted that they were sharpened like razors and his skin was so pale his blue veins showed.

"Please, eat." He gestured. "It really is insulting to deny food your host has made."

"I will not entertain this farce, Mordën." I pushed my plate far from me and glowered at him. "This whole charade, posing as my dead friend, is really in poor taste."

"I own the dead." Will smiled. This time it was a leering joyous grin. "More flock to my ranks every day this joke of a war goes on. I gave you a chance to yield. Do not say I am without mercy."

"Is that why you're here, in my dreams? You think I'll be the betrayer your servant spoke of and like last time, let you possess me so you can destroy all our hopes?"

"You seek hope where it cannot be found. It is cowardly to remain behind when all that awaits you is certain death."

"It's cowardly to turn and run." I met his gaze without flinching.

"Is it cowardice to spare lives?" He leaned forward and the orange light revealed the scars and gashes in his face. His left eye was a scarred ball of flesh. "Is it cowardly to separate the living from the fallen? Was it cowardice to die alone and forgotten on a bed of agony? Will was a coward, then. What glory comes of a burning city? Will its ashes and flames be a rallying cry for your honorable dead? Shall your warriors let their lives expire on this, the Eastern Ward's flagstone?"

"You said yourself, you own the dead. Until we become the fallen, you have no power over us. I think you fear what that represents. You like to march your armies and show your drakes, but deep down you recognize

that if there remains living, breathing people with a fighting spirit, you will always be at war. This battle is not a victory for you. It's the beginning of your defeat."

He laughed. "Big words from the bairn who even now sleeps because I let him. At my call, my armies will flood your second tier and within minutes, you all would perish. Perhaps you should be asking yourself why I allow you to live."

"I'm not a bairn." I slammed my open palm on the table and stood. "My name is Phoenix Rather."

"Phoenix Dunnigan Rather, I know." Will stood and paced the far edge of the table, pausing when he stood directly opposite me. His buzzcut hair and wide glasses felt out of place in this setting. "You will know suffering." He placed a cold hand on my cheek. "Before this is all over, you will know pain. You think the horrors of your past can even remotely measure up to the bone-splitting agony of your future? I will personally see to it that every waking moment you are in hell. Every dreamless sleep will drain you more than if you'd not slept to begin with. The curtains of rain will fall on your head and your heart. Then the world will see the true colors of the DarkBairn. Your real name is worthless. You will only ever be the answer to a prophecy of my return. They will see how you shatter. Your pieces will fly to the corners of the world. Your blood will anoint my right to reign over these lands. Your name will be a chanted curse on the lips of my armies. We shall march and the shadows of fear and death will be our banners. Woe to those who see us on the horizon. There will be no peace. The light is cold. There is no warmth in the sun. All good things perish beneath the storm of . . . my wrath." He snarled the last words and spittle flew in my face. "In darkness I was cast down, betrayed, and lost. You shall feel this same torture. Before the end you will clamor for the merciful kiss of death. You will feel the double-edged sword of betrayal from your own flock. You worry it is you, who will betray your people? You've done that already. You've done more damage than a simple backstabbing could hope to achieve now. No, I have far greater plans for you than that."

We waged a silent mental war as the lights dimmed slowly. The seven figures stepped closer behind me. I could feel their hissing chant. My vision turned red with pain. I gripped my temple, determined not to show how much it hurt. When I looked up, Will was gone and Mordën stood before me. The table had vanished, and I was strapped to the same torture bed from long ago. Pain arched like currents up and down my back. I felt my blood leaking out of me, drip by drip.

"I have something you value more than anything else." His voice was velvety soft as his clean fingers ran up and down my neck. His black eyes burned holes in my head.

"You have nothing I want." I gritted my teeth. The veins on my body strained like I was under extreme pressure.

He leaned over me. His cracked pale lips pressed against my temple. A kiss of death. He pulled back and studied me. His skin was pulled tightly over his bony skeletal face. It looked like one rapid pull would snap it in two. His perfectly manicured hands and sculpted hair did nothing to hide the vile odor that wafted off him. It was a mixture of rotting death and embalming fluid. A single strand of his black hair fell to the pull of gravity and tickled my lips. He smiled.

"I have the . . . only . . . thing you want."

I struggled but try as I might, I was secured without hope of escape to the bed. Whatever was piercing my skin, nails or shards of glass, dug deeper. I groaned and screamed at the same time.

"The only thing I want right now is for you and your armies to leave these lands and never return." Sweat gushed down my face.

"Think clearer, bairn." He smiled till the skin pulled tight. "I am offering you one final chance. I will give you what you most desire if you but bend the knee."

"My desire to return home is lessened of late. You're too . . . late . . . cur," I spat and strained against the bonds holding me down.

"Deeper," he cooed, "much, much deeper. Consider what you have and remember what you could lose. You forget, I know every thought in your head. I've thought them all when I was you."

"That was a long ago." I forced the tears back as the pain seared. "You don't know anything about me now."

"It's true," he mused, "you've probably changed much since that day two years ago. But one thing I'm certain has not changed. One thought among the rest has not changed. If anything, it's grown in intensity."

The sharp objects dug deeper. It was a strange thing to happen, but a hysterical laugh burbled from my tightly pressed lips. I wanted to stop but I couldn't force it down. I laughed loud and hard as if I'd never laughed before.

"Whatever you hope to gain by having me here," I gibbered, "I'm prepared to disappoint you."

"Perhaps I was mistaken," he said almost to himself. "I thought you would leap at the chance. Oh well. Dying on the battlefield is a much more storybook ending, isn't it? So be it."

My vision spun and then went black as a deep hysterical laughter echoed against the darkness.

Night blossomed to golden bloom which aged swiftly until once again the dying embers of the sun shed a cold flickering light through the grey clouds. Fear kept everyone high-strung and irritated as patrols swept from the northern alleyways which led to the furthest northern part of the city down into a sweeping valley still behind the walls. Great weeping willows and thick oak trees had been planted in the swooping hills to cover the hidden paradise within. Brooks babbled to themselves as they weaved between lush bushes and cut fields. It was here, in the Northern Quarter, that several times a year, celebrations would be had for all the bairns and maidens of the city who were maturing into adulthood. It was a time of momentous occasion and often warranted delegations from the free races to offer their salutations and well wishes to the lucky youth. It was a time-honored tradition that began with the Drucodians of yore and continued into modern day. South of that in the tiered buildings south of the second level's gates, long low buildings sprawled out haphazardly. On the main level, taverns welcomed in with warm light and boisterous noise the cold traveler alien to these parts. If the tavern was well known, it would include a small inn on the second level. If it wasn't, the tavern barkeep and his staff would sleep above. In the most well-known taverns like The King's Tavern, the third level would be reserved with sleeping quarters for dignitaries and during rare events, even the king himself. Rumor had it, the oldest tavern in the Southern Quarter, Ale's Bargain, on the second level, had once hosted the High King Temporal in the Second Era. There wasn't much stock in it, but the beefy barkeep promoted it like Temporal himself still resided there. It was here, in the broken rubble of the oldest tavern, that the wounded and weary gathered under the watchful eyes of sparkling stars overhead. Flickering torchlight was the only warmth they felt, for inside and out was the cold gripping fear of anticipation. Some cursed loudly while they shivered beneath threadbare blankets. The wounded moaned and wept throughout the passing hours and either succumbed at long last to their wounds, or slowly drifted off in feverish delusion. Blood was everywhere. Pools of it gave birth to maggots and insects which buzzed like miniature horns beneath the heads of injured. Water barrels were brought, and cups of rationed water fed to the thirsty. Those not injured fidgeted with their weapons. Here and there a random log burst into a shower of embers as it succumbed to the flames. Wind howled around the mountain peaks in tumultuous cacophony. The second tier of the city waited in growing anticipation of the fight to come, yet it was slow to arrive. Trees swayed hauntingly and debris was blown along empty cobblestone streets. Alleyways birthed shadows of evil which whispered in the ear of those who skirted through. Beyond the wall, into the main level of the city, darkness held control. The fires had long since gone out and a brooding darkness hung like a poisonous gas cloud over the empty windows and abandoned merchant stalls. It was creepy and goosebumps raced down my arms every time I stared out at it.

There was no sign of the enemy. We'd done several tentative scouting trips along the wall, which stretched dutifully from the Northern Quarter through the residential and merchant squares into the furthest point of the Southern Quarter. Nightfall only worsened our inability to see the Varglarian and Nightshades we knew hid out there. The Rever Drake and remaining Rachnadons were missing in action or hidden by the swirling fog bank which hung just outside our gates.

As the witching hour deepened, I hugged my arms to my torso and felt my grip on the spear in my hands lessen.

"They mean to starve us out," Kissinger grumbled, his palms on the stone of the wall. His back was straight as he stared out into the taunting darkness.

We'd been assigned watch duty the moment the sun dipped below the horizon. Flashbacks to the Outpost raced through my mind as Kissinger stood on my left and DarSheer on my right. It was not lost on them either the irony of our predicament.

"If only," DarSheer said darkly. "We have the rest of the city *and* the Ethero Basin at our backs. Food is not a concern, for we could have shipments from The High City brought across the water. No, there is some other reason why."

"Then why isn't he attacking?"

"Psychological warfare," I said softly.

"What?" Arabella rubbed her eyes from where she stood next to Kissinger and blinked blearily at me.

"He means to drive us insane by anticipation. We'll spend all our last moments tensed up and jumping at shadows until finally either from pure exhaustion or despair we allow ourselves the commodity of sleep and rest. Then, when our guards are down, and we have no fighting spirit in us, he will attack and meet little to no resistance. He holds all the power as he always has."

"Someone's cheery," Kissinger muttered.

"What else should I be?"

"A little less gloomy."

"Why don't you try it?"

"Settle down," Arabella said soothingly. "Fighting each other will only worsen our resolve. Save this energy for the fight to come."

The wall was silent now save for the weeping of the wind. The empty houses and forgotten streets appeared more ominous than before. If I strained my ears, I could hear laughter and the running of small feet on stones. The ghosts of the families who had once lived here was palpable. Shadows twisted around broken columns and licked out like serpents about to spring. I'd never felt so nervous. As I was allowed this moment of respite, my muscles began to seize up and the trauma of what had occurred over the last day truly sank in. I knew it could not be easy for the others, especially Kissinger, who was now prone to long moments of sullen silence. When he did speak, he snapped or ground his teeth. DarSheer, weary and exhausted as he was, had slept even less. His bloodshot eyes roamed the empty streets. His hair was bushy and unkempt. He smelled like the rotting bodies just feet outside the perimeter of the wall. We'd tried to force him off for a hard scrub, but his loyalty was to the wall and he would not budge. Even Arabella, radiant once, mirrored a traveling hobo who had not bathed or eaten in days. Her body was covered in scabbed wounds and her hair was tangled. At some places, it was even cut from a rogue blade. She leaned against Kissinger and closed her eyes. He made no effort to express his appreciation, but I saw the faint smile that flitted across his cracked lips. I also saw him take her hand under the cover of his blanket.

The muscles under my tunic twitched sporadically and without my command. My skin was simultaneously clammy and flaky. One moment I was dizzy, another I was nauseous. It took everything I had to not throw up over the edge of the battlements. The smell here was unfavorable, made worse by the bloating corpses of horse and free race alike. Maggots appeared and burrowed under flesh, in discriminatorily of who it was. They did so to the actively dying so to look upon them was to see their flesh moving like small waves. It was entirely vile and miserable at the same time.

Right below the overhang of the wall, the stones had already been discolored by vomit from the occasional watchman who couldn't handle the odor. The more I stared at the bodies and inhaled the toxic fumes, the more I considered emptying my stomach of whatever measly breakfast I'd managed to force down. The food was scarce and the water scarcer. At least there was some minor humor in the idea that we lived so close to a body of water and were starving ourselves out.

We stood shoulder to shoulder, watching over the ruined city below. There was no need for words. There was nothing to be said anymore. Words hurt to say. Throats were scratchy and sore from tears and screaming. The peace below was not disrupted by swords singing in the air. The hours of the night continued to clomp past until the darkness was broken by a softer grey. Movement behind us alerted me to the pending watch change and I shook the sleep from my limbs and the morning moistness from the folds of my cloak.

"This is despicable. All this fighting, all those deaths just for us to stand idly by awaiting our turn to perish. It's cowardly." I yawned and jostled Kissinger awake. He slapped my hand away and muttered some unintelligible complaint as Arabella stirred her head against his neck.

DarSheer, who had remained vigilant throughout the whole night, folded his arms. "The love of war is a great evil. Seeing the innocent with their throats slit as they sleep and their blood run down the streets is a terrible sight to behold. When you see the fire-ravaged wastelands of villages and the burned corpses of their occupants, you begin to understand. War changes things. To yearn for a simple thing such as home is to hold on to the idea that this war will end. It's a sign of hope. I would not so dismay at the thought if I were you."

"Why would you think I yearn for home?" The guilt of my nightmares flared up. *Did he know?*

"When faced with great calamity, all wish for simpler times. I'd take a garden to weed or a calm lake to fish over this." He gestured randomly about.

"But we cannot."

Those three words silenced the rest of the conversation as we took to brooding. Katy mounted the aged flight of stairs and smiled at me. Her eyes were wide, refreshed from a long night of sleep. Unlike the others, she'd used her time to her advantage. Her hair was back in its usual ponytail and her face was scrubbed free of grime and blood.

"You're tired," she grinned at me.

"You talk a lot," Kissinger muttered.

"What?"

"Sorry, I thought we were just stating obvious facts. We've been up since the blasted nightfall. Where have you been? You were supposed to go on watch with us. They pulled some gold . . . Elfin from the barracks to cover for you."

"King Elharan can excuse my absence." She flicked a single strand of hair back from her eyes. "Since when did my location mean so much to you?"

Below in the courtyard, horses were led by the bit from makeshift stalls and readied for combat. King Elharan and DarSheer had concluded that Mordën could not ill afford to wait any longer. The more time he gave us to prepare, the better we'd last. The High City could, not that they would, send thousands of reinforcements over the basin and what once would have been a slaughter would instead be a fierce battle. He couldn't afford that. Torches were lit and braziers roared to life. Men strapped their armor on and sharpened their blades against strategically placed whetstones. Horses snorted and pawed at the ground as they were scrubbed and fed. Groups of Elfinian bowmen jogged by on their way to the northern edges of the wall. A troupe of Ebyian hammermen slipped from shadow to shadow and out of sight.

"Where's the king?" Kissinger rubbed his eyes.

"He makes plans in the makeshift command tent." She pointed to a single white tent barely visible in a copse of trees up the road. "DarSheer, he wishes your presence."

DarSheer only nodded and trudged off. I sheathed my sword and lowered the spear I'd been tasked to hold back against the wall for the next watchman. The day grew lighter until an angry orange burst over the horizon. Kissinger, relieved of his watch, hurried off to get sleep or as he put it "rest with both eyes open and two swords in my hands." I noted how Arabella slipped off after him. There was something happening there, and I felt relieved.

After being assured I was not also needed, and giving Katy a quick embrace, I hurried to the barracks. Inside, wounded slumbered while some men chanced their luck in a card game over an upturned barrel. They paid me no heed as I stumbled in and collapsed on a free cot. I laid my head down on the thin blanket that had been waiting there and tried to silence my mind and slow my breathing but a thousand fears and hopes and nightmares took control. The stars above had no longer been visible. A thin blanket of fog moved again over the city. It was like staring into an empty void. A void that swirled and shifted in varying shades of black. I tossed and turned and grunted and sighed until sleep overtook me. It came and went in flits of dreamless bliss. In that manner, I slept . . . slept, that is, until the screams and sounds of flesh being rent asunder woke me from my slumber.

The first scream was high-pitched and guttural, like an animal as its limb was being ripped off. I was on my feet before the second blood-curdling scream severed the morning's rest. The men in the room were gone save for the most grievously injured. I threw the door wide and stepped into complete and utter pandemonium. Horses bolted past, their riders barely hanging on. Fires raged hungrily on the roof of a nearby house. Several Elfin tried to battle it into submission but gave up as Nightshades, bearing torches and swords, marched into view.

"The gate was opened!" An Ebyian rushed past.

"Stand! Stand, you dimwits!" Ir'Landi rode past and corralled his Ebyians. "Rally to my voice. We ride to aid Parod. Rally to the Ebyian banner."

I pawed at my eyes as the last shreds of sleep vanished. My body was alert and adrenaline coursed through me. Kissinger, sword in hand, raced into view. Several Elfins jogged with him and together, they were dispatching a horde of Varglarian who had snuck past the Drucodians.

"Kissinger!" I waved one hand as my other drew my blade. "What news?"

"The gates were opened in the night." Kissinger wiped the blood from his blade as he paused at my side. "They attacked us. DarSheer and Elharan stand with Parod fighting elbow against elbow in the courtyard, but it is clear it is a slaughter. The Drucodians hold the line but as you see, they are unable to stem the flow. More and more slip past them and run rampant in the city itself."

"How did the gates open? Who opened them? Did a Shade slip in through the shadows?"

"We do not know; it happened at the guard change," Kissinger grunted.

"Where are the others?" I felt the strength of my sword in my hand. I yearned for combat.

"Katy and Arabella retreated to the section of road overlooking the courtyard. They pick off what they can, but their arrows run low," Kissinger grunted as he deflected a clanging blow from a Varg and side-stepped the next swing. I parried off a Nightshade's snarling stab and watched as Kissinger easily beheaded the creature.

I ducked down and leaned against the trunk of a tree, gripping my blade even as a third scream and a fourth split the air. A horn sounded wildly. Somewhere, a body thudded. I'd turned to find Katy rushing down the road toward me when a horde of Nightshades erupted from the shadows. She hadn't seen them in her haste to reach my side.

"Katy!" I bellowed as a new attacker stepped up immediately to my right and swung its huge sword. I leaned back so the blade cut cleanly through the air where my head had just been. Thrown off-balance, the Nightshade stumbled. I drew one of the daggers strapped to my waist and watched the creature drop lifelessly to the ground. Its flesh made a sucking sound as it retrieved my knife. Its body twitched on the ground. A second leapt from the low-hanging limbs of a tree onto my back, snarling. Saliva trickled down my cheek and neck as I wrestled to toss it off. The creature spun me in several directions before I was able to slam it into the trunk of the same tree it had leapt from. I limped forward and again reared back so the Nightshade was slammed, headfirst, into the tree. Its grip weakened as it became dizzy beyond the point of recovery. I wiped its blood off my blade as it sagged into a fetal position.

The courtyard was in utter disarray as warriors tripped over fresh bodies and Nightshades swarmed anything that moved. Fireballs erupted overhead. Everything was moving so quickly. Bells rang and horns sounded. Screams bellowed and metal clanged. Somewhere, someone roared a warning and in the next moment, I was on my back, ears ringing as rubble rained down around. Fire rimmed my vision. I groaned and slowly rolled to one side. A second fireball hurtled overhead into the edge of a waist-high wall. I coughed up dust and phlegm.

A deep booming filled the air as a long line of grey bodies appeared through the mist and haze. The Drucodians chanted in a baritone hum as they locked shields against the screeching and snarling Varglarian hordes that pushed them back. Parod, at the front, was wielding his blade with blinding speed and agility. They were holding the line even as they slipped a few inches back at a time.

"Phoenix!" Arabella slid over the gravel and rubble to my side and helped me up. Her hair dangled in front of her eyes as she checked me over. "We have to fall back. King Elharan is injured and DarSheer says the city is about to be fully overrun."

"Where were our defenses? How did they surprise us so easily?" I tried to shake the humming from my ears. Blood trickled down my temple and dripped down into my eyes.

Her words still hadn't sunk in as we staggered toward the final tier of the city. All around, Elfin and Ebyian dying groaned under blocks of stone. Random severed appendages decorated the road. A horse without a head festered in the blood of its rider. A dozen arrows appeared out of its flanks. Further up, a long line of bristling bowmen readied for the charge that was sure to happen.

"Ebyians, to me!" Ir'Landi rallied his Ebyians into a long line. "Parod, duck!"

The Ebyian bowmen let loose a shower of projectiles as the Drucodians fell to their chests. The rushing horde was caught unawares and fell motionless. Behind them, the survivors took shelter behind rubble.

"My gratitude," Parod rumbled.

I rushed the scene even as Kissinger and Arabella appeared. Katy had her arrows ready as we stood to the side of the road. The battle was intense as a fresh wave of Varg appeared. I watched as dozens of Elfins fled, leaving their weapons, and hurtling toward the final level of the city. Some carried the more grievously injured on cots and stretchers. Berëthelluïn was one of them. His eyes were shut and dried blood stained his temple and crown. King Elharan rode into view behind them and swung his sword in the air.

"Ride! Retreat to the basin!"

Arabella forced us both down as a wave of arrows hissed overhead. I turned and saw the line of Varglarian scum drop twitching to the ground. Behind them, Elfinian stragglers limped and hobbled forward.

"Rally to the king!" the cry went out, and a large force of Elfinian spearmen rushed their ruler. They made a wall between him and the charging Varg.

"No!" I protested weakly. "You're blocking the bowmen. Get out of their line of fire! We can hold them off. Get out of the way."

Arabella cried out as an arrow appeared in her thigh. It happened so quickly that I barely had a moment to register it before she was on one knee, grunting out in pain. Blood stained her leg. Elharan moved past without seeing us. In moments, we'd be on the front lines again and staring down a fierce horde of Varglarian as the line of defenders retreated. I pivoted and reached a hand out to help her. When she tried to put her weight on the leg, her eyes widened, and she nearly collapsed.

"I can't walk," she said. "I can't, Phoenix." Her voice quaked with fear.

"Arabella!" Kissinger abandoned his fight and hurried up. "Are you badly injured?"

"I can't walk, Kissinger." She winced.

"I'm getting her out of here," he told me with no room for argument.

"Phoenix!" Katy struggled as a Varg picked her up by the throat and slammed her full force into a stone wall. She slumped into unconsciousness.

The Drucodians were choking on their own blood as they became decorations on the ends of polearms. The Varglarian were in no rush. They had won. All they were doing was cleaning up the city. It wasn't long before the dreaded banner was brought forth and an ugly chant began to ripple out like thunder on the edge of a thunderhead.

I pushed off an inclined slab of rubble and slammed into the Varglarian before it had a chance to end Katy. My body was ready for a fight. Every fiber in my being was on fire. The vermin stood no chance as I turned away from its corpse and cradled Katy's head. Kissinger stopped and stared.

"Take her," I pleaded. "Take her to the Basin and get out of here. I'll meet back up with you on the docks. Please, Kissinger!"

For a long moment he eyed me but nodded as Arabella gestured. She held a long sword under her armpit like a crutch and as Kissinger picked Katy up, they began to hobble away.

"Phoenix?" Her voice was so soft I barely heard it.

"I'll be with you soon." I rubbed her arm and kissed her forehead. "Go with Kissinger. He'll protect you." With that, they were off in the flood of retreating warriors.

The line of bowmen broke as the Varglarian raised their shields and charged. Parod roared out.

"This is our moment! We stand so we may die the same way as our forbearers. Unite under the banner of our people. Let our last stand be one for the storybooks. I command you all to stand and feel no fear. Breathe in the sweet aroma of death. We go now into the shadows of the south. Our city shall weep no more. No longer do we hide as thieves in the night. To war!"

I watched as the group of less than a hundred Drucodians, the last of their race, bellowed out war chants and planted their feet firmly in the dirt. One by one, they fell to sweeping blades and snarling Varg. Parod filled the street around him with bodies as he roared and swung his great and mighty weapon.

"Curse it," I muttered and charged.

A Varglarian bore down on me. Its smooth iron mask held more emotion than my own face. Through the eye holes, its eyes blazed angrily. I could practically feel its hot breath rolling over me through its thin slits. Before I had any chance to raise my sword, though, an arrow hissed through the air and imbedded in its chest. The creature stopped running and stared down at the quivering bolt. With an ominous growl, it snapped the projectile in two and roared into the sky.

"Back up quickly now, quickly!" DarSheer shouted as the Varglarian stomped toward us. He fired a second dart into the creature's neck this time. Blood gushed out of the wound as the monster stumbled but kept advancing. DarSheer released another arrow; this one rang off the metal and did no damage. Finally, the fourth arrow found its mark in the creature's eye and the Varg dropped to the ground.

"Thanks," I breathed heavily.

"Parod!" He waved one long arm. "Fall back. Fall back!"

Parod turned and I saw in his eyes his response. "This is our last stand, Broadsword. Carry our legacy with the injured fallen. We go now. Be at peace."

From the direction of the gates, horse's hooves thundered over broken stone. A tremor in the ground began as a dozen mounted riders rode into view.

"What of Ir'Landi?" I clamored. "Where is he? We can't leave the Drucodians here. They're dying, DarSheer."

"I have eyes," he snapped. "But I cannot force them to flee. They find the death of a warrior a finer death than perishing while they run. Parod and his have made their choices. He's allowing us the chance to fall back without enemies right on our tail."

"He's sacrificing his people for us?" I turned and watched as Parod dropped to one knee, an arrow in his stomach.

DarSheer grabbed my arm and pulled me. "Come, bairn."

I watched as a single Drucodian was placed on a stretcher and hurried past. The rest were abandoned on the field as they were slowly beat down.

Pain erupted in my side and my vision tinted red as a black knife sunk into my gut. I quickly kicked the Varglarian back. It was one

I'd thought was dead but had used its last strength to crawl to me. Reaching one hand down, I felt the blood oozing out around the edges of the blade. Without thinking, I yanked the dagger out and cursed loudly. Blood gushed out and down my legs. A small pool began to form next to my boot.

An Elfin medic dropped next to me with an arrow in his throat. I clumsily reached over him and found his bag of supplies.

"Dagger to the gut," I gasped painfully as DarSheer paused.

The road was filled with warriors abandoning the fight and fleeing toward the gate. From the shadows, a Nightshade shrieked. It swung a sword as long as I was tall. The tip cut into my tunic as DarSheer thrust me out of the way. They battled back even as he spun and kicked off a nearby tree, launching up and on top of the brute. I turned away as he stabbed a dozen times until the creature lay a motionless heap to be forgotten.

I rotated enough to glance behind. The city was in flames. Not just a minor house on fire or a tavern eaten by a blaze. Nearly every structure, every tree, and every corpse that was visible was burning. Orange light climbed high into the sky. It made a horrible rumbling as wind carried sparks around. Embers rained down around like a rainstorm of fire. The Rever Drake was stomping about the lower city levels, roaring, and crushing everything in its path. Rachnadons moved in circles, snapping their mandibles at unseen fighters while their riders, gripping the reins to their mounts, shouted encouragements. They had been ready. They had been waiting.

DarSheer grasped at a lone horse and hoisted himself up. He reached down even as the last Drucodian collapsed. He yanked me up in front of his mount. If we'd waited a few moments longer, we'd have been overrun.

"Get out of here!" I shouted to Parod who knelt in the center of the street. My vision darkened.

Without speaking, DarSheer tore a piece of his cloak and handed it to me. I accepted the cloth and pressed it to my side. Pain flared up and I thought I would pass out, but the jolts of the horse brought me back to reality. We rode hard over the swoops and hills of the second level.

"Don't leave me to their blades," an Elfin wept on the side of the road. Both his legs were missing, and he pulled himself forward inch by inch. "Somebody, help me please! I can't walk. I won't be a burden! Someone have mercy!" He gurgled out a wet scream as a knife imbedded in his back. The Varg on top of him began feasting.

"I have a bairn," a man said as he staggered out from the trees to our left. His face was ashen. An arrow protruded from his stomach. "Take me with you!" This he directed at us as we rode past. When we didn't stop, he simply stood motionless with a stricken look in his eyes as a Nightshade dragged him back into the shadows.

"Curse us all!" An Elfin lay on his back against a stone. His eyes were turned upward, and he blinked through the flood of blood that trickled down his face. His stomach had been cut open and his entrails hung out. "Erëthuil take us to your hallowed halls so there we may be free of this misery. There is no hope for any. Mordën has won."

An Ebyian leapt in front of us and without stopping, DarSheer rode him down. I tried to choke out a horrified scream as the crunch of bones echoed the din of hooves on stone. The body of the Ebyian slumped in the middle of the road.

"There is no hope; there never was!" A man missing both his eyes staggered into view.

"They'll eat us alive." A second wept as he surveyed his missing foot.

"I'm ready to die. Take me, Erëthuïl."

"I'll never see them again. I've made mistakes. I pray they don't suffer because of that."

I willed the cries to subside as tears threatened to flood down my cheeks. The silent watch of just a few hours past was a graveyard of the dead and the dying. Blood was more common than water. Those who wept, wept till tears were no more.

"We must help them!" My voice broke with emotion. "DarSheer, we cannot leave them to die."

"If we stop, we all die," DarSheer growled. "Just keep your eyes shut and shove your cloak into your ears."

"We condemn them to a fate worse than death," I said hollowly as I slumped forward and leaned against the neck of the steed. Brenneth's face flashed through my mind, and I saw again his pained expression. "We must help them." I saw his body hung on the pike as it was marched forward.

"We cannot." DarSheer was warm around me. His arms prevented me from sliding off the stallion. "Erëthuïl has decided their fate. This is the result of war."

We quickly reached the third terrace and any hope I might have harbored about making a stand here fled with the wind. The gate was already broken down. I knew with certainty that our only hope now lay in retreat. *We've been betrayed.* Guilt racked me as I let my mind wander. Injured tried to keep up with the mass of retreating bodies. It had all gone so wrong so quickly. There were no words to boost morale. No speech was given from the ramparts. No one fought anymore. All that anyone cared about now was self-preservation. Even up here, the homes and taverns and inns were ablaze. I slid down from the mount as we cantered to a stop. DarSheer helped me stand. My wound leaked blood through the fabric but for the time being the blood didn't gush out. I was light-headed but not nauseous. It was a temporary fix, but a fix nonetheless. Thankfully, the blade that had buried into my side was not a long one.

"We move for a final meeting in a glade just up ahead." DarSheer helped me as we moved hastily.

The glade was considerably longer to get to than DarSheer had led me to believe. But when we finally arrived, Elharan was waiting. Scion and Ir'Landi also awaited us. Bereth was nowhere to be seen. The Elfin King welcomed us with a terse bow before addressing the gathering.

"My friends and allies gathered here before the fall of this noble city, we are overrun, and our positions compromised. I fear most shall perish before they make it to the docks. Such is our last stand, if it must be one; we shall all be on the front lines guarding the docks till the last ship sets sail. It is my decree to my people, none of the highest-ranking commander down to officer shall step a foot on a boat until every injured soul attempting retreat is aboard. We've lived our lives of luxury. It is their turn to survive."

"Your words are wise but misplaced," Ir'Landi muttered softly. His eyes were dark with grief, and he bore many wounds. But his head remained high as he stared out toward the carnage. "My people spilled their blood below to ensure a retreat was open. Grace us with this request, that the last of my kin go down in the east with blood on their sword and a war cry on their lips. Give us this honor, King Elharan. The Ebyians will stand on the docks while you ride for safety."

"My friend," the Elfinian royalty stared somberly at him, "you and yours have given enough in the sacrifice of this city. We cannot ask it of you."

"It's not a request we make lightly." Ir'Landi adjusted his belt and the two Ebyians who flanked him did the same. "We simply cannot see ourselves sailing west over the basin while our brethren choke on their blood and perish here. It is simply not honorable. You wish to honor us for our sacrifice? Let us defend the final retreat over the docks. The last of our blood shall be spilled giving Ëonë a fighting chance. If the Western Ward loses its commanders and king, they shall scramble in disarray. We are not so crucial. We've lived a life of isolation free from impact on your world."

"It pains me to add fire to the burning choice," Berëthelluïn hobbled into view, "but we must make a choice, my king. The Varg have pushed the Ebyians back and the last of the boats are moored up for their occupants. We must go if we are to ever flee."

"What says the king?" Ir'Landi stood.

Elharan stared at the other with a mixture of grief and determination as his gaze flickered over the creature's short stature. The Ebyians, once thousands in number, now numbered in the hundreds.

"I will not allow it," Elharan said loudly. "Enough blood has been shed for my people and this city. I will not allow it! You and yours will ride the ships to safety and there meet up with your people. The dark days are still to come and every fighting spirit shall be needed."

"Please," Ir'Landi begged as the sounds of chaos drew near.

"I . . . will . . . not . . . allow . . . it," Elharan ground out.

"As you wish."

Elharan turned to the rest of us and said: "I am honored to have stood alongside such warriors as you all. These are days and nights of chaos. More death and ruination shall be bestowed upon us ere our hours are finished. Erëthuïl is drawing our lives out, like a rope over jagged stone. Our days are numbered, and I do not blame any who runs. Not all who run are cowards. The old times of Ëonë are of the past. The wind of filth blows through the mountains and descends in madness upon our cities. Run for your life depends on it. Run with the foul breath of our foe at our necks. Run as my last command to you. To the docks . . . RUN!"

As the Ebyians and Elfins scattered in full retreat, the Varglarian lines appeared around a sharp corner. A few Drucodians remained to prevent them from fully sprinting toward us, but it was clear they were weak and tired. Those fleeing abandoned anything that slowed them down till a road of armor and weapons littered the ground. A vessel with seven unfurled sails and a blustering captain was in the process of pushing off the docks as Ebyians and Caldonanites fell from the gangplank into the water. Several Elfin tried to leap the distance and slammed into the side of the ship, crying out in frustration as they plopped into the frothing waters.

"Commanders to your legions," Elharan turned and rushed off with his entourage of guards.

DarSheer pivoted on one heel and gestured emphatically. Smoke spiraled up from the tops of burning buildings. Trees crackled and keeled over. Near every alleyway and street, Varglarian and Nightshade ran unchallenged. Though they fought with blinding speed, the Drucodians were not enough to handle the thousands of swarming vermin that flooded throughout the city. Parod, somehow still standing, cried out in pain as a black blade pierced his shoulder. He doubled over and with a resounding roar, stood tall and bashed the creature high into the air. A second sword slashed his face and he stumbled back. My stomach did summersaults as I looked about, wondering my course of action. It seemed inhumane to abandon them to their fate, yet Elharan had made his orders clear. Screams erupt from one end of the city to another. Acrid smoke spilled through the city.

The ground shook. Dust and ash coated every surface. My blood raced, for I knew what time had brought. Death and bloodshed shook the deep core of the world. The once unyielding lands recognized a new master and ceased resisting. Poison of an ancient origin seeped into the deepest caverns of the world. The darkness rose with a million chants. Eyes of crimson malice and venom flickered from the shadows. They had one purpose. They served one master. There was no song nor mourning for the honorable dead. The time to defend had departed. Now was the time to survive!

The docks of Avalon, tethered to the gracefully undulating ripples of the Ethero Basin, were now under a siege of their own. Great vessels bobbed slowly in the clear water with a lazy weariness. In quieter times, they were solely used to shuttle dignitaries and persons of great important from the Western Ward's docks to Avalon's swooping shores. Now they were floating hospitals as injured were practically hurled in. Blood sloshed at the bottom as Men and Elfin and Ebyian lay groaning in various positions. There weren't enough medics nor tools to save everyone. It was chaos. Screams and howls and weeping cries for help battled with metal clanging against wood and stone. Those uninjured supported their allies into boats until the ships were so weighed down that they began to slowly sink. At that moment, a few uninjured would leap off and back onto the dock to prevent the craft from capsizing. Burdened down, just barely above the waterline, the boat would then be shoved off with long pikes and frantic grunts as all put their muscles to the task. Vessel after vessel successfully cleared the confines of the shipyard and were soon dots on the horizon of the basin. Every time one cleared danger, the docks would let out a moralizing cheer. Fewer victims for their enemy to butcher. More warriors for the days to come.

DarSheer helped me stumble toward the last vessel still tied to the decks. It was a smaller ship with a massive sail. The golden archer illustrated the fabric. The wood was made to point upward toward the heavens. Small windows in the sides hinted at cabins below deck. The ship was already filling up fast as panic erupted. Too many clung to life in their feeble positions on the shoreline, waiting their chance at a ship. When word spread that the last ship in the entire basin was preparing to push off, pandemonium erupted. Brother turned on brother and knives were pulled.

"I've secured your passage," DarSheer was saying through the roar. "When you make landfall on the other side, move with haste and purpose to The High City."

"You're coming too, surely?" I stared at him as we neared the gangplank.

"Of course." He gave me a side glance. "Now Arabella and Kissinger and Katy should be onboard. Your other friend, the one who sulks a lot, is nowhere to be seen. If he is not present when the last ship departs, he will be lost."

I felt another familiar flare of guilt. In all the chaos, I'd only been focused on Katy and the others. I hadn't even given him one thought. I craned my neck about, hoping against hope to see his form burst from the shadows and hobble to the ship. But he was absent.

"Phoenix!" Kissinger's curly head appeared over the edge of the ship. His eyes were frantic. My stomach plummeted. "Phoenix, she's gone."

A dizziness rushed into my head as I stumbled. "What do you mean gone? I told you to watch her!"

"We got separated in the darkness. Nightshades. From the shadows. I thought she was right next to me when we finally made it out, but it was Arabella. I can't find her. Phoenix, I can't find her!" His voice was hysterical.

DarSheer tried to hold my arm, but I yanked from his grasp. My heart beat rapidly. Somewhere, out there in the chaos of death and grief, Katy was alone. My pain lessened considerably as I sprinted back up the docks. I was shoved and jostled by the horde of trapped seeking to get on the ship. Some cursed at me as I shoved past them. Others elbowed me. Most ignored my small form for their insatiable desire for the safety of the last docked vessel was far stronger. King Elharan and his Elfin guarded the gangplanks and only allowed injured in or the few bearers of cots or stretchers to pass. Before I could reach the shoreline, the sand exploded in fire and the sound of a whirlwind hitting. I flew back and tumbled till I came to a stop against a small post. Many were not so lucky. Those on the docks flew into the water or spun end over end out of sight. Those on the shoreline or still moving from the darkness of the city lay scattered about missing arms and legs.

My vision blurred then refocused as Katy stumbled into view. Her eyes were full of terror as she slashed a sword behind her. I heard her gasp and tried to stand but a wave of dizziness and nausea overcame me. Blood oozed from my bandage. All I could do was watch, horrified, at the dark form that was chasing her. From here, sprawled on the docks, it was impossible to make out if it was a Varglarian or a Nightshade. She was clearly struggling and losing. The form following her swung at her till her sword flew from her hand. She tripped over a body and rolled into a panting mess at the bottom of the docks. By this time, the docks were empty of those seeking passage. All were either dead or onboard. King Elharan and his host moved up the gangplank and into the vessel as DarSheer stood, waiting.

A knife appeared in her hand, and she rolled just in time to avoid being cut in two. Over the waving heads of trees and the lifeless buildings, the Rever Drake appeared. First it was an ominous black shape against the golden glow of the wind and fire storm. Its glowing eyes were like two massive balls hanging in the air. The fires that had started sporadically about the beach shed light ono its glistening teeth. It roared and spittle flew out. I couldn't see its rider, but I knew Mordën was here.

Kissinger's hands were on my shoulder now. *How had he made it here? Wasn't he supposed to be on the ship?* He tried to drag me back as DarSheer bellowed for us to board. He shouted something unintelligible. I struggled defiantly. He cursed at me but was undeterred. Arrows hissed out behind us as several standing Elfinian bowmen took shots at the figure chasing Katy. Hope surged back in me. Whoever it was, whatever it was, it couldn't survive an arrow. Surely.

"We need to help her!" I snarled. My tongue felt thick.

"You need to get in the blasted boat," Kissinger pleaded. We were moving inches at a time. "Phoenix, please!"

Utter lawlessness. The scene unfolding was one that stayed with me for the rest of my days. From the edges of the city, Varglarians poured in uncountable numbers. They leapt onto the bodies of the injured unable to make it to the ships and I gasped as they tore into the fallen with animalistic hunger. Guts and blood spurted up. The pale gold of the sand ran red. Katy still battled fiercely to avoid her attacker. She spun, dove, twisted, leapt, rolled, pushed, slashed, ducked, stumbled, screamed, parried. The fires shed light on the figure, a disfigured form in a flowing red cloak. Its black eyes were trained on her. It stalked toward her. The figure slashed and parried, cut and plunged, blocked and stabbed. With a last desperate kick, Katy put some distance and turned to face me. Her eyes were crazed with fear and her face covered in blood. The creature raised its blade as a single arrow appeared in its eye. I whirled about. DarSheer, arms shaking with exhaustion, lowered the bow and turned back to the ship. Katy hobbled closer.

We were almost to the gangplank now. DarSheer had boarded and finished assisting the last of those uninjured. The ship was clearly overweight as it sank lower than normal. The guards on the docks and the seamen waiting stood without movement. Their faces were directed with horror at the beach. No one shouted for them to push off. No one demanded they leave us behind. Not even when the Rachnadons finally appeared, their long legs slamming into friend and foe alike. They didn't even sound the cry to push off when Nightshades appeared from the shadows and swarmed the beach. They simply watched in growing fear, frozen in place.

Katy had made it halfway down the docks, a few yards from reaching us. Behind her, dozens of shapes flitted about the shadows.

I chalked it up to the pain, but I saw clearer than I did before. Maybe *that* was because of the pain. Eyes open, mouth agape, I struggled to slip from Kissinger's iron grip. Every part of me wanted to run to Katy and help her. My heart seized.

Katy had stopped. Sweat glistened on her clammy face. Her hair, clumped and tangled, hung in front of her eyes as she saw me. For a moment, as if time itself had stopped out of respect, we made eye contact. I wasn't sure if the tear that fell from her was from sighting me or what happened next. She opened her mouth and closed it again as she lowered her sword. Behind her, a shadowy figure had appeared as if from the air itself. It stood inches from her. It wasn't making any sense. Why wasn't she running? She just stood there. My voice cracked.

"Katy, get out of there. *Run!* What are you *doing*? Why aren't *you moving*? Come to me!"

It was like I'd entered some nightmare. With a strength I didn't know I had, I shoved off the dock. My tunic caught in Kissinger's hand. The strings to untie it dangled tauntingly at my side. The same side was coated in my blood. I should have been weak. But I wasn't. I should have been nauseous or faint . . . but all I felt was fear, grief, and rage. A power flowed through me. She remained planted to one spot. It didn't make any sense.

"Phoenix, get back here!" DarSheer roared. He had leapt onto the dock and slipped in a pool of blood.

Sounds . . . quieted. Speed . . . slowed. Katy brushed the hair from her eyes and took a step toward me. The figure took a step back. She just stood there. Her eyes took years to slowly look down at the curved black steel that protruded from her stomach. Tears blinded me and plummeted to the dock. My body shook. My head erupted into a buzzing nausea. It was all a horrible blur. Sound and smell and touch mixed into a venomous concoction of blinding speed. The wind rushed through my hair and up my nose. It was like I'd forgotten the figure, the Varg, Nightshades, the entire blasted conflict. All I saw, in that moment, was her slow realization. Blood appeared as a single dot on the tip of the blade then blossomed into a trickle down her torso. She dropped like a stone, as if every bone in her body had turned to jelly. No matter how I ran, I couldn't reach her before her head cracked with blinding reverberation against the wood. I screamed, or I thought I did but I couldn't hear my own voice. I couldn't hear anything save for the beating of my heart. It was as if my body was shutting down all my senses to keep from overloading my brain.

Nonsensical words echoed behind me. Her eyes swelled shut, hair matted with blood. Some previous injury cut a long and deep gash from her left temple to her chin. I could see bone. When she gasped for breath, I could see her blood-stained teeth and my hearing returned in full as she coughed a watery cough. Katy stared ahead with no emotion other than a dazed frown. But all that paled in comparison to the steel blade impaled in her gut. The point of the weapon glinted in the burning fires beyond, mocking. Debris and bodies covered the docks. Small fires had begun to build in ferocity and parts were going up in flames. The roaring wind above only aided in the quickly spreading glow. An animalistic scream bubbled out from between my cracked lips. I let my legs give before I'd even reached her side. I felt no pain as I slid to her motionless body and reached out.

Hands shaking, I scooped Katy up and held her cradled in my arms. By instinct, I went to grab the knife's handle but was met with a warm hand on mine. I looked down at the tear-streaked beautiful brown eyes of the woman I loved. She was crying. I felt her squeeze my shaking hand and she smiled ever so faintly. A tear of my own dropped on her cheek. I brushed a strand of her hair from her face as more tears plopped down on her.

"No, no, no," I gasped shakily as I ran my fingers through her hair. "No, no . . . *no!*"

"We both know how this will end, my love." Her voice was full of pain. "Thank you, thank you for everything. For the smiles . . . the laughter. For the good moments . . . and the . . . bad." Her voice was broken in sharp gasps of pain. Her face was so pale. I saw the flecks of ash and soot in her eyes as it rained down about us.

"Katy, what are you talking about?" My brain struggled to understand what was happening. "Don't talk like this. There's good medics, amazing medics on the boat. They can help. We just need to get you to the ship. It's just over there. We're *so* close! We still have so many memories to share." I choked out between grieving howls. My tears flowed down my cheeks.

"We'll share a fantasy of memories," she whispered. Her eyes had begun to drift away. "When the wind calls and the oceans sing the songs of sirens, I'll be there. I would not give up any moment of this if it meant I lived."

"I love you," the tears were flowing now. My voice was pitiful and weak. "Don't you get *it?*" My voice dropped to a low octave as I begged. "*I love you, Katy.* Please don't leave me here alone. Don't make me survive in a world that you're not a part of. I lived that life once. I survived when I *assumed* you were out of reach. I can't do it again. I can't live *knowing* you are beyond my embrace. Don't. Please. Erëthuïl save her. Take me instead!"

Her eyes flitted slowly like a butterfly's wing. She tried to say something but couldn't as blood dribbled from her lips. I looked down at her wet head and scared face. She slowly opened her eyes and looked up at me, wordless.

"No, no, no!" I brought her face close to my breast. My arms shook. "Do not cross between worlds. *You can't.* Okay? You're supposed to come home with me. Remember? Home? The mountains from your house? The blue bear? I was going . . . I was going to ask you to . . . Katy?"

"It hurts. Phoenix," she gasped suddenly. Her eyes flew open. The calm murmur was replaced with a fearful pleading. "Why can't I see? I can't see anything. Phoenix? Help me. Help! I don't want to die. I'm not ready. Why can't I see you? I'm not ready. Please! *I'm not ready to die.*" Her tears mixed with the blood on her face.

"I'm right here, my love." I wiped the grime and moisture from my tears off her face. Her broken look twisted my heart like a sponge. "Katy, I'm right here. I'm not going anywhere. Feel this." I gripped her hand to my chest and let her fingers slowly feel my heartbeat. "I'm here." Sobs shook my body. "I'm not leaving."

She spoke like one just having woke from a deep sleep. Her chest heaved as she coughed blood. "Phoenix, I can't feel anything. I'm so cold. It's so cold. Why can't I see you? Don't leave me here." Even as her glassy eyes strained about, tears trickled down.

I wept bitterly as her hand slowly lost strength and her fingers curled involuntarily. Her eyes slowly closed now.

"I can't keep going if the only reason I have left for fighting is you," I whispered. "I can't leave you behind. *Don't become a memory*. Don't take your piece of me." I blubbered like a newborn, big fat tears rolling down my moist cheeks like diamonds. Snot ballooned in my nostrils. "*No!* Katy . . . Help! DarSheer? Kissinger? Somebody, help!"

"Please don't leave me here. I'm scared." Her words brought me back as I looked down.

"Why can't you see me. It's me, your Phoenix." I hugged her body tight and stroked her hair. The point of the dagger pressed my own chest and without thinking, I let it draw my blood. "Do you remember? That summer? When we couldn't decide if we were going to drop out and travel the world or enter high school like all the others? And you told me, 'Don't you ever leave me. A million things can happen—our schools can be altered, our lives can be disrupted—but don't you ever leave me, you hear?' I won't be leaving you, Katy. Not now, not ever." My voice choked.

"I . . ." she choked, her eyes dimming. Her touch became softer as the strength left her. "I . . . love you. Please don't hurt him. He's not himself. He hasn't been for a long time. He would never do this of his own accord. It's *him* controlling his thoughts. That I know." She swallowed her blood. "There is still time to change. I know this to be true."

"Who? Mordën?" Confusion colored my tone. "Katy? Katy, wake up. Please!"

I had no clue how much time passed, if it was a year or a second, before I realized she'd grown still in my arms. Not just the motionless from a deep sleep but the stillness where her chest remained quiet. I didn't feel her weak exhalation on my face anymore. Her hand dropped from my cheek and came to a stop on her unmoving chest. A single strand of her hair blew about in the wind. And something inside of me broke. Shattered. Imploded. Ended!

"You can't go; no, it's too soon," I murmured in a hollow voice. "What am I fighting for? Everyone I love leaves me. Why am I even here?" I eyed a discarded dagger nearby and for a horrible moment let the urge wash over me.

"A life, for a life," a voice said above me.

I finally looked up, still holding her lifeless body to my chest, and stared into her killer's eyes. The shadowy form that had plunged the knife into her back towered down at me. His hair flowed out behind him as flickers of light revealed small patches of his identity. A final surge of wind blew light over his face. The docks behind us were in full blaze. Timothy Brestdon stood over us, his hand flexed open and shut while his steeled gaze took in the scene. Something about him was off. My scrambled thoughts took a long moment to register what was happening.

"He will cleanse this world of those who do not deserve to live," Tim said. "Because of you, Temper and Will lost their lives. A life for a life. You will die, Phoenix, and all you love will perish alongside you."

"Tim," I stammered, "she's dead. You have to help me!"

Tim didn't move. His gaze remained riveted on her lifeless body. The light in his eyes was gone and replaced by a darkness. His tangled hair hung around his massive shoulders. It took him a very long moment for him to look at me.

"We have to get her to the ship," I pleaded with him as I stumbled to my knees. Katy hung in my arms.

"So naive, so eager, so young." There was an ancient pain in his voice. "Doesn't even know. Can't tell. Blinded."

"What are you talking about? Help me!"

"Help you? You both betrayed me, left me in the wake of your love." Tears of his own rimmed his eyes. *His eyes.*

Fear bloomed in my chest as I stared with growing horror at his eyes. They were no longer his. There were now only black orbs as dark as night. *His* eyes.

"Tim? What have you done?" My strength was gone as realization hit.

He looked at me, an anguish in his voice. "What *I've* done? Think about what *you've* done! What about all the people you've hurt, all the pain you've caused? You never should have been allowed to live. You should have died and stayed dead. It's what we all wanted. She said it herself. Do you know what went through my mind as I lay strapped to that bed? How every sound, every footstep brought a surging hope wondering if I'd see your face or Will's or Katy's? You speak of hope, but you took that from me. You put a knife in my back and bled me out like a stuck pig. I thought I would be saved. I realized I was left to die, nothing more than a tool at your disposal. I might as well have been. My only friends . . . abandoned me." He pointed a long finger at Katy. "She was the only one to return for me. And she betrayed me in the end by loving you."

The silence was heavier and louder than a grieving mother's scream. I was having trouble processing any of what he was saying. None of it made any sense. All I could focus on was the weapon in his hand. *He wants you dead. He always has. There would have been no hope for saving him.* I looked down briefly at Katy's face. She looked like she was suspended in a nightmare. Her face twisted in pain. I looked up at my former friend. My ears buzzed. It was finally sinking in.

"I could not be there for you, Tim, when you lay in that cave. Do you not think I would have if I could? Has it not crossed your pea-sized brain that everything that has happened has happened because of *him*? What have you done? You've killed her . . . because of what happened in the past? I was tortured as you were. We all were, and we finally had a chance to return as friends. To stand in defiance of evil. United! Instead, you've sided with him. You've killed her!"

"Your love?" His voice dripped with hurt. "Funny thing about love . . . you think it's there to make you happy, to feel happy. But really, it's there to spread pain. That's what's different between you and me.

You're a man in love with a broken heart. I'm a man with an army at my back and the strength of an ancient evil in this world. Now tell me, who do you think survives to write this tale? Who will the bards sing praises of? The broken cripple? Or the dark prince heralding in a new era, a kingdom of blood and tears? I've been promised much. I will *take* everything!"

DarSheer and Kissinger were quickly advancing. Both had swords ready as they took care not to attract his attention.

"You really think he will share power with you? You're a tool, and he will cast you aside the moment he gets what he wants. You think Mordën speaks truth? He lies in every breath. He is the father of lies." I leaned against a supporting post in the deck and slowly inched my way to a standing position. Katy was still in my arms. Her head lolled to one side. "Tim, has he damaged you so much that his falsehoods ring as truth? You speak of your agony, yet you deal the same to all who are forced to your company. The suffering you have given to *her* will rain down ten times on you." I spat out the last few words and felt hatred surge through me. All pretense was gone. He was gone. His black eyes seemed to glow a radiant energy. The Tim I knew was no longer there. He had been killed as clearly and brutally as Katy had. The husk of a man that stood before me was a vessel. "And you, Mordën, will pay, this much I swear to you. I hate you."

"And I loved you," I continued. "To think, I considered you a brother."

"It seems we both made mistakes then, weakling."

Tim gripped his dagger and took one step toward me. His focus was entirely on me. "You believe me weak in his presence? I am myself. My mind is sane. And this promise I make to you, bane of my existence: that shall the day come, I will strike you down and bathe in your blood. You shouldn't be making promises you can't keep. It's in bad taste."

"Now!" DarSheer's clear voice rang out.

Kissinger was at my side in a flash. He stooped and picked Katy's legs up. Her body hung limply in our arms. Part of me wanted to shout at her. *Move. Why are you so silent? Squeeze my hand. Raise your arm.*

Do something! DarSheer, on the other hand, had blocked Tim's downward thrust. My former friend snarled his displeasure and kicked DarSheer's knee with violent incensed rage. They fought, or more accurately, Tim advanced on him, and his blows hit so hard that DarSheer was unable to keep his sword up. I'd never seen Tim that powerful before. I'd never seen DarSheer seem so powerless. Tim's stint in athletics was always a source of pride for him, but now he was something else. The power of another being flowed through his arms and lent weight to his savage cuts.

"We have to get her to the ship," I said, my words tumbling out.

"I know, Phoenix." Kissinger blew sweat from his eyes as we staggered toward the gangplank.

Hands reached out and with a final heaving gasp, we swung her into the safe arms of those already onboard. Pain erupted in my stomach, and I doubled over. The adrenaline had been keeping pain the furthest thing from me, but now that Katy was safely aboard the ship, it returned in dizzying intensity. I clutched my stomach and threw up over the edge of the docks. Metal hitting metal brought me back to my senses and I looked up in time to see DarSheer turn and bolt for the ship. The gangplank was being removed as Kissinger helped me aboard. DarSheer took a giant leap and crashed into us as the men onboard pushed the boat away from the docks. They dropped the pikes used to launch us and began paddling with long oars. Bowmen unleashed arrows of fire on the docks, and we all watched the last bit of wood go up in flames. In the shadows and flickering flames, Tim stood, scowling, facing us. The Rever Drake landed on the beach and Mordën dismounted. The giant dragon had one talon in the shallow end of the basin and rumbled softly to itself as it watched us. I knew one command, and we were finished. *Maybe that is preferred to a life without her.* She'd grown cold. Icy cold. The blood had begun to dry into crusty patches on her face. As time went on, she looked less and less like the Katy I knew. Her face sagged. A disgusting combination of phlegm and blood congealed at the back of my throat and every breath was loud and wet.

I collapsed into a wet mess in the center of the boat. I didn't care that I wasn't being helpful or that the others glanced at me with alarm. Arabella sat next to me, one arm over my shoulder while I wept. It was Kissinger's turn to vomit, which he did so thankfully into the basin. His pale face resurfaced as he stared at Katy's lifeless form. I rocked back and forth where I sat, tuning out the grunts of the oarsmen and the rippling of the sail. A man shouted for more strength. We were not moving nearly fast enough.

"Strange the power one can have over another. It consumes you, changes you. Your life choices become as mirrors of theirs. Then you are forgotten." Mordën's voice cracked out over the water like a whip. He spoke clearly, like he was sitting in the boat with us. "Information is power. The more you know, the more you control."

Arabella pressed her body close to mine. I appreciated her warmth. She leaned in and lay her head on my shoulder.

I whispered, "This visage of a fearless bairn facing down all the evils of this world is a carefully crafted illusion. A lie to paint over my fear."

She didn't respond, letting me weep bitterly into the night. Fell voices chorused before the growing darkness. Varg and Shades filled the beach. They roared and bellowed and snarled. Some slapped their swords against their breastplates and howled into the night. The image of a thousand dark shapes with glowing amber eyes burned itself permanently into my nightmares.

The entire city was in flames. Nothing was spared, from the tallest spire to the lowest hut. Homes and taverns and stables and inns all burned bright in the night. The light glowed orange like the sun. *Avalon, The Golden City. Avalon, The Burning City.* The truth hit me like a punch to the gut as we sailed far out of reach. We had failed. Avalon was in flames. The battle was lost.

The Eastern Ward . . . had fallen.